SONGS
from the
FOREST

ZHANG WEI

Translated by
Haiwang Yuan

SINOIST

Published by Sinoist Books (an imprint of ACA Publishing Ltd).
University House
11-13 Lower Grosvenor Place
London SW1W 0EX, UK
Tel: +44 (0)20 3289 3885
E-mail: info@alaincharlesasia.com
Web: www.alaincharlesasia.com

Beijing Office
Tel: +86 (0)10 8472 1250

Author: Zhang Wei
Translator: Haiwang Yuan

Published by ACA Publishing Ltd in association with the People's Literature
Publishing House

Original Chinese text © 刺猬歌 (Ci Wei Ge) 2007, People's Literature Publishing House,
Beijing, China

English Translation text © 2020 ACA Publishing Ltd, London, UK

ALL RIGHTS RESERVED. NO PART OF THIS PUBLICATION MAY BE
REPRODUCED IN MATERIAL FORM, BY ANY MEANS, WHETHER GRAPHIC,
ELECTRONIC, MECHANICAL OR OTHER, INCLUDING PHOTOCOPYING OR
INFORMATION STORAGE, IN WHOLE OR IN PART, AND MAY NOT BE USED TO
PREPARE OTHER PUBLICATIONS WITHOUT WRITTEN PERMISSION FROM THE
PUBLISHER.

Paperback ISBN: 978-1-910760-98-7
eBook ISBN: 978-1-910760-99-4

A catalogue record for Songs from the Forest is available from the National Bibliographic
Service of the British Library.

SONGS FROM THE FOREST

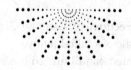

ZHANG WEI

Translated by
HAIWANG YUAN

SINOIST BOOKS

LIST OF PRINCIPAL CHARACTERS

Liao Mai - Husband of Mei Di, father of Liao Bei. Sworn enemy of the Tang family

Mei Di - Wife of Liao Mei, mother of Liao Bei, and adoptive daughter of Liangzi and a hedgehog spirit

Liao Bei - Daughter of Mei Di and Liao Mai, also known as Beibei

Tang Tong - Chief executive of Tiantong Group and son of Tang Laotuo and a she-ass called Jenny

Tang Laotuo - Mounted bandit turned businessman and father of Tang Tong

Lord Huo - Largest and wealthiest landowner in Jiwo, descendant of a wild ass

Liangzi - Handsome stranger who mysteriously arrives in Jiwo. Father of Mei Di

Shanzi - Beautiful and intelligent woman, later known as Lady Shan and Old Woman Shan. Mother of seven adoptive sons

Scarred Apricot - Pretty daughter of Maroon Lips

Maroon Lips - Head of three villages, mother of Scarred Apricot

Xiu - Female classmate of Liao Mai

Qi Jin - Male classmate of Liao Mai

Maoha - Son of a dugong, delivered by Shanzi, adopted by Huo Er'er

Huo Er'er - Servant girl of the Huo family, married to the headman Xiao Shuai

Golden Lock - Trusted hotel manager of Tang Tong

Yuyu - Daughter of Huo Er'er

Shaliu'er - Daughter of Yuyu and noted Fish Opera singer

Rabbit - Villager, former soldier and enemy of the Tiantong Group

Chatterbox - Drunken sailor, also known as Xu Haunches

Jin Tang - Provincial official

ONE

YOU ARE DRENCHED WITH TEARS

"Liao Mai, you're a really fine man. / I'll love you for the rest of my life. / I love you so desperately that I bite and kick you, / And I draw you whooshing into my arms. / Liao Mai! Oh, Liao Mai!"

Mei Di chanted this doggerel just to tease him, her voice first low, then high. She called his name again and again, but he was lying face-up like a corpse. His breathing was inaudible. He remained like this for quite some time before he stirred and started gulping for air. As the wings of his nose widened, two blasts of warm air brushed her face, her throat and her ample breasts. She was crouching on the *kang* bed-stove, gaping in alarm. She remained gazing at him and held her breath for a long time, before chanting the doggerel in his ear again while reaching out to caress him tenderly.

Who has ever seen a man faking death and deciding not to live a good life in the hot summer month of August? A strong, young guy only two decades before, he now adamantly refuses to take a single pill even when suffering from a fever of 39 degrees Celsius. The poor head of our household! My naked sweetheart!

Kneeling on the *kang*, Mei Di looked at him and then out of the window. The wheat fields near and far were cut as short as the stubble on a man's face. A couple of willow trees cast flickering shadows on the fields. Good God! The scorching sun resembled mercury once it rose above the horizon. Like the owner of the endless fields, it had a temper as hot as an electric iron. Over the years, there had been a succession of different landowners. First it was someone called Huo, then it belonged to the Commune and, today, who was it? Mei Di murmured to herself with the breath of a young chick: Tang…

Kneeling in front of the man, Mei Di gently bit his nipples, which were as hard as broad beans. She pressed her ear to his chest, trying to detect the thunder that was rumbling closer from afar. She heard nothing. To prevent her thick hair from covering her eyes, she tied it together with a thread. She measured his chest, arms and thighs with her handspan and paused at his firm lower abdomen. "Oh, Liao Mai, my fine man. My child's father. Are you dying?" She stood up in panic, at a loss what to do. She looked around and suddenly bent over to bite his arms and his muscular thighs.

The man lying on the *kang* opened his eyes into slits, from which a light of chilling strangeness shot out as if from another world.

"Hey, you scared me to death!" she shuddered. "Talk to me now."

Hearing her scream, he shut his eyes again. She stooped to bite him afresh and increased the intensity by increments. His skin tanned by the August sun gave off the smell of baked pancakes.

"I'm anxious, Liao Mai. Do you know how anxious I am? We can't go on without a head of the household. But you've been in a stupor now for three days and nights. We can overcome anything. I'll listen to whatever you say, to whatever you say, all right?"

She mumbled between bites. Her mouth, slightly larger than normal, opened and closed, leaving a trail of moisture on his forehead and throat. He slowly opened his eyes until they were as wide and bright as their normal state.

Staring at her, he asked: "You'll listen to me?"

She nodded as she hung her head low and knelt there without any intention of getting up, like a Japanese wife.

"Then, tell me, tell me everything from the very beginning."

Three days' high fever had made his voice hoarse and feeble, but each of his words sounded like a piece of iron ore striking her face and chest. She had to place her hands over her steaming chest to protect it. "Oh Liao Mai, the fever must have muddled your head. What do you want me to tell you?"

"You know what to tell me. I want you to tell it from the beginning."

Mei Di ran her hand over his head and kissed his chapped lips, but he remained indifferent. Clenching his teeth and twitching the muscles of his cheeks, he fixed his razor-sharp eyes on her as if to demand an answer: Are you going to tell?

"What do you want me to tell, naughty boy? Look at your head! It's as hot as a pancake fresh from the oven." As she planted kisses on his forehead, she tried to pull him up by grabbing his shoulders. Now, either through exhaustion or having become submissive, he leaned his head against her breasts and sat up with the momentum of her exertion. Sweat broke out like rain, drenching his forehead, chest and lower abdomen. His body smelled like something burned, his face turned ghastly pale and his eyes glistened with menace. Mei Di's smile melted away, and she swallowed the few words she had meant to utter. Before she could speak, the man reached out his big hand and grabbed her hair in order to pull her head back, further back. She endured the pain in silence.

From above, Liao Mai looked at the beautiful hair in his hand: flowing down from the back of her ears, it was as thick and dense as the fibres of velvetleaf. Her mysterious hair was now in his grasp but, however hard he tried, a tuft or two would always escape through his fingers. Look at her! She was still a fashionable woman, her hair dyed golden yellow here and scarlet red there. To be frank, she just yearned to have a taste of a Western lifestyle. In fact, her long bob had always caused him to swallow and his blood to surge as if he were a young man. But enough was enough, and the good old days had to be forgotten. Winding the thick hair over his wrist, he tugged it backwards. Instead of screeching in pain as he had expected, she remained stoically silent. He shoved the back of her head and neck hard, dragged and shook her, and dug his knee into her back. Covered with a generous layer of fat, her back emitted so much heat through its moist skin that his knee was seared. For a full quarter of an hour, he held her hair motionless, only watching her from above. He watched her wide open mouth that revealed white teeth, moist red lips, a slightly plump chin, and tears streaming in a torrent from her long eyelashes, down her cheeks and onto her cream-coloured blouse to gather at her cleavage. Her prominent breasts were full and firm even without a bra. The rage that he found hard to harness in all circumstances flared up at the sight of her breasts. The fire of anger shooting through his body now burned his arms, his shoulders and finally his neck. He began to pull her hair with greater force, thinking of how to inflict more pain. The hair was so deeply rooted that he would not be content until he pulled it free. She remained silent. Liao Mai opened his eyes so wide that he felt his eyeballs nearly popping out of their sockets. He turned her around and let her go, and she fell thumping to the floor, tearing her blouse and shorts in the process. While falling, she leered at him, and her astonished eyes appeared to ask: What are you doing? What are you up to?

Liao Mai picked up a plastic sandal from the floor, pressed his knee against her torso, and slapped her hard below her lower abdomen, where a red mark immediately appeared in the shape of the sandal. Another slap! She bit her lip and closed her eyes. Then, when she could bear the pain no more, she started screaming like a wounded animal. She spread her limbs out and tried to keep still so that Liao Mai needed to exert less effort while beating her. He could hardly distinguish the sweat splashing from his arm from the tears flowing from her eyes, but he was aware that Mei Di had reached her pain threshold. He knew it because she started screaming.

"God! I've really got hold of my man!"

Upon hearing these words, Liao Mai dropped the sandal. He knew that she always screamed like that in the throes of passion.

STEWING A GOLDEN-SCALED CRUCIAN CARP

A hot day had almost spent itself. Only when the mercury-like rays of the sun started to fade did Mei Di assist her husband out of the house. A gust of warm wind sprang up from the ground. The bodies of a few sparrows killed by the terrible heat were lying nearby. Casting his eyes over the dead birds, Liao Mai said: "Looks like we're having the hottest summer ever." While saying this, he looked around, seemingly ignoring the presence of his wife limping alongside him. The surrounding fields covering an area of about two hundred *mu* (about thirty-three acres) were enclosed by wattle walls. The plants growing on mounds of earth, the winding paths and the log house constituted a scene worthy of a landscape scroll painting. In the west were fruit trees and grape vines. In the east were the uniformly ridged fields, where green shoots were already fifteen centimetres tall. Irrigation sprinklers sprayed streams of silver whiskers back and forth, as if an invisible hand were tirelessly pencilling the earth's moist eyebrows. Behind them was the L-shaped ranch house. The house was surrounded by tall, thick pines, firs, Canadian poplars and Chinese parasol trees. A few dairy cows were lounging in the shade of the trees. A hundred metres away in front of the house was the glittering lake, regarded as the eye or heart of the fields. At the corner of the lake there were blooming water lilies and erect flowering narrowleaf cattails, on which goldfinches with bright, piercing eyes perched.

Smacking his lips, Liao Mai closed his eyes and came to a halt.

"I can't walk on, either," said Mei Di as she pressed her cheek against his arm. "Let's go back to the house. We should be lying in bed now."

He seated himself on the ground, paying no attention to her. Mei Di meant to crouch down against him. But as soon as she stooped, she fell and had to support herself with both hands. She endured the pain and only whimpered. Liao Mai ran his hand over her head with tenderness and said: "I beat you too hard, but I couldn't help it. I couldn't stop no matter how much I wanted to."

Looking into his eyes, Mei Di replied: "I knew you must have become muddle-headed after you'd been suffering a high fever for three days and nights, with nothing to eat or drink in the meantime."

"I have never been so clear-minded," he sneered. "During the three days of stupor, I roamed the underworld, where I reached the bottom of our lives both in this world and the next. Everything was clear. That's why I asked you to tell me your story from the very beginning. You'll tell me sooner or later."

Mei Di silenced him by pressing her lips to his mouth. With tears still in her eyes, she turned her face towards the setting sun. But Liao Mai turned it towards him again and, staring into her eyes, asked: "Is this our home?"

She nodded.

"That won't do. You must say the words."

Rubbing her eyes, she said aloud: "It is our home."

Liao Mai swallowed and said: "We've devoted all our sweat and blood to building this farm, first you alone, and then we together.

We were like little birds carrying twigs in their beaks. But you! You're going to sell it to Tang Tong..."

"Maizi![1] I have no alternative, you know that. No one else does, either. Everything around us belongs to Tang Tong now."

Liao Mai clenched his teeth so hard that they chattered, as if he were still feeling the effects of the fever. "I overheard you saying to yourself: 'This is our last summer.' That's what you said, right?"

"Yes, I said it. You know Tang Tong's people have come twice, including some with official titles. We've even had visitors in uniforms."

"I'm talking about you! For a whole month you kept on muttering to me about selling our land. You've been collaborating with that local despot and acting as his mole."

"Oh my God!" Mei Di screamed. "What are you thinking! Are you serious? My child's father, you can never think that way. Never!" She held him in her arms and continued: "You can do whatever you want to me, but you can't think that way. Good Heavens! You've said a lot that I'm sure you didn't mean. You've been upset by them these past few days."

Liao Mai gazed at the lake motionlessly. He was stooping on his long legs with his big, veiny hands on his knees. His dried lips were bloodied and covered with cracks. His silhouette appeared golden in the twilight and made his outline appear more distinct. The days of high fever had taken their toll on him; his eyes were more sunken, his brow ridges more pronounced and his cheekbones more prominent. His eyes spewed the occasional sparks of anger. The day he regained consciousness from his stupor, this hot-tempered man, built of the strongest intertwining tendons and veins, had turned boisterously foulmouthed, his voice as loud as thunder and his clenched fists as fierce as iron claws. As a result of his beatings, Mei Di still felt pain in her abdomen, her legs and around her genitals. The pain seemed to be aggravated ten-fold by the light-iodine-coloured afterglow. She moaned gently as she leaned against him and held him close.

He sensed her body odour in the hot air, that most familiar odour. He looked down at her hair dishevelled by his grasping hands, at the blue veins meandering from her neck and disappearing at her breasts, and at the faintly discernible bruises on her abdomen. He stroked her thick hair and pinched the long lashes protruding from her closed eyelids. As he was doing so, he gurgled a faint sigh from his throat: "You're a real jewel."

Mei Di feared that he might hear her thumping heart and see her tears that were welling up. She had heard many nicknames and terms of endearment that this guy had given her over the years. She looked up at him and turned her face to take in the movement of his big caressing hand, ready to receive his first act of affection since the good beating, in the form of a light touch on her lips by his own chapped, blood-clogged lips. However, he only edged closer to her and blurted in her ear: "Big Loose Woman."

"That sounds awful! That sounds too awful!"

"But I like to call you 'Big Loose Woman'."

"So, call me that then. Do as you please. Do whatever you want. Beat me if you want to."

He tore open her cotton blouse to examine the bruises, and muttered: "I beat you too hard, Big Loose Woman. No matter what, I shouldn't've beaten you so hard."

"I'm your wife after all, aren't I? After wandering for the better part of my life, I realised from the day I returned... I realised what we mean to each other in our lifelong relationship."

"What do you think it means?"

"You beat me to death, and I love you to death."

Clenching his teeth, Liao Mai fell silent. He suppressed what he had wanted to say: That would be great, but we may not be so lucky! He lifted her chin so that she looked up. He rubbed her broad forehead with his thumb, as if wiping the fuzz off a peach. He couldn't help feeling amazed at the fact that, although she was nine years his junior, she was still almost forty. But her face had always been a glowing, mysterious apricot-pink colour. This was a face no one could forget, so it became the most dangerous thing on this small plain by the sea. None of her physical features – from the wrinkles on her thin lips to her purplish-black eyes and large breasts – could give men the peace they needed to go to sleep. Despite their lengthy separation, they had been husband and wife for the past few decades. Why did they have to face so many temptations? He had loved her every second since he had returned, but he just found it hard to trust her.

"Big Loose Woman, do you know why I've given up everything to come back to live with you, even at the risk of my life?"

"Because you missed me, thinking of me every day."

"Good answer. But there's something else. I'm telling you now – I want this farm. I want to own it for the rest of my life."

"You also want my hair. You like it and have always been thinking of uprooting it..."

Liao Mai was silent. He wanted to correct her: he depended on her more than he wanted and liked her. He did not know when it had started. As soon as an unbearable anxiety seized him, he would find immediate relief by burying his face deep in her thick hair.

Sinking her head in his chest, Mei Di took in his salty taste. She ran her hand over his entire body, and when it reached his face and lips, she giggled: "Beat me. I know I owe you and deserve your beating for evermore. I can endure the pain. When I can't, I'll scream like I did before. But I can't do it now because your beating has injured me. Hey, my fine man, do as you please, my really fine man. You're still as strong as you ever were, and you've become more handsome!"

Liao Mai said to himself: That's strange. Her meekness and submissiveness are killing me! She's always been meek and submissive, so much so that a vigorous man like me has lost his wits. I can do nothing but beat her violently. This is true!

They returned to their house before nightfall. Liao Mai lay down on the *kang* and, looking at the ceiling, said: "Tang Tong's men will storm in again until I kill one or two of them. But look how weak I have become. You must make me stronger. Go and stew me a pot of golden-scaled crucian carp. Hurry up!"

Mei Di had been limping a minute before, but now she suddenly became nimble. Looking up at him, she responded with a categorical "Yes". Then she rushed into the next room to get the fishing rod and hand net.

The golden-scaled carp is a rare species. An adult measures about seventeen centimetres in both length and width and is the colour of copper. They live among pebbles in strong currents and like to break the water surface at dusk. Eating the fish had helped keep Liao Mai alive during his wandering years, something he would never forget for the rest of his life. A soup stewed with the fish is believed to have the properties of correcting the 'five strains and seven impairments'. According to traditional Chinese medicine, the 'five strains' refer to the weaknesses of the five yin organs, namely the spleen, lungs, heart, liver and kidneys; and the 'seven impairments' refer to the ailments caused by the seven emotions of grief, joy, hate, love, happiness, anger and desire. In this way, the soup can enable a person confined to bed to rise again, to clench his fists and to walk with the vigour of a tiger. The first thing he did after returning to the farm was divert water to the lake, line its bed with white sand and stones, and try to raise the golden-scaled crucian carp. He was keeping them for a rainy day. He seldom disturbed them, that is, he did not catch them even once in a year. Walking by the lake, he enjoyed the sound of the ripples and the sight of their glistening copper forms when they broke the surface in the setting sun. Each time, he would give a thumbs up and say: "Good job! Grow healthy and become more potent for me. It's about time. Yes, it's around the corner."

Mei Di returned from the lake about half an hour later. Lying on the *kang*, he heard her taking off her big rubber boots and the golden-scaled carp thrashing around in a bowl. He also smelled gunpowder. That's right, he said to himself, the golden-scaled carp doesn't smell like ordinary fish. He had etched the pungent odour in his memory during those wilderness years. He began to praise his wife in silence. Damn, she's really something – capable and yet submissive, as courageous as a female warrior and prepared to kill people for the sake of her loved one. Look how skilful she was in catching the fish. In ten minutes, she'll slit its belly open and throw it into a boiling pot.

Lying on his back, he felt slightly worried. He had taught her goodness knows how many times how to make fish soup properly, but he was still concerned. He struggled up, staggered to the outer room by holding the doorframe and lay down on a bench with a back rest. He needed to make sure that he heard the sound of chopped spring onions popping in the hot oil.

The boiling oil was searing the chopped spring onions, minced ginger, star anise points and Sichuan peppercorns. They bobbed up and down three times before this big-hipped woman grasped a handful of minced pork belly from behind her and cast it into the oil. Steam sizzled up as the fat in the pork was rendered into lard and blended with the oil. She stirred the ingredients constantly with a steel spatula before inviting the main character, the golden-scaled carp, to come on stage. As soon as it went into the oil, the guy gave off a loud cry: Decease! A whiff of purple smoke rose instantly with the strong smell of gunpowder that irritated the eyes and nostrils. But the big-hipped woman didn't even pause to squint. She pressed the spatula on the belly of the fish, allowing it to jump three times on each side. The golden-scaled carp had been killed in a salt solution before it was cooked. In doing so, Mei Di had bestowed it the last bit of her mercy. As a hero of aquatic animals, this type of fish has nine lives. It would jump three times and cry three times even when placed in a wok of boiling oil. They were indeed the cries of the fish, not the sharp clanking of the wok with the spatula. At last, it went to the dreamland of eternal slumber, from which it embarked on its journey to the other world.

Wielding the steel spatula in her hand propelled by her strong wrist, the big-hipped woman produced sparks as she stirred this old chap in the wok sufficiently quickly to get it seared but not burned. By charring the fish black, she would have invited a big slap on the face from her husband. The stir-frying demanded great strength and skill. She eventually boiled away both the water and the oil, with purple smoke enshrouding the pot, and managed to get all the minced pork into its belly. Losing no time, she put the steel spatula down and picked up an earthen jar filled with spring water, which was kept as cool as possible. The best temperature was like the icy water that collected behind the house in midwinter. She poured the water into the wok with a splash, and now the soup was more than half-finished. Liao Mai could see in his mind's eye the soup being as white as snow and as smooth as milk. Damn! This Big Loose Woman had succeeded once again! What came next was to wait patiently for half an hour, to add seasonings such as vinegar and white pepper, and to enjoy it till beads of sweat broke out on his forehead.

"Why aren't you having some?" asked Liao Mai as he stared at her.

"I," she replied, wiping her hands, "I don't like the gunpowder flavour."

Liao Mai let her alone and gulped down three bowls in succession. He began to crack his knuckles. Mei Di gazed at her husband with pleasant surprise, her eyes sparkling like stars. After finishing the last morsel of fish soup, Liao Mai rose, rubbing his hands together. He walked beside the door, stuck his hand into the wet hand net and took out a black plastic bag.

"You're going to eat this fish," he demanded. "I've long smelled its fishy odour. But you must cook it and enjoy it yourself after I go to sleep."

THE ADULTEROUS FISH

Liao Mai shook the fish to the floor from the bag. Strangely, with its eyes wide open, it was lying motionless on its stomach. The fish had a muddy-grey colour, a large, round head and a small, lean body. It gazed at people with its fins holding its lower jaw like a person propping their chin on their hands. The fish also pressed its upper and lower jaws hard like someone biting their lip. The appearance of the fish was abhorrent, evoking immediate disgust. This kind of fish had existed in the lake before Liao Mai's return. He often saw them lying on their bellies in the shallows at the edge of the lake, staring at the workers in the fields. One day, he caught such a fish in a hand net and cast it onto the dry dirt. But it remained alive for a long time, fixing its round eyes on him. He had been so irritated that he kicked it, but all it did was roll in the dirt a few times and stare at him, seemingly determined not to return to the lake. He had remembered that Mei Di had come by just then and, giving off a gentle scream of compassion, picked it up, blew the dirt off its body, whispered some words of comfort and placed it back in the water.

Feeling the air to be permeated with their stench, he said: "We must wipe out these ugly, wretched fish and chop them up for duck food."

Mei Di pouted her lips and said: "Don't. Don't say that."

What happened later amazed Liao Mai. During supper, Mei Di ate two of the ugly fish, and as a result she became inflamed the whole night. Like a drunkard, she leered at him, flushing, and kept biting him. He had to dodge her since blood began to seep from his shoulders and back. He wiped some blood with his hand and looked at it in the lamplight, veins throbbing on his forehead. Before he could fly into a rage, she had already huddled in his arms like a kitten and kissed him incessantly.

Early that morning, straight after getting up, he went to the lake to stare into the eyes of an ugly fish lying on the bank. He cursed it maliciously and menaced it with his hand in the shape of a cleaver. The fish, however, remained undisturbed in the rays of the morning sun. Starting from that moment, he began to devote his attention to the study of this bumpy, ugly breed of fish.

He found no record of the fish in any dictionary. He went through all the handbooks and charts of aquatic products but to no avail. One day, he ran into a tramp who happened to be something of an autistic savant. His face was greasy and dirty, and his hair was heavily clogged. However, he appeared to know a lot, and at a single glance and without thinking, he blurted out: "Adulterous fish!" It seemed to be the name for this ugly species. Liao Mai then sent a picture of the fish to a friend, who was a fish expert in remote southeast China. Along with the picture, he attached a detailed explanation. A month later, the expert replied, affirming the identity of the fish as a rare 'adulterous' species found in both the Orient and the West. He also sent him a copy of a stanza from a poem written by the French poet Du Bartas. The stanza, which was about an adulterous sea fish named Sargus, read:

> The adulterous Sargus doth not only change
> Wives every day, in the deep streams, but – strange!
> As if the honey of sea-love delight
> Could not suffice his raging appetite,
> Goes courting she-goats on the grassy shore,
> Horning their husbands that had horns before.

For a long time, Liao Mai sarcastically referred to himself as the "husband of a she-goat". He jotted down the words and ruminated over them. After taking a steaming shower together, husband and wife would read the stanza together beneath the floor lamp, each reading a line in turn.

Tonight, while lying in bed, Liao Mai listened to Mei Di clinking her spatula against the wok in the kitchen. He knew that she was preparing a sumptuous dish for herself. He was mulling over the origin of the adulterous fish in the lake. Could it be that someone had stealthily slipped them in? He had asked Mei Di about it before, but she had replied: "Well, they've been in the lake from the beginning. They are native to it."

Liao Mai had said nothing, knowing that Mei Di was the true owner of the farm. During the past decade, she first had it on a short-term lease and later purchased the right to its use, for a fifty-year period. What a woman! She really resembled a sword-brandishing bandit on horseback. But at the time, she had been a charming single woman. If their story was to be told from the beginning, it would be a miracle in a world of misery. He had instantly been mesmerised by the thirty-two acres of barren land: its borders had been fenced, the fields had been laid out in squares and bounded by ridges, and the trees had begun to form into groves. And the lake had a surface area of more than three hundred acres, with plenty of wild aquatic plants growing in it. The first time he had seen it, they had rendezvoused there secretly.

Their farm had then only recently been established. Instead of a comfortable house, it contained only a two-roomed hut made up of plank walls and a thatched roof. One of the rooms was used by their daughter Beibei as her sleeping quarters. Liao Mai had just sneaked back. Soon after entering the farm, he had taken Mei Di out for a stroll towards the lakeshore. They walked hand in hand on the ground covered with silvery frost. By the lake that night, there was a clump of fresh, raw-smelling Jerusalem artichoke stalks, which had been cut down about ten days before. Despite the thorny hairs on the stalks, the two had laid upon them. This place in the farm was closer to the sea than to the town. There, they cuddled in silence for a long time, each of them in ownership of the other. Out of nowhere, she let out a scream that hushed the aquatic creatures in the lake. In fact, they both forgot everything around them.

"Oh my God! I'm really getting hold of my man!" she screamed while holding him tight, her tears streaming all over him and the Jerusalem artichoke stalks underneath. After they had got up and walked back towards the thatched house in the moonlight, he looked at her and found her back, abdomen and crotch all bruised by the stalks.

Before dawn that day, they tiptoed to the bedside of the slumbering Beibei and stood there for a full hour. As they stepped out of her bedroom, Liao Mai asked: "Is this really my daughter?"

"Of course, you fool!" she replied, looking at the greyish whiteness on the eastern horizon. "Of course. Only we could give birth to such a beauty. She's fantastic, perfect."

That adventure of sneaking back had made him determined to give up everything and come back home. He would come back to live with her through thick and thin, to fix the farm, and to love her day and night. Life is short, he said to himself, and I can no longer wander outside my native land. Never again. I'll return. I'll come back even if it costs me my life.

His return, however, had proved less dramatic. Soon after he last left home, an overjoyed Mei Di had told him the good news – he could come back because Tang Tong had lifted his vicious ban. Mei Di said he could really return this time.

THE WORD 'KILL' IS UTTERED

Tang Tong, owner of a gold mine and chief executive of the Tiantong Group, was the son of Tang Laotuo. He might have been thought of as an elite member of society during this time, but he was also considered a bad human being, even worse than a beast. Since ancient times, residents of this mountainous area by the sea had never loathed animals. On the contrary, they coexisted with them and even intermarried. Which of the elderly villagers on the coast could not tell a story or two? Who could not identify the names of a few who had been reincarnated from, adopted by or even born of wild beasts? Some of them were the descendants of wolves, others were relatives of wild boars, and one of them was even the firstborn of what the villagers call a 'sea hog' that had crawled ashore one midnight. Though formally called a dugong, a 'sea hog' is not the same as the well-known, adorable porpoise. It is a rare species of aquatic animal seen only by local fishermen. Like a female bear, it is covered with black hair all over. With its fins functioning as legs, it slowly roams the beach waiting for the moon to descend so that it can deliver its cub on a clump of cogon grass. It was going to give birth to a son for a single old man who had been a fishmonger all his life. Some men were too impoverished to have wives. Therefore, they wandered the plains or in the mountains by the sea and mated with whatever creature they ran into so that they could procreate. The offspring of such liaisons looked exactly like humans when young, but their appearance would change as they advanced in age, and their temperament and features increasingly resembled those of their beastly mothers. Some had the face of a wolf, some had the ears of a rabbit and others even had a pair of fish eyes. As for people with fox or sheep faces, they were so many that no one regarded them as odd. What animal had Tang Tong been incarnated from?

None of the villagers could figure it out. On the boundless plains and in the mountains, strange beasts abounded. It was often said: "That guy is a terrifyingly strange animal. His former life must've been strange as well."

During his days of acute anxiety, of his obsession with returning and of his subjection to frenzy, one fact Liao Mai neglected the least: how could she, Mei Di, have built such an attractive farm in the vicinity of two such powerful and influential beasts? Everyone knew that the father and son of the Tang family were man-eating creatures with iron mouths and steel teeth. They ate people whole, not even bothering to spit out the bones. A sweep of their tails could destroy a wood; a stomp of their hooves could change the course of a waterway or even collapse a dam. What kind of magic powers did Mei Di possess to enable her to settle down here, overcome adversity and rear his 'illegitimate child'?

At that time, Liao Mai was a fugitive obsessed with endless troubled thoughts. He was extremely cautious during the early days of his return, always walking on tiptoes. So much so that his wife yelled at him: "What're you afraid of? This is your farm. You're on your own territory. You're the king here, and whatever you say matters."

He nodded, coughed noisily and raised his head to look around. The hazy outline of a mountain loomed in the southwest. That was Gold Mountain, the stronghold of the Tang family for generations. Today, Tang Tong had left the mountain and claimed most of the plains as his property. Not only did the Tang father and son exploit the blood-dripping gold mine, but they also engaged in almost every other business. They dug and explored frantically on the coastal plains as if trying to turn the entire world upside down and siphon off all the water from the sea to expose its bone-laden bottom. Tang Laotuo eventually died as a result of this huge, wasteful operation and passed away at the age of ninety, leaving his only son Tang Tong behind to continue working like mad.

"Mei Di, our daughter's mother, you've been through such a lot. How did you manage to develop this big farm in the wolves' lair?" asked Liao Mai, gazing at the stars outside the window one quiet midnight.

She stooped over to gaze at him and found his eyes more beautiful than the stars. "What can I say? We have both been trying to escape the jaws of death. You had run away and left me behind, but I had to survive and stay alive while waiting for you to return. There used to be only a tract of land with waterlogged, saline-alkali soil. Apart from reeds and silvery wormwood, nothing could grow in it. In winter, the north wind brought seawater up to flood the area. In spring, sandstorms heaped sand dunes and prevented people from opening their eyes. I worked alone among the dunes and in the saltwater marshland while taking great pains to bring up our newborn myself because none of the villagers would want me as their neighbour since they treated me as a bad woman. I built a hut as a shelter and begged them to spare me and our daughter so that we could eke out a living. Otherwise, they would have driven us into the sea. I opened a small plot in the fields, then another, and planted trees near the seashore as a windbreak to check the advance of sand. Some kind-hearted villagers came to help, and I reciprocated by giving them the cowpeas and turnips I grew. Later, I leased the marshland that none previously wanted to possess.

"At that time, Tang Tong and his men could never have imagined things turning out like this."

"No, he couldn't've imagined it. Neither could've the people from the small village nearby."

Gnashing his teeth, Liao Mai sounded muffled in the dark evening as he went on: "What's harder for me to imagine is that Tang Tong should allow me to return and spare my life."

Running her hand gently over his forehead, Mei Di said comfortingly: "You may set your heart at ease. You should know that everything's changed in a decade. How does he have the time to care about what happened in the past and what happened between you and his father? He's as busy as a…"

"But I care. I remember everything clearly."

"Well, you're different. Maizi, my good husband, my really fine man. You must hold me tight every night. You must do what you've promised me."

That night, Liao Mai did not sleep well. In fact, he could not get to sleep at all. He gazed at the night sky as though he were looking at his own fate. He had a feeling that he was still living in a kind of dream. Sometimes, he was dumbstruck by what was happening under his nose, unable to believe that it was real. In those years, Tang Laotuo had been one of the town leaders. He had earlier served in the armed forces and had had the experience of being wounded. After his discharge, he had become invincible locally. When Tang Tong had grown up a bit, father and son surrounded themselves with many militiamen and village thugs. During the stormy decade, they had run amuck, and on his say so, his men could have beaten someone to a pulp. Liao Mai would remember that moonless night in midwinter for the rest of his life.

Mei Di had been the cause of everything that had happened to him.

At that time, the little girl brought here by her forest-ranger father had grown into a young woman of considerable beauty. She was like a flower blossoming quietly in a corner. At first glance, Liao Mai was dazed by her beauty as if his eyes were burned by the sun. He first froze at the corner of a brick wall and then covered his eyes with both hands for a full quarter of an hour. He slowly lowered his hands and stared at this dazzling flower, gaping like a fool. Standing opposite him, she reacted in nearly the same manner – entranced and motionless, allowing his eyes of flame to scorch her face.

Going to school some distance away, Liao Mai had been unaware of what had been going on in town. He had never imagined that the father and son of the Tang family would have been coveting this young woman. Tang Tong had been considering marrying her in a few years. As if ensnared by a strange spirit, this long-legged Liao Mai had been leaning against, or rather, glued to that corner of the wall for the next three days and nights. On the fourth night, he heard footsteps as soft as those of a cat and closed his eyes to wait for the fateful moment. The cat's paws covered his face, and then the onslaught of a wildflower's fragrance overwhelmed him. Even at the last moment, he had no idea where he had directed his hands before they eventually fell on her short blouse adorned with purple flowers and trembled in her young cleavage. She kissed his forehead and mouth and was fascinated by his soft, young beard. Time was like a pile of bashful petals fallen on the ground being swept away by a reluctant broom. The broom was sweeping and sweeping for no one knows how long when several torch beams struck them like lightning, and a rusted bayonet was thrust against their chests.

Liao Mai had spent the next few nights suffering in a cellar. Five to six village thugs took turns to watch him and torture him using every means possible. He never forgot the ordeal that they inflicted upon him. They tied him to a post at a crossroads for public view. He was stripped of his clothes so that his genitals, mangled by the scourging, were exposed. He hung his head low and shut his eyes in the bright sun. He really wanted to die and end this public humiliation once and for all. However, he kept himself alive by thinking of her eyes, hands and cleavage. He could no longer contemplate separating from her.

He also thought again of the day when he had bidden an eternal farewell to his father. Before breathing his last breath, the old man had held his hand and secretly passed him a paper slip. Liao Mai wailed and wailed and did not open the crumpled paper until he had laid his father to rest. He found it to be a request that he return a hidden package to a lender. The lender was a gold miner. Sure enough, following the instructions on the slip, Liao Mai found a securely wrapped parcel in the location indicated.

He went to the gold mine, gingerly carrying the parcel, to ask about its owner. He remembered being stopped by a red rope. Many passers-by were waiting for a big explosion. Someone was waving a small flag, and immediately the mountain and the earth began to shake. In an instant, a picturesque mountain slope was erased from existence. "Wow! Such power, Kick and Kick, Kick and Kick!"[2] shouted a toothless old man.

All the other onlookers echoed with amazement: "Kick and Kick! Kick and Kick!" The image of the collapsing mountainside and those three words were etched in his memory... With great effort, he finally found out the identity of the parcel owner. It was an old miner, a personal enemy of the Tang father and son. He had died in the mine shaft three days earlier. At dusk that day, Liao Mai went back home, knowing that he couldn't fulfil his father's request to return the parcel to its original owner. On his way, he had opened it at a place out of public sight. He had been stunned by its content – "Kick and Kick!"

Liao Mai was tied to the post as a public spectacle under the blazing sun during the day and thrown into a cellar at dusk. He stayed up all night over the remaining few days, always thinking that, had he survived, the old miner would have taken the parcel to the Tang father and son and detonated the contents. Liao Mai's father had tried to stop him from doing so, only to end up in misery himself. The old miner should have lived, Liao Mai said to himself.

He tossed and turned, causing his scabbed genitals to bleed again. His face and ears had scratches all over them. Another day broke, and he was kicked out of the cellar again.

Pointing at his forehead, Tang Laotuo said: "Go to work in the mine in three days." Each word sounded like a thunderbolt to Liao Mai, who knew that a lifetime of penal servitude was about to begin.

He had only three days left. So, before the village thugs escorted him to Gold Mountain, he decided he had to flee. But prior to his flight, he needed to accomplish two things: first to avenge his father and that poor old miner, and then to see Mei Di. After making up his mind, he refused to eat or drink. He no longer felt any pain. Only two faces flashed alternately before his mind's eye: his father's and Mei Di's.

It was pitch-dark. Mei Di would remember that dark night all her life. After the barking of the last dog died down, no sound was audible. In fact, it was frighteningly quiet. Suddenly, a screech broke out, followed by a mixed commotion of gunshots, shouts, the clash of bayonets, and the clacking and thumping of footsteps. The entire town was thrown into chaos. Mei Di knew that something grave was happening. She waited as she leaned against the small window, shivering. As soon as someone tapped on the window in earnest, she pulled open the latticed window panels.

A man with his face smeared with soot crept into the house. As soon as he entered, he hugged her tight. His panting was scary.

"You did it?"

"Yes, I did it."

"What happened?"

"It was a close call…"

"Good Heavens! You'd better run. Hurry!"

"Wait for me."

"Hurry and run," a crying Mei Di begged him.

On his soot-covered face, Liao Mai's eyes shone particularly bright. "You must wait for me. You promise."

Holding his leg, she said: "I promise."

"Say it again."

"I promise."

Liao Mai leapt out of the window. Meanwhile, Mei Di heard the commotion coming from Stone Street. She also heard Tang Laotuo struggling like a dying old animal as he kept moaning loudly and hoarsely: "Aargh! My God! He can't get away! Aargh! We'll hack him with axes and stab him with knives, and we'll dismember him when we catch him. Anyone who sees him can kill him!"

A BLOOD FEUD OF TWO GENERATIONS

A staunch and swarthy figure always entered Liao Mai's dreams. The guy was sturdy and of medium height. He always looked at him amiably without saying a word. He used a pistol-shaped lighter to light his cigarette, and before starting smoking, he would always offer the cigarette to him as a gesture of courtesy. Liao Mai found the face familiar but could not remember his name. He woke from the dream breaking into a cold sweat. He was convinced that this guy was trying to do something in his dreams. Sure enough, he later found him sneaking away and pretending to wash his hands by the lake. He then produced a few mud-grey fish from his pocket and released them in the water. With a scream, he charged towards him, brandishing a three-pronged fork. But the guy vanished in the blink of an eye. Liao Mai was wide awake, sitting there slapping his thighs and cursing his bad luck aloud. Each time, Mei Di had to calm him down by wrapping him into her bosom like a baby. He would always struggle out of her arms and gaze out of the window in the direction of the lake, muttering: "That type of fish is by no means native. They must have been slipped into the lake by Tang Tong!"

Mei Di was silent. What could she say? Tears swelling in her eyes, she felt sore once more in her lower abdomen. "My really fine man, I'm afraid my injuries and pain will linger. I can't make you feel good any more."

Liao Mai did not seem to hear her and muttered in the direction of the window: "My only regret is failing to kill Tang Laotuo that night. But I could do nothing better at the time because I was too young, and my master had died earlier."

"Master? What master?" asked Mei Di. Liao Mai did not respond but lay face-up on the big *kang*, cracking his knuckles once more. He regretted not having met the old miner earlier, thinking that he must have been an expert. He believed that he had hated a man before he breathed his last. That was his father, the miner's old friend and principal of the village's elementary school.

The old miner, when he was alive, had always confided everything on his mind to the old principal and asked him for advice. His only son had been embroiled in a dispute with a village thug over the construction of his house. Tang Laotuo then had him bound and escorted to the upper-level authorities. Two days later, he had been taken back and plunged into a dungeon-like cellar permeated with the smell of blood. The old miner's only son was short-tempered. Each time the village thugs battered him, he cursed Tang Laotuo. Eventually, the enraged Tang father and son tortured him themselves. They changed the mode of punishment each day. When the old miner and his wife had sneaked into the cellar to visit their son, they had found him so skinny that he no longer quite looked like himself. They had also found his body covered with cuts and bruises. They dropped to their knees before Tang Laotuo and begged for mercy, refusing to get up until Tang Laotuo gave their son back to them. But seeing his half-built house demolished, their son collapsed, spewing blood from his mouth, and he was never able to rise.

After burying his son, the old miner went to his old friend, saying: "I'm so poor that I've nothing left but a package of Kick and Kick."

Grabbing the package from his hands, the principal stopped him: "You can't do this. You can't. Let me write you a charge against them for you."

Two weeks after the indictment was delivered, it ended up in Tang Laotuo's hands. Stomping at a crossroads, he shouted: "It's a rebellion! A revolt! The hoodlums are revolting!" The Tang father and son reserved their greatest hate for intellectuals and were convinced that it was the principal who had incited the old miner's son to carry out something that was beyond his capability. The village thugs prepared a long, narrow table and Tang Laotuo sat at it, flanked by men carrying rifles with bayonets. As soon as the old principal was brought before him in this kangaroo court, Tang Laotuo slapped a gavel on the table. Each time he slapped the wooden block, a village thug would come up to kick the principal on the back of his knee. "Kick and kick him! Kick and kick him!" Laotuo slapped and roared. "I can't believe he won't confess and tell me who his accomplices are. We'll round up the names he spews up and string them together. Kick and kick them! Kick and kick them!"

They kicked and kicked until they mangled the front and back of his knees, and he was unable to stand up. In the last few days of the kangaroo court, they had to drag him in. They locked him up in the cellar, feeding him nothing but a bowl of stale rice. Knowing his days were numbered, the old principal made two requests: having his glasses returned to him and meeting his son in the cellar for one last time. Learning of his requests, Tang Laotuo came to the cellar humming a tune and casting the glasses to the floor. Before the old principal could pull himself forward to reach them, Tang Laotuo crushed them with his foot while yelling: "Want to see your son, eh? A son doesn't like a rebel. If you want to die a quick death, you'd better confess and tell me who your accomplices are."

The old principal clammed up.

"Confess or not?"

The old principal closed his eyes. Now, the only thing on his mind was to die. However, he was still worrying about his son. Once he closed his eyes permanently, his son would never be able to see him. His good boy would never imagine that his father had been tortured to death. He also thought of his old friend and of the package he had concealed for him. He gritted his teeth so hard that they clattered.

"Anybody there? Pry open his mouth of old teeth," screamed Tang Laotuo.

A gang of village thugs who had been waiting outside the cellar swarmed in, followed by Tang Tong. Tang Laotuo was so wrathful that he twitched the corners of his mouth further apart. Panting and pointing at the old principal, he roared: "Pull him up! Hang him! Only allow his toes to touch the ground. Do it!"

The old principal was hung on a wooden frame in a corner. Tang Tong went over and felt with his hands to make sure that only his big toes were in contact with the ground. Then, he asked: "Dad, what do you mean by hanging him like this?"

"He can live on for a few more hours this way."

It was midwinter, and it was starting to get bitter cold. The old principal died.

Before his death, he was finally able to see his son. Liao Mai's mother had died when he was very young. His father had raised him alone. Liao Mai had hurried back home only to see his father absent. So he dashed to Stone Street. In the cellar, he saw his father's mangled legs. Holding his father, he cried himself out of breath. The old man could not speak any more. Breathing heavily in his son's ear, he produced a paper slip with great difficulty and uttered a few words: "Kick and Kick..."

'A SECRET HISTORY OF THE JUNGLE'

Every living thing in this world has its prime, whether it be a thriving Jerusalem artichoke flower or a pony with bright shiny hair – each has the chance to enjoy the most flourishing stage of its life. Liao Mai was a late bloomer; his good days came when he was almost forty years of age. Hold on to what you have in your life, he said to himself. Hold on to what has been haunting you in your dreams for more than two decades, that is, the woman who you can neither forget nor escape from no matter how hard you try, like a tramp who's suffered from hunger and cold for half his life is unwilling to let go of a flaky pastry he's already stuffed into his mouth. No one knows what he would have done if he had been eight or ten years younger, but now he could only let her huddle in his arms so that he could enjoy the unique scent emanating from her entire body. A woman of purplish-black hair, of apricot-pink complexion and of lustrous skin. Now she was looking at him with her eyes as innocent as those of a lamb.

Running her hands over the stubble on his chin, she said: "Oh Maizi, we'll never separate for the rest of our lives. For this day, I've died several times, but each time I came back to life again. I've been through all the ordeals there are in this world. I gave birth to your child and kept her alive so that she was able to wait for her loving dad to come back. This day has finally come. We've won. Raise your head and look around. This is our home and our farm. And our family of three are all together here."

Liao Mai remained silent while he listened. He had always been thinking of the day of his return and would never forget her teary scream. He was amazed at her steadfast yearning for her loved one, and for him she had been able to withstand humiliation and starvation, to take lashings and kickings, to struggle on year after year, and to dash around under the threat of bayonets. No one would have thought of the bayonets as real without seeing them in person. Yes, she had won. They had all won. The day had finally come, and starting from that day, she suddenly became new and turned herself into an eternal bride under the sun.

They had devoted ten years to the project of putting their farm in good order. It had to be flawless, every tree and every inch of land had to be touched by the hands of the man and the woman. The lake had been formed naturally by a depression filled with accumulated rainwater. Liao Mai reworked it by digging a canal to allow water to circulate, thereby eliminating silt and aquatic weeds. He planted water lilies, comparing their white blossoms to his wife and their extending green leaves to her dress. He designed a new house with an attic, which, as he had planned, would serve the sole purpose of allowing him and Mei Di to lean close side by side against its windowsill to enjoy a view of the sea and the vessels sailing on it. Every day, he conversed with sheep, goats, cows, Chinese parasol trees and roadside oxeye flowers – anything that was living. He could not believe that a human being should have been able to reap such a great reward. For more than a decade, he had led the life of a fugitive tramp. Meanwhile, he had entered a college on a faked identity and eventually became a government employee. All the while, though, he was restless, spending every waking hour thinking of Mei Di and home. Even in his wildest dreams, he could not have imagined that things would have turned out so amazingly, thanks to Mei Di, his almighty woman. Miraculously, she had forced Tang Tong to rescind his order to kill, taken care of this huge farm and raised their daughter.

"I have treated this home and everything in it as a dream for the past decade. Now, the dream's about to come to an end. Damn it! Look! Tang Tong's really going to take the land away and drive us out," said Liao Mai, gazing outside the window.

Mei Di was out of breath and looked pale. "Maizi! Maizi! Tang Tong's not taking the land away for nothing. He's offering a competitive purchase price."

"How much?"

"Don't know yet... But it's reasonable. You know he's going to expand his factories, all the way here."

"I don't want to sell," Liao Mai said sneering. "This is my life."

"I also wanted to hang on and delay the sale, too..."

Liao Mai stared into her eyes with an aggressive intensity that caused her to look away. He then looked out of the window again, murmuring to himself: "Mountains, sea and plains all have lives like humans. In a matter of seventy to eighty years, an endless woodland has been turned into a wilderness. From the coast, walk twenty-four hours nonstop to the south, to the west and then the east, and you can hardly see a single tree standing tall, not to mention a grove. No wildlife has survived. Their extinction is a harbinger of the end of humanity. This is true. My father said so when he was alive."

"Maizi, oh Maizi! You're mincing words again. Please don't. Please don't put it this way."

"You know I have had a dream to record what's happened in this area over the past seven or eight decades, to write a book called *A Secret History of the Jungle*. But Tang Tong's driving us away just after I've settled down and sat down at my desk. Now, he's going to force me to wander again."

Mei Di bit her lip and shook her head, saying: "No. When we move west of the big river, we'll have a bigger and newer farm. Besides, we can have a study in our house so that you can read and write whatever you want since that's what you really like to do. But you can't mince words like this. Don't forget how your father passed away – being clever with words only invites disaster."

"Yes, I'll record everything from beginning to end. That is my dream. There's no doubt about it. I'll write *A Secret History of the Jungle*."

"What are you going to include?"

"Everything, from beginning to…"

"Maizi! Oh Maizi!"

"There's no doubt about it. I'll record everything from beginning to end."

TWO

SOME GOOD ANIMALS

DOMESTIC ANIMALS ARE KEPT in pens, and wild animals are scattered in the forests. There are no domestic animals without wild animals, no humans without animals and no wild animals without forests. From the perspective of heaven up above, this area looks like the antler of a spotted deer thrusting into the sea, surrounded by water on three sides. Both its plains and mountains used to be covered with trees. Mountains and hills in the south and the west rolled into the sea, eventually tapering into a plain. North of the hilly area was the densely populated old village by the name of Jiwo, which means 'a nest of thistles and thorns'. Every one of its residents had a history with the wild animals of the forest.

It had been a tradition for the residents of Jiwo to associate with wild animals. It was believed that the second maternal uncle of the biggest landowner in the village, Lord Huo, was a wild ass. Some of the villagers who had seen the wealthy and powerful Lord Huo gossiped that he had a long face and a pair of exceedingly big ears, which would twitch endlessly when he heard something interesting. Besides, his chin looked whitish and felt extremely soft. Lord Huo had had the Huo Mansion constructed. Made of black bricks and tiles, the buildings were situated in a hilly area connected with a plain. The Huo family claimed all the trees and waterways within this area as their private property. Someone mentioned that he had run into one or two foxes while taking a walk one morning. When he asked them who they were, they replied without hesitation: "Our family name's Huo."

With incalculable wealth, Lord Huo had long stopped being an extreme penny-pincher. Everyone has their hobbies and foibles. Lord Huo had a penchant for women and some female wild animals. Without knowing it, he spent his innocent and artless life in the hills and the plains. He wandered here and there, running around with various beautiful beings, sleeping with them wherever he set foot. Consequently, he sired some grotesque-looking children. They and subsequent generations oversaw the farms and forests according to their talents and preferences. Some of them were responsible for the rivers, while others appropriated a large grove of oak trees.

Being rich and powerful, people from the Huo Mansion were bound to bully the poor. They captured and shackled those who were prone to violent anger. They had to arrest anyone who rebelled and hurt people in the middle of the night, then bagged and carted them to a river into which they were thrown. The Huo Mansion kept a few hundred retainers, all dressed in military uniforms with the character 'Huo' printed on the chest. The most violent of them had the blood of aardwolves running through their veins. These young retainers walked quietly, bared their fangs, exhibited more tendons than flesh and leered at people. Lord Huo disliked those retainers. Passionate and compassionate, he judged individuals not by their wealth but by their appearance. All the good-looking people and animals were his friends. He even formed a close attachment to the occasional tall and beautiful tree that he ran into, such as a poplar, a Chinaberry or an oak.

A few years before his death, Lord Huo's life had become well integrated with Nature. Wherever he went in the forest, he was followed by a number of animals including white goats, foxes and spotted dear. Whether mutually reinforcing or neutralising each other, all of them lived closely and harmoniously. In his late years, Lord Huo built a huge *kang* and slept on it with wild animals on his left and right, along with one or two of his wives. Before going to sleep and getting up, he always planted a few kisses on the little lips of his rabbits. Starting from the age of sixty, he cut out all meaty food from his diet and began to eat grass as his staple food, the same grass grazed by wild animals.

He became so kind-hearted and lecherous that people from the Huo Mansion could only beat or kill people behind his back. Good-looking women were reluctant to appear before him because they considered him too old, so much so that they could smell the stench of death whenever he opened his mouth. He went around carrying a load of silver dollars that he used for the purpose of bribery in times of urgent need. In the last years of his life, people in the mansion often happened to see him stuffing money in his maidservants' hands while groping them all over. The maidservants and other women in the village said: "Lord Huo couldn't actually do much, but he was a pesterer and wasted our time."

Time sped by. Lord Huo was no longer in this world. This grinning old man was missed by everyone in Jiwo and the surrounding hills and plains. In the first two or three years after his death, the forests lost their tranquillity at midnight. Countless squalls and sobs were heard, rousing the villagers from their beds. Elderly men and women simply gave up going back to sleep. Whereas the former smoked one puff after another, the latter sewed their outsoles stitch by stitch. While doing so, they could discern the sounds made by different animals – foxes whimpered, badgers hiccupped and hedgehogs wailed. Everyone in the village knew that hedgehogs were the most romantic of the forest animals, and some of the female ones were particularly charming, tenderly attaching and reluctant to quit yearning for their loved ones. These characteristics of theirs, however, were not to be publicised.

It was believed that Lord Huo held a lifelong ambition to take a boat out on the sea to visit a few islets. A fish spirit had appeared in his dream to deliver a message that his reputation had also spread across the sea and that the islets boasted both breathtaking scenery and some exquisitely beautiful mermaids that were expecting to see him. At the time, Lord Huo had lost most of his teeth and he staggered when walking. Nevertheless, he arranged for the construction of a castle ship, known in Chinese as *louchuan*, literally a floating fortress. Hearing the hammering sound of shipbuilding, he exclaimed: "I didn't think of going to the sea before my death. I am, after all, a rich local man born at the foot of a mountain."

Lord Huo died when the castle ship was only half-completed.

The entire population of Jiwo, which had long since become a large town, breathed a deep sigh of relief, because anyone, whether from the Huo Mansion or elsewhere, could do either good or bad deeds without fear of repercussion. They felt relaxed before being seized with grief as they began to prepare for a grand funeral. It was such hard work that a dozen young and middle-aged men died of exhaustion merely in the process of finding the right wood to make his coffin and preparing for the banquet to be held after his burial. Luckily, someone suggested that they finish building the big castle ship, place him on a bed as if preparing him for sleep, and launch the ship into the sea with a few children accompanying him.

The villagers immediately espoused the idea and acted upon it. When the moment of truth came, the riverside was teaming with people. The big castle ship was enshrouded with colourful curtains and festooned with lanterns. Young girls, dressed in robes of red and green and with their hair in double buns, waved on deck at the port and starboard. The ship sailed into the wind to the sound of long wails uttered by the wild animals lurking in the verdant woods along the banks of the lower reaches of the big river. As the ship moved along, the trees swayed and rustled as if swept by a hurricane. Wild geese, swans and hawks soared into the air. The villagers who had been looking on along the river sighed: "What more could a man ask for, having enjoyed such an affinity with the wild creatures?"

The tables of the grand banquet after the burial ceremony stretched for a length of five kilometres. Residents of the town and beyond were all invited. They said that that was Lord Huo's last act of generosity. The guests came from all walks of life and were strangers to each other. Among them there were certainly some animal spirits from the woods. More than one human attendee found some of the inebriated exposing their long, thick tails or hairy faces. Some of them were so frightened that they couldn't stop their wine-cup-holding hands from trembling. Unaware of his exposure, one bushy-tailed guest was tearfully recalling the past deeds of the deceased Lord Huo: "I miss him so much. One time, he spent all night running his hands through my beard and tickled me so much that I giggled breathlessly. That's not what a lord is supposed to do, but that was him. He never put on airs."

Another said, rubbing her eyes: "I must induct the child I had with him into the Huo Mansion, where he'll find his roots, right? Right? The boy looks so handsome with his big eyes, though he's a bit hairy."

As the animal spirits gossiped, a young retainer of the Huo Mansion was about to pull his sword from the sheath on his back when a sharp-eyed and agile old butler stopped him by grasping his wrist. A tall and fair-complexioned woman drank a mouthful of wine as she bent her head back and, wiping away her tears, said: "I used to be a young poplar tree by the river. The lord had set his mind on marrying me. I said to him: 'Dear Lord, I'm wooden while you're human. How can we be compatible?' As we were both feeling awkward, an old physician came over, scratching his goatee beard. He persuaded me by saying: 'According to the principles of traditional Chinese medicine, the liver organ in a human being has the properties of wood. So, do as the lord asks.' So, I got married to the liver of Lord Huo and lived in harmony with it for the past thirty years."

An elderly woman at the banquet was wearing a straw raincoat. She was not in the mood to eat or drink, and her mournful appearance was rather touching. It was puzzling to see her dressed in that raincoat on what was a fine day. It rustled whenever she took a step. Later, the old butler found out that the woman was none other than a hedgehog spirit. She had been Lord Huo's favourite animal wife.

EFFICACY ENHANCER ADDED TO MEDICINE

The castle ship went without a trace. The moment it entered the estuary, a fog suddenly appeared, as if an invisible hand had pulled a vast curtain to envelop the ship. That night, clouds driven by the wind rolled in with full force. According to some of the villagers who had followed the boat to the mouth of the estuary, the sea surged throughout the night, and whitecaps leapt more than three metres high and rushed towards the mouth of the river. Their rumbling did not die down until daybreak. Nothing could be seen nor heard of the ship. The entire town of Jiwo was shocked, wondering if Lord Huo and the pretty girls on the castle ship had all been swept to the bottom of the sea. Some villagers shook their heads and objected: "Nah! The waves meant that the sea gods held a ceremony to receive Lord Huo and the girls passed to him by the river god, and the sea gods would in turn pass them on to each of the other gods. The higher the waves, the better it was because they were produced by the sea gods beating their drums." The young men of town, however, were always preoccupied with the pretty girls, still counting the days until their return.

Many years later, when speaking of Lord Huo's death, the town's traditional Chinese medicine physician sighed with grief: "It was such a shame that the wrong medicinal efficacy enhancer was used!" It turned out that when Lord Huo was short of breath in bed, the emergency medicine was prepared minus the fresh urine of a young boy that had to be added as an enhancer. That morning, patchy fog had just descended. When the old physician left his house carrying an earthen bowl, a boy came along gesticulating with his hands and feet. The physician hurriedly stopped the boy and obtained his urine. He brought it into the house, mixed the urine with the emergency medicine and fed it to Lord Huo. The patient had just swallowed a greater part of the medicine when the colour of his face changed, and a layer of sticky sweat broke out on his brow. The old physician panicked. He tested the urine enhancer in the earthen bowl only to find it tasted fishy. The bowl slipped from his hands and smashed into pieces on the ground. He realised that the boy from whom he had obtained the enhancer had not been a human boy at all.

In reality, the farsighted old man, whose vision was further hindered by the fog, had misidentified the little being walking with the light gait. It was actually a turtle spirit that had just crawled out of a creek. Although a centenarian, it was of a small and thin stature and had a smiling face. That was why the old man had mistaken it for a boy. He had never noticed the deep lines of wrinkles on its small forehead.

The old man decided to conceal the secret in the recess of his heart. Only when he met the owner of the creek in the forest did he confide his grievances to her. In the forest, all waterways, be they rivers, streams or creeks, had their owners. Each of the ravines and gullies was also overseen by a particular spirit. A tree could appear in someone's dream with a message before its death; an old bear could see the physician when it fell ill. These facts were well known to the residents of Jiwo. The owner of the creek was a black eel. She had been friends with the old physician for more than two decades but kept the relationship platonic. She had had a crush on the physician when young. On several occasions when he was checking her pulse, she had the urge to pull his hand from her wrist to her chest so that it could press against her breasts, but each time she suppressed it. They sat cross-legged, face to face by the creek, talking about the trouble that the old turtle had made. The black eel considered the turtle to have made an innocent mistake but "acted in disrespect of the seniors". She did not elaborate and stopped short of telling the old man about the turtle's lechery – it had waddled by her with an intentionally loosened waistband on several occasions.

Without their owner, the retainers became unrestrained. Maidservants, and even the lord's wives, often disappeared at midnight. A rumour circulated that mounted bandits had emerged in the forest and taken the women away with them. In fact, it was the retainers who colluded with people over the mountain to traffic the women. Fully aware of their scheme, the loyal old butler wanted to get rid of the evil-doing retainers, but he had no solid proof. Therefore, he felt forced to go to the forest to visit Lord Huo's animal descendants and friends and tearfully tell them about what was happening in detail. Tears had never dried on the faces of these creatures in the past six months, and now they finally had a chance to weep their hearts out in the company of the old butler. Afterwards, they held a banquet in the forest and invited all the retainers. At first glance, they all appeared similar in their uniforms with the character 'Huo' printed on the front, but when seated at the tables spread with meaty morsels, each showed its true nature. Those who bared their canine teeth and ate with ferocious table manners were the descendants of aardwolves. At the end of the banquet, desserts made of mulberry paste were served. The nimble wild creatures in the forest had poisoned the desserts with the juice of lethal mushrooms. Consequently, all those who walked quietly and had canine teeth succumbed on their way back to the Huo Mansion.

Peace had just reigned in the Huo Mansion when the grownup descendants of the poor in the hills and on the plains who had been killed by the retainers rose up in rebellion. They came, iron forks in hand, to avenge their former generation. In the past, it had been the offspring of aardwolves that would have fired their blunderbusses over the buttress walls and suppressed the rebellion in just a few hours. Today, however, the remaining retainer guards dressed in their uniforms emblazoned with the 'Huo' character opened their sheep eyes wide and trembled so hard that they could not hold their blunderbusses level. In the end, they were all captured by the rebel villagers. After repeated turmoil, the descendants of the Huo family found it hard to safeguard its heritage. They simply left the Huo Mansion with their share of the properties and established their independent nuclear families. Consequently, members of this reputed Huo family scattered across the whole region.

Before long, a gang of mounted bandits really did come to the hilly areas. Every one of the armed men was frighteningly strong, and each had a blunderbuss in hand. Their horses were all male and kept their penises erect day and night. Silence reigned in the hills and on the plains. Even the creeks and brooks muffled their gurgling. Having one foot in the grave, the senile butler of the Huo Mansion made a last-ditch effort to stand up to the bandits: he asked the old physician to go to the forest with him to discuss the matter with the creatures that were there. They sneaked into the forest, ducking their heads to conceal their identity, only to find most of the wild animals disheartened. Even the river god and the creek goddess softened their voices when they spoke. The black eel, owner of the creek, being already very old, had a piece of moss bandaging her head. She was suffering from toothache. Patting her swelling cheek, she said to the old physician: "Give me a cure. I'd have gone to see you in normal days."

The old physician prescribed a medicine with an efficacy enhancer called 'pouring out your heart'. "Pour out everything in your heart," the physician said. "Don't let your thoughts weigh on your mind. Take this medicine, and you'll surely recover."

After cursing him, the black eel had to tell him everything from beginning to end: "The situation's terrible. From now on, we're doomed. The mounted bandits will be stationed here as firmly as nails. They'll never leave."

"All the townspeople, plus you guys in the forest, are martial arts masters with unique skills," the old butler responded. "How can we fail to beat them?"

Spitting out a flood of saliva after coughing awhile, the black eel countered: "You're really a country bumpkin! We'll do well simply to survive. If something should happen, all of us could be exterminated. Fuck those mounted bandits and their eighteen generations of ancestors!" With this, she held up the bowl of medicinal soup and gulped it down in one go.

The vast mountain forest was as silent as the dead. However, when the bandits swooped from the mountain forest, their horse hooves could be heard in all corners of Jiwo. Everyone bolted their front door while a few single men peeped at the erect penises of the horses through the crack of their doors and said, clapping gently: "Could they be our army?"

Sure enough, news came a few days later that the mounted bandits were the rarest people in the world. They had destroyed all seemingly invincible strongholds in their path. The chieftain of the bandits had acquired a particular elixir that required an efficacy enhancer – killing seven rich men wherever they went, and taking the medicine three times a year. The entire town was terrified. Bulletins were put up saying clearly that every household was required to declare its assets, with its land and houses to be calculated in terms of silver coins.

The day the bulletins were put up, nearly everyone with the surname Huo ran away.

The town was desolate, and all its businesses were dying. The few households with the surname Huo that remained categorically refused to admit their affiliation with the Huo family. When asked, they would reply: "My last name is Hao."

HANDSOME

During the years of desolation and random killing, if there was one refreshing note, it was the emergence of a handsome young man. His appearance, though disregarded at first, was gradually more noticeable and eventually became a local phenomenon. The young man would undoubtedly feature in the town's chronicles one day. While his presence was no longer an illusion, his merits and demerits became more blurred than distinct as time went by. His case was different from that of Lord Huo, who became known publicly as a harmful person one or two decades after his death. Except for some of the wild creatures in the mountain forest that still said the occasional good thing about him, none of the other living beings would come up with a single word of praise. Unable to tell right from wrong, those wild creatures were beasts after all.

The handsome young man was called Liangzi. No one had paid any attention to him when he was young, not caring about his family background or even his family name. Consequently, whether he was related to the Huo family could never be determined. For decades, the verification of one's blood relationship with the Huo family had been a big deal in town. Initiated by the mounted bandits who had occupied the mountain forest, this tradition continued after they were driven away. The tradition should have long been discontinued, but strangely some people carried it on and even to the extreme. To prove a person's identity, they investigated his three previous generations. In a situation like this, various kinds of investigation methods were bound to surface. A barefoot doctor invented the method of checking one's belly button or little toe. For a time, all the townsfolk, men and women, old and young, had to take off their trousers or shoes at least once. The results of the investigations were all registered. It was said that for a while, the handsome young man Liangzi held his trousers up with a rubber band as he was asked to take them off so frequently. The successive town heads, particularly one who had just assumed office and had to work hard to prove himself, hurriedly summoned him to come to the town's big house to pull his trousers down or take off his shoes whenever they thought of doing so. As time went by, things became worse. Investigation became more rigorous and meticulous. Even elderly women and female leaders concerned with politics began to treat him in the same manner. It was a common occurrence for a middle-aged woman carrying firewood to stop him on his way, saying: "I'm going to check you up."

At sixteen, Liangzi's elegance had begun to ravish the eyes of beholders. They had never seen a man so handsome. His muscles and tendons were firm and balanced, his complexion slightly tanned, his eyelashes long, his eyes watery with a tint of heroism, his stature tall but not lanky, his waist soft and elastic, his hair resembling the fleece of a black lamb in spring, and his lips angular and piquant. He was so reserved, honest, courtly and cultured that he did not seem to be a native of the hills. The townspeople gossiped that he was born with courtesy and did not need to attend school because he was self-cultured.

One day, I will have a relationship with Liangzi. I was his girl by birth. Don't believe me? Wait and see! The more mature girls in town would all talk to themselves in this manner. When they first caught sight of this young man, they gasped. They tried their best to hide their fluster. Whenever they laid eyes on him, they would tremble all over, their brains would lose control of their mouths, acting as if they were experiencing a high fever. A few days later, there was still a look of confusion and stupefaction in their eyes. Their mothers scuttled about looking to find a doctor for them, but they soon realised what had happened to their daughters when they ran into Liangzi themselves. One mother came up to him and whispered in his ear: "If I were twenty years younger, I'd give you a hard slap!"

Perplexed and scared, Liangzi asked: "What, what did I do to deserve this, Aunty?"

Holding her breath, the woman responded: "I hate you so much that I want to punch you to death and eat your flesh." Upon hearing this, Liangzi turned and took to his heels.

There was a young woman named Shanzi, who was delicately charming and always reserved. She was known as the smartest beauty. While still a girl, a chief of the mounted bandits had a crush on her but ended up being killed in a fight over her with a fellow bandit chief. With the departure of the bandits, she grew up. Swinging her hips as she walked down the street, she claimed to be a proud virgin. She intimidated all other girls of a similar age, trying to prevent them from getting close to Liangzi while she clung to him all the time. Although younger than Liangzi, she appeared ten times more mature. She liked to tell stories and did so vividly. She often good-humouredly scared him by saying: "I'm a descendant of the Huo family!"

Liangzi understood the significance of these words and was so scared that he dared not look up. Shanzi then said in a hushed voice: "Let me tell you this – only those closest to you would confide such a secret because it could be a capital crime!"

After his initial shock faded, Liangzi began to study her and expressed his suspicion. Without hesitation, Shanzi showed him her belly button, saying: "This is the hub of the entire body. It'll reveal everything if you can read it." On her instruction, he stooped over only to find three distinct vertical lines crossing her L-shaped navel. Then it was time for her to scrutinise Liangzi, a practice to which he had become accustomed. Staring at his abdomen, she rubbed and pressed it while her teeth began to chatter as if it were midwinter. "Let's get up," she said. "We can examine each other however we want in future."

At first, Liangzi did not get what she meant but soon realised the significance when she became head of the women in town. He was surprised by her transformation after she assumed this position. Previously soft-spoken, now she walked with her hands on her hips. She also learned to smoke cigarettes and pipes. Sometimes, she sauntered at a crossroads with a bronze water pipe in her hand, which instantly reminded senior townspeople of Lord Huo in previous years. She would beckon Liangzi over without any reason, saying: "Let me check you up. Let me check you up." Sometimes, she wouldn't even bother to avoid public notice and untied Liangzi's waistband as pedestrians walked by. If any female dared to inch close to take a look, she would threaten to gouge her eyes out. If she overheard a woman talking about Liangzi, she would say: "Is Liangzi a name you dare mention?"

One bright moonlit night, groups of people were thumping and pounding along Stone Street with blunderbusses rattling in their hands. No one knew who they had caught, having only heard the shouts. Not long before, a descendant of the Huo family had been discovered. It was an old widower farrier fixing ass hooves. He had betrayed his identity under the influence of alcohol. They tied him up and subjected him to a series of interrogations that proved his slip of the tongue to be the truth. He was beaten to a pulp and locked up in a dungeon, his fate left at the mercy of the senior authorities. Two weeks had elapsed, and no word came from the senior authorities. Tang Laotuo, who had just become head of the town, said: "What're we waiting for? Kill him. Kill him now."

On the day of execution, all the locals turned out, filling the area at the bend of the river. When the moment came, all the women, except Shanzi, covered their eyes with their hands. Holding her water pipe, she paced up and down as if nothing were happening. Afterwards, people gossiped: "What a pretty girl. But what a cold heart she has! Let's wait and see how Liangzi will put up with her."

Everyone was worrying about Liangzi.

PATIENCE NEEDED TO SLEEP WITH A HEDGEHOG

The handsome young man tantalised many women. One day, however, he suddenly left and was nowhere to be found. When the news broke, a group of people with blunderbusses passed by Stone Street. In their wake, plodding in the sun, was Shanzi, without her usual water pipe and with her hair in a mess. Slapping their knees, elderly women sighed: "Nowadays, anything can happen. A cooked duck can fly. A sure thing's slipped through her fingers!"

After Liangzi fled Jiwo, Shanzi was in no mood to be the leader among the women. She became reticent again and lived in the seclusion of her own home. Now, people began to rediscover her beauty with her large, deep-set eyes on a full, tight small face; she simply looked like Liangzi's biological sister. But she soon had enough of her isolation and came out into the open again, before quickly slipping into the forest. Good Heavens! It was simply unthinkable for a young woman to go in and out of the vast forest that extended from the hills and dales all the way to the seaside.

The vast forest had remained quiet during the past several decades since that band of stalwart mounted bandits were stationed in the mountains. It seemed that humans no longer dared to run around with the wild creatures of the forest, and, for their part, the creatures rarely dressed like humans only to unwittingly reveal their tails at banquets after getting drunk. Folk would say: "They've been spoiled. Spirits fear villains, so next time, if any of them dare to reveal his tail, we townspeople will shoot and kill him." However, it was easier said than done. The vast forest was still revered and even dreaded in secret. Besides, the townspeople had had blood relationships with the wild creatures in the forest for generations, and those ties could not be severed easily in just one generation.

It was impossible to completely ignore the immense existence of the forest when there was such an interest in hearing news from it. For example, a man accidentally ventured a few steps deeper into the forest when he was out collecting medicinal herbs in a peripheral area and ended up being discovered lying in a clump of grass, naked and drained of his vital essence. Not feeling in the least surprised, elderly people would say: "He must have been laid by a fox spirit." Another man was chopping firewood when he suddenly heard heavy breathing nearby. He looked up only to find a strange creature ogling at him with affection. He had never seen such a creature before; it had a face resembling both that of a wolf and a man. It also had deep-set eyes and fierce buckteeth. Its hands, when opened, appeared like claws. The man screamed and passed out. When he came to, he had permanently lost his senses and become a half-wit.

The way Shanzi was behaving reminded people of the handsome young man who had gone missing. They assumed that he must have fled into the forest. Only after being deeply loved could a woman become as grieved and courageous as Shanzi, who would probably be bent on finding him even at the risk of her own life. It was really strange that the young man should have been cornered by his own good looks. Many times, Shanzi was seen emerging from the forest with unkempt hair and clothes, her matchless beauty still visible. Looking stoical, she gritted her teeth and remained reticent. Some saw her hands and the front of her garment covered with blood and concluded that she had killed some creature, or rather, some man in the forest. But it turned out that she had delivered a female leopard of its cub. The truth is that wild animals also suffer while giving birth and even risk death from labour dystocia. Public interest in some of the secrets hidden in the forest was rekindled by a word or two from Shanzi. For example, they now knew that the desperate screams coming from the forest at midnight were let out by a wild sow in its pang of giving birth. The dull, staccato whines streaming from the fog-enshrouded seaside emanated from a large female dugong delivering its baby on the beach.

Milling about in the forest, Shanzi looked for the handsome man but to no avail. But she ran into wild animals in labour again and again. Each time, she would crouch down to deliver their young and often appeared bloody-handed when she walked out of the forest. Various townsfolk concluded that she had changed her disposition from aggressive to placid. Some ventured to propose marriage, only to trigger a barrage of curses from her mouth. From then on, no one would think of doing so, knowing that she was still determined to give her heart to that 'regular customer'. Apparently, she had not given up on him.

Those who really knew the secrets of the forest were the

strange people traversing the town and the hills and plains. Their presence could be traced back to antiquity. They tramped everywhere in rags, each carrying on his shoulders a blackish bedroll, their only possession. When they smiled, white teeth would gleam from behind their filthy faces. They were gossipy and indiscreet, although much of what they said was incoherent. They went begging from door to door. The locals called them 'foolish beggars', reserving the term 'great foolish beggar' for those who were extremely filthy and always uttered a disarray of words. The foolish beggars collected wild fruits in the forest and shellfish on the beach. They slept in nests of dry grass that they assembled on the ground and drank from brooks and creeks. They were believed to have made friends with the wild creatures, who were certainly not the ordinary kinds but, instead, the incarnated spirits of the beasts. It was said that some of the great foolish beggars were very capable and talented, having acquired their bewilderingly varied skills from the wild beings, or rather, their incarnated spirits.

When they wandered into town, the foolish beggars were invariably accosted by local residents trying to learn from them what was going on in the outside world, particularly in the forest. These filthy-faced and gibberish folk often said something that even they themselves could not comprehend. The listeners, however, would always get what they wanted to understand and isolate the truth from their gobbledygook. The foolish beggars said: "You think that Lord Huo has died? Nah! That dirty old man just took a pill that an animal spirit of the forest had given him so he could fake his death. Then, he floated straight out to sea on the big castle ship. All these years, a succession of good things have happened to him, and he's now enjoying a carefree life."

"You think he's willing to give up such a big mansion plus the endless mountain forest and land?"

Rubbing at his dirty face, one of the foolish beggars continued: "On the contrary! He left because he heard the mounted bandits were coming. He knew he couldn't keep his great fortune any more, so he just relinquished his life on land and departed. The beauty of all this is that mermaids vied to jump onto his castle ship and into his arms, giving him the ultimate pleasure. Isn't he enjoying himself?"

Gazing at the foolish beggar, the audience were in a state of half-belief and half-doubt.

"Whenever fog comes down, that castle ship secretly pulls in to shore. What does it do? Nothing but pick up wild creatures, the dirty old man's intimate friends. I often lie on my stomach at the seaside and watch through the fog. I saw with my own eyes pretty women getting on and off the boat. Some held babies in their arms, some were well endowed and some wore a *qipao* that exposed their chests. Each of them was as beautiful as a flower, and just looking at them made you break out in a sweat all over. They didn't care about each other and one by one kissed the dirty old man again and again at the port or starboard…"

"Tell us something about Liangzi. Is it true he's in the forest?"

"How can it be false? He's a smart guy. Foregoing one or two girls in town, he got all the wild beings in the forest! You think he's short-changed? To be frank with you, even I have dated a dozen of the beauties. I'm telling the truth. Well, I can't help feeling aroused. Why? It's hard to give up those you have a relationship with. Foxes, spotted deer, muntjacs and all the other wild animals have their incarnated spirits. They all want to run around with people so they won't get bored. They may not be humans, but they can be wild once they get horny. Take the old rabbit spirit, for example. When you hold her in your arms, there's no chance of getting any sleep. She'll keep on kissing until you pass out. The wild boar spirit is another example. She may smell a bit foul, the stench of her urine may pique your nose and she may be a little rough, but she can also be affectionate. The spotted deer are just great. They're real beauties. Naturally pretty, they still like to dress themselves up, always wearing a spotted short cape and smelling musky all over.

"But the most lovable beings are hedgehogs. They're shy and sway their hips when they walk, just like young ladies from genteel families. They always have something lurking in their thoughts that makes them blush hotly. Each of them has a pretty face. When she's being intimate with you, she cuddles you closely. Just think how nice it would be if a hedgehog spirit held you by the shoulders with her tender hands while you two were intertwined in a passionate embrace and lovemaking! It's said that Lord Huo's favourite animal-companion was none other than a young lady incarnated from a hedgehog. Hedgehogs are quiet, and their coughs are gentle and soft. While they're submissive, you mustn't hurry when you want to sleep with them. Why? Because they've got hidden spines all over their bodies. Of course, their chests and bellies are soft and tender. If you're in a hurry, you might accidentally hurt them and piss them off. They'd shudder involuntarily and turn themselves into balls of spines. Then, you'd suffer terribly. Your private parts will prick and bleed badly. So, to sleep with a hedgehog, you must be patient."

I AM A MOUNTED BANDIT

What family name now prevailed in Jiwo? It was Tang. The rocks, the trees, the streets, the dogs running in the streets and the tracts of farmland – all bear the family name of Tang. It was just like before, when everything bore the family name of Huo. This fact was pointed out by an elderly man smoking a pipe in the sunshine. One day, he was saying it when Tang Laotuo strode over and, brushing the pipe from his hand, yelled at him: "Son of a bitch! What nonsense are you talking? Are you comparing me to a despot landowner?"

Having finished his tirade, Tang Laotuo went away with his blunderbuss. Staring at his back, the elderly man grumbled: "You're so powerful, and you're still telling me the town is not named Tang!"

Tang Laotuo had left the village when he was young. Now, none of the younger villagers knew anything about him. The elderly, however, knew he had been a mounted bandit. They would say: "By going to a faraway place, Laotuo was acting in accordance with the old saying: 'A rabbit doesn't eat the grass by his burrow.'" By quoting the saying, the elderly meant 'A villain doesn't harm his neighbours.' Nevertheless, when a group of bandits passed through town one day, many of them thought that one of the bandits on a big horse resembled Laotuo, though they could not be sure. That day, the bandits looted a lot of money and grain from the townspeople. They also killed a few fat local residents to offer as sacrifices to their banner before their departure. As usual, the women all made themselves less attractive by smearing their faces with the soot scraped from the bottoms of their cooking pots before the bandits' arrival. However, they had never expected that the bandits would ignore them completely. Since then, the townspeople realised that not all mounted bandits were the same. These bandits avoided women as a sick person is supposed to avoid certain food when drinking traditional Chinese medicinal soup. So women were their taboo, and they eventually left them intact.

The last band of mounted bandits to occupy the mountain transformed Jiwo. These bandits were extremely powerful. They cut down trees and, like the bandits before them, searched everywhere for the people from the Huo Mansion – only that they searched even harder. Even though the members of the Huo family had fled, leaving the town more destitute for a time, the bandits from the mountain still would not let them be. They would catch them even if it meant digging the ground to a considerable depth. Disguised as beggars or collectors of medicinal herbs from the mountains, they chatted with every household in order to discover the whereabouts of the Huo family members. Through a month's open and secret investigations, they caught all the Huo descendants hiding near and far as well as in every obscure part of town. They captured a total of thirty-three men and women who had been reluctant to leave their native town, betting their fate on luck. Strung in a file with an iron wire, they were paraded along Stone Street, with their escorts shouting "Kill them! Kill them!" on the way. The thirty-three men and women of different ages were taken into the mountains, and none of them came back alive. It was a miserable night of foul wind and blood. Wailings could be heard throughout the forest. The chieftain of the mounted bandits said: "Both the domestic and wild animals were collaborators of the Huo family. Let them weep a little now – the time for them to cry their hearts out is yet to come. Pick a date and burn the forest, and see where you can build your nests."

Once he had finished yelling, the forest was utterly hushed. Later, the mounted bandits did set fire to the forest. As smoke rose, large hawks shrieked, soared into a cluster of white clouds and disappeared. The whistling wind swayed the trees, followed by loud rumblings that dropped from the sky to the earth, bringing with them incessant downpours that doused the terrible conflagration in the forest. Angry beyond control, the bandits swooped from the mountain and forced everyone in town to fell trees, saying: "Cut down the ones that survived the fire. Keep cutting until the trees are gone. As for the wild creatures, leave them to our blunderbusses."

The townspeople worked without a break throughout the winter and spring. By the time all that cutting had cracked the hands of the loggers and exhausted their bodies so much that they could not rise from their beds, they had managed to clear a peripheral edge of the forest.

Early one morning, as the townspeople were cutting down trees, the mounted bandits suddenly left. After a moment of silence, what remained of the forest was alive with the sound of twittering birds of all kinds. Foxes ran out singing, and even reclusive hippos walked up to the banks of the river belching. Everyone in town knew that the world had changed.

However, six months after this episode, Tang Laotuo returned with his blunderbuss, followed by a few fierce-looking thugs armed with either iron maces or sabres. They first singled out those who had been the town heads and held them in custody for a few days before recording their confessions. They then made them put their thumb prints on certain documents and shoved each of them in a jute sack. This last practice was very familiar to the townspeople who had seen the retainers of the Huo Mansion throwing people into the river in the same manner. Sure enough, the sacks were taken to the riverside and cast into the water one by one.

Tang Laotuo gathered the whole town for a meeting, at which he enumerated the crimes committed by the Huo family, saying that he would go after their descendants relentlessly in the future.

An elderly man could not help saying: "You've just killed thirty-three Huo family members, and they've all died without a single descendant left."

"What you are referring to were the mounted bandits," Laotuo roared. "We're the busters of mounted bandits! You're fucking confusing the two armed forces!"

The reprimand sent a chill up the elderly man's spine. As he really could not tell the difference, he did not dare to speak up any more.

"Go and cut the trees," Laotuo yelled again. "Cut them down! Cut them so we can see the light of the sky. There're two things I hate more than anything – one is people wearing glasses, and the other is trees. We'll cut down the trees so we can grow cereal crops in the fields. Take his spectacles off and replace them with a donkey blindfold."

"He still claims he's not a mounted bandit," someone murmured, "yet everything he does makes him look like one." Unfortunately, the person who overheard this comment was one of Laotuo's spies. He reported him immediately. Laotuo tore his shirt open to bare his chest as bony as a tortoiseshell and thumped it with his hand as he moved close to the man. "I *am* a mounted bandit!" he said. "You bastard, take a close look at me! But whatever you do, you must do as I tell you. I don't have many methods of governing the town except this one – killing!"

The next day, an order was issued, and all the dogs in town were slaughtered. The reason given was that, when troops marched through the streets, barking would expose their presence.

After the dogs were wiped out, the recruitment of soldiers began. Since there were not enough blunderbusses, the recruits were each armed with a thick club. Therefore, townspeople nicknamed them 'rustic clubs'. Jiwo was placed under curfew every night, and secret question-and-answer codes were made up and issued for communication. The codewords that changed every day included 'Owl', 'Beaver', 'Mountain Lynx' and 'Ungeo Spirit' – all names of living creatures. A townsman who got the code mixed up for the one issued the previous day was beaten to a pulp. Laotuo gave the thugs who carried out the beating a thumbs up, saying: "Good job. Orders are orders. They must be as firm as mountains."

A 'rustic club' reported to Laotuo that no one in town dared to wear glasses any more except for the old man with the family name of Liao, who taught in the elementary school. Hearing the report, Laotuo flew into a rage and yelled: "Drag him here!" Sure enough, the old man turned out to have a pair of glistening glasses on his nose. Before he could say anything, Laotuo grabbed the glasses, tossed them to the ground and crushed them with a few stamps. The old elementary teacher shouted in protest. Sticking his forefinger to the old man's nose, Laotuo said: "If the superior authorities were not forcing me to set up a school, I would…" Instead of finishing the sentence, he made a slicing gesture by forming his hand into a sabre.

The old man Liao was so stubborn that he put on his glasses again soon afterwards. Laotuo demanded that he be dragged to him again and crushed his glasses as he had done before. After the process was repeated another three times, Liao finally gave in.

During this period, the women in town had another female

leader. She was an Amazon with the nickname of Jenny, meaning 'female donkey'. She had eloped with an army low life in earlier years and returned to town soon after his death. She knew how to use a blunderbuss, which was an attribute favoured by Tang Laotuo. One day, Laotuo felt hot and dry after drinking and happened to see Jenny coming his way. He dragged her down to the floor and mounted her. The she-ass protested silently, and Laotuo responded with a sharp slap on her face, saying: "I'm not in the mood to do this for fun! I'm old and I want a son. You'd better behave!"

The next year, Tang Laotuo did indeed have a son. He was called Tang Tong.

CLAY EATERS

Many years later, the people on the hills and plains would record Tang Laotuo's three major accomplishments in the town chronicles: chasing and routing the descendants of the Huo family, exterminating people wearing glasses and cutting down trees.

Tree felling was the most laborious of the three because the vast forest, handed down from previous generations, was too big to remove. Descendants of the Huo family and those who wore glasses were in the minority after all. Trees, trees, damned trees! They were so verdant and endless that they looked frightening and so detestable that the sight of them caused people to grit their teeth audibly. And there were so many living creatures jumping up and down among them, ready to revolt!

Slash and burn was carried out as smoke rose and covered the mountains and the open country. They worked so enthusiastically, as if they were firing mountain guns and blunderbusses, that they just stopped short of shouting the earth-shaking word "Charge!"

Trees were felled for nine years in succession until there was nothing to block the view. The only thing that grew back where the trees had once been were bushes. The only trees around were a few saplings visible in the distance. All good things had to come to an end. The days when the townspeople and the wild creatures in the forest depended on each other, visited each other and mingled with each other were gone once and for all. During the last days of the gradual deforestation, Tang Laotuo had a large public loudspeaker mounted on a high tower to broadcast three days and three nights nonstop to the depth of the forest: "Listen carefully, all you wild creatures! Before all the trees are gone, you must hurry and change back to your human forms, then we'll let bygones be bygones. If you want to beat it, don't wait. Don't wait till we lift your cover and find your hairy animal bodies, then things will get nasty. There aren't many days left. Hurry up! Don't wait till it's too late and blame us for not warning you. OK?"

After the broadcast, only a few strange faces appeared in town. The animal spirits that had been thought likely to surrender to the town did not do so. "Laotuo must have tried to trick them into town because he needs labourers," went the gossip. "They must have feared his blunderbusses. Pull a trigger, and one will go off like thunder. It can make cats and dogs shudder and take to their heels. How differently would the wild creatures in the forest react?"

"Where are they fleeing? The remaining edges of the forest don't have enough room for all of them, and there are no forests elsewhere as big as ours in Jiwo."

"Who knows? They may have fled to foreign countries. Foreigners have blue eyes, and most of them were transformed from wild creatures."

Under the governance of Tang Laotuo, Jiwo had achieved the three major accomplishments. But it did forgot one small issue: food. One morning, it was apparent that there was nothing to eat.

It was the only time that Tang Laotuo felt disheartened as town head. He muttered to himself: I didn't expect to capsize in a stream having sailed on big rivers. He was so hungry that he did not have the strength to carry his blunderbuss. He was not rejuvenated until his wife Jenny butchered a wild cat and cooked it up for him and their son. As a result of the food shortage, all the chickens, ducks, geese, dogs and the few remaining cats in town were cooked up and eaten. Then, the leaves and bark of the surviving trees were also consumed. It was only at this point that they regretted cutting down all the trees. Jenny, who was naturally lanky, was so starved that she could hardly keep her trousers from falling down. "You good-for-nothing!" Laotuo scolded her. "The hungrier you are, the more coquettish you become!"

Pulling her trousers up, Jenny rebutted: "Hey Tuo, watch your foul mouth. Our kid's old enough to understand what you say now. How about going out and trying to get us some food?"

Dragging his blunderbuss, Tang Laotuo went out. Three rustic clubs followed him but collapsed dead halfway. When Laotuo returned three days later, he found over forty of the townspeople starved to death and more than half the survivors to be unconscious. He himself, however, glowed with health, his eyes radiating with vigour and his blunderbuss slung over his shoulder again. Jenny hurried to greet him and was about to say "Help" when her legs gave way. Propping up his wife with one hand and his son with the other, he shouted at those lying on the ground and gazing at him hopelessly: "There's an old saying: 'Everything comes from the earth.' So, why can't we eat clay? This is what I've learned from my visit outside. From today on, let's eat... clay!"

The townspeople looked at each other in silence while Laotuo showed them how. He crouched down, scraped off the topsoil with his hands, scraped again and cast away a piece of rusted iron mixed in the moist dirt, and continued scraping. The clay here is too coarse, he cursed. While shaking off the dirt from his hands, he asked for a spade and started digging. Not until he reached a depth of about a metre, where a layer of the gingerroot-shaped calcareous nodules were laid bare, did he see the dark, oily clay. He took a piece, rolled it into a thin strip in his hands and put one of its tips into his mouth. The whole town started laughing.

Two days later, all the townspeople began to eat clay. On the third day, however, a report came to Laotuo, claiming that more than half of those who had eaten clay were dead. Tang Laotuo was so angry that he burst out: "Those pigs. They ate too much and too fast as soon as they saw something edible. Fine. Some of them were descendants of the Huo family three generations ago anyway, and their stomachs and bowels were too delicate to take clay. They deserved death."

As he was scolding, Tang Tong came and told him that his mum was dead, too. Glancing at the dead Jenny holding her belly with her hands, he sighed: "How come I didn't know that you were a secret descendant of the Huo family?"

Many years passed before the townspeople stopped eating clay. Nevertheless, they were unable to adapt straight away to a grain-based diet. Therefore, they had to mix in some clay. "Those years of starvation will remain imprinted on my mind till I die," said Tang Laotuo to his now adolescent son Tang Tong. "They were actually a good thing in disguise. By starving bad people to death, we now have better ones left. All the descendants of the Huo family are now gone."

Blinking his eyes, Tang Tong asked: "Not a single one left?"

"We can't let our guard down," responded Laotuo, looking to the north in all seriousness. "Didn't that Lord Huo fake his death and sail out to sea on the castle ship? Perhaps, he'll come back from the sea."

Many years later, an event that merited mention in the town's history occurred: Liangzi, who had been missing for decades, came back. He was not alone. With him, there was a girl of five or six – it was said that the woman in a straw raincoat had accompanied them to the outskirts of town, stooped to kiss the girl and left for good.

Most of the elderly townspeople had been starved to death, and the ones that survived no longer recognised Liangzi because he had been away for so long. Look at how this vagabond appeared today! His beard had greyed, his hair was dishevelled and his face was covered with deep wrinkles like withered bark. He was wearing no clothes because he was covered in bark and rags that were strung together. The girl by his side, however, was a different story. Her large, watery eyes, never seen by anyone in town, were unforgettable. She was wearing a small straw raincoat that was woven from dried Indian aster. The glistening raincoat looked exquisite on her.

Since no one could recognise Liangzi, Tang Laotuo did not trust him and his daughter and refused to accept them. He had his kangaroo court table set and interrogated him for three days, during which the only questions he asked again and again were: "Where have you been all these years?", "What did you do for a living?" and "How did you get this girl?"

"I couldn't stay in town at that time," Liangzi answered. "So I volunteered to be a ranger. As for this child, she's an orphan I picked up in the forest. We depended on each other for survival."

"That's bullshit. I won't believe it till I die," said Laotuo, smoking a foreign cigarette.

Tang Tong had been staring at the girl, who was so scared that she hid behind Liangzi. Laotuo continued: "There's nothing to prove you haven't come from the sea and are descendants of the Huo family."

Liangzi shook both his big hands vehemently and replied: "No! No! We're not at all... I'm Liangzi. I just want to return to my ancestral home like leaves must eventually fall to their roots."

At this moment, Tang Tong stooped and whispered something in his father's ear. Laotuo smirked and yelled: "Anyone there? Go and dig a handful of clay for me!"

With the clay, Laotuo said: "In our town, anyone who's not from the Huo family has the guts to eat clay."

Looking around and frowning, Liangzi reached for the clay. He blew on it carefully, culled a few grains of sand and then began to eat slowly.

THREE

TO A STUNNING BEAUTY

"Maizi! Oh, my Maizi! I know what's on your mind. I know there's no more stubborn man in the world than you."

"Good for you."

"When you have a whim, you'll stick with it to the end."

Liao Mai sat up, stared at Mei Di and lay down again, resuming his gaze at the stars outside the window.

"Isn't what I said true?"

"No, it isn't a whim. You think it's like sleeping together, which we do on a whim... No, it's not like that."

"Then like what?"

He moved his gaze from the window and onto her face, which revealed only a pair of sparkling eyes in the gloom. As he got used to the light, he noticed that she had added a little weight and had the makings of a double chin. He ran his hands over her shoulders and arms, then he quickly withdrew them and turned his face away. Looking once more out of the window, he said: "Let's borrow the literary word 'faithful', that is, my faith in myself and in my own heart. Don't laugh at me and say I'm mincing words. If I don't say it this way, I can't find the right words to make myself understood properly. I have only two choices – faith or death. That is, I would rather die if I discovered I was betraying myself."

Mei Di was speechless for a moment, containing her anger by biting her lip. She knew that she might not be as eloquent as her husband, but she fully understood what he meant. She was also aware that he could be really desperate at a crucial moment. She only prayed silently for that moment not to come or, at least, to come at the last second. But she did not know how to stop him, and that was her deepest fear and pain. She had never been so fearful. She feared that her husband did not know what she was afraid of, nor the extent of her fear. However, she knew from the bottom of her heart how much she loved him. She loved every bit of him and for eternity, finding it hard to leave him. Something had certainly happened in their relationship, but it was not enough reason to negate her love. Absolutely not, particularly in these difficult times.

He bent his head behind her, his entire body enshrouded in the dark shadow. He seemed to be asking this nightly darkness though directed the question at Mei Di: "So, you think this farm of ours will really – or definitely – be sold to Tang Tong?"

"I've said we'll put up a desperate fight. We'll fight till the last minute, unless… We must fight with determination."

Prompted by these words, he reached out to touch her mouth and found her teeth clenched shut. What beautiful teeth. White and smooth. A glance at them would stir one's heart. As he felt her mouth, he could hardly contain himself, for his fingers were now held gently between her teeth and caressed by the tip of her tongue. He sat up and huddled in her bosom as if looking for the loaf of bread that he could perpetually claim as his own. Huddled like this for a while, he was surprised by something moist. It was the dripping of her tears. He tried to comfort her but to no avail.

"I'm sorry I beat you so hard the day before yesterday. I'd never normally do that, but I was really confused. I do apologise, my darling. If our Little Beibei knew about the beating, she would never be close to me. What the heck did I do?"

"Our daughter will never know for as long as she lives."

He stroked her back. "I may have been confused. I may have even been crazy all these days. My heart breaks to see Tang Tong eating up all the farmland in the hills and plains, watching him encroaching the villages, fields and pools. Since he became CEO of the Tiantong Group, this gold mine owner has become an omnivorous monster. Look around us! Who can stop him? He has rows of police cars with armed guards marching behind. It's too late to cry. He was already being lenient to us when he asked people of power and influence to come to our door to lobby us – this is too much of a favour. I know he acted this way for your sake. As for me, I've always been his foe."

Mei Di suddenly stopped shedding tears and said: "Please, please stop it, OK…"

Liao Mai had been enjoying his wife's love. In fact, they had been together like this for only ten years, during which time she had been his bride every day. Their happy days came too late and were too hard-earned, with blood and sweat, so to speak. My mysterious jewel that I love so passionately, said Liao Mai to himself. Why is your heart thumping so hard? You're feeling sad? Hopeless? Indignant? No, you must be filled with boundless love, which is the rarest thing in this age. Tonight, it's seducing you and me.

It was late at night, but they could not sleep. They had been like this for days. However, the usual soothing, heart-pouring tone had been replaced by a note of gravity and yearning. Each time they were together like this, he began to mince his words. Fortunately, she was used to it.

"I've been wandering for too long," he said, "and I've got injuries all over, scars upon scars. During the most hopeless days, I was thinking of nothing but you, plus our daughter later on. I was a fugitive and an orphan. Eventually, I entered college and became a government employee, something that would have been unthinkable before. But I couldn't stop wandering because my heart was still hurt. I only knew that, when I found you, I found my home… How many hardships I've endured! You're really special. You've not only survived but also built such a big farm, one that even has a large study just for me. I knew if I were able to come back, I wouldn't care if I had to work harder. It was because we could restart our lives from scratch and exist like human beings again. We'd build our farm like an embroiderer sews a piece of fabric stitch by stitch or an author writes a story word by word. We felt neither fatigue nor hardship. We worked another ten years and have now turned our farm into how it looks today. I've never felt so content and happy, but you already know that.

"I'm reading whenever it rains, day and night. And I'm jotting down some notes. My handwriting's so awful that you may find it illegible. I don't expect you to read it anyway. I told you a few days ago that I'd write a book called *A Secret History of the Jungle*. I'm not kidding, because if I didn't record what's happening in the hills and plains, it would exist only in our dreams. So would our home as well as my experiences of life and death. When things are gone, they'll never come back. I'll record them. I'll record every incident. This wish has been hidden in my mind for thirty to forty years. I believe my father would do the same if he were alive. He'd put on the glasses that would have been crushed by the Tang father and son as they had done time and again before and record every word. Today, his son's going to do it. I'll dedicate the text to one person. When I was taking notes letter by letter, I always had that person in mind."

The night was getting darker and quieter. Splashing sounds came from the distant lake. Liao Mai knew it was his golden-scaled crucian carp, which were fidgeting as much as he was tonight. Yes, only this kind of fish can jump high deep into the night.

"That person? What person?"

Liao Mai was still following his train of thought and said affirmatively: "Yes, I'll dedicate what I've written to that person."

"Who on earth is that person?"

"A stunning beauty."

"I see. She's… Is it true?"

"Yes, it's true," said Liao Mai, sitting up. "But we haven't seen each other for twenty-one years."

"I'm really jealous of this person. Fortunately, you haven't seen each other for twenty-one years. You've been with me."

Mei Di moved her body a little, thereby unwittingly allowing the starlight through the window to shine on Liao Mai's face. She turned to look at her husband and remained silent for quite a while. Another series of sloshing sounds came from the lake. She smiled, but it was an awkward smile, and one that was hardly visible to Liao Mai on this dark night. As she spoke, her white teeth glistened: "So, she's really that good-looking? I've never heard you praise a woman in such a tone."

"Not only is she good-looking, but, as I said, she's also been in my heart, and I'll never forget her. I'll use what time I have left to do this for her, to do it on my own farm."

Mei Di wanted to get off the bed, but whenever she moved, she felt a stab of pain, particularly in the groin. She pressed her hair gently, but her scalp also hurt. It seemed that the pain prompted her to say: "If we must leave our farm, your reading and writing may have to be delayed."

"That's why I'll stay here. You'll see how I do it." Liao Mai's statement was so loud that the night trembled.

What remained of the night was only darkness and silence. Neither of them dared to break it. It was as if a string was stretched in the night, and it was stretched tighter and tighter, threatening to snap. Mei Di could not recall her husband being so seriously sick in the decade since his return. It was truly scary this time. He himself knew that it must have been life-threatening. That was why he asked her to fix the golden carp soup. He had a superstitious conviction about this gunpowder-flavoured fish.

Mei Di recalled something important. But once she asked about it, her question suddenly and unexpectedly eased the tension in the air for the rest of the night: "I want to know where that woman is now."

Liao Mai shook his head. "This is probably the last thing you want to hear – she's dead. The bad news came gradually from different sources, convincing me that she really had passed away."

Mei Di had been holding her breath all the time, but now she breathed a deep sigh of relief.

OVERJOYED

The word 'weekend' sounded so exhilarating and powerful that even a man in his late forties would succumb to it. Whenever it was mentioned, he would become excited, and his eyes would sparkle with joy. "It's the weekend in two days," he said. "My Little Beibei's coming home again."

He always looked forward to seeing his daughter. Nevertheless, his expectations had been dashed of late. She had not returned home for two weekends in a row, something that rarely happened before.

"Our daughter's a grown-up," Mei Di said. "She's now head of a department. You can't imagine how busy she is."

What Liao Mai could not imagine was how an extremely naive little girl had suddenly become a decision-maker. So he gave up imagining and simply relished the image in his mind's eye of her being calm and happy and relished the memory of her growth from a pre-teen to an adult. He never got tired of it. He admired Mei Di's tremendous achievement of giving birth to such a daughter. For this achievement, he would be able to forgive any mistake she might make in future. But he had only thought of the word 'mistake', not 'crime'. He only tried using the term 'crime' in secret. What if it was a crime? His Little Beibei was twenty years old, but her maturity far exceeded her father's expectation. In his eyes, she was always a little girl and an untouchable, delicate flower with dewdrops quivering on the edges of its petals.

Mei Di commented in Beibei's absence: "Our daughter's prettier than I was at her age. She's much better than her mum. She's incorporated both our best attributes."

Liao Mai did not know what to say. He had exhausted all figures of speech used to describe her because smothering love and tenderness could plunge anyone into confusion. Mei Di said to him: "Look how shapely she is with her long legs. Look at her dainty and slender hands. Look at her purple-grape eyes. Until now, I only described others this way figuratively. Our daughter's like a spotted fawn that remains quiet when she's supposed to be quiet and kicks her little legs with 'hoofed feet' when it's time for her to jump around – Maizi, did you notice how pleasant she smells? As soon as she enters a room, she fills it with that smell. It's not the scent of some cologne or rouge..."

Liao Mai enjoyed listening to his wife chattering in this manner, admiring her perception and impartiality. But he never understood why Liao Bei smelled so pleasant if she did not wear any perfume. How come she smell so good?

"What else could it be?" Mei Di said assuredly. "It's her body odour. Out of a thousand or ten thousand girls, she smells the best."

Liao Mai could never forget her expression of assertion and self-confidence along with a certain timidity. "Will she always smell this pleasant?" he asked.

He remembered Mei Di lowering her eyes and murmuring: "Who knows. Normally, a girl won't change at all before her marriage..."

Her remark reminded him of her own body odour when she had been an early teen. That odour was indeed unforgettable because it consisted of the smell of the wilderness, the fragrance of fresh grass, all mingled with a little deer musk. What a fascinating and alluring combination. It had been ubiquitous, emitting first from her armpits and then spreading in a colourless and formless mass to enshroud her whole body. When evening came, all the molecules of the smell were stowed in her thick hair, which had allowed him to bury his face in it for as long as he desired. After she grew more mature, particularly since the night when he had first sneaked back and impregnated her, her body odour intensified – so much so that it nearly caused him to faint on several occasions. What happened after that? He tried hard to recall and piece together the original odour. But he found it very difficult to accomplish. He remembered Mei Di masking the evil smell of the ugly fish that she had been eating more and more excessively with large doses of perfume. He could detect the stench despite the perfume because it was produced from her sweat glands. Whenever she screamed "God! I've really got hold of my man!", a gust carrying the smell of fish, mud and algae would permeate the air around him. He would feel as if this thick odour had lifted him in the air or left him wallowing in mud so that he struggled, drifted and eventually lost the chance of a soft landing. He would crash like a deflating balloon, the air escaping from multiple punctures. He could not help asking his wife what the matter was. His wife kept planting one kiss after another on him with puckered lips that made her big mouth small.

"My silly baby, do you have to ask? Your wife is one of the working class, toiling in the muddy water all day long. How're you feeling? Dizzy? Lightheaded? It's because you have such a great wife! Your wife's not going to brag and say things like 'You can't find such a good wife anywhere else'. You! You lucky guy, wallowing in a jar of honey!"

This was not the first time that Liao Mai found Mei Di transforming into a wild, arrogant and domineering lady of the house while they were enjoying such a sweet, tender moment. He, by contrast, was pushed into a corner, a corner reserved for a clumsy bookworm. Perhaps it was because of this that his wife had told him more than once that he read fewer books or scribbled fewer words, which, she said, were bad habits that he had formed at college – habits that he now had to employ to relieve his boredom.

Little Beibei liked to share whatever was on her mind with her mother. While mother and daughter were chatting away, Liao Mai would always feel a sense of loss. In such a situation, he would inch closer to her, and only then did Beibei pay attention to him. Occasionally, she would hold him by his neck, rub her cheek against his stubble and scream a little. She was almost as tall as her mother now, but she could still make faces. "Beibei! Beibei!" he would call her. He picked a few books in his study for her to read. When she saw him cautiously remove one from the collection, she burst into laughter.

She was a flower in his heart, an eternal flower.

Her musk-like smell perfumed the entire family. This association with the musk deer gave her the nickname 'Little Fawn's Hooves'. Except for her graduation and employment, she had never been a cause for concern to her parents. She had started college a year ahead of schedule. After passing the entrance examination, she was enrolled in a private college to study as an undergraduate. "She was too playful," Mei Di would complain. "Otherwise, she could have entered a top university."

For a long time, she refused to take her 'failure' lying down. She became more anxious when it came to her daughter's employment. Eventually, they breathed a sigh of relief when Beibei found a job in a fairly good joint-stock company. However, about a year later, the company was purchased by the Tiantong Group. It became part of the Tang family in a blink of an eye. After learning of this development, Liao Mai decided that Beibei should leave the company.

"Where will she go? You must first listen to what she thinks," said Mei Di, a bit vexed.

"Well, our daughter can come back home. We've got a farm of a few dozen acres, and we need a helping hand."

'Little Fawn's Hooves' did not take her father's decision seriously. She kissed his ear and showed particular interest in a scar that she had found there, saying: "It must have been left by the frostbite you got when you were wandering in the big mountains."

Her father gave a bitter smile, not being in the mood to talk about his scar. "Daughter," he said, "as soon as the owner of the company changes, you'll have to leave."

"Why?" Beibei laughed. "The staff will still be the same. The change is only nominal. Who knows who that 'Lao Tong' is? Besides, the Tiantong Group has purchased countless companies and enterprises. It won't have much impact on a junior employee like me. We'll still clock on and clock off as usual."

Liao Mai found Mei Di siding wholeheartedly with their daughter. She even said: "All companies are the same. Besides, Beibei's making a little more money now."

That weekend, he barely talked apart from repeating to himself the same sentence: "No, it's not the same."

Time flew by, and more than six months had passed. Beibei was promoted to the head of a department in her company with her salary doubled and her bonuses increased several times. Beside herself with joy, Mei Di said: "Our daughter's really different from others. Now do you see?"

Liao Mai pointed out to her with all seriousness: "She hasn't come back home for the past two weekends."

"It's no big deal. It only means she's busy."

Liao Mai, however, stressed each of his words with bluntness: "I want her to come back home every weekend like before."

The next weekend, Beibei came back. As soon as she entered the house, she rushed to her father's study, shouting: "I heard that someone at home's been mad at me."

"Yes," replied Liao Mai, trying to put on a poker face.

A thick wave of body odour caused Liao Mai to flare his nostrils. Looking up, he found his daughter had gained some weight and was wearing a pair of glistening pendant earrings. She hugged him and was about to leave when he stopped and said: "You're pretty enough not to adorn yourself with gold. It's such a shame that my otherwise perfect daughter has her ears pierced."

Beibei meant to say something but stopped short when, raising her head to look at his gloomy face, she caught sight of a film of tears forming in her father's gloomy eyes. Oh my, she exhaled as she froze with astonishment. Then, she gently removed her earrings.

Beibei never wore any jewellery from that day on.

Another weekend came. A maroon car rolled onto the farm at dusk, startling a few pigeons, which sprang up and then landed behind the vehicle.

"It's Little Fawn's Hooves!" Having sat next to the window for some time, Liao Mai had been expecting her arrival and blurted out her nickname upon seeing the car. He strode out of the room only to feel dizzy, and he slowed down his steps since Mei Di had anticipated him and was already standing in the hallway.

"My Little Fawn's Hooves, come. I've got something important I want to discuss with you."

After dinner, Liao Mai called his daughter to his study. Beibei's pretty face seemed a little pale. As soon as she entered, she sat in the high-backed wooden chair, trying to hide the fatigue that she was feeling behind her beaming face.

"Well, here's what I'm going to discuss with you," said Liao Mai sitting opposite her. "You may have heard that Tang Tong is forcing us to give up our farm, to drive us away. He's going to build his factories, which will extend from the west and the south all the way to the coast. Our farm is in his way."

"How much compensation will he offer us?" asked his daughter. Her smile now vanished.

"Oh, it's far from being a matter of money, my good daughter."

"But we must make sure about the purchase price. As far as I know, Boss Tang paid only a few thousand yuan for a 6.7-acre plot of land like ours around here, which is absurd. On that basis, we'd only get about a million. Of course, our house, woods and other properties would yield some additional money, but perhaps not a lot. With the same amount of cash, we couldn't even buy an equivalent-sized area of wasteland. It's simply not on."

Liao Mai was amazed at his daughter's business acumen. He gaped a while before nodding and saying: "This is an act of bloody plunder. He's been plundering like this all the time. As a last resort, we'd have to abandon our farm and either go out to look for temporary work or find and lease a tract of wasteland in Xihe."

Beibei widened her eyes and said: "Lady Shan has a few houses at the estuary in Xihe. From there, a little over ten kilometres west, there's a water-soaked depression that is uninhabited…"

"Yes, it's there, ten kilometres west of Lady Shan's residence. Tang Tong wants to force us there and has promised much more money than you've calculated. But, my daughter, this is by no means a matter of money."

"How much is it exactly?"

"That, my Little Fawn's Hooves, you must ask your mum. I've said my piece. It's not a matter of money."

"Then what is exactly the… matter?"

Eyeing the still discernible pierced holes in her earlobes, Liao Mai sighed. He held her slender hands in his. When she was young and still in a dreamland, he had seen her only once. He had touched her, and she had held him by his hand with one of her fingers, the forefinger. She remained fast asleep, and he was motionless. He could still clearly remember that moonlit night. He coughed, let go her hands and directed his eyes outside the window. The moon was hidden behind the clouds.

"My daughter, you should've known a little more about the past and about what's happened to the hills and the coastal plain. It's because you've grown up so quickly. The world's changing really fast."

"I often hear you and Mum talking about the past."

"No, that's not enough. Far from enough…"

A RED PUPA

The waning of the period of hunger during the beautiful and mysterious years meant bidding a gradual farewell to the days of eating clay. Many people believed that gods and spirits had been healing the world with a special hunger therapy, that is, to get rid of those with the blood of the Huo family flowing through their veins. During the most difficult times, the townspeople had expected to survive by eating tree bark and leaves. But in the following years when the mounted bandits occupied the mountains and the succeeding few years when Tang Laotuo ruled over the town, there was not a single tree left along the alleys and streets. Viewed from a distance, one or two tall trees were still visible in some of the small villages in the plains. The townsfolk had seen those trees as marks of disgrace to their town. Later, when the magical door had been opened to clay eating, the number of people with glowing, ruddy cheeks began to increase. Unfortunately, these people only appeared puffy and healthy while they were, in reality, extraordinarily feeble. For example, they had to watch the bushes growing wild around them without being able to cut them as they didn't have the strength to lift their hoes.

At that time, young Liao Mai always carried fingertip-sized, fried clay pellets in his pockets. He popped them in his mouth all day long. One morning, he stepped onto the street, only to find the men and women that he had seen the day before all lying on the cold slab-stone pavement. He shook and called out to them, but none woke up. From then on, he learned that an eternal dream meant death. A person who slept without waking up would become an obstacle and had to be removed and buried under the ground. Liao Mai had lost his mother at an early age, so his father tried every means to keep his only son alive. Finding him having difficulty swallowing clay, he fried them into pellets and turned them into much better-tasting treats. Liao Mai became happy again.

Chewing the clay pellets, he rushed out of town and went to the seaside. There, he ran around freely through the bushes where neither humans nor large wild animals lived. They had vanished with the disappearance of the forest. According to rumours circulating among the townspeople, they had transformed into blue-eyed humans and relocated to places on the other side of the ocean. The small creatures in the sand such as lizards, grasshoppers and butterflies became his bosom friends. Each time he came to the bush grove, he would bring a celebrative atmosphere to it. The small creatures would rally around him chattering, trying to learn from him about what was going on in town and watching him unbuttoning his trousers to pee with great curiosity. Gazing at his small, protruding tube squirting water, they exclaimed: "What! So that's the way floods are caused!"

The hedgehogs appeared with their sparkling eyes and blushing little faces. They were even wearing spiked armour. Their appearance pleasantly surprised young Liao Mai. They took him to tour the most hidden parts of the grove, where they found the sweetest berries. As all the bears had left two years earlier, the wild honey available on the beach now belonged to young Liao Mai. Whenever they found a store of honey, the hedgehogs would sing aloud, their singing both as hoarse and as warm as the willow leaves rustled by the wind. Upon hearing it, one could not help collapsing and lying intoxicated on the warm sand, reluctant to rise again.

Young Liao Mai was never able to find wild honey by himself. To do so, he had to rely on the hedgehogs. He would never forget the sweet taste that was sourced from the endless beach and the irreplaceable nectar that could satisfy his eternal craving for sweet things. Its flavour enabled him to appreciate his powerful taste buds for the first time and that the biggest secret in the vast wilderness was nothing but the hidden wild honey.

He had to be taken around the places by the hedgehogs, and he enjoyed all the fun amid their singing and clapping. One day, he was lying on the warm sand for several hours, listening to the hedgehogs coughing continually – whenever they stopped coughing, they were nowhere to be found. He looked up at the drifting white clouds while seeing in his mind's eye his father stealthily putting on his glasses, peering out of the window from time to time and then stowing them away at the mere sound of something astir. As he hallucinated, he felt hungry. He reached into his pocket for the clay pellets but in vain. He yearned for the wild honey so much that his heart ached, and his hunger was gnawing him to the bone. He dug and scraped the sand with both hands to search for any clay pellets he might have dropped accidentally. He dug and scraped until he found something glittering and the colour of magenta. He dug a little deeper and the entire thing was exposed in the sun: a moth chrysalis as big as a thumb and as red as a jujube fruit with three eye-like dots on its body. He gingerly scooped it up and held it in his hands. As soon as he pressed its bottom, its sharp head began to wiggle gently. He was convinced that it was talking in its own language as a mute man communicates with his hands.

"Where can I find my hedgehog friends? Please help me, little red pupa. If you can move your sharp head in a certain direction, it would be as good as someone pointing with their finger."

He begged and gazed, and saw it really moving its sharp head, pointing to the southwest. In the direction the red pupa pointed, he walked and walked until he saw two large hedgehogs. They were hugging each other tight, busying themselves in mating. That was why they did not have time to visit him. They asked him very shyly to look away, saying that what they were doing was pleasant but laborious. "Of course, you can't understand it fully at your young age…"

He faced the other way for half an hour. Every now and then, he couldn't help peeping back, which annoyed the hedgehogs very much. They said later: "If we weren't good friends, we wouldn't forgive a Peeping Tom like you. This is a very important matter and requires courage, caution, care and love. What we did doesn't happen all the time, but when it does, it can't be disrupted by either wind or rain. Anyway, you're too young to understand what we've been saying." Concealing his unhappiness, young Liao Mai hung his head down as he listened to them complaining.

After venting their anger, everything went back to normal, and they led him on their search for wild honey again. While enjoying the honey, little Liao Mai asked something that he immediately regretted: "Which is more pleasant, eating wild honey or doing what you did?" The hedgehogs seemed to take offence again as they snorted and belched. But they eventually forgave Liao Mai, putting his indiscretion down to his young age.

"Only imbeciles and foolish beggars ask such a question or make such a comparison. Nothing in the world is more pleasant than the thing we did."

Young Liao Mai looked at them bewildered and departed while licking the honey from the corner of his mouth. He carefully held the red pupa in his hands. Each time he kissed it or touched it with his cheek, it would wiggle with excitement.

He talked to the red pupa and blew on it as he walked. Thinking that it might be feeling cold, he held it close to his chest. When it touched the skin of his chest and abdomen, it began to wriggle shyly. The wriggling gave him a kind of unspeakable sensation as smooth and cool as jade. What a miraculous beach, it turned out to have everything! He looked up at the fuzzy bushes merging with the remote outline of the mountains and the sky. He looked around and suddenly felt that he had lost his bearings: "Where's the north and south. What direction is town?"

He panicked, his heart pounding hard and fast. He was afraid that his father was worrying about him because the same thing had been happening to every family lately: a child goes out never to return. They walk and walk until they suddenly drop dead and become 'road fall', so to speak.

Then he thought of the jewel next to his chest. So he picked up the red pupa again with three of his fingers and said: "My good friend pupa, please help me. Please point to the direction of town. I don't know how to go back home now."

The red pupa leaned towards his face as if to gaze at him for a while and then twirled its sharp head, which eventually stopped moving and pointed in the direction of a cluster of dark, low-lying clouds. With tears in his eyes, he said: "Now I know! I know!" He strode towards the clouds.

Young Liao Mai returned home before dark. Upon hearing the door squeak, his father quickly put his glasses away.

From that day on, young Liao Mai could traverse the vast wilderness without concern or fear. Led by the red pupa, he ran into more pairs of hedgehogs in the middle of their lovemaking. He could not help complaining about them, saying: "You're always doing this. How much time have you been wasting?"

"We can't help it," the hedgehogs rebutted. "It's the season. We can't miss the season." They moaned as they humped.

Unless they were disturbed for no good reason, the hedgehogs were pretty friendly and happy, either singing songs or reciting verses. One day, they were particularly joyful. They sat in a row around a willow tree, clapping in unison while chanting: "We hedgehogs are happy. / Together we're lucky, / Hand in hand we seek honey. / Mind your skin if you touch me."

"Why do we have to mind our skin?"

"Because we have spines all over."

Early one evening, Liao Mai was sitting on the white sand and talking to his red pupa when he was startled by a mass of burning heat. He turned to look, only to see a woman peeping from behind a tree. He immediately recognised her as the girl named Shanzi who lived in the same town. She had become plump, beaming with dimples on her cheeks. She had been gazing at the red pupa in his hand. Now she sat down close against him.

Young Liao Mai would never forget that evening. On subsequent occasions, whenever he closed his eyes, he would be able to hear his heart thumping as loud as the remote rumbling of spring thunder. He feared her eyes, her mouth and her breasts, each as large as a baby's head. He wriggled, trying to escape as soon as he could. "You can't move!" she said, reaching her hand out and asking if she could take a look at the red pupa. Liao Mai hid it hastily. Then, she said panting: "Hey, how about this. If you hand me your red pupa, I'll let you touch them – here!" She was pointing at her breasts.

That moment, or rather the afterglow of that moment, was so hot that it was almost melting young Liao Mai. Gazing at her breasts, young Liao Mai shook his head violently. But she caught one of his hands before he knew it and pressed it against her bosom where she moved it in a circular motion. "You touched them! You touched them! So, give me the red pupa!"

With that, she put her weight on his legs and abdomen. Bent on getting hold of the red pupa, she unwittingly tore his trousers in the commotion. As he struggled, young Liao Mai carefully protected his precious pupa, murmuring to himself: Good Heavens! Oh, gods of the beach, please help me quickly! I'm being bullied by a female mounted bandit.

His prayers were answered. He felt his teeth growing in bulk until he finally could not endure the pressure and he bit down, in the process catching her chest in his mouth. What a fleshy chest! The female mounted bandit gave off a scream and catapulted herself from him. Stretching her legs in agony, she fell upon her back.

Young Liao Mai took to his heels.

From that experience, he learned that the beach was too vast to be comprehended and that not all the big animals had been decimated. His belief was reinforced by an incident that took place later. One day, his red pupa stubbornly pointed in the same direction for some unknown reason. He felt compelled to walk as he was directed. He walked about an hour till thick fog began to fall. Gradually, he could hear the sea rumbling and animals singing their hopeless songs. He was stunned and rushed forward. As he ran, he felt the oncoming fog rubbing at his cheeks and making them sore.

The coastline loomed through the dense fog with a rising, rumbling wall of white-foamed breakers. Seagulls and some other nameless birds fluttered up and down and screeched. But all their screams and screeches were drowned out by the roar of the waves and the wails of an animal. Only then did he realise why the gulls were crying so sharply. He found them circling above something below. They were terrified by that big thing, so terrified that they kept screaking their warnings to each other.

Young Liao Mai finally plucked up enough courage to walk up close. He saw a huge black creature near the surging breakers. It had the broad face of a human being and four fins or hands spreading in all directions. Its belly was large and prominent, and white liquid oozed from the nipples on its purplish-red breasts. Next to the huge creature was a person, kneeling down. Rubbing his eyes, Liao Mai saw clearly that it was a woman, and she was none other than Shanzi. She was attentive, her hair ruffled by the wind and waves.

Whenever hair covered her face, she would utter a curse. It turned out that she was attending to the big sea creature's private parts, which were opening and closing rhythmically with the red and yellow hairs around them. Fresh blood seeping out of the creature smeared Shanzi's hands and arms. Liao Mai gradually figured out what Shanzi was saying: "Take pity on the 'sea hog' mother. Take pity on her, you nautical and heavenly gods and goddesses. Help the mother and her baby. Take pity on them."

That day, the misty fog was imbued with the smell of blood and the terrifying wails of the dugong. After a quarter of an hour, her wailing stopped. Young Liao Mai saw Shanzi, covered all over with foam, sand and seagrass, bending her upper body down as if to pray in prostration – she was biting off the umbilical cord with her teeth. A crying young life gesticulating with its short limbs was born. She held it up and looked it over, seemingly trying to tell its gender. At the same time, young Liao Mai saw clearly what that newborn monster looked like; its eyes were closed, its face ruddy, its body ginger-yellow and its two pairs of fins like hands and feet. It also had sparse whiskers around its gills.

This incident happened between late autumn and early winter. For the rest of his life, young Liao Mai would remember the rolling waves, the wails of the dugong and particularly the blood-stained Shanzi. From that day on, he no longer seemed to hate that woman.

That winter was especially cold. Throughout the season, young Liao Mai protected the red pupa from the cold air by placing it in his bed or in cotton wadding. It wriggled against his skin at night. It rubbed against him rhythmically and he responded by rubbing its smooth body with his cheeks while talking to it.

He snuggled with it until spring slowly arrived. After eating clay pellets throughout the autumn and winter, Liao Mai found the nights darker and his sleep deeper. When he woke up one morning, he saw the sky already brightening with the light of dawn. As usual, the first thing he did was reach for the red pupa – but it was not there any more. He rubbed his eyes and looked out of the window. "Gosh!" he blurted out. "What a big, colourful butterfly." It was perched on the windowpane, its open wings made transparent and glistening by the sunlight that was shining upon them through the window paper.

Tears welling up in his eyes, he knew that spring had arrived, and that the creature would fly away. He would have to say goodbye to it that very morning.

GOLDEN STRAW RAINCOAT

Amazing news always spreads quickly. In just a few hours, the whole town had become aware of the return of Liangzi, who also brought with him a little girl that he had adopted. When asked "Who's Liangzi", the elderly had to tell his story from the beginning. But it was a difficult story to tell because it was a complicated legal case as well as an obscure historical episode.

"Son of a gun! How can a man be so showy?" said the young people, not knowing the whole picture. They then all rushed to the big house on Stone Street to see Liangzi with their own eyes. Unfortunately, Liangzi's troubles did not end there. The door to the big house remained closed, and the Tang father and son were still interrogating Liangzi to get to the bottom of his disappearance and reappearance.

Rubbing their eyes, elderly women said: "What's the matter with him. What does he think our town is? How can he come and go at will? I'm afraid that he needs to spill the beans."

For two days in a row, Liangzi and the little girl stayed next door to the big house. They were in fact under house arrest. In addition to their identification, their residential registration was also problematic. Liangzi had been registered before, but it was later annulled automatically.

"Why?" asked Liangzi. "I'm not dead yet."

Tang Laotuo snorted: "The wild creatures jumping up and down in the forest are not dead, either. Who would register them as residents? To my mind, you've given yourself up to the wild beasts these past years."

Liangzi was speechless.

As Liangzi was able to eat clay without incident, he was finally able to demonstrate his lack of association with the Huo family. Then they had to figure out who the little girl was. A few days before, Tang Laotuo had also had some clay brought over and served to her, but she sniffed it with disgust and ran away screaming.

"Eat it. Open your mouth and eat it!" Laotuo had yelled with anger. The little girl burst into tears.

Liangzi begged him: "Please spare her. She's still a child."

All the while, Tang Tong had either stood aside looking here and there or loitered around the little girl. He spoke up for her: "She's too young to know anything. How about asking her to eat it in a few years? She can't escape anyway."

Laotuo relied heavily on his only son for assistance, so he snorted, waved his hand and finally relented: "So, let's wait a while then."

Since first setting eyes on her, the townspeople noticed that the little girl was always wearing her straw raincoat, whether she was eating or sleeping or even answering nature's call. When she went to the toilet, the prickling hair over her straw raincoat glistened in the morning or evening light. Rubbing their eyes, a few 'rustic clubs', namely Tang Laotuo's thugs, wondered what it was that was blinding them. Curious about what was going on in the coastal forest, they dragged the little girl over and asked her a lot of questions, none of which she refused to answer. Speaking of the straw raincoat, she told them that her mum had made it for her from a kind of golden-leaved aster plant that her mum had collected with her own hands. She said that her mum also wore the same kind of raincoat. Someone vaguely remembered seeing a woman in a straw raincoat accompanying her and her father to the outskirts of town before leaving them. "So that was your mum?" The little girl shook her head and then nodded. When she found their attention momentarily diverted, she dashed back to the big house.

The story about the little girl with the glistening straw raincoat and about a woman in a similar raincoat accompanying her and Liangzi back to town spread in an increasingly bizarre fashion. Someone shared his doubts with Tang Laotuo, saying: "Originally a romantic young man, Liangzi was bound to interact with the spirits of the wild creatures in the forest where he'd been wandering for so many years. The little girl may have been the offspring of a relationship between him and a hedgehog spirit. Now that the forest's gone, they've got nowhere to live, and they have no choice but to resettle here."

Taking a deep puff of his pipe, Tang Laotuo responded: "Well, that does makes sense." To dispel his suspicion, he repeatedly sent for Shanzi to examine the father and daughter. She could identify Liangzi simply by sniffing him with her eyes closed, but as she had grown into Lady Shan today, her affections for him had chilled to permafrost.

At the mention of the name Liangzi, she could not help sneezing and added a "Pah" when she finished. As for whether the little girl had been born to a hedgehog spirit, Shanzi said to her inquirer: "There's no mistake about it. It'll be clear when you take her clothes off."

After Tang Laotuo told this to Tang Tong, the son punched his fist in his palm and said: "Shanzi's the smartest. Let the barefoot doctor examine her, and we'll watch nearby."

The barefoot doctor was old. He spoke in a muffled voice due to a cleft palate, and he lisped due to his unusually large tongue. The Tang father and son liked him because he was prone to prescribe large doses of medicine. All the other townspeople would halve the prescribed dose before daring to take it. The barefoot doctor separated the father from the daughter and gave him a brief checkup by looking at his pupils and the coating of his tongue and then by pinching his testicles a few times. In the end, he waved a hand to signal an end to the procedure.

Now it was the little girl's turn. She was initially reluctant to undress, but after persistent coaxing by the barefoot doctor, she finally gave in. She was, however, captivated by the doctor's stethoscope. All smiles, she took off her floral upper garment and eventually her pants. Right at that moment, the Tang father and son burst into the room. As soon as they entered, they cast their eyes on the girl's naked body, oblivious of the horror written on the old barefoot doctor's face. The father and son were truly stunned by the sight of her body, which was covered all over with a layer of velvet fuzz exuding fluorescent hues in the dim ambient light of the room. The fine hair formed a V shape at the base of her spine and spread around to form a dense mass over her lower abdomen. She seemed not the least bashful as she looked at the people beside her in a friendly and somewhat curious manner. Tang Tong could not close his gaping mouth as he massaged her entire body with his eyes. He then fixed them on her chestnut-size breasts before moving them to her lower abdomen and crotch. The glistening velvet fuzz in those areas now appeared finer and yet darker.

"It can't be more obvious," said the old barefoot doctor as he took off his stethoscope and stepped out of the room with the Tang father and son side by side. "The fuzz on her back was transformed from the spines of a hedgehog. The fuzz on her abdomen, well, can be counted as pubic hair."

Laotuo had been pleasantly surprised. But now, drawing a long face, he gazed at the skyline in the west and said: "I wonder if we'll bag her and sink her in the river today or tomorrow..."

Tang Tong's mind had been diverted by lust. When he overheard his father's suggestion, he blurted out: "Dad! Don't do it! Keep the little girl for me no matter what. Let's deal with her when she grows up. Otherwise, it'd be too late to have regrets. We'd mess things up. We'd mess things up big time."

Seeing his son so stressed that his eyes widened and his face reddened, Tang Laotuo gave up on the idea. When the three went back into the room, the little girl had dressed herself and was wrapped in her glistening straw raincoat again.

With a blunderbuss slung over his shoulder, Tang Laotuo shrugged and grumbled: "Damn it. Why do you have to wear that thing all day long?"

"Let her wear it," said the old barefoot doctor. "Let her wear it. Taking it off is as good as skinning her."

KICK AND KICK

Since then, the town boasted a girl named Mei Di. In her glistening straw raincoat, she played games with other girls such as shuttlecock kicking and hopscotch. Later, she went to school. She was popularly referred to as 'The Hedgehog Kid'. Everyone had seen her, and they were all amazed at her unique beauty, saying that her complexion and features were all one of a kind, different from those of any other girl they had ever seen before. Her eyes, in particular, would be etched in their memories. "This is a sprite! A little sprite!"

Lady Shan had now become a recluse in town. Only occasionally did she appear on Stone Street. She lived most of the time at the estuary in Xihe, where there were a few connected mud houses that were inherited from her late chief-fisherman husband. Perhaps she began to stay in town after he had gone fishing at sea. Tang Tong often tagged after her like her shadow, following her through Stone Street and to the big house at the estuary. One day, he was sauntering with her on the street when he saw a crowd at a crossroads. When Lady Shan asked him what was going on, Tang Tong told her that people were teasing the little Hedgehog Kid and asked if she would come along to take a look. Twitching her lips and snorting, she said: "I'd better not. I'd get so angry on seeing her that I might tear her to pieces. I've seen enough of this type of half-breed on the beach."

Tang Tong was aware of her deep hatred for Liangzi. She would not forgive him even in death.

Tang Tong also liked to ramble alone with his blunderbuss, shunning the company of even a single rustic club. He leaned against the wall in an alley leading to the elementary school for a while and then paced up and down it. Night fell, and the moon rose. The schoolchildren streamed out. Mei Di walked into the alley by herself. Tang Tong blocked her way, but she was not intimidated at all. He then coaxed her to an abandoned livestock pen, where he demanded: "Let me check you up. I'd like to see how the glistening velvet fuzz looks today."

Little Mei Di nodded and removed her school backpack. Seeing her acting too slowly, he tore open her blouse, his eyes glowing like a wild beast. He found the fine hair on her back a little sparser though not having shed completely. Only the hair on her lower abdomen looked the same as he had seen before. He kept rubbing and caressing it, enjoying the feel of its velvet-like smoothness. He could also sense the distinct coolness of her small breasts, which resembled two peaches hanging from a tree in late autumn. Panting heavily, he cast his cumbersome blunderbuss away and hurriedly took off his trousers. Pointing to his robust manhood, he asked: "Do you know what this is?"

Little Mei Di glanced at it and then looked up at him in the moonlight. She answered honestly: "Yes, I've seen it on donkeys, too."

Tang Tong burst out laughing: "Let me tell you. This thing is more powerful than a blunderbuss!"

She looked confused. He hugged her closely for a while. Then, he said trembling: "Grow quickly and put on some weight. You belong to nobody but me. Do you realise that? My dad gave me permission. If anyone dares to lay a finger on you, I'll strangle him to death. No, I'd bake him in a pan. I'll bake him till his fat burns to smoke."

Tang Tong stretched out one of his legs and rolled up his eyes to make his point with the gesture of death, which gave little Mei Di a shudder.

Mei Di was growing fast and seemed to have instantly matured into a young lady. She would be going to a new school out of town next year. Having grown out of that shrinking straw raincoat, she stowed it away carefully. Before long, her adoptive father Liangzi died of illness. On the day of his burial, she cried so much that she fainted. It was a chilly and wet autumn day. The mourners gradually left the burial ground. She opened her eyes, only to be frightened by a heavy woman standing nearby. She was fixing her red, swollen eyes upon her.

Later, Mei Di learned that the bulky woman at the burial ground was Lady Shan.

Mei Di became an orphan. She tried desperately to avoid Tang Tong. Carrying his blunderbuss and wearing a pair of leather boots, the stout young man had more than once chased her, yelling: "Do we have to wait for the wedding day to be together? A popular saying goes: 'You need patience to sleep with a hedgehog.' Dammit, I'm so impatient. You're going to torture me to death!"

Liao Mai's handsome face had flashed by Mei Di once but left no impression on her at first. As a result, she was shocked when she met him later in that alley. She exclaimed to herself: Good Heavens! Who's that? Look at his features. When my father was young, he must have looked the same. Look at this guy! His eyes are frighteningly beautiful, his nose is straight and his lips regularly angulated. Such a wonderful young man could only appear in my dreams. I wish he was my biological brother. Then I wouldn't be an orphan any more... As she was contemplating these thoughts, her heart thumped. She blinked her eyes and then fixed them on his face. Her feet appeared to be nailed to the slab stones on which she stood.

The same sensation was true for Liao Mai, who felt as if he was scorched by the sun.

Over a period of days, they became better acquainted, to the extent that they were inseparable. When they held each other in their arms, they knew intuitively where to direct their hands. Liao Mai finally learned about everything. For the rest of his life, he would be grateful to her for her generosity and trust, baring her life to him without reservation. He would always remember her wild-honey-coloured complexion and her lingering kiss. Finally, when he caught her off guard by suddenly placing his hand over the dense and fuzzy golden hair below her abdomen, she looked up and asked: "Don't you feel disgusted?"

"I, I seem to have dreamed of you waiting for someone on a brilliantly golden grassland, and that someone is me."

Tears rolled down her cheeks.

Tang Tong showed up on the third night of their rendezvous. A dozen or so blunderbusses with rusted bayonets were held level against them to prevent them from moving. After a little while, they were escorted to separate places. Liao Mai was dragged away a few steps when Tang Tong gave him a hearty slap on the face along with a barrage of expletives: "Are you courting death? Is that a proper place for you to touch?"

Tang Tong shut himself with Liao Mai in a dark room for fifteen minutes, determined to establish what exactly had been going on. When he learned that they had done nothing but hug and chat, Tang Tong jumped with laughter.

That night, Liao Mai was pressed to the ground by a few thugs and stripped of all his clothes. At Tang Tong's command, a thug brought in a wire brush and struck Liao Mai hard in his crotch. Each strike broke the skin in numerous places, and the area was soon covered in blood. Liao Mai gritted his teeth. As he was holding his breath, veins bulged on his forehead. But despite the pain, he did not make a single sound.

He was tied to a pole stark naked. Tang Laotuo arrived, followed by a throng of thugs. Pointing at Liao Mai's lower abdomen, the old man explained to them with a smirk: "Do you see? Do you know why he's bleeding? Because he's too bold for his tender age. He dared to sleep with a hedgehog but was pricked by its spines." The frightened thugs looked down at the wound before bursting into laughter.

Everyone except the Tang father and son had left. Laotuo asked his son to untie Liao Mai and pushed him against a wall, and then demanded: "I want to know who you think you are, a member of the Liao family who dares to eat from my son's bowl?"

Liao Mai glared at him and clammed up. "Answer me!" screamed Laotuo, flying into a rage. Liao Mai covered his ears with his hands. After Laotuo pulled them away, he put them back over his ears again. Laotuo was infuriated and yelled: "Anyone there?"

The thugs tied Liao Mai again as he struggled fiercely. Puffing out a circle of smoke, Laotuo produced a rusted nail, moistened it with the tip of his tongue and ordered the thugs to pin Liao Mai's ear to the wall. Bang! He drove the nail into his ear, and blood dripped from it. Now, Liao Mai could no longer turn his head.

Laotuo then shouted in his ear: "You son of a bitch! Sooner or later, you'll die a more miserable death than your father did. You tried to cover your ears, eh? Now you have to listen even if you don't want to. Fuck you, son of a bitch! You've dreamed a fucking daydream and got nowhere. That woman is reserved for my son. He can sleep with her whenever he likes, and you can only look on helplessly. Listen clearly and carefully, or you won't even be able to fart your report to the King of Hell!"

Laotuo screamed and jumped. His wrath even scared Tang Tong standing by his side. After he finished, Laotuo stepped aside to catch his breath, sweat streaming down his shrivelled and hardened chest. His eyes darting from his father to Liao Mai, Tang Tong exploded as if he had just awakened from a dream. He charged screaming towards Liao Mai and began to kick at his ankles. He kicked and kicked until they were mangled. Patting his knees, Laotuo cheered his son on, shouting: "Kick and kick! Kick and kick! Kick and kick."

Liao Mai's ankles were lacerated, exposing the bones. Blood oozed from his feet.

"Kick and kick! Kick and kick! Kick and kick…"

FOUR

A GREAT FOOLISH BEGGAR

IN FRONT of him was the dark night near dawn. Behind him was a blaze of firelight. Rushing wind buffeted Liao Mai's ears; twinkling stars lit up his eyes. Columns of chilly autumn air descended from the sky, attempting to extinguish the demonic fire and scatter the diabolic smoke all over the ground. He ran nonstop, like crazy. The only thing on his mind was to shake off the fire dragon hot on his heels – it dashed from Stone Street and nearly caught his fluttering shirt. He could not afford to look back or stop to rest for a second. The Tang father and son had mobilised three generations of aardwolf descendants to chase him from all directions armed with blunderbusses. They were ready to tear him to pieces after forcing him into the centre of their encirclement. With a final glance, he caught sight of Tang Laotuo, lantern in hand, shouting repeatedly in the distance: "Oh, my God! I was lying on the *kang* having a smoke when the rebel nearly cut off my face. Oh, my God! It really hurts. This rare seed of a rebel! This damned son of a bitch! Catch him and bring him back to me. I'll chop him up and boil him. I won't spare his life."

Tang Tong echoed: "Will not spare his life. Will not spare his life."

The aardwolf descendants followed suit: "Don't spare his life.

Don't spare his life. We'll lasso him with our leather loops and catch him with our iron hooks. We'll bring him to Lord Tang. We'll chop this son of a bitch in half."

Ah, dense autumn frost, fall harder. Quickly fall and kill Laotuo's fiery dragon. Drive the mad aardwolves back to their den in an instant. Liao Mai was so anxious that blood almost seeped from his eyes. The fiery circle was closing in around him. He could see the blunderbusses now. He opened his desperate eyes wide and saw the firelight and, through it, Tang Laotuo's cheek, which was covered with blood running down to his neck and dyeing a large patch of his shirt red. Beside him, Tang Tong levelled his magic weapon, a blunderbuss equipped with a round magazine for rapid firing. Once activated, it could spit a volley of bullets to riddle its target with a sound that went takka-takka-takka. Even the nimble spotted leopard could not dodge them. What am I going to do, Liao Mai asked himself. He had been driven to the last ditch, from which there was no escape. He looked about anxiously, wishing to leap onto a tree – but, unfortunately, there was not a single tree in the entire town of Jiwo. He was now cornered to the edge of a cliff, facing imminent death. Widening his bloodshot eyes and screaming, he darted towards the cliff edge with an endless abyss down below.

He would rather smash himself to pieces with his eyes wide open than fall into the hands of the Tangs. He was about to reach the edge when the magic weapon with the round magazine began to sound takka-takka, kicking up a wall of dirt and dust behind him. At the same time, a miracle happened. He saw a snow-white roe deer dashing out beside him at the clifftop. He jumped after it. The roe deer looked up into his eyes while he was falling. Then, arching its body, the deer received him and leapt back to the top of the cliff carrying him on its back.

Later, whenever he recalled his escape from the deadly encirclement, Liao Mai would first remember the dashing white roe deer. Carrying the blood-stained orphan on its back, the deer scurried and scampered, shaking off the pursuing aardwolf descendants. "I recognised you as a member of the Liao family," it said. "You used to stroll on the beach all day long. But when I heard the reports of the blunderbusses, I knew you were going far away."

He could hardly distinguish his thumping heart from the chattering of the roe deer along the way, but what was more distinct was the rushing wind, drowning everything with its whistles. Carrying him on its back, the white roe deer darted like an arrow and soon left the valley and the windy mountain pass behind. He could envisage Tang Laotuo milling around like an exasperated dragon. Now, he himself was riding away on the gently undulating clouds. Suppressing tears of gratitude, he kept murmuring: "Oh, White Roe Deer, I'll never forget you, my saviour. One day I'll return and avenge myself and my father. Besides, I've promised Mei Di that I'll definitely come back."

Mumbling in this manner, he started to feel dizzy and lose consciousness. In his dream, the white roe deer gently licked the top of his head and his cheek, stood a little while and departed slowly, wagging its tail.

A whole day or a night? Liao Mai did not know how long had passed. But anyway, it was already daybreak. Liao Mai felt sore lying in the sun. In fact, it was the pain that awakened him. Wondering where he was, he was alarmed to discover bloodstains on his arms and chest. Looking further down, he saw his calves mangled and covered with shrivelled blades of grass clogged with dried blood. After removing the grass, he found his skin split and his flesh torn, exposing the ankle bones. He closed his eyes and inhaled through clenched teeth to fight off the pain. Keeping his eyes closed, he recalled the long days and nights and remembered what had caused the bloody wound to his ankles: a hard leather boot that kicked and kicked at them while he was fixed to a wall with a rusted nail driven through his ear.

He remembered everything, including the desperate escape, but he did not know when he had blacked out, how long he had remained unconscious and where he now was.

He sat up with great effort and then clambered to his feet by grasping a false indigo-bush plant. Any further movement risked opening his wounds. His ankles hurt even more. The pain was becoming unbearable. He strained his neck to look around, trying to figure out how far he was from town. He could not see a great distance since the area was surrounded by a succession of mountains and valleys. All around him were nothing but clods of earth, bushes and white rocks glaring in the sun. Managing to calm himself down for a moment, he figured out that he had been running in a southerly direction the whole night. He knew it because the plain and beach were to the north of the town. He felt lucky that he had run in the right direction; if he had gone to sea, it would be the end of his life. He just had no idea where he was now and he was concerned that those aardwolves might pick up the scent of his blood.

Gnawing hunger pangs dulled the spasms of pain. He was aware that he had to prevent the wounds on his legs and ankles caused by the kicking from cracking and bleeding. He was desperate for them to continue to function since his fugitive life had only just begun. He knew that a kind of green artichoke growing in the wild could stop bleeding. So he started searching. He limped a few steps and saw Chinese plantain, shepherd's purse and false bindweed, but there was not a single artichoke in sight.

"Where are you hiding? Please help me. If I keep bleeding like this, I'll pass out and die in this valley."

As he muttered to himself, he stooped down and pushed aside the bushes and the cogon grass that were in his way. His hands were soon pricked by the thorns of a Maackia hupehensis bush. His face brightened as he saw something growing in a patch of moist, rocky soil: they were indeed artichokes! There were only three plants with withered leaves, but he was so happy that he hummed. He hung his head down like a lamb and chewed the roots and leaves into a paste. He then pressed the paste on his ankles. A sharp pain made him scream. Gritting his teeth, he tore a strip from his clothes and bandaged the plastered wound. After completing the task, he felt his forehead streaming with perspiration and his clothes drenched with sweat.

Throughout the day, Liao Mai plodded towards the sun. This is the path of my life and the path of my return, he told himself again and again. I'll come back along this path one day. His mind gradually became clearer, and he continued telling himself: You must bite the bullet and survive. Only then can you go back to Jiwo.

Liao Mai came to a brook, and he drank greedily. A small fish swimming near the bed caught his attention and he gazed at it for a while. He scooped some water to wash his face, but once his ears got wet, they started hurting badly, and he remembered the long lacerations on them. He wanted to pee but found his undergarment stuck to his lower abdomen. He had to wet it bit by bit with the brook water and carefully separated the fabric from his mangled genitalia. As he closed his eyes and inhaled with pain, he gulped in mouthfuls of cold air, which caused his whole body to shake violently.

Please get me through this day and let me sleep in a stack of hay on my first day of hiding. As long as I can sleep, I can regain my strength. But now, I can't move any more. Despite holding these thoughts, he continued walking. He told himself to trudge on while he was still breathing. Climb over the hill ahead as soon as possible. You may find shelter from wind and rain on the southern side and enough food to keep you alive.

It took him a long time to clamber up the big slope and over the ridge. The hill was harder to climb than it had first seemed. Thistles and thorns grew amid the dirt-covered rocks, and they soon pricked his hands and feet. But he had no time to worry about such things because he had to press on and run for his life. By now, the fog at the foot of the hill had mostly dissipated. He could see figures in the distance carrying their burdens, walking on the winding dirt road. They might be going to market, taking manure to the fields or carrying firewood back home. He did not know whether to mingle with them or keep his distance. After watching for a while, he staggered to his feet, and only then did he find it so hard to take a single step. He stumbled as soon as he lifted his foot, and once he closed his eyes, he would never want to open them again. He began to wonder if his time was really coming. He feared that the ominous moment could be approaching. He opened his eyes wide with what strength he had left to scan the area down the hill. He knew that he could survive so long as it was not owned by the Tang family.

But the biggest obstacle on the path to his survival was hunger. A ravenous wolf had sneaked into his body and, since the night before, had been gnawing at him and eaten everything in his stomach. Now, it began to bite his spine. I have to feed it something or it will break my backbone, he thought. But what to feed it? He opened his mouth, but there was nothing to chew. He was feeling anxious when he heard a familiar voice that seemed to come from the unseen world. It clearly belonged to his father. His father was shouting hoarsely: "My son, don't hesitate any more. Hurry. Use the last resort known only to us Jiwo townspeople – eat clay." After swallowing the first mouthful of clay, Liao Mai felt the world going black.

He would know later that the long path of life could sometimes darken abruptly. The darkness could be scary, inky and primordially chaotic.

When he woke up from this long and yet short, dark night, he still had the piece of clay in his mouth. It prevented him from speaking. Sitting opposite was a white-haired old woman, who was carefully removing the clay from his mouth. She had been looking at him hopelessly when he opened his eyes. Slapping her knee, she exclaimed: "You've finally come to... Good Heavens! Where did you come from? How did you manage to crash to the bottom of the cliff and hurt yourself like this? My good boy, why don't you say anything? Can you hear me?"

The old woman continued working to get the clay out. After a long while, he could finally utter in a drawl: "I..."

"Whose child are you?"

"I..." Liao Mai was still unable to speak due to the clay. With great effort, he opened his eyes, only to find himself lying on a clay *kang*. He coughed and stuck his tongue out but still could not complete a sentence. The grandmother pried his mouth open, sighed and took out another clog from under his tongue. "You can't speak because your mouth's full of clay. Are you a 'foolish beggar'?"

This time, Liao Mai heard every word of what she said and, looking at her, nodded. Then, dropping his eyelids, he went back to sleep. When he woke up, it was close to dusk. The grandmother returned with a bowl of hot soup. She lifted his head, laid it on her crossed legs and fed him one spoonful after another. Liao Mai could not determine the flavour at first, but as he savoured it bit by bit, he found it the best soup he had ever eaten. A strong taste of umami surged into his chest, swirled around his stomach and rippled out in the lower abdomen. As it warmed him up he could almost hear the cracking of ice in his body, and, while gaining the freedom to move his limbs, he felt as if a spring melt was gushing out of his nostrils and eyes.

"What a good boy you are. You've got such long eyelashes and a perfectly erect backbone. Even if you are a foolish beggar, I couldn't let you die. Now tell me, my good boy: Are you a foolish beggar fortune-teller wandering about?"

Gazing at the grandmother feeding him, Liao Mai suddenly had the impression that she was the mother he had never seen. He nodded thoughtfully.

Sleeping fitfully, Liao Mai did not know how many days had elapsed. He sat up at long last one day and found his legs, belly and other parts of his body plastered with brown herbal medicinal ointment. He examined the surroundings and found the building he was in to be a two-room house built of mud and straw. It stood on the sunny slope of a mound with a rivulet meandering on the right. He looked into the distance from the window and saw the rivulet curve not far in front of the house, forming a large L-shaped body of water, on the edge of which whisker-like aquatic weeds were growing. At the time, the grandmother was working on something with a rod and a hand net. Liao Mai gazed without blinking and caught sight of a flash – a fish more than fifteen centimetres long landed at her feet.

The grandmother spent the rest of the day making a soup with the fish. He learned later that the fish she had caught was called *huanglin dabian* (literally 'yellow-scaled big flat'), a kind of golden fish with yellow scales and a broad belly. This type of fish only lives on the pebbles and stones beneath rapids. When cooked, it is reputed to have the power to save lives... The thick fish soup was ready for Liao Mai by late morning.

What a magical soup! After only a few days, Liao Mai's eyes began to shine, and his wounds started to scar. Bursting with warmth, he hopped from the bed to the floor.

"A good boy can't die! At first sight, I knew the King of Hell would drive you back to this world with his club." Running her hand over Liao Mai's dark glossy hair, the grandmother added tearfully: "Something must have scared you badly. That's why you, my good boy, dare not speak. Are you really a foolish beggar, a great foolish beggar?"

Liao Mai nodded and dropped to his knees before her.

BLUNDERBUSSES IN A STRANGE LAND

"You disgraceful thing, you're wasting our food here," said his escort, a red-nosed young man. After giving him a few shoves, the young man walked ahead. The man being shoved perked up when he heard the command for livestock "Yeah! Yeah!" coming from nearby, and then he could smell domestic animals. Sure enough, he was pushed into a stable.

The blunderbuss-carrying young man summoned over a lame stableman, saying: "The boss wants you to watch him. Be on the alert. This guy was caught on the other side of the hill. Don't know who he is."

The young man and the lame man worked together to shackle him with rusted iron rings, and then they left. The rings were chained to a wooden pillar. The chain clanked every time he moved. A large white horse that was feeding stopped to gaze at him. The lame stableman returned before dark and stirred the fodder in a few wooden troughs. Then, together with the white horse, he also gazed at him, hands on knees. "Where did you pop up from, you beast?" he asked. "Wandering at such a young age, you must be a fugitive."

The lame man licked his reddish-brown beard with the tip of his tongue as he spoke. "Answer me!" He suddenly raised his voice and picked up a big iron ladle, looking all fierce.

Liao Mai did not want to look him in the face. Instead of hitting him, the man scooped a ladle of the stale beans used as fodder, shoved it under Liao Mai's nose and left cursing. Liao Mai shoved a handful of the beans into his mouth. While he was eating, someone came next door with the ringing voice of a young woman: "Dad!" It turned out to be the lame stableman's daughter. They mumbled something briefly before the young woman went out. She leaned on the doorframe to look at the chained man. In order to see him more clearly, she found a kerosene lantern and held it up and down before him. She was quiet and, as if frightened by something unknown, tiptoed away. In the ambient light, however, Liao Mai caught a glimpse of a young woman with a round face featuring a pair of large eyes and bushy eyebrows. She seemed a few years his senior.

The next evening, a skinny man in his fifties came in. He had a blue-tinged face and wore a fur-collared overcoat. Accompanying him were a number of armed men. He coughed loudly as he entered. Liao Mai assumed him to be the village head, that is, the "boss" mentioned by the stableman. While coughing and spitting, he interrogated Liao Mai angrily. His questions only amounted to where he had come from and what unlawful acts he had committed. Liao Mai adhered to the same answer: "I've been wandering over the hills and plains since childhood, and I live by begging food from every household."

"So, you mean you're a bastard. A hero can come from bastards."

The skinny man's jeering remarks made the others laugh heartily. The exhausted Liao Mai was about to sit down against the pillar when someone shook the chain vehemently and pulled him up. They tortured him in this manner for another half an hour before unfastening him from the pillar. Leading him by the chain, they said: "Time to go. We've something going on this evening, and you're at the right time and right place."

Liao Mai had already regretted leaving the grandmother the night before. But he had told himself not to stay in her home in case it was not sufficiently far from Jiwo to shake off the aardwolves that could have tracked him down easily. When he was able to walk again, the first thing that came to his mind was to run. He did not imagine being captured by a night militia patrol soon after he had trudged over a mountain ridge.

A few people dragged Liao Mai to a threshing ground stacked with wheat straw. He saw a wooden frame erected and two white wooden desks set in front of some shining kerosene lanterns. A large crowd seemed to be expecting something. When they saw a stranger escorted over, they immediately strained their necks and started chattering. In an instant, silence reigned again, and Liao Mai was pushed aside. It appeared that the crowd was still waiting; men were smoking incessantly while women were stitching outsoles, cutting paper patterns or twisting threads in the bright light of the kerosene lanterns. Before long, some people began to move about in the shade. Then, the skinny man shrieked in an extremely high pitch – just as the old saying goes: 'The shorter the person, the higher-pitched the voice'. With this guy's bugle-like scream, everyone on the threshing ground went silent in expectation.

Several blunderbuss-wielding young men dragged three people and rushed them to the front of the wooden desk like a blast of wind. Before the three could steady themselves, the young men had bent their upper bodies down forward by pressing their heads and shoulders, their execution of the procedure being amazingly slick and skilful. Liao Mai saw the three people consisting of two older men and a middle-aged woman. After the young men bent them for a while, they tilted their heads backwards to reveal their faces. Liao

Mai was taken aback by the sight of a photo stuck on the forehead of the woman. It was a picture of a man with indistinct features.

Led by one individual, the crowd on the threshing ground shouted slogans continuously. Few of the women in the crowd were able to concentrate on their needlework. They watched their male peers going up one by one to slap the three people on the face. As they watched, the women either clicked their tongues or scratched their heads with the blunt end of their needles. Not having the heart to see the woman being beaten, Liao Mai turned his face away. Then someone suddenly remembered him and came over to push him, saying: "You were caught trying to escape. You can't be up to any good."

The three people were humiliated until the middle of the night. They were then hung from the wooden frame. The woman's clothes were tattered so that half of her chest was exposed. The wild screams of the crowd on the threshing ground propelled the rally to its climax. Some of the spectators grabbed the ropes and belts over from other spectators' hands and slashed the three hard. Others suggested hanging Liao Mai up, and the skinny man consented. As a consequence, Liao Mai was also pulled above ground while the chains and the rings around his ankles were still held by someone.

"Quite a handsome young man," a woman in the crowd exclaimed, which immediately invited a barrage of rebuttals.

"These days, you can't judge people by their appearance. A man may look like a film star, but what does it say about his character? He may steal here and there or run his hands over a woman's breasts while watching a film at night."

"You're right. When a man is horny, he can't even buckle up his waistband."

The skinny man held up the chains attached to Liao Mai and gave them a tug. The chains clanked amid his repeated screams: "Confess or not? Confess or not?"

It was not until shortly after midnight that Liao Mai was led back to the stable, with ligature marks on his wrists and abrasions on his ankles. The abominable screams of "Kick and kick! Kick and kick" rang again in his ears. He said to himself: You must tough it out. If you let out a single word, they'll send you back to the Tang father and son.

The white horse moved its head over and rubbed Liao Mai's

head gently with its lips. He was afraid that it might start munching his thick hair as if it were grass. But the white horse only placed its chin on his head as if to kiss him, and it stayed motionless for a few minutes. He thanked the white horse heartily. The moon rose and poured its silvery light through the window.

Liao Mai was awakened from his brief nap. He looked up and caught sight of someone, the lame stableman's round-faced daughter. She was standing before the white horse and kissing it while placing her arms around its neck. Liao Mai was flabbergasted. He watched while holding his breath. With her eyes closed, she kept rubbing her cheek against the horse's face, causing the animal to shiver. Its large mouth moved over her eyes and nose while she was moaning. She moaned gently before suddenly stopping, seemingly remembering something. She turned around to look at Liao Mai with her eyes widened. She gazed for a while but still looked worried, so she let go of the horse and walked over to take a closer inspection. When she was certain that Liao Mai was fast asleep, she returned to hold the white horse again.

About an hour had passed, and the round-faced young woman still found it hard to tear herself away. She was exhausted and sat down opposite Liao Mai, without saying anything, but he could sense a whiff of boiled polenta sweeping across his face. She sized him up and reached to give his eyelashes a pinch. He opened his eyes.

"It's said that you're pretending to be a foolish beggar," she said with a broad smile.

After rubbing his eyes, he found the young woman soaked in sweat and her breasts featuring prominently. He turned his face away to look at the moonlight and was certain that a silvery frost would cover the ground tonight.

Flaring her nostrils, the round-faced young woman said in a hoarse voice: "It'd be quite something if you turned out to be a real foolish beggar."

As if to confirm her suspicion, she ran a hand over his chest, pinched his lips and pressed his nose. She did so for a whole quarter of an hour. Fixing her eyes on his mouth, she seemed to be making a bigger decision.

"I'm not a foolish beggar," Liao Mai blurted out.

She first moved away a little as if frightened, but then she leaned over again, saying: "So what *are* you, handsome young man?"

She spoke these words in a gentle whisper. She hugged him while breathing heavily. He remained motionless and pleaded: "Could you please unfasten the iron rings shackling my ankles? I have been wronged. I'm a simple traveller."

"No, I can't do that," she said, still smiling. "You'd only run away."

Liao Mai stopped speaking, his eyes harsh and cheerless. She kissed him like a chick pecking at food despite his efforts to evade her. "Who says I'm hard-hearted," she sighed. With it, she rose and went next door. Perhaps she had gone to find the key to his shackles from the pocket of her sleeping father. As soon as she returned, she busied herself in freeing the chains from the pillar. She led Liao Mai by the chains out of the stable and then towards the outskirts of the village.

The dogs seemed to tremble in the moonlight because they only whimpered a few times and remained passive. She took him to a haystack and paused.

"Let me go, please," Liao Mai begged her. "I won't forget you."

"I want to elope with you and follow you wherever you go."

"But I'm a married man."

"You're lying! Look how young you are."

"My marriage was arranged when I was a little boy."

The young woman's round face fell. Biting her lip, she was anguished. The dogs started barking behind them, and then came the sound of thumping footsteps. The sharp-witted young woman quickly pressed Liao Mai onto the ground.

Someone ran by quickly, and Liao Mai recognised her as the woman being hanged on the threshing ground. She didn't even have time to remove the picture from her forehead. In her wake came the pursuers, three or five blunderbuss-carrying people led by the skinny man. Their hubbub went something like: "Stop or we'll shoot."

The woman refused to stop and the skinny man yelled: "We'll shoot. We'll pull the trigger."

The others held their blunderbusses level. The skinny man waved violently to give his order. Fire spat from only two of the four blunderbusses, as the other two contained duds. They fiddled with them, stamped angrily and cursed. The skinny man scolded: "The decent blunderbusses have been issued to other fucking villages. The ones we have can't even shoot birds."

They cursed some more and went back with their heads hung low in dismay.

Meanwhile, Liao Mai noticed that the round-faced young woman was wiping tears from her eyes. Continuing to cry, she removed the rings from his ankles. Then, she pressed his face against her chest and said: "Hurry. Don't wait for me to change my mind and alert my people."

DRINKING THE MILK OF A LUNATIC

The sweet potatoes, sorghum plants, melons and jujubes that were grown all over the mountain slopes were God-sent food for a vagabond. Sustained by them, he did not have to lean on one doorframe after another and cry out: "Kind-hearted aunties and uncles, please spare me a morsel of food."

If a fit and healthy teenager did the same, instead of alms, he would receive curses such as: "You damned lazybones! Why are you begging at such a youthful age? Why don't you earn a living?"

Liao Mai was deeply ashamed. He had never thought of begging before, but the heavens just teased him by giving him no way out. To work as a helper, to hoe the fields or to quarry in the mountains, he would have to be interrogated with questions like "Where're you from?" and "Do you have a pass in your pocket?" In such a situation, he would have to run away as fast as possible. There were too many busybodies who could stop and ask questions these days. When asked, he had to say something convincing unless he pretended to be a foolish beggar who could answer "No" to any question without suspicion. Not regarded as normal, a fool could do nothing but beg on the streets, and it would be most unlikely for him to give personal information such as his name or family background. Therefore, Liao Mai would always need to appear with his face smeared and his clothes tattered.

But it was no easy job to be a foolish beggar on this land. Even if you did not have a name or any possessions for that matter, you still had to go through endless interrogations and detentions on a daily basis. Sometimes, a piece of cow dung would be smeared on your mouth to see if you were really deranged. Liao Mai had no alternative but to lead a life of constant fear and anxiety, a life he resented very much. He was aware that no matter where he hid, be it in the wilderness or in the alleys, a gun could be pointed at his forehead at any time.

Those vagabonds wandering in groups in the autumn wilderness, who always held their heads high though dressed in rags, usually had their leaders. Each leader stowed in his pocket a paper slip with a red seal on it. The slip contained the date of issue and the reason for permitting its holder to earn a living as a wandering vagabond – such as the occurrence of a disaster or a sudden turn of events – the request for local authorities to give special preference and a concluding salutation. A fat man with a tuft of white hair on his head and a chain whip around his waist possessed such a paper slip. He had in his fold more than a dozen men and women of different ages, as well as children. Carrying a huge iron pot and other utensils, they cooked their meals wherever they took a break from wandering. Bold and self-confident, they treated other vagabonds roughly so that a lone tramp would always dodge them. One day, the fat man ran into Liao Mai and asked him right in his face: "Want to join us?"

Seeing the tuft of white hair, Liao Mai was scared and took flight. The white-haired man scolded him behind his back: "You little son of a bitch. I'll break your legs one day."

Liao Mai kept running on his long legs, not daring to look back. After living in this stressful manner for several days, he began to regret his decision to flee. By the end of autumn, despite his lingering angst, he decided to turn around to catch up with the gang led by White Hair. He raised his head to search the wilderness for the smoke of a cooking fire and finally found White Hair drinking by a battered iron pot.

Liao Mai said hoarsely: "I want to join you."

White Hair did not budge. He only bent his head sideways and yelled: "Take this greenhorn in!"

With a "Yes", three young rogues with filthy hands and feet came up and hustled him aside. They searched all his pockets and asked him a lot of questions. When they tried to pull off his trousers, Liao Mai withdrew and demanded to know what they were up to.

"This is our routine. To join us, you must share everything you have with us. Last time, we found a guy hiding money in his crotch. Our boss was so angry that he almost castrated him."

Liao Mai had to give in but insisted on taking off his trousers himself and exposing his naked body away from the view of the women nearby.

The gang went about their daily activities erratically. Whether to move or to sleep was down to the whim of White Hair. In addition to begging, a few younger rogues stole domestic fowl from villagers and collected autumn berries in the wild. Sometimes, they could haul back a pig. The white-haired boss made some of the women prepare food, pick out lice from his body and even sleep with him. One of the gang members was a deranged woman of forty-some years, her breasts sagging like sacks. She was said to be the wife of a paternal cousin of White Hair. She cooked for the gang all day long in a state of undress. One midnight, she went berserk and jabbed White Hair in the testicles with a stick used as a stove poker. White Hair's shriek in the dark night was terrifying, so much so that the blunderbuss-carrying people from the nearby villages were drawn to the commotion. Since they were all acquainted with the gang members, they smirked and left, but not before drinking a few mouthfuls of the liquor from White Hair's bottle.

The few young rogues at White Hair's disposal would go wild after drinking. They would steal and force Liao Mai to collude with them. One day, they made him eat food that had gone bad after being set aside for a few days. He was so furious that he knocked over the bowl.

"OK, we'll help you vent your anger. But don't blame us for being unpleasant."

After exchanging glances, they pounced upon him at once, pulling his hair, kicking him in the crotch and rolling up their sleeves ready to remove his trousers. White Hair watched without intervening. After a while, he waved them off and said to Liao Mai: "Hey newbie, I think that was your fault."

His face covered with scratches and a tuft of his hair pulled out, Liao Mai glared at the boss in a towering rage.

"These sons of bitches grew up on the breast milk of the deranged woman, so they're all lunatics," White Hair said. "You can't fight them unless you're a lunatic, too." As he spoke, he pouted his lips at someone nearby.

The deranged woman was gazing at Liao Mai. She was grinning from ear to ear while holding her breasts in her hands with milk dripping from them.

Liao Mai was often sleepless at night. Fixing his eyes on a particular star, he believed it to be above Jiwo Town, which, not anywhere else, was home to all the reasons for his forbearance and survival. He repeated the name of Mei Di silently in order to endure all the hardships. He knew that she remained in Jiwo, living in the jungle of blunderbusses. But he was convinced that she could survive because she would, like him, be constantly repeating the name of her loved one…

The filthy and dishevelled gang drifted eastwards like a debris-encrusted mudflow coursing over an autumn wilderness. As it moved, the group constantly attracted new recruits, who were immediately placed under the protection of White Hair as well as at his disposal. A woman joined with her toddler, but the child cried uncontrollably at night. So she took a chance and fled with her child. What surprised Liao Mai the most was White Hair's fondness for reading aloud. Before supper, he would produce a rumpled little red book and read a few passages from it to his gang members, who were not supposed to do anything but listen attentively. Even the deranged woman was no exception. Holding her breasts, she was all seriousness.

"How can we not study these passages?" White Hair said. "If we hadn't done so, we would have died long ago."

At dusk, a few young rogues dug up from somewhere a dead pig with a horrible stench. While others covered their noses, they did not care at all and insisted on cooking it with alcohol. When the pork and liquor were served, Liao Mai wouldn't touch it. After staring at him for a few seconds, White Hair could no longer contain his anger and yelled: "We have a dandy boy among us!"

The young rogues, taking their cue from the boss's wink, spat out what they had in their mouths, sprang up and took hold of Liao Mai. They forced the food into his mouth by pinching his nose, and called the deranged woman to hurry over and feed him her milk. The woman came quickly and did as requested.

Liao Mai coughed violently but failed to throw up anything. He huddled on the ground in despair.

Drinking a few shots of alcohol, White Hair said: "Anyone who's eaten the lunatic's milk will become a lunatic himself. But so what, I like lunatics."

The deranged woman crouched down and watched Liao Mai fearfully. In her anxiety, she urinated and the stench awakened Liao Mai. As he jumped up, he picked up a piece of rock.

"How do you feel? Now, it's your turn to go crazy, eh?" jeered White Hair while staring at him.

Liao Mai nodded. He felt the alcohol forced into his stomach burning his guts like fire, and the heat caused his scalp to numb and itch. He tried wiggling his neck, exhaling a couple of breaths and blinking his eyes a few times.

"Looks like this guy's really going to become a lunatic," said White Hair, winking to the rogues beside him.

Before White Hair finished grimacing, Liao Mai sprang to his feet and smashed the rock on the part of his head covered by his tuft of white hair. Blood instantly covered his face. The rogues around were momentarily stunned by this unexpected turn of events. After a few seconds, they hurried to look for something to use as a weapon. But before they could find anything, Liao Mai hit them with the rock one by one. Leaping among them as nimbly as a leopard while striking and screaming, his prowess was unstoppable. "The guy... the guy's really gone crazy!"

Covering his face with one hand, White Hair was trying to remove the chain whip from his waist with the other when he gave off a loud cry and collapsed sideways – it turned out that, during the commotion, the deranged woman had once again stuck the stove poker stick between his legs.

In the dark night when the moon was hidden behind clouds, Liao Mai scampered through the autumn wilderness with his tattered clothes fluttering in the wind. "I'll become a real lunatic from now on because I've drunk a lunatic's milk! I'll fear nothing. I'll be bold enough to kill aardwolves and jump through a series of fiery hoops. I'll storm back into Jiwo even if it costs me my life."

Liao Mai kept running, unfazed by the prospect of anyone chasing him. Now, no one, not even a bullet, could catch up with him.

The moon showed her face from behind dark clouds. When she laid her eyes on Liao Mai, she was amazed and screamed: "Look!

Where does this young man come from? How handsome he is! What long legs he has!"

A LOVELY FACE

In this hilly area with a circumference of twenty kilometres, everyone regarded Scarred Apricot as the prettiest girl around. Her mother was the head of three small villages, which sat in a triangle on the top of a small hill, only half a kilometre apart from each other. The head was nicknamed Maroon Lips. She had a kind heart despite her fierce looks. Having been widowed for a long time, she placed all her hopes on her daughter. She wanted Scarred Apricot to marry a high-ranking military officer in future. This was known to all the villagers, including the children, who improvised a riddle: "A high-ranking officer – how high? A high-ranking officer – as high as an ass is long!"

Over the years, those who dared to make negative comments about Scarred Apricot's appearance all suffered a miserable fate. An old woman once said that Scarred Apricot could have been prettier if her mouth had been smaller and her breasts fuller. As a consequence, she got a slap on the face in the dark, which caused a malignant boil to form on her lips. Despite treating it for six months, she still succumbed to the infection. Another woman had bragged about her daughter's outstanding looks and suggested that she was the finest beauty. Then, several armed young men came and took her daughter with them. They were putting on a touring show, a significant part of the seasonal celebration, in which she was made to play a role. The girl did indeed look beautiful in her make-up and costume, but unfortunately, she could neither sing nor speak well, and she simply did not have the voice necessary for theatrical performances. A winter's ordeal plunged her into depression. Eventually, she became as thin as a skeleton, and her hair fell out in tufts until she was nearly bald. Her mother then ceased to brag about her beauty.

Under the protection of Maroon Lips, Scarred Apricot's beauty was becoming even more apparent. "A big flower will bear big fruit," said Maroon Lips, who was smoking a cone-shaped roll-up while gesturing with her hands in a masculine manner to her superiors coming to the village to inspect her work.

All the higher-level administrators from outside the village leaned nearer to look at Scarred Apricot closely. They were amazed and lavished compliments on her beauty, regretting seeing her too late at their advanced age. A senior official had come to visit after hearing about Scarred Apricot's good looks. The villagers remembered him carrying a palm-sized blunderbuss outside his waistband. The blunderbuss had been kept in a brown leather holster. That day, he fixed his eyes on Scarred Apricot for a while with his hands on his hips and then pinched her hands and feet tentatively. He also praised her clothes. Grappling her breasts beneath her blouse and weighing them in his hands, he said repeatedly: "This material's not bad, not bad at all."

Scarred Apricot kept crying, thereby embarrassing Maroon Lips, who said reproachfully: "Why are you crying so terribly? What important people hasn't the senior official seen before?"

Hating reading, Scarred Apricot had dropped out of school at an early age. Maroon Lips said: "It's fine if you can just write your name. You know, nine out of ten teachers are nothing but asses. It's better to stay away from them." She made her daughter crotchet lace on the *kang* all day long. Sheltered from the sun and rain, her skin was all the more delicate, ready for marrying a high-ranking military officer.

One morning, the ground was covered with heavy frost. As a matter of routine, the blunderbuss-carrying youngsters were supposed to get up early to patrol the streets. On a frosty day like this, they would be more successful in finding fugitives. The fugitives had to keep warm by huddling in the dried grass swept into the ditches by the wind or in the haystacks on the outskirts of the village. But by doing so, they became sitting ducks. The same thing happened today. About six o'clock in the morning, the militiamen found a lunatic sheltering in a haystack. This big-eyed man seemed startled when he was dragged out. He glanced at each of the youngsters and made several attempts to flee, but he was caught each time.

Having had no cases to try for a long time, Maroon Lips felt bored and had an itch to conduct one. She had the lunatic escorted into a room. With a roll-up in her mouth, she slapped her hand on the desk as a scare tactic and said to the young lunatic: "If you should make me mad, I'll make you wear those!" With that, she pointed at a pair of iron shoes beside her. They were often forced onto an interrogee's feet after being heated deep orange in a coal stove; usually, the mere sight of the heated iron shoes would elicit a confession. In reality, Maroon Lips had never had anyone wear them. Known for her bark rather than her bite, whenever an interrogee cried after being beaten, she would turn around and shed tears. One day, someone in the village had plotted to revolt, and she had had no choice but to have him hung up and beaten till he was bleeding all over. The bloody scene caused her to cry the whole night, so much so that her eyes became swollen. This time, however, at the mere mention of the iron shoes, the young lunatic hurried over and thrust them on his feet. Maroon Lips burst into laughter, saying: "It's true! You are indeed a foolish beggar, and an impatient one at that! The shoes aren't heated yet."

Interrogating him for a while, Maroon Lips assumed that he was a deranged vagabond beggar instead of a criminal fugitive. Most important, she took a liking to this filthy young man after a few more glances at him; for the smears on his face could not conceal his handsome features. She took a closer look at his eyes and burst out: "You motherfucker! It's such a shame for those eyes to be wasted on your face. You son-of-a-bitch fool! You know nothing but to eat and wander. How I wish I could reach out my hands to tear you to pieces!"

The lunatic was locked up in a vacant room. As usual, the militiamen brought him some pig or dog food in addition to some murky water. This time, however, Maroon Lips asked them to take in some decent food, saying that she would keep him well for a final decision to be made by superior administrators when they came to try him.

News that a handsome lunatic had been captured spread like wildfire among the villagers. Scarred Apricot could no longer sit crocheting. She came over to look at him. Leaning against the window outside the room for an hour, she still found it hard to tear herself away. Maroon Lips arrived to get her home.

"I like him," the daughter said.

Maroon Lips scolded her: "Shame on you! Who wouldn't like a man like this? But he's a lunatic. What's the good of him being handsome?"

Scarred Apricot curled her lips and told her mother: "From his looks, I bet I can tell he's not a lunatic at all. All of you've been taken in."

What her daughter said alerted Maroon Lips. She looked again at the detained lunatic, and the more she gazed, the more suspicious she became. Feeling a chill creeping up her spine, she thought: It's terrible! If he is faking lunacy, then this could turn into a big incident.

She admired her daughter's perception. Clicking her teeth, she had the lunatic escorted in for another round of interrogation and asked her daughter to sit in to observe.

During the interrogation, Scarred Apricot winked wordless messages to her mother and the interrogee. Several times did she find him responding with a blush or a drop of his eyelashes.

Seeing the interrogation lead nowhere and her mother moping and sighing at the fruitless result, Scarred Apricot suddenly had an idea and shared it with her mother: I'm a grown-up now, not a kid any more. I can distinguish between public and private interests and important matters from trifles. "How about having the armed men stand on guard outside the room while leaving the lunatic to me?" she suggested. "I'll make him reveal his true nature within two or three days."

"So what would you do if his true nature is exposed?" asked Maroon Lips with scepticism.

Making a gesture of a ring with her hands, Scarred Apricot replied: "With a clank, we'll cuff him."

Maroon Lips heaved a sigh of relief.

In the pink room where lace was crocheted sat a freshened-up Scarred Apricot. Beside her was the quiet young man.

"Tell me the truth. What's your name?"

He almost blurted out the truth before biting his tongue. He found it the hardest thing to do under heaven to keep a secret from such a genuine beauty. Look at her! Her face, hidden in the hills for years, was round and featured a nose bridge not too high and a pair of eyes black and wide. Due to lack of exposure to sunlight throughout the year, her face looked rather pale, but the skin was as tender as cream. Like the skin on a peach grown in sandy soil, it was covered with a layer of pink vellus hair. Fine blue veins crawled from her forehead down to her neck, so clear that they evoked an urge in the beholder to take good care of her. Above her distinctly black and white eyes were eyelashes fluttering like butterflies.

"I'm in fact…" Liao Mai stopped short.

"You're in fact what? Who are you?"

"I'm thirsty. I'm now a thirsty lunatic."

Scarred Apricot got off the *kang* twice and each time got him a bowl of sugar solution. She sat closer to him and picked out a few grass blades from his hair, along with a ladybird and a small web-building spider.

"What a poor man you are! You ate and slept in the wild and had no one to mend your tattered trousers. Covered in rags, you didn't know where to get the next meal. When you were thirsty, you didn't even have dishwater to drink."

Sighing and frowning, she placed her cotton-soft hand on his masculine body and blinked her dark eyes that harboured a burning temptation. "Where in the world are you from?" she asked. Tilting her head sideways and pouting her lips, she stared at him playfully.

His nostrils were filled with so much of her pleasant scent that he began to sneeze. He felt his heart pounding in his chest. He was about to turn his head to evade her gaze when she suddenly held up his face and planted an abrupt and yet targeted kiss on his forehead. Liao Mai wiped his face in a hurry as he moaned. She quickly pulled his hand away and pressed it to her chest. Kick and kick! Kick and kick! Liao Mai repeated these words silently with eyes closed. He was struggling so hard to resist the temptation that he was sweating all over.

"From the moment I first saw you, I realised you were no lunatic. You are the smartest and most handsome young man. I'm just not sure what you did unlawfully. You saw with your own eyes that my mum was the queen of this place. It would quake at a mere stomp of her foot. When she's happy, she can wrap you up in cotton, so you don't freeze in midwinter. I'll place a fire-pit bowl with burning willow charcoal on the *kang*, and we can read poems, make paper cuts and eat sweet potato pies and eggrolls with spring onions. My mum has a sharp tongue but a soft heart. She'll forget to smoke her cigarette when she lays her eyes on a handsome young man…"

Holding his hands in hers, Scarred Apricot murmured. He listened and listened and was getting fascinated, so much so that he could not help asking: "So you can read poems too?"

"Of course! I wasn't lying."

Like a child, she began her recital with her squinted eyes looking up while rocking her head from side to side: "Lift her satin bed sheets / Smell the odour she excretes… A girl at the age of twenty-three / She's growing more and more busty."

Liao Mai uttered a slight 'Hah', wondering where this silly beauty learned all these vulgar rhymes. He felt his throat tighten and his palms moisten. He stood up, but she pressed him down and said something in his ear. Liao Mai could not hear her clearly, partly because she spoke so softly and partly because his ears were ringing and buzzing. She was acting in a rather fretful manner. After clapping her hands for a while, she pushed him down on the *kang* and covered him with a floral quilt. Then she crouched by him, watching.

Liao Mai felt sorrow deep in his heart. He kept his eyes tightly closed and cried in silence: Oh Mei Di! I've been stumbling down a path of escape over mountains and rivers. I've tried hard to survive the smoking muzzles of blunderbusses. The calluses on my feet are as hard as iron, so hard that they're thorn-proof. My stomach has been toughened by clay and grass roots. But the trouble is, I've met a good girl who's provided me with such a fine quilt sleeping bag. No matter how ungrateful I am, I can't say a bad word about Scarred Apricot. I'm really, really tired. On my journey of escape, whenever I lay down to rest, I would miss you and see you in my mind's eye. I repeat your name every day, I've evaded bullets, I've become immune to cold and illness, and I'm safe and sound. But I'm so tired. Too tired. Please allow me a few nights' sound sleep in this kind-hearted young woman's home. Please allow me to have a sweet dream beneath her fragrant floral quilt sleeping bag. I'll dream of you hugging me and of you kissing and biting me with your tender mouth…

As he muttered in silence, he fell asleep and began to snore.

Scarred Apricot, who had been crouching beside him, was initially taken aback by the resonance of his snores and then felt pleasant again. She tiptoed out of the room and gently unbolted the door.

Maroon Lips had been waiting outside all the time. As soon as she saw her daughter, she asked: "What were you chattering about in there? I couldn't make out a single word. Has he confessed?"

Scarred Apricot placed a forefinger to her mouth and said in a hushed voice: "He's asleep. He was so tired that, after so much talking, he went to sleep and then started snoring. I covered him with the floral quilt. Place your ear against the crack of the door and listen: 'Snooooring, snooooring'. That's how he's sleeping."

Maroon Lips listened and heard the snore. She drew her eyebrows tight and reproached her daughter: "So, this is your brilliant idea?"

Holding her mother's face with both hands, Scarred Apricot pleaded: "Mum! Everyone knows you're kind-hearted. Please let this nice young man have a good sleep. When he's slept well and yawns towards the rising sun, I bet he'll tell us everything."

Maroon Lips had no option but to tell the blunderbuss-carrying young men to watch the door closely, add a lock to it and stay put. Then she walked out of the courtyard with her daughter, and they sauntered in the streets until dark. They returned to listen against the door only to hear the snores continuing. So they went out for another brief walk. The mother and daughter had separate bedrooms, one in the west wing and the other in the east. That night, since they couldn't go back to their bedrooms, they had to find a vacant room and went to bed in their clothes.

Neither of them had a good sleep. Scarred Apricot dreamed of the handsome lunatic holding her in his arms. Despite his filthy face, the kisses he planted on her were as sweet as honey. Maroon Lips had a different dream. She dreamed of the crazy young man trussed up tightly, vowing that he would rather die than confess. Eventually, she had to have him wear the iron shoes heated red-hot; he plodded in the shoes while gritting his teeth. He walked and walked and took off the shoes only to find his feet badly seared.

Maroon Lips was the first to wake up from her dream. Gazing at the dense darkness, she said: "My heart ached when I saw him in the iron shoes. But what else could I have done?"

FIVE

MOUNTAIN OF GOLD AND SILVER

ON A SPRING MORNING five years before Tang Laotuo's death, his son had wakened him. His face covered with sweat, Tang Tong said in his father's ear: "A fox spirit appeared in my dream and told me there was gold in this mountain."

"Frack!" Tang Laotuo responded, looking up.

"Mountains of gold and silver."

"Frack!"

Tang Tong knew that his father had no choice on waking up but to swear a couple of times in order to clear his throat. Only then could he speak in complete sentences. He waited while eyeing the scars on his neck and upper arms inflicted by a knife.

Squinting his eyes, Laotuo repeated: "Frack! The upper-level administrator told us that ages ago. Stay away from fox spirits." He was aware that his son had been hanging out with Lady Shan in recent years and was very superstitious of ghosts and spirits under her influence. He was therefore worried about his ability to accomplish anything after he himself gave up the ghost.

Rubbing his hands together, Tang Tong went on: "I dreamed of gold and silver piled up in mountains in our courtyard. Those who helped carry the gold bricks included not only the townsfolk but outsiders speaking different dialects. There were also various kinds of wild creatures among them. They wore red waistbands to ward off evil spirits."

Laotuo got up and, picking up his pike, muttered: "Everyone craves gold. I don't think the government will allow us townspeople to have a hand in it. From ancient times, the tradition has been that each gold bar is guarded with a blunderbuss."

"We have blunderbusses!" said Tang Tong, raising his voice. "We, too, have weapons that we can shoot."

Laotuo closed his eyes. He was recalling a gold-looting incident when he was young. Seven or eight stout men were lying by the roadside in wait for a truck loaded with gold. When he heard the truck come rumbling, he became tight all over and he instantly stopped sweating. His cock became erect, something that always happened whenever he was faced with a life-threatening danger. Because of his fearlessness, he naturally became the leader. As the truck appeared, they detonated the mine. The eruption of fire and pungent smoke made the two-dozen good-for-nothing young soldier escorts blanch. As they jumped from the vehicle, five of them were killed by bullets and four were beheaded by broadswords. A dozen or so survivors tried to clamber to nearby trees and take up their usual position of crouching on one knee in order to return fire. They had never expected their attackers to be indiscriminately murderous mounted bandits. Brandishing their swords half naked, they cut their heads off, saving themselves the trouble of firing their blunderbusses.

During that raid, Tang Laotuo's left leg was accidentally injured by one of his own swordsmen. Pressing a hand on his wound, he scolded: "Fuck you! Fuck your whole family!" His roaring curses still rang loud in his ears today.

Old age has made me a good-for-nothing, Laotuo said to himself. My humble son Tang Tong is rustically swarthy and stout. Whenever he speaks, it's always about fox spirits. Frack! Laotuo was known to be the most flatulent man in town. Now he lifted the quilt, and the stench sent Tang Tong staggering out of the room. That morning, he vowed to move the gold mountain home. It would be illogical for gold to be taken by others when it's on my doorstep, he reasoned.

Sure enough, the upper-level administrator dispatched a group to open up the mountain. When they first came, they wore pith helmets and sunglasses. Among them, there were some delicately pretty young women who busied themselves flipping books and filling in forms. Tang Tong barely paid them any attention. Representing the townspeople on Stone Street, he entertained the outsiders. Emboldened by alcohol, he said to a bespectacled young woman in a white dress: "These are impressive!" When asked what, he pointed unequivocally at her prominent breasts.

The woman was so scared that she dropped her wine glass and darted into a lavatory before fleeing back to her dormitory. "Motherfucker! She thought she could dig the gold for nothing! She thought my liquor was not potent!" In a drunken frenzy, Tang Tong smashed his own liquor cup to the floor.

Afterwards, Tang Tong tried every means to get his hands on the gold. Leading a group of people, he dug a large quantity of ore from the edges and corners of the mountain. Six months later, he opened the town's gold mine. Laotuo panted over to his son's ore mill where he gazed with his eagle eyes at the rumbling ore crushers. He was pleased to see his son, with his hands on hips and his feet in riding boots, behaving like the chieftain of a mounted bandit gang. Laotuo thought of his long-deceased wife Jenny, convinced that his son combined his boldness and her unruliness. The only baffling thing was that he and Jenny were by no means lustful; they were mere lovers of blunderbusses and broadswords, but why in the world had they brought forth such a lascivious child? This son of his was tenacious as well as wild; he devoted ten years of his life to one woman! Good Heavens!

Grabbing the arm of his son pacing by the crushers, Tang Laotuo said: "Remember. Without an iron fist, you can't hold wealth. Veteran blacksmiths all have iron hands. I've sensed something. The people you must be vigilant against may still be the descendants of the Huo family."

Thinking his father senile and confused with chronology, Tang Tong had laughed at him in silence. Then, a few years later, his father died, and his lust for wealth was put on the fast track. The gold mine was divided into shares, and he acquired the lion's share. Then, on the other side of the mountain, one company emblem after another was erected, and people who had shares in them emerged as his challengers one by one. He began to lose sleep at night. He was startled and sat up in bed when he suddenly remembered what his father had told him. He concluded that those who could afford to purchase equipment and property, those who could compete for the gold mountain with him, may well have been the descendants of the Huo family that had survived by concealing their identity – only they were good at doing business. He yelled in a muffled voice at the darkness of the night: "I'll kill them!"

The woman in the white dress who had been here a few years before returned joyously in the capacity of head of an exploration team. After traversing so many mountains, she managed to retain her youthful looks, only that she had become rather plump. She had totally forgotten the previous embarrassing encounter. As soon as she saw Tang Tong, she reached out to shake his hand, saying: "Hello, Board Chairman Tang."

Tongue in cheek, Tang Tong replied: "You guys are just like rainfall after a drought. We really need people like you. Hurry up and find us the gold with your magic power. We'll pay you back even if it means being reincarnated as asses or horses in our next lives."

"You're too polite," the woman responded with a wave of the hand. "This is what we experts are good at."

Tang Tong gave a grand banquet in honour of the exploration team. When he was half-drunk, he shouted at the top of his lungs: "Woman expert, I must let you know that in previous times only Lord Huo could hold a lavish banquet like this. He did it to entertain fox spirits and other wild creatures. I'm doing it for the sake of 'goldie'." Here, he was referring to the name he coined for gold that he thought would please the female guests. The white-dressed woman did not gulp the alcohol in the manner he did. She only sipped while urging this swarthy-faced man to drink several cups in succession. Tang Tong knew clearly that this woman was expecting him to make a scene. How could she know that after I drink half a bottle, another cup will make no difference?

He leaned nearer to another woman who, though a little older, still retained some looks. He mumbled a toast to her. Now arching his brows, now pressing his lips, as if he were wronged and befuddled, he flattered her: "I was amazed when I first met your ladyship two years ago. I wondered how your skin could be as tender as young onions even though we all eat the same grains. Look at your soft hands, your moist lips, your swaying gait as if you are strolling on clouds, and your body as curvaceous as a sparrow... Talking of features, we have one here in Jiwo that really is something. Whoever catches sight of her would roll on the ground with envy – I mean, your ladyship, I didn't mean you're not... Your ladyship..."

The middle-aged woman was the leader of the team, but the team members still customarily called her Engineer Ji. For days, Tang Tong kept calling her by this title as he followed her around the mountain and into the pit and watched her marking each of the identified mineral veins on a chart. When they were alone in her hotel room one day, he pressed a gold ingot as big as a bar of chocolate into her hand.

"We experts are the last people to do such a thing!" she blushed.

Tang Tong insisted and stuffed the ingot into her pocket. She went to the lavatory and washed her face. When she returned, her blush had disappeared, and she looked as usual. After Tang Tong held her down on the bed, she blushed again, saying: "We experts are the last people to do such a thing!"

A month after the woman's departure, a gold mine of the best quality was dug out. The news came to Tang Tong, who pressed his index finger to his lips and rushed out of his office. He climbed a corner of the mountain in one breath and paced briskly in front of the pit. Then, he ordered the foreman to lead a group of strong young men into it. A few days later, the labour force in Jiwo was exhausted. Tang Tong dispatched someone to recruit a few hundred people from nearby provinces. Rumbling reports of TNT explosion could be heard all over the mountain. The townspeople commented: "Tang Tong is more capable than his father and those mounted bandits that occupied the mountain before. Kick and kick! Kick and kick! This time, he'll end up kicking the whole mountain over."

A few days later, the foreman came and broke the news with his hand over his mouth to muffle his voice: "The pit's caved in and killed about a dozen miners."

"Hurry and seal them in the pit," Tang Tong shouted. "If you leak any news of the accident, I'll throw you into it."

The foreman dashed back to the work site.

LIKE AN INFANT

"Ji! Oh, Ji! Once you leave home, you're not coming back. You're going to that gold mine almost every day. You no longer take care of your home. Neither do you take care of your husband. The violet on the balcony is almost dead."

Engineer Ji's mother complained as soon as she saw her daughter returning from the east. She loved her only daughter so much that she would do anything for her. As she mumbled, she gently ran her hand over her daughter's hair.

Ji said nothing and, after putting away her suitcase, she went to take a bath. Her face looked as glossy and glowing as an apple. Wearing loose pyjamas, she cuddled up to her mother on the sofa, playfully stroking their cat's nose and hugging her mother. "Boss Tang's invited you to visit him when you've time," she said.

"You've got to be careful," her mother warned. "Got to be careful. You mention him too much."

"Really? I don't think so."

"But you *do* mention him too much."

Lying on the sofa, she held her mother's arm. The cat scampered away. She pressed her cheek on her mother's arm and said: "I wish you had seen the boss. Then you wouldn't be worried. He's like a baby, not stern at all. He's not crafty, either. Even though he's an adult, he tags after me wherever I go. But he does everything in a hurry, more so than my college tutor. If he wants to do something, he can't wait even for a minute. He's also got a hot temper, simply too hot. But Mum, all those who achieve great things are like that. They all have a powder-keg temper, but none have an ounce of malice in them. Whenever he has the time, he'll chat with me. What we talk about would be too much for you, it would make you laugh to death. Like a child, he loves to watch TV soaps. The meaningless storylines always reduce him to tears. Never in my life have I seen someone so simple, soft-hearted and gullible. He believes in whatever I tell him. Sometimes, he tries to take me in, but, as I said, Mum, he's as innocent as a baby. I can tell from his face if he's telling the truth. You see, with a boss like that, what's to be worried about?"

"But you can't be travelling to him so often that it becomes a habit. People will talk."

Ji made a face and cuddled against her mother again.

"Times have changed. Such talk is only sour grapes. Nowadays, not many people have grapes to eat. This is a job that deals in gold, nothing but gold! The boss trusts me and has delegated all responsibility to me. When I see him anxious, I want to shed tears with him. Think about it – such a big company, the mine, and the employees numbering in the hundreds and thousands and coming from various parts of the country. What a tremendous job! He must feed them, take care of their families by giving them monthly wages. I hang out with him from time to time. Once, I sat on his sofa and looked down at him – he likes to sit on the carpet and behave like a child – I found the hair on the top of his head thinning badly, barely able to cover his scalp. Before, his head was a mass of thick, curly hair, like the wool of a lamb… He often acts up. When I make him angry, he'll seethe for a long time. Even when he calms down, he'll ignore me for an hour. He's generous and often quite surprising. He occasionally produces something from his pocket and says: 'Ji, close your eyes! See what I can conjure up for you.' He's no magician, he's just being playful. Once, he slid something onto my chest and left it there, making me scream with terror. It was as cool as a snake, but once I grabbed it, the present belonged to me…"

"You're a married woman," said her mother, twitching her mouth. "Make sure you don't hurt someone."

"Haha. Mum, you talk like someone from the nineteenth century. Family is nothing to people like my boss. Family, hmm! How different men are! The bespectacled guy in my family, a burp from him would make my heart sink… In a word, trust me. Where moral character's concerned, my boss is outstanding. His honorary titles are no baubles that he's picked up from the street. I told my colleagues: 'A gold digger must have a heart of gold.'"

"He's a gold mine owner, not a gold miner."

"Why can't he be both?" For the first time that night, she sat up straight and gazed at her mother in surprise. "He may not dig gold by wielding a pickaxe or lighting the fuses of explosives, but his contribution to the mine is far greater. Without him, there wouldn't be a gold or silver mountain. A slap of his palm on his desk shakes the earth. A simple command from his mouth accomplishes everything. I've seen it with my own eyes all these years. Mum, your daughter's in a perfect position to say this. Please don't misunderstand him. I'm a witness to all his feats. His courage makes him a real man in the true sense of the term. For the sake of gold, he is not afraid of death!

"On the other side of the mountain, there was a man as fierce as a highwayman. He led a gang to the mountain and started digging gold. My boss rushed over to confront them without hesitation. I was really worried that day. Really! I knew both sides were armed with guns and swords, as well as iron-toothed hooks. You may not believe what I'm telling you, Mum. There are indeed people who don't fear death under the sun. My boss tossed his shirt aside and bared his chest, his eyes widened, his shouts rumbling and the veins on his neck intertwining into a bulging mass. The mere sight deterred the opponent and effectively took their minds off the gold mountain. That incident makes me understand the meaning of the saying 'Wherever there are struggles, there will be sacrifices' and tells me what it takes to be a real man. When he's angry, he must fear nothing. During the confrontation, his hair stood on end, the few remaining curly hairs stood erect in the wind. To tell you the truth, I too was scared by his appearance."

Mother shook her head sighing: "No matter what, you're still a woman. You must be cautious and make sure you know what you're doing."

"Of course, I won't do anything that might cost me. I've been working hard all these years. I studied first as an undergraduate and then as a graduate. I later worked in a research institute before going to many places prospecting. So what kinds of people haven't I run into? There've been those who made advances, but I gave them no chance. That advising professor of mine years ago, he might have wasted a lot of nonsense on me, but eventually I did what I needed to satisfy him just enough. He has nothing to complain about, even today. He should've felt satisfied. You saw the professor that summer vacation, a fat man who stuttered a bit. How scrupulously polite he was to you! He was respectful and humble. Who is he today? If he's only one finger, my boss would then be the ten in comparison. All he possesses is worth less than a wheel on my boss's car.

"You worry too much. Just think about it, Mum. Being the big boss of such a big company, what can he ask of me? Both his feelings and intentions are genuine. To be frank, even if I've devoted all I have to him and given up everything for him, how much can I help him? Not much."

"You! Poor daughter. You've been running around there for too long. I can't understand what you're saying any longer."

Ji giggled and shook her mother by her arms as she said: "Don't worry. I won't get involved in any money-losing business. I know how to judge people. I won't deal with those who are ruthless no matter how powerful they are. Such a good character like Boss Tang is rare. His masculinity, well, can be scary, but he's a man who can open up a gold mountain and yet still be so amiable and prone to tears. When he cries, he looks like a little child. A real rascal, Mum. Indeed, he sometimes lies on the floor seething, kicking his legs and wailing loudly like a boy. He boohoos and acts like he's drunk, though he isn't. On those occasions, he'll take his cue from me. Whenever I draw a long face, he'll be intimidated. Then, he'll bribe me with sweet words, whimpers and tears. I'll relent every time he does so."

THREE FOXES SNEAK INTO WEST MOUNTAIN

Tang Tong gave the foreman three slaps on his face and three kicks on his behind. The foreman endured the strikes without moving. Tang Tong removed the tie he had been wearing the whole morning and tossed it onto the desk. He spat and then heaved and puffed for quite a while before beginning his harangue.

"How many times have I told you? You must choose the right people. Don't hire good-for-nothings! Don't hire the soft-hearted! Don't hire those who can't handle blunderbusses!"

Listening to him enumerating the three 'don'ts' in one breath, the foreman kept mumbling "Yes" and nodding his head. Tang Tong kept a lid on his anger but nevertheless went on with his diatribe as he panted heavily.

"Let me tell you. You must hire blunderbuss carriers as Lord Huo recruited his retainers in years gone by. You must find those who have triangular faces, who leer at people with their heads slightly lowered and who skulk or slink as they walk. They must have aardwolf blood flowing in their veins, and when needed, they can be ruthless. Look at those losers you've got. How many of them could be useful, eh?"

A few days later, the foreman selected a number of miners and took them to Tang Tong for interview. He sent them away cursing: "Those sons of bitches each have a broader face than the last one. I've already told you – those who have faces wider than a handspan must be good-for-nothings. As for their table manners, they eat like pigs with drooping ears. Those who are strong must show their gums when they bite and side chew their food. Like this," he said as he demonstrated to the foreman.

After venting his anger with a fit of cursing, Tang Tong went to the mine shafts to select for himself the people he most favoured. He enlisted only three after making a tremendous effort.

"These days, all men seem to be castrated, as soft as noodles," he sighed. "There aren't enough tough and ruthless men. In my father's time, people were like flammable spirit. 'You'd better climb up in one breath / Loneliness leads to the brink of mental breakdown / Dance and dance... Don't stop! Don't stop! / My heart's like an explosion.'" He hummed as he pounded a fist into his palm. He had learned the song from a bitch in the karaoke hall. These particular lyrics were his favourite.

I must get well prepared. The fox spirit's going to visit me in my dream with a message, said Tang Tong to himself. He really did dream of a fiery red fox sitting on the edge of the *kang*. She was gesticulating her prediction of imminent vicissitudes in his fortunes. "Duh, you bitch! I knew that anyway. As the proverb goes, mole crickets can tell the weather. I've already sensed that something will happen in three months."

He did not know whether to love or hate the fox spirit because his father Laotuo used to detest wild creatures, believing that they were associates of the Huo family. Nowadays, with the surrender of the land to the Tang family, the wild creatures had also given themselves up. Wait! What about that daughter of the hedgehog spirit? That wench is still resisting me... Whenever he thought of that woman, he became listless. Sometimes, he would confine himself to bed for a few days. He cursed in silence and burped in rage. He refused to get up no matter what. Like a typhoid fever patient, he would clatter his teeth and make one lewd gesture after another as he gazed in a particular direction.

One day, he was making the same obscene gestures when he was taken aback by the sudden arrival of the foreman.

"Jeez! It's me," said the foreman.

"Get out!"

"The thing is..."

"Get out!"

The foreman dropped to the floor, determined not to leave, and continued: "Boss, something terrible has happened. Indeed, it's terrible..."

Blinking, Tang Tong sat up and glared into the foreman's small eyes that resembled black-eyed peas: "What? Mm-hmm?"

"Boss, it's like this. There's a car parked a hundred steps away from the back door of your house. It's been there for two days."

"Smash it with a hammer!"

"It's eerie. The more I think about it, the more uncomfortable I feel. The car is locked. The plate is fake. It's a pile of junk, worth almost nothing."

Biting his lip, Tang Tong replied: "Then let me go to the back door and take a look."

"Boss, I beg you to go through the front door. We figured that the car may be meant to hurt you. There's something fishy about that car."

"Mm-hmm?" Tang Tong sprang off the *kang*. As he put on his clothes, he murmured: "Hmph, I told you something would happen within three months. Dammit! The fox spirit's prophecies are always accurate. They come true all the time. These days, people follow this or that religion. If I must believe in something, I'd rather choose the fox spirit."

"Where're you going, boss?"

"I'm a fox spirit believer!"

The foreman was so anxious that he nearly burst into tears.

"Boss, I meant the car may have something dangerous attached to it in order to ambush you."

"I knew it. The fox spirit already told me in a dream. You stay here, and let's wait and see what's going on together."

Tang Tong made several phone calls. When he finished, he took some chocolate from the refrigerator and started eating it. He also cast a bar to the foreman.

About ten minutes later, the sirens of police vehicles were audible. Viewed through the windows of the office, some armed men wearing steel helmets rushed out, and each took position in a horseback-riding stance.

"Such awesome young men! And damn interesting!" Tang Tong leaned over the back window and watched, his hand around the foreman's shoulder. He saw the helmet-clad men running here and there far away from the vehicles. They had also brought military dogs.

"These guys can never do a proper job because of their drop crotch trousers." Tang Tong made this remark to the foreman while pointing out of the window after he tossed his head up and gulped a mouthful of water.

Things did not quieten down until three hours later. In the meantime, more cars came along with some more fat dogs, as well as a few big shots. The car under investigation was towed away while the armed men remained on guard. Eventually, a senior official came to knock at Tang Tong's door. Tang Tong winked at the foreman, who opened it. His face clammy with sweat, the senior official said on entering: "Good Heavens! The thing we found in the car would have blown up the entire town of Jiwo. This guy was really merciless."

"Merciless? He can be nothing but a useless country bumpkin. A pro would never have done it this way."

While carrying on the conversation, Tang Tong heaved a sigh of relief. Handing a cigarette to the official, he continued: "Your helmeted guys in drop crotch trousers did a good job. You must entertain them with some good food and wine in addition to some whores."

The senior official coughed huskily: "You're being too courteous, and you're very funny, too."

"I'm not being funny. I'll pay for the restaurant bill and all the other costs."

The official beamed: "It's very generous of you. But we have iron military discipline."

"Of course you do. Your people will have learned the martial art of 'iron crotch' in a few years. This means they won't be afraid of being kicked between the legs. Let's go for a drink and get wasted."

"Boss, do you not have any lingering fear after the incident?" asked the foreman three days later.

Tang Tong shook his head: "I'm trying to figure out who did it. I think it must be someone from the other side of the mountain. As you know, there're many people who're faster to act than I am in the front and at the back of the mountain. That's why I asked you to recruit the right people. The day we need them appears to be far away, but in reality it's right under our noses."

Hearing these words, the foreman hung his head down. Tang Tong immediately sensed something wrong.

"What else has happened?"

"Well, well…"

"What?" asked Tang Tong, staring into his eyes.

"It's through."

Grabbing his collar, Tang Tong persisted: "What's through?"

Looking up, the foreman shouted: "The gold pit is through. The wall between our tunnel and the one on the other side have been dug through. It's incredible! Theirs is really rich in ore. Unfortunately, they had more people, and they have been relentless. They closed the opening hands down. We dug it open again, and they plugged it up once more. They also started a smouldering fire and choked some of our men into unconsciousness…"

Tang Tong fell silent. He paced back and forth in the room for more than ten minutes while occasionally glancing up at the foreman. Sweat broke out all over the foreman's forehead. When Tang Tong finally stopped in front of him, the foreman was so frightened that his teeth chattered.

"It's OK to chatter your teeth so long as you don't pee in your pants," Tang Tong laughed. "Let me check to see if you've peed or not…"

"Ouch, you're killing me!" shouted the foreman.

"Killing you? If you can't cut off the hands thrust over from the other side of the tunnel, they'll castrate you. See how happily they're working now!"

After Tang Tong tweaked his ears a few times, the foreman followed three men out and returned to the tunnel. The three men were emotionless, their faces triangular and their lips livid.

That night, the fox spirit visited Tang Tong in his dream again, with the message that gunfire had been heard in the tunnel. It had been the three skinny men who had raised their guns and aimed at the people on the other side, yelling: "We're cutting you down! We're cutting you down!"

Tang Tong's dream was prescient. It turned out that the miners on the other side of the tunnel knew that 'cut down' meant 'shoot to kill', but they only thought it a bluff. Who would have expected that the three men should really pull the trigger? Several of them dropped to the ground with the gunfire. Their bodies were dragged away and buried in the remotest tunnel. At the time, there were a few other miners nearby, and, stupefied with fear, they were not able to speak for a long while.

The foreman lectured the miners on site and promised them hefty rewards. What worried him most was that the soldiers in drop crotch trousers and steel helmets would come sooner or later, and so would the senior official. The foreman's apprehension was confirmed later when these very people caught wind of what had happened and easily traced it to the four miners on site. They cuffed them and hauled them away.

Tang Tong was impatiently trying to contact that senior official when the latter came to him. As soon as he entered, he asked with a sneer: "What about the guns? And the men?"

Tang Tong rolled his eyes and made a face.

"Don't fool me around. They've confessed to me."

"Sir! Listen, sir. I know – I'll pay the fine no matter how much it is. You can't fall for the gibberish of a few illiterate shitheads."

The official smirked: "The four men all told me the same thing."

Twitching his mouth, Tang Tong replied: "Everyone knows the four dudes have been enchanted by fox spirits. We've three fiery foxes here. They sneak into our West Mountain all day long. They also appeared in my dreams with their messages several times. So, sir, how can you believe what they say? You'd better order them to be brought here so we can conduct a 'three-party cross examination' – what do you think? Do you dare?"

Unable to bear his grimaces, the senior official finally nodded in agreement.

The four captives were escorted in by the helmeted army men. After everyone else withdrew from the room, only the foreman, Tang Tong and the senior official were left with the four cuffed men. Tang Tong hopped and stomped with rage and, his eyes bloodshot, he lunged towards the four men, yelling: "Tell me everything! You all tell me the truth! How long have you been followers of the fox spirits? How did they teach you to trick people and talk rubbish? If you don't confess, you'll have to wear these cuffs till you die. If you do, you'll be feasted with sumptuous food."

The four captives exchanged a knowing look with one another and said: "I'll confess. I'll confess…"

"Have you been influenced by fox spirits? Are you haunted by those from West Mountain?"

"Yes! Yes!"

"Just confessing is not enough. You must sign your name and press your fingerprints with red ink on your confessions," shouted the foreman.

GRAINS FOR SURVIVAL

In such a big company with hundreds if not thousands of employees, there were millions of things that required the attention of its boss. But sometimes, Tang Tong proved elusive. He did not answer the phone and could not be found in his office.

Who would have imagined that Tang Tong, his face and hands covered with fine sand, should be crying in a bush on a sandplain a few miles from town? Some gerbils were watching curiously through the foliage, and even the wild pigeons perching on a tree nearby and ravens on another further away trained their eyes on him. They knew that a lame vixen would come to him soon. She would always hide in a photinia bush behind Tang Tong, begging for alcohol and listening to him weeping and talking nonsense. The man with fuzzy hair would cry like a baby every once in a while.

The vixen limped over, then peed under the photinia bush. She gave her whiskers a few strokes and waited for her favourite drink.

"You motherfucker! Crouching and peeing, are you going to kill me with your stench? You shameless creature! What can be done with you? Here's the liquor. I've only taken a few sips. Life's so boring, I'd rather die. I tried all I could think of, but I'm still in despair. How can I get out of what's snared me from above and down below? You old, bitchy fox, you're experienced and knowledgeable. Please help me find a way out…"

Tang Tong huddled in the sand, handing the vixen the hip flask and then chattering with his eyes half-closed.

After taking a gulp of the alcohol, the lame vixen smoothed out her whiskers before giving him a pep talk: "Don't take things to heart. There's an old saying: 'One can't eat piping hot tofu in a hurry.' You must be patient. You can't rush her. What's more, this time you're going to sleep with a real hedgehog – the offspring of a hedgehog spirit."

"You're right. My dad and I searched her body when she first came out of the forest. She had golden fuzz all over her, I mean all over her back. They had originally been hedgehog spines. Since then, I seemed to have been bewitched. I'm always seeing her dainty looks in my mind's eye and calling 'Mei Di! Mei Di!' I shouted until I was foaming, for which my dad laughed at me, saying that my birth was an atonement for the sins committed by the previous eight generations of our family. Despite his foul words, my dad loved me very much. He gave me a lot of ideas and regretted not having killed the guy named Liao Mai at the beginning to dash any hope she has for his return. Who can deny what he said is true? We have ourselves to blame. We were too kind-hearted. Just as the song performed by the slut singer in the karaoke hall goes: 'Too kind-hearted. Too kind-hearted!' Well, there's no use crying over spilled milk. You'd better give me some ideas as to how I can start a relationship with her."

"You were indecisive at the start. How can you be so tender-hearted when you chase after chicks? Why don't you have your men tie her up with a hemp rope and force her into your bridal chamber? Then, you can do whatever you want."

"What're you bullshitting, you slut! You think she's a chick? If you keep on shitting Mei Di like this, I'll sell you to a country bumpkin or a fur trader! She is the apple of my eye. Everything I do is to please her. A smile from her would make me forget sleeping and eating. She's my food for survival. I can't live this life without her."

"Umm, haven't you been tormenting her enough all these years? You pushed her to the brink of suicide several times."

Tang Tong burst into tears again, saying: "Please don't mention it any more. Each time it's mentioned, I feel distressed and remorseful. I wish I were an ostrich and could bury my head in the sand. I was so confused then, so impulsive and so unwise. I was, as it were, at a loss what to do. What did I do! Luckily, I didn't do anything more stupid – you know someone, that is, my tutor, who suggested that I drug her and have her hands pressed by a few rough elderly women who were ready to help. Her suggestion was tempting, but I was indecisive and eventually didn't carry it out. Why? Because I know it's easier to claim her body than her heart. It would be a waste of my time and energy. I want her to volunteer her pouted lips to me and throw herself into my arms with a smile. Since I made this decision, I've never done anything silly except secretly curse her and gesticulate a bit in the direction of her residence while I was lying on my *kang*. Whenever I ran into her, I would greet her by nodding and bowing as if she were a senior official. But my heart thumped and thumped. What kind of miraculous motherfucker is she? Am I enchanted again? When am I going to escape her spell?"

Streams of his tears moistened the sand. The lame vixen sighed in sympathy and reached out a hairy paw to pat him. "Tang," she said, "looking on the rosy side, you've slept with a lot of women and sired a number of bastards. You can't hide what you've done from others. Can you still claim that you love her wholeheartedly?"

"I admit that I have a short fuse. When I want something, I can't wait a minute. I sleep with other women only to release my stress. But the stress remains because the more women I sleep with, the more I think of her. It's like that song: 'To drown one's sorrows in liquor / One feels all the more sorrowful.' It's useless. The name 'Mei Di!' 'Mei Di!' 'Mei Di!' has caused a callus to grow in my ears. I sat on a wall of her courtyard and wept nonstop for the whole night. I also lay on the snow in front of her house after drinking a lot and eventually hurt my lower back. Three times I tried to commit suicide with poison I had prepared for myself. You know I've suffered more than a human can bear… My merciful tutor grabbed the poison and tossed it away during each suicide attempt. She talked the whole night trying to dissuade me from taking my own life. Do you know who my tutor is? It's a woman, an extremely good-looking woman. She's devoted to me, so I do whatever she tells me. My tutor's never jealous of Mei Di. I learned of this later. Holding me in her arms at midnight, she said: 'Tong, my darling, you can't go on like this. We must come up with a perfect plan.' Despite what we've said, we're both at our wit's end. We're helpless."

"I, too, am worried. I'm not drinking your booze for nothing. You know, I've talked with Sister Weasel. We thought it was the easiest thing to do because weasels are natural enemies of hedgehogs. The only trick a hedgehog can play is to turn itself into a spiked ball. What else can it do? When a weasel runs into a hedgehog, it doesn't have to hit or curse it. It only needs to edge closer and release its foul-smelling musk, and the hedgehog has to extend its body – then its soft, warm belly will be exposed, and you can do whatever you want with her. It would have been a cinch, but you simply won't let us do it..."

"Of course, I won't! You'd destroy both of us in the process. As I said, I want her to run around with me voluntarily. I've heard songs with lyrics such as 'I will love you till I die'. I reckoned they were nonsense. Who would have thought they're true, damn true. There's nothing fake about it. I can't do without her! The thing that's called 'love' does actually exist. I've been living it. I would have never believed it if someone had told me about its existence before, not even if it meant facing death or being forced to believe it by the provincial governor. This time, things are getting terrible. This lovesickness thing befell me. It's been dogging me for the last decade or two. In theory, I have money and blunderbusses as well as a gang of people who can come to my aid whenever I give them a holler. If I settle on a woman, I can just grab her over, spread her legs and voila, it's done. But this time, I can't do that. I simply can't do it. You know I only vent my anger behind her back. I wish I could do something about her, like tearing her dainty legs into pieces. But what's the use of getting pissed off in secret? Whenever I see her little face and gaze at her deep-set eyes, I melt. My hands tremble, my heart beats hard, all the savagery in me dissipates, and my bones will crumble...

"Good Heavens, every person has his own fate. Why did I have to run into a creature like her? Could it be that some formidable wizard has cast a spell on me or dispatched this soul-snatching creature from the beach to harm me? I heard elderly people talking about using the blood of black dogs to exorcise evil spirits. So I slaughtered two and smeared their blood on my body and my doorframes – to be frank with you, I also rubbed some on my crotch. After two months, however, not only did the wizardry fail to work, but things got even worse. I've slept with all the horny women that came to town, including a foreign one. I've done everything I can, but nothing's worked. Even my tutor's puzzled, saying that I'm suffering the 'ultimate bewitchment'. She says there's nothing I can do except, Good Heavens, killing the slut Mei Di. With my own hands! But it's easier said than done. Only thinking of killing her would shorten my own life, not to speak of taking her life as well. Killing her would be as good as killing myself. I immediately covered my tutor's mouth with my hand, but then she moved my hand down to her huge breasts. Those fatty things can be suckled by people during the starving years or by men who had a hard time finding women to marry them. But I've already got food in my stomach, so I don't feel hungry. I'm a man who's suffering from that 'ultimate bewitchment'. Oh, my God! My God! When it comes to this issue, I want to die! I want to die…"

Tang Tong cried heartily, wriggling and kicking in the sand, and in so doing, he smeared his entire body, including his head, with a layer of white sand. He kicked so hard that he left two deep furrows in the sand. Glancing at the sky in the west, he gasped for breath.

Scared, the lame vixen put the hip flask on the ground and felt his pulse and chest. She kept patting him tenderly and said: "Lao Tong, no one can help you if you act like this, you poor bewitched thing. I'm your auntie, and you're getting worse and worse right under my nose. You're losing control of yourself so much that your trousers almost fall to the sand. If a stranger passed by and saw us, he might think I was greedy not only for your liquor but also for your body. Well, well, what can I say? I'm not going to complain any more, because I may just as well treat you as a child. Now I must make you feel at ease."

As she mumbled, the lame vixen placed his head on her thighs and his mouth on her shrivelled breasts. She pinned him to the sand by holding his listless hands tight with her hind legs.

Tang Tong felt as if he were in a dream in which his hands were held tight. He sucked vigorously and wondered whose milk it was because it tasted so dry and unfamiliar. A whiff of urine and sheep caused him to open his eyes wide, spring out of her grip and vomit some of what he had in his mouth.

"You're so ungrateful! You've been cuddling in my bosom, and now the minute you leave my arms you start puking. How can you behave like this after taking advantage of me?" The lame vixen was rather vexed and returned to the back of the photinia bush, where she picked up the hip flask.

Wiping his mouth, Tang Tong said: "What did you say? It's hard to say who took advantage of who. What you did to me was like 'robbing me while my house is on fire'. That song has it right: 'I'm an unlucky guy…'"

He pushed back his hair, looked around and listened to the sound carried by the north wind – splashing, splashing.

"From the waves of the sea? Huh? But the sea is still far away…"

"From the sea waves for sure!"

"'Oh, sea waves, rock gently the ships'," Tang Tong muttered and then hummed another tune.

I DREAMED OF YOU AGAIN

The foreman had been bringing Tang Tong good news for several days. "We've been kept so busy with all the 'goldie' there is to dig that we don't even have time to pray and offer incense to the Goddess of Gold."

But Tang Tong was not in the mood to listen because his mind had been wandering elsewhere since he got up that morning.

"Good news! Good…" shouted the company's office associate at the door.

"What do you know about 'good', you son of a bitch? Get out!" scolded Tang Tong while pretending to fumble for the short blunderbuss beneath his pillow by the bedside. Seeing this, the associate scurried away in fear.

In fact, Tang Tong was living in a state of self-retribution. For a long time, he had not visited his tutor, Lady Shan, who in her advancing years was now known by all the townsfolk as Old Woman Shan. None of the possible reasons – a hectic work schedule, living in a dangerous world, the honorary titles that were amassing or the gold arriving at home in piles – justified him not going. For many years, he had been visiting her regularly. He had to do so as time-honoured experience told him. He had thought it the right thing to do even when his father, Tang Laotuo, had been alive. Old Woman Shan neither requested his visit nor sent for him. It was he who could never resist going to the estuary. The older she grew, the tougher she became. Tang Tong, however, increased his solicitude for her with each passing day, not for her body but for something else.

He was worried that she might have new insights but forget

them before he could find time from his busy schedule to visit her and listen to her telling them to him in person. It was like someone who had so many treasures that he was no longer aware of their true value and would often toss them away. Old Woman Shan had innumerable insights of great value. She was the only person in his life who made him feel inferior, and therefore she garnered the most respect from him. He subconsciously treated Old Woman Shan as a mother.

He dreamed of her again last night. "Damn it! So many days have passed in a flash. She knocked at the door in my dream when I failed to visit her as I should've done," mumbled Tang Tong, slapping his knees. He did not know since when he had begun to pay more attention to the dream world than the real one. He had never dreamed an unrealisable dream. To him, there were only unrealised dreams, and no unpredictable ones. Dreaming was his secret weapon. One night, he dreamed of killing his most favoured and reliable friend and woke up before the blood on his hands had dried. When he had reflected on the dream, he brushed it aside as unbelievable. Nevertheless, he was horrified when the dream became a reality six months later, when the friend died mysteriously at home soon after having a squabble with him.

Of course, not everything happened exactly as in his dreams, but they had not been too far off. "Damn it! Wouldn't my life be easier if everything in broad daylight turns out as true as in my dreams?" he often exclaimed.

It was sunset. He thought he had to see Old Woman Shan today no matter what. He asked that something be prepared for him to take to her, though, in fact, she was in need of nothing. As he had not visited her for so long, he had to show his sincerity. But in actuality, even this show of sincerity was unnecessary as both he and Old Woman Shan were aware of their emotional intimacy without admitting it openly. They could accurately gauge what the other was thinking most of the time.

What kind of a person could live in that place? It was not a question answerable by a mortal. He could never have answered it if he had not known her for the past fifty years and been involved with her both emotionally and physically for the past three decades. Ahh, it's so strange, so odd, he would exclaim repeatedly to a total stranger.

Old Woman Shan lived on the barren estuary a few dozen kilometres from town. She had chosen to live here several decades earlier. The place was known for its wild forest, flash floods, lush reeds, flying seagulls, roaring waves and violent winds, in addition to small, low-lying mud houses. But many changes had taken place in recent years. For example, the wild forest had become sparse and wild creatures nearly extinct, whereas the number of mud houses had multiplied. The most remarkable change had been Old Woman Shan's marital status. She had given up her singlehood by cohabiting with a chief fisherman before reverting to her single status following his fatal accident. As she grew older, she adopted seven sons of different ages. They all became helping hands in her newly established sea cucumber farm. Together, they owned seven shabby and yet powerful boats of varying colours. Being propelled with oars, they might seem to be as slow as a plough ox. But, as Tang Tong realised, the boats could lose their temper, and once they did, they could roar into the depth of the dense mist in a breath.

Fascinated with the boats, Tang Tong called them 'sweethearts'.

It was the mud houses, however, that fascinated him the most. They appeared to be a cluster of low-lying houses grouped in two or three connected courtyards lying in a zigzag pattern. However, the actual layout of the houses was far from being that simple. Even Old Woman Shan's adopted sons did not have access to every nook and cranny of the house complex. Only Tang Tong was allowed into the most secret and intriguing room.

Her seven sons lived in another two small, connected courtyards, the conditions of which could not be better. One of them contained piles of boat-repairing tools, machine parts disassembled from the boats and defence weapons such as three-section staffs, iron maces, sabres and firearms, which were either heaped or hung on the ground floor. There was also an electric generator, which, despite the availability of public electricity supply made available nowadays, was still maintained to a good condition. The other courtyard was home to the seven brothers. While the house had several spacious rooms, they somehow chose to sleep in a single room on narrow bunk beds. Other rooms were furnished with all the necessary amenities such as a game table, electronic appliances, a large wooden bathtub and even a sauna.

Old Woman Shan's small courtyard was surrounded by the two

courtyards. Each of the mud houses in this courtyard contained an exquisite skylight equipped with a sound ventilation system and a sunscreen-adjusting device. The rooms were well lit and spotlessly clean. The best feature was the acoustic insulation. They were so soundproof that, despite the roar of the wind and waves outside, the clink of a needle could be heard when it fell on the floor. Furnishings included cloth tapestries, leather sofas and handmade carpets. A covered corridor led to a peculiar little home cinema, where thousands of films and TV series could be played and where Tang Tong would weep to his heart's content as he watched them.

This courtyard within the courtyards was forbidden to anyone except Old Woman Shan and Tang Tong. One of her sons had once entered without permission, and Old Woman Shan had had his legs broken by the other six sons. While the boy was rehabilitating, Tang Tong saw him lying obliquely on a bunk bed with his legs in plaster casts. He did not raise the slightest complaint against the punishment. Instead, he made a slicing gesture across the pelvic region of the trunk and said: "The boss should have cut my legs off here!"

Running his hand over the guy's bald head, Tang Tong responded: "Next time."

Tang Tong became excited as soon as he approached the mud houses. At night, he dreamed of the seven skinny sons staring at him in silence, biting their lips. Their nominally adoptive mother came from her courtyard, wearing a large blue cloth as a scarf. Despite the absence of wind, banks of breakers rolled on the dark-blue sea.

Everything was like in a dream. The seven young men, who were not out at sea at the time, were fiddling with fishing nets when Tang Tong arrived. Pressing their lips together while busying themselves, they pretended not to see him as usual. A side wooden door at the end of the courtyard did not squeak until he approached it.

Pushing open the door was none other than Old Woman Shan. Still wearing the blue cloth scarf, she gazed at him at the door and gave a huge yawn.

SIX

A CURSE OF THIRTY YEARS

OLD WOMAN SHAN clearly remembered the day when she lost her sweetheart. It was autumn, when crows were cawing all over the marshes and when the wild creatures were scampering and leaping throughout the forest. At the time, she was incredulous of everything. When news came, she was smoking her water pipe. She flew into a rage upon hearing the first word and felt like striking the messenger on the head with her pipe. Several days passed, and there was no news of Liangzi's whereabouts. After murmuring that he must have wandered away, she got up and went to the forest.

In those years, the endless forest still retained its original splendour, with trees towering into the sky and standing firm in the ground. A tree's crown could be large enough to accommodate a family of three generations of wild creatures. The ground was traversed with brooks and streams and overgrown with stumbling vines. Wild creatures with body lengths measuring about a handspan scurried squeaking in the grass while grimacing and gesticulating at the people who invited themselves into their habitats. Shanzi's beauty was testified in the wild forest as well when a few male animals tagged after her, drooling and making obscene gestures at her. Armed with a short blunderbuss in her waistband and a leather-handled dagger from her hip, she had no trouble in killing a few little lives. What's more, she was in a bad mood and anxious to draw blood from a few breathing creatures. However, she hesitated after holding up the little blunderbuss, blew over its dark muzzle and looked around.

Shanzi felt lonely. Various animals were gazing at her in the trees, from behind bushes and by streams. She finally realised that, if she fired her blunderbuss, she would be torn into pieces by the creatures. A few reckless male ones could press her to the ground and violate her before ending her life. Shanzi had never been so scared in her life. Dodging the gaze of the glowing blue eyes, she threw her blunderbuss to the ground after screaming: "Liangzi, you're so cruel!"

It had been a dreadful autumn because she had lost not only Liangzi but also her short blunderbuss, both her irreplaceable favourites. It was in order to find these two things that she had repeatedly ventured into the forest alone that season, convinced that the ungrateful fugitive must have been in the forest along with her short blunderbuss. "I must grab you and hold you in my hand even if you've transformed into a quail flying between the trees or into a mushroom hiding in the shade. I'll pluck your feathers or boil you in a pot – this time, I must make you feel comfortable and let you know my prowess as a young woman. With one stamp, I'll squeeze blood from your nose and mouth so that you'll scream and die! I've never come across such a rude bastard that takes a virgin like me so lightly. Even the murderous mounted bandits weren't able to do so." As she swore, she plunged herself deeper into the forest.

A mounted bandit crossing the mountain noticed her, pulled her onto his horse and took her to a place a few kilometres away. There, he bared his hairy chest and uttered a string of swear words. But eventually he failed to carry out what he had planned because she managed to enlist the help of a senior mounted bandit who was later killed by one of his buddies.

"Neither of the two bandits succeeded in violating me. If you don't believe me, Uncle Laotuo, you can check me." The then unrestrained Shanzi asked Tang Laotuo to give her a physical examination.

"Damn it! Why do I have to inspect your private parts?"

Jiwo Town had seen many a valiant visitor, including soldiers and scholars. Each coveted her beauty but did not have a chance to get close to her. Thumping her chest while smoking her water pipe, she bragged: "Now they should know what a pretty girl looks like, right?"

She despised the women who had been victims of rape, saying: "What's the use of your teeth? And your feet? You should've bitten them or kicked them to death!"

Exchanging knowing glances, elderly women proclaimed: "My word! We now have a chaste shrew in town."

The shrew had roamed the streets after dark with her glowing eyes, and they happened to shine on Liangzi. "Didn't expect there'd be such a handsome man in Jiwo. Look at his poker face! He's not talking to anyone. He's not carrying a fountain pen in his suit pocket. He's looking at people with his big watery eyes. Well, I'll make him a lucky man today since he's run into me."

Being confident and fearless, she shouted at him half-jokingly and half-seriously: "I'm now taking you as mine."

She milled about in the forest with her hair untidy and her face smeared. Before long, all the wild creatures began to feel a great affinity with her, agreeing to help her look for the short blunderbuss. "Let's find that destined lover of mine first," she said. She described the appearance of the man with the help of gestures, and as she was doing so, she felt so grieved that she dropped to the sand with teary eyes, reluctant to get up.

Some female animals tiptoed away and, exchanging a knowing glance, said: "Let's hurry and look for him. But don't let her know when we find him!"

During her years in the forest, Shanzi found herself on a path of despair. She realised many years later that she would never see Liangzi again and she began to curse him all the time. She had been doing so for the past three decades.

At the beginning, Shanzi's curses were punctuated with frequent memories of the good old days. "You ungrateful, heartless and shameless scoundrel! After all, you showed me your naked body when I was still powerful and resourceful and when I had a lion's heart in a woman's body. There was no way you could have refused to lie down and go through corporal punishment. Capable of calling for wind and rain, I could even make Tang Laotuo bow in trepidation. I regret not throwing you into a boiling pot so that you would become a featherless chick unable to fly away with a flutter of your wings. You son of a bitch didn't recognise the decent person that I was! You motherfucker washed your face with pig manure but your bottom with a honey solution. Damn you mean bastard! You'll be unlucky for the next eight generations because you have the eyesight of a snob! To this day, I'm still a kickass virgin!"

Shanzi's tears dripped into a creek that joined a stream, causing the black eel, owner of the stream, to feel sorry for her. This was because the eel herself had been forsaken by a catfish when young. Crawling up to the bank, she said comfortingly: "Big sister, don't cry any more. Very few of the male creatures are good. My catfish ex, proud of his beautiful whiskers, sneaked to the bosom of a small goldfish. Today, however, he may have long been cooked into a fish soup."

Shanzi was taken aback and gazed at the black eel with secret admiration. She found that the wild creatures here were far better at imprecating than the townspeople.

The black eel suggested that Shanzi live in the forest and find a job like the yam king or the goji spirit. "It's always better to have some responsibilities and authority," she said. "You'll have endless trouble in life being one of the common people."

Patting herself on the chest, Shanzi asked: "What about me, my body? Whom shall I give it to?"

The black eel was nervous when asked such a pointed question, one that she had been asking herself without an answer. She burst into tears and confided what had been weighing on her mind to a townsperson that she had never met before. "Big sister, to be frank, there was a time when I desired to give myself up to an old physician. Later, after careful consideration and reconsideration, I eventually suppressed the desire."

"It was fortunate that you suppressed it," Shanzi said, chuckling. "How did you know that the physician was even worse than an accomplice of the late Lord Huo? Our Tang Laotuo is thinking of cutting him up."

Looking up at the west sky, Shanzi was still contemplating her own past, her teeth clattering. She said to herself: Liangzi, wait and see. Not only will I curse you out loud, but I'll also condemn you physically with my body. I'll make you suffer and reel under the pain of the two-fold curses. You'll reel into hell. To hell! To hell! Go to hell!

A REAL BEAST

Shanzi had made up her mind to find her lifetime partner in a walking beast, a real beast in the wild. She had found that there were too many fake beasts, each pretending to speak inhumanly, eating like pigs and putting on the air of a highwayman. However, when cuddling in the bosoms of women, they would reveal their true nature. Those good-for-nothings then became soft-hearted, vowing to be great lovers for the rest of their lives.

Shanzi told herself that such a beast must have a waist measuring about two metres, a swarthy face with eyes pointing upwards and a pair of callused feet tough enough to withstand thistles and thorns. A guy like this must have killed someone in his early teens, and preferably be a rapist or an arsonist. He must have the guts to cheat his parents and siblings and to fuck a black ass. Can't we find someone like that? Have guys like this already become extinct in our land full of good-for-nothings?

After smoking a water pipe and drinking a bottle of strong alcohol, Shanzi began shouting at elderly women on Stone Street.

The men in Jiwo all walked around her. She spat and called out to them: "Who do you think you are? How much are your chicken-bone skeletons worth?"

Some men from leading positions came, attired in uniforms and with neatly parted hair, and they tried to give her some advice. But before one of them could speak, she handed him her water pipe and said: "You must have been castrated before emerging from your mum's womb, right? I need to check you out and see for myself!" With that, she reached out her hands towards his crotch and sent him scurrying away screaming.

Tang Tong often gazed unblinkingly at Shanzi's breasts, wishing to be nestled there and to be pushed back and forth in the grip of her hand. Having been wild and reckless since childhood, Tang Tong touched her, making her feel ticklish all over. She immediately squeezed his neck between her thighs and would not relax her grip until he was red-faced and short of breath. After half an hour, Tang Tong lay on the ground exhausted, looking sideways, breathless for a long time before being able to gasp for air, and matted with beads of sweat on his forehead.

"You're too young," Shanzi jeered. "You'd better add some beef shank to your diet before you'll be up to it."

Tang Tong responded with a "Huh" and left with fear written on his face.

Spring arrived, and a Chinese parasol tree began to bloom. This was the only tree that had survived in Jiwo due to an oversight on the part of the town's residents, and it grew in the harsh environment before its final felling two years later. Bees and butterflies circled the flowers and leaves before flying away. Soon, people began to exchange glances and gossip in whispers. Several looked out of their windows in search of the source of the thumping footsteps, loud and heavy. They came from the entrance of an alley, moved down Stone Street and finally stopped in front of a small courtyard built of yellow cobblestones. Now people could clearly see a typical great foolish beggar. He was over six feet tall, stout but not a hulk. However, he was filthy and greasy, the hair on the top of his head dishevelled and curly with the rest hung over his shoulders in separate tufts. A pair of bucked teeth pressed down onto his fat lower lip. On his forehead was a glistening scar that pulled his eyes a bit sideways under dashing eyebrows. His long ears looked like those of a rabbit. He was carrying a black-cloth bedroll, and when he walked, he tended to hold his hands into fists, his wrists protected by spiked bracers.

"Jeez, the guy looks as if he's come to Jiwo for a martial arts contest. It's quite something for a great foolish beggar to be so cavalier. Doesn't he know what era we are living in now? If it were in the early years, our Laotuo would've ordered blunderbusses to be trained on him." The gossipers did not know that, as they gossiped, Tang Laotuo and his son Tang Tong were leaning out of a window and also looking at the new arrival. Tang Laotuo decided to wait and see since the guy's appearance in town must have something to do with Shanzi.

Standing in front of the cobblestone courtyard, the great foolish beggar shouted something like his name and where he had come from. After a while, a small window was opened ajar. It must be Shanzi eyeing the stranger from head to toe. Minutes elapsed, and it was hushed all around. The window banged closed, causing the great foolish beggar to flex his fists and stomp his feet. Then, the window opened again. No one knew what gesture the person in the window had made – later, many of the spectators vowed that Shanzi did not beckon him in – but anyway, the great foolish beggar went straight into the courtyard, walked up the steps, pushed open the door of the house and entered. It was strange that the doors in neither the courtyard nor the house were bolted that day.

Then, the most intriguing and incomprehensible thing came to pass. But whatever it was, it would become a mystery forever since it transpired within the confines of the house. All the townspeople, particularly those right across the cobblestone courtyard, leaned out of their windows, each of them cherishing inexplicable and self-contradicting hopes. A quarter of an hour had passed since the great foolish beggar's entrance, and nothing could be heard. Perhaps to correspond with the quietest morning in town for a century, none of the dogs or chickens along the streets made any noise. A miracle happened in those fifteen minutes: at least more than a dozen people witnessed this exciting event, which was still worth talking about and ruminating again many years after its occurrence.

The first sound was a 'bam'. Some said that it was the house door opening while others claimed it was a punch that Shanzi delivered because the stout but speechless great foolish beggar backed out of the house and fell on his back as soon as he stepped out of the door. He kicked his strong legs a few times, perhaps trying to pull himself up to save face. However, Shanzi dashed out of the house in his wake and gave his crotch a good kick. The raspy, long shriek and the groan of extreme dejection and grievance lived long in the memory. The event was considered significant enough to be recorded in the town's chronicles.

Under the gaze of the townspeople, the great foolish beggar left with his head hanging low and carrying the same black-cloth bedroll that he had come with. From the rear, he looked far less strong than when he had first arrived. Nor did he appear as tall.

That was the whole picture of the incident remembered in perpetuity by the townspeople.

Shanzi never mentioned the visiting great foolish beggar. No one ever asked her what had gone on in the room during those fifteen minutes.

If it were not for what happened in the hot summer that followed, the great foolish beggar would have been the object of interminable gossip. But the various details of what had happened to him before were overshadowed by the new incident.

The heat of high summer was not recorded in the town's chronicles, but it was said that a similar hot summer had hit Jiwo only once in its history. According to the elderly, it had been so hot that sparrows dropped to their death during flight, and dogs and chickens sought to drown themselves in water wells. The heat resulted in an abnormal collective behaviour that still made the townspeople blush today; when the temperature cooled down a bit in the middle of the night, moans of pleasure and dirty talk came from the windows in more than half of the residential houses. The sounds merged into an increasingly loud symphony that contrasted with an extremely languid and tranquil dawn over Jiwo.

This was the second hottest summer in memory. In the early afternoon, every household would open their windows to let in the breeze so that they could relax in a wooden chair or on a bed by the small window in the north wall. Most of them would not move until four o'clock in the afternoon. But that day, as if in a unified call for action, more than one person abruptly ended their siesta and stuck their heads nonchalantly and yet earnestly out of their rear windows in search of a stranger.

This was an old man whose age was hard to tell. He was climbing a gentle slope on Stone Street with slow but purposeful steps. With each step, he bobbed his large head forward. He might have a stout, bony frame, but he was shorter than average. Due to the hot weather, he wore only a pair of shorts and a small, buttonless cloth waistcoat with only the front and back parts connected on both sides with bands, which fully revealed his saggy skin and protruding ribs. He had a hard, concave forehead, which was glossy and covered with wrinkles. His appearance, coupled with his slow, bowlegged gait, reminded beholders of a certain reptile: a turtle. From that afternoon when he was first seen, he acquired the nickname 'Old Turtlehead', which would stick with him forever.

After pulling himself up the slope, he wiped the fine sweat off his forehead, looked around at those peeping out of their windows along Stone Street, and asked in a rare, raucous voice: "Excuse me, may I ask if there's a young woman here named Shanzi?"

The windows were shut quietly. The old man asked a few more times without getting an answer and resumed his journey. After he had passed, all the small windows opened again, allowing the residents behind them to see that he had already reached the yellow cobblestone courtyard house. He was looking up in a way to suggest he was dazed by the glare of the sun. The bedroll on his back looked exactly like the shell of a turtle. This time, the small window in the cobblestone courtyard house opened without much ado. Later, everyone called it a miracle, saying: "It was so strange! Just as if everything had been calculated in advance, Shanzi, dressed in her brand-new floral garment, was waving, all smiles, at the window!"

Saying nothing, the old man stepped into the house slowly and yet forcefully, and the door and windows were shut behind him. Apparently, the owner of the house did not care about the summer heat. Residents peeping out from their windows along the street found the door and window of Shanzi's house closed tight until sunset. When night fell, they saw warm light reflected on the paper windowpane, on which there appeared two shadows that once merged. Three days passed like this without sound or movement. Neither of them came out into the courtyard, either. "Strange! They should've come out to buy vegetables or fetch water by now. Had she stockpiled provisions ready for the old man's arrival?"

The townspeople became increasingly confused. On the afternoon of the fourth day, when it was so hot that an egg could fry in the sun, the door finally opened. Old Turtle Head, though dressed like before, looked rather pleased with himself, his upper lip with that long, deep philtrum drooping heavily. Supporting the old man with her hand, Shanzi glowed with sweetness, admiration and respect. Above all, she looked very complaisant. She accompanied the old man along Stone Street and stopped to whisper a while with him at the crossroads. When the time came to say goodbye, the old man was seen moving his bowlegs to the kerb. He unexpectedly stooped and picked a false bindweed flower. He might have been expected to place it in Shanzi's hair, but instead he planted it in her cleavage with his quivering hand. Shanzi looked down at the flower while the old man patted her cheek with tenderness.

That was how they had parted.

Shanzi was standing on the outskirts of town, watching the old man plodding towards the misty vastness of the west and then turning in the direction of the rolling mountains in the south. The false bindweed flower quivered on her breasts. Afterwards, the townspeople had to compliment Shanzi, saying that she deserved some sympathy as she had been standing there for a long time, her breasts appearing like ripe pumpkins in the blood-red afterglow.

As everyone said, it was by no means hearsay. The fact was that Shanzi enjoyed her three wedding days and nights during the hottest part of summer. From that moment on, she was no longer a virgin. After the three days, her blush faded and her new life began.

Rumours about the somehow mysterious, turtle-like old man circulated among the townspeople, to the effect that he had been a rare talent with some extraordinary martial arts skills acquired during half a lifetime of seclusion. The old man must have been attracted by the reputation of Shanzi's beauty, but he never went back to Jiwo. As the saying goes: 'A smart horse never returns to graze on an old pasture.'

TAKING AN APPRENTICE

The residents of Jiwo came up with a doggerel to describe the state of Shanzi's life after her marriage: "After the three-day wedding / A scene the girl's making / She lays a jackass by day / She smokes her pipe at night." She might have always been vixenlike without equal, but she had her principles with regard to sex. After giving herself to Old Turtle Head, she had totally changed.

She rested in isolation for a few days during that unforgettable summer. Then, claiming that it was too hot, she kept her door and windows open day and night and went in and out in a state of undress. Her nudity caused passers-by to scream with surprise: "Wow! What a fair-skinned young woman! She scares us farmers to death without worrying about capital punishment!"

Life on Stone Street had since lost its tranquillity. The elderly in every household banged their windows shut and repeatedly told their children not to crane their heads in order to peep at her or, when they went out, to bypass the yellow cobblestone courtyard, the residence of a jinx.

Tang Laotuo learned everything about Shanzi. To bring peace back to the scorching town, he went to the small courtyard with his blunderbuss and shouted with his eyes closed: "Put on your clothes!"

A response with an invitation into the house came from within the courtyard, and Laotuo continued with his eyes closed: "I'm here to call on you for business purposes. You must come out to answer me."

Shanzi came out in a reddish silk blouse. Tang Laotuo said admonishingly: "Well, you've been a woman head and you've used a blunderbuss, and you should know the time-honoured principle that a military command carries as much weight as a mountain. So, let me tell you this – I don't care if you perform somersaults on your bed till your backbone snaps. But if you expose yourself in public, my blunderbuss may lose its temper!"

Shanzi kept nodding and said: "OK. But don't expect everyone to be always strong enough to carry his blunderbuss."

Young armed men on patrol were often called into her house by Shanzi to drink with her. For this reason, every young man in town loved to be on duty. Those who were not supposed to make the rounds took to hanging about on the street. Any man coming out of the yellow cobblestone courtyard admired her from the bottom of his heart. They admired her not only for her body but also for her wisdom and temperament, which stunned them into hopeless submission. During the precious hours of being together with her, she gave them a brainwashing lecture that transformed an unlearned and provincial Jiwo man into a yes-man. The men felt so diminished in front of her when she gulped down her liquor and laughed without restraint; when she put her long, shapely legs on the mat over the *kang*; and when she chattered with assurance and eloquence while holding her bronze water pipe.

"In our lifetime," she said, "it's better to see for ourselves than to hear from others. There's a mountain beyond the next mountain, and the grass is always greener on the other side."

All the men who stepped out of her house did so with an inexplicable mixture of ecstasy and awe and the same feelings of fright and trepidation that an explorer has after an adventure. As for revisiting that courtyard, they found it essential to first pluck up enough courage and conquer their sense of inferiority.

"I'm coming too!" These were the first words that Tang Tong uttered one midnight when he entered the courtyard carrying his blunderbuss.

"You've come at the right time," Shanzi said, grinning. "Have you had your supper?"

The veins throbbed on Tang Tong's forehead, and his teeth

chattered. He dropped his blunderbuss clanking to the ground so that the cotton ball stuffed into the muzzle was dislodged on impact. Shanzi was about to turn and reach for something when he pounced upon her, snarling and hissing like a leopard tearing its prey. Shanzi chuckled and poked him a few times until he was sapped of energy. While Shanzi was getting him a flask of alcohol, he swooped at her from the rear and held her neck in his mouth while ferociously banging her rounded buttocks. At first, Shanzi leaned her head over and over with the pull of his mouth. She then bumped him to the floor with her ample bottom. It was too late for him to struggle because she had sat on him with the full weight of her body, leaving him with no chance to fight back. She wiggled her body a few times. Tang Tong was still lean in those days, and he found himself suffering from the misery of being crushed. He could even hear his skin and subcutaneous tissue snapping. An indescribable pain radiated out from inside him. Tang Tong instantly grasped the true sense of 'being trampled upon'. His anger overwhelmed all his shame, and he opened his mouth to the widest extent. Had her back not been just an inch out of reach he could have bitten off a piece of flesh. But with her body as heavy as a crag upon him, it was impossible for him to overcome this small distance. He was not even able to wipe away his tears of humiliation. He wanted to swear: Fuck you! Fuck you stinky slut a thousand times! But in fact, what came out of his mouth was: "I beg you... I'll never... dare."

By the time Tang Tong finally became submissive and had buried his calabash-shaped head in Shanzi's bosom, it was approaching dawn. Patting him comfortingly, she said: "It's better to behave, to be a good boy. Genuinely decent men are rare in our Jiwo. You're one of them. Be good. See how much you've benefited from being a good boy."

Shanzi kissed his teary eyes and briefly placed her double chin on the top of his head where there were two whorls. Soon after the departure of the turtle-like old man, she gained weight, and the trend was unstoppable. Her once stout legs, prominent breasts and plump bottom became more pronounced. Both their colour and shape exuded a sort of finality and unquestionable obstinacy, possessing a kind of accumulated, preconceived and absolutely subjugating quality. She subdued the young leopard not with the strength of her arms or the weight of her body but with this quality stored up within her. Now, he quietened down. As she ran her hand through the smooth, natural curls on his head, a pang of sympathy welled up from her heart.

"You're just a child. You're not supposed to be rude and unreasonable. Just now, if it had been anyone else, I would have crushed a couple of his ribs with my wriggling butt. See how well you're behaving now. Have a drink of the heated spirit to expel the chill of the night. Once the alcohol has warmed up your tummy, I'll cuddle you against my chest and smother you in kisses. You've seen eagle chicks in their nest and wild boar piglets in their den, right? Their feathers, their hairs grow bit by bit. You can't hurry growth!"

Tang Tong nodded, feeling that she was unequivocal and he was lucky. She could have crushed two or three of my ribs, he said to himself. Good Heavens! She's really frank. It's as the old saying goes: 'A life's spared when affection intervenes.' It was like fighting on a battleground where I initially considered myself an arrogant mounted bandit but, in reality, find myself unable to dodge her darts when the battle's engaged. The identity of the winner is crystal clear.

Dawn set in. In the crimson first light of morning, Shanzi held the flask to his mouth like a mother bird feeding its chick. After drinking, Tang Tong took off his clothes item by item. She used her handspan to measure his waist, buttocks, upper and lower body, as well as his feet and the distance between his nipples. Finally, she said: "Grow up quick and it'll take you only a few years to become a despot, able to dominate this town. Now, you only have to tell me one thing – are you a virgin?"

Shaking and nodding his head alternately, Tang Tong hemmed and hawed: "I've long lost my virginity…"

Shanzi directed her gaze out of the window, feeling sad and grieved. Pouting her lips, she said: "As the old saying goes: 'A master teaches an apprentice the skills, but it's up to the apprentice to achieve perfection.' It'd be nice if you could forget the first person you fell in love with."

Tang Tong enjoyed an unforgettable night, particularly the part before dawn. For the rest of his life, he would remember the pink room, where they had been lying naked in the rays of the sun cast upon them through the window panes, and he had felt his shyness recede. At that moment, her large, watery eyes glowed like those of a cat, then like those of a lynx and finally a fox. Her firm, plump body exuded odours that were as pungent as star anise, which he gulped down into his lungs, and he felt himself maturing like the rising sun outside the window.

During their languid breakfast, Tang Tong tentatively asked about the man who had taken away her virginity, the strange old man who had walked like a turtle. Hearing the question, Shanzi burst into a laughter that was imbued with genuine happiness and pride.

"No other man will match him. If I had known that such an encounter was likely, I would have built a *kang* twice the size. The wisdom he taught me during those three days and nights will benefit me for the rest of my life."

What wisdom? Tang Tong meant to ask but decided not to. He began to realise that it was better not to ask silly questions.

A LOVE AFFAIR WITH A CHIEF FISHERMAN

Soon after the death of the man that Shanzi had been cursing as a heartbreaker, half of the yellow cobblestone courtyard mysteriously collapsed, and Shanzi refused all offers to rebuild it. The little house in the courtyard was also built of cobblestones. Sitting at the end of Stone Street for a century, it was, in fact, the only cobblestone house in town. However, after the stormy funeral, the courtyard wall crumbled and cracks began to crawl over the walls of the little house. Tang Laotuo dispatched his blunderbuss-carrying young men to help her repair the walls, but Shanzi declined.

"I'm not sure when the house may fall and crush you two," Tang Laotuo told Shanzi as he pointed at the little house with mixed feelings, knowing that his son had been enchanted by this woman.

"It's none of your business," Shanzi snorted.

She began to spend increasingly more time out of town. She went straight to the west and the north, trudging in the endless bushland formed after the trees had been cut, and roamed to the seaside to watch the waves heaving and rumbling. She preferred going out in inclement weather. When violent wind came howling from a murky sky to darken the earth, and when everyone outside covered their heads and scurried back home, she would stride into the open air alone.

"This slut has blubber ten centimetres thick to fend off the chilly winds," jeered the townspeople behind her back.

Shanzi did not wear many clothes. For the better part of a year, she wore a pair of elastic-waist trousers as Liangzi had done. It was convenient for her to pull them down when needed. She always wore her upper garment partially covering her body, with an intent to show off her firm, oily skin. The late autumn north wind brushed her bare chest and turned it fiery red. That was the place where youngsters desired to warm their hands. Nevertheless, Shanzi became more restrained as she grew older. She simply confined herself to her house with a cold, repelling look after Liangzi passed away. People came to the conclusion that the man she had been cursing had taken part of her life with him.

The place where she most liked to stand and stare blankly was on the coast, where huge tidal waves lapped the shore. Too close to the edge, she was almost swept out to sea on several occasions. Some townspeople said that she might be obsessed with the town legend: that Lord Huo was still enjoying his leisurely sea journey and, on days of wild wind and huge waves, would moor his castle ship by the seaside to let off and pick up some land-based creatures. Shanzi must have been waiting for the vessel so that she could spend the rest of her unrestrained life at sea.

Some townspeople claimed to have seen Shanzi delivering wild creatures of their babies and said that she would avail herself as a midwife on the wilderness several times a year and adopt the babies when they grew up. They speculated that she might want to become the most influential person in the area by having a large number of adopted sons. Tang Laotuo took the gossip with a grain of salt, but he was fully aware of the power wielded by Lord Huo, who had been working with the wild creatures. But Tang Laotuo, who was already senile, could do nothing about it. He was now relying on his son Tang Tong, who was fortunately hand in glove with Shanzi.

Having left the cobblestone house, Shanzi was reluctant to return. The house was impregnated with too much odour, which she filtered whiff by whiff every midnight until she detected the smell of a single person – Liangzi. Today, however, this man was buried in the ground, and she saw with her own eyes the heaping up of a brand-new mound above his grave. Facing the rolling mountains of waves, she bared her breasts to match those of an expecting dugong, which were huge, dark purple in colour, and encircled by fuzzy hair and bursting with milk. Shanzi felt the heat of the flames beneath her breasts increasingly fanned by the chilly wind from the North Sea. She scooped some seawater and drank it like the most pungent bitter rice wine. She roamed further west, and only when she was blocked by a meandering expanse of water did she realise that she had reached the estuary of the big river.

There was a little mud house on the estuary, vulnerable to being smashed by the huge waves. Shanzi broke into a smile, for she had found her permanent home.

There lived in the mud house a chief fisherman who had a genuine red beard. He used to be a strong man among a coastal fishing tribe. Countless legends were told about this man who had become a head fisherman even in his early teens. He himself remained after his tribe's migration to the west. One rumour went that he was abandoned by his people due to a crime he had committed. Another said that he simply loved his new trade and lived on the estuary of his own will – the trade in which he was currently engaged, farming sea cucumbers. When Shanzi entered the house, the guy was eating a dish of sea cucumbers boiled with seaweed on a blazing stove. The moustache of his red beard bobbed up and down as he ate, and a roll of seaweed quivered in the corner of his mouth. He was half naked, his skin glowing with a certain greenness. When he looked around and saw Shanzi, he quickly swallowed what he was chewing and grabbed another handful of seaweed and stuffed it into his mouth.

"You remind me of a greedy horse," said Shanzi standing by.

He wiped his mouth, scooped a spoonful of the sea cucumber soup and gulped it down with a toss of his head. "You remind me of the wife I had a dozen years ago."

A ripple of a smile circled the corners of Shanzi's mouth. "Where's she now?"

"I crushed her to death with a single blow."

Shanzi guffawed and reached for some sea cucumbers. She put a handful in her mouth; they were as tough as rubber. She chewed hard for a while and swallowed them with such effort that tears swelled in her eyes. She came out with a string of swear words.

Leering at her, the chief fisherman nodded, murmuring to himself: She's not bad!

The wind outside howled into the little mud house through its rickety door and windows, further lowering the temperature reduced by the extinguished stove fire. Shanzi felt so cold that she looked around the room and found only half a mat on the *kang*, along with a filthy quilt sleeping bag. Training her eyes on the half-naked Red Beard, she was astonished to find beads of sweat dotting his forehead.

At night, the wind blew harder over the sea. A dugong could be heard shrieking. Then, something was banging the door, and tufts of brown hair stuck through its cracks. Casting a glance at Shanzi, Red Beard shouted at the creature outside: "Not tonight. I've a guest."

With that, the banging stopped, and the ensuing footsteps were heard shuffling into the distance. "Nothing but wild creatures," he murmured as he jumped onto the *kang*.

Shanzi sat alone, adding fuel to the stove to the irritation of the man on the *kang*. Hopping from it stark naked, he yelled: "Are you trying to roast me to death? I'm so hot that the heat crawls through my body like a pea worm, and it's tilting my ding-a-ling up. Are you blind?"

Looking at him in the firelight, Shanzi almost blurted out: This guy is certainly well built, without the slightest flab. He has knots of muscles all over. His arms, particularly his abdomen and thighs, are all covered with brownish-red hair. His feet are thin and oval, pinning him to the ground, and they would patter with each step... Her eyes glided down to his private parts, and before she had a chance to say anything, he had already swept her onto the *kang*.

There, they entangled themselves into a ball. In the night air, all that could be heard were the sounds of heavy breathing and two people hitting each other. Shanzi rolled him over by wiggling her buttocks as big and firm as those of a horse and then poking his lower abdomen hard with her chisel-like fingers. As he bent over to cover his lower abdomen with his hands, she bumped him with one knee down to the floor and on his back. Using all the adrenal strength summoned by her anger, she applied her entire body weight and her naturally strong fists to this recumbent man. She was fully aware of the significance of the first night. If she did not have the upper hand, she would in future become a miserable underdog, suffering day and night in this man's hands. What irritated her further was the glimmering blue eyes that she saw peeping through the cracks of the door and windows. They belonged to the wild creatures that could have spread the bad news of her defeat throughout the wilderness and lead to her ultimate disgrace.

However, everything that happened was beyond Shanzi's anticipation. As long as he held his breath, the guy's knotted muscles were able to harden like rocks. Therefore, he never tried to fend off her attacks. Neither did he dodge them, except for the crushing buttocks that put a degree of fear into him. She soon gasped for air like a giant animal and sweated all over beneath her garments already shredded in the fight. She was launching another strike with the full force of her body when he received her into his arms using her momentum. He held her tight and did not allow her to break loose for a total of six hours. Now vibrating, now bristling, his beard prickled her face, giving her the feeling of a cold, authoritative air supposedly assumed by an invincible conqueror. Only then did she give up all attempts to prevail and allow him to own and engulf her entirely on that windy night.

Day broke, and the sea resumed its tranquillity. A naked Red Beard got off the *kang* and fished a handful of seaweed and sea cucumbers from the pot over the smothered fire. He walked up to the bed while chewing. Eyeing her plump body bearing the scratches he had inflicted, he exclaimed: "You're like a bottle of powerful liquor."

MY JEWEL

"From now on, I have a good wife and you have a strong husband. Can I put it this way?" said the chief fisherman sitting on an abandoned sampan that had capsized on the beach. He was eying her while smoking his pipe.

She was sitting on a patch of dry sand, fiddling with the sundried sea cucumbers while chewing one or two tiny dried fish that she had picked out. She had stayed in the little mud room for seven days and started to help with his work since the day before. Her hair was the texture of jute and looked purplish in the sun, so appealing to the chief fisherman that he couldn't help reaching out to stroke it from time to time. She looked up and nodded, her eyes falling upon his oily, muscular body.

"Then I'll have a fucking plump wife in my arms for the rest of my life. Working here alone, I couldn't know what I might run into. At midnight, a wild creature smelling of urine might come to spend the night with me, but early the next morning, the stench would make me throw up everything I'd eaten. You fatty woman, time to tell me something about your previous life. I'll do the same."

As he spoke, he was massaging his grotesquely big feet and sniffing at his fingers time and again.

Shanzi detested this behaviour of his as well as the smell of scorched rubber that his body gave off at midnight. "The early days of my youth were simple," she said. "I was a virgin. As for what happened later, I slept with a couple of men, but they're all gone now, not a trace to be found. Just pretend nothing's happened, OK?"

"So, you didn't chomp up the men you slept with? They were really lucky!"

"Everyone has his or her vanquisher. His arms, once holding me tight, turned into a confining iron hoop. His skin was so thick and tough as leather that I didn't know how to bite him. We made love for three days and nights. You couldn't imagine it even if you were to rack your brain for a whole day. You don't understand how that lovemaking made me feel, Red Beard!"

Stroking his beard, he said: "The dude must have been a jackass. Don't expect me to run into him. If I do, he'll be finished, he couldn't survive. I'll fill his belly with sand and cast him into the sea."

When the weather was fine here, it was really pleasant. The sun warmed up the white sand along the entire beach and people liked to linger. The calm sea appeared as blue as a gigantic piece of sapphire. Mumbling Red Beard wrestled Shanzi onto the sand, where they both lay face up gazing at the white clouds. After a while, he went back to the mud house and took out a bottle gourd filled with liquor, which they began to drink by turns. Leaning against the sampan was a black blunderbuss that he used to shoot gulls for fun.

"Our life's not bad. I've fucking seen fortunes and misfortunes in my life. Don't be scared if I tell you about them, my fat wife. I was the captain of a pirate boat, enjoying countless looted treasures and the best women that could be taken. I killed the stubborn ones by slitting their throats. I enjoyed robbing big ships the most because they had more good wine and women, in addition to gold and silver coins. I really enjoyed fucking those sluts. I really enjoyed screwing them."

The chief fisherman began gulping down the liquor without offering it to Shanzi any more. He soon drank up a gourd-full and went back to get another and resumed his drinking. He capered on the sampan and screamed into the seas, brandishing his fist in a menacing manner while slinging out a torrent of terrible swear words through his red beard. Shanzi chattered her teeth gently to conceal her astonishment, realising that she had finally met someone who had a dirtier mouth than she did. This guy could randomly rearrange swear words into more bizarre ones and cast them into the calm sea, string by string.

"I yanked the delicate women dressed in floral garments from the arms of their seemingly faithful men, and none of them dared stop me. If they upset this old man, I'd give him a slit with my knife. I placed gold coins in big-bellied earthen pots and buried them in the ground." Red Beard stopped his prattling and turned abruptly when he caught sight of Shanzi doodling something in the sand. He whistled a while, picked up the blunderbuss and aimed it at the seagulls.

In the evening, the chief fisherman asked Shanzi to munch the sea cucumbers and seaweed as he did, but she wanted to vomit as soon as she ate the first morsel.

"Hey old lady, if you want to live as long as your old man, say, a hundred years, then you must eat this stuff in big mouthfuls. Sea cucumbers give you energy, but if you eat them like you eat your average meal, your nose and mouth will bleed in a few days and you'll get hopelessly sick. What's the trick? It's the seaweed. If you chomp it together with sea cucumber, you'll be fine. Go ahead. Help yourself."

Shanzi managed to stuff a mouthful of the filthy, coarse and pungent seafood down her throat and flatly refused to eat any more. At midnight, the chief fisherman hoisted her above his head and dropped her to the *kang* face-down. With one foot on her buttock, he banged her endlessly. Clenching her teeth, she endured a terrible and yet affectionate onslaught, which was punctuated with a melee leading eventually to a tuft of her hair being pulled out of her scalp. Every night, the chief fisherman paced the floor holding her under his arm, sometimes peeping out of the window, sometimes standing stupefied and sometimes pausing by the door as if he were on night patrol. The tide was flowing from the endless expanse of the seas with a myriad of breakers. A nocturnal bird let out a cry on the roof of the mud house. He massaged her dark, bright eyes gently with his teeth, wishing to bite or lick them off in one breath. After laying her on the *kang* again, he rubbed her breasts, arms and crotch so hard that tiny drops of blood began to seep out. At every such moment, the chief fisherman would moan and groan, uttering something like a lullaby, which mingled with the rising rumbling of the tide into a symphony of resonate rhythms. Each time, she was amazed to be sought by a man who was constantly digging and searching into her sensual being. Her eyes closed, she would feel intoxicated, carried into a state of ecstasy of near death or immortality. Her moans gradually turned into screams of passion, which would at a certain point bring the chief fisherman back to this world.

The chief fisherman foolishly grinned from ear to ear, unwittingly showing a chipped tooth in his big mouth.

Shanzi, on the other hand, took a deep breath and said: "Old man, sometimes you really know how to talk big. Do you really have those pots and pots of gold coins? You're daydreaming, aren't you?"

"I'm not bragging at all. Why didn't I follow those fishermen? I just wanted to stay and keep an eye on the treasures…"

"I won't believe you unless you can dig up a pot and show it to me. Then, I'll be convinced that you're not talking in a daydream."

The chief fisherman felt sleepy. He shook his head and said with closed eyes: "No, I can't. The treasure was either kept for you or no one at all. It depends if you're lucky."

SEVEN LEAVES

"I dreamed last night that the cobblestone house in town had collapsed," Shanzi said to the chief fisherman. "I must go back and take a look."

The chief fisherman gave her consent with an "Mmm".

Shanzi was about to step out of the mud house when she heard a cry of pain. She looked back and saw him holding his foot and mumbling: "Come back soon. Come back. I can't be without you for too long."

Shanzi rushed to Stone Street. As the town skyline came into view, she realised with amazement that she had really settled away from it, and she had left it for so long. She hurried onwards, but as she stepped onto Stone Street, she began to walk gingerly and slowly as if it were a minefield. Before, the townspeople had not cared for her coming and going, but this time, they gazed at her with a strange look.

From the expressions on their faces, she could tell that the cobblestone house had really collapsed.

Sure enough, following a rumble on the stroke of midnight last night, the house had been reduced to a pile of cobblestones. Tang Tong had had his blunderbuss-carrying men stand guard around the pile before dawn. He also ordered his men to salvage things of value and place them in a wooden trunk. When it was stuffed, there was still a lot left to pack. Suddenly, he thought of a coffin left unused in the stable and had it carried over. When Shanzi entered the courtyard, she caught sight of people collecting what they had recovered from the rubble and casting them clinking and clanking into the casket. Seeing this, she felt her heart skipping a beat.

That night, Tang Tong put Shanzi up in the stable and kept her company. He cried and touched Shanzi's breasts again and again with his wide-open mouth cast from the same mould of his mother Jenny. But he felt something wrong. Holding up a kerosene lamp to shine upon her, he saw several bruises on her naked body.

"Good Heavens! What arsehole could have been so audacious? Did he eat a leopard's gallbladder and believe he had become a leopard himself?"

Running her hand over the curly hair on the top of his head, Shanzi replied: "You'll know who it is when you send the stuff to the estuary tomorrow."

As soon as day broke, two horse-drawn carriages, escorted by Tang Tong and some of his armed men, rolled out straight north, then turned to the estuary in the west. After nearly half a day, they approached the little mud house. When they drew near, Tang Tong gasped in an exaggerated manner and stood in front of the house with his mouth wide open, panting like a dog.

The chief fisherman stood in front of his house, hands on hips, without stepping forward.

"These people are from town," said Shanzi. "And these're my – our belongings."

Stroking his beard with gratification, the chief fisherman sized up each of the escorts. As soon as he caught sight of the coffin on a carriage, his legs and hands trembled. He walked up to Shanzi and grumbled: "Who… who's dead?"

Shanzi was taken aback when she saw his ashen face and each hair of his beard shivering. Tapping the coffin, she answered: "Oh, no one. It just contains our stuff. They used it as a temporary container."

After realising what had happened, the chief fisherman rushed to the carriage, grabbed the reins of the horse, pounded the coffin repeatedly and said: "What're you doing? What're you up to? What…"

Shanzi calmed the exasperated chief fisherman down with great effort. However, from that moment on, he was sapped of energy and spirit. He leered at the casket from time to time while the others were busying themselves unloading the miscellaneous articles and putting them in order. The chief fisherman examined each item and picked up a small, red *dudou* – a traditional Chinese one-piece, backless halter top – a big, buff bra and two pieces of pumice stone used for sanding off heel calluses.

"What the fuck!" he said.

"Stop dawdling there!" Shanzi responded. "Now that we have so many guests from your bride's family, go and get a decent dish to entertain them."

Without a word, the chief fisherman left with a hand net and a trident.

Tang Tong was shocked by the simplicity and crudeness of the mud house.

"This fucking bachelor is a good-for-nothing!"

After Shanzi whispered about the hidden treasure, Tang Tong jumped up, only to be slapped back to his sitting position by Shanzi's large palm.

Tang Tong was unable to remain composed for the rest of his stay, his eyes searching every inch of the one-room house, before going outside to look around and stamp his feet here and there.

The chief fisherman returned with three fish, each as thick as a man's calf. "Want to pee? We don't have a toilet here. Pee wherever you want."

Tang Tong unbuttoned his trousers while his eyes were still fixed on the wall footings and the wrecked sampan filled with a pile of miscellaneous items.

Tang Tong returned three days later carrying a half pig on his shoulder.

"Your wife's family's worried about you both since you seem to be living such a hard life," he said. This time, the chief fisherman drank a lot and showed off his trick of munching sea cucumbers and seaweed.

Winking at Shanzi, Tang Tong said to him: "You're a hero, a real man!"

"Actually, I didn't use the trident to catch them. I used my bare hands." With that, he led them to the seaside.

The wind had swept the waves up, and the colour of the ocean turned dark blue. The chief fisherman dived into the water and started swimming.

Glancing at the man in the sea, Tang Tong tutted and said to Shanzi: "If this guy lingers here all day long, we won't be able to find the treasure." Shanzi did not respond; she had been focusing her eyes on the black dot of the chief fisherman on the crest of a big wave. Tang Tong went on: "Wouldn't it be great if he got a shot from my blunderbuss!"

Shanzi leered at him, and he turned his face towards the high seas in the distance, muttering: "If I shot him now, no one would know what happened. He'd then never be able to return."

During the rest of the day, Shanzi wore a long face. The black dot on the wave crest was increasing in size until his features became visible to them. He paddled the water with one hand and wiped his face dry with the other.

Shanzi whispered, as if to tell herself: "Now go and pick the leaves in the forest."

Tang Tong sprang up saying: "OK. An old cow would bleed from its nose after eating them. I'll get you a big handful."

"You don't have to. Seven leaves will be enough."

That evening, the chief fisherman ate some sea cucumbers wrapped in seaweed. He grimaced as he munched on them. He hoisted Shanzi up and down with his big hands and shouted: "A slut like you can only be enjoyed by me." He kissed her and teased her by flicking her head with his fingers as if she were a little girl.

She touched his brawny body and flattered him: "You're as strong as a big water buffalo."

The next afternoon, the chief fisherman took his sampan out to sea to release juvenile sea cucumbers in the sea cucumber farm. Shanzi sauntered along the river on the east bank towards the south and finally sat on a rock. She waited until she finished smoking a pipe of tobacco before Tang Tong came along with sweat covering his face.

"I came earlier," he said. "I'd been here earlier." With that, he shoved a handful of slender black leaves of considerable length. Shanzi took only seven of them, those darker in colour, with a thicker cutin and a finer, smoother surface. She cut the leaves into fine shreds, mixed them in the seaweed and rolled some sea cucumbers in it. The seaweed roll that she made looked much prettier than the one the chief fisherman had made himself. As soon as he came back from the sea, the first thing that caught his eye was the seaweed roll, and he immediately exclaimed: "You damn old lady, you've learned a lot."

He drank some water and began to chew the seaweed in a disgusting manner. This time, it took him ten times more effort to finish eating. Shanzi sighed while the chief fisherman complained as he stroked his beard, with tears choked out by the seaweed in his eyes.

"That was fucking bitter! Maybe I'm getting old. I find it harder to eat with each passing day."

Shanzi offered him a bowl of cucumber soup and patted him on the back, saying: "After you drink this, my Big Water Buffalo, you'll never have to eat the seaweed."

"I'll have to eat it. I'll have to."

"No, you'll never have to. You'll never have to."

After the moon rose during the wee hours, Shanzi went out of the mud room and sat with her shirt draped over her shoulders. Some wild creatures leaned over the windows and doors screaming aloud. She let them alone.

"Grooowl! Grooowl!" Several large wild creatures scampered along the wave-lapped coast growling and howling fearfully and desperately.

SEVEN

SILVER MOON

AN OLD WOMAN turned around and busied herself with something after casting the terminal tackle into the water and tying the other end of the line to a Populus cathayana tree. She pulled a bunch of narrowleaf cattails from the shallower part of the pond and rinsed off the mud that had collected on their roots. She placed chunks of narrowleaf cattail roots that looked like dried ginger in a basket half-submerged in the water. The small calabash attached to the fishing line as a float bobbed a little and caught her attention. She looked up – the calabash moved gently and reared up a few times before everything returned to normal. She stooped down to resume collecting narrowleaf cattail roots and young leaf shoots. Then, the calabash gourd shook violently, rocked back and forth, and glided in a diagonal direction. She rose from a kneeling position with the support of her hands, pulled the fishing line, raised it and hoisted it above her head. A small, silvery wave rippled and dazzled on the dark surface of the pond. The wave was spreading out to the size of a large bowl when suddenly it splashed and sprayed, and from the middle of the spray shot out a golden light, which then somersaulted in the air.

A short time later, a large golden fish lay on the narrowleaf cattail leaves and roots in the basket. Holding the basket in her arms as if it were a baby, the old woman headed towards a small house. The late afternoon sun cast its rays on the narrowleaf cattails and sedges by the pond. Pygmy bee flies danced about in pairs. What a glorious day. The old woman was seized by a pang of strange and conflicting feelings of agitation, jubilation and anxiety. Later, she realised that she had indeed been expecting something. However, she had never been notified of the arrival of a guest. She thought that what she had been waiting for was nothing but another day, and that no one would come into her small house. Now, she was quietly alarmed by something unusual, something that was so strong and apparent that it caused her to feel unsettled from time to time. She sat dumbfounded on one end of the *kang*, trying to figure out what had caused her discomposure. After racking her brain for a long while, she finally remembered her dream of the night before. She was able to recall every detail of the dream in the middle of the night, but when she sat up in the morning, it simply vaporised into oblivion.

These strange feelings must have something to do with that dream. Previously, she would have ruminated on the dream teary-eyed, but now she was no longer so impetuous. The dream, however, still weighed on her mind as she walked to the edge of the pond carrying the basket and fishing line.

She had dreamed of a slender boy, naked, with closely-cropped hair and eyes twinkling like stars. He was leaning over the window peeping in, with dewdrops seeping into his clothes. She spotted him and, looking at him outside the window, asked: "Where're you from? Aren't you cold leaning over here naked at night?"

"I'd like to go into the room," the boy responded. "I was going to crawl in from here."

"Who're your parents? Where's your family?"

"I'm your son!" the boy answered hoarsely. "Mother, do you not recognise me? I'm home. I'm Silver Moon."

A wave of warmth swelled up from the bottom of the old woman's heart. She sat up, awakened from her dream.

It was only midnight. She felt the windowsill on which the boy had been leaning. She opened the window, only to see the moon so bright and clean that it seemed as if it were expecting her. She sat by the window until fatigue overcame her once more. Her snow-white head slumped down...

Day broke, and the window was still ajar. The old woman closed it. She knew her only child Silver Moon would never return. He had gone with a fellow villager to northeastern China to look for his father. Now that ten years had passed, she finally gave up her faith in miracles. The man who had led him away had been a villager. The woman who he left behind put a black gauze band on her left shoulder the next spring. The band hit the old woman like a thunderbolt, for it was a traditional symbol of mourning. The old woman wondered if her husband was dead. Then, what about Silver Moon he took with him? She became crazy and ran wildly and arrived at Bankou's house at the end of the village. She banged on his door. The then young Bankou came out still sleepy. He widened his eyes at the sight of the old woman, then frowned and consoled her by saying in an assuring tone: "Silver Moon's fine! Silver Moon is Silver Moon after all."

The full silver moon was hanging in the sky, and the old woman could see it once a month. Yes, Bankou was right, she said to herself, Silver Moon is Silver Moon after all.

This lonely house at the foot of a hill was half a kilometre from the small village. It had been built by her husband as their marital home. Now that both men had gone, the house became their shadow.

"Auntie, how about moving back to the village? Then, we could easily take care of each other." Bankou came several times trying to persuade her to relocate. The old woman shook her head. How could she leave the house? Doing so would be as good as leaving her husband and son. She decided to continue living here and wait. While waiting, she farmed and erected fences, and bit by bit transformed the few acres of weed and rocks at the foot of the hill by the pond into picturesque fields. Bankou often came to help, promising that he and the fellow villagers would not see her starve. But she still worked hard.

"She's missing her loved ones," the villagers said sympathetically. "When you think of your loved ones, you'll keep yourself busy and work and work."

The more she lived in the house, the more she realised why her husband had built it here: he loved the deep, cool pond. While collecting edible plants near the narrowleaf cattails and the white sand, she always regarded the pond as one of her loved ones that could protect and help her for the rest of her life. The pond was a mirror and an eye, as well as a composed man – yes, a man, a heroic man. For a time, she had the habit of sitting by the pond day and night, recalling the past. She collected edible plants by the pond such as shepherd's purse, amaranth and cowbane and also fished as her husband had done. The fish she sought had a flat, broad cross-section and was covered with golden scales. Her husband used to call it "a big flat fish with golden scales". It was believed that this crucian had the properties of producing great strength and energy. Later, she found the narrowleaf cattails here exuded a particularly fresh smell and their roots were not only edible but also sumptuous. A rice dish mixed with the nutritious narrowleaf cattail root and a soup made from the tender shoots of narrowleaf cattails could be fit to entertain the goddess of the moon if she deigned to visit.

She fixed a good meal and laid the dishes on a white wooden table. A bird with a large, round face hopped into the house, attracted by the smell of the food. She fed it a spoonful of rice. The bird's face and chest reminded her of her twenty-something self. Soon, magpies and collared doves were perching on the windowsill, and she fed each of them. She had long been acquainted with the birds and could even understand their dirty words or witty remarks.

She sat and waited instead of enjoying the delicious meal. She waited until the moon rose and the pond gurgled. She was not hungry at all. Sitting by the window with her palms held together, she gazed at the sky and the pond that gradually started to turn crimson. Then, she really did see someone walking on the water surface – she rubbed her eyes and leaned forward to peer at the figure, but it turned out to be the reflection of a shaking poplar. The tall, slender poplar tree swayed and swayed and then split into two, one slanting forward and the other standing where it was. The swaying part of the poplar moved by fits and starts and as it turned around, its leaves were rustled by the wind. But they turned out not to be leaves but the long, thick hair of a man! Now, the old woman had a clear view. Repressing her desire to shout in amazement, she leaned over the windowsill. Good Heavens! It really was a tall, slender young man. It seemed that he hadn't had a haircut in over a year. Look at his long, unkempt hair! In the gloom of the early evening, the young man milled about by the pond as if he had lost his bearings. Leaning hard against the window panes, she nearly broke the wooden lattices with her tightly balled hands.

"Silver Moon!" the old woman shouted. "Silver Moon! My child…"

The hirsute figure seemed pinned to the ground near the pond. He stood there motionless for a quarter of an hour before he suddenly dashed over to the little house.

LIQUOR OF NARROWLEAF CATTAIL ROOTS

He coughed incessantly before trembling violently all over and choking till his face turned a purplish-red.

"My child, oh my child! You've caught a cold. You're too tired."

She rubbed his back and chest and fed him with a traditional Chinese medicine soup in separate doses – the soup was a concoction of twelve kinds of medicinal herbs she had collected by the pond. It alleviated the coughing and turned his face to a healthier colour of rose. She began to feed him the first spoonful of her fish soup.

While he slept, the old woman examined the scars on his ankles, ears and shoulders. The sight of so many scars made her heart ache. To this day, she still remembered clearly how she had saved this boy's life with his mouth filled with clay. She had found the worst of his injuries to be on his lower abdomen, which was mangled and bloody. It seemed that some scoundrels had almost beaten his intestines out… She counted on her fingers and realised that three years had passed. Those wounds had since healed, and he was healthy and strong. Where had he been hiding all this time? Where did he get his food? The young man had grown taller, and the hairs on his upper lip had turned darker. However, he had lost weight. In fact he was so skinny that his eyes were sunk in their sockets, giving him the appearance of someone who had stumbled all the way here having endured many trials and tribulations.

"My child, how many places have you been during these three years? Where have you run away from?"

"Mother, Mother, Mother…" He opened his bleary eyes but could not utter a coherent sentence.

He went back to sleep straight away. She sat by all along, content to just watch his chest heaving and pushing up the quilt rhythmically with each breath. This is a strong young man, the old woman said to herself. When he's better, I'll have him take a hot bath in a wooden tub and eat a few meals of golden-scaled crucian carp soup, and he'll surely recover. Looking at his long, dense eyelashes as he slept, she had a feeling that every part of him resembled Silver Moon. Only then did she realise with amazement that this was the same Silver Moon that she had dreamed of!

He woke up at midnight, by which time his coughing and fever were gone. His eyes sparkled. "My child, you're well now. Sit tight there."

The old woman got off the *kang*, kindled the fire in the stove and heated the left-over fish soup. She carried it to him and fed him spoon by spoon.

Knitting his brows, he said: "Mother, this has that familiar gunpowder flavour. It's the same kind of fish you fed me that year, isn't it?"

"Yes, it's the golden-scaled crucian carp."

She cut the young man's straggly long hair short. He was fully recuperated from his illness. Then, she asked him to jump into a wooden tub filled with warm water.

"If the weather were warmer, you could dive into the pond to wash there," she said as she turned away from him and went to the next room to wait. After he had finished bathing and changed into his clothes, she found him a transformed young man. Silver Moon's father had left all his clothes home, and they fitted the young man perfectly. He looked heroically handsome in them, his eyes bespeaking tenderness and affection. He said to the old woman: "Mother, from today on, I'm going to work in the fields."

The old woman tried to stop him but to no avail. He repaired all the damaged bamboo fences extending from the pond to the waist of the hill; removed the overgrowing weed in the fields; irrigated the fields with water drawn from the pond; harvested some of the narrowleaf cattails; and filled and plastered all the cracks in the little house with cob.

"My child has accomplished in the past seven or eight days more than I can achieve in several months. Luckily, I had some of the villagers to help me. Otherwise, all the crops would have died in the fields." Her chatter tapered into a murmur. "Oh Silver Moon! My Silver Moon's grown up..."

They agreed that she would call him Silver Moon in future, and he would call her Mother. Liao Mai felt obliged to call her Mother because she had saved his life three years before. He had never seen his biological mother since childhood and had grown up with a father who had gone through multiple misfortunes. Today, however, he finally had a mother. At night, they shared the *kang*, and he told her everything about his father. With his glasses taken off and crushed on the ground again and again by the head of his village, he had had to put them on in secret when he taught him to read – his old man's eternal wish was that he read widely. "Books are the best, the best things in the world," his father kept telling him. In the dead of night, Liao Mai eventually told the old woman about the miserable death of his father. The old woman sobbed and sobbed.

The old woman did not sleep that night. Instead, she gazed at the moon, while occasionally feasting her eyes on him. "Your dad was right," she said. "A good boy must keep learning. Do as your dad wished. Don't worry about anything while living here – we have a different village head. Our Bankou is a kind man. Silver Moon, I'll tell Bankou in the village tomorrow that my son has returned from northeastern China."

The old woman was a doer. Early the next morning, she went out and came back with a man in his sixties. Erect and vigorous, he walked with heavy steps and had a pair of caterpillar-like brows. The old woman talked on and on, weaving a flawless story: her son finally returned, he'd grown up in the blink of an eye and she now had someone to support her for the rest of her life. Bankou coughed, smoked, nodded and finally pulled Liao Mai out of the house. They sat by the pond.

Bankou smoked silently for a while before abruptly tapping the burned tobacco out of the pipe bowl onto the ground. The old man ran his hand over Liao Mai's shoulder and looked at it, then he asked him to take his shoes off and examined his toes. Bankou lit his pipe again and started smoking. He said to himself in a low voice: "Silver Moon had a mole on his shoulder, and the little toe of his left foot was injured by a vehicle. The boy died at eight in a boat wreck, but the whole village kept the news of his death from her."

Liao Mai held back his astonishment and listened with his head hanging down.

Tapping his pipe, Bankou continued: "It's a good thing that she has adopted you as a son. I'm not going to ask where you're from. I'll register you as our permanent resident tomorrow. But you must be honest and grateful. If she lost another son, it'd definitely kill her."

"Uncle Bankou…"

"It'd definitely kill her!" Bankou cast a significant look at him and stood up. Stooping slightly, he peered at the little mud house nearby and walked away with his head down.

Liao Mai sat by the pond alone.

It was on that day that Liao Mai made his solemn vow to treat the old woman as his own mother for the rest of his life.

The old woman asked him to pursue his studies outside the village. He said that he would buy some books and teach himself because it was still too close to Jiwo. He said that he had to hide, continue to hide.

"So long as you remember your father's wish and study hard," the old woman said. "Don't let your father down – you have a bright future. It's fine if you leave this little house someday. Just so long as you come back, I'll be content."

"Mother, even if I travel to the end of the world, I'll come back."

It was getting cold. Leaves began to fall.

Liao Mai gazed at the sky with wide open eyes until midnight. He was reticent. The old woman wiped the sweat off his forehead again and again. He suddenly grabbed her hand saying: "Mother, I must pay a visit to Jiwo, or I'll become a real lunatic, a real great foolish beggar."

The old woman did not say anything. She went to the window and looked out at the narrowleaf cattails swaying in the dark. Shaking her head, she said: "Be patient, my son. I'm afraid. I can't lose you again."

"But I can't get to sleep. I haven't seen her for three years. I think of her day and night. I promise I'll be back after a brief visit."

Wiping tears from her eyes, the old woman said: "I can understand. You can pick a dark night and go – I just want you to be safe. I won't allow you to get hurt from falling. You must get back home by daybreak."

The darkest evening finally came. Counting on her fingers, the old woman calculated the time of moonrise, then she said that he could go. But it was a windy evening, with the gusts whistling at a terrifying rate. He gave a shudder as soon as he opened the door. The old woman went out before him, took a look and returned to ask him to leave the next day. Liao Mai shook his head stubbornly. The old woman went around to the back of the house and returned with a black pottery jar.

As soon as she opened the lid, a unique bouquet washed over their nostrils and permeated the entire room.

"This is narrowleaf cattail-root wine that my husband taught me to brew. You can't go out into the cold wind without first taking a drink. Have some, my child."

"But I'm not used to alcohol. During my escape, someone forced me to drink and it made me choke with tears."

The old woman poured the light golden liquid out of the jar and into a bowl until it was half-filled. Liao Mai took a sip gingerly and felt a hot sensation flowing down his chest, causing his ears to ring joyously as if the whole room were filled with the song of narrowleaf cattail. He took another sip, still another and finally the rest of the wine in one gulp. As their flowers flew everywhere, the narrowleaf cattails sang and danced like crazy. The song was so loud and unconstrained that his eardrums started to hurt. The shout of "Kick and kick! Kick and kick!" rang in his ears again – the source of the shouting was none other than Jiwo, the town of his personal enemies as well as his loved one. Kick and kick! Kick and kick! Oh Mother, I'll be drawn towards the town by the song's forceful and compelling beat. "Mei Di, Mei Di! The Mei Di who's just reached puberty, the Mei Di who's as gorgeous as a flower or a jade stone, the Mei Di who's made a vow to marry me, the Mei Di who must one day be my wife. Please wait for me this evening."

As soon as he stepped out of the house, Liao Mai plunged himself into the north wind. When he said goodbye, the old woman stuffed a flask into the front of his garment. He wrapped it close, ducked his head and made his way towards the hill. The sandy wind whistled through him, but he did not feel chilly. Before long, flames rose in his body, and he felt so warm that he had to tear open his shirt to expose his bare chest to the north wind.

He trudged on the seemingly endless, twisty mountain paths

with the wind rushing by his ears. On this moonless, pitch-dark night, innumerable wild creatures were stunned by the sight of this young man dashing north. They first remained quiet, then commented loudly: "Yes, I saw him. Yes, I saw him. He's galloping again tonight! He must be going to do something big, something important. Shall we run after him?"

"Run after him! Run after him! Tighten your waistbands and fasten your shoestrings. Follow him and run fast." The wild creatures swarmed after him. Liao Mai felt only the grass rustling and the trees waving. He heard cries and shouts everywhere, but he continued to race northwards, murmuring a name.

The night was so dark that Liao Mai could see nothing; the mountain paths, either wide or narrow, were completely invisible. Fortunately, a rabbit was leading the way. Leaping over bushes, it looked so gorgeous with its four legs in the air. As it ran ahead, it called: "Follow me, good man. I know clearly where you're heading. We became friends at the beach, and my dad traded his pile of jujube wood with you."

A fox behind chimed in: "You're lucky to have us as your escorts. Even bullets will miss you when you're following us. But don't forget us when you drink your wine."

With that, it reached out for his flask. Liao Mai placed it to his own mouth and took a big gulp before giving it to the fox, and it was passed among the creatures in a relay. When it was handed back to him, he shook it only to find a few drops left. "Now, I'm not going to give it to anyone. This wine's mine!"

No one knew how long elapsed before dawn. When Liao Mai lay down on his stomach on the outskirts of Jiwo holding his breath, the wind suddenly stopped. All the wild creatures following him had vanished. Their disappearance caused him to suspect that he might have been accompanied by the whistle of the wind, and the creatures had existed only in his imagination… The town in the dark of night appeared like a giant monster. Neither barking nor crowing was heard except for the occasional long moo and grunt. He took out the flask and finished the narrowleaf cattail-root wine. Like a slow-burning blue flame, as soon as it went into his stomach, it heated his entire body. He opened his eyes so wide that their corners barely cracked. He let his mind race, trying to figure out which was the best alley leading into to the downtown area to bypass Stone

Street and where the blunderbuss-carrying thugs known as 'country clubs' would be on patrol.

"Mei Di, are you still living in the little bluestone room with the low mud walls overgrown with green foxtail grass?" As soon as he closed his eyes, he would recall the waving foxtail grass on the walls. Afterwards, the scars of previous injuries would begin to itch and hurt.

It was too dark. Meteors streaked across the sky from time to time. It seemed that something grave was happening up above, corresponding to the chaotic situation on Earth.

Roosters began to crow, heralding the break of day. Liao Mai finally managed to sneak to the wall of the courtyard. As he leaned against it, he felt the entire wall trembling. He was quite capable of climbing over it with a single leap. He had just put his hands on top of the wall when he heard footsteps. He had to lie down again, over a clump of velvetleaf. He placed his face close to the plant. He could vaguely make out some figures coming his way. It was a man and a woman, each carrying a blunderbuss. As they walked, they kissed, their hands around each other's shoulders. When they reached the little stone house, the woman paused and leaned against the wall. Meanwhile, the man walked a few steps and looked around, then returned to her, mumbling in a very sorrowful tone: "I haven't studied philosophy for more than a dozen days."

The woman stamped reprovingly, saying: "You've been horsing around, haven't you? You're finished! You're kidding, aren't you?"

The man shook his head and tried to kiss her again, but the woman dodged him and in her anger decided to ignore him. Just then, another set of footsteps was audible. The man turned around and, wielding his blunderbuss, asked: "Who is it?"

"Who are you guys?"

"It's Xiao Gouli and me."

The man who had just arrived was dressed in a tattered, cotton-padded coat. Smoking a cigarette, he smirked: "I just saw two dogs trying unsuccessfully to mate by a haystack." Casting the cigarette butt to the ground, he left, saying: "I'm doing another patrol."

The two hugged each other in silence for a long time. The woman whispered: "You're finished if you give up studying philosophy."

Staring at the back of the man walking into the distance, the man cursed: "Pah, you motherfucker!"

"If you don't study, you're finished."

The man and woman finally left. All the while, Liao Mai had been trying his utmost to contain himself as the alcohol in his body kindled the blue flames again. How he wished to pounce on them and knock the blunderbuss-carrying pair to the ground.

After climbing over the low-lying wall, he found the little bluestone house empty. He tapped each of the windows and called in a hushed voice, but it was dark everywhere, and there was no response. Fine sweat broke out on his shoulders and hands. He flopped to the ground.

"Mei Di, oh Mei Di! Has something happened to you? Where in the world are you?"

He was so nervous and agitated that his forehead became covered with beads of sweat and his clenched teeth chattered. He had never expected Mei Di to leave this place. Where could she be? She didn't have a second home in town. Nor did she have any loved ones who lived there.

What he feared the most was that Mei Di, unable to stand up to the bullying from Tang father and son, had taken flight to the beach and disappeared once and for all...

Dawn had yet to set in. Liao Mai was crouching by the small window, knowing that a miracle would not happen tonight. But he would not leave, because he sensed Mei Di's smell before the window and in the whole courtyard, a smell that began to mingle with wine that lingered on his breath. Oh, the narrowleaf cattail-root wine, it rekindled the blue flames in Liao Mai. It caused the veins on his forehead to throb and his hands to clench into fists. He wanted to lift all the paving slabs from the surface of Stone Street and smash them to pieces. He yearned to retrieve his own life, that is, his Mei Di.

I'll look for you a thousand times, ten thousand times. I'll look for you forever, he pledged to himself. I'll continue searching for you. As long as I live, I'll search for you.

THE REMOTEST PLACE

"This is not a dream at all. Look at yourself! You've lived up to your father's expectation this time," Liao Mai said to himself aloud.

At a time like this, he preferred being alone in a quiet place, where he could contemplate. Since early morning, he had been taking deep breaths from time to time. Bankou and other fellow villagers were in the next room. They were here to congratulate him because he was the first in the village to have passed the entrance examination and been admitted to university. Seeing the old woman sobbing among the villagers in the next room, Liao Mai could not bear to leave her alone and came over to her.

But soon Bankou began to ask him a lot of questions. "Where's the university? Is it far away?"

Liao Mai told him that it was in a city in southern China – far, far south, and straight south. To get there, he had to cross several big rivers. It was really far away, the farthest place. "Damn, I've never even dreamed of such a place," enthused Bankou. Liao Mai nodded.

"Silver Moon's a born sparrowhawk that can soar high," said some of the elderly women, smiling and patting the owner of the little house. "He can't fly low. He went to live in northeastern China when he was a child, and now he's going to the very south."

The old woman brought out the narrowleaf cattail-root wine to treat her guests. As soon as he saw the wine, Bankou hopped away, shouting: "I had some when I was young, and I nearly lost my blunderbuss. It would've been a capital crime if I had."

The villagers did not leave until dusk. The old woman pulled her grown-up son over so that he sat opposite her. She kept stroking his hair. Since his return, the old woman had taken on the role of his hairdresser and always gave him the same butch cut: the top and upper part of the back and sides trimmed to an identical length of a little more than three and a half centimetres.

"Mother, I'll finish my studies in a few years. No matter where I go, I'll take you with me."

"How silly! If I were to leave, who'd watch the house and fields?"

For a while, he could not find an answer to her question.

The time for him to leave was drawing near. A few days prior to his departure, Liao Mai tossed, turned and sighed on the *kang* throughout the night. Each night, he was thinking of Jiwo, particularly the little courtyard encircled by low-lying walls.

After midnight, the old woman suddenly said: "My child, I'll go and take a look. No one knows me anyway. If I run into her, I'll try to take her out – you must meet her before you go."

Liao Mai kept shaking his head, saying to himself: Mother, you can never imagine how cruel the Tang father and son are. You've done way too much for me already, more than I can pay you back for the rest of my life. "Now the darkest night comes again," he said aloud. "Mother, wait for me at home."

That night, Liao Mai went to two places. He climbed up to the east slope of Jiwo, where he knelt before his father's grave, murmuring in silence: Dad, I'm going south, to a faraway place. A place your son's never dreamed of. I won't forget what you told me. I'll remember it forever.

He shut his eyes abruptly on hearing the whistle of the wind blowing his way, which caused his heart to thump hard. He expected something often told in legends to happen in the graveyard on a dark night with no one but himself around – something like the encounter with his father's spirit coming from the other world. Sure enough, he really felt his face being looked at hard, so hard that he became short of breath. He prayed with his eyes closed, first silently and gradually audibly: "Your son's leaving without knowing when he's going to come back, but you may rest assured that I'll never lose my bearings no matter where I go. I'll be your good son, and I won't forget the wrongs our family has suffered."

To his surprise, the wind died down as soon as he finished his prayers. Only then did Liao Mai open his eyes, and he saw nothing but the solemn grave. He pulled himself up.

Tonight's Jiwo was not peaceful. A few dogs kept barking while the alleys were constantly traversed by people. Liao Mai had been hiding outside the walled courtyard encircling the little bluestone house for a long time, waiting for the sound of people astir in the alleys to fade into the distance. He had even heard bayonets being detached from blunderbusses and overheard armed men conversing in hushed voices. Once the hubbub faded into the distance, he tiptoed to peep into the courtyard, supporting part of his weight by his fingertips clawing the top of the wall. He had hoped to see a ray of a lamplight through the small window of the house. But he neither saw nor heard anything. It was all darkness and silence. He peeped in this manner for half an hour before making the difficult decision to climb over the wall into the yard.

The paper windowpane appeared new, which gave him a shudder of excitement. He tapped the window grille gently and called in a muffled voice: "Mei Di! Mei Di!" It was extremely quiet inside. He waited awhile and was about to move to another window when he heard something astir. He pinned himself to the ground, his chattering teeth barely audible. He fixed his eyes on the little door, convinced that it would open ajar and that her face would appear, and her eyes would drive away the darkness of the night…

The squeak of the opening door was almost imperceptible – Liao Mai shook a little, ready to throw himself into the receiving arms. But when he looked closely, the only thing to appear was a blunderbuss and a pair of rat-like eyes. His heart skipped a beat, and without hesitation, he sprang up and sprinted across the courtyard and over the wall without even knowing how he managed it. He seemed to see a throng of the wild creatures hiding themselves outside the walls including the rabbit, the fox and the weasel. They sprang up at the same time. He could think of nothing but the urge to run.

He heard a hoarse yell behind him: "Hurry! I saw him this time! I saw him. Hurry! Someone's climbed the walls of the courtyard! I saw him with my own eyes. Listen to the big feet pattering and pattering. Hurry! Hurry up!"

In the wake of the shouts, footsteps could be heard in the alleys. It sounded like people were rushing over from all directions. Torches scanned the sky and the ground. Carried by his long legs, Liao Mai was able to cover a considerable distance with each stride. He soon left the boisterous folk far behind. He dashed out of the alleys and Stone Street and began to climb up to the edge of the cliff in the east of town. The pursuers were further behind, and their pace had slowed down. A man began to scold: "Why didn't you open fire and shoot him? You think he's a good guy? We don't have to pay with our lives if we kill anyone."

The raspy voice was carried to Liao Mai by the wind, and he could tell that it belonged to Tang Tong. After reprimanding his people, Tang Tong started cursing in all directions: "Listen you son of a bitch! We're on constant alert. We've cast a big net for you. You can't get what you want even if I happen to be asleep. So long as you step on our territory, I'll find you and tear you to pieces. I'll cut you with a blunt knife! You think I don't know who you are and how many times you've come? The blunderbuss in my hand hasn't tasted human blood for two years. If you're a real man, I dare you to come out to satisfy its appetite."

Gusts of wind cut the cliff with dull echoes of their whistling. Liao Mai stood on the cliff. Overlooking the dim and sparse lights of town in the distance, he found it hard to drag his feet and move on. Which of the lights is yours, Mei Di? Or have you been staying in the darkness all these years, in a satanic place without even a gleam of light. Did you hear my call tonight? Can you imagine that I'm going far away and that I've come to tell you I'm travelling to a distant place? Mei Di! Mei Di! I'm about to leave here and make that journey by bus, train and boat. But wherever I go, I'll worry about you. I'll never forget what happened tonight. I may have to be gone for several years. I'll remember everything that I come across in the south and come back to share my experiences with you. What I'll see must be the most unique and grotesque...

The day of departure finally arrived. Liao Mai put on the black cloth shoes and blue cloth socks that the old woman had sewn for him. With his square bedroll, he got on the horse-drawn cart arranged by Bankou. It would take him all the way to the long-distance bus station.

This was the first time that Liao Mai had made such a long trip. After the bus ride, he took the train, then crossed the Yangtze River on a ferry, and took another train before catching a final bus.

He travelled south and then further south. Gradually, he began to see palm leaves and a seemingly bigger sun. Everyone was talking in an exotic dialect. He found men and women with concave foreheads.

I've really ventured into southernmost China and am seeing what's described in books about the concave foreheads and dark, round eyes. Mother, Mei Di, Bankou and my fellow villagers, I'm seeing them now, and I like them!

DESTINED TO BE MY WIFE

I'm twenty-eight now. I'm a man who must find a job and establish a family, said Liao Mai to himself while shaving in front of a mirror. He had already become an employee of a government office after graduating from college. This city was a day's train ride from Jiwo. Time flew so fast that six years had elapsed.

During those six years, several significant events had come to pass.

The year after his enrolment in college, his mother became critically ill. After receiving the bad news in a telegram from Bankou, he travelled back for a day and a night and was able to see her. That had been a day of overwhelming grief. Seeing his mother's white hair on the pillow, he realised that life was but a dream and that everything could disappear and become meaningless. His mother's breathing became shallow and tenuous. Before taking her last breath, she opened her eyes and took out a paper package with great effort. It contained a small stack of money, which Liao Mai took from her, biting his lip. He knew that the money was her life savings, in addition to the amount he had posted her as a college student in monthly instalments of five yuan, the money that he had saved from his food allowance and that his mother had been reluctant to spend on herself. Looking at his mother, the image of the golden-scaled crucian carp came to him. As he grabbed the fishing hook and hand net, Bankou stopped him, saying: "It's no use, Silver Moon."

During his four years at college, Liao Mai had made lifelong friends with two classmates and established an unforgettable acquaintance with one of his professors.

One of the two classmates was a young woman called Xiu, a local resident of the city. Her concave forehead, dark, round eyes, small and delicate stature were all characteristic of a native of southern China. Constantly writing poems, she had a sunny temperament. When she broke into a smile, she revealed her deep-set dimples and bright white teeth, and her delicately sweet face somehow presented an image to Liao Mai of a crunchy, juicy fruit. Having never left southern China since birth, she was interested in everything about the north. So much so that she even wanted to borrow Liao Mai's handmade socks to try them on.

"I've never worn such thick socks before."

When debating certain topics from their textbooks with Liao Mai, she could become so excited that tears would frequently well up in her eyes, or sometimes she would even storm out of the room. While she was reciting poems alone in the cool moonlight, Liao Mai could see her white scarf fluttering in the distance. Xiu, Liao Mai and a thin, dark-skinned male classmate called Qi Jin were friends. They spent time together debating, studying, picnicking and hiking. When Xiu lay on the grass, she looked like a little girl, except for her large breasts that betrayed her maturity. She could drink half a bottle of wine and still remain completely sober. She also smoked in secret. In their company, she was surprisingly frank and capable of touching upon topics considered to be taboos. Liao Mai regarded her as a stoic, never crying except when she was writing or reading poems. The sight of her being lost while reciting poems would remind Liao Mai of the sophora flowers blooming white and fragrant in northern China.

When alone with Xiu, Liao Mai felt his own hands become chilly. On discovering this, Xiu held them in her own little hands to warm them up. All the while, she remained silent.

On the eve of his graduation, he and Xiu leaned against a railing above a small pond. When she leaned forward a little, he had to hold her back.

"Northerners are really fine people. Northerners are strong. Northerners are poetic to their bones."

For his part, when he was holding her, Liao Mai could not help admiring her petite and perfect body. When he accidentally put his hand on her breasts, she moaned and exhaled these words: "I'm already twenty-two…"

He did not know why he responded "Yes". He could hear that his voice was hoarse and raspy and feel his body shivering. Looking up, he was stunned: the pole star appeared to be dancing. He bit his lip for fear that he would blurt out the words: Mei Di! Oh, Mei Di! I'm here. I'm still yours. You must wait for me. I must take you as my wife.

Qi Jin was a bookworm and a young man of few words. He was known on campus as an eccentric. Coming from a big city, he was regarded as mysterious, cold and somewhat awe-inspiring. He never revealed his family background nor anything about his past.

He picked friends on the basis of a rigorous judgement of their eyes. He looked into Liao Mai's eyes and concluded that he was unyielding, evasive and innocent. He was never interested in prying into others' privacy.

His dark complexion and bony stature were a result of a strict diet and regular physical exercise. He was an expert mountaineer and a voracious reader. He could read books in English and had translated quite a few passages into Chinese. He spent one holiday travelling alone with a simple bedroll to the loess plateau along the Yellow River, and soon afterwards, he embarked on a trip to a coastal area in east China and did not return until the new term began. These long and laborious journeys made his tanned skin even darker but also caused him to be more taciturn.

Before graduation, Liao Mai asked to be assigned a job in northeastern China, and the closer to a mountainous area, the better. Xiu remained in her native city while Qi Jin was determined to go to the loess plateau in west China – he did not care what the job involved.

A long time after graduation, Liao Mai still remembered Qi Jin's corner in the dormitory. It consisted of the bottom half of a bunk bed, a small desk against the window, a makeshift bookshelf and simple yet tidy piles of bedding, books, notecards and hard-bound notebooks. During the day, most students spent their time out of the dormitory, either in libraries or in flower gardens, but Qi Jin remained in the dorm and, when everyone else returned, he went to the empty classroom. His desire for solitude, his thoughtfulness, and his somewhat opaque decisiveness – all of these Liao Mai had felt but could not explain. The day before graduation, Liao Mai talked about their job options and career prospects with Qi Jin.

The usually reticent Qi Jin told him: "Nothing's more important than the evaluation and examination of oneself. Only by doing so can a man be strong. I'm suspicious of all life that has been conceptualised. I'm a little afraid. I'm afraid that one day I'll be destroyed by abstract ideals."

He stopped short of saying anything further. Liao Mai might not have fully understood him at the time, but he did not discuss the matter with him further. That, he considered, might be something to be regretted. In the years to come, what Qi Jin had said often flashed in his mind.

It was the summer after the devastating death of his mother. A professor had invited Liao Mai to go on a tour during the long summer vacation. The professor was in his forties and was somewhat different from his colleagues on campus because of his profound knowledge and full beard. He showed particular concern for Liao Mai, who was in turn very grateful and regarded him as a big brother. The generous professor took him from one city to another, where they always stayed in luxury hotels. He bought Liao Mai whatever he liked. Afterwards, the embarrassed Liao Mai always declined his kindness.

In a lakeshore hotel, the professor returned from the front desk in haste and said to Liao Mai: "They don't have enough rooms. We need to share a room tonight." They stayed in a spacious single room with a bathroom. The bed they shared was king-sized. Everything was fine until, as Liao Mai remembered, about eleven o'clock at night, when the professor propped himself up in bed in order to chat with him. He reached out his hairy hand to fumble here and there in an attempt to touch him intimately. As he did so, his body gave off the odour of a buck goat. Liao Mai buried his face in his pillow. Thinking him shy, the professor started giving him patient, seductive advice and guidance. Liao Mai at first suspected that he might have misheard his professor. Then he sat up abruptly, staring blankly at this man whom he had previously held in such high esteem.

The professor's black beard had somehow turned purple in the blink of an eye – it had turned purple indeed! Liao Mai remembered it clearly. He had been as perplexed as frightened. The professor, however, only uttered a "Hah" and, giving his beard a stroke, begun to fix his eyes on his student. His teeth chattering and his chin quivering, he said: "You, you must... Come on!" Only then did Liao Mai notice the professor's powerful deltoid muscles, sturdy hip bones and buttocks as large as those of a bull.

The memory of this incident lingered in Liao Mai's mind for a long time. He remembered that he had felt the joints of his fingers itchy and tense. At the time, however, he restrained his anger and jumped off the bed, shouting in a muffled voice: "Professor!"

Once he had landed on his feet, he grabbed his clothes and, after putting them on and picking up the backpack, he took flight. By the time the yelling professor chased him downstairs, he had already dashed out of the door and leapt onto the street.

He walked the whole night. At daybreak, he was still walking.

Although he had enough money to take a bus or train, he insisted on getting back to campus on foot. Did he intend to do so as a self-imposed punishment? Even he himself did not know the answer. Whatever the reason, it took him a dozen or so days to get back, striding along on his long legs during windy days and sleeping on dew-laden nights. That summer was etched in his memory.

The faces of his classmates and professor would occasionally reappear in his mind's eye even after four years had passed.

In the September of the sixth year after his graduation, he finally sneaked back to Jiwo. It became the most important season, or rather, moment of his life. The ownership of the moment would permanently change the course of the rest of his life.

He returned in secret. He settled himself in an extraordinarily luxuriant false indigo bush to the west of town. He made a bed out of soft satintails. The dense branches of the bush above formed a natural dome of a roof that shielded nearly all the heavenly bodies in the sky. At first glance, he decided that it was the best place for his future prospects, for treasure hunting, for success and rebirth. Liao Mai had never been so confident and adamant. He was not going to doubt himself any longer. The place was only half a kilometre from town lying to its east.

He made several attempts at venturing into town. Each time, he was delighted beyond expectation, for there were no longer armed patrols on Stone Street. To him, this was a reflection of the changing times. Indeed, everything was changing quietly. But on the first night, he still watched cautiously in hiding. He did not want to take any unnecessary risk. He waited till the following dawn, the quietest moment of the day, before finally climbing over into the small courtyard.

In the steaming-hot, little bluestone house, there was indeed someone who had long been waiting. It was too dark to see anything, but the permeating body smell told Liao Mai everything. It was almost too strong for him, so much so that he nearly fell on his face. Enshrouded by Mei Di's fragrance that saturated the night air, Liao Mai bent over and, for a moment, was unable to tell where he was. He blurted out a cry as if he were faced with a calamity, but he immediately covered his mouth with his hands. He crouched by the side of the *kang* to allow his cheek to touch Mei Di's hair hanging from the pillow.

In the darkness before dawn, he and Mei Di decided not to waste time. They left the alley hand in hand, and after the dogs ceased barking, Liao Mai scooped her up into his arms, where she nestled closely, panting like a little bird. Carrying her, he strode across the cobblestone road in the west of town and plunged into the dense false indigo bush.

When the southerly wind swayed the stems of the bush, the sky in the east began to gleam silver-grey.

LISTENING TO A HEDGEHOG SING

If you have a lot to say, then don't say anything; if you aren't a fool, keep your mouth shut. Hands, eyes, skin, arms, feet and even hair were now expressing themselves in unison. The thick, tough hair tangled their necks, causing their throats to burn and feel hoarse even though they were not saying anything. The branches of the false indigo bushes produced a hot wind, carrying a pungent smell of the wild to ignite their hair, clothes and everything. As he started to climax, Liao Mai looked up and saw the sun sifting through the gaps of the bush stems and foliage, dancing on her wild-honey-coloured skin and radiating countless golden arrowheads. Her large eyes gazed at him like forget-me-nots, her breasts that had previously been shy now greeted him with boldness. Their bodies smelled like cooked rice and the young shoots of narrowleaf cattails, like the bouquet of narrowleaf cattail-root wine, like the silent eagerness innate in aquatic plants when they spread their spores in the southerly wind, and like the moans emanating from the depth of a flowing stream – all gathered into a single mass crowding around their mouths, ears and nostrils. He reached out to hold her and felt her spine that was still as soft and supple as a child's and her legs so silkily feminine that they accelerated his agitated heartbeat. She covered her lower abdomen tight with her hands while placing her chin on the top of his head. Her chin was covered with an imperceptible layer of golden fuzz. Her lower abdomen was a mass of silk threads, its golden colour flickering on her skin.

"This is really a hedgehog child," exclaimed Liao Mai, his face pressed against her chest. He held her close.

Their new house was destined to be built on this wilderness, and it marked the end of his seemingly endless trek. Pairs of invisible eyes flashed from gaps between the trees, and their gazes were full of fear, surprise, joy and advice. Running around to inform one another, all the seaside creatures learned what had happened before dawn and rushed about on the sandplain with the little cash gift that they could afford as tokens of affection. As the old saying goes: 'A mother is always concerned about her travelling child', no matter how old the child is. Mei Di was the daughter of this vast forest. Though the forest had disappeared, its soul remained there. It was doing everything it could to prepare her a dowry, as if to say: Look! The white-sand beach is warm and cosy; the satintail is smooth and supple; the thick foliage of the Chinese scholar trees shields the scorching sun; and the scent of the grand wormwood grass is repellent to all those annoying ants and flying insects. You naked boy and girl, enjoy your hugs and kisses here. Neither wind nor rain will disturb you because no clouds are visible in the vast sky.

"Hey good fella! Awesome guy! Don't think you've covered thousands of kilometres on those long legs of yours so that you can act without restraint. Our hedgehog child has needles hidden in her attire of floss. Her little hands can reach into the tip of your heart and put an end like a gust of wind to what you have become after so many trials and tribulations. You must protect her as the most delicate flower petal. You must blow warm breaths onto her body five times and sprinkle dewdrops over it three times a day. If you should act imprudently and allow your reckless moves to hurt her, then you can't blame her for pricking you with her hidden spines. It's not worth injuring yourself on a day of great joy. We're being frank. Pardon us for not lavishing fine-sounding words and good wishes upon you. Anyway, all the wild creatures throughout the beach are here to congratulate you. You've taken away from us at one stroke the most gorgeous and tender hedgehog spirit that best knows how to care for and love a man. This is the day when we've lost the queen of virginity in this area. Lord Huo or so-and-so others would absolutely hate you. So you must be wary of stormy days, when Lord Huo's castle ship may stealthily pull into shore and rob you of your bride. As you know, he's been a greedy and lascivious man all his life, searching for beauties both on land and at sea."

Unable to cover his ears at such a moment, Liao Mai simply allowed himself to take in all the sounds and voices of the wild. It was inevitable that they would offer him garrulous advice. He could not blame anyone because he himself was a child of the wilderness. He found his bewitchingly charming bride quietly metamorphosed into a new person on the boundless backcountry. Her irresistible sense of shame had weighed like a thousand-pound crag so that she was unable to raise her head or open her eyes. Now, however, she stared at her groom with a smile that revealed her white teeth and held him by the hand, guiding it in a search of all the treasures that her body could offer. Like a queen wearing a floral crown, she rose in pride while keeping him down on one knee, ran her right hand over his head and lifted his chin so that she could gaze at his open mouth for a long while as if to count all his teeth. After doing all this, she closed her eyes and, in the process, unwittingly shed a teardrop of farewell from her long, flushed eyelashes. She lay down slowly.

"We hedgehogs are happy / Together we're lucky / Hand in hand we seek honey." A row of hedgehogs sat on the sand, singing against the warm southerly wind while clapping their little hands. Liao Mai had never heard a song like this sung in such a clear voice. For a moment, he felt himself carried onto a cloud, which was fleeting above the North Sea, now low, now high, and allowed him to hear the waves splashing and to travel through the stars whooshing. What a dizzying trek! A trek through torrential currents and colliding stars. Several times did he cry out for fear of falling off the cloud. However, there was no response all around, nothing but clouds whistling by and waves soaring up. He felt an irresistible force pushing his whole life forward – to the abyss, real and fathomless.

He closed his eyes.

A VOW BY THE LAKE

Liao Mai did not have the heart to think about it for long. Nor did he have the heart to imagine Mei Di walking up and down Stone Street with her swollen belly. This was his lifetime of pain and guilt.

He always said to himself: Wait, you'll be punished for this. You will for certain.

He thought that he should not have hesitated at that time; he should not have yielded to Mei Di, who had insisted that she stay in town until he gained a footing in the city – like owning a small house – before taking her away with him. This should have been an attainable goal in the short run, but unfortunately it was never achieved – and then its realisation became unnecessary.

Mei Di's pregnancy shocked the entire town of Jiwo. She had to summon all the courage she had in her petite frame. This was also true of Liao Mai. For his part, he had thought of various plans but found none of them feasible. He still bore the name Silver Moon, and if he should have broken into town at all cost, he would have been treated as a fugitive and subjected to severe punishment – then Mei Di and their daughter would have had to endure hardships throughout their lives. Liao Mai no longer trusted Jiwo. He did not think that any force could protect him – he had had no faith in the town before, nor did he have any now. He would distrust it for the rest of his life.

With the birth of Beibei, Mei Di was plunged into a worse predicament that was impossible for her or her daughter to escape. Tang Tong's people were flabbergasted and kept a close eye on her. She had to live through the misery until things eased up a little. By then, however, she had given up her desire to escape simply because she was exhausted. She wanted to cling to Jiwo all her life. Neither Mei Di nor Liao Mai could figure out why she did so and they came up with the hypothesis that she was obsessed with the land – an enchantment that had attracted Liangzi to return and later would lure Liao Mai to come back as well. All of them were victims of this fatal force.

Liao Mai was not able to see his daughter until a few years later. At that time, she and her mother had left town and resettled in the wasteland by the sea. The girl was lying on a small bed woven from vines in a shabby straw hut surrounded by the wilderness. In the cool moonlight, he clearly saw her sleeping face. He touched her, and she grasped the forefinger of his left hand in her dream. He stood motionless.

In order not to disturb their sleeping daughter, he and Mei Di came to the lakeside, where they had long conversations one precious night after another. The wilderness provided an open field of vision; the view of the long coastline and the vast land overgrown with swamp grass was unimpeded. It provided an easy escape from any risk or danger. Liao Mai knew that Mei Di had chosen to live in this wilderness soaked in salt water partly for the purpose of self-imposed exile and partly to facilitate a tryst with her husband. But there had been more to it, which Liao Mai only came to appreciate later – Mei Di had wanted to fight a life-or-death battle with her own fate and to devote her life to a piece of tangible land, where, though more than half of it was immersed in bitter brine, she would stay with him until her final day.

He stared at the boundless wilderness and exclaimed in his heart: Mei Di, how similar we are to one another! We share the same qualities of staunchness and tenacity.

Facing her own man, she felt so proud and affectionate. These emotions were reflected in the look with which she gazed at the wasteland and the tone with which she described it. The whistling night wind carried over the smell of fish and putrid grass from a swamp where filthy bubbles formed on the surface. But she would say: "This is our lake." Her reference, however, reminded him of the old woman's pond. In silence, Liao Mai was planning to build the area into a farm consisting of a vibrant body of water and a tract of paddy fields where the most beautiful and valuable plants could grow. The moon was now casting a brighter and clearer light on the wilderness and illuminated an unparalleled beauty with her generosity. Indeed, this young woman who had suffered so much was now gradually recovering and, in the process, was becoming more mature and plumper than before. She gave off the rich aroma and searing warmth of a baked pancake, making it impossible for him to resist clinging to her and loving her. Each time he came close to her, he would be pushed to the hopeless extreme of happiness. On that occasion, the Jerusalem artichoke by the pond bloomed so boldly and vigorously that it enabled the entire hopeless situation of their love affair to look so splendid and horrifying that he felt scared. He feared that being ensnared in great happiness, he might forget all the contingencies that might arise.

That night, staring at the gentle ripples, Mei Di said: "I'm not going anywhere. I'll settle our family of three in this wasteland, a place that nobody wants. I'll fight desperately and even risk my life to wrest permission from Tang Tong for the return of my child's father, my husband. He must return. He's not going anywhere. He's supposed to come back home. His home isn't in the city but here by the North Sea. It's simply because this is the place where he grew up."

Liao Mai never forgot that remark of Mei Di's, knowing that it was her personal proclamation.

She would pay the ultimate price to fulfil the pledge.

She was just doing that. She would do it anywhere because she was more strong-minded and fearless than had been imagined. She would do that.

EIGHT

AN ACCOUNT TO SETTLE

"MY VERY FINE MAN! If it weren't for you, this land of a few dozen acres would be lying waste, and becoming less and less possible to farm."

In the early autumn sun, Mei Di licked her teeth with the tip of her dainty tongue while squinting at him, at the fields with verdant shoots just starting to appear from the ground, and at the glistening ripples on the L-shaped lake. To Liao Mai, while her weight gain was unstoppable, her temperament became increasingly like that of a child – a sly child.

"You've been lying waste just like the land," Liao Mai joked. She took him by surprise by biting her lip and then holding him tight. These days, they spent more time chatting, hugging and making love than working in the fields.

"This is not right," said Liao Mai, patting her. "We must figure out how to stop being so amorous."

Mei Di broke into a smile, saying to herself: This is what I want. This is what I want.

Seeing him looking into the distance with his sleeves rolled up to reveal the glistening hairs and bulging veins on his arms, she regarded him as a real man. How can a woman do without a man, she asked herself. She'd be lying waste, or rather, feeling empty and lonely. She'd be agitating as if her heart were turned into a wasteland, overgrown with weeds. Look at what's happening now; with this fine man here, all the weeds have been removed blade by blade, clump by clump. "You brilliant man, I can't love you too much. I'll bite you so much that you'll run around and around."

Liao Mai worked without a break, sometimes covered in splashed mud. On such occasions, she would find it hard to get close to him. After his return, it took him only a week to learn how to tinker with all the agricultural machinery. During the second week, he accidentally drove the tractor into the lake and could only pull it out with the aid of a few cows and some hired hands. Usually, they employed several farmhands during the busy seasons. He admired his wife in secret and felt indebted to her. The largest debt that he owed her was the time when he left her alone, and alone she had brought up their daughter while attending to every detail on the farm.

"You're wonderful," he would often say. "Truly wonderful. In fact, the farm was already in good shape without my involvement. I can only imagine what kind of a life you went through, how hard you worked and how tired you were."

"I said I wouldn't use your absence as an excuse for the land to lay in waste. So long as you were in my heart, I wouldn't allow the large farm to lie desolate. I went all out, telling myself to work hard in order to give him a decent place to settle after his return. So I hired people from town and elsewhere, and I counted every penny when I planned the budget."

Liao Mai became reticent. For a long time, he had been troubled when it came to hiring workers. He had several unpleasant conversations with Mei Di with regard to this issue. Even though he compromised at the last moment each time, he knew that the problem was not solved, far from it. The issue was still weighing on his mind. In fact, since his return, the appearance of the farm had completely changed: the muddy water that had previously been running unbridled was now forced into the L-shaped lake, and the area had become a vast tract of beautiful and profitable paddy fields that were ideal for growing narrowleaf cattails and lotus roots. The remaining two-thirds of the area was transformed into fertile farmland, half of which was planted with vegetables and the other half with various fruit trees. On and around the lake embankments, the field ridges and the drainage ditches, poplar and pine trees towered, interspersed with glossy privet and cherry trees. The labour invested in them was enormous. Liao Mai was grateful for the hired hands, particularly the few who worked here all year round. What disturbed him was the fact that their earnings were no higher than the going rate. The profits from the farm, on the other hand, kept growing. The annual income from the paddy fields alone reached a hundred thousand yuan. He wanted to implement a new wage system across the farm on a trial basis, that is, to make their income and expense accounts transparent and distributing the fruit of labour as fairly as possible. "Otherwise, we'd become part of a band of new exploitative farm owners. That is something I will not countenance," he told Mei Di.

"So, what's your new system? What in the world are you going to do?" Mei Di held up her head and flared her nostrils as if she had a cold.

"I haven't thought it through yet. Probably a new way of grouping the workforce. Otherwise, we'll still have a wide difference between the input and output of labour, which isn't equitable."

Mei Di smiled. She smiled without saying anything.

"From the perspective of long-term development, this new system is more dynamic. When the workers treat the farm as their own, they'll naturally be concerned about it. This system can be dubbed 'mental fusion'. But now, everyone knows that the farm belongs to us two only. The current income distribution system is obviously unreasonable," said Liao Mai while rubbing his hands together.

Mei Di withdrew her smile, saying: "Apparently, your idea's nothing new. It's still like the concept of 'communes'."

"No. It has nothing to do with concepts. It's based on solid accounting…"

"Really? Then let's go through the accounts. How many years have we been separated against our will? How did they treat me after I was pregnant? Besides, think of the nail holes in your ears. Let's do our accounts and add all this up together with the expenditures on land lease, chemical pesticides and machinery. Let's count each of our bills and incidents – if you can figure out the balance, fine! I'd accept an equitable distribution of our income and be 'mentally fused' with them."

Mei Di's rebuttal was as coherent as it was eloquent, but the words she used hurt Liao Mai. Although by no means persuaded, he decided not to argue with her; he just did not want to be a farm owner, and he meant it. He just wanted to put the problem to one side for the time being.

While he was silent, Mei Di stroked his stubble and said in a reproving and yet affectionate tone: "My really good man would be perfect if he didn't mince words all the time. I can't love a bookworm like you enough. But you have to choose your moments. You can only be 'mentally fused' when you're with your wife and daughter rather than anyone else."

Liao Mai broke into a bitter smile. He meant to rebut her by saying that they must be one heart and soul, not get 'fused'. But he stopped short because what he wanted to say would be ten times more complex than that, and he found it impossible to make himself understood in a succinct manner. At this moment, he thought of his swarthy-faced classmate Qi Jin. Yes, if he were here, how much I could discuss with him! They could engage themselves in an in-depth discourse. Liao Mai was convinced that this pressing issue of income redistribution concerned not only himself and his family but also the workers. However, the time was not right. The person that he loved was right beside him. He could not shake off this plump companion who was liable to come up and plant a kiss on him at any time. With her, nothing serious could be discussed.

A CRYING FISH

Liao Mai was a believer in the strength of wind because it was ubiquitous and capable of making or breaking everything in the universe. Winds from all directions share the same strength. An individual is oblivious to the changes caused by the wind after it penetrates their body in stealth but that is not the case for their loved one – provided the loved one genuinely and unconditionally loves the person affected by the wind. Not long before, Mei Di had still looked like a young girl, with her supple, slim body resembling that of a bird. But the wind, sometimes blustery, sometimes gentle, came from all directions and cut through her physical body – these shapeless winds of silk threads, finer than the fuzz on a peach, could effortlessly penetrate the skin and flesh, taking away elements such as calcium and colloidal substances and leaving behind things like yeast. As her body became more supple, her hips became wider. While her stomach was still flawless and femininely attractive, the skin around her navel, as Liao Mai observed, rippled out and became plumper and more accommodating. It was apparent that her buttocks, the centre of her body's gravity, were unquestionably more pronounced and eye-catching. From all her changes, he could feel it – the strength of the wind.

The winds in May, blowing gently through the Chinese scholar tree blossom and hovering among the gaps between young cattail shoots, could sometimes repair other winds – the hot winds coming unchecked from more distant places. Even those friendly winds might also secrete a kind of substance similar to alcohol to inebriate her, making her feel dazed and erotic. Liao Mai could often discern the effects on her from her sparkling eyes at midnight and her slightly parting, childlike lips. At this point, she had no idea what she was saying or doing, and she was inclined to be peevish, naive and extremely attached to him.

Liao Mai had considered her a young woman only a decade before. But everything had changed since then, chiefly because of the effect of the wind. Now she had become quite strong. Sometimes, she could be seen flexing her biceps. When she placed her arms around him tight from behind, he would feel her suffocating strength. She moaned and screamed: "God! I'm really getting hold of my man!" The scream seemed to be coming from the depth of the vast wilderness and from the hollow of a cold wave-cut cliff, carrying with it the prickling hairs of wild creatures. The scream had initially stupefied him, making his chin shiver and become sore. At such a moment, he nearly melted into this call of the wild.

Today, however, a decade later, having returned and calmed down, he wanted to recall the cry from its beginning. He wanted to trace it to the exact date of its utterance, though it was no easy task. If his memory served him well, Mei Di had begun to manifest her significant and gradually obvious changes nine years, oh no, eight years or even seven years before their daughter Beibei was born. She became bold and vigorous, even to the extent of rudeness. From that moment on, she ceased to be a shy little hedgehog.

He remembered one chilly autumn night, a night so important that he deemed it necessary to regard it as pivotal and a basis for analysing and remembering his life. It had been a night after he had made several attempts to sneak back to the farm – like before, Little Beibei was still sleeping in the hut, and they first walked on a ridge in the fields and then embraced each other. But because a few helping hands were staying in some rickety sheds on the other side of the lake, they had to be cautious.

Later, Liao Mai was still baffled by Mei Di's behaviour that night. She had been so brazen that she disregarded his repeated reminders and eventually let out one scream after another – yes, this had been the first of her screams in Liao Mai's memory. He could recall it because it made him so nervous that he looked around and tried to fend her off several times, but to no avail. That was also when he first experienced the strength of Mei Di's arms. She was determined not to let go of him and succeeded in keeping him, at least for the time being.

They sat there deep into the night. Huddling against him and holding his arm, Mei Di mumbled: "My really good man, don't be scared for no reason. Haven't you heard others say that times have changed? You know people think of nothing but money today. They care for nothing but money. Being so obsessed with making money, how can they pay attention to us?"

Liao Mai turned to stare disapprovingly into her eyes, saying: "How far has your negotiation with Tang Tong progressed? Since he doesn't care, you can tell him clearly that I'll be back for good."

This was the only topic to make Mei Di's body tauten all over. "I'll ask Tang Tong," she said. "What else will you do to us after so many years and after we've suffered all these undeserved hardships? We have only one thing to ask of you – our family reunion…"

As she talked, tears swelled in her eyes, and she pressed her head on his shoulder. "This is our business, also the Liao family's business," Liao Mai said. "There's been a feud between the Liao and Tang families for two generations. Tang Tong was fully aware that there will be a day of reckoning between us. I'm afraid it's down to me to settle the account."

Mei Di raised her head abruptly, and apparently frightened by his remark, she trembled all over. "Maizi! Silly Maizi!" she shouted. "You have your wife and daughter to look after. You're not alone now. I've told you I'll negotiate with him and lay our cards on the table. I'll try everything I can to make him revoke his licence to kill..."

"Let's wait and see."

Grabbing his shoulder, Mei Di sat up and said with confidence: "You can rest assured, my really fine man. I'll take care of it. You'll be back home soon."

"How in the world have you been negotiating with him? And what did he say?"

Liao Mai wanted to know everything in earnest that night, but Mei Di seemed either to have difficulty explaining things clearly or was trying to keep them from him. She only said: "My husband, my really good man, pack your luggage when you go back. If I say 'soon', it'll be soon."

But he had to tell her in all seriousness: "We must be careful not to fall into his trap. The Tang father and son are the kind of brutes that eat people without spitting out their bones. They can do anything they want."

Massaging his heaving chest, Mei Di said: "Don't worry. Tang Laotuo's already dead. We're only dealing with Tang Tong. The father and the son are as different as a wolf is from a badger. We can't fall into his trap."

"They may be different, but I think each generation down is craftier and more vicious than the previous one."

"Perhaps. But... but people say times have changed. Things are totally different now. Let's be happy, Liao Mai. Let's be joyous."

"It's true," Liao Mai said, looking into her large purplish eyes in the moonlight. "But Jiwo still belongs to the Tang family. That hasn't changed."

A short while after that night, about two weeks or so as Liao Mai remembered, he got the good news – he could return home safely. To him and Mei Di, as well as to their daughter, the world had indeed gone through an epoch-making change.

He returned home just like that. It was almost unthinkable that they finally held their happiness in their own hands. The homestead – the farm, his wife and daughter, the verdant fields and the rippling lake – all tried to share their new life and hopes with Liao Mai, a man who had spent half his life wandering. He was intoxicated by all of this, as if he were floundering in thick, wild honey, with a sense of drowning in a kind of sweetness. From that day on, be it midnight or dawn, Mei Di would let out those screams. And it was in those moments that Liao Mai could feel the strength of her thickening hands and arms and sense the power of time and the wind.

Meanwhile, he also noticed a kind of unique fish living in the farm lake. He was trying to figure out the secret about the fish and what it had to do with his tumultuous relationship with Mei Di. He discovered that Mei Di's screams were subtly related, to say the least, with this exceedingly ugly kind of fish. She and the fish did communicate with each other because more than once he spotted Mei Di crouching by the lake saying something intimate, and when he walked up to her, she lapsed into silence while the surface of the lake rippled with a streak of bubbles, evidence of the fish having dived to the bottom of the water.

He saw that kind of fish more than once. It had a mud-grey colour, a large head with spiny ridges and small eyes that always seemed to fix their cold gaze on people. To his surprise, Mei Di made herself a soup with the fish. When a strange stench started to permeate the room, she would light some silver wormwood to mask it. Eventually, he came to realise that each time she ate the fish soup, she would let out these barbaric screams.

Liao Mai tried catching the fish but failed each time. Bait and a hand net didn't help much. However, while this was going on he saw a strange phenomenon: every time Mei Di neared the lake, the fish would bubble up to the surface, forming a streak with their short, small bodies and flex joyously back and forth. Liao Mai tried to eradicate them from the lake, removing any prospect of them surviving. However, these guys were blessed with amazing fecundity. The ova of each fish formed a sticky mass like the strings of toad eggs, and once they adhered to aquatic grass, the grass would eventually wither and die.

Since it was hard to catch the fish, he attempted to remove the ova, but it was an extremely difficult task; masses of sticky eggs tangling themselves with the narrowleaf cattail roots and putrid aquatic grass would spawn very quickly, and the fries appeared very much like tadpoles. If he had not taken the decision later to raise ducks to eat them, the consequences would have been unthinkable.

Mei Di, however, hated the ducks paddling on the lake. "They're ruining everything," she complained. "They quack noisily, crap as soon as they get out of the water and destroy things under its surface. How can we put up with them?" But instead of explicitly advocating their removal, she quietly allowed the workers to catch and eat the ducks – she felt content so long as she could smell duck soup wafting over from the work sheds.

One night, Mei Di's forehead, lower jaw, neck, arms and lower abdomen were all covered in a rash. She gasped for breath and rolled her eyes. Her symptoms frightened Liao Mai. Holding her in his arms, he called to her and patted her, and after a long while, she let out a deep breath. He wanted to take her to the hospital right away, but she refused. She recovered quickly and soon held him tight in her arms and kissed him incessantly. Her bites began to cause him pain like they did before. Her screams were so penetrating that they worried Liao Mai very much. He feared that the workers in the sheds could hear her clearly. Sure enough, the dogs outside the house were startled and barked continuously and, in the end, their barks turned into inexplicable groans and moans. Before dawn, Mei Di felt thirsty and drank one glass of water after another.

"I must have scared you last night, mustn't I?" she said. "I screamed too loud."

"No, you were sleeping all the time. It was the fish that was screaming."

It was dawn, but Mei Di did not get up. Liao Mai went to the kitchen alone to prepare breakfast. From the fish bones wrapped in a bundle of a newspaper, he assumed that Mei Di must have eaten too much of that ugly fish the day before.

A FEAST OF YOUR LIFE

It had happened six months prior to Liao Mai's return. He had been having a hard time in a government office. It was the second occasion that his department director had urged him to pay a visit to the senior official at his home. It was an embarrassing and objectionable request but one that he did not have the courage to refuse. In fact, the errand was just to deliver a book on floriculture, but he still had to subject himself to all kinds of interrogations conducted by the guards at the gate in the subdivision and then by those at the gate in the smaller courtyard before he was given access to the senior official's house. The department director told him that the senior official's wife had been notified of his visit beforehand. However, when he arrived, he was again asked a lot of questions; the only thing missing was a body search. Where was the senior official's wife, the woman who had supposedly asked for the book? Liao Mai was pondering this when a young female janitor came out to receive him, and then she led him to another young woman.

"Where's the senior official's wife? Where's madam?"

It soon proved to be such a silly question and one that he would come to regret asking.

The second young woman was none other than the senior official's wife. She was really young, dressed in loose white clothing. She was rather plump and had bright, upward-slanting eyes. Taking the book, she offered him a cup of tea and said in a straightforward tone: "Well, well, we've much to talk about."

Liao Mai found her temperament akin to that of his university classmate Xiu, except that she did not have her concave forehead and was not as tall. But she had the same dark, sparkling eyes and spoke with a similar accent.

The department director asked him to deliver books for a third and then a fourth time, and he returned to Mei Di once in between. His final delivery errand had been only two weeks before he received the exciting news of being able to return home. During that fortnight, he became distracted and absent-minded, but this only made the senior official's wife take more of a fancy to him. "He's like a big boy," she observed.

The department director was passing the senior official's wife's observation on to Liao Mai and added excitedly: "Hey, your absent-minded demeanour is proving irresistible!" The director was a southerner, a fellow townsperson of the senior official's wife.

Liao Mai did not give his remark too much thought because he was preoccupied with silently conversing with Mei Di day and night. He was always able to sense her smell – he could tell it better than anyone else.

I can't stay here alone any more, said Liao Mai to himself. I'd die pining and craving. I'd turn into what I was ten years ago – a 'great foolish beggar'. I'm already accustomed to being held in your arms, having my hair chewed wet and with your scratch marks dug into my back. Since I left our farm, each of my tendons and veins has become a jubilant clock spring wound tighter and tighter from time to time, animating me with unstoppable excitement with its stored energy. I want to hold you, kiss you and breathe on you. I want to look at you without blinking. I'll never separate from you... Yes, you were right when you said that I must go back to my birthplace – returning to it nearly cost me my life, but neither of us can leave this birthplace of mine. I'm but a guest sojourning in a metropolis, or rather, an ant struggling to exist in a hot pot. I must return immediately. I would go back even if it meant becoming a tree as soon as I stepped on that native land. That's not a bad idea, a tree. The secret is unknown to everyone but you, and you can build a house around that tree so we can stay together day and night...

The department director talked with him again. This time, he was unable to conceal his excitement as the centre of his forehead turned from red to purple as he spoke: "Listen! Congratulations on being selected by the senior official to serve as his secretary. Go and prepare a dossier. Staff from the personnel office will talk with you soon, very soon."

He stared at the director dumbfounded, and after a while, he shook his head.

"What? Cheer up! It's an opportunity. An opportunity..."

This time, Liao Mai could hear him clearly and told him: "I may soon return to my native place, back to the farmland."

"What? You're pulling my leg," said the beaming director while giving him a gentle punch.

I've been longing for our reunion, pondered Liao Mai. The next time we meet, we'll never part from each other again. The heavens can be cruel and generous in equal measure, sometimes uniting and other times separating us. But our days of separation will soon come to an end. I dreamed of you so often. I dreamed of you smiling each time and being so eager to tell me everything. What a farm and what a life we're going to build! You are my world! My world...

Each morning, Liao Mai would recall every detail of his dreams.

Sometimes, he could not distinguish his dreams from his actual encounters with her.

"There's a difference between a personal secretary and an office secretary. We've finished our investigation of you," a middle-aged man with hairy hands and bulging eyes was telling a distracted Liao Mai.

Perhaps the senior official wanted to have a talk with him in person. A car drove him to the closely guarded subdivision and the courtyard. This time, his eyes were caught by some fig trees that he had never noticed before. The senior official was not at home, and he was received once more by his wife.

She had clearly just taken a bath or was about to take one. Her hair was hanging down, and she was dressed in a loose gown. Her eyes were red. They had either been exposed to water or she had been crying.

"We can give you a key in future so you can come and go as you please... since we're of one family now," she mumbled. "Don't stand on ceremony. Yes, I'm the one who insisted on recommending you work here. I can't let him have his own way. I just want..."

Liao Mai could not help noticing that the breasts of the senior official's wife were struggling hard against the thin fabric of her garment.

His voice might be hushed, but he enunciated each word assertively: "I'm going to return to my farm soon. Mei Di can't take care of it all by herself."

The senior official's wife turned a deaf ear to him. Either that or she had no interest in what he was saying. She held her head high and put on an air of naivety. "Look! This is an orchid. This is a plantain lily. And this is a lily. I bathe in water strewn with their petals."

Liao Mai smelled a fresh fragrance coming from all around, given off by Mei Di's body. "My really good man, a good man who's suffered all this hardship for my sake. From now on, I'll soak you in my honeypot all day long. You'll feel like you're being treated to a feast every day! Every hair on my head and every strand of fine hair on my body will belong to you. They're all yours. I'll let you be my great mounted bandit – mine only. You'd better bully me till I cry. I've kept all my tears for the day when I can happily sprinkle them on your chest, your face and belly. Look at you! How strong you are!

How straight your back is! The corners of your eyes have something that reveals what a real fine guy you are. You big rascal! You sweetheart! My man! My child's father! The head of our family."

Mei Di had been lying half-naked on the narrowleaf cattail grass, with some of its wind-blown flowers stuck in her hair. The moonlight added a darker shade to her wild-honey-coloured skin and gleamed on the fuzz on her abdomen. He rubbed her arms and other parts of her body where his hand was drawn, and wherever it touched, a distinct smell would slowly emanate. "My lifetime, lifetime," he stuttered.

"What about your lifetime, my really good man?" asked Mei Di.

"You're my lifetime," he sighed," my lifetime feast!"

Mei Di heard Liao Mai's remark clearly this time. Pressing her tear-streaked face against him, she said: "My husband. We've been separated for too long. If heaven should separate us again, that would be worse than death."

The senior official's wife held a large handful of flower petals and showed them to him, saying: "Look! These flowers were picked when they were still fresh and before the buds had opened. You know, you must pick flowers when they're fresh. You must be swift and pick and pick decisively."

"It would be worse than death." Liao Mai was repeating what Mei Di had said, his eyes burning at the corners.

"Ouch!" the senior official's wife exclaimed, and the petals were jolted out of her hands and scattered all over the floor. "What do you mean by 'death'? You're crying? Oh, look at the tears! Well, well!"

The official's wife found a scented handkerchief and handed it to him, even wiping the tears off him with her hand while standing on tiptoe. "You're still young," she said beaming. "In short, everything will be fine."

Liao Mai felt Mei Di's tears on his cheeks, too much for him to wipe away. Tilting her torso back slightly above him in the moonlight, she said in a buoyant tone: "I'll build a spacious study for you, big enough to accommodate all kinds of books. I'll install the best bathroom so you can wash away your two decades of hardship and fatigue in warm water full of fragrant bubbles. If there's anything else you want, don't hesitate to tell me. Don't hesitate."

Stroking Mei Di's velvetleaf-fibre hair, Liao Mai said: "We'll plant trees, many trees. We'll add a sunroof to our new house. We'll floor it with the false indigo bush and place in it the softest hay we can find to make it into a wedding bed of our lifetime..."

"Haha, my really good man! You are so imaginative. OK, we'll do everything as you wish and as you command. I live to make you happy! As you said, I'll exert all my strength and use up all my energy to give you a lifelong feast. Remember what I said in the moonlight because it was as good as taking an oath: 'The words I said tonight won't change even if, in future, everything changes or is swept away by the winds from the sea.'"

The senior official's wife picked up the petals from the floor and held them again in her hands. She gazed at him with her hot, black eyes – eyes peculiar to a southerner, eyes that reminded him once more of Xiu. He suddenly had the feeling that the world was made up of only two kinds of material: misfortune and love.

Liao Mai called Mei Di's name in silence: Yes, I hear you, Mei Di. Your words will never change!

A MAGNIFICENT PLACE

Mei Di was a miracle worker and a person who always surprised Liao Mai. In the blink of an eye, she took out a sketched plan of a new house and courtyard, down to the minute detail. She had loved drawing since childhood, and this was an opportunity to show her talent. Her mastery of perspective, the decorations and the room layouts stunned Liao Mai. Some of the caption texts, markings and furnishing details were both puzzling and amazing at the same time. He wondered how a woman who had never stepped out of Jiwo could have imagined such an elegant house, particularly when the design required a deep understanding of and appreciation for modern household goods and appliances. This knowledge and ability was far beyond what might be expected of her. As he went through the plans, he could not help looking up from time to time at the designer by his side – and she was just standing there, smiling.

"Maizi, here! Especially here," Mei Di explained while moving her forefinger on the sketched plan. "These are our living quarters, which consists of three rooms – two bedrooms and a living room, spacious but not too big. The room to the side is self-evident as it has only an ordinary bed and a bath. The double bed is two metres wide of course, and the bathroom isn't very big, measuring six-and-a-half square metres only. Next to it is the main bedroom, which contains this sixty-square-metre chamber with a glass roof and a big bathtub. I did the drawings exactly in line with your idea. To provide the right microenvironment for the two rows of false indigo bushes to grow lush and thick, sunlight and ventilation are needed here. We must also allow water in and feed the bushes with a special kind of odourless fertiliser. This type of plant emanates the true scent of the wilderness when exposed to sunlight, but they can only flourish in the sun. Set amid the bushes will be our big bed. I want to have a straw mattress specially made for us. The straw will come from what the locals call cotton grass. There will no doubt be lots of bugs, mosses and butterflies in the bushes, but we'll kill them all except the Chinese bush-crickets so we can enjoy their chirping. I want to have a pumpkin plant by the bed so that the bush-crickets can feed on its flowers..."

Liao Mai laughed: "Are you really going to grow shrubs indoors and set a big bed among false indigo bushes?"

"Why not? Isn't it wonderful? And this is all my fine man's original idea. You may not have appreciated the significance of what you once said. It's interesting. It took a lot of effort and no little skill to drawn the plan."

"Not an easy job indeed. It's nothing less than a sophisticated ecosystem! I just said out loud what I was imagining. But it would be too extravagant to turn it into reality. Mei Di, I think we've got to give up the idea. Really, it's too sophisticated and luxurious..."

Mei Di bit her lip, which she did whenever she was unhappy. But in doing so, she only succeeded in making herself look lovelier in Liao Mai's eyes.

"I know you're concerned about the funds," she said. "In fact, I've worked out a sound budget for the project. We've got more than enough money. Besides, I'll enjoy spending money on it. I really want to spend a small fortune on us. It's worth it because we're building our nest."

Shaking his head, Liao Mai looked out of the window at the L-shaped lake a hundred metres away. A row of simple and crude work sheds stood on the other side. "Above all, it's not a matter of money. Hey, look over there. We all do the same job during the day, but at night, we live in very different places. Our living conditions are pretty good now. I just want to add one or two rooms plus an attic – with good insulation, it would provide us with a pretty decent living environment. It would be the house of my dreams."

Mei Di made a face. "To make do is one thing, but to compare us with the workers – temporary migrant workers – is quite another. Then, we can't do anything. Nothing! My silly bookish man, you're driving me to my wit's end…"

Liao Mai shrugged, saying: "They're living on our farm, too close to us. You see, this is not a matter of comparison."

They stopped arguing. Mei Di planned to go to the food processing factory the next day. She and the factory had a close business relationship because it was buying the half-processed produce from her paddy fields. This time, she suggested that Liao Mai go with her so that they could inspect one or two guest houses and hotels on the way to broaden their horizons. Liao Mai agreed.

The food processing factory had been state-run before becoming a private company that was later purchased by Tang Tong. Liao Mai became concerned after Mei Di told him about her close business relationship with the company because she had an exclusive deal to sell them all the produce from the paddy fields. He suggested that they set up their own processing and marketing system, but Mei Di said that that would be too difficult. She argued that their original export and domestic sales network had been successful for more than twenty years.

Leaving the processing factory, Mei Di drove him all the way to a hotel in an imported pickup truck. Sitting in the passenger seat, Liao Mai suddenly felt that his wife had become a totally different person as she deftly steered the car to negotiate bends and overtake other vehicles. Moreover, she looked serious and spoke tersely with the company's staff. What impressed him the most was the scene that took place when they approached the hotel, where the porters dressed up in their ridiculous and awkward uniforms all came to meet her at the same time and kept calling her "Boss Mei".

Built on a small plot of flat land to the left of the mountain, the hotel occupied a large area. It looked like a castle in a dream world. If he had not seen it himself, Liao Mai could have never imagined that there would be such a luxurious facility near the town of Jiwo.

"Boss Mei," he teased, "could you please tell me who owns this hotel if you don't mind?"

Mei Di grinned. "Of course it's the Tiantong Group. They own most of the deluxe hotels and gourmet restaurants around here, as well as all the amusement parks."

As they proceeded through the hotel, they were greeted by various people, and several of them smiled at Mei Di in particular. It was apparent that they had known her for a long time. Sure enough, when she asked a lobby manager if she could take a look at their guest and function rooms, the manager was very courteous and immediately ordered a young female employee to show them the way.

The hotel interior was gilded here, there and everywhere. Wherever they looked, they could not escape the sight of gorgeous vulgarity: the imported bath taps; the sets of silver cutlery; the marble surfaces; mahogany furniture; oil paintings; pseudo-classic bronze ware; and the *guqin*, a plucked seven-string musical instrument. The largest hall serving Western-style food, measuring about three hundred square metres, was dominated by gold-plated chandeliers and snow-white linen tablecloths. Then there were the fireplaces and the rich aroma of coffee. Mei Di hushed her voice when she spoke here, quite unlike how she behaved on the farm. She wanted Liao Mai to see a deluxe master suite. In addition to the high ceilings and large bathroom, there was a separate, partitioned bedroom to put up a guest, along with a walk-in wardrobe and study. The floor was covered in an expensive handmade carpet, while a pond fed with flowing green water was situated outside the window.

"Look," said Mei Di. "We can do something like this ourselves, so long as we can divert water in from its source." Liao Mai realised that it was the beautiful pond that Mei Di had really meant him to see.

After the master suites, she took him to look at the presidential suites. From there, she led him to a small home cinema via a short corridor. It was beautifully appointed and quiet, and the carpet was extremely thick. The seats, totalling a little more than twenty, were all armchairs except for the one in the middle. That was a love seat with an exquisite side table with shelves. Liao Mai had just sat in one of the seats when the young female employee turned on the sound system. It was virtual surround sound. There could be no doubting its gracefulness and sophistication.

Stepping out of the home cinema, Mei Di's face suddenly turned fiery red. Liao Mai stared at her awhile before she came up to him and took his arm in hers, saying: "Maizi! I've been thinking of getting us a home cinema like this one – of course, it doesn't have to be as good…" Liao Mai chuckled and she went on: "How do you like this place?"

She looked into his eyes with her head tilted to one side.

"It goes without saying that it's magnificent."

"It's all because of him – them, the gold miners," Mei Di said, looking into the distance. "They're the Tiantong Group!"

Smirking and shaking his head, Liao Mai said: "I didn't realise that we Jiwo people had such capacity for imitating and learning. They can copy something as soon as they've absorbed how and make it look exactly like the original!"

"Absorbed what?"

"They're absorbing everything quickly."

A STEEL BLADE CANNOT STEM FLOWING WATER

It was Liao Mai's first long trip away from home after his return. He had to go simply because he found it hard to stay. His mind had been thick with something that made him agitated day and night. However, it was something that he couldn't put into words.

"I want to travel a while," was all that he said.

To his surprise, Mei Di embraced the idea. She even predicted that this was bound to happen sooner or later. "My really fine man isn't like me. My fine man has a pair of feet that can cover a thousand miles, so he's sure to get sick confined to his home all the time."

She joyfully helped him pack his luggage and gave him some precautionary advice, which included one sentence in particular: "Come back home as soon as you feel homesick, and don't dawdle on your return."

He told her about his reasons for leaving in some detail. He was visiting his two former classmates, Qi Jin and Xiu. He particularly wanted to see Qi Jin, the guy with a swarthy face and profound and yet cold eyes. He had been pondering the trip for some time.

This image of Qi Jin was associated with many unforgettable memories and questions. It took time for the friendship between classmates to become established. It was recently weighing so much on his mind that he often endured sleepless nights. He had to admit that Qi Jin was the most unforgettable of his college classmates. Without him and without the atmosphere and environment they had shared before, it would be impossible for Liao Mai to carry on thinking in a very meaningful way. As for Xiu, that was a little different. It seemed to be a unique yearning, something like nostalgia for all he had experienced in southern China and a comprehensive remembrance and reflection of bright days, hot weather and transparent sound quality. Whenever he felt the cold, damp sea wind in northern China, his mind would go back to the clumps of camellia, the large-leaved trees, as well as Xiu herself.

He planned to visit Xiu first, and from her he would be able to hear more about Qi Jin before going to see him. Then, he would stay with him for a while – what a reunion it would be! How many deep conversations they would have! That would require some considerable time, not a brief visit. How important it is in one's life to communicate and argue with another person, to consult others, to experience different lifestyles, and to examine and appraise oneself and others. For quite a while, Liao Mai had been feeling confused and even hurried, a feeling he had never had even during his fugitive life thirty years before. This made him hanker after the journey now – a desire different from yearning to return home. Well, it was time to pack up and hit the road again.

After graduation, Xiu remained in her native city and managed to find a job in her alma mater. Liao Mai found that he was so eager on the journey there that he was secretly thrilled. However, he knew that the prospect of seeing Xiu was not the sole reason for this feeling. There were other inexplicable reasons. Leaving his genuine home for the place where he studied and where he could take in the sights and smells of southern China, made him feel elated, light-hearted and relaxed. Nevertheless, as he got nearer, he felt a sense of disappointment because he found the intense emotional stirrings and wonderment that he experienced years before were now absent. The country, from the north to the south, had become so crowded, clamorous and turbid. Hubbub, restlessness and a sense of melancholy – all this ensnared the beautiful land like an oppressive net.

He was somewhat more forgiving as he approached the city. He rushed to his old university, only to become hesitant at the gate, as if he were too shy to see his former professors and friends. He had called Xiu beforehand, and she was waiting at the gate, trying to identify him. Then she spotted him and ran over, waving her hands.

They stayed together for three days, three unexpected days.

Despite the passing of so many years, Xiu had not changed much. She was obsessed with poetry, nothing but poetry, as if poetry were her ultimate secret to eternal youth. Her large, black eyes had the same sparkle, her wide mouth, when she broke into a smile, still revealed those familiar white teeth. As soon as they met, she grabbed him by the arms and exclaimed: "Good Heavens, my ex-lover!"

Liao Mai meant to correct her but bit his tongue, as if he did not have enough reason to do so. Now, he found her excessively concave forehead a little comical and lovely – if she had really been his ex-lover, then this forehead would have been the most appropriate place for him to plant a kiss. But he was aware that he had only one lover, whether yesterday or today. She was now busying herself in a place where the sea wind cuts through incessantly day and night.

Xiu found him a room in the university's guest house, but he spent most of the time in her cosy, well-lit house, having accepted her invitation. Xiu's husband had gone abroad two years before. She had visited him but returned home as she found it hard to settle there. After much reflection of the past with him, Xiu said: "You seem to have grown taller."

He knew this was impossible. Perhaps he had lost weight. She held his hands, envious of his calluses, saying: "Among my friends, you're the only one with such hands." She knew everything about why he had left the government office for his hometown, where he had been living as a farmer. She even showed him a poem she had written, in which she referred to him as "my lover in northern China". Liao Mai turned his head away, afraid of seeing such words.

They ate dishes from southern China and drank some wine. Meanwhile, they kept talking about Qi Jin. "I would have married him if he hadn't been running about, and if he hadn't been torturing himself. You know how important you two are to me." Her lips were made more prominent by the colour of her lipstick so that they looked like the thick flesh of some fruit. To avoid smudging her lipstick, she was extremely careful when she ate and drank. The excessively long, false eyelashes over her already full, natural lashes blinked like the navigation lights used by ships at night, and the message read: Are you Liao Mai? I love you. Yes, as I did before.

She now changed the topic of conversation from Qi Jin to her husband. "He's stereotypical. He gives you a perfect first impression because he's absolutely normal. But as you spend more time with him, his lack of inspiration will give you a headache. By the way, I do get headaches – it's not a metaphor." With that, she produced a bottle of painkillers, flashed it before him and shook out two pills. After swallowing them with her wine, she said: "I can't help it. I'm addicted to them." Then, she lit a menthol cigarette. As she puffed, she explained: "I never use tobacco. I only smoke one or two cigarettes when I drink with my best friends."

That night, they drank too much without realising it. Liao Mai meant to return to the guest house. After lounging on the couch for a while, he was too tired to budge. Before leaving him, Xiu kissed him while holding his face in her hands. He hurriedly turned his face aside. "Don't be afraid, fine man!" she said. "It's nothing serious." After saying goodnight to him, she headed back to her bedroom. She had taken only two steps when she looked back saying: "Everyone has their merits. My husband, for instance, is a decent *guqin* player."

Nothing improper happened between them during the first two days although they talked a lot. Xiu said: "In a word, both you and Qi Jin were quiet. When we were together, I talked all the time. And I have a medium build while you're both tall. In the eyes of southerners, you're very northern."

Speaking of Qi Jin's life during these years, Xiu clicked her tongue and said: "While he's a bookworm, he's also a man of action. He's active every minute of the day. He used to teach in the western region, and because he looked so lonely and austere, local ascetic monks took notice of him, or to be more exact, kept a close watch on him. They would not divert their attention away from him. Eventually, they took him to live in a tent deep in the mountains. He told me that he left the west later just to escape the monks."

Stunned, Liao Mai tried to imagine life in a tent deep in the mountains with the monks before eventually having to flee. Chuckling, he asked about Qi Jin's marriage.

"It didn't work out," she giggled. "His better half pestered him like a cat in heat, screaming and meowing. It would have been fine for a day or two, but behaving in this manner, she drove Qi Jin crazy. Sure enough, he eventually made the hard decision to run away. You know, people are different. Some are not fit for marriage."

"Where's he now? Where can I find him?"

Xiu scratched her temple with her little finger. "The last time he contacted me, he used an address that read 'Trident Island'. He was doing a temporary job there. If he's still there, that'll be four years. He's a good man, very funny. But he's destined to lead a hard and miserable life. I really like that guy."

Xiu was in something of a fluster when the time to say goodbye was approaching on the third night. While she tried her best to hide her emotion, Liao Mai could still sense it. Since he was going to set out at dawn the next day, Xiu was reluctant to move. She kept reading poems to him until midnight. They both drank too much like on the first day. While saying goodnight, Xiu put her white scarf over Liao Mai's neck – the scarf that had fascinated him many years before – and pulled him closer and closer towards her and gave him an exaggerated kiss.

Liao Mai slept on the same couch. Before dawn, he felt a bit chilly. He wrapped himself tight in a thin quilt, but it didn't help much. Just then, he heard the door squeaking, and Xiu came out with a blanket over her. She hopped onto the couch saying that she was feeling terribly cold. She huddled against him and held him tight, trilling her tongue in a wild, high brrr. She snuggled closer and pretended to snore. He did not move. She curled up a bit and resumed snoring. Between the snores, she began to sob: "You're about to leave, and you're not saying anything to comfort me."

"You were fast asleep."

She rolled over abruptly, placing her face close to him and gazed into his eyes, murmuring: "It's getting serious this time." She gasped and placed her hand on his chest to feel his heartbeat, and, through chattering teeth, said: "It's really cold. We have no alternative but to do this. It's impossible to stem flowing water. I... we... can't cut it off. Oh, Liao Mai, you big northerner! What're you waiting for? After so many years, why are you waiting? You don't trust yourself? How much I trust myself..."

Liao Mai tried hard to resist her but eventually found they had gone too far. She appeared to be holding him with no fabric between them. His underwear somehow seemed to have slipped off.

She fell into silence, nestling close to him like a small bird.

A LITTLE HOUSE

"Such a small mud house. Is this really the house of those years?" Mei Di asked as she got out of the pickup truck. She looked forward and then back at him with wide-open eyes. Liao Mai was also rather surprised to find it appear now as small as a sparrow perching on the lower slope of the hill. They walked closer, running their hands over its cracked mud walls. They looked around, knocked here and there with a piece of stone, and undid an old lock with great effort.

It was true that the little house consisted of only two rooms. The foundation was built of pagodite and the walls laid with mudbricks. The house had not collapsed thanks to the occasional care bestowed on it by some of the villagers. There was a fireplace for cooking and some firewood in the outer room. In the inner room, there was a *kang* with a flue system leading to the fireplace. In those years, Liao Mai and his mother used to sleep on it. Liao Mai and Mei Di stood there motionless. Mei Di's gaze shifted from him to the *kang*, evidently doubtful how this small bed-stove could accommodate such a stout man. The quilts were folded as neatly as before. They were thin and covered all over with repair patches.

Mother, oh Mother, Liao Mai said to himself, sighing. Your Silver Moon's back with Mei Di – you worried about her too in those years. She and I, particularly I, should have come to see you more often. Today, I find the fences dilapidated and the fields by the pond laid waste.

He surveyed everything, the tattered bedding, the small table clock that had stopped ticking, along with the rusted pots and the small stool. He would not have been surprised to turn around and see his mother sitting in front of the cooking fireplace.

Coming out of the house, they climbed up the hill along the path by the pond. Standing on the sunny side, they scanned the small village nearby and moved on. The most important thing for them to do on this trip was pay tribute to the old woman in her tomb.

After they came down the hill, Mei Di did not want to go into the house immediately. Instead, she gazed at the pond for a long time. Its dark green colour gave her the impression of fathomlessness. At the northwestern corner of the pond, there was a patch of narrowleaf cattails, and it was just the season for them to be in flower. A fish leapt out of the water and a grey-capped greenfinch landed by the pond.

"What a wonderful place. It's all because of this pond. The location of the house is also good as it sits against the hill and faces the pond. It's a shame the house is too small and shabby," Mei Di said.

Immersed in his recollections of the past, Liao Mai did not hear her.

"It's really a shame." She looked around and crouched down with her arms crossed.

Liao Mai went back into the house, leaving Mei Di alone by the pond. He mentally absorbed everything in the house. He lay on the *kang* and closed his eyes. He seemed to step into the past instantly – he had left here, stepped forward along the small path by the pond, and then went straight ahead and further on.

Mother, I'm really afraid of getting lost – I'm back. I'm back once more. It was here in this palm-sized house that you saved my life, and here where I ate the golden-scaled crucian carp and drank the narrowleaf cattail-root wine.

Silver Moon! Silver Moon... Who was calling him from the unknown world? The calling seemed to come from afar but was getting nearer and nearer, before landing by his pillow. He was expecting it with his eyes closed tight. Sure enough, a hand, a shadow and the increasingly distinct face and white hair... A white-haired old woman opened the door and entered silently. She glanced at him on the *kang*, snuggled the quilt under his chin, then went to sit on the small stool in front of the fireplace and began to pump the bellows. Steam permeated the house, and the aroma of fish soup filled his nostrils. He heard porcelain bowls clinking and the soup being ladled into one of them.

The old woman walked gingerly towards him, holding the bowl

of piping hot fish soup. She blew on the soup and set it by his pillow.

He reached out his hand.

A skinny and calloused hand ran over him and pressed his forehead. He was motionless...

Outside the house, Mei Di was shouting loudly by the pond. It soon got a bit raucous. Liao Mai opened his eyes slowly. He sat up, looked around, got off the *kang* and went to the room with the cooking stove.

He felt the small stool, and it was still warm, as if someone had been sitting on it. He also felt the wooden pot cover, which had been washed white by the old woman. He lifted it, only to find the pot empty. It's been thirty years, Mother. Silver Moon's going to tell you he may have achieved his wishes, but he's never felt so confused. Could you please tell me why? Why?

Looking at Mei Di out of the window, he was hesitant. For days, he had been thinking of telling her something. He had been trying to make up his mind.

He had planned to visit the small house for two purposes: apart from paying tribute to his mother at her tomb, he wanted to unload a heavy burden from his heart. He could not conceal what had happened during his trip to southern China. He decided to confess to her here and now.

He stared briefly at the stopped clock on the small wooden table, pushed the door open and strode towards the pond.

"You look pale, Maizi. Are you feeling alright?" As soon as she looked up, she noticed the colour of his face. She hurried to him, pressed her hand on his forehead and patted him.

"Yes. I want to tell you something today about Xiu..."

"You're fine," she interjected. "You don't have a fever." She held his hand with excitement and led him to the pond. They walked a few steps, her eyes unusually bright.

"Mei Di!" He swallowed and continued: "I have been back for a long time, and I've always wanted to tell you what happened at my alma mater. I..."

Carried away by her excitement, Mei Di had no intention of hearing what he was going to say. She interrupted him again: "My really fine man, I know you're called Silver Moon in this village, the returning son of the old woman." With that, she suddenly became serious and lowered her voice: "You have full inheritance rights – I mean the little house and the pond should all be placed under the name of Silver Moon, right?"

Liao Mai was stunned and asked: "So what?"

"Silly you! My little unthinking fool. The house may be small, but the pond and the surrounding land is valuable! Think about it. As travel's getting more and more convenient, it's not too far to drive here from our farm. We can replace the little house with a decent-sized one and then put up a fence around the pond. It'll become a great resort. We can come here to stay for a few days with our Little Beibei every other week or month. Our family of three then…"

Liao Mai did not say anything.

"Did you hear me? You fool!"

Liao Mai looked as if he had just woken up from his reminiscences. "Yes, I'm listening. What other plans do you have?" His voice was low and suddenly became hoarse.

"Yes, the new house will look a bit antique, and the furnishings will be cosy. The cosier, the better – I like it that way."

Liao Mai's face suddenly clouded over, but he did not interrupt her.

"But you," said Mei Di when her eyes fell upon his face. "You're feeling ill, aren't you?"

Liao Mai remained silent.

"Did you hear what I said?"

"I'm listening," said Liao Mai, gritting his teeth.

"I'm talking about the house."

"I know… I know you're talking about the house."

NINE

THE SON OF A DUGONG

As soon as Mei Di reached the edge of the lake, she was frightened by what she saw. She took a step back and turned her face away several times, but eventually she could not help moving forward to take a closer look. The workers had come up to the lake shore long before, and the small pickup truck used for transporting goods had also been driven away. But this guy remained, fast asleep on a pile of cattail stems and leaves. He was apparently a temporary worker hired during the peak season. But whatever his circumstances, he should have been sleeping in one of the sheds. So she went to wake the huddling sleeper and say hello, but as she approached him she was hit by the sight of his webbed feet. As he had just come out of the water, his long hair was matted to his face, and as a result, his age could not be estimated. He wasn't wearing too many clothes except for something that looked like a rubber raincoat or cloak. It had been used partly as a bedsheet beneath him and partly as a blanket, thereby revealing most of his dark-brown body covered with dense, maroon-coloured fuzz. The two pairs of breasts lying shrivelled among the dense hair on his chest astonished Mei Di. His thighs were thick, but his calves were as thin as a child's. His genitals stuck out of his tattered shorts, covered with sludge from the lake along with bits of moss and aquatic grass. Mei Di gasped. She had to tell Liao Mai, and tell him quickly.

She tiptoed away and went to the work sheds. The workers were eating there. When asked about the strange person, the foreman immediately signalled her out with a gesture. In a hushed and terrified voice, he told her: "This weirdo has come from some island. I didn't think about it much since we all get the same wages. Who would have thought that he was capable of doing as much alone in the lake as several of us combined? He can stay under the surface for ages like a fish before coming up for a breather. When he's hungry, he'll simply eat some fish and shrimps. We can still see fish scales in his mouth when he gets out of the water. Look at his chest and feet. He's simply a monster! I don't know if we need to report him to the authorities or not. But he's really a good worker."

"Shush," said Mei Di. She told the foreman not to spread rumours and turned to look for Liao Mai.

Liao Mai was repairing a machine in the garage, his hands covered in oil and grease. Upon hearing her account of the strange man, he rubbed his hands clean in the sand and headed towards the lake.

Mei Di followed him a dozen metres behind and then stopped to watch from a distance. She saw him crouching down by the guy, and after a while, the guy stood up. They conversed and gesticulated for more than ten minutes before the stranger seemed persuaded. He picked up the bedroll that he had used as a pillow and followed Liao Mai as they walked towards Mei Di.

In fact, they walked past Mei Di and, after Liao Mai waved at her, continued walking forward. It turned out that they were heading for the garage. Mei Di now realised that it contained a vacant room used for accommodating the mechanic that they occasionally sent for to repair their pickup truck. Liao Mai was probably taking the guy there to rest.

They remained in the garage from early afternoon till sunset.

That night, Mei Di waited for Liao Mai for a long time, curious and worried. It was almost dark, and she saw from the shadow on the garage window Liao Mai carrying food and drinks into it and closing the door behind him. The moon rose, another two hours passed, and it wasn't until dawn that Liao Mai returned to her. But he left again soon afterwards, taking something with him.

The men stayed together for two days and nights. When Liao Mai returned to Mei Di on the third night, she found his eyes brimming with vigour and without any trace of tiredness.

"Maybe we've run into a freak?" Mei Di asked tentatively.

Liao Mai remained silent for quite a while. He looked out of the window. From this angle, he could see clearly the lamplight in that room by the garage. He shook his head slowly and said: "A man like him is rare. I still can't figure out if he's a great foolish beggar or not."

"What do you mean?"

"I mean, I want to know how much of what he told me these few days is true and how much is false. I'm really confused. But everything he told me is so coherent that I find some of his stories hard to disbelieve. As you know, I'm planning to write *A Secret History of the Jungle*. There's so much I need to include. A lot of the things we've heard as myths are corroborated by his accounts. I can't ignore what he's said…"

"But he really looks like a freak! Where's he from?"

"He said he came from Trident Island – far away from the mainland. It's been neglected for many years. It's like an extra-terrestrial enclave. He was a poor orphan but was lucky enough to have been adopted by someone on the island so that he was spared the common fate of being thrown to the bottom of the sea with stones tied to him. Many of the islanders refer to him as the illegitimate son of a dugong and a mainlander. His adoptive mother was a kind-hearted old woman who saved his life almost at the risk of her own. Before her death, she told him to look for two people across the sea – a man and a woman. It's on this mission that he left the island."

"No wonder! He looks scary, like half human, half beast."

"It's already unfortunate to be deformed," said Liao Mai, shaking his head. "Let's not talk about him in this way. The question is what happened later – I was surprised when he mentioned two people. I had to listen carefully. He said that the man was called Qi Jin, who had lived on the island for four years. In the meantime, the daughter of an old woman fell in love with Qi Jin, but then he disappeared never to return. The girl was devastated. Mei Di, you know Qi Jin's my classmate and my best friend. And I know he's lived on Trident Island. It can't be anyone else. As for the woman the guy's looking for, she's none other than Old Woman Shan, who lives near the estuary."

"Old Woman Shan? Then why didn't you tell him about her?"

"We don't have to. He's just escaped from her. He headed straight east along the coast a few days ago and finally ended up on our farm. He said he'd been crying all the way and wished to kill himself by bashing his head into a tree. He didn't do it because he thought of the old woman to whom he owed a great debt of gratitude. He also thought of her dying request. Up to this point, he's found no one."

"How come? He's already found one. You can help him locate the other. But what happened to Old Woman Shan? Why did he go to her in the first place?"

"You're right. I asked him the same question, but he wouldn't answer me. I finally agreed to help him find Qi Jin on condition that he'd tell me the whole truth. That was how he ended up telling me everything."

"It's really amazing," Liao Mai continued. "I could barely believe what he was saying even though I heard him with my own ears. He said the old woman on the island had told him before she died that he was indeed a dugong's son. Someone had handed him to her years before – and that someone turned out to be Old Woman Shan, who lives on the estuary across the sea. According to the old woman, they met on the beach across the sea, and Old Woman Shan was covered with blood. She told the old woman she had delivered a dugong of the baby, and the dugong had gone through a difficult labour. After giving birth, the dugong vanished. Old Woman Shan meant to cast the hairy offspring into the sea. The old woman, who didn't have the heart to see her doing so, offered to adopt the crying infant and carried him to the island and reared him... the old woman had been dreaming the same dream a few days before her death and told him about it in detail again and again.

"She said caringly: 'I'm about to leave this world. Then, there'll be no one to take care of you here on the island. Go to the mainland and find your relative, who'll definitely adopt you. That person's also old, and she's childless. She'll probably need you to provide for her when she's too old to take care of herself, to attend upon her as she's dying and to give her a proper burial after she passes. Go! Hurry up!'

"Therefore, he crossed over and asked about the two people along the way. After many trials and tribulations, he finally located the estuary. For some reason, he burst into tears upon seeing the mud houses. He knelt on the ground for a long time, without any intention of getting up. He had suffered so much during his search. He was crying when a narrow-faced young man spotted him and interrogated him. He told the narrow-faced young man about the old woman's words and added: 'I'm from Trident Island. My name's Maoha. I'm here to look for my mother called Shanzi.' The narrow-faced young man drew his face even longer, saying: 'She's your mother? Your biological mother?' 'Something close.' Narrow Face went away and, in a little while, helped Old Woman Shan out of her house."

Mei Di listened intently and then exclaimed: "Maoha, a dugong's son... My God!"

"Maoha said that, as soon as he saw Old Woman Shan wearing a blue cloth scarf and looking so old, he had hardly been able to stop shedding tears. For untold reasons, he wanted to call her Mother once he laid his eyes upon her – and so he called her aloud. He was still regretting doing so because Old Woman Shan immediately turned hostile. He would feel frightened by that look for the rest of his life. Maoha then recounted to Old Woman Shan what the old woman had told him in detail. He singled out her dreams. Old Woman Shan stood there listening for about ten minutes without saying a word. She stood silent for a while with a long face. He thought that she would reach out to hold his hand, but instead, she scolded him: 'You beast!' Then, she turned around and walked away. No matter how often he called out to her, she refused to look back. The narrow-faced young man caught up with her and followed. But Maoha would not leave. He lay by the estuary waiting and watching, wishing that Old Woman Shan would relent and take him with her. He waited there for three days, in fits of sleep and wakefulness, and kept mumbling: 'Mother! Mother!'

"On the third day, it was windy and the water was rough, and as soon as he opened his eyes, he saw the narrow-faced man coming out of the mud house with a rifle in his hands. The man prowled about, in an apparent attempt to approach him. At first, Maoha thought he was going to hunt birds, but then he realised that something was up – he had just craned his neck to take a peep when a bullet whistled over, nearly skimming his head. It was a really close call. Aware that the man meant to kill him, he gave a loud scream and plunged himself into the choppy water. He swam nonstop for half a day and managed to stay alive in the end."

"That sounds terrible," Mei Di said. "But I kind of don't understand."

"That's why I'm saying his story sounds like a myth. Luckily, Old Woman Shan really does exist."

Both fell silent. Mei Di stared out of the window for a while, murmuring to herself: "How did the old woman on the island know Old Woman Shan? And if he was born by Old Woman Shan, Maoha must be her illegitimate son. She must hate letting the cat out of the bag, right?"

"But the entire town of Jiwo knows she's childless. So there's no need for her to kill him even if she doesn't want her secret to be divulged. She's not that stupid."

Mei Di shook her head and pouted her lips. "Well, how many days has she stayed in town during her life? What do the townspeople really know about her? He may actually be her biological son."

"It was just a wild guess. Maoha said too much, too much…"

"Are you really going to help him find Qi Jin?"

"I must prick up my ears and get to the bottom of this before I can give him a helping hand. It's not difficult to locate someone."

WATER DUNGEON

Maoha's adoptive mother was a native of the island. Her appearance there had been connected with a well-known shipwreck.

It would be too difficult to delve into the origin of the old woman. Why? Because she was dead, and a dead person tells no tales. "Damn it! Damn it! If only one of them had survived. Why couldn't one of them have lived?" yelled the headman called Lao Shuai while he was tearing up and down the wreckage of the boat. The cold weather that day nearly killed him.

That was what happened that day, according to the elders of the island. It was related to a marine accident, in which a rare gust of wind smashed a ship of unknown origin and swept away nearly all the wreckage and belongings except for a few odd objects. Though small in number, these objects could still identify the ship's origin as being from a wonderland; for each of them, being delicate and elegant, exceeded the islanders' wildest imagination. The only survivor was a teenage girl, who, dressed in her best, looked pretty and adorable. Unfortunately, she was struck dumb with terror, unable to speak coherently. She was holding a chest tight in her arms, allowing no one to touch it.

The dumbstruck girl was rescued by some of the islanders and resettled in a rickety Buddhist temple. Then, after she gradually regained consciousness and was able to speak sensibly, Lao Shuai took her to his home. He did not have the heart to see her crammed into a place exposed to the wind. But there were also rumours that Lao Shuai was coveting the chest that she held in her arms. No matter how much treasure there was in it, it would eventually be known to the public.

The girl said that her name was Er'er and that she used to be a servant girl of the Huo family by the big river. Her family name was Huo because everyone in the Huo Mansion, including the buildings, plants and animals, all bore the same surname. Lord Huo's mountain properties were larger than the whole island. His mansion was as magnificent as a royal palace, with so many exquisite objects for entertainment that no one could see or enumerate them all. While the lord's family members enjoyed rare dainty foods and even their servants could have steamed bread and meaty dishes, Lord Huo himself grazed like a horse. This was because he was already a demigod who had become an integral part of nature. After becoming tired of the luxurious life on land, he had a big castle ship built and went out to sea. Lying on the ship, he fell into a permanent slumber, attended to by his girl servants. The ship cruised for three days and nights until it found itself at the mercy of fog, wind and rain. Two days later, the little servant girl Er'er was picked up by the islanders. "I'm missing the Huo Mansion, missing Lord Huo," she said before bursting into tears as soon as she learned where she was.

Lao Shuai's intention became known to the islanders a few years later because two years before he passed away, he married his adoptive daughter Er'er to his only son. The Lao Shuai family were well-off, but a few years after Lao Shuai's death, his son Xiao Shuai suddenly became rich. He bought land and built a large number of houses, which the islanders nicknamed the Shuai Mansion. "It must be the chest held in the girl's bosom that's given him the magic power. Lao Shuai was really shrewd," commented the islanders in private.

The heyday of the Shuai Mansion was cut short by Xiao Shuai's premature death. However, he died a lucky and smart death – at that time, a gang of pirates had fled to the island, where they ran rampant. Xiao Shuai and his fellow islanders finally had enough of their oppression, and he sneaked out of the island to get help. Knowing the sea route well, he led soldiers to the island on several armed junks by circumventing turbulent currents and promontories. Xiao Shuai's heroism led to the soldiers' eventual annihilation of the pirates. But unfortunately, before the soldiers made landfall, he was stung by a venomous fish, collapsed soon afterwards and perished along with the pirates.

The liberation of Trident Island would always be associated with the Shuai Mansion, and the islanders would always feel indebted to Xiao Shuai. After his death, his wife Huo Er'er and their daughter, along with the servants, were given preferential treatment to varying degrees. However, the soldiers enforced a new law of equal wealth distribution, resulting in the demise of the Shuai Mansion. Even so, subsequent generations of the Shuai family were still respected. People said that the family had treated them fairly during its prime. It was regrettable that things were changing too fast. Later, not only was wealth distributed equally, but the islanders had to repeatedly denounce the rich – it was said that platforms were set up in more populous places outside the island, and there were cases where an entire village mobbed a platform to scold their wealthy fellow villagers in tearful voices. Sometimes, when their grievances went out of control, they even killed the wealthy one by one.

Those were the days when Huo Er'er and her daughter lived in fear. Luckily, all the residents of Trident Island were grateful. Feeling indebted to the Shuai family, they did not have the heart to scold them. When put in a position where they had to do something, they did it in a perfunctory manner. Some of them said: "Aunt Huo, when I went to your mansion to eat melon and bread, you guys forced me to eat it all up. That was as good as coercion!"

Another said: "Hey, Huo Er'er! You gave me second-hand clothing to help tide me over that winter. But if I'd known I had to suffer because of your generosity, I would rather have frozen to death. You meant to hurt me, didn't you?"

Huo Er'er and her daughter lived in peace with both overt and covert help from the islanders. A year later, a deceitful woman suddenly appeared on the island, and her presence proved disastrous to Huo Er'er and her daughter. It was impossible to finish recounting in three days and three nights the hardships that they would face. Their ultimate survival was deemed a miracle.

The deceitful woman was a few years younger than Huo Er'er. She had wanted to become Lao Shuai's daughter-in-law but lost out to a person that she went on to detest, so much so that she cursed her every day. One day, she found a cellar in the vicinity of the Shuai Mansion. The cellar was connected to a fissure in a coastal cliff. When the tide rose, the cellar became flooded with waist-deep water. Sitting by the opening of the cellar, an idea came to her. She went to an official dispatched from the superior authorities and said to him: "After much consideration, I'm determined to tell you about it."

Though puzzled, the official prodded her to go on. "Tell me about it."

"I'm really going to tell you."

"Go ahead then."

The deceitful woman dragged him to the cellar by his hand. When they crawled in, the tide was just rising, and the bubbling saltwater half-filled the cellar. The official gasped and stared at the woman in bewilderment. The woman burst into tears. As she sobbed, the man said: "Don't be afraid. We'll uphold justice for you."

The woman wiped her eyes so that they swelled in no time. Pointing at the cellar, she said: "Now, can't you see? This was the water dungeon the Shuai Mansion used in those years."

"Water what? A water dungeon?"

"See the black holes in the wall? That was where I was hung from spikes. I was thrust in the water twice a day. My clothes were soaked rotten so that my body was exposed. Xiao Shuai the beast then touched me with his hands and lashed me with a whip. I would've... have died in the water if you had not come."

Shocked and scared, the official gasped in the cellar's cool air and kept asking: "Why? Why did he do that?"

"What other reason could there be except for his lust? I was young and good-looking at the time. Besides, I had a fair complexion. But I was poor and was locked up simply because I couldn't afford the levy on a few pounds of fish."

"Why didn't you make a public complaint against them?"

"Why? Because I was shy. I would've complained if I weren't a woman."

The official, who had placed his hand on the rock wall to support himself while listening, now formed his hand into a fist and pounded the rock with it. Blood dripped from his hand.

"Good Heavens! Good Heavens! You guys from the superior authorities are so easy to provoke... You must uphold justice for me!"

"Certainly! Certainly!"

A GIRL WHO SWALLOWED A GOLD KEY

Huo Er'er's only daughter was called Little Yuyu. She was fifteen years old. That was the year when the deceitful woman made up that horrible story, which stunned the whole island. Some elderly islanders came forward to call the rumour into question. They said: "Good Heavens, we've never seen such a thing as a water dungeon on our island. Could it have been brought in by someone – someone from outside the island with a big ship?"

"Most probably. Most probably."

But before long, these dissenting voices disappeared, and no one else would say anything. It turned out later that all those who had questioned the existence of a water dungeon had been dragged into the shadows and given a slapping. Young people jeered: "No wonder you got slapped even though you're adults. You insisted on speaking when you were not supposed to. Don't you think you really deserve to be slapped?"

Seething with anger, the youngsters did not even sympathise with the older generations in their own families.

It was time for the mother and daughter to suffer. Being tortured in interrogations day and night, Huo Er'er had to tell the truth: "I don't know. I've never heard about our family ever building water dungeons."

Her torturers took her to the site, but she still shook her head.

"Beat her! If you didn't beat the slut, the wife of a fishing overlord and moneybag, she will never confess." But she clammed up. "Beat her! Kill her!" came a shout, and immediately someone acted accordingly. No one knew why the young and middle-aged men were so angry and why they were the most enthusiastic. Several of them assaulted her by grasping her hair and yanking a few tufts from her scalp.

Her daughter was locked up at home, but whenever she was let out, she would throw herself upon her mother and bite anyone who dared to lay a finger on her. Since she had bitten two people already, whenever they escorted Huo Er'er out into the open air, they would have to lock the little girl up first. When they were separated, Huo Er'er would always shout: "Little Yuyu, don't cry. Mum will be back before long."

The water dungeon was soon sealed off, and access to it was denied to the public. A few outsiders came to the island and busied themselves with something beyond the public's comprehension in the sealed-off dungeon. It was known later that they were dungeon experts who had come to renovate the cellar meticulously. They worked a whole winter in this manner. When the cold, windy days were gone, and the seal was removed, a new dungeon appeared and was reopened to the public.

The day was regarded as a holiday on the island. Many people came from outside – as elated as angry. Learning of this rare site from unknown sources, they wanted to be the first to see it and see as much of it as they could. They filed into the cave gesticulating with indignation. The renovation, which involved the installation of a staircase and wooden handrails, made the descent to the dungeon easier. When visitors arrived on a platform, they could feel the increased moisture level and hear the burbling of the water dripping all around. Rusted spikes and hooks stuck out from the walls like ferocious fangs. The visitors were all horrified, sometimes yelling and sometimes gasping.

Whenever there were visitors, the deceitful woman was on site to serve as a guide and interpreter. After many sessions, she became increasingly fluent and eloquent, and gradually developed her fabricated story into a full-blown narrative that included how old she had been when she was first thrown into the dungeon, what she looked like, how she felt about her genitals and breasts being soaked in the filthy water, how the fishing overlord entered lantern in hand, how she kicked him in the crotch, how leeches crept up her legs while she was in the water for so long, how snakes crawled into her pants before dawn, how she missed her relatives every night, how she was sexually assaulted by the beastly lord in the darkness, how she was reduced to a skeleton of skin and bones after years of torture, and how she was abandoned on the street as an object of loathing.

The gaping audience said in unison: "Seeing's believing!" At the conclusion of each session, a group of young women, who were junior guides and interpreters lurking behind the visitors, would step up and start shouting slogans. The visitors chanted with them. Thanks to the excellent acoustics of the cellar, the echoes of their chanting rumbled so loud that they themselves felt scared, so much so that they would later have nightmares.

The deceitful woman had become a star on the island and beyond. She now considered herself above the task of interpreting for ordinary visitors. She was invited to recount her personal experiences to audiences on the other side of the strait. Returning to the island from each trip, she would attract crowds of spectators from the entire island with the state-of-the-art gadgets that she often brought with her. The novelty of the gadgets was betrayed by their glossy packages. One day, she opened one of the cartons and produced a curious cubic box with knobs, a turn of which would make the box talk and sing. Only a few young people were able to identify what it was, and they vied in crying out: "Ra – radio!"

The deceitful woman began to wear different clothes from before. Some elderly people went up close to her and felt her glossy clothes, saying: "Wow, these are terrific! Like they're electroplated." She also looked a decade younger than her sixty years. Not only did her face shine, but her breasts also started to bulge.

Someone else whispered: "This glib-talking slut has probably been running around with quite a few youngsters and taking in a lot of their vital essence." Not knowing what "vital essence" meant, young islanders asked repeatedly, but no one would answer them.

Shortly afterwards, a few bespectacled men were sent to the island by superior authorities. Their arrival told the islanders that something new would happen to the water dungeon. Sure enough, these men hung around with the deceitful woman day and night.

They also went to the water dungeon repeatedly and visited Huo Er'er and her daughter from time to time. One of them tried to touch the little girl's cheek, but he had just reached out his hand when she caught his finger between her teeth. Despite his hysterical scream, she would not relent. When she finally released the finger at her mother's scolding, it was already bleeding like a dripping tap.

It turned out that these people had been assigned to create a big drama on the island along the lines of the story of the water dungeon, that is, a Fish Opera, popular in the region around Trident Island. This genre of opera was only put on in small productions, and no one knew how many centuries it had been performed. With its spoken parts written and spoken in ancient vernacular, the opera had not been staged for decades. The string and percussion instruments used in the opera all came from marine creatures, such as fish skin and bones. The characters and events depicted in the opera were almost all related to marine creatures. The tunes mimicked the sounds of fish drumming their swim bladders, boatmen rowing with their oars and fishermen singing their sea shanties. Nevertheless, those who could perform the Fish Opera were a rapidly declining number on Trident Island.

The bespectacled men took turns to write. They came and went over a period of a few months. They worked hard on the script by day and slept on the same *kang* with the deceitful woman at night. On the bed-stove, in addition to the essential bedding, there was a short-legged table with pens, ink and paper set on it. Scripts were said to come to their minds at any moment, even in the middle of the night. Therefore, whatever dawned on them had to be committed to paper immediately. Scripts pass through the mind without giving one a second chance to capture them, no matter who one is, what official position one holds or how learned one may claim to be. After a hard day's work of fishing, curious young islanders flocked below the window of the deceitful woman's house to overhear the conversations she had with her guests and caught them fooling around and giggling. The young fishermen were particularly fascinated by the deceitful woman singing a line or two from a classic Fish Opera: "I say, my fishing lover / Wait till I've undressed. / Why are you so perplexed?"

The young men were indeed perplexed by what one of the men said: "We're going to rescue a genre by rescuing an opera." The eavesdroppers fell silent because the word "rescue" alone indicated the extreme gravity and urgency of the matter.

No one knew how many viewed the water dungeon and then paid special visits to the mother and daughter. Pointing at them, they said: "See? This is the concubine of a fishing overlord, and she's still alive!"

"How can she be so shameless as to keep on living? She simply watched her man raping an unmarried girl!"

"A concubine of a fishing overlord like her should have been screwed by the fishermen who work at sea all day long!"

During the early days, Er'er always yelled: "Our family has never built a sinister dungeon. This is a lie someone's made up to hurt me. I was never a concubine. I was the only wife of my husband."

When she screamed loudly in defence, the jailor would give her a few slaps on the face. With the elapse of time and the increase in the number of visitors, she simply left them alone – she would sit quietly with her daughter's hand in hers, letting the sun shine on her white hair, her face furrowed with deep wrinkles. At night, while caressing her daughter, she would admonish her: "Little Yuyu, listen to Mum. Don't bite people any more. They could pull your teeth out – those beasts can act on whatever they say. Good girl, it's for you that Mum's struggling to stay alive!" Little Yuyu nodded, without tears in her big eyes. But every time someone reached out to insult her and her mother, she would bite them without hesitation.

A worse ordeal was in store for Little Yuyu. As news about the water dungeon spread far and wide, especially with the creation of the Fish Opera, efforts intensified to investigate Huo Er'er's past life. Some people began to interview elderly folk on the island, asking them about every detail of that tempestuous night and the wrecked castle ship. In the end, they focused on the chest held tight in Huo Er'er's arms, wondering if it really contained silver and gold, if there was anything else and where in the world the chest was now.

The interrogation of Huo Er'er resumed: "If you don't speak, we'll hand you over to the youngsters who've long been asking us to do so. As you know, they can be reckless and indiscreet."

Huo Er'er's response remained the same: "Where can I find the chest after so many years? Besides, it belongs to Lord Huo, so it must be returned to his descendants."

"You moneybags' slut! You scum servant! You're like a viper that remains venomous even after it's dead."

Eventually, they were at their wit's end and passed her on to a few youngsters who had come to the island. They were joined by several other young native islanders. They tried every means to torture and interrogate her. They first used a stratagem known as 'physical pain', which involved lashing her with a rope soaked in the salty seawater, pinching her private parts and hanging her so that her feet could barely touch the floor. They then employed the ruse of 'shaming', or removing parts of her garments in order to expose her breasts and genitalia to public view. Old singles peered at those areas with their reading glasses on while children placed creepy worms into the holes... After all the torture proved fruitless, they racked their brains and suddenly came up with another idea. Slapping his thigh, one said: "I've got it!"

They threw Huo Er'er into the dungeon again and left her in the water for a month. They escorted her out only a few times to get fresh air and see sunlight for fear that she might die. "It's your family water dungeon, but you don't like it?" jeered the youngsters. Eventually, her knees became blistered, her hair was overgrown with moss and her body was covered with numerous water bugs. Even her heels were stuck with true oysters. Seeing her barely alive in the water dungeon, the young people had to transfer her to a stable for imprisonment.

For two months, she was separated from her daughter Little Yuyu, who was locked up alone elsewhere. A group of people with steel drill rods made a thorough search of their house, leaving no stone unturned. But they still found nothing. Then, someone thought of the *kang*. "Tear it apart!" he shouted. "Tear it apart!" But after demolishing it, they found nothing. When they thrust a drill rod into the ground at the foundation of the mudbrick *kang*, they laughed because they discovered a porcelain jug with a lid. When the lid was removed, the chest presented itself.

But the chest was made from a special metal. Small and delicate in appearance, it was extremely sturdy. It had a keyhole, but there was no key to unlock it. "Fuck! We can neither cut it nor hammer it nor damage the contents inside. It's baffling," said the team leader.

They hurried to look for the key, but due to its small size it was ten times more difficult than looking for the chest. They searched for several days but without success. Someone thought of Little Yuyu and had her pressed down. While taking every precaution not to be bitten, they stripped her. They all found Little Yuyu's naked body to be as lovely as that of a slippery fish. She was wearing a red *dudou* – a one-piece, backless halter top – and a golden thread around the neck. Yanking the thread off, they found something glistening and burst into exclamations. It turned out to be a gold key. The assailants were beyond themselves with joy, so much so that they did not even know where to place their big hands. Before they composed themselves, the girl had struggled from their grip and bitten the man who was reaching out to touch the key. While the man was screaming, she took back the key, held it in her hand and hid it behind her. The men forced her into a corner. As she stepped back, she looked around and suddenly placed the key into her mouth.

The men tried to pry her mouth open, to dig for the key in it and tickle her by reaching a feather into her throat, but all their efforts were in vain. "Fuck! She's swallowed it! She's swallowed it!" cursed the team leader, rubbing his slimy hands together.

A MAGIC NEEDLE

Little Yuyu was confined in a closely guarded wing-room, with the head of the guards staying in the next room. The wing-room was against a sea cliff, so that the rumbling of the surf pounding the rocks was heard as loud as cannon shots, making it hard to sleep. The sleep-deprived head of the guards was all the more fidgety. But he had to put up with the noise because the little girl needed to be locked up here – people could defecate more easily and frequently when exposed to the sound of pounding waves according to Wandu (literally 'Curved Belly'), who was famous for being the only doctor on the island trained in both Chinese and Western medicine. It had been suggested that laxatives be applied to the girl, but Wandu said while stroking his silver beard: "This is not the right way to do it. If she discharges her loose stools too fast, that thing could get stuck in her stomach or bowels. Then, we would have to operate on her. That wouldn't be a smart move."

Sure enough, the head guard started frequenting the outhouse from the first day of his posting here. Before tying his waistband, he left the pit, rushed to the armed guard and asked: "Has she been to the toilet yet?" The guard would always shake his head. The head guard peeped at the girl through the window and saw her face peaceful and solemn and her eyes, filled with hatred, trained towards the sea from time to time. She kept pacing in the room. She must be thinking of going to the outhouse, he wondered.

"How many times does she go to the outhouse each day?" asked the head guard.

"She just peed three times," a guard answered.

"Damn! That's strange. It's no good," mumbled the head guard as he returned to his room. He ordered the guard to notify him as soon as the girl defecated, be it day or night.

"Yes, sir," responded the guard.

The pit toilet in the outhouse used by the little girl was rebuilt especially for her. A bucket with a big iron strainer placed in it was set in the deep pit.

Day or night, as long as he was awake, the head guard would lean over the windowsill to watch her pacing. To his amazement, she slept little but paced a lot, doing nothing but pacing. "Fuck, if she isn't bursting, what else does it tell me? So, I'll be waiting, and you'll release what you swallowed sooner or later." He ordered the guards to serve her more fatty fish bellies and added: "Let her eat. It'd be better if she screams for being too full!"

At three o'clock in the morning on the fourth day, a guard woke the head guard as if he had great news to tell him, although the head guard had just nodded off after being tormented by sleeplessness for the better part of the night. He rolled up, rubbed his eyes and saw the young man carrying the bucket in one hand and the strainer in the other, his mouth distorted and his nose wrinkled. The strainer had a big, cone-shaped mass sitting in it, golden and pleasing to the eye. "Wow, the brat did a pretty good job!" The head guard examined it closely while flaring his nostrils and walked around it several times. He then took the strainer over and gingerly carried it outside the room. Fiddling with a gourd ladle, he mumbled: "I must rinse it carefully." He reprimanded the young guard by his side at the same time: "This stuff is not smelly at all. Why are you standing so far away? Raise the lantern higher. Even higher." The result, however, was utterly frustrating.

Another two days passed, and two examinations were conducted in the same manner. But the outcome was the same. Drawing a long face, he asked Wandu what to do. Wandu responded with tears streaming down his cheeks: "She has to go under the knife."

"Is the operation complicated?"

"A cinch. As easy as taking something out of a pouch. I just need you to leave the island and buy me two surgical instruments. I also need some helping hands. But," said Wandu wiping his face before continuing, "it's a shame that she's such a nice girl and has a cute belly. Surgery would..."

"Well, we've no alternative. She deserves it anyway. Does it really hurt?"

"Nah. I have my secret weapon – the magic needle. With it, I don't even need an anaesthetist. How about the morning of tomorrow or the day after? My eyes are better in the mornings."

Wandu set up his operating theatre in a room away from the waves. He smoked the room with silvery wormwood for a few hours and sprinkled some sanitising liquid onto the walls. He asked people to stand on guard some distance from the house to prevent others from passing by. He also asked the head guard to issue an order to all the islanders: during the surgery, no one be allowed to speak loudly, chant sea shanties, shout in unison when they launch a boat into the water, or clatter their pots and pans.

"Why? Didn't you tell us it was as easy as castrating a piglet?" asked the head guard.

"When did I say that?" said an irritated Wandu. "I said it was as easy as getting something from a pouch."

"What's the difference?"

"It *is* different. No one is allowed to startle my scalpel. It's our business, me and the girl – my professional skill and her perfectly healed belly. If anyone should disturb me during surgery, I'll cut off his ding-a-ling with the scalpel!"

What can be done with him? He's our only hope, the head guard told himself. He's the only doc with both Chinese and Western medical training. Biting his tongue, he held back the curse: Damn you, motherfucker!

When she first entered the room, Little Yuyu, ignorant of what was going on, was in good spirits. She kept sniffing the silvery wormwood that suffused the entire room. However, when she spotted the old physician and his men wielding knives and scissors, she began to sense danger. The old physician pulled her aside and informed her of the surgery. He told her that she could die of a possible stomach perforation if the gold key were not taken out. If that should happen, it would be too late to save her life.

"Then, I will die!" Little Yuyu responded.

"But you would not be able to see your mother."

Little Yuyu hung her head. After a while, she looked up and said: "I would rather die than give them the key."

Shedding a few tears, the old physician said: "My child, it would be easier to get the key from a dead body."

He then tried talking her into accepting the surgery in a soft, slow voice, saying that he would use the best technique in the world. A few pricks with some needles and a cut with a little knife would be no more painful than being stung by a bee. "Don't worry about having a big ugly scar because I've been thinking hard, my child, of how to perform the operation. I'll make a cut as small as the mouth of a goldfish and sew the cut edges together like a skilled embroiderer. When it heals in a month, I'll plaster it with some herbal gel, and in fifteen to twenty days, the scar will be invisible even with the help of reading glasses."

Looking into his eyes, Little Yuyu asked: "Are you telling the truth?"

"I am, indeed. I'm so old that I could be your grandpa. How could I talk nonsense? I love children."

Little Yuyu fell silent and lay down in the makeshift operating theatre.

The old physician first had someone make her swallow a few white pills. After she fell asleep, he took off her clothes himself. As a child, she did not have a single scar on her plump, flawless body. Her small breasts looked like two small apples, a sign of early puberty. Her navel was adorable as well. He was examining her body carefully when he turned his head and caught sight of the head guard peeping through the window. He waved a warning at him.

Little Yuyu's hands, stomach, legs, feet and head were covered with quivering acupuncture needles. She was still fast asleep. When she started snoring gently, the old physician said: "We can start now", and he held his hands out level. An aid put rubber glasses on his hands and a mask over his mouth.

During the whole operation, almost nothing was audible except the faint clinking of surgical instruments being cast into an iron box.

SOMETHING THAT TAKES A LONG TIME TO DECIPHER

The mysterious chest was opened, but what it contained was completely beyond expectation; for there was no treasure at all. All it contained were two pieces of brown paper with spaced-out characters written on them with an ink brush, and beside the characters, there were marks the colour of cinnabar.

Few people were on site, as opening the chest was considered a confidential operation. Those who saw the contents after it was first opened included the head guard, his superior and two of the Fish Opera playwrights. At a relatively close distance, stood the deceitful woman. But eventually, she was pushed a few steps further back for the reason that she was 'not entitled to the privilege in her ranking'.

Their emotional trauma went through the stages of astonishment, confusion and agonising frustration. They sat motionless around the chest, each with his brows drawn together. They had sat like this for a long time when the head guard slapped his own forehead and said: "Aha, it's a list of names for revenge!"

Each of the other three shifted their eyes from the paper to each other and said nothing. They did not believe it because they found no records of money on the paper. They considered the conclusion impetuous. The head guard prodded his superior to look more closely, and it read: "a lamb's hoof, a wild boar's foot, a pink-nosed deer, a floral girl, a fine-skinned calf, a doxy, a white hare..." After so many years, the ink had become heavy and some of the cinnabar marks conspicuously red.

"This is apparently a list of animals," said the superior official, a bit disappointed.

The head guard smirked and said: "To my mind, this is the moneybags' ruse of 'throwing dust in people's eyes', that is, intentionally nicknaming the people to be avenged by their descendants after some animals. The nicknames don't have to be known to anyone but their descendants."

"Then what do the red circles and dots mean?"

"They indicate either heavy debtors or great personal enemies that they expected their descendants to decapitate... Well, I'm getting a bit confused, too. But, anyway, I'm certain this is a list of people used for revenge. We must send the list to the superior authorities at top speed so that they can find some experts to decipher it. As the old saying goes: 'What's difficult for a layman may be a doddle for an expert.' Professional decoders see it as plain as the nose on our faces. Right? Right?" The head guard gesticulated with a hint of complacency.

Having no further comment to make, his superior just demanded that it be put away and said that he would report it to the superior authorities as soon as possible.

Many years later, the theory of 'a list of names for revenge', though proved and then disproved alternately, remained unconfirmed in the end. The chest was passed from one city to another outside the island and even to experts farther away. Published articles on research into identifying the contents of the chest led to more complicated hypotheses. One assumed that it could be a list of rare animals jotted down by a wealthy person with a peculiar interest. Another argued that texts so painstakingly kept must be significant, and they had to be the code names of secret society members in the mountain forest and the back country. The marked names had to be those of the ringleaders because the moneyed landowners at that time had been hand in hand with the local secret societies. Still another concluded that it was a map of bandit liaisons. Other interpretations of the name list included undercover hatchet men, mercenary head guards and artisans of various trades.

Notwithstanding the diverse theories, the few Fish Opera playwrights adopted the assumption of 'a name list for revenge' and wove it into the water dungeon story. Eventually, they made up a pathetic and gloomy Fish Opera comprising a few acts. The leading character was the most gorgeous woman on the island. Coveted by a moneybag, she was forced to part from her lover. The opera was performed on the island for three days running. It was so moving that, as they watched, the audience were weeping while pounding their chests and stomping their feet. Elderly men and women made up the most loyal audience. They did not so much watch the show as try to relive the past by listening to the familiar tunes because they often appreciated the singing with their eyes closed.

"I haven't heard such tunes for so many years. Wow, wow, wow! It really satisfies my artistic hunger and scratches my emotional itch." They swayed their bodies to the rhythm of both the instrumentals and vocal music, and unwittingly crushed many a chair beneath their wiggling buttocks.

The amused youngsters sneered: "The older they are, the heavier their backsides grow!"

There were two aspects of this Fish Opera show that particularly exasperated the elderly men and women. One concerned the characters. In a real Fish Opera, they were mostly aquatic creatures. Only occasionally, human characters were called for in case they were emotionally involved with fish spirits or dragon princesses. The characters of this particular opera, however, were exclusively humans, and they had to sing and dance like fish, which made them look as awkward as clowns. The second disappointing aspect was the woman protagonist portraying the deceitful woman on the island. Although she was homely in real life, the character on stage was turned into a breathtakingly beautiful fairy. As their opinions converged to a consensus, they could not stop themselves from speaking out. Consequently, those who dared to do so almost risked being detained. Senior officials said reprovingly: "So you still want superstitious shows to be put on again? So you want the old stuff to be restored? So you think the story's not real? So you want to cover up the evil deeds of fishing overlords? We'll do a thorough investigation to identify those who're talking nonsense!" Then, everyone was hushed.

Being prevented from seeing the hidden contents of the chest still rankled the deceitful woman. She neither ate nor drank and took a boat from the island to complain to the official of the superior authorities. "How could they treat me like this! People like me can look at everything, right? I may be illiterate, but I could tell what it was just by smelling it. Then you, as an official of the superior authorities, would not have to be bothered in such a big way."

The official then reprimanded those who had kept her from viewing the contents of the chest and immediately ordered a special person to take her to the specified location to crack the code. Holding the chest to her bosom, she sobbed for a while, saying that only wealthy landowners had such a high-quality casket. She sniffed and felt the two pieces of brown paper, sneezing incessantly. Finally, she said: "Brutal! Brutal!"

When asked why, she answered: "What good deeds can rich landowners perform? They're the names of those they killed! Look at the red marks! They mean – they were killed!" Everyone was shocked.

For a time, a rumour circulated that the Huo Mansion had left an astonishing record of murdered people. Whether the rumour had originated from the deceitful woman was unknown.

In a flash, a few decades had passed. Many events happened in the meantime. The spread of various rumours about the brown paper in the chest never stopped. At Huo Er'er's persistent request, the chest was finally returned to her, but the two pieces of brown paper were evidently replicas. Even though the originals were nowhere to be found, Huo Er'er was still so excited that she again locked the papers in the chest.

Little Yuyu still had a distinct vertical scar running down her abdomen, contrary to what the old physician had promised. Luckily, the centipede-like scar was far from being unsightly. Trying to explain away his failure, the physician said: "It was all because the medicinal herbs were tainted. One of the herbs had lizard's pee on its leaves. That was how the accident took place." Later, he applied some ointment to her abdomen. Since the scar had already formed, the ointment did not make much difference. What happened later saddened the old physician – it was the year when Little Yuyu got married. The old physician grounded a new preparation of herbal medicine for scar removal and hurried to her bridal room with it. There, he was lifting Little Yuyu's garment off without saying a word when her husband rushed in and roared as loud as thunder.

It was perhaps for the sake of the secret contents of the chest that Huo Er'er left the island in the same year as the chest was returned. While there was no way of knowing whether her trip had solved the secret or not, she did something that stunned the entire island: she brought with her a little boy with webbed feet.

But no one knew what on earth the relationship was between her and Old Woman Shan, who had returned the boy to her.

TEN

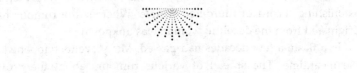

A PACING SHADOW

LIAO MAI HAD to leave the management of the farm to Mei Di while he concentrated on taking care of Maoha for the time being. For him to stay in the little room by the garage all day was no easy job. Mei Di attended to the miscellanies alone and sent food to the garage every evening. Several days had passed, but the workers remained excited at the mention of 'Maoha'. They still nursed a grudge against this strange man who had come and gone so hurriedly. Whenever they saw Mei Di, they would become rowdy: "God! That guy can lie on the water surface without eating or drinking for half a day. Maybe he's really an incarnate of a fish spirit. No one knows where he is now. He may be hanging around nearby."

"How can such a wild man stay in one place?" said Mei Di. "He may have returned to the sea, riding on its waves."

One morning, an emaciated man appeared among the temporary workers. He asked a few questions with a poker face, all about that man with webbed feet. After someone told Me Di about this skinny man, she hurried to the work sheds by the lake. Sure enough, she saw the stranger there. He had a long oval face and looked morose. He stared at her with clenched teeth but had no intention of saying anything.

"Are you here to work for us?" asked Mei Di.

He did not answer, only casting a glance at her, which made her cheeks burn with pain. "I'm here to hire people," he said eventually.

"What on earth are you doing here? Headhunting my people?" Mei Di felt her heart thumping hard as she intentionally raised her voice.

The oval-faced man hurried off without responding to her question.

Mei Di watched the man leave the farm and made sure he had headed a good distance west before she returned home. Still feeling uneasy, she walked back towards the garage to see Liao Mai.

The small window in the little house by the garage had recently been boarded up, and the door had been bolted securely. She tapped on the wooden door panel rhythmically a few times, and the door opened. The strange man called Maoha was sitting on the *kang* with his hands holding his knees, while Liao Mai was seated opposite him. Both were silent. While his hair was still a mess, the sludge on Maoha's face was gone and he had changed his clothes. His trousers, in particular, no longer had holes. The thick, brown hair on his chest, however, was still visible from his neckline. Perhaps he knew who had showed up. Instead of making eye contact, he stared at his webbed feet, biting his lip. After whispering with Mei Di for a little while, Liao Mai followed her out of the little house by the garage.

After a few minutes, Liao Mai came into the little house and said: "Maoha, maybe we need to be more cautious. The guy who fired at you came to our farm today."

Maoha looked up to reveal his large, round, glistening eyes. Liao Mai suddenly had the feeling that they were the eyes of a marine animal. Maoha stared in the same manner for a while and, rubbing his nose a few times, said: "Brother Liao, you'd better send me back to the estuary – maybe my mum's regretted letting me go. I've always felt Old Woman Shan to be my biological mother. As soon as I saw her that day, I had this feeling – she may take me in. I'd better go back to her."

Patting him on the shoulder, Liao Mai said: "You can't go back until you've figured out what she's really up to. If she'd been kind-hearted, she wouldn't have allowed that man to shoot at you – instead of taking you in, she was apparently trying to take you down!"

On hearing Liao Mai's words, Maoha snarled with a raspy, somewhat high-pitched voice, similar to the cry of a large marine mammal. As he listened, tears streamed down his cheeks and onto the brown hairs on his chest. "Please stop talking like this," he said. "Please. I've told you it was not her. It was her adoptive son who fired at me. Maybe she doesn't know about the shooting... I can't stay here. I must go to her. I really think she's my biological mother."

"Then you're bewitched. You have no evidence whatsoever..."

"Evidence? Where can we find evidence for a matter like this? Mother Huo could only tell me this much. She could've told me more, but she didn't have the time and then she passed away. I waited and waited at the estuary that day. Half a day seemed as long as a year. Finally, Old Woman Shan came out, and my heart skipped a beat when I saw her face, her eyes, the blue cloth scarf on her head. I couldn't help crying out 'Mum'. I'd rather she was my mother, my biological mother."

"I don't believe a biological mother would be so cruel to her son. It was impossible for her not to know about the shooting." Trying desperately to talk the strange man out of visiting her, Liao Mai continued: "That Old Woman Shan has nominally adopted seven sons. They all do her bidding. Without her command, they dare do nothing. Besides, having seven sons already, how can she take you in?"

"But I don't think she'll see me as one too many."

"You're different from them!"

Maoha hung his head. "I know I'm too... ugly."

"No, that's not the reason. There must be other reasons – maybe we can get to the bottom of them in future. But whatever you do, you mustn't approach her place now. The shooting incident was really life-threatening."

Maoha cried and his nose started running: "Then let me die by the estuary. I can't return to Trident Island empty-handed like this. Maybe I should've died by her side..."

Liao Mai was at a loss as to how he could persuade him. He had to wait till he calmed down. Liao Mai felt this guy to be quite different from those who lived in the coastal or mountainous areas. Perhaps he had been in the deep sea for so long that he became pig-headed and began to hold extremely queer thoughts. It was hard to reason with people like him. After a while, Liao Mai changed the topic to the Fish Opera in the hope that it might cheer him up. He said that he would like to listen to him singing a tune in his peculiar voice and pitch.

Liao Mai's request had an unexpected effect on Maoha. He stopped shedding tears and instantly became cheerful. He nodded and said that Mother Huo's granddaughter was the true beauty and the best Fish Opera singer on the island. He said that Liao Mai needed to go to Trident Island if he wanted to hear her singing.

"That's something I'll do in future. But for the time being, can you sing a few lines?"

Maoha hesitated. "I can, but I must think hard." As he said these words, he ruffled the hair on his head and started to scratch the brown hairs on his chest. Eventually, he began to sing while rolling his big, round eyes:

A squeaking little turtle, don't be so muddle-headed.
I, an old man, am going to lift a couple of pieces from your shell.
It's clear the tide is rising and roaring.
I, the dragon king, am coming to the crystal palace.

Striving to reach a high pitch, he grabbed his throat with his hands. Liao Mai burst into laughter.

"Maoha, can many of the islanders sing?"

"Most of them can sing a few lines, but very few can perform an entire opera. No one in the world can sing as well as Old Sister Yuyu's daughter, Young Shaliu'er." At the mention of the name Young Shaliu'er, he turned his eyes aside and pounded the edge of the *kang* in frustration.

"I must go and look for that guy Qi," he continued. "I must find that son of a bitch and get him back. It was he who caused Young Shaliu'er to cry like that. I really want to strangle that red-faced son of a bitch. But Mother Huo wanted me to look for him. What else can I do?"

Liao Mai could tell that while liking, or rather, loving the girl that could sing the Fish Opera, Maoha had to carry out a mission to get his love rival back. It was perhaps because of this that he was confused and sometimes dazed, and he was at a loss what to do.

Liao Mai pressed his brawny arms and large hands with caring sympathy.

"The fucking bastard of a shrimp mother! The rotting-tailed turtle that can't even afford to eat foul jellyfish! The old white bream strangled by nine coiling sea snakes! This tail of a Japanese grenadier anchovy! This fragment of dried shrimp! This yellow croaker spread with soybean paste before being cooked in a pot! How nice it would be if you were dead. Then, I wouldn't have to travel a thousand kilometres to look for you, you turtle!"

Maoha's shouts gradually faded into a mumble. His volley of curses both surprised and amused Liao Mai, and he tried to calm him down by saying: "You don't have to worry. Leave the job of looking for Qi Jin to me. Trust me. Your biggest concern right now is to get yourself better and then go back to the island healthy and strong."

Maoha fell silent and lay down at an angle. But within a minute, he raised his head and flared his nostrils towards the door as if he had smelled something.

Liao Mai opened the door and went out at once, only to find it already dark. The wind was a little chilly, and the waves rumbled louder. He was about to turn around and go back to the house when he noticed something strange about the row of poplars thirty to forty metres away in the west. The otherwise erect trunk of a poplar tree now appeared to have something on it. When he peered harder, he found a lanky figure dashing between the gaps in the trees. He stooped to pick up a hoe and rushed over. He walked around the poplar trees several times but found nothing. He suspected that he might be seeing things.

They finished the food that Mei Di had delivered to them very late as they always went to sleep at midnight these days. For the next few days, Liao Mai meant to talk about the Fish Opera and what had happened to Qi Jin after he scurried to the island. However, he did not have the heart to pick up the topic once more, knowing that the mere mention of the names Qi Jin and Young Shaliu'er would upset him.

Dawn set in. Before going to sleep, Maoha talked about Mother Huo again. "I still don't understand why she was dreaming the same dream for several days in succession before her death. And the dream agitated her so much that she urged me to leave the island."

While speaking, he flared his nostrils towards the door again as if to sniff something in the air, looking nervous and edgy.

Grabbing a torch, Liao Mai dashed out.

The beam of the torch scanned across the poplar trees, then the surroundings of the garage and the bushes in the north. There was indeed something moving among the randomly swaying trunks and branches. It was a dark figure.

A RECURRING DREAM

"My children, I think it was Lord Huo who came to visit me in my dream. I dreamed of us girls being together with him on the castle ship. He was sleeping beneath his vermillion satin quilt, and no one could shake him awake." This was the third time Yuyu heard her mother Huo Er'er recounting this story. To make her mother feel better, she let her keep on saying it – again and again until the day when she would take her last breath. Yuyu had felt very sad for her mother.

"I'm not sure if they were dreams or my recollection of the past. When people get old, they sleep less and have trouble telling if they are asleep or awake. Even though a few decades have passed, I still sometimes feel I'm being tossed on the crests of the waves and struggling to cry out for help when I wake up. That disaster scared the hell out of me and made me forget everything about it. I remembered something now and then but found it hard to connect them. Luckily, they're all coming together in my dreams."

The white-haired Huo Er'er rubbed her eyes and asked Yuyu and then Maoha the same question: "My children, tell me why I have been having this dream. Every night I'm startled awake by the same nightmare."

The castle ship was a rare thing. Not only did it boast winding corridors, decorated pillars, ornamental engravings and carved mythical birds and animals, but its port and starboard sides were covered with various colourful designs. The contents of the ship were equally impressive: countless gold and silver vessels and utensils, floral carpets, and tassels of gold threads tied to the curtains and screens. All the passengers were teenage girls except Lord Huo. Selected from a million candidates, the makeup-clad maids were there to serve the lord.

While Lord Huo was sleeping in the huge canopy tent, no one was supposed to utter a sound lest it startle him. He was not to be awakened for the three meals each day as he had cultivated himself into an immortal requiring no mortal food or drink. He had been like this even during his time in his mansion. He would have drunk some grass soup or chewed a couple of almond bars when in a good mood. Otherwise, he would pull some clumps of grass and stuff them into his mouth. What he found indispensable were beautiful females, be they humans or animals. When he was home at any time of day, he would have his old butler get them ready. In his bedroom, as soon as he cleared his throat with an "Ahem" and said "Fix me up with one", a female human or animal would have to be delivered to him.

In his old age, Lord Huo was never seen without a book or person in his hand. While sipping his green grass soup, he would run one hand over a female being while holding a book in the other. He had a favourite bitch. For several years, people in the mansion could hear it panting in the lord's bedroom. He also had a pretty young woman with a prominent bottom and fine complexion. She came in and out of his bedroom carrying a box in her arms every day, claiming that she was entertaining him with 'peep shows'. She was heard shouting from inside: "Let's see this picture, and this one." But in fact, the lord had no interest at all. One day, when the old butler entered to deliver fresh grass to the lord, he accidentally looked up, only to detect a long tail sticking out of the bottom of that slut's long dress.

The head of the female servants often told them: "When the lord wakes up and hollers, whoever he calls mustn't feel bashful. All of you will be his woman sooner or later anyway. I went through this when I was young. Initially I sobbed, fearing that the lord would think me ugly, my skin not milky, and my body too plump or too skinny. In reality, I found out in the end that the lord was easy to attend to. He's never picky so long as you're a female and know how to kiss. The lord's big mouth is thick and soft, as warm as polenta hot from a pot. Even at our young age, we're no match for his avidity. Putting aside his grass soup, he'll turn around and nearly kill you with two or three of his kisses! Of course, like the ancient saying goes, a gingerroot becomes spicier the older it gets.

So, let's be prepared to chomp this old gingerroot to our hearts' content on the ship in the coming years."

The head of the female servants handed an exceptionally exquisite chest to Huo Er'er and told her: "Guard it closely. The lord meant to stow it beneath his pillow but felt it digging into the back of his head. Wear its key around your neck and keep it close to your belly. Don't ever give it to anyone."

Huo Er'er remembered every word. The castle ship sailed with the wind for three days without stirring the sleeping lord. A servant mumbled: "Why isn't he waking up? He's killing us with anxiety!"

The others jested with her, saying that she was eager to win the lord's favour since she was tired of being a virgin. Huo Er'er held Lord Huo in great esteem. Though having caught a few glimpses of his lanky frame, she had not yet had the chance to see him up close. She knew that he was kind-hearted and affectionate, though his waist band was a bit too loose. It would have been a blemish for others, but for him, it was just about right because it made him look like a naughty boy.

"What a great lord! He frolics with anyone regardless of their age," murmured a female servant coming out of Lord Huo's bedroom while rearranging her clothes. She was overheard by Huo Er'er who was walking by in the corridor.

Huo Er'er would blush and fluster at the mere thought of Lord Huo, not knowing if she was happy or scared. Leaning over the starboard railing, she feasted her eyes on the vast blue sea, wishing that the lord would wake up soon and that she would be the first to enter his canopy tent. This was like a battle, and the one who charged first would be regarded as a hero or heroine. But he just would not wake up, and she had to hold the chest all the time, even when she went to the toilet.

Wind sprang up that night, rocking the ship so much that everyone aboard vomited. After throwing up on her clothes, Huo Er'er was worried that the lord might be repelled by her appearance should he see her. At last, the light of dawn appeared on the horizon. Peering into the near distance, a mid-sized boat could be seen heading towards them. Huo Er'er rushed to the port to watch with the others, but then she felt like vomiting again and went to the toilet.

The boat approached the ship in a matter of a few minutes. A stout, red-bearded man beamed at everyone on the castle ship. Before the spectators knew what was happening, two grappling hook ropes had already been cast over and caught the castle ship. Red Beard immediately withdrew his smile. As soon as he whistled his command, several men pulled themselves over on the hawsers. The head female servant turned out to be a leader after all. While the others were trembling with horror, she picked up an axe and applied it to the hawsers – unfortunately, she did not have enough strength to sever them. Instead, she was cut down with a swooshing sword wielded by Red Beard.

All the female servants were stupefied. Leading his men onto the castle ship, Red Beard shouted: "Kill everyone except the women. Kill every man as usual." He ordered his men to search everywhere and soon gathered up all the female servants on deck. Huo Er'er was so scared that she huddled in the toilet, peeping out from a small crack and trembling all the while.

Then she heard a hoarse voice: "Chief, we've searched everywhere on board and found only one man. He's lying stiff, playing dead."

Red Beard pulled his sword from its sheath and rushed to the canopy tent. The man who had just spoken to Red Beard said with laughter: "You don't need your sword any more."

Ignoring him, Red Beard went into the tent anyway. It was quiet in the tent for fifteen minutes. Then, Red Beard kicked a partition panel open and came out carrying the stiffened body of Lord Huo level in his arms and went straight to the starboard side of the boat. The others watched, biting their fingernails. Even after all this time, Huo Er'er still remembered how Lord Huo's splendid attire was ruffled by the wind; the glistening silk fabric of red and green fluttered like undulating waves.

"Go to hell!" Red Beard screamed.

Red Beard cast the stiff body of Lord Huo effortlessly into the sea.

Huo Er'er was stupefied by the scene. But she still held the chest tight against her bosom.

Red Beard took the lead in collecting all the valuable items aboard the ship, tore up the pictures on the walls and seated himself in Lord Huo's canopy tent to rest. He lay down and sat up several times, laughing and shouting: "I'm the lord now. I am the lord. Get me some tea! Hurry up."

After Red Beard and his men sexually assaulted all the female servants, they tied them up, threw them in their black boat and set fire to the castle ship.

As soon as a strong wind blew away the castle ship, a rainstorm struck and doused the fire. The boat capsized, and bobbed upon the raging sea.

A MAN IN THE MOUNTAIN

South of the city where Qi Jin lived, a mountain range extended fifty or more kilometres. To Liao Mai, the mountain near Jiwo Town was like a small hill in comparison. What surprised him was that, while embracing such a large modern metropolis, the mountainous areas were so desolate, impoverished and isolated. Perhaps these attributes were necessary for the area to preserve a kind of mystique and power inherent in nature. He was convinced that this power had something to do with Qi Jin's choice to settle in this mountainous area. The guy had been good at achieving his goal in a devious way. He had walked away alone in silence and arrived in a faraway place. After leaving the city in southern China, as well as leaving Xiu, Liao Mai had been anxious to look for Qi Jin. Having promised Maoha, he felt it all the more urgent to do so.

In the wrinkles and cracks of the mountains, innumerable animals were crawling, shifting and crying, which gave Liao Mai the feeling that the world was fresh and vibrant. Unfortunately, this natural scene had irreversibly disappeared in today's Jiwo and most other places – this is the worst of our generation's luck, thought Liao Mai. We have no alternative but to address the problem. We have to find the worst terminology that we know to describe the predicament in which we find ourselves.

When Liao Mai finally located him after a long, exhausting journey, he pounded Qi Jin's shoulder with his fist. "Qi Jin, you swarthy-faced bag of bones! You've made it so difficult for me to locate you! You've become a hermit in a cave. If you want to relocate or change into something else, could you please let me know beforehand?"

But Qi Jin did not smile. With his rough, gnarled fingers, he rolled a cigarette and puffed on it unhurriedly. "Can't help it, I'm afraid. I've formed the habit of smoking and drinking a little bit." His voice seemed to be lower and harsher than before. It was through this voice, not anything else, that Liao Mai suddenly recalled a friend from the depth of his memory, as if he had reached out a hand into an unfamiliar, chaotic and barbaric place to get hold of him and pull him close to his face.

Liao Mai entered the hermit's den. This guy was living in a deep, vast mountain cave.

Liao Mai noticed how special his residence seemed to be. It was a large cubic cave halfway up the mountain, and a simply built, three-room house was connected to it from outside. Put together, the house and cave formed a huge space. It turned out that the cave had accommodated mountain people three decades before. They had vacated it after the government persuaded them to relocate. Qi Jin had built the house outside the cave and more than doubled the living space. He explained to Liao Mai: "While I only need one room, I use the other rooms to house my friends who come to visit me. The spacious cave is used for teaching."

Liao Mai noticed the many seat cushions on the floor as well as a big blackboard. The large cave opening allowed ample light to enter. This was evidently the classroom. Pointing to the scattering of little stone houses at the bend of the river, Qi Jin said: "There's a school there, where I'm going to teach. Sometimes, the children will come up to the cave on Sundays, and I'll tutor them here in the cave. I'm planning to set up a library for the village down the mountain. It's beginning to take shape."

"So you're living here alone?" Liao Mai was keen to get to the point, but he also remembered what Xiu had told him about his divorce. These years, the best and worst parts of the population were starting to separate from their spouses.

Qi Jin nodded and then shook his head, saying: "I'm currently living here by myself. Most of the time I live here alone." He then suddenly asked: "You've met Xiu, right?"

Liao Mai nodded, blushing.

Qi Jin glanced at him and said: "She's a good girl. She's a bit too warm and enthusiastic, though. But there's nothing wrong with that, because the world is too cold... Our classmates are now scattered everywhere. After one or two decades, everyone has changed alarmingly."

Liao Mai meant to seize the opportunity to explain that Xiu had in fact not changed, but he held back.

Qi Jin told him about all the classmates that he knew; among them were officials, businesspeople, teachers, writers, artists and performers. Needless to say, some were more successful than others. A few of them went on to become international human traffickers, drug kingpins, pimps and hired propagandists. "Look at them! They used to be all enthusiastic and aspiring, but today, each picks a different tree on which to perch, like a bird. Unfortunately, some had long ago become bad birds."

Going over all the occupations and trades in his mind, Liao Mai was not sure in which category he belonged. He thought of the thirty-two acres of land on his farm, of Mei Di, of their repeatedly compromised and wavering life, and of their disputes over income redistribution. If he told Qi Jin all of this, Qi Jin would ask pointedly: Are you faltering? And then he'd assert that it was but an excuse for escape. Liao Mai felt his cheeks scorched by blushing. He now found it difficult to discuss topics such as new ways to organise labour. Besides, Liao Mai had a pressing problem that had been torturing him for a long time, that is, his affair with Xiu. He wanted to get his advice on how to deal with Xiu and how to tell Mei Di everything about it. He plucked up the courage, but before picking up the topic, he digressed once more: "I heard you couldn't stay in the western region mainly because you had to shun those ascetic monks. Is that true?"

Qi Jin looked up and stared towards the west for a long time. Then, hanging his head down again and puffing on his roll-up, he said: "They were actually people of great importance. They wanted to fight the commonplace with their lives. Of course, there were a few con men and rogues among them. They found me to be a pretty good performer under tremendous pressure, a tough guy who could endure hardship and a 'polar bear' that could swim in cold water. So, they misunderstood me. I respected them, but as you know, I'm suspicious of all stereotyped lifestyles. People can be rude and violent when they try to embrace an abstract ideal – those people wanted me to collaborate with them. When I declined, they tried to tie me up and drag me to their tent. They wanted me to join them."

With that, Qi Jin chuckled. Casting away the cigarette, he continued: "They were too hospitable and self-confident, adamantly believing that only ascetic monks could accomplish things... only they could deal with this corrupted material world, and that they were the greatest people in the entire world. Maybe they were, but I had no evidence. So I just ran away. During my escape, I thought of things more concrete and closer to us in this world. They're more difficult to accomplish and require more courage, willpower and stamina."

Liao Mai nodded. He had been pondering deeply while Qi Jin was talking, and now he said to himself: Intelligence and benevolence should give us strength. Awe and mercy should give us strength.

Qi Jin ran his large hands over Liao Mai's shoulders and picked up the thread of their discussion. "For example, I'd been running here and there for so many years, for hundreds if not thousands of kilometres. But when I looked back, I realised there was so much for me to do here in the southern suburbs of my native city. Why didn't I realise this? Because it was too close. It was right under my nose. People usually think that things of great significance lie in the distance, in faraway places. But they forget that, in the eyes of others, we are also in a faraway place, aren't we?"

As he listened, Liao Mai felt tears welling up. Once again, he had the feeling that there was no secret that he could not divulge with this big brother. Therefore, he confided in him all the details about him and Xiu sleeping together.

His confession did not come as much of a surprise to Qi Jin, who snorted and asked: "Do you regret it terribly?"

"Frankly speaking, I can't forget either Xiu or that night. But I've always been thinking that this was unfair on Mei Di. You know she's suffered a lot for me, or rather, for us. I felt not only shameful and indebted, but also... Up to now, I haven't had the guts to tell her about it."

In saying this, Liao Mai's mind flashed back to Xiu with her large, bright, black eyes looking into his and the warmth of her breath in his ear. Until then, he had never imagined that the outspoken Xiu could have been so gently affectionate, warm and simple, and could have been so romantic, which is characteristic not of a poet but a person, or rather, a woman... In short, the Xiu of that night was the real Xiu. She was incredible.

Qi Jin remained silent for quite some time, apparently perturbed. He gazed at the mottled marks on the cave wall. With one of his big hands in the other, he sometimes shook his head, sometimes pouted his lips and sometimes knitted his eyebrows. After a while, he mumbled: "Damn it! We don't know how to handle such things. And there's no wizard beyond this world that could arbitrate the problem. Damn it! It's really a nuisance."

"I blame myself and debate with myself, trying to find a reason that either convinces or confounds me," Liao Mai said. "I ask myself how I'm able to resist and avoid everything in hard times but gave in like this today. I can't figure it out."

"No, no! What you went through was not exactly 'hard'. Brother, the real hardship has only just begun."

While saying this, he looked up at Liao Mai, whose face revealed a mixture of expressions: despair, confusion and intransigence. Qi Jin and Liao Mai had both been born in the mid-1950s, while Xiu had come into the world a bit later. Oh, fleeting time! Oh, mysterious time! This gap in time might explain the most important things in one's life.

They had many things to discuss but found it impossible to tackle any of them.

Liao Mai thought that it was time to stop talking about himself for the time being. He should really pick up the topic of Maoha; there was still the entrustment given by Grandma Huo on her deathbed. He then recounted from the beginning how Maoha had run into danger at the seaside and what his purpose was in leaving the island. Qi Jin listened attentively and finally hung his head down. He murmured despondently: "The old mother's gone... She's gone."

Liao Mai could tell the devastating impact the news had on Qi Jin. He stood up, paced back and forth and looked into the distance, coughing violently. As he was walking back to the cave house to get tobacco, Liao Mai said: "You'd better pay a visit to Trident Island. The greatest concern of the dying old mother was her granddaughter. The girl's been leading a miserable life."

These words apparently had an undertone of censure. Qi Jin sat down, puffing and coughing hard, and then crushed the cigarette butt with his fingers. For a considerable time, Liao Mai did not hear Qi Jin say anything. The news, as well as the topic of conversation, might be weighing too heavy on his heart. But what could Liao Mai do? He had to tell him about it because he was convinced that Qi Jin should never have walked away and evaded his responsibility.

"I was really surprised when Xiu told me you were on Trident Island," said Liao Mai. "I had no idea why you suddenly left the western region for that island. Your deep emotional entanglement with the girl went beyond my imagination. It was really not like you… For a time, I didn't even believe Maoha's words."

Pouting his lips, Qi Jin seemed to have suppressed his urge to speak. But then he finally gave in, his voice light and yet grave: "That was true. Maoha told the truth."

"What made you think of going to the island? What for?"

"For the Fish Opera. I meant to collect the repertoires of an opera on the brink of extinction. I became fascinated with it." Qi Jin's eyes began to sparkle, and he continued: "Think about it. The characters' roles in the opera are all fish. Whether they talk, sing or move around, they must act as if they are swimming. What a beautiful opera! In my scope of field research and in my sphere of knowledge, I can't think of any theatrical performance in the world that is more sentimental than the Fish Opera."

A GLISTENING KEEPSAKE

The residents of Trident Island got panicky because the tide had never risen so high in their memory. On several recent occasions, however, it had begun to quietly flood the streets and alleys. The islanders had to consider relocating to higher ground. At the highest point of the island were three hills, their bases extending into the sea like three fingers. Only the level parts of the island at the base of the fingers were connected and formed the centre of the island.

Rising along with the tide was the revival of the Fish Opera, which had not been staged for years. It brought solace to the anxious islanders. Originally, no one except some elderly folk could remember the tunes. They had even forgotten the lines of the few opera repertoires that had been popular years before. It was strange that, in recent years, not only were people able to sing a few lines, but one traditional opera after another began to be performed again.

Gradually, a prototype of a Fish Opera troupe took shape and even became a hit on the island and beyond.

During high tide one night, the islanders congregated on the central ground of the island despite the risk of being swept away by the raging waves; for, being the flattest part of the island, the central ground was also at the lowest altitude. An ancient stage was built right in its middle and had been the busiest and hardest-to-forget place over the past hundred years. It was a source of pain as well as joy. This stage was where Huo Er'er had been denounced by the entire island and where a modern Fish Opera about her had been staged. Tonight, the islanders could not wait to satisfy their curiosity. They seemed to have suddenly rediscovered the long-lost performing art that was so beautiful and realised that they had been deprived of it for several decades. They wondered how they had managed without it all those years; it was as bad as living their daily lives without cooking oil or salt. Young people, who were exposed to a Fish Opera performance for the first time, blushed to the ears after sitting close to the stage for only an hour. Elderly people, on the other hand, were immersed in their memories as they listened with their eyes closed. Sometimes, they would hum along to the tunes being sung on stage, oblivious to the tears streaming down their cheeks.

One night, the tide rose again. A Fish Opera performance was reaching its climax on stage. Transfixed by the show, the audience was unaware of the seawater rising onto the beach to the accompaniment of frequent drumbeats and sad, sweet melodies. Their passions intensified with the rumble of the waves. Fixing their tear-blurred eyes on the young mermaid singing and performing her swimming dances on stage, they were so thrilled that they held each other's hands unknowingly and, trembling all over, cried in a hushed voice: "Oh, Heavens, pray let them get married. The suspense is killing us! It's an ordeal that no human should endure!"

By the time the seawater reached the area around the stage, it was exactly midnight. However, the people both on and off stage were oblivious of the danger. Those staying at home, awakened by the clamour of drums and gongs, opened their windows and gazed up at the moon. But once they looked down, they saw a large expanse of white water encircling the stage. They gasped and rushed out screaming but found themselves blocked by the water.

They had to cup their hands around their mouths and shout at the top of their lungs. Only then did they succeed in getting the attention of the crowd who had become so wrapped up in the story of the opera. But it was too late to escape.

That night, the entire audience swam like the fish characters on stage as they retreated, calling one another. Their clothes were soaked, and some of their belongings were missing, but they were more scared than hurt.

The same thing happened again on several occasions before the decision was taken to move the old stage to a higher place. Its relocation meant a sea change, equivalent to bidding farewell to the only square on the island. Every inch of the soil here had been sprinkled with tears of joy and sorrow. Who could have thought that the theatre for the Fish Opera would be rebuilt in such a place – halfway up the slope of a hill! From a distance it appeared like a hanging cradle, small and delicate. This location benefited the residents on both sides of the stage. It was so close to them that they could have grabbed the colourful costumes of the performers by simply reaching out their hands. From that day on, they could enjoy the shows just by leaning over their windowsills.

In the spring after the relocation of the stage, a swarthy-faced migrant worker came to the island. During the day, he worked with those on the kelp farm on boat and on land. At night, he interviewed elderly islanders about the Fish Opera. "He held a little book and jotted down what we said. With each word we uttered, he drew a few strokes."

The old men and women told each other about this newcomer and what he was doing. Slapping their knees, they said: "Yes, he reminds us of the three men who came to write an opera script about the 'water dungeon'."

"Well, those three dudes were up to no good. Although the tunes were quite pleasant, their script was nothing but nonsense and did a great harm to our Aunt Huo."

"This swarthy man's not so bad. What he dictated was all the dialogue from the classic operas that you and I told him. If there're things we can't remember, he'll find them elsewhere outside the island."

"Not bad at all. He's a hard worker. He lives in a hut by the sea in winter, all by himself."

In midsummer, Maoha came into public view on the island. This adoptive son of Huo Er'er was inseparable from the Fish Opera collector. Later, they shared their sleeping quarters. Huo Er'er had lived on an open depression before moving to the hilltop. Her house was connected with that of her daughter Yuyu. The old woman and Maoha lived in her spacious three-room house. After Yuyu lost her husband three years before, she lived in the company of her only daughter. Maoha had gone to see Qi Jin in his seaside hut at the instruction of the old woman, but he took the migrant worker home without saying a word. As soon as they came in, the old woman Huo Er'er opened a very exquisite chest. But she had called in Yuyu beforehand because she had that glistening key hanging round her neck. Yuyu asked her daughter to take out the two sparsely scribbled sheets of brown paper. It turned out that she wanted this learned young man to decode the secret that had been haunting her for the best part of her life.

As soon as she opened the chest, Yuyu stowed the key away and stayed for only a few minutes. But her peculiar eyes and wilful look were etched in Qi Jin's memory. He remembered that on her blanched face, her eyes, like fathomless pools under delicately dark brows, had blazed with a cold light and shot him a most distrustful glance.

At night, Maoha told Qi Jin a considerable amount about Yuyu. Her life was full of misery and had gone through all kinds of ordeals since childhood. Later, she finally married and had a child as beautiful as a fairy but then she lost her husband at sea. "A strong wind blew up that day and crushed... crushed his boat to pieces. It was winter, so it was impossible for him to survive in the water." With that, Maoha burst into tears and, with his mouth wide open, he cried like a baby.

Qi Jin could not decipher the two sheets of brown paper. He found them to be mostly animal names. The old woman told him that she did not have much time left in this world. She just wanted to solve the two mysteries that had directly impacted her life over the years. One was the origin of the water dungeon, and the other was recorded on the two sheets of brown paper. The truth about the water dungeon had been brought to light a few years before; it was nothing but an abandoned cellar for storing yams that was left unused by the older generation of the Huo family. It had long been sealed and was not in use after seawater flooded the chalcopyrite-encrusted floor due to the cave's proximity to the sea. This simple cellar, after being fictionalised into a vicious tale by the deceitful woman, had plunged Huo Er'er and her daughter into a calamitous ordeal that nearly cost them their lives. The story had also been adapted into a Fish Opera performed on the island and beyond.

"These two sheets of brown paper contain the only unsolved mystery that I have. What in the world is written on it? If I can't figure it out, I won't be able to close my eyes when I die."

Unable to decipher the scribbles, Qi Jin copied the text and returned the paper to Huo Er'er.

He resumed his work collecting Fish Operas. Yuyu's daughter Young Shaliu'er was the best Fish Opera actress on the island. Her given name, appropriately enough, meant 'lark'. Qi Jin's interest in the opera was closely related with watching her performances. While she was Ms Popularity on stage, without her makeup and costume, this petite, charming young woman was even more attractive. Qi Jin had traced the Fish Opera from where he had first watched it being performed to Trident Island, without knowing himself what had attracted him over. Perhaps he was bewitched by the intrinsic charm of the opera or, instead, captivated by the singing of a lark.

A year later, Qi Jin came to realise that he had travelled to Trident Island neither because of the Fish Opera nor because of its performers. It was because of a more miraculous fate – and its power was irresistible.

What frightened him was that he found himself taking a liking to Young Shaliu'er's mother and not to her. It was hard to understand that everything had happened before they had a chance to say a word to each other, though this widow was several years his senior.

At that time, he had been scribbling in his notebook what Young Shaliu'er was telling him. He barely asked any questions nor challenged anything she told him. However, he was awed by this plump young woman's memory of the dialogues, monologues and lyrics of so many of the Fish Opera repertoires. He thought of her as having been born for the opera. When she became too excited, Young Shaliu'er would sing and move her hands a little. Her singing would disturb her mother Yuyu, who would come out of her room, stand by the door and leer at them in silence.

One evening, Qi Jin discussed the Fish Opera with Young Shaliu'er for quite a while and he was ready to leave for Maoha's residence. He was about to step out when Yuyu called out to him.

"I hate Fish Opera," she said. "I never want to hear it again for the rest of my life."

"But how pleasant they are! Besides, your daughter's the best inheritor of the operatic tradition." Qi Jin found himself unable to say anything more. He did not understand how anyone could hate the opera. It could be that the opera had been used to depict the water dungeon in those years, thereby bringing added insult and humiliation to her.

"I'd like to ask about the brown paper," she said, not wanting to bring up the subject of the Fish Opera any more.

Qi Jin shook his head and knitted his brows.

"A task my mother entrusted me with is many times more important than the Fish Opera." After she finished speaking, she returned to her room.

That night, Qi Jin could not sleep. Maoha slumbered beside him before being startled awake by a gust of wind. He sat up abruptly, leaned out of the window and watched for a long while, mumbling: "The high tide's rising again…"

Neither of them were in the mood to sleep again. Qi Jin asked him about what had transpired a long time before regarding the water dungeon and the two sheets of brown paper. Maoha's answers were all irrelevant. Crossing his arms in front of his chest of brown hair, and widening his eyes with fear, he continued dwelling upon the high tides. "It looks like the dragon king is angry and plans to take our Trident Island back."

"It's said that someone locked Mother Huo up in the water dungeon because they wanted her to give away the secret hidden in the chest."

Maoha turned to look at him and said: "My mother told me about it. She hadn't yet adopted me at the time. If I'd seen her persecutors, I would have strangled each of them." Maoha made a gesture of strangulation with his big hands. Hanging his head down, Qi Jin noticed his webbed feet, and Maoha immediately withdrew them into his quilt.

The wind died down after midnight. The crashing sound of the waves also faded. But viewed in the moonlight, the level ground at the foot of the hills was covered with white water, which merged with the sea. Qi Jin gasped, knowing that the only way to access other alleys on the island was by boat. Only the three hills were above the water, making them look like three disconnected islets close to one another. Luckily, the seawater would subside at dawn.

"Sister Yuyu bit them, and they were all afraid of her. She held them fast in her mouth and wouldn't let go," said Maoha, gazing out of the window all the time.

Before they went to sleep, Maoha told Qi Jin how Yuyu had swallowed the gold key and how they had cut her belly open. Qi Jin listened quietly, gritting his teeth. He finally managed to fall asleep before daybreak and dreamed a dream that he would later remember clearly: a pale middle-aged woman standing by his bedside, her hands covering her white belly. He pulled her hands off and saw a small vertical scar, which was actually quite attractive. He planted a few kisses on the mark of her wound.

It was broad daylight. Outside the windows some islanders were running and shouting. The tide had gone out. They swarmed out of their houses with hand nets and baskets in their hands and were now on their way to collect fish, shrimps and shellfish that were stranded on the square.

While working with Young Shaliu'er, Qi Jin found himself less engrossed than had been before. He would often interrupt her melodious singing and mention things in the past that related to her mother and grandmother. Pouting her lips, Young Shaliu'er complained: "Well, well, well! Those things happened many generations ago. You're boring me to death." She often focused her eyes on him, calling him 'Blacky' and was only keen on asking him questions about events taking place outside the island.

One day, she said: "Since you like the Fish Opera so much, why don't you live on the island – live here for the rest of your life? Then I'll sing for you every day!"

Qi Jin did not respond because his attention was distracted by the dream he had had during the night of the high tide. Somehow, he was scared by a hunch that the dream might one day come true.

Young Shaliu'er became impatient. She sometimes paused while singing, staring at him with lustful eyes.

At the same time, he found himself being detested by Maoha, who had been leering at him in silence for several days running.

What Qi Jin found unbearable was that Maoha would rise and pace up and down at midnight, chewing some raw fish or shellfish, whose choking smell pervaded the entire room. After chewing a while, he would lie on his back and fall into a deep sleep, snoring and exhaling the same intolerable stench. Qi Jin had no alternative but to pinch his nose. When catching him doing that, Maoha would say: "Don't like it? Have you got a problem with me? What can I do – I'm the son of a dugong. You should count yourself lucky. One year, when I woke up confused, I gave someone sleeping by me a bite and gnawed a big hole in his belly."

Qi Jin knew that it was time to leave Trident Island. But he could not forget that blanched face, the cold glare that shot from her eyes and the odd dream. He tried to put up with Maoha's insolence and stay on and as long as he could.

The third spring arrived. Qi Jin felt that he had to leave.

It all started one day, when Maoha and Qi Jin took a sampan to sea. They went to a nearby black reef to untie a few hawsers in a fish farm. The sea was calm, but Maoha started breathing heavily, and his face turned livid after he had propelled the boat a short distance out to sea. He steered the boat in such a manner that it rocked and rolled violently.

"Are you feeling OK?" Qi Jin asked.

Maoha did not respond. When it made a turn and neared the black reef, the sampan unexpectedly darted towards it. As Qi Jin screamed, Maoha thrust the scull against the reef and jerked the boat up on one end, throwing Qi Jin into the sea. A sudden, unendurable chill penetrated his whole body. He was floundering, shouting for help and searching for Maoha. He could see nothing but white foam all around. Before he became completely exhausted, the sampan turned around from behind the black reef. Qi Jin struggled to emerge from the surface of the freezing water and reached out both his arms as he caught sight of the scull that Maoha was offering to him. But as he was about to grab it, the sampan seemed to be caught by an undercurrent and veered sideways. The scull fell upon his shoulder with force, and he was submerged again and swallowed a few mouthfuls of the bitter brine. At that moment, a feeling of despair took possession of him. He instinctively dodged the quivering scull shoved maliciously at him. But in the end, he was cornered by the scull and had to take hold of it, determined not to give it up until he clambered back into the sampan.

The day he said goodbye to Yuyu, Qi Jin gingerly made a request that he take the key to the chest with him and promised that he would keep on trying to decipher the enigmatic scribbles written on the brown paper.

This was apparently an absurd request. After hearing it, Yuyu became silent and hesitant. She prevaricated for about half an hour before she slowly turned around in front of the window and started to undo the two buttons on her collar. She tried to pull the red silk ribbon out with considerable effort. In the end, to make things easier, she had to take off her thick, cotton-padded jacket, but in doing so, she revealed a shirt of very thin fabric embroidered with a design of a cockscomb flower. The silk ribbon and the key had got caught in the shirt, and as she was trying to pull the ribbon up, her snow-white skin was unwittingly exposed. Though the exposure lasted only a few seconds, Qi Jin clearly saw the vertical scar.

It was very, very small, just like a centipede.

ELEVEN

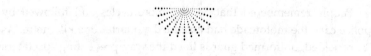

A LARGE RAMPART COMPOUND OF PURPLE SMOKE

IN THE MEMORY of the elderly folk of Jiwo, the only foreigners they had previously seen were immigrant Russians and Western missionaries, and that was more than six decades ago. Today, a group of blond-haired, blue-eyed men and women, or to be exact, three men and two women, suddenly appeared in front of them. They had to rub their eyes again and again to make sure that they were indeed foreigners. Accompanied by a group of officials, the foreigners got off from a motorcade and kept saying a few greetings, but unfortunately, the officials could not understand a word. Neither could Tang Tong. His curly, black hair was glossy with wax, and a strip of fabric hung around his neck. Early that morning, all the people involved had decided to put on this thing, which looked like a tongue sticking out of the corpse of a man who had died of strangulation. Tang Tong beckoned over a young interpreter locally referred to as *tongzuizi*[1]. The *tongzuizi* jabbered for a while with the foreigners. Then, mimicking Chinese actors playing Japanese soldiers speaking awkward Chinese, Tang Tong said to a hefty foreign man beside him: "This place is great, great good!"[2]

An official whispered a reminder to him: "There's no way he can understand you. He's not Japanese."

"Dammit! This is all too complicated. It's a pain in the neck!"

Beads of sweat broke out on his forehead, which he tried to wipe off repeatedly. Luckily, there was the translator whose mouth would always bloom into a smile when he turned to the foreigners. He soon translated very fluently what Tang Tong had said and would repeat to the foreign audience. Tang Tong was exceedingly happy. Patting the guy's shoulder, he complimented him: "You're damn good. I bet you can pull the most beautiful girl in the world! Great! Great!"

People remembered that, led by motorcycles and followed by police cars, the motorcade had extended a quarter of a kilometre. As it proceeded, uniformed guards lined the way, preventing spectators from getting too close. The motorcade drove around the complex of the Tiantong Group. The delegation spent half a day in the large glass building before being taken on a tour of the hills and plains, particularly the arid area by the beach. Who could ignore Tang Tong's glass building in town? It was said to have everything, including restaurants and entertainment facilities, as well as girls lining up nodding and bowing in their *qipao* dresses with slits up to their waists. They walked clackety-clacking on the floor in their high-heeled shoes. One could imagine the foreigners being dumbfounded as soon as they sneaked into the building and saw the girls. The townspeople witnessed them swaggering into the building one by one like big fish, rubbing their hands together with joyous excitement.

"Sons of bitches! The things in there will blow their minds. Tang Tong won't let them off so easily."

Throughout the morning, crowds gathered at the intersection in the west part of town. It was a vantage point where they could see the parked vehicles of the motorcade. They knew that, as long as the motorcade was not moving, the passengers would be enjoying themselves in the glass building, and Tang Tong would no doubt be bringing his talent for hospitality into full play.

"They must still be drinking in there," the crowd said from a distance. They were all aware of the 'artificial sea' – a huge pool with a sand beach, in which plastic palm trees were planted. After drinking, the foreigners would pass through the shade of the trees and plop naked into the water, followed by the *tongzuizi*, then the officials and Tang Tong. "All the big deals are said to be negotiated in the water. Just think about it – as they goggle at all the naked bodies, how can they begrudge a few pennies? Tang Tong must have made another big deal." In saying all this, they had no idea what kind of a deal might be involved.

Not until about six months after the foreigners' departure did the townspeople find something amiss. They said to one another: "Now there's starting to be action on the big deals."

Workers wearing sunhats and sunglasses began to appear, anchoring surveyor's tripods to the ground here and there. They reminded the townspeople of the scene right before the goldmines had been opened and speculated that something big was about to happen. Based on their previous experience, the townspeople paid special attention to the women wearing jeans or floral skirts, with pencil stubs pinched between their fingers. Those who revealed their cleavage proved to be the most capable, as in the case of the female head of the prospecting team many years before. Leading her team, she took measurements while scribbling notes in her book, resulting in something amazing: a big mountain had nearly been toppled! Oh, around-the-clock, rock-blasting sounds! Oh, the thundering explosions that could chisel away a promontory! T-N-T, Kick-and-kick! While saying meekly "Yes, sir", these delicately pretty women could kick and kick in a big way with their dainty hands and feet. They especially enjoyed breaking ground where Tai Sui[3] was located. After much comment and gossip, the townspeople concluded that Tang Tong possessed an exceptional talent for recruiting women with a penchant for revealing their cleavage. They might be, as it were, too frail to stand a gust of wind; they might talk as faintly as a buzzing mosquito; they might grin with their mouths as wide as those of a pike; and they might walk as if skimming the surface of water; but they all had the experience of battling with heaven and earth. Whoever wanted to break ground had to go to them first. It was like seeking the help of *tongzuizi* when negotiating with foreigners.

Before long, excavators and heavy trucks could be heard rumbling. Among them there were huge vehicles with more than fifteen axles. It was at this point that the townspeople realised that Tang Tong was up to something big this time. Ground was broken at the foot of the hill and the areas up to the east and the north were planted with colourful flags. Whereas some of the small villages had to be relocated, several of the bigger ones were surrounded by all kinds of vehicles, which, viewed from a distance, appeared like a pack of dholes gnawing at the corpse of an elephant.

"Since our ancestral soil has now been moved, the heavens must be getting really offended."

"How can we continue to farm? Can it be that more gold has been discovered in the ground?"

The villagers panicked, knowing that Tang Tong, a gold digger, would never have been so desperate if he had not seen gold here. "He's opening a large tract of fertile farmland like a butcher slits a pig's belly."

But no gold was dug out. It transpired that they were digging a large pit with concrete piles driven into the ground and reinforced cement concrete spread on the footing. Sometime later, a structure emerged, first vertically and then horizontally. No one could figure out what this huge structural complex was. They had never seen such a thing, even in their most bizarre and horrifying nightmares. They watched this dark and stiff edifice grow day by day, appearing like a half-collapsed hillock; like a sheer precipice; a celestial cellar; or a monster's head that had been chopped with a broadsword for an entire night, baring its terrifying teeth. Still, no one could tell what it was used for. During its construction, foreigners came again, followed by at least three *tongzuizi*. Tang Tong accompanied all of them – this time, he stunned the foreigners. Instead of wearing the tongue of a strangulated person, he changed to an outfit worn only by a corpse lying in state in a coffin: a short upper garment of red satin that opened in the front, with a large-size character of 'longevity' printed all over it. Staring at his curly hair, the dumbfounded foreigners kept babbling and prattling. The male and female *tongzuizi* took turns to interpret and finally made sense of the melee of voices. The foreigners broke out into a guffaw, and Tang Tong laughed heartily as well.

Vehicles rumbled, welding arcs sparkled, colourful flags fluttered and *tongzuizi* came and went. All this hustling and bustling went on for a year and three months. As a result, this tall and vast colossus grew up from the ground, like a monstrous house or a mountain being 'kicked and kicked' by TNT. Damn! Whoever claimed that we farmers had not seen the world were plain wrong! Didn't we watch this freak rising from under our noses? Weren't we there when its completion was celebrated? The scene involved a motorcade, guards along the streets, foreigners, *tongzuizi*, officials and a steel scaffolding stage, on which there was sometimes the beating of gongs and drums and sometimes the setting off of smoke and firelight like the ancient signals rising at border posts to warn against the approach of invading enemies. Suddenly, out of the smoke and firelight, half-naked girls appeared, opening their bloody red mouths to sing at the top of their lungs. The song that they were chanting was entitled *A Song Dedicated to CEO Tang*. Everyone knew that it referred to Tang Tong. Combing his curly hair with his hand, he stood up and went on stage, where he saluted to the left and bowed to the right. He broke wind in his excitement, to the astonishment of the foreigners, and then burst into laughter. The foreigners started murmuring among themselves. A *tongzuizi* proclaimed loudly and in haste: "Our foreign guests said this is typical, very typical Oriental humour!"

The whole event broadened the townspeople's horizon as many wondrous things happened to them for the first time in their lives. But the most memorable and unforgettable episode was still that Oriental humour.

Soon, it became apparent that this kind of humour was a foretaste of things to come. It would become the theme of this land for the next fifty or even a hundred years. This theme was determined by an odour known to everyone.

From now on, as soon as they raised their heads, people in the hills and plains could see the dark-grey building compound swelling above the ground and purple smoke rising from the small openings in its protruding parts. As long as they turned their noses up, they would smell a familiar stench. "Good Heavens! We're finished! Our land will be filled with the smell of farts all day long!" People groaned and looked around in panic.

Instead of hyperbole, the smell was real. It definitely originated from the Large Rampart Compound of Purple Smoke – the locals customarily referred to colossi lower than mountains but taller than hillocks as 'large ramparts'. From that day on, the townsfolk remembered that the reference to ramparts was a kind of 'Oriental humour' and a monstrous building constructed by using so much labour, and the building contained a farting machine that Tang Tong had obtained from foreigners.

From this time on, the people of the hills and plains began to enter a time of real dejection. They were left frustrated not because of hunger and poverty, not because of chaos and turmoil, and not even because of humiliation and oppression, but merely because of an ancient smell that permanently saturated the land and was too shameful to mention.

DESCENDANTS OF AARDWOLVES

Old Woman Shan would occasionally confide in a man that she trusted the most. Now, most of what she was confiding to him was the recollection of her prime years, particularly the last few of her youth. One day, she came up with a witty remark on a whim: "Those were the years when I was rolling my youthful body on the edge of a blade." Later, either she herself or others agreed that this remark best summed up the prevailing spirit.

At that time, Shanzi had put on a bit of weight but still retained the vitality of a virgin. She had free access to anywhere in the hills and plains, where she had been able to order nature around, so to speak. Many a time, she had concealed her sorrows and singlehandedly done things unknown to others on the vast sandplain and in the dense forest. She had predicted that she would never have her own children. Therefore, she had wanted to learn more about the secret of life during her early years. Whenever a living creature went into labour, she would observe closely. She cherished the blood that accompanied the birth of new lives so much that she would put off washing away the slimy placenta blood stains on her hands and clothes for as long as possible.

For a time, she believed that the most appealing job was to become a midwife. She tried being one several times, all in secret. She was fascinated by the process of large wild creatures giving birth. She wanted to observe up close wild mothers that were either gentle or savage. She would scrutinise their heaving and rolling bellies, their expressions of pain and happiness, and their swelling and generous breasts. Crouching by their side, she would burst into tears at the sight of those hairy little faces emerging from their mothers' wombs.

This was all true. She could unmistakably trace to a straw nest in the forest where a wild creature was in labour merely by its odour. It was a medley of the smells of blood and milk, as well as the stench of fish mixed with a faint fragrance of chrysanthemums. As soon as it assailed her nostrils, it would twitch the nerve of her tear glands. Then, she would pick up her pace and run towards the source of the smell, crying "Aww, aww". Her ever-growing breasts were more excited than her thumping heart, and several times she heard them calling eagerly. Trying to calm them down by patting them, she said: "Hold! You'll have the chance to make your contribution." She had, in fact, long made up her mind to put her breasts into full play for the rest of her life. "I'm the greatest mother in the world even without my own children! Once I'm nursing a baby, I'll be incredibly generous. I'm as good as a dairy farm. My gushing milk can feed forty babies at once, and the leftovers can be sundried into two cartloads of milk powder. I'm a legendary, carefree daredevil of a virgin. Had I been born at the right time, I might have become a woman famed for dying as a defender of my celibacy!"

Lying on the grass, a narrow-faced woman was about to give birth. She waved her arm at Shanzi like a dog wagging its tail. Her foul stench reached Shanzi's nostrils even from a considerable distance. Going up to her, Shanzi stared at her forehead for quite a while until she could make out three vertical furrows with fuzz. Her face was covered with fine brown hair like ink bleeding on a sheet of paper in a traditional Chinese ink wash painting.

Yikes, a female aardwolf! Shanzi exclaimed silently while suppressing her surprise and fear. She sat down to deliver her.

Oh, aardwolf in difficult labour, your lifetime of suffering was all tangled up in your narrow hips, Shanzi said to herself. You're so miserable, so pitiable, having passed out three times and come to three times. You're staring at me with a ferocious look, but it's a look begging for help. Shanzi did everything she could, pushing, stroking, tapping and patting her. Finally, she took off her coat and gesticulated, trying hard to give her a hint: Oh, aardwolf! Where's your savagery and greed? You must summon up all your brute strength and – bang-bang – give birth to a cute pup and feed it the first mouthful of milk before sunset!

Shanzi's hands, stomach and genitals were all stained with the aardwolf's blood. It looked as if she herself were giving birth. The groans of pain shook the earth and mountains, scaring all the other wild creatures out of their wits and sending them scurrying five kilometres away. Oblivious of everything around her, Shanzi busied herself meticulously, her sleeves rolled up to the elbows. She was so tense that she involuntarily passed urine in a torrent. When the urine seeped onto its crotch, the aardwolf's thighs started shaking violently. It grabbed Shanzi with its sharp claws so tight that they plucked a piece of flesh off her forearm. With Shanzi's agonising scream, the pup was born.

"It's got to be my child! It felt like I gave birth to it."

It was a male pup with sharp, canine teeth and glowing blue eyes. It was capable of biting as soon as it came into this world, capable of finding its mother's nipples and capable of grunting and yipping. "Beastly son of an aardwolf bitch!" cursed Shanzi while removing the placenta and the slimy membranes from the pup and helping it locate the tiny nipples among its mother's brown hair. The aardwolf's breasts were much smaller than her own. After losing blood and having perspired heavily, the aardwolf felt thirsty and hungry. Now, she was staring at Shanzi with her upper lip scrunched up to reveal her front teeth. Shanzi pulled her trousers up, fastened her coat and grabbed a handful of sand, ready to throw it into the aardwolf's eyes in case it sprang up to pounce upon her. At the same time, she also pulled her upper lips to bare her teeth and growled back her threat. The aardwolf blinked.

Shanzi wandered along the beach all day long, searching hopelessly and mysteriously. Many a time she thought of giving herself up to a big, ferocious male beast, as long as its teeth were sharp, its legs strong and chest brawny, as long as it could stare down all the other animals, and as long as its organs stood firm and erect in a menacing posture. But she would always balk at the last minute. She still desired to give her virginity to a man on their first encounter and unburden herself of all the pent-up feelings. That would be the voice of a true woman, a voice unintelligible to the beasts scampering on the grassland.

Over the past few years, she had delivered goats, foxes, badgers, wild asses, spotted deer and earless seals. She had to admit that the fox was the most impressive of them all because its resourcefulness, lucidity, tenderness and appearance always eclipsed the other wild creatures. Therefore, when the wind of religious conviction came sweeping across the land many years later, and when her only disciple Tang Tong asked what the best would be to follow – Jesus

Christ, Confucius or Buddha – she replied without hesitation: "Believe in fox spirits."

The consensus she and Tang Tong reached was that anyone who did not have faith in fox spirits must be an imbecile. Many years later, he was still grateful for her generous counsel. But he feared for his father who had slighted wild creatures during his lifetime. The fear often made him breathless with anxiety. He was convinced by her assertion that fox spirits, the most sagacious of all wild creatures, had been the cause of all the fortune and misfortune in her life.

The process of delivering a fox had given her a chance to condition herself for a better personality. Unlike ordinary creatures in the wild, each of the foxes had both a small, artistically painted face and a docile, playful temperament. Even during a difficult labour, they would still put on an air of beauty and never reveal their tails. Each had a honeyed mouth that could soften the hardest heart. Whenever they spoke, they would call her 'Big Sis' or 'Auntie'. They would say: "A kind-hearted and virtuous person is here to offer a big help and, together with us, to continue our family line." The two long, horizontal rows of tactile hairs on their faces were now retracted into less visible fine hairs shimmering in the sun, and from them, beads of sweat were dripping. At a moment like this, Shanzi genuinely wished that she had been a man. Their breathing and groaning evoked heartache and loving care in Shanzi. She knew that those uncivil and uncaring young women had better receive some tutorship from the foxes. Even in the throes of labour, they remained sweet and charming, holding Shanzi's arm tight with their little hands while pushing hard in silence. After a cub was born, and if it was a male, Shanzi would secretly make a small mark on one of its little toes.

Many years later, Shanzi summarised the first half of her life to the first man that she had the luck to meet – the turtle-like man known to all the townspeople. She used scholarly terms to describe her past: "I admit that I have gone through trials and tribulations." Running her hand over his soft, wrinkled neck that resembled an empty bag, she shed all her tears on his hard, glossy forehead. Age had whittled away the old man's curiosity. While she was revealing her secret feelings, he only acted out his love attentively. He looked adorable when he pouted his lips to kiss her, the radiating wrinkles around his lips seemingly contributing to his effort. At the peak of her excitement, she said to the old man: "I know there's something we can't do, but we'll have many children and grandchildren in a few years."

That turtle-like old man never understood what she meant. With a large generation gap and different life experiences, they lacked effective means of communication except their highly coordinated physical contact. They could easily take each other's hints from winking and gesticulating.

In that intolerably hot summer, Shanzi and the old man lost their virginity. Since then, she had changed completely and become increasingly sedate. She soon settled down in the mud houses by the river and covered her head with a blue cloth scarf. She seemed to become Old Woman Shan overnight. She was expecting the children that she had helped deliver to come to her, counting on her fingers from time to time and knowing that they had now become orphaned grown-ups. While expecting them, she was also searching the wilderness and the villages for them. She observed their features and took off their shoes to examine their little toes. At night, she would sit by the door, facing the bright moon and hearing the pounding waves at her back. "Fox spirits, please help me," she prayed repeatedly. "Please let all those sons of mine return home. I have prepared baskets of food for them to eat and a *kang* for them to sleep on."

Sure enough, those reticent young men came converging to her from all around. They each had narrow faces and their eyes had grey and yellow hues. They also walked without a sound. "We've come to the seaside for work," they said as they took off the small bedrolls from their backs after entering the house. Afterwards, they fell quiet again. For the first few nights, they went to sleep without greeting each other and lay on their backs on the *kang* that were lined up in a row in one of the mud houses. During the wee hours, panting came from the house followed by the commotion of fighting, which aroused Old Woman Shan from her sleep. She stepped out of her house nearby, listened a while and went back to sleep again. For three days, she left them alone. Nor did she provide them with anything to eat or drink.

At dawn on the fourth day, Old Woman Shan listened by the door and heard nothing but snoring. She opened the door and found only seven young men sleeping. The others were all gone. She took a closer look and gasped; she saw blood stains on the door, the windowpanes and the mat. She knew that the sleepers had killed, swallowed or driven away all the others. Only the seven survivors were the real descendants of aardwolves.

She awakened them from their sleep by shouting and pointing here and there at the mess in the room. "Well?" she asked. The seven young men hung their heads down. Without saying anything, they started mopping and tidying, not daring to look up. They worked arching their backs, their spines jutting out like knife blades.

SOBBING

There were several mud houses on the beach, forming a U-shaped courtyard. They appeared deserted against the lapping waves. It was quiet here, as the seven young men were always silent no matter what they were doing, whether casting nets, taking the boats to sea or coming in and out of their house.

Though they lived in the same mud house compound as Old Woman Shan, they barely saw her even once or twice a week.

When Tang Tong visited the mud houses, he always drove a car with a leopard's head painted on the bodywork. He parked the car outside the courtyard and went straight to the house at the bottom of the U-shape. The young men came out of their house, stared at the leopard's head awhile and started wiping the dust off the vehicle until it shined. Then, they drove the car into the yard, parked it and covered it with a tarpaulin sheet.

Dressed in a loose gown, Old Woman Shan was pacing up and down on the carpet barefoot. As soon as Tang Tong entered, she would, as always, give him tea made from four sea cucumbers and a clump of seaweed and serve it in an earthen bowl. He had to eat it all up, like a dose of bitter medication that must be taken at regular intervals. He cursed as he reached for the bowl. He first ate the sea cucumbers and then chewed the coarse seaweed like a rabbit. Having chomped it all up with great difficulty, he gasped. And after gulping down a bowl of boiled water, he flopped onto a couch, letting out a barrage of four-letter words at the same time.

Old Woman Shan tried to leave him alone during the first half of the night because he would lie on his stomach and cry "I'm dead!

I'm dead!" if she tried to touch him. Afterwards, he would remain motionless as if he had really given up the ghost. Once, she was wheedling him and trying to turn him over when she was taken aback – this dude looked quite ghastly with his eyes rolled up so far. "Young Tong! Young Tong!" she had to call and pat him for a long time before he opened his eyes and started laughing.

"Good boy, I know you're tired from running that business empire of yours. You've become a fucking elephant's tusk, a rhino horn, a shark's fin. You've become so rare and precious that you could be a guest to the grandest banquet laid on by the governor's father. But it takes more effort to manage a big business. Look at you! You're so exhausted that you're as thin as the bony hips of a rabbit, your eyes are as deep-set as a monkey's and your little ding-a-ling's as limp as a dried spring onion. As your tutor, I must do something to nurse you to health," mumbled Old Woman Shan as she continuously rubbed his forehead until red spots appeared between his eyebrows. She put a snow-white bib around his neck.

Tang Tong panicked and implored with his hands clasped in front of him, saying: "I beg your mercy, Ma'am! Fishy smells make me puke. I can eat anything but your clam powder, abalones and seaweed."

Without saying a word, Old Woman Shan yanked his head towards her chest and picked up the soup bowl with the other. The soup consisted of three pink jellyfish and the freshly removed intestines of sea urchins. With a cry of "Oh, Good Heavens", he shut his eyes. A morsel was enough to choke him to tears. Wiping his mouth, he screamed: "Oh Ma'am, when shall I fuck you to death? I suffer each day when you're alive." As he cursed, he huddled against her chest and soon fell quiet and into a slumber.

After he woke up, they went to the home cinema and stayed there for ages as usual. There were several large boxes containing rolls of various kinds of film and digital videodiscs of old and new TV series. Tang Tong would watch them twenty-four hours when in a good mood, and Old Woman Shan would always sit beside him. They heaped a lot of snacks along with drinks, both alcoholic and non-alcoholic, on the coffee table in front of them and lounged on the couch without getting up. Tang Tong would crack a few jokes at first, but within thirty minutes, he would focus on the screen, craning his neck and breathing quietly. He would not avert his eyes even when he ate or took a pee. Old Woman Shan had prepared a blue-and-white porcelain enamel spittoon for that purpose. Less than an hour into the show, he would begin to sob, feeling sorry for the characters. He kept consuming the snacks and drinks, taking a pee and shedding tears. Time and again, Old Woman Shan had to wipe his tears and pat him on the back.

"My good boy can't bear to see good people suffer and bad people doing evil. My good boy's heart is as soft as cotton velvet." Old Woman Shan sighed as she planted a kiss on his forehead. She took pity on him when she saw him sob harder and harder until his shoulders heaved.

Still focused on the screen, he said to Old Woman Shan: "I'll shoot and kill this guy if I run into him some day. I won't spare his life even if I'm put in jail or sentenced to death."

"But it's only a show. The actor and the character that he plays are two different people…"

"That's the actor's bad luck then. As long as I bump into him, I'll kill that son of a bitch! Make no mistake about it."

Old Woman Shan fell silent. She had a hunch that he meant what he said.

On several occasions, Tang Tong could not help standing up, rushing to the screen, cursing loudly while pointing with a finger, and making various obscene gestures at the villain character. He jumped up and down for a while and flumped onto the couch again, his eyes reddened from excessive crying. Running her hand over his head, Old Woman Shan was startled, for his curly hair was soaked with perspiration.

When they left the home cinema, it would always be in the early hours. Constant eating and drinking had inflated Tang Tong's belly and reddened his face. Having sobbed to his heart's content, Tang Tong was very meek. Holding Old Woman Shan by the arm, he was beaming and whispering whenever he spoke. He would not raise his voice even at the mention of things that would normally annoy or irritate him. Instead, he would talk in a gentle and languid manner. "Old Fifth Brother in West Village is a daredevil. He led his entire village to block my way. He'd rather die than listen to me, regardless of my carrot-and-stick tactics," he said with a grin that revealed his recently cleaned teeth. "It seems this guy needs your guidance. I'm not smart enough to deal with people like him."

"OK, I'll remember," said Old Woman Shan, patting him. "I'll remember. Who else has made my boy unhappy recently?"

Pouting his lips, Tang Tong continued: "There're also Lao Zhou, Li Spectacles, as well as that swarthy woman and her father, in addition to that pockmark-faced guy at the customs. They're all troublemakers. They listen to neither advice nor flattery. When they're biting a lousy bone in their mouth, they wouldn't trade it for anything I offer them. They'll kill me sooner or later by ganging up to bully me..."

"I'll keep what you told me in mind. Don't cry any more, my good boy, it's bad for your health. You've gone through a lot over the years. It's not just the gold mine any more. That whole big group is at your command. It wouldn't surprise me to see you with a semiautomatic tucked into your wide waistband and clomping along in a pair of heavy leather boots. Look at you now, haggard and bony, going out without bodyguards. Even an average townsperson could mess around with you. Don't you know it's a different time you're living in? Even after high-ranking officials came and shook hands with you and you put up bedsheet-sized posters made from the handshaking pictures along the street, the townspeople still don't take you sufficiently seriously. Now, when you're caught up in this and that trouble, you're still dumping them on me, so that I have to do the dirty work like wiping your arse clean after you've taken a crap."

Tang Tong nodded and, rubbing his sleepy eyes, said: "You're right. I'm much wealthier than Lord Huo ever was, but I'm nowhere near as happy. I heard that Lord Huo was at least one level higher in rank than all the officials he met. He could kill anyone without having to sacrifice his life and could sleep with anyone he fancied. He dared to walk on the street stark naked just on a whim... Well, comparisons are odious. I'd better stop complaining."

While undressing Tang Tong, Old Woman Shan coaxed him to bed. But he insisted on drinking a bottle of wine. Unable to talk him out of it, she got him a cup and put the bib back around his neck. Tang Tong took the bib and his clothes off together. He was drinking one cup after another, naked and with tears in his eyes. He paced up and down the big *kang*, occasionally stopping to huddle in the bosom of Old Woman Shan. She wanted to cuddle him longer, but he would not behave and often struggled out of her grip. All the wine that he had drunk turned to tears, and the more he drank, the more tears he shed.

"Looking back at my life, I've done in all the people I wanted. I've made all the money I've craved and screwed all the women I fancied. I'm in want of nothing, but it's strange – whenever I relax, I still feel I've been treated unfairly. I feel awful, so awful that I want to cry day and night. I'm always thinking of coming to you for advice. I want to know why," he sobbed.

Shaking her head and biting her purple lip, Old Woman Shan tapped him on the top of his head covered with hair the colour and texture of lambswool. "Even a tutor like me can't answer this question of yours," she said. "To tell you the truth, I can't figure it out myself. If I were eight or ten years younger, I'd put my nipples into your mouth and let you drink until your belly is swollen. Then, you wouldn't be whining like this. Well, I'm too old for all that now."

Tang Tong rose with a pensive look on his face and strode to the other end of the large *kang*, facing away from Old Woman Shan.

"The construction of the Large Rampart Compound of Purple Smoke must continue," she said. "You must have an iron hand and leave the dogs in the manger to me. They're like a child refusing to get off a potty. They should've got away by now!"

"But some of them... well!"

"If you're soft-hearted, you can't accomplish anything. You're far more incompetent than your father! He was a much better person than you are."

"But I..."

"You don't have the heart to hurt Liao Mai because of his wife," Old Woman Shan chuckled. "Whenever you see her – that hedgehog spirit – your legs shake!"

Tang Tong turned around to face her, made a menacing gesture with his hand and crouched down with his head hanging low. He remained silent in the same manner for a long time. When he looked up, he scared Old Woman Shan. Tears were streaming down his cheeks like a torrent, washing his chest shiny clean.

"Christ," exclaimed Old Woman Shan.

Tang Tong rose stiffly, leaned close to her and whispered: "Could we, could we stop talking about her? You know I hate people talking about her. You can talk about anyone except her.

Please don't! Just don't... I don't want you to mention her. No, I don't."

Old Woman Shan fell silent.

A RABBIT IN THE WHEAT FIELDS

Two kilometres to the west of the mud houses by the estuary, a few stone dykes extended out into the sea. After years of erosion by the tidal waves, only a section of each dyke remained and they were all covered over with moss. Jutting into the sea like broken arms, they were the legacies of someone's dream in those years, a dream to build a fishing dock. The project had just begun when it was thwarted by a strong tide, leaving behind the remains of the dykes and a run-down house on the beach. As fish, crabs and sea cucumbers often took refuge beneath the remaining stone dykes, the narrow-faced young men living in the mud house to the east came here now and then and took possession of the dilapidated house. They reinforced it and locked it up with numerous instruments that no one had ever seen before.

It was getting increasingly hot. The narrow-faced young men never ventured out unless it was early morning or late afternoon. Now, the seaside was silent, as if all living creatures had been suffocated by the heat. A few remaining seagulls were flying lethargically, taking off and landing by the dyke remains without the strength to squawk. The house by the dykes had a flat roof, and, without a decent window, it was as oppressive as an oven inside. At around five or six o'clock, one of the narrow-faced young men strolled over. He undid the big lock, and a gust of hot air swept out, nearly knocking him off the ground. Finding it dark inside, he opened the door wide enough to make everything visible. It turned out that there was a big fellow with his arms tied behind him to a horizontal wooden pole, his yellow shirt covered in blood stains and dirt smudges. He was wearing a pair of shorts. His eyes were shut and his face inclined to one side with his nose close to touching an iron bowl secured somewhere above his head. The bowl contained some spoiled food.

Soon after entering the house, the narrow-faced man poured what he had in his hand into the iron bowl and then jerked the big fellow a couple of times by the hair. The big fellow did not open his eyes. The narrow-faced young man took a puff on his cigarette and pressed its burning end against the armpit of the fellow. He screamed, opened his eyes wide and stared at the narrow-faced man.

The young man then left the big fellow alone. He sat down, took a knife from the back pocket of his trousers and started to whittle something. He was making a handle to attach to a harpoon spear fork, with which he was going to catch some fish by the dykes. After finishing the handle, he tapped the iron bowl with it, but the big fellow did not respond. He then poked his chest with the sharpened end of the handle, and immediately something red and moist seeped through the fellow's shirt. Looking down at the blood-stained handle, the narrow-faced man had an urge to sharpen it again. Holding his breath, the long-legged, tethered fellow furtively pulled back his right foot. His feet, just reaching the ground, were the only moveable parts of his body. He pulled it back further and further, his face growing purple with the pain and physical exertion. The narrow-faced young man could now hear the big fellow holding his breath, but just as he raised his head, the big fellow kicked hard at his temple. He fell thumping to the floor.

The big fellow repeatedly reached out his foot to bring over the fallen knife. He tried to work it onto his instep but failed several times. Sweat broke out on his forehead. After repeated attempts, he finally succeeded. He turned it so dexterously with his big toe that it fell flat upon his instep. He flipped his foot and tossed the knife into the air while throwing out his chest to receive it. He then juggled it slightly on his chest until he could pin it with his chin to prevent it from dropping. He moved his mouth bit by bit until he could bite the handle.

The big fellow leered at the man lying unconscious on the floor and cut the rope by drawing the knife up through it with tremendous effort. He eventually managed to free his left arm, and after that, the rest was relatively easy. He severed the last rope and relaxed himself a bit by rotating his wrists, bending his neck, stretching out his knees, and massaging his back and shoulders. Then, he leapt over the man sprawled on the floor and darted towards the door. On exiting, he looked back at the dark room and the man lying prostrate and then limped towards the south.

The big fellow intended to plunge into the bushes before dark.

He ran for a while and, seeing the sun setting, sat down to tighten the cloth strips bandaging his left leg. Just then, he heard something. It was the sound of a vehicle. He could see nothing but bushes all around. He was worried that the narrow-faced young man had regained consciousness and had called for help through his walkie-talkie. He punched the sand with his fist, regretful for having been too careless and kind-hearted. He should have thrown that man into the sea before leaving the house. He knew that the vehicles might not be able to drive onto the sandplain, but those hooligans would definitely loop around from the seaside and from the west and south of the bushes – in two hours, dogs would start barking, and when the beams of powerful torches began to scan the forest, he would be in big trouble.

The big fellow was still sitting there. He tried to calm himself down so that he could think straight. He had been escorted here four days before, sometime around midnight. He had been handling a stack of paper when suddenly some strangers stormed into his room, took the paper from his hands and yelled: "You son of a bitch! You want to sue us? Let's see what's written on it. Hurry and search the house inside out." They left nothing unturned in the house and smashed all the breakable utensils.

"We've found nothing."

"Fuck! Take him with us. Cuff him, of course! He learned martial arts some time ago…"

They pushed him around, slapped his face and tied him up before throwing him into a truck, which rolled straight to the north. He was thus locked up in the small house by the sea. He did not know their names but was fully aware that they must have been from the Tiantong Group. From the moment they had thrust him into the woodlice-infested dark house, they began to torture and interrogate him, forcing him to reveal whom he had recently contacted, how he set himself against the Tiantong Group, what he had being doing, what had happened around the Large Rampart Compound of Purple Smoke and who was the mastermind behind the riots. As he clammed up, they threatened to throw him into the sea. Knowing the hooligans' brutal nature, he never doubted their ability to do so. When the gang left, only the narrow-faced man came to the house occasionally. This strange young man tortured him in silence, his face sullen.

After a brief calculation, the big fellow reckoned that the only way to escape was by the river, where the water was at its deepest, preventing the hooligans from crossing it. He chuckled, picked himself up and limped towards the riverbank.

The sound of barking dogs was now distinctly audible. Torches swept along in the north, the west and the south. The big fellow knew that everything was happening as he had anticipated. They quickly mobilised for action, and this time, they were bent on catching him. He felt as if he were like a rabbit in the wilderness being chased by hunters from all directions.

Those rushing over from the north were drawing nearer. When the big fellow threw himself into the river, they failed to spot him and kept on running in the direction of the bushes. Later, a few dogs began to bark at the water's edge, attracting three or four of them to return, yelling and cursing. By this time, the big fellow had swum to the middle of the river. "Are you afraid of getting hit by our fucking bullets?" they shouted from the bank. "This time, we'll fire for real." They continued to shout for a while before gunshots rang out, seemingly aimed high above the water surface.

Those on the bank were whispering, probably discussing how they could get to the other side of the river to block him off. The people hurrying from the south and the west were also arriving here. The big fellow swam harder, knowing that the motor vehicles could only cross the river by driving around to the submersible bridge at the end of the river. The stone bridge in the south was further away.

The big fellow swam vigorously upstream. The wheat fields on the other side were soon in sight, appearing white in the dark of the night and emanating an ever-intensifying aroma of bread. He looked left and right and was astonished to spot a jeep dashing over from the north and about to pull up in front of him. The high-powered spotlight on its roof illuminated everything on the bank. He felt his heart nearly jumping out of his throat, and the corners of his bulging eyes were about to crack. As soon as he reached the dirt on the bank, he arched his body, sprang up and darted into the wheat fields. Meanwhile, the jeep vroomed by near the bank. He might have been crushed to pieces if he had been a minute later. The big fellow leapt and hopped over the water that had collected in the furrows and charged desperately into the depth of the fields. The jeep with the spotlight ploughed into the wheat fields with the beam trained on the big fellow all the time. He managed to lie on his stomach to escape detection. With the beam still searching for him, he bent low and sprinted with all his might... The sound of the engine and the occasional discharge of guns soon drew the surrounding villagers over. They mistook the commotion for a game of rabbit hunting. An old man shouted at the jeep in front: "What are you doing? You're destroying my crops. It's a crime to ruin my wheat crop for the sake of a rabbit."

The jeep barged on along the bumpy wheat fields, its roaring sound drowning out the hubbub of the people. It followed its target closely to an aqueduct, which, spanning over the fields, allowed pedestrians and vehicles to pass under it. The beam of the spotlight was aimed at the fugitive, and the passengers in the jeep could see clearly how he was galloping, jumping and stumbling to the aqueduct.

The jeep blitzed out of the wheat fields, raced to the aqueduct and screeched to a stop. Two people hopped out cursing and yelling, anxious to get hold of the fugitive.

"Jeez, this son of a bitch has gone again."

"He was here a moment ago, a moment ago..."

BROTHERS

Mei Di was awakened at midnight by the sound of barking dogs. She saw the beams of light sweeping across the sky through the window. Instead of bothering Liao Mai, she slung a coat over her shoulders and went out. She headed due south since that was where the hubbub was coming from. The shouting and barking became increasingly loud. Her own dog was barking back at the dogs outside the fence wall, and it flopped to the ground wagging its tail when it saw her coming.

"What's wrong, Big Tiger Head? Don't bark for nothing." Mei Di reached out to run her hand over its head. She felt it tremble and noticed it staring at something in a nearby haystack while cautiously moving towards it.

Mei Di walked up to the haystack, but before she got there, a dark figure sprang up and darted towards the lake along the fence. She was about to call out when she caught sight of Liao Mai. Her long-legged husband had presumably stepped out as soon as he heard the commotion. He blocked the way of the fleeing black figure. Mei Di heard the two men talking in booming voices, which they soon lowered to an indistinct muttering. Meanwhile, the men and the torches were pressing closer beyond the fence, and the barking of the dogs got even louder. The clanking of metal was audible in the air. With it, two men armed with rifles climbed over the fence. Another man encouraged the dogs to jump over the fence, but Mei Di stopped him.

The two uniformed riflemen each held a powerful torch in their hands. They said to Mei Di: "Someone jumped over the fence a moment ago. We must search your place for him."

"You can't. This is my farm. Besides, I didn't see anyone hopping over."

The taller of the two men moved ahead anyway and whispered to the other: "Don't waste your time arguing with a woman!"

The two headed for the L-shaped lake, shining their torches here and there randomly.

"What are you doing? You're so rude!" said Mei Di, raising her voice intentionally and feeling certain that the southerly wind would carry her warning to Liao Mai's ears. Taking Big Tiger Head by the leash, she stood on guard at the fence, determined to prevent anyone from climbing over, particularly the two lunging dogs on the other side.

The rifle men searched the work sheds and every part of the house. Liao Mai could not stop them from doing so because they claimed that they were conducting official business. While they searched meticulously, three more men jumped over the fence, each carrying electric shock rods and rubber rods. They were sweating all over. The five men began to search together. Eventually, they reached the two-roomed house by the garage and surrounded it with the illumination of their torches. Liao Mai glanced at the hut and fidgeted with anxiety. Standing in the front and at the back of the garage with Liao Mai, the men urged him to open it.

"There's nothing but a rickety car and gas canisters. The next room is empty."

"You must open that, too."

When they swarmed into the room on the south side, Liao Mai's heart was about to jump out of his throat. He saw one of them shine his torch into the room in a circular motion and then crouch down to direct its beam into the space under the bed.

"Let's head west, go to the lake embankment and the poplars. Now the guy's sneaked in here, he can't expect to escape…"

They searched the farm for ages but found nothing in the end. They left cursing and rubbing their hands together.

Not until the torches disappeared into the distance and their beams could only be seen waving outside the fence did Liao Mai lock the garage again. He was taken aback at the door of the adjoining room in the dark: out of it there came a long-legged man, about a handspan taller than he was.

"You were there a moment ago?" Liao Mai asked with great alarm.

The man nodded. Liao Mai grabbed him, and the two dashed back into the room and shut the door behind them.

The man asked for a cigarette in great earnest, so Liao Mai went to find one. Just then, Mei Di arrived leading Big Tiger Head. He signalled her to get some cigarettes and meanwhile took over the leash and tied it to a nearby poplar tree. Mei Di soon returned with a pack, and Liao Mai went back to the room and shut the door.

The man lit a cigarette and started puffing away. Only once he'd satisfied his craving for nicotine did he begin to tell Liao Mai the whole story. In the darkness, Liao Mai listened without comment. Liao Mai learned that this guy lived close to the Large Rampart Compound of Purple Smoke, or to be exact, a village about five kilometres away to the southeast. After his demobilisation from the People's Liberation Army, he managed a reed farm in his village and lived a fairly good life. The Large Rampart Compound of Purple Smoke, however, ruined him. It not only acquired half of his farm but also made the remaining half infertile by contaminating the source of irrigation water. The entire village had no clean drinking water, and more and more people became mysteriously ill. All the villagers expected him, a man who had seen the world, to lodge a complaint on their behalf. On three occasions he brought the case to places far away from their village but to no avail. He was stopped from making his trip when he tried a fourth time. After the fifth, he was beaten so badly that several of his teeth were knocked out. From then on, strange things happened to him. He would be beaten up by strangers who broke into his house in the dark of night for no reason at all; he was detained over some bizarre allegations; three of his ribs were somehow broken; and few of his remaining teeth were left intact.

"I'm so lucky that I've escaped them this time," he said with his head hanging down. "They've been chasing me in the wheat fields for several hours. They tried to run me over and shoot me in the leg. The villagers around thought they were chasing a rabbit." The man took another puff of his cigarette and continued: "When I was in the army, I ran so fast that they nicknamed me 'Rabbit'. So, Brother, you may call me that as well."

Liao Mai surveyed his arms and brawny chest and then bent down to look under the bed. He was incredulous: was he capable of making himself invisible? The man demonstrated how he had hidden himself by hanging and pressing his body tight against the bed board underneath. This was how he made his narrow escape.

This guy's truly awesome, Liao Mai exclaimed to himself.

Grinding out his cigarette butt, Rabbit asked: "Is this large farm yours? Under their nose? Bro, you're incredible…"

Liao Mai did not want to explain how and why. He just listened.

"You wait and see. The Large Rampart Compound of Purple Smoke will expand to the east, to the north and spread back here. Our good days are numbered. We've at least been able to breathe before, but now it's impossible. The air is filled with a foul odour, and every drop of water has been contaminated." With that, Rabbit punched the bed board with his fist.

"Only beasts build large rampart compounds of purple smoke around here on such fertile farmland," said Liao Mai.

"No, Brother, they're worse than beasts. A time of suffering is coming. Trust me."

Liao Mai had learned that the big fellow was only a year his junior. Upon hearing his words, Liao Mai felt flames flaring up inside him, and his chest suddenly heated up. In the dark night, he could see Rabbit's eyes sparkling. Suddenly remembering something, he shut the window, lit the kerosene lamp and began examining the injuries on his body.

Good Heavens! Liao Mai said to himself. He's still smiling and talking with such composure despite being wounded so badly. This is really some man!

He put the kerosene lamp down and said: "I'll get you some

medicine and food." Rabbit nodded 'yes' to his suggestion of venturing out.

In the meantime, Mei Di had been standing under a poplar to the west of the garage, worrying about the pair. As soon as he came out, Liao Mai caught sight of her and went up. After he whispered something in her ear, she went away.

Liao Mai waited for her under the tree. Rabbit also came out and stood by his side. Gazing in the direction where Mei Di was heading, Rabbit said: "Brother, she's dynamite! You've got yourself a real good wife."

Liao Mai did not say anything.

Rabbit repeated what he had said.

Liao Mai then remembered to ask about his family. The man fell silent and, after a long while, said in a hoarse voice that his wife had divorced him and remarried, taking their only son with her.

"It's better this way, better for her to leave me," Rabbit said as he rubbed his hands together and then pressed one of them against the wound on his chest.

Footsteps were heard in the deep night.

"Mei Di's back," Liao Mai whispered.

TWELVE

A HEART ROAMING THE WILDERNESS

THE WIND FROM THE SEA, the wind from the plains and the wind from
the mountains merged into one, now gentle, now violent, but it
could never blow away what transpired that night – a night of
vengeance, of pursuit and of farewell. From now on, the best man in
the world began his life of vagrancy away from home. From now
on, the Tang father and son began searching for their personal
enemy with their eyes wide open and calculating ways to harm him
day and night.

"Argh, he's dangerous. Argh, that sinister rogue! He almost blew
me to hell!" Tang Laotuo was still cursing on Stone Street a long
time later, his chest and arms bandaged with thick gauze.

The curses hushed the whole town. The residents dared not
breathe aloud while chickens, dogs, geese and ducks all kept their
mouths closed.

"Surround… encircle this murderous brute! Make the
encirclement as watertight as a tin bucket! Use a horse-tripping rope
to trip him and capture him as soon as he falls to the ground. This
time, I'll skin him, slice him and pull him apart alive!" Tang Laotuo
would bark at whoever happened to be carrying a blunderbuss
when he came out to inspect the sentries in the middle of the night.

Mei Di was never afraid again. Putting up with the hue and cry every day, she no longer felt a shudder of fear when she heard the hustle and bustle of activities around her. She came to realise that Tang Laotuo's screams only affirmed Liao Mai's successful escape from his chase. She prayed in silence: My really fine man, run as far as you can, never to return. Don't worry, nothing will happen to me here. Just run with your heart at ease. Run straight to the depth of the wild mountain. Make a big, soft nest of hay so you can lie there and wait for me.

Late at night, she often rehearsed different scenarios of their rendezvous, all for the same purpose: hugging her really fine man tight and vowing to be together for the rest of their lives. In such a future, they would hang out together all day long with plenty of time on their hands. What to do with the time? Mei Di asked and then answered herself: Nothing is set, but it's only natural to include kisses and physical contact. This will be enough to make my face burn, my body shake, my eyes freeze and my tongue get tied in knots. I'll bite him gently whenever I see him. Good Heavens, how can I help it when you're so handsome? You're simply killing me by causing me to miss you like this. How can I help it when you have a pair of such thick, angular lips? Whenever I put my mouth upon yours, I'll feel our warm lips, and it will make me terribly bashful. I'll stroke your hair, your collarbones, your chest, your back, your arms and your belly button… and there's something that's too shameful to think about. Anyway, we'll never separate for the rest of our lives. I'll be your woman for as long as we live. This is an unshakeable fact. If you doubt it, wait and see and find out who's more unyielding and resilient. I will never beg for mercy even if I were burned at the stake. I want nothing because nothing's valuable. I could toss a mountain of silver or gold into a ditch. All I want is the long-legged really fine man who can leap several feet in the air in a single jump!

Hearing Tang Laotuo cursing and hurling his diatribes around her house, Mei Di regarded him as the most stupid, vicious old beast in the world. She said to him in silence: You think you can force me to be your daughter-in-law just because you have a blunderbuss over your shoulder and a sword in your hand? You think I must be trapped in your tigers' den just because I'm an orphan? You're daydreaming! Even if you chop me to pieces, my flesh and bones are still mine. You may have subdued many others, but you can't crush me. I share the same stubborn temperament as my really fine man.

Being together with Liao Mai that night made her grow up. She told herself time and again that she had to be prepared to wait for a hundred years, for systematic torment, for forced labour and for eating clay – all the different forms of punishment that the Tang father and son could think of inflicting upon her. She would fear none of them.

To Mei Di, being lovesick was both a torment and nourishment. She could see him with her eyes either open or closed. Her heart was following him as he ran through the wilderness day and night, without eating or drinking, without feeling hunger or fatigue. She only hoped that he would look back and smile at her, which she took as her best reward. She could absorb every aspect of the smile and understand its mysterious message and wonderful pledge. Deep in the night, she would hold her quilt tight and cry "Liao Mai" as if she had touched his head, eyes and cheeks. She would ask him and answer for him at once: "You're the worst really fine man!"

"I am."

"You hurt me when you bite me!"

"I just want you to feel it when I bite you."

She babbled with little sleep the whole night and yet got up the next morning still radiant with vigour. She tried on her best clothes, including the ones that her father had left her. She fumbled through them and found that she could no longer fit into most of them. The golden straw raincoat was the most fascinating, and it was still hanging there ostentatiously. She buried her face in it to feel its proximity and sniffed the scent of the wilderness that exuded from it...

When Mei Di went out on the street, she would always be followed by blunderbuss-carrying figures. They followed her very closely at first and then from a certain distance. When she tried to veer off at the crossroads, they would hurriedly stop her from going further.

In the first few days, she did not venture out and did not want to do anything anyway. Later, she stepped out to carry water with buckets hanging from a shoulder pole and caught sight of the blue sky at the end of a lengthy alley. She instantly yearned to run away and disappear. Tang Laotuo had someone pass a message to her: "You rebellious vixen, don't expect to go anywhere because your case isn't closed."

"Then close it quickly," she replied.

Tang Laotuo agreed and had her escorted to a big house. As soon as she entered, she sensed the previous day's atmosphere, which reminded her of the time when she and her father were interrogated there after returning to Jiwo. She particularly remembered what had happened in the past that had made her deeply angry and resentful. That was when Tang Laotuo's son and the barefoot physician stripped her on a wooden board and examined her body. She also did something more foolish, when she naively allowed Tang Tong to see her naked body when she started primary school. She tried shutting her eyes a few times, ashamed and hateful, in the hope of never seeing the big stone house again.

Tang Laotuo coughed while fiddling with the gavel. She looked up and saw a long wooden table set between her and Tang Laotuo. He was flanked by his curly-haired son and two haggard young men, who, with their chests thrown out, were each carrying a blunderbuss over their shoulders.

Tang Laotuo waved the two young men beside him out of the room. Now that only he and his son were facing Mei Di, he banged the gavel and said: "Let me ask you. Do you know what you are and what crime you've committed?"

Mei Di did not respond. She suddenly felt that the father and son were animals incarnate; for she saw the black hair covering Tang Laotuo's hand and his eye sockets surrounded with thick fuzz of the same colour. As for his son Tang Tong, the look in his eyes and the curly hair on the top of his head also reminded her of an animal – a badger crawling out of a burrow. She tried to suppress a laugh.

"How dare you laugh, you slut! Attempting to murder an upper-class man with your adulterous man, you've committed a capital offence. It would not be an over-reaction if we decided to chop you into pieces with an axe!"

Having heard a new term for the first time, Mei Di asked with curiosity: "What do you mean by 'upper-class man'?"

Pointing to himself with a thumb, Laotuo said: "It's me, you ignorant slut." With that, he turned to his son. "I don't understand what this filthy bimbo is good for. The Tang family is so powerful that we can call the wind and command the rain. What do we need her for? I'll have someone find you a round-faced girl tomorrow."

"No, no!" Tang Tong replied in a teary voice. "We've decided on her, haven't we? I've been seeing her growing up little by little. We cannot change our shared history."

"You hear him, you slut. Every word my son has said carries weight. It's your good fortune. But to me, you must cultivate yourself for another two or three generations before you can be part of our family. Up to now, the stench of wild creature spirits is still assailing my nostrils. Our family thinks you are too filthy to be likeable. You've only just shed your straw raincoat, and your origin is by no means decent. Between you and me, on the day of your consummation with my son, you must behave. If you dare to be rude and hurt my son's private parts, I'll kill you with my peeling knife and sell your big hedgehog skin to a pharmacy. I'm warning you now..."

What Laotuo said made Tang Tong exceedingly happy, so much so that he couldn't help fidgeting on his feet while coughing from time to time.

An amused Mei Di asked: "Who's marrying me to your son? Since my parents are no longer alive, I'll decide my own future. I've never agreed to marry him."

Laotuo flew into a rage: "You slut! Since your father took you back to town, your marriage with my son has become a town decision. Your father has passed, and your mother is a hedgehog spirit. Wandering around on the beach, is she able to take care of you? If you're going to reject him, then put on your straw raincoat and go back to your life as a wild creature!"

Mei Di immediately took up the thread of his words, saying: "Fine! I'm going now. I'm leaving." With that, she headed out.

Tang Tong blocked her way and begged his father: "You can't let her go. Her case isn't closed yet."

"Yes, there's an outstanding case against you," Laotuo said, squinting his eyes, "and you can't expect to go anywhere in this life..."

Mei Di's heart sank, wishing that she could find herself in the wilderness. As she widened her eyes, she pictured her long-legged fine man. As a consequence, she could neither hear what was said nor see anyone around her.

Seeing her in a daze and unresponsive to any of their questions, Tang Tong went up to her and waved his fingers in front of her wide open eyes. But she still showed no sign of reaction. "Oh my! Dad, do you think she's dead? She's like a possessed fool!"

"Let me take a look." Tang Laotuo left the long table and came up to her. He also waved his fingers in front of her as his son had done.

"You slut, can you see me?"

Mei Di was silent.

"Well, well, she's a fool. She's really possessed."

UNDER THE WINDOW

Whenever Mei Di ran into Tang Tong when she was out, Tang Tong would smirk at her while gesticulating and mumbling. Mei Di would say: "I'm going to the market out of town."

Tang Tong shrugged, a blunderbuss over his shoulder, and said: "Your case is not closed yet."

"When will it be closed?"

"That's up to you."

"Do it in a hurry."

"Fine. You're asking for it!" said Tang Tong, clapping his hands.

"Where to close it?"

Stomping his feet, pouting his lips and scratching his head, Tang Tong muttered: "Well, well, we'll close it on the *kang*, of course."

She no longer paid any attention to him.

How much Mei Di wanted to go out on moonlit nights! But she could only step into the courtyard. Leaving the yard would be difficult, since young armed men would stop her again and again.

She would shout: "I want to go to Stone Street. I want to go to the riverside."

"You're daydreaming! You're daydreaming! You'd take a hike as soon as you stepped out of town. Then, as government employees, we'd be in big trouble. You'd better hold your horses."

She had to watch the small, nocturnal creatures like lizards and beetles at night. A bat flew as low as the door lintel, skimmed above her shoulder and soared into the sky. "Oh, my really fine man, live well under such a bright moon. Rest all you like and play as you will. Make sure you don't trip up or bump into anything and hurt yourself. I'm now as good as jailed by the Tang family. But I've said I'm afraid of nothing. I'm waiting for you to come back with all my heart."

It was midnight. All the armed men had withdrawn to the entrance of the alley under an order given by Tang Tong. He jumped over the wall and into the courtyard and settled under the window. There, he crouched down and occasionally stood up, calling Mei Di all the time. He even answered his own questions from time to time. He did this tirelessly night after night. Mei Di could see his talking and gesticulating shadow cast by the moonlight. Sometimes, he remained silent for hours. Mei Di would then open the window ajar to peep out, only to be taken aback: Tang Tong was fast asleep on a blanket he had spread on the ground.

When Mei Di had returned to bed and was about to roam into her dreamland, the guy outside the window woke up again and started to talk gibberish at varying pitches. Sometimes, he sounded hoarse due to a constricted throat; on other occasions, it was high-pitched like a sobbing soprano.

"You think I've never seen beautiful women? I saw many buxom, good-looking women when I went to the market and the range where a military skills competition was going on. They knew who I was and they ogled me. But once I placed my hand on them, my brain would go blank. Why? Because I thought of you! Good Heavens! I often toss and turn in bed praying to the gods and goddesses. I ask them to deliver me from your spell or castrate me when I'm fast asleep. Otherwise, I couldn't stand the ordeal. The fire of my lust would bake me to death like a seared fish. I can't go to sleep for nights on end, imagining your pretty face, your golden-haired back and your plump belly. I've been so anxious that I don't want to live any more. I won't be able to figure out why until I die. I just don't get it. Why would such a smart broad like you be lured into a relationship by a weirdo? Besides, what's the use of waiting? You should know he can't expect to come back to town alive. Once he shows up, he'll be chopped to death."

Tang Tong stomped his feet, thumped the ground with his blunderbuss and gritted his teeth so loud that the sound reminded Mei Di of a rat sneaking out at night. After a long while, he suddenly changed tone and began to talk gently and softly: "Oh, my darling, my jewel! If you join my family, you'll be very, very happy. Can you imagine the good life you'll enjoy? Maybe not. I'll have several floral quilts made by the best embroiderers in the neighbourhood. Each of them will have a satin lining and silk facing. I'll have the *kang* heated up. I'll have delicious food served to you – muskmelons, jujubes, stewed pork, steamed buns and all kinds of alcoholic drinks. In future, I'll be at your disposal. When angry, you can slap my face, and I won't get offended. I'll amuse you by doing handstands or by singing a song from a folk opera. I'll carry you on my back and wander the streets to pick pockets. Tell me whatever you'd like to have. From the day we come together, you'll become the real head of town, and my dad will be a fake. We'll pretend to obey him, but in secret, you'll be in charge of twenty-eight people armed with blunderbusses. If you want someone killed, just signal me with a cough. If you should catch a cold and can't stop coughing, I'll keep on chopping people's heads off. You want wheat, I'll give you wheat flour. You want watermelons, I'll give them to you with the seeds removed. If you want me, I'll slip into your sleeping bag. I may be a rustic guy who is handy with a gun, but I can also sit on a small stool and recite poems. Listen: 'A good wife causes her husband less misfortune. / When birds are twittering hither and yon, I awake.' Such a beautiful line... Li Bai, wasn't it?"

Mei Di knew the first section of the line should have been "On a drowsy spring night, I slept until daybreak", and it was not a poem by Li Bai, but she kept quiet.

Tang Tong continued: "It's said that the old brothers known as Li Bai and Du Fu were poor and banal. Those dudes ran helter-skelter from south to north leading a poor life. They had nothing good to eat or drink except a flask of rice wine and a dish of cucumber salad."

Unable to go on listening, Mei Di shouted: "I want to leave. I'm going to the riverside tomorrow."

"Sure, you can go. As my own jewel, you can do whatever you

want. I'll have someone accompany you when you go for that walk tomorrow. You can also go to the beach if you like. Hey, you've become a queen without knowing it. Haven't you noticed that you're guarded by armed men night after night? What a spectacle it is! You may say: 'Pah! You're doing this to prevent me from escaping!' And you may be right, but just think about it. Why am I not afraid of others running away? It's because I hate to let you go. I truly like you and must marry you. I know you're the daughter of a hedgehog spirit, and you can mangle me with your prickles. But I'm patient and know how to smooth your spines and make you feel so happy that you'll lie on your back and scream with joy. I know you have steel spines on your back but fuzz hairs on your belly. I'll cuddle you face to face and massage your belly gently. So, just think, what obstacles can exist between us? Then, you won't regret falling in love with me and holding me tight in your little arms and paws, preventing me from going to sleep. It's true what they say: 'Each family has a tune hard to be sung by others / Until the end, a couple in love won't…'"

To drown out this stream of abusive language, Mei Di kept crying out in silence: Oh, my really fine man! Do you know there's a monster outside the window? To guard myself against him, I carry a pair of scissors at all times.

Leaning against the window and gesticulating, Tang Tong resumed his prattle: "My sweetheart, it's chilly outside. Please open the window and let me in. Why can't I hear you? Are you sleeping? How can you sleep on such a moonlit night? Don't you want to listen to me singing a tune from a folk opera?"

He cleared his throat and started chanting:

My good sister, don't be nervous
I'm taking off my clothes piece by piece,
First the dark blue coat opening in the front
Then the vest to reveal my stomach.
Now I'm untying the black silk leggings.
Loose are my trousers with a folded top,
A jade talisman from a red thread hangs
Down the crotch, it keeps swinging.

Mei Di could feel tears streaming down her cheeks. She cursed him in secret: You're a beast worse than a dog or a hog! I wish you were struck by a thunderbolt."

My good sister, don't be anxious
Don't back to the wall on your dainty feet
I'm a real man of significant stature
And a handsome face with a big mouth.
Now, my heart's thumping like a drum
Holding out my hands with long fingers
I'm here to propose marriage to you, dear.
A real man mustn't be shy and reserved here.

Mei Di covered her ears and closed her eyes, but she could not help shedding tears. Then, she heard the paper windowpane being torn. She opened her eyes, only to feel dizzy: something was being thrust through the hole. Gritting her teeth, she raised the scissors and, with all the determination she could muster, drove the blades hard into it.

"Ow! You're so cruel! It was lucky I anticipated your move and used a stick instead of my hand. I could have bled to death! Jeez! You're the cruellest person in the world. You're not my woman any more! I don't want you any more! Anyone can fuck you she-demon with your savage, stubborn nature…"

Tang Tong snarled like a wolf caught in a trap. His shrieks soon attracted hasty footsteps.

ENDLESS TORMENT

"You can't live here any more. You must come with me." The female leader urged Mei Di repeatedly while rubbing the two purple marks left on her forehead by the cupping therapy.

"This is my ancestral home. Why are you driving me out?"

The leader was a tall, stout woman. Whenever she grinned, she revealed two rows of large teeth that scared Mei Di. Seeing Mei Di stand there with her arms folded in front of her, she went up close and pinched her crotch.

"Ow! You dragon!" Mei Di screamed as she stepped back against the wall.

"No matter what names you call me, I'll be your mother from today on." She then reached her hand out again to threaten her.

"You're disgusting," said Mei Di as she spat on the floor.

The seesaw battle lasted for a long time until Mei Di realised that she could no longer stay there. The door squeaked again, and several women stormed into the courtyard, each carrying a blunderbuss over their shoulders.

Mei Di hesitated and agreed to move out. She was getting her bedding ready when the female leader pulled her hands away, saying: "You can't take anything with you. I have everything for you."

The leader escorted Mei Di out of the room and stopped the two armed women from following her. "You guys stay here to tidy things up and lock the door behind you," she ordered.

From then on, Mei Di began to live with the ogress in a two-room hut next to a stable with a few cows and horses for company. The ogress used the larger room as her bedroom, leaving the smaller one to Mei Di. The two rooms were partitioned by a wall of sorghum stalks plastered with mud. As a result, Mei Di could clearly hear the ogress snoring. Mei Di had to cut fodder with a scythe and clean the manure out of the stable during the day and get up twice to feed the beasts of burden at night. With her slim arms, she had trouble handling the scythe and carrying the large iron container of fodder. The ogress grinned at her so broadly that she revealed her purple gums, all the while feasting her eyes on Mei Di's breasts.

During the first few nights, Mei Di couldn't sleep, not only due to the snoring coming from the next room but also because of the filthy, smelly quilt. For sanitary reasons, she went to bed fully clothed each night. Finally, she had enough and decided to wash the quilt and bedsheet. The ogress caught her doing so and stopped her, yelling: "How dare ruin my bedding, you savage slut! You're too audacious!"

Eventually, Mei Di became so tired that she was able to sleep. But then, she was stirred by the hubbub coming from the next room. A man was talking in a muffled voice. Later, he was heard battling with the ogress, who kept groaning and begging: "I'm dying! I'm dying! Wow, what a sleep! It's good for the slut to overhear us!"

Mei Di gradually realised what they were doing. Whenever the two were battling with each other, the beasts of burden would react with a commotion of kicking and neighing and mooing. Holding her breath, the ogress would shout: "You slut can do nothing but sleep. Why don't you take care of the unruly cows and horses?"

Mei Di had to go to the stable, where she was so scared that she covered her mouth with both hands. A large, chestnut stallion, which had shaken itself free of the reins, was covering a white mare, and the two were battling each other vigorously, neighing and sweating all over. "Good boy! Good girl! Please don't fight any more. Please..." The horses calmed down a bit but soon resumed their battle.

Mei Di stared into the darkness night after night, thinking of her little stone house. She began to worry that her really fine man would sneak back and find it empty. The more she thought about it, the more heartache she felt. She could not fall asleep even in the small hours. The ogress in the next room did not snore but coughed occasionally. She was smoking, and the smell of tobacco leaked through the many cracks in the mud-and-stalk partition. Soon, the door in Mei Di's room was pushed open. There stood the ogress stark naked, cigarette in mouth. Mei Di turned away.

"Sleeping with your clothes on, little slut. Do you think my bedding's dirty? I've given you the cotton-padded quilt with a new floral cover and new lining. Why don't you appreciate my kindness? You ungrateful wild slut! Until the day you marry into the Tang family, you'll be under my control. That is, unless you can waggle your arse to someone who can take you with him. Then it would be, as the old saying goes: 'A daughter married out is like water poured out.' In that case, I would unleash you. But I can't do it right now. For the time being, you must take it lying down and submit to my control." With that, the ogress cast the cigarette butt to the floor, ground it with her feet and jumped onto Mei Di's *kang*.

Mei Di sat up instantly. The ogress smelled like a dead rat. Her heavy-set, naked body was scary to look at, and her breasts that Mei Di had accidentally glimpsed were so big that they caused Mei Di to gasp. One of them was drooping more than the other, and the nipples appeared like curved thumbs. "Good Heavens! Am I having a nightmare?" Mei Di blurted out and turned towards a corner of the room with her hands covering her face.

The ogress pulled her hands away and tore her clothes open. Mei

Di was terrified. When the ogress moved her coarse hand up to her mouth, she bit it hard. "Aww, that really hurts! Aww, I'll beat you to death!" The ogress kept pinching Mei Di's crotch. While Mei Di was trying to fend off her repeated attacks, the ogress pressed her with her knees and quickly stripped her, first the thin layer of her outer garment and then the smaller underwear.

"You're as bony as a weasel, you little slut. You look pitiable. Look at your chest bones! All your ribs are showing! You really know how to bundle yourself up. I'm going to strip you of all the layers of clothes."

Mei Di wriggled, struggling with all her might to free herself from the ogress's grip. But she could not budge an inch because the ogress's knees and feet were as firm as an anvil and as heavy as a rock, and her hands gripped her as tightly as a pair of pliers. In the blink of an eye, she was stark naked under the sharp scrutiny of the ogress. Mei Di made a great effort to hold back her tears. Whenever she attempted to cover her chest with her hands, the ogress would slap them off, saying: "I must examine you little slut carefully and figure out the little beast that is your body."

She raised a kerosene lamp to shine on her front and back. She pulled Mei Di's thighs open and pushed her head back. After moistening her finger with the saliva in her mouth, the ogress pinched Mei Di's dainty breasts and her back while muttering: "Well, well! You're nothing but a little beast with fuzz hair all over and a smell that hurts my nostrils. Fuck!"

As soon as the ogress loosened her grip, Mei Di sprang up. The ogress then said with hands on hips: "You little slut, the offspring of a beast! I really want to chomp you and swallow you into my stomach. But tonight, I'm going to spare you for the sake of the Tang family. From now on, you'd better be more obedient. If you try to buck me, I'll hold each of your legs and pull you apart as I do with a little frog."

Mei Di trembled with fear, being in no doubt of this woman's prowess. In the flickering light of the kerosene lamp, Mei Di noticed something wriggling like a nest of snakes beneath her greyish-yellow skin. Good Heavens! she screamed in silence, filled with despair. I've fallen into a dry well. I'm afraid I'll never see my really fine man again.

The ogress did not leave until three o'clock, before dawn. For the rest of the night, Mei Di cried a bitter cry and then gazed into the darkness, yearning for her really fine man. She kept thinking of him, if only to cheer herself up.

During the day, the ogress ordered some armed women to clean the stable of manure with Mei Di. Seeing Mei Di unable to lift heavy loads, the ogress said: "You can carry that weight on your back by crawling. Isn't that how a hedgehog moves?" With that, she was about to press Mei Di down when she looked up and stopped. Mei Di also raised her head, only to find a swarthy-faced man standing at the door. It was Tang Tong.

Tang Tong had been standing there for a while. Instead of entering the room, he just watched from outside.

"A cat has three kitties in each litter, a dog has four, and a hedgehog may have about the same number. I'm not sure how many she can conceive for each pregnancy. My superior, you'd better find some help. This little slut's breasts are as large as autumn peaches and she's horny inside out. With so much libido, she gets so impatient that she bites people!"

As she finished, the ogress went over to him. She raised her left hand and pointed out the bitemark on the back of her hand to the man outside.

But Tang Tong focused all his attention on Mei Di, as if he had not seen the ogress at all.

DREAM INTERPRETATION

Counting on her fingers, Mei Di found that she had been living miserably in the stable for a year and three months. In the late spring of that year, she finally returned to her little bluestone house. Breaking down in tears, she said to herself: I'm mortal, released from a she-demon's den. She nearly chewed me up.

On examining her bedding on the *kang*, she found the curly hair of a man. Enraged, she made up her mind and took the bedding to the yard and burned it.

A cloud of smoke rising into the sky soon attracted a group of armed men. Leaning over the wall of her courtyard, they watched in silence.

The next day, someone brought her wheat flour and pork and

told her that they were gifts from Tang Tong. On the third day, another man came to inform her that if she wanted to go out, she could just let them know, and two or three escorts would accompany her wherever she liked. Mei Di felt almost suffocated. She pushed the door open and stormed out of the yard regardless of the warning. As soon as she stepped onto Stone Street, she broke into a trot. A few blunderbuss-carrying men started following her closely, shouting: "Hey, big girl! You're running too fast. We're so tired, we can't catch our breath."

They tagged after her all the way to the riverside and then to the sand beach. She galloped and walked alternately. She grabbed some bush branches and pressed her cheek against them. The fine, white sand also gave her tremendous joy, so much so that she threw herself upon it. She did not saunter back to town until sunset.

"She's really wild in nature," the escorts whispered.

She wandered out on each of the next few days and returned exhausted each time.

Before going to bed, she would always think of her really fine man and talk to him until she fell asleep. Even in her dreams, she would follow him to the wild, where she hopped and ran. She saw his image in one dream after another. Once, she dreamed of him walking in the fields when, all of a sudden, he fell over the edge of a cliff. He had been lost in thought and missed his footing, thereby putting his life at risk. Luckily, there was a deep, shiny river at the foot of the cliff. But in her dream, she forgot that her really fine man was a competent swimmer. She screamed in anxiety and watched him turning into a dot among the breakers of the waves. The dot bobbed and bobbed and eventually merged with the horizon, where the water surface and the sky met...

She could no longer go back to sleep. She was uncertain as to whether her really fine man had been drowned or safely swum to the other side.

She was still worrying at daybreak. She even wondered how strange the dream was or whether Liao Mai had visited her in her dream with a message. She was so anxious that she could feel her heart thumping. She mumbled to herself: Oh, no! Oh, no! Maybe he's in big trouble and is so anxious that his soul comes to me in my dream!

That day, she was not in the mood to do anything. She did not event want to eat or drink. The only thing on her mind was to rush to the wilderness and search for the cliff that she had dreamed of. Lying on her stomach on the *kang*, she cried.

She lay on the *kang* dizzy and sleepy for most of the day. At dusk, she suddenly thought of a woman who lived on a backstreet and could interpret dreams. She hopped onto the floor, threw a blouse over her shoulders, locked the door and dashed to the backstreet. She didn't even glance at the men who ran after her.

The backstreet oneirocritic was seventy years old. She had white eyelashes and grey eyes. When she raised her head to look at the visitor, she bent her head forward till their faces almost touched. Feeling that she was being sniffed rather than observed, Mei Di stepped back a little. With quivering lips, Mei Di told the old woman her dream and asked her to interpret it. The old woman slapped her knees and said: "You're causing me trouble, child. You're putting me at risk. Who has the nerve to do something like this these days?"

Mei Di begged repeatedly: "Kind-hearted witch, take pity on me! I'm an orphan. I have only this loved one, who's on the run."

The old woman was silent, incessantly blinking and looking out of the window, not to be swayed.

Mei Di entreated her again with teary eyes.

With a sigh, the old woman reached out and lifted her chin a little. She gazed at her and snorted: "Good girl, your looks are matchless, prettier than me when I was young – I was also an attractive young woman then... Well, you've lived a hard and sorrowful life. But you may have a lucky thing coming your way once you reach twenty or so. Oh, no. It'll be a big, happy event. Look, your forehead may be cloudy now, but when it's clear..." The old woman paused and counted on her finger joints before resuming her interpretation: "At least in two or three years, the happy thing will happen to you."

"What happy thing?"

"Not something concrete, but it's happiness anyway. There are various ways you can be happy, like making a fortune or having someone who loves you. All can be counted as 'happy'. A human life can't be the same all the way through. It's sometimes dark and sometimes bright, sometimes windy and sometimes rainy."

That dream was Mei Di's top concern. Therefore, she told it in detail again. Biting her upper lip, the old woman rolled her eyes, as if to look into the unknown celestial world. "Well, dreams are all contrary to what they indicate. It depends on how you interpret them. Like undoing a crocheted cap, you must grab the end of the thread to unravel it little by little... Well, well, falling off a cliff means something good. It means he's gained his footing. As for swimming in the water, it means roaming around. Alright, my child, wait patiently and set your heart at ease. From now on, he's travelling farther away."

"It means he's not drowned?"

"Drowned? Nonsense! The young man is able to cover several feet with a single stride!" The old woman adjusted the cap on her head and fell silent with her eyes closed.

Mei Di was so happy that half-shed tears glistened in her eyes. Holding the old woman's hands in hers, she pleaded: "Dear witch, may I trouble you to tell me something more about the dream? Where's he now? Is he having a hard time?"

The old woman counted on her finger joints again with her eyes rolled far up and her eyelids opening and closing at an increasingly rapid rate.

"Of the four compass points, he's been to the south and the west, and now he's heading towards the east and the north. Well, well, I dare say he's getting close to you after travelling here and there. So, don't go anywhere. You're destined to wait for him where you are, wait till the big happy event occurs."

Mei Di trembled with gratitude, her face reddening and her tongue tied. Finally, she bowed deeply and dashed out.

From that day on, Mei Di was ensnared by a variety of colourful dreams, most of them pleasant. One night, she even dreamed of him waving at her, shouting in a hushed voice: "Come over! Come over to me, and let's get married!"

Stomping her feet with frustration as she watched the gushing river, she asked: "How can I cross it? I'm so anxious." Liao Mai was smiling and waving his hand instead of crossing over to pick her up. Eventually, Mei Di was awakened by anxiety. When she opened her eyes, she found that she had shed a lot of tears. The dream had been so vivid; her really fine man's facial expressions and the wrinkles around his lips had both been extremely distinct. Mei Di could not help pushing the door open and rushing to the backstreet. This time, the old woman would not open her eyes.

"Tell me the dream from beginning to end," she said coldly.

Mei Di did so hastily and, holding her breath, watched the old woman listlessly counting on her finger joints, rolling up her eyes and sighing for a protracted time without saying a word.

"What in the world has happened?"

Slapping her knee, the old woman seemed to have finally decided to divulge something important. With her eyes closed, she said: "He's passed."

"What? What do you mean?"

"That river was a boundary line between this world and the next. This world is on this side and the netherworld is on the other. By waving, he meant to ask you to cross the river to meet him in the netherworld."

Mei Di collapsed to the ground. Her eyes clouded over and she could see nothing. Nor could she hear anything but a banging noise in her head. She instinctively covered her ears with her hands. She did not cry out until a long time had elapsed.

"You're talking nonsense! You're fooling me! Liao Mai couldn't bear to let me drown. He'd never harm me. He won't for the rest of his life. You must have misinterpreted the dream. Your interpretation today contradicts the one you did last time."

No matter how Mei Di shook her arms, the old woman refused to say another word. After a while, she rubbed her eyes and started her interpretation anew, counting on her finger joints while shaking her head and sighing.

"Good girl, there's nothing I can do. I know you deserve a great deal of sympathy, but the dream tells the truth. I can't do anything about it."

"But you told me last time I'd get a big happy thing when I reached twenty years of age. This is what you told me in person."

"That's true as well. This big happy thing is a gift from someone. And in fact, this someone is a good man. But it's you who's blinding your own eyes. With this respectable person, you can afford to wear gold and silver jewellery and hold a treasure bowl in your hands."

Mei Di stopped crying immediately and stared at the old woman: "What does this respectable person look like? His head must be covered with curly hair, right?"

Counting on her finger joints, the old woman said: "Absolutely right! Absolutely right!"

"Pah!"

A DREAM COME TRUE

For a long time, the oneirocritic remained Mei Di's most hated person. Luckily, she believed only in the first version of the old woman's interpretation and treated the second as pure nonsense.

But in less than two years, she would be twenty, when the 'big happy thing' would happen according to the prediction. It was the year when she turned twenty that Tang Tong began to lead his blunderbuss-carrying followers in prospecting gold. Their absence from the alleys and streets made the town more relaxed.

Liao Mai had sneaked back several times. Sure enough, Mei Di's waiting paid off. The return of her really fine man was the 'big happy thing'. Mei Di was amazed when she thought of the old woman's prophesy. It's a dream come true! It's a dream come true! Mei Di's hatred immediately gave way to gratitude. She now realised that the old woman had had no alternative but to come up with the second version of her prophesy; Tang Tong and his men must have forced it into her mouth. They had coerced the old woman to deceive her.

Oh, what a magnificent autumn! Mei Di's belly started to bulge when winter came. She was so happy that she became short of breath. She talked to her baby in her womb and her husband in her mind's eye all day long. She told her really fine man far away: Get a nest ready quickly, a small one is fine. I will fly there to hatch our little chick soon.

Unfortunately, it was all too late, and she would rue the delay for the rest of her life.

That day, she was carrying retted kenaf with others. When she turned, she found herself in someone's way. It was none other than the ogress, who had been watching her. Mei Di ignored her, but the ogress followed her all along, first to Stone Street and then to her bluestone house.

"What're you up to?"

"I want to see when the hen will lay her egg."

"You're a disgusting woman!"

"You may curse me, but at least I don't have an illegitimate child!"

That night, armed townsfolk surrounded the little house. The ogress stormed into it with two women, followed closely by Tang Tong. The two women pinned Mei Di down. The ogress then lifted up each layer of her clothes while panting loudly. Mei Di screamed and cursed, but the women went on examining her as if they had not heard her.

"Shall we send for a doc?" asked the two women who were pinning Mei Di.

The ogress leered at them, clapped her hands a few times and went up to Tang Tong.

"What's the use of sending for a doc?" she said. "She's evidently pregnant."

"Ah?" Tang Tong uttered, staring at Mei Di in a daze and cold sweat breaking out on his forehead.

"I told you!" said the ogress. "A field goes to waste if you don't till it. And weeds will certainly grow..."

Tang Tong waved all the women to leave and edged closer to Mei Di. He asked in a lowered voice: "Whose child is it?"

"It's Liao Mai's of course!"

"Ahh! It's this bastard's indeed, this bastard's... I was too negligent. Fuck, a gentleman can never accomplish anything! I should've listened to Old Woman Shan."

Tang Tong slapped his thigh, groaned and paced up and down the room. He then turned his back on her and looked out of the window. When he turned around, his face scared Mei Di, for it was covered with tears, his nose was running and his lips were pressed hard.

"Listen to what I'm saying," he said. "Listen carefully. You'll be sorry for what happens today for the next two generations. As righteousness doesn't make a man wealthy, so benevolence doesn't turn a man into a general. I've been too fucking tolerant. You'll be going to hell from now on. You know you're a woman with an illegitimate child. You're a daredevil! You're a rebel! Aww, you're really revolting..."

Tang Tong gasped. His tears had dried up. For a while, he was tongue-tied. The beads of sweat hanging on his forehead now began to splash to the floor. He stomped his feet, pounded the wall and howled in grief like a wolf. He wielded his fist at Mei Di but stopped short of letting it fall upon her. Afterwards, he walked around Mei Di with his head held high and said through clenched teeth, spacing the words for emphasis: "I assume you're not going to see your child born."

"I'd rather die if not!"

"Go and die, then. Die as soon as possible. You, a slut and the offspring of a wild creature, are a bane of this town. My father was right, totally right. You'll soon trip over your own legs and drop dead on the dry dirt. Then someone will pick you up by pinching your legs with a pair of tongs and pull you to a sewer with a big hook tied to your mouth! Then, it will be too late no matter how hard you cry. Sluts like you are two a penny, no one will have you any more. Even dogs treat... treat you as ugly! You, neither dead nor rotten yet, exasperate the living. You slut and rogue, murderer's accomplice, will see your days of sorrow coming."

Tang Tong cursed until he sweated all over, then he turned around and left without looking back.

It was quiet during the first half of the night. Mei Di murmured to Liao Mai: You'd better not show up now. They've cast a big net to catch you, and they'll vent all their frustrations and anger on you. Don't worry about me. I can endure anything that lies in store.

For the rest of the night, she was thinking of only one thing – how to escape Jiwo. She told herself: You must have the heart to give up this ancestral bluestone house. Your home should be where the father of your child is, where there is a nest for three. Don't waste a second. Whenever there's a chance, run as fast as you can... Her biggest regret was that she had not fled this town earlier, thus turning herself into the biggest fool and the most miserable woman in the world.

She was sleepless the whole night. Several times did she step out onto the frosty ground and towards the door in the courtyard. Each time, she heard people pacing and coughing outside.

As soon as dawn arrived, the ogress came with a cigarette in her mouth. She took off her shoes and mounted the *kang*. Sitting cross-legged, she said: "I told you I was your mother and should've kept you under control. See, you've caused such big trouble only a few days after you left me. I think, you and I, daughter and mother, must talk it over and find a way out before the town knows what's going on. Then, everything's going to be fine. We'll put it all behind us so that you can start all over again."

Mei Di had been staring at her purple lips.

"If you cooperate, then I haven't wasted my time saying all this."

"What're you up to?"

The ogress clattered her teeth and said: "Let me, your mother, get rid of your child before it's too late."

Mei Di immediately picked up the scissors.

"Ugh, you're revolting! This woman was daring enough to thrust a knife into a mounted bandit, and now you think I'll be afraid of you slut with a body as small as a sparrow? I can reach my hands out, grab your feet and pull you apart hands down!"

"Go ahead, then. Bring it on!"

A lock of her hair fell to cover her face, and she caught the tip of it between her teeth.

The ogress peeped out of the window twice, snorted and swallowed, her Adam's apple bobbing with anxiety. Mei Di said to herself: This woman's like a man! She's so rough and imprudent that she can do anything.

Mei Di focused on her while holding the scissors tight in her hands before resuming her silent soliloquy: Oh Liao Mai, I'm going to kill, too! I have the guts to drive these scissors into her for the sake of our child and let her blood splatter all over the *kang* and the walls of the room.

The ogress blinked and, with her upper lip curled, said: "What're you doing flowering those scissors? Tang Tong's armed men can fill the entire town. I won't do anything without his command. It'd be too tiring to do something to you. I just want to have a good chat with you."

Holding the scissors above her head, Mei Di said: "Listen carefully then and tell Tang Tong when you get the chance. The day my child is hurt is the day I'll die. I can always bump my head into a crag."

A FLEDGLING IN THE WILDERNESS

"Ma – ma!" a little girl called her mother, gesticulating adorably with her curved fingers.

"My sweetheart, my beloved everything!"

Whenever she saw her toddling Little Beibei, tears would swell in Mei Di's eyes. The baby girl ran out of the thatched hut in the bright sun to catch a butterfly perching on a reed stalk with her clumsy little hands. Her hair appeared purple against the intense light.

"Baby, you look just like your daddy. Every feature looks like him."

Little Beibei blurted out: "Da-dada."

To the baby girl, the beach wasteland was her entire world. After several recent upheavals, no more than a few decent trees survived here. Nothing could be seen apart from puddles of accumulated saltwater, swept-up dunes, and various grasses and weeds. Aside from inclement winters, the place was still beautiful and impressive – at least in the eyes of Mei Di and her daughter. Here, they could enjoy larks soaring and twittering in the sky – a sight they had not been able to see in town.

"This is a windflower. This is orange peel. These are common madder berries." Mei Di identified each plant in the wilderness while never letting her daughter stray a single step from her.

In the past two or three years, Mei Di had survived thanks to the townspeople's financial help and the alms they had been able to beg: a handful of rice, a piece of vegetable and a smile. Even the oneirocritic in the backstreet secretly gave her some brown sugar. She recorded every item and penny that she had borrowed in order to pay her creditors back in future. One sunny day, a year after her daughter's birth, Mei Di carried her in her arms out of town. She went straight west and then north. She suddenly had an urge to see the endless sandplain as well as the sea. She trudged and trudged. The blunderbuss-carrying men had long disappeared from the streets, and no one was there to stop her from going anywhere.

She went straight to the seaside. She had never dreamed that the closer she approached the sandplain, the more desolate and even ugly it would appear. Everything had been ruined in the space of a little over a decade. The tides had pushed the filth and brine up the beach for more than a dozen kilometres. What the ebbing tides left behind was only an expanse of rust-coloured water.

It was on that day, while standing on the endless, desolate sand that she thought of her father and came to appreciate a startling fact: her father had been a very handsome young man who had left town without looking back and began wandering on the sandplain ever since. His move was prompted solely by his entangled feelings of boundless despair and hope. Planting a few kisses on his daughter's forehead and looking at the distant horizon, he said: "I'll follow your grandfather's example. I'll leave town like him and become a man of the sandplain. I want my daughter's father to belong here as well someday."

Coming back from the sandplain that day, Mei Di began to prepare for moving out of town. Having been engaged in the gold mining business, Tang Tong was no longer in the mood to put a tight lid on the town like a tin can. Armed men disappeared altogether from Stone Street for almost the whole day.

Eventually, Tang Tong learned about the thatched hut that Mei Di had built in the wilderness. He drove to it along the river. Then he had to trudge the remaining five or six kilometres on foot as the place was inaccessible to vehicles. He was astonished to see the thatched hut, and he felt as awful as when he had first learned of Mei Di's pregnancy. He plodded for some time over the uneven ground and the twining tropical kudzu vines, panting hard, his curly hair tangled with blades of grass and beads of sweat, and his face covered in perspiration.

Mei Di ignored him.

Tang Tong walked a few steps around the thatched hut and, having peeped at the child fast asleep, said jeeringly: "I know you two are too ashamed to stay in town. But freezing winter claims one or two lives each year here. In spring, you can be buried alive after a sandstorm. Do you want to risk your daughter's life in order to wait for that adulterous man?"

Mei Di remained silent, busying herself with what she had been doing.

Tang Tong lit a cigar and began to puff furiously.

"You think this lousy place is not owned by anyone? It does have an owner, from a small village in the south. One word from me, and they could drive you out of here. Besides, that bastard you're waiting for, we can still catch him. His case isn't closed yet. I'm warning you – as soon as he shows up, I'll have his head chopped off! Mmm, that's what I'm going to do. Don't cry."

Tang Tong paced around the thatched hut for a while and did not leave before he had deliberately urinated on its shady side.

Mei Di knew that this tract of wasteland was under the jurisdiction of the seaside village fifteen kilometres away. The head of the village had tried to dissuade her from settling down here. He had said: "Good Heavens! You, a woman with a child, are going to live here? To reclaim the wasteland? You're crazy!"

While Mei Di could not sufficiently articulate her reasons, she entreated him and expressed her determination to open up the land and settle down here to the bewilderment of the village head. He finally gave in, simply because no one else would have claimed the wasteland, and her terrifying tenacity persuaded him to grant consent to her request.

Laden with the bitterest brine, this wasteland might be a killer of corn, but it was favourable for the growth of cowpeas and sweet potatoes. She tested it and found it also hospitable for false indigo bush. For a time, she worked ferociously on cultivating the land, growing bushes and digging furrows to divert puddles of water from the land. To cope with the horrible wintry weather, she found some helping hands from the small village to reinforce the little hut and build a big fire pit inside. Luckily, fuel was never in short supply, which was the biggest solace to her. As long as it was sunny, she would go out in search of firewood. Before winter arrived, she had already stacked dry branches and hay all around the thatched hut. They were helpful in her fight against the bitter cold. She also had an assortment of medicinal herbs and Chinese patent drugs ready for dealing with the most worrisome thing: her daughter's health. It was, however, strange that she and her Little Beibei had been extremely well from day one. Colds or fever were rare, too.

What a terrible winter! It was unavoidable. Despite the heaps of hay and firewood, snow covered everything. Mei Di wished that spring would come soon, but when it finally arrived it was still frighteningly cold on the seaside, by which time every bit of fuel was exhausted, and the remaining hay was frozen in ice. The long winter was still reluctant to retreat. Her greatest concern was to make sure that her daughter would not freeze to death during the cold nights. She had heard that, so long as a child's chest was still warm, she would be alright. Therefore, before going to bed, she would pull out the cotton from her padded shoes and coat and bind it around her chest and back.

On one wintry night, a whirlwind sprang up and had increased in velocity many times by midnight, howling like wolves. She cuddled her daughter tight in her bosom, fearing that the little thatched hut was about to topple over in the wind. Sure enough, a large piece of the thatch peeled off and the window came crashing to the floor at the same time. Immediately afterwards, a beam fell only a foot away from her. A petrified Little Beibei burst into tears. Mei Di scooped her up, bundled her up in a quilt and fled the imminently collapsing house. That night, she crouched by the thatched hut and blocked the wind with her body while cuddling her daughter tight. By dawn, the wind had died down. The hut had not completely crumbled though half of it had been blown away. Holding her daughter, she forced herself into the house through the debris, and the first thing she did was look for the small straw raincoat. Good Heavens! It was still there! She pressed it close against her cheek…

Coping with numerous winters like this would make anyone fearless. The roar of the sea became deeper and sounded more powerful in winter, giving the impression that it could engulf everything at any moment. Many a time, even this shelter shivered with fear like a human being. On wintry nights of this nature, the bitter cold would drive all bandits and monsters away so that they would leave the mother and daughter alone on the wasteland.

The period after the inclement weather was one of recuperation and imagination. Sitting on the warm *kang* and holding her daughter in her arms, she was missing Liao Mai and expecting spring to arrive.

Spring did finally arrive. As it progressed, flowers bloomed and larks began to soar in the sky again. Larks never seemed to feel fatigued.

Little Beibei was still bundled up, looking clumsy and yet lovely as she wobbled around on the wasteland. "My little fledgling. Wait there. I'll dress you up like a little hedgehog, like your mum when she was small."

Little Beibei ran around and wallowed in the clean sand, as playfully as a boy. While Beibei was entertaining herself, Mei Di set to the task of pleating a straw raincoat for her with the long blades of satintail grass she had picked.

Little Beibei liked the satintail raincoat so much that she wanted to wear it day and night. "Sweetheart, you can't wear it all the time," Mei Di said. "Others might call you the child of a hedgehog spirit!"

"I a hedgehog."

"Little hedgehog, you're missing your dad, aren't you?"

"I missin' dada…missin' mama…. I a hedgehog."

THIRTEEN

A CASTLE SHIP LAUNCHED TO SEA

LIKE MANY OTHERS IN TOWN, Tang Tong also began to enshrine and worship the Buddha. He built an elaborate family hall for worshipping the Buddha and connected it to his bedroom with a dimly lit corridor. Entering the hall via the corridor, one would be dazzled by the brilliant lights and the glistening radiance of the golden Buddha statue. As soon as he stepped into the hall of worship, he would assume a serious expression. Even his heart would start beating more heavily. After offering incense, he combed his curly hair repeatedly before casting a side glance at the Buddha statue. He then began pacing in the hall, first quickly, then slowly while murmuring: "You didn't answer my last prayer. If I weren't devoted to you, who else could be in this world? I know you may find it hard to grant what I pray for and you don't have the heart to do it. But sometimes, things aren't so difficult to accomplish after all."

Later, he moved the bust of his father Tang Laotuo to a shrine next to the statue of the Buddha, claiming that it was more convenient to offer incense to both of them at the same time. In fact, he meant for his father to keep an eye on the Buddha or, at least, to monitor Him in the dark. After many prayers went unanswered, Tang Tong resorted to a fox spirit whenever he had a bad day. In two instances, the fox spirit's prophesies came true. These experiences taught him to shop around where worshipping was concerned, avoiding the risk of putting all his eggs in one basket. In the end, he also moved the effigy of the fox spirit into the prayer hall.

A geomancer happened to enter his prayer hall and blanched with fear. He admonished Tang Tong in a hushed voice: "How can you do this? You're mixing together the three worlds of gods, ghosts and immortals! You're taking a big risk. You're more audacious than anyone I know."

Tang Tong moved Laotuo's bust elsewhere and set up a separate hall for the fox spirit. You've been really silly, he admonished himself. Praying is a private matter. How can you put them together? From then on, he prayed separately, making a different request of each one. He prayed to the Buddha in cases of grand events, to the fox spirit in cases of rare problems that defied easy solutions and to Laotuo when it came to the most secret plans and schemes.

He stared at his father's bust, finding his eyes sharper than they were in real life and his pressed lips revealing unshakeable self-confidence. In the middle of the night, he seemed to hear again the old man shouting in the underworld: "Kill him!"

"I hear you. Your son Tong is always decisive. Following the success of the gold mine, I've built the Large Rampart Compound of Purple Smoke as a joint venture with foreigners. I'm currently planning to build a second and a third. After taking over the family business, I must expand it. We're going to surpass Lord Huo during his heyday. Sometimes, I try to do things like he used to do. One day, I pulled up a clump of grass and tried to chew it, but I puked immediately. With its strange flavour, it's only suitable for rabbits. I wanted to be intimate with some wild creatures, but I can't bear their fishy smell. Besides, it's not easy to bang them when they're always kicking, bucking, staring and snarling. Their body hair and bristling whiskers make things worse.

"Anyway, we simply can't beat the Huo family yet in some areas. I know you're still preoccupied with them. You were always vigilant against them and worked hard to go after the Huo descendants. And you're right, the Huo family built a castle ship. Lord Huo fled on it while faking his death and was accompanied by a group of pretty girls. He was really a treacherous and crafty moneybag. He launched the ship onto the sea and sailed with the wind. He took all his valuables and the best-looking girls after he learned that his good days were numbered in Jiwo. A few decades after Lord Huo's departure, his descendants may have built several more castle ships. I know this is your biggest concern. You even planned to take a boat out to sea to investigate, but you didn't have the time to do it. Don't worry. You have me, your son Tong. I've long been planning to build a castle ship. I'm going to act on it in the near future. Just wait and see!"

Sure enough, Tang Tong hired some shipbuilding technicians and artisan painters. He had them draw a blueprint before building the ship, which was to be big and beautiful.

"How big is it? What does it look like?" asked the technicians and artisan painters one after another.

"I don't care about anything else, but it must be bigger and better than Lord Huo's ship," Tang Tong replied.

His answer put them in a very difficult position because they knew neither the size nor the appearance of Lord Huo's ship. They discussed the subject again and finally gathered some illustrations of ancient castle ships. They also suggested to Tang Tong that he purchase a medium-sized passenger barge for modification. The shipbuilding project finally started.

The townspeople turned out to watch and gathered around the newly established shipyard. Day after day, they saw a golden castle rising on the deck and acclaimed with amazement. An elderly man commented: "All the richest families build their castle ships."

"What for?" a young man asked. "For sailing on the sea?"

The elderly man shook his head: "Touring is only an excuse. They're actually going to search for the elixir of life. That was exactly what Lord Huo did in those years. Ships must be built in a hurry, or it will be too late." The remark stunned its listeners, who looked at each other speechless.

A magnificent and gorgeous castle ship was moored on the river about five kilometres to the west of town. For days, all kinds of cargo were shipped along the river and loaded onto the vessel. It was said that the hall in the ship's castle was more splendid than the one on land. It was fitted with wool carpets and decorated with rows of huge porcelain vases. Its corridors were festooned with caged canaries, and even the toilets were gilded. More than a dozen of the prettiest girls aboard were dressed in *qipao* dresses with slits on the side up to their waist, in addition to heavy makeup and hair done in a bun. Whoever saw them would be dazed. There was also a Buddhist hall of prayers on the ship, with incense exuding a strong fragrance all day long. The chefs on board were first-class and capable of preparing a different variety of dishes each day comprising the delicacies of land and sea.

It was said that Tang Tong had boarded the ship a few days before it set sail. He had to do this in order to try out the lavatories, taste the food and drinks, and enjoy the view of the pretty girls. He would not go out to sea until he found everything satisfactory. Each day of delay was a testimony to the ship's unreadiness.

The townspeople had thought that it would take a couple of days for the ship to be ready. However, they had never imagined that ten days had passed, and the ship still showed no sign of moving. Cargo trucks had long stopped coming; only sedan cars came and went. Since the access roads to the shipyard were all blocked by security guards armed with electric batons, the average person had no idea what was happening on and off the vessel.

At a time like this, the last person that Tang Tong would leave behind was Old Woman Shan, who eventually boarded the ship like the others. She brought one of her narrow-faced adoptive sons with her. Her cabin was on the deck below the hall but connected to it by a staircase covered with a red carpet. The two ate and worshipped together. Sometimes, they even bathed in the same tub.

The topic they discussed the most was the real reason for going to sea, to seek immortals. At that time, Old Woman Shan spoke with Tang Tong with a sullen face, treating him as a disobedient child. Sometimes, she simply ignored him. Making a slight bow with his hands folded in front, Tang Tong entreated: "My tutor, please accept a bow from your disciple!"

At night, Old Woman Shan dragged him to the bathroom fitted with an extra-large bathtub. She filled it with water, tested its temperature and took off his clothes piece by piece. She then rubbed his chest and back with a loofah. She gently pressed with her hand his lower abdomen as plump as that of a spider, measured his hips with her handspan and kept sighing.

"Before the castle ship is launched, you must bathe and brush yourself, the cleaner the better. You must avoid eating meat and coming into contact with charming women. You can't even hold their hands. You must stay away from anything filthy. You must remember everything I'm telling you."

Old Woman Shan gave him a stare with each sentence. Tang Tong kept his eyes down, submissively allowing her to poke him while she was babbling. Meanwhile, he kept muttering: "Why the fuck do we have to go through so many damn rituals? There're too many of them!"

"We've no alternative. This is a matter of going out to sea to seek immortals for the elixir of life. Besides, if we offended the gods of the sea, there wouldn't be peace on our ship."

Tang Tong shut his eyes, secretly feeling a bit fearful. He feared that he could not resist the taboos. Once, Old Woman Shan was rubbing him in the bathtub when he brushed her hand off him and said: "Aren't you a woman of charm?"

Old Woman Shan shook her head.

A few days before the ship was launched, a stage was set up on the riverbank, and an opera show was performed for three days in a row. The place was crowded with people, and a hundred acres of farmland was rendered infertile under their trampling feet. The elderly asserted that this grand event was probably the first of its kind in a hundred years. Even Lord Huo was not able to match this. When he launched his ship, he only had a Daoist ritual performed amid the beating of gongs and drums and a show of lion and dragon lantern dances. Today, however, in addition to enjoying the opera, spectators could appreciate the view of the magnificent castle ship as well as the qipao-clad young women standing in line on the deck. The crowd commented that times had really changed, for the girls on board were prettier, taller and more shapely than those that had been on Lord Huo's ship.

"Look at them! Each has a pair of dimples. Their faces are as full as steamed buns, chests as well-rounded as hills and waists as slender as willow branches. Each looks more delicate than the other! When the ship finally set out to sea, the god of the sea will surely be tantalised to death. Maybe Tang Tong will offer them as gifts to the god of the sea."

"I think so. Today, heaven and earth are the same. You must get a rich bride ready if you want to accomplish something big. There's no arguing about it."

It was a fine day when the ship was launched. Colourful flags fluttered on the riverside. As cannon fired three times in salute, the ship slowly set sail amid an uproar of cheers and firecracker reports. Those who cheered the loudest were all from the Tiantong Group. Dressed in their uniforms and each holding a bouquet of flowers, they stood in squads and shouted rhythmically after their leader: "Happy, happy! Happy journey! Happy, happy! Happy journey!"

As the ship's horn sounded, a few spectators began to cry for no reason. As they kept rubbing their eyes, someone whispered: "Don't cry any more. This is a happy event. How can you cry?"

"I don't know, but whenever there's a boisterous rally or a ceremonial event, I feel like crying. I just can't help it. It's an old habit of mine – a habit since the days of Lord Huo."

A VOYAGER'S VERSION OF JAPAN

"None of my ancestors have been to sea," Tang Tong said. "The people of Jiwo always feel queasy at the sight of the waves. Those who live by the sea only know to eat fish detritus. Very few of them have ever ventured onto the ocean on big boats. Ooh-la-la! I'm the first! Like the first child of the dragon king, I'm learning to dive and swim in the waters."

Tang Tong began to have some weird dreams long before the completion of the castle ship. The dreams were filled with indistinctly flickering scenes of mountains and jewelled palaces inhabited by immortals. He asked the oneirocritic in the backstreet to interpret them. After counting on her finger joints continuously, the old woman finally told him: "You'll make a fortune at sea."

Today, the oneirocritic looked very old, with her cheeks sagging like a turkey's wattle. Her voice sounded as if it came from the netherworld: "Sooner or later, you'll acquire a mountain inhabited by immortals. Then, you'll be a king both on land and at sea. A king! A king!"

As she spoke, the old oneirocritic shed tears, which astonished Tang Tong. Asked why, the old woman claimed that she was happy to see a respectable person before her.

That day, Tang Tong rewarded her fabulously.

While the castle ship was being built, Tang Tong hunted for sailors everywhere. Someone recommended a retired captain, saying that this man had been drifting at sea all his life and had even been to the remotest Kingdom of Java and that he had seen more of the world than any king. That someone also told Tang Tong that he would be able to work for him as a captain if he could pay him decently. Tang Tong had imagined him to be a handsome and debonair man, but he was taken aback when he saw him. He looked exactly like a big fool. He was not very old, and neither was he a captain. He was a sailor who had been fired for negligence of duty due to excessive drinking at sea. When found, he was lying inebriated on the street, his body partially exposed under his tattered clothes. Tang Tong had someone feed him a soup with sobering properties. When the man became more clear-headed, Tang Tong started a conversation with him on the topic of seafaring. They talked from two in the afternoon till exactly midnight. Once he started talking, the man was unable to stop. Finally, Tang Tong patted him on the shoulder and said: "Chatterbox, you'll be my captain."

Chatterbox talked a lot about the weird happenings he had experienced at sea.

"It's too darn boring to spend one's entire life on land. A man of real mettle and ability must venture on the high seas. The sky and the sea are the upper and lower parts of a chaos, equally large and mysterious. The sea teems with treasure, immortals and exotic plants, and in addition, and most important, there are innumerable beauties. I've seen mermaids crawling up to the islands with my own eyes on several occasions. So, they're by no means legendary. Their skin is slimier than that of fish, their bellies are white and soft, and their navels are as round as copper coins. Generally speaking, the concubines of the island kingdoms' princes are all mermaids, their musk glands emanating a scent like the fragrance of Cape jasmine. But be warned, never offend them. When they're angry, they neither cry nor wrangle, but they only shed blue tears that give off a pungent odour. As soon as a man inhales it, he'll become impotent. I may be a heavy drinker and have other bad habits, but I've never lusted after women. The women on the islands at sea, Good Heavens, are totally different from those on land. These beauties of all ages, guess what, all eat fish and shrimps as their staple food, which contributes to their libido. As for their disposition, years of seafaring has made them loose, so much so that they can take off their trousers and underwear and pee anywhere they want. See how open-minded they are! How unrestrained! How straightforward! How bold! Think about it – how can we mountain people deal with these horny women? Anyway, so long as they take a fancy to you, they won't hesitate to unbutton their tops and bare their snow-white breasts. Slapping their chests, they'll throw themselves upon you. When I was young, I was handsome and smart. I could hardly escape being 'lustfully hijacked', so to speak, by the women, be they young or middle-aged, once they happened to lay their eyes upon me. Think about it – you'll be scared out of your wits when you're being followed with the sound of their big feet pitter-pattering behind you.

"Why was I so panicky? It was because everyone had their own hobby, but womanising was just not my thing. Think about it – they may be promiscuous without ill intentions, but what about me? As soon as they put their arms around my shoulder and placed their warm lips against mine, I would immediately be turned off. It's hard for a man to restrain himself away from home. Coming from the same land as Confucius, shouldn't I be a bit more civilised? Besides, I couldn't offend people on a daily basis because I wanted to survive in the wide world. So even though I was hurt emotionally, I had to put on the air of a lecherous man. I often pretended to say things like how much I craved them and how much I lusted after them. Then the best of the best girls would throw themselves into my arms, and I had to put up with them. Busying myself with them during the day, I often wanted to cry on my hammock at night. I often prayed to the vast sea, saying, oh gods of the seven seas, please save me! Or let me run into many hot babes or turn me into an out-and-out lech. What I feared the most was to be caught between being loved and being unable to love, an ordeal more than a human being could suffer. During those days and nights at sea, I had to smear my face with soot from time to time to make myself look unattractive. Unfortunately, it didn't work because those pretty sluts were so smart that they could see through the ruse. Besides, even the blackest soot could not mask my extremely handsome features. Well, well, well, what could I do? When the situation became critical, I had to buy some liquor to knock them unconscious so that I could beat a hasty retreat."

Seeing Tang Tong gaping with awe, Chatterbox became even more garrulous.

"I don't know if Master Tang lusts after women or not. Well, I won't ask further if you don't tell me. But from your curly hair, I can tell you're a heartthrob courted by a million girls. You may not have noticed your charm. As the saying goes: 'A respectable fellow is apt to be forgetful.' Now, let's talk about me again. I can't tell how much good food I've eaten in my life, but I'm still a virgin. Look at your blinking eyes, Boss. You must be in disbelief. Unfortunately, even the best doctor can't certify it for me.

"So much for that. Let's talk about the island kingdoms. One year, I landed on a small one, smaller than Jiwo in terms of area. You may not know it, Boss, but whatever the size, so long as an island is ruled over by a king, you must get down on your knees as a subject to salute him. It's not surprising that a princess fell in love with me at first sight. But I didn't expect her to take me to the beach one moonlit night. She undressed herself and lay stark naked on the sand. Good Heavens! Let me tell you, Boss, her skin was the colour of sand and glistened shyly in the moonlight. Her big black eyes, curling up at the corners, sparkled with blue light. There was not a single blemish on her legs, belly or anywhere else on her body. Besides, she also emanated an indescribable fragrance. Aww, you're crying, boss! You're crying. You must be thinking of some sweetheart. Anyone who lives in this world has their own sweetheart. Good Heavens, the boss is crying... Let me go on. I've said I'm not lusting after women, but I had a close call this time. Barely able to resist the princess, I felt my gums numbing and my feet turning cold. I had to kowtow to her – as I was much older than she was, I shouldn't've done it – but you know, being with the best beauties, age was nothing. I've seen with my own eyes that men in their seventies and eighties stare unabashed at pretty girls, their mouths watering and then dropping to their knees. There's nothing wrong with that.

"Now, let's get down to business. I'm telling you something about the 'Three Mountains of Immortals'. You may have heard about that bloke Xu Fu, right? A man of modern times? Nah! He was of the same generation as the First Emperor of Qin. His birthplace is neither remote nor close – it's right by our seaside. The First Emperor of Qin lived in Xi'an and was always thinking of living for eternity. He had heard about the Three Mountains of Immortals in the East China Sea – the mountains of Penglai, Fangzhang and Yingzhou, all habitats of immortals. He then took the trouble of traversing far away to the east. Xu Fu told him that there was no problem in visiting the mountains and promised that he would go ahead for an inspection and, if convenient, ship the elixir of life as well as the immortals back to him. The emperor was happy and admired this otherwise hidden hero. The emperor then decreed that Xu Fu set sail on a big castle ship with all kinds of grain and all sorts of artisans, along with fifteen hundred boys and fifteen hundred girls. As a matter of fact, the Three Mountains of Immortals did exist, but Xu Fu was not a fool. You think he'd reveal the things he found himself? Boss, you're a smart man, you can figure out what really happened later. Today, well, I'll throw caution to the wind and, in the presence of a big boss, I'm not trying to hide any more. I confess that I'm a descendant of Xu Fu."

THE DESCENDANT OF XU FU

"Is Xu Fu a god?" Tang Tong asked. "Shall we erect a tablet in his likeness so we can worship him?"

Chatterbox shook his head and then nodded. "He was only a fisherman from a small coastal village. But he did something big later. He found a fairy mountain, saw the immortals and ate their elixir of life pills. Do you think he was a god or not?"

Tang Tong pondered for a long time before saying: "Then, we'll place his tablet for worship along with the fox spirit." Rubbing his nose, Chatterbox did not say yes or no.

Chatterbox was treated to good food and alcohol every day, but he was still unsatisfied. Tang Tong had only one flask of liquor served to him each time, but it was just enough to stimulate his craving for more. Then, he became smart. He would abstain from drinking for two days and then down three flasks together on the third. Tang Tong had a captain's uniform designed for him. He put it on and looked at himself in the mirror. He blanched: the cap had a badge that was as big as a man's fist, the epaulettes were decorated with three stars and tassels, and the cuffs, the collar and the rubber buttons were embellished with designs of wheat, leaves and anchors. Besides, many of the designs on his uniform were embroidered with gold and silver thread… He tried walking a few steps but nearly stumbled. "This won't do. I must try hard to get accustomed to it." After wearing the uniform for three days and nights, he began to move his arms and legs normally. He looked at himself in the mirror again and found his image to be perfect. He thought that he should have a pair of binoculars around his neck and a sword on his waist. He told Tang Tong about it, and Tang Tong thought it made sense.

Boarding the ship in his splendid uniform, Chatterbox requested that the girls in *qipao*, the chefs and everyone else salute him at all times. He declared it to be a rule of the ship. Later, when he met Tang Tong, he fixed his eyes on the latter's hand. Seeing that it showed no sign of being lifted in salute, he showed frustration.

"Hey Chatterbox, don't put on airs just yet. Tell me something more about your time at sea."

"Boss, I know a respectable person is apt to forget things. My name is a bit hard to remember, so how about calling me Xu Hou? 'Hou' means 'descendant'. I'm an offspring of Xu Fu anyway."

Tang Tong burst into a guffaw and said: "I am indeed forgetful. A grander name is easier for me to remember. So I'll call you Xu Haunches." Chatterbox drew a long face.

Before the ship set sail, Tang Tong rallied everyone on deck to address them.

"As the old saying goes: 'Everything has its vanquisher.' Aboard this ship, you must all obey your captain Xu Haunches when it comes to the steering of the vessel. And you must salute him when appropriate."

One day, Xu Haunches went to Tang Tong and said: "Everyone acts according to the rules except the old lady below. She doesn't salute me."

Tang Tong told him that she was Old Woman Shan and was different from the others. "She's supposed to kick your ass when she sees you." With that, Tang Tong gave him a good kick up the rear.

"My ancestor Xu Fu was learned in both astronomy and geography and well versed in the yin yang and five element theories, as well as the *Qimen Dunjia* divination techniques. He really screwed the First Emperor of Qin at the time. As he was growing older and older, the emperor became increasingly desperate for elixir pills of immortality. He rushed over here on his horse-drawn carriage three times, and the bumpy journeys nearly shook his bones loose. As soon as he reached the coast, he asked for the elixir pills before taking a pee. My ancestor kneaded some fishbone powder into a ball and, with a high-pitched 'Your Imperial Majesty, here's the pill', thrust it into the emperor's mouth. After munching it, the emperor cast a pleading stare. My ancestor said promptly: 'No more. Things as delicious as the pill are hard to come by. To find more of this magic stuff, we have to climb up to the Three Mountains of Immortals. Unfortunately, big killer whales block the way. We must build a ship big enough to carry archers, delicate girls, vigorous boys and plenty of good food.' The emperor was thus taken in by my ancestor. He granted him whatever he requested. When everything was ready, my ancestor steered the ship out to sea, never to return. The emperor waited by the seaside for the elixir pills month after month. Burning with impatience and not being acclimatised to the local conditions, the emperor eventually succumbed to a serious illness. He died on his way back to the capital Xi'an."

Xu Haunches could be garrulous when he took off his uniform, but he would say little once he put it on.

Tang Tong asked him with a smile: "What happened to your ancestor?"

"He became king of an island. He was ranked the same as the First Emperor, both were national-level leaders."

Hearing that, Tang Tong paced up and down in the hall, pressing his lips tight. He sometimes scratched his curly hair, sometimes took a glance at Xu Haunches.

"My ancestor had more than enough good food and wine. He was a picky eater and ate only the maws of Japanese Spanish mackerel, the eyes of sea bream, shelled oysters and eggs taken from living sea urchins. At night, he slept with girls by calling the numbers assigned to them. He had a jar of elixir pills by his side so that he could take them when he felt light-headed. He met immortals on equal terms, practising sword martial arts, playing Go and exchanging elixir pills with them. The weasel spirit was the smartest of all the immortals. With her intriguing, blackish face, she won my ancestor's favour by flirting with him. The fox spirit had a pretty face and was a heavy drinker. When intoxicated, she would unknowingly reveal her big tail, which, being a good material for a scarf, he always thought of acquiring from her squashed body. The hedgehog spirit, with a small and round body, might have a gentle personality but felt prickly when held close. The wildcat spirit was the largest of the beauties in the world. No one could resist her coquettish gaze, brief as it was. The island was covered all over with lilies and prone to strong winds imbued with a fishy odour. Anyone who stayed there long enough would become lustful. No one could help it. If you, Boss, don't believe me, try living on it for some time. I guarantee you'll be fooling around with the women there every day."

Tang Tong grinned from ear to ear and rubbed his hands together. "Xu Haunches, you're really straightforward. I picked the right person to be my captain. We can't just talk without taking action. Let's set sail and follow the route of your ancestor. There must be great scenery all the way. I won't short-change you if we succeed in finding the Three Mountains of Immortals."

That morning, an event took place that merited inclusion in the annals of Jiwo Town. With three reports of gunfire from salute cannons, the castle ship started to sail slowly. Xu Haunches had put on his uniform early and was now standing magisterially on deck. Tang Tong had just taken a pee in the toilet and was disoriented when he came out. He saluted Xu Haunches without thinking and subsequently regretted it. A few sailors hustled and bustled back and forth. The girls in *qipao* lined the deck with smiling faces. Tang Tong had been standing on the starboard side of the deck and felt extremely excited when the ship pulled out of the estuary and into the endless sea. He found Old Woman Shan, accompanied by the narrow-faced young man, and said to her: "Whenever you have time, give that guy a kick. And kick hard." When Old Woman Shan asked why, he answered: "No reason. When I stepped out of the lavatory, I got muddle-headed and somehow saluted the guy."

Old Woman Shan laughed. The narrow-faced young man looked sullen and did not say a word.

The sea was calm, and the sky was clear. Seagulls chased the castle ship for a while and flew up and down nearby. It took an age for the sight of land to disappear. Now the castle ship seemed to be suspended in the air with nothing but water around. Tang Tong was a bit nervous. He looked around and pretended to be composed, though murmuring: "Good Grief! If the wind whips up, who shall we ask for help?"

He rushed to Old Woman Shan's cabin, his face blanched. Seeing him scared, she scolded: "You're from the mountains after all. We're only just out to sea. You're scared like this and it's still broad daylight! My ex-husband Red Beard lived on the high seas for most of his life. What storms and waves didn't he experience? He was so different from you."

Tang Tong fell silent. To mask his awkwardness, he whispered a horrible dirty word to Old Woman Shan and walked away quietly.

The night was pitch-dark. Nothing was visible on the vast sea. Only the lapping sound of waves was audible. Tang Tong could not stand it any longer. He went to Xu Haunches and said: "Stop! Stop! How can we sail at night? Let's set sail again at dawn."

"That won't do," said Xu Haunches while fondling the binoculars hanging from his neck. "As the old saying goes: 'Let the rider but not the horse rest.' We can let the ship sail while you, Boss, just go to sleep as you wish."

To help himself get over the fear of the vast sea, Tang Tong asked the chefs to fix a grand banquet and had a big table set in the hall. In keeping with Western style, he also had knives and forks laid out and candles lit. He began to make frequent toasts yet he still complained that a Western-style banquet was incomplete without foreigners and a translator. "It'd be better if we had a fucking *tongzuizi* with us." Some girls stood by attending to them. Though the half-inebriated Tang Tong patted their buttocks more than once, they were still putting on their smiles of content, looking neither overbearing nor self-effacing. Their smell of cheap perfume diffused the air.

It was the smell of alcohol that wafted into the pilot house and attracted Xu Haunches to make several trips down the bridge and into the hall. Each time, Tang Tong drove him away cursing: "You son of a bitch! If you don't attend to the ship, it may run aground. If that should happen, I'll chop your head off!" But half an hour later, Xu Haunches was back again. With a winking hint from Tang Tong, Old Woman Shan went up to Xu Haunches and tried kicking his behind. One of the kicks was right on target, causing Xu to screech in pain.

Tang Tong drank until two in the morning and, as a result, he did not wake up until two in the afternoon, aroused by the hubbub on deck. Captain Xu Haunches followed a sailor, whose face was red with excitement, down to the corridor from the deck and to Tang Tong's cabin, where they knocked on the door repeatedly. Upon entering the cabin, the sailor opened a nautical chart and said to Tang Tong: "What route are we following? It's already been twenty-four hours, and we're still milling around. If we go on like this, it'll take us a year to reach the high seas."

Pointing at his forehead, Xu Haunches said: "You must salute me first."

Seeing him so obstinate, the sailor reluctantly moved his hand to the side of his headgear. Xu Haunches continued: "You've been talking out of turn. You're just a beginner who has been exposed to the sea wind for a few days while my ancestor sailed out to the ocean as far back as the Qin dynasty. We're following the route of Xu Fu – excuse my imprudence, ancestor – you think we're out to catch fish or crabs?"

As he spoke, Xu Haunches glanced at Tang Tong, who had taken over the nautical chart and was yawning repeatedly. Then he said to the sailor: "You little turtle! You must obey the captain."

During the three days and three nights of their voyage, the only land they saw was a shadowy big island with the strobe light on its lighthouse flashing. Tang Tong ordered that they make landfall. Xu Haunches raised his binoculars and said: "How can an island with a lighthouse be the Three Mountains of Immortals? Besides, it's just one island, not three, and it's so close to the mainland."

Hearing this, the sailor smirked and Tang Tong ordered: "Pah! Move on!"

After they sailed another two days, the sailor complained that the ship had come around to where they had been before and that it was not far from the mainland. In fact, it was even closer to the mainland than the big island they had seen previously.

"What the fuck do you know, you little turtle?" Tang Tong said. "If you go on messing with our voyage, I'll make you salute him all day long as a punishment." Biting his lip, the sailor spoke no more.

On the sixth day, they ran into a fishing boat, on which everyone wore shiny oilskin trousers and looked at the approaching ship in surprise. Standing on the starboard side, Xu Haunches shouted: "Who is the captain?"

"We don't have a captain on our small boat," someone on the fishing boat answered. "Spill it if you have something to say."

"Let me ask you, have you heard of the Three Mountains of Immortals, that is, three islands not far away from one another?"

The fishermen looked at each other. Then, one of them slapped his knee and said: "Do you mean Trident Island? That consists of three islands lying in a row. But we're not sure if there're mountains of immortals on them – Trident Island is not far ahead."

"See! You damn see!" Xu Haunches was beside himself with joy. He snapped his fingers at the crew on the fishing boat and rushed into his pilot house. With a series of resonant toots, the castle ship sailed forward, breaking the waves against the wind.

Tang Tong followed him into the pilot house. He attempted several times to ask for the binoculars to look into the distance. But each time Xu Haunches rejected him, saying: "This is a crucial moment. Besides, they are vital for our navigation. I'm terribly sorry."

Tang Tong regretted not having brought his own binoculars and gave up the urge to scold him when he noticed him scrutinising the nautical chart and the course.

Amid the fog, three small islands gradually came into view. Hurrahs sprang up from the deck.

At the same time, a few large fish appeared in front of the castle ship's bow. They swam and jumped with their dorsal fins knifing the surface of the water. The sight caused those on board to exclaim, and their commotion caught Xu Haunches' attention. He rushed to the bow and looked, and he suddenly turned white.

"Aren't... aren't these the killer whales that tried to block my ancestor's progress in his time?" he screamed while stepping back. "But we don't have archers among us! What shall we do?"

The others had no idea why Xu Haunches had become so agitated.

"Why don't you concentrate on steering the ship?" said Tang Tong. "What're you out here for? Go back to your pilot house!"

Pointing into the waters, Xu Haunches cried: "Killer whales! Killer whales!"

The narrow-faced young man who had been with Old Woman Shan all the time leaned over the bow and produced from his upper garment something blackish. It resembled a flechette launcher. He fired a few darts at the killer whales, but they did not appear to be affected. Instead, they continued leaping forward, drawing beautiful arcs in the air. After having their fun, the killer whales gradually vanished in the vast expanse of the sea.

Xu Haunches looked on, his face covered with beads of sweat and appearing as pale as death. Seeing the killer whales disappearing, he heaved a heavy sigh of relief and returned to the pilot house.

The three islets were close at hand. They appeared full of vigour and covered in lush vegetation. A flock of seagulls appeared again, like messengers dispatched from the three islets, circling up and down and mewing their warm welcome to the visiting castle ship.

Everyone aboard was standing on the starboard. They whispered: "Three Mountains of Immortals, Three Mountains of Immortals..."

DANCING WITH KILLER WHALES

"I don't give a damn about anything else. I just want to find this man called Xu Fu," Tang Tong mumbled as he escorted Xu Haunches onto one of the islets of Trident Island. A glittering, golden boat with a richly ornamented castle moored in the bay near the islet naturally became a sight of attraction for all the islanders. As soon as he climbed up to the peak of one of the islets, Tang Tong grabbed the binoculars from Xu Haunches and surveyed the streets and pedestrians below. He was greatly disappointed.

"Where's the sign of immortals?"

"It's said that a man of great talent never reveals his appearance," Xu Haunches answered. "Maybe we shouldn't be too hasty."

They clambered up the stone steps, gasping for breath. His uniform drenched in sweat, Xu Haunches watched in pride as an increasing number of the islanders followed him.

"Wow, he must be a high-ranking officer!"

"Look!" said another as the islanders crowded around Xu Haunches and Tang Tong. "He's got a curly-haired bodyguard with him."

Seething with anger, Tang Tong bawled Xu Haunches out,

saying: "Fuck you! Don't you have a mouth under your nose to explain things to them? Let's get on with looking for your ancestor."

Xu Haunches had to ask the followers: "Do you have someone named Xu Fu on your island?

"Never heard of such a person."

"Think hard. He must be on one of the three islets."

"High-ranking officer, may I ask when this Xu came to the island?"

Xu Haunches glanced at Tang Tong with a look of complacence and answered in a raised voice: "In the Qin dynasty."

The islanders were all taken aback and began to wag their tongues: "My God! How can he be still alive?"

"I'm afraid not. After more than a thousand years, he may have long been laid to rest."

Xu Haunches turned to Tang Tong with a disheartened look. "Well, damn it! It's impossible to deal with illiterates. As the old saying goes: 'A scholar can't argue with a solder.'"

They covered the entire first islet, wandering here and there, and found it truly beautiful. From passers-by, Tang Tong learned that the three islets used to be connected as one large island. In the past decade or so, the low-lying land gradually submerged in the seawater, and one island turned into three. Prodded by Xu Haunches, Tang Tong went to the other two islets by boat and found them more or less the same as the first one. Everywhere they went, they looked for Xu Fu as well as his descendants. All the islanders confirmed that there was not a single person by the name Xu.

"Boss, it isn't unusual when you think about it," Xu Haunches whispered to Tang Tong. "After so many years, they must've changed their family name long ago."

"Why must they?"

"Well, Boss, a smart man like you can get confused occasionally. It's only too obvious that, having fleeced so many of the First Emperor's valuables, my ancestor's descendants would become either princes or aristocrats of great wealth. The poor people would have smashed them to death if they'd revolted. So, it would be unthinkable if the descendants hadn't changed their names. It's like the case of Lord Huo in Jiwo. How many of his descendants still dare to bear his name today?"

Slapping himself on the forehead, Tang Tong realised for the first time that the babbling Xu Haunches could make a lot of sense. His thoughts then turned to Lord Huo who had taken his castle ship to sea. He immediately started asking the islanders if any of Lord Huo's descendants were living there.

"People with the surname Huo? Yes, we had an old woman whose name was Huo Er'er, but she's already dead."

"What? Doesn't she have any children still living?" asked Tang Tong.

"Yes, she has a daughter and a granddaughter. The granddaughter's name is Young Shaliu'er, a famous Fish Opera actress."

"What's Fish Opera?"

"You don't know? It's been handed down by our older generations. It's so good that when you prick up your ears to listen, you'll forget to eat."

Tang Tong snorted, nodded and looked around, picking his nose. He was thinking of meeting this descendant of the Huo family and listening to her singing the Fish Opera. It would be a cinch if he were in Jiwo because an opera could be put on any time at his holler. But he had no idea what to do on this strange island. He instructed Xu Haunches: "Go to the head of the island in a minute or two. Tell him that someone from the castle ship will pay handsomely for a block booking of a Fish Opera. The sooner, the better – tonight even!"

When it got dark, they returned to the castle ship exhausted. Tang Tong had meant to stay on the island, but none of the stone houses were good enough. Old Woman Shan had already retreated to her cabin to rest after touring the island accompanied by the narrow-faced young man. All the girls were excited after the ship moored in the bay. They spent quite some time on their makeup, and with the permission of their supervisor, took turns to land on the island. They hung about in groups, one after another, for about an hour altogether. Their appearance unsettled the town and caused the young fishermen to toss and turn at night. Up till then, they had only seen such beauties in pictures. These slightly plump young women, with their large chests and long legs, looked as if they had been cast from the same mould.

"Good Heavens, could there be a beauty-producing machine on the southern coast? Look how uniformly pretty they are! They're coming to the island with their chests thrown out and their steps thumping. What a pitiable life we islanders lead, with neither a castle ship nor shapely girls like them! Well, at least we've got our Fish Opera and the little mermaid Young Shaliu'er."

Tang Tong had a good sleep and, as usual, did not wake up until late morning. He had brunch and strolled on deck in his thick pyjamas. The surface of the sea was as calm as satin. Flocks of seagulls circled in the sky mewing in innocent, rapid staccato. A few girls leaning over the port railing wowed and screamed alternately. Tang Tong went up and made way for himself by pushing the girls aside, his hands brushing their breasts. He watched and instantly joined in the screaming.

The sight that confronted them was hard to believe. The killer whales that had faced the castle ship as it approached the island were now swimming over again. They jumped about three metres high above the water, plunging back in the path of an arc, or standing straight up on their tails on the surface of the water waving their upper bodies at the castle ship. The spectators were even more astonished to see a hirsute man emerge by the killer whales. He squirted a stream of water at the whales, grasping their dorsal fins and frolicking with them. The killer whales appeared to be his playmates, kissing each other, rubbing against each other's faces and chasing each other. The hairy man's swimming ability, as good as that of the whales, was the most remarkable thing of all. He could swim with the whales under the water for more than ten minutes without coming up for air. The people standing high above on the castle ship witnessed every scene.

The sight dazed Tang Tong so much that he did not realise that his trousers had dropped below his waist. When he was clapping, stamping and shouting to the sea, a girl who happened to lower her head spotted his exposed flesh. Blushing, she pulled his trousers up while he, unaware of what had happened, was still screaming and clapping.

That night, everyone except for a few guards left the ship for the Fish Opera show on the island. Situated on the waist of a hill, the theatre's space was limited, but by taking advantage of the topographical conditions, it still allowed everyone in the audience to watch the performance. Tang Tong sat by Old Woman Shan on the seagrass cushions laid out in the front rows, seats that the islanders had prepared especially for the honoured guests from the ship. Wearing insufficient clothes, Tang Tong covered his thighs and knees with Old Woman Shan's woollen sweater. Whenever he stretched his arms and legs, the sweater slipped off. Old Woman Shan would then put it back on him. The opera began. The exotic sound produced by the percussion and string instruments, in addition to the extraordinarily sweet and agreeable tunes and melodies, enraptured the visitors. Tang Tong gaped, raised his brows and followed with his eyes the pretty little mermaid on stage. She was dancing like a swimming fish in a mesmerising manner.

Oh, my, he exclaimed in silence. So this is Young Shaliu'er! Each place has its own talent. An unrivalled beauty. There can be no punishment for killing me by your tantalising beauty!

After the performance, Tang Tong insisted on inviting the main actors and actresses to a late-night party on the ship. Finding it hard to turn down his earnest invitation, the theatrical troupe accepted but insisted that they take off their makeup and costumes before boarding the ship.

Tang Tong would not hear of it. "Come with me now. Let's go! What's the problem eating with your makeup on? Don't waste time."

Seeing him so persistent, the performers had to go with him. Xu Haunches strutted with a swagger all the way, his white uniform being particularly eye-catching. Walking alongside him, Young Shaliu'er looked at his uniform with curiosity. Pointing at him, Tang Tong ordered: "You little turtle, go to the front to lead the way and tell the chefs to get on with it!"

The castle ship was ablaze with lights. The actors and actresses couldn't help acclaiming the luxurious decorations. Tang Tong took Young Shaliu'er away from the crowd and gave her a detailed tour of the ship, especially his grand suite with the spacious bathroom and big tub. He even sat on the ivory-yellow toilet as a demonstration. In the guest hall, he pulled a lily stalk from a vase and presented it to her with both hands, saying: "Madam, thank you so much for your performance." As he spoke, his eyes swelled with tears.

Young Shaliu'er found the boss to be as peculiar as he was polite. She sat down warily, unsmiling. Holding his breath, Tang Tong leered at her in the unusually bright light. He uttered a faintly discernible comment: "How true the old saying: 'Seeing is believing.' Lord Huo's descendant is really unique – the slim waist, the dainty features and the face painted like a Chinese pearleaf crabapple. Mwah, how much I want to kiss her..."

"Boss, what're you murmuring?"

"Me? What am I mur-muring?" Tang Tong replied, mimicking the high-pitch voice of the Fish Opera and improvising the gesture of a swimming fish. Young Shaliu'er broke into laughter.

The party, complete with sumptuous food and drink, did not end until midnight.

The next afternoon, Tang Tong felt a sense of loss and seemed to be in a trance. A girl served him a sobering soup, but his hands shook so violently that he spilled some onto her chest. Old Woman Shan came over, tweaked his mouth and ran her hand over his curly hair. He calmed down a few minutes later but still mumbled: "What a great actress, a dainty beauty! Our Tiantong Group can afford to hire her at a decent salary. What a waste of talent to leave her here on the island."

Old Woman Shan nodded. "Money can buy anything. I'll send for her so you can have a talk with her."

Young Shaliu'er was invited to the ship again. To Tang Tong's surprise, she looked more gorgeous and charming without her makeup. His eyes remained wet from the moment he first saw her. He found himself a bit tongue-tied and stuttering. It was only through great effort that he finally made his intentions understood that he would hire her at a high salary. Young Shaliu'er had been listening attentively, showing a faint sign of amazement but no intention to speak.

While he was talking, a commotion came from the deck and increased in volume. Tang Tong was angry. Striding up to the corridor, he yelled: "Who's talking so loudly outside the hall?"

Xu Haunches came wearing his combination cap sideways and placing his hands on his hips. He was followed by two sailors who held tight in their hands a man covered with brown hair all over. Tang Tong was taken aback. The hairy man had sharply bright, round eyes and a protruding lower lip that made him look as if he were ready to chew. His feet were thin and long, as well as webbed.

"You, you creature!"

He had just uttered a few words when the hairy man screamed:

"Give me back my niece, you motherfucker! If you lay a finger on her, I'll give you a good kick in the balls!"

Hearing the hubbub, Young Shaliu'er ran out calling "Maoha!". She told Tang Tong that he was her uncle. Tang Tong was stunned. When they let go of Maoha, Xu Haunches recognised him as the guy who had been playing with the killer whales that afternoon. He took two quick steps back, hissing audibly.

Old Woman Shan, who had been sleeping a while, was startled awake. She was also drawn to the deck by the hustle and bustle. She had just moved a few steps towards the hubbub when Maoha caught sight of her and immediately screamed: "Mother! My mother! My mother has come here, too..."

Maoha threw himself upon her. In dodging him, Old Woman Shan lost her balance and plunked herself down on the deck. Crouching on one knee, Maoha reached out to help her up. Old Woman Shan, however, gritted her teeth with a pallid countenance.

"Mother! My biological mother! I recognised you when I first saw you at the estuary. Mother Huo told me about her dream repeatedly. When she was dying, she asked me to look for you outside the island. My biological mother!"

Old Woman Shan shook his arm off and stood up, saying: "You've got the wrong person."

"Yes, yes! Mother Huo asked me to look for you at the estuary. She had told me about Red Beard again and again. She remembered everything before her death. Mother, please accept me!"

Maoha cried heartbreakingly, with tears streaming down his cheeks. Everyone was astounded, not knowing what was going on.

Ignoring the eyes of astonishment, Old Woman Shan turned to the narrow-faced adoptive son and winked him a signal. "Son, get this fool out!"

Narrow Face went up to Maoha.

Turning his head, Maoha saw Narrow Face and instantly cried unintelligibly. Pulling himself up, he grabbed the edge of the starboard rail. Narrow Face inched a step further with his eyes fixed on the guy.

After searching for Old Woman Shan one last time, Maoha leaned back, lifted his legs and plunged himself into the sea.

MASTER OF AN ISLAND

After several setbacks, the Tiantong Group finally purchased Trident Island. Now it was clear how ridiculous and comical the first voyage of the castle ship had been. Following the route of the Qin dynasty alchemist Xu Fu, the ship had milled around several times at sea while Trident Island was actually situated only an hour's sailing from the mainland. Besides, there was a small wharf just five kilometres to the east of the estuary. From there, one could cross the strait aboard a passing cargo-passenger ship. Although strongly suspicious of the island's identification as the island of immortals that Xu Fu had discovered, Tang Tong made the best of the misidentification and bought it anyway. He planned to turn it into a tourist spot and market it in a big way by sensationalising the legend of Xu Fu. He had many of the crags and rocks on the island inscribed with the text: "Xu Fu searching for immortals". He also had Xu Fu statues placed in some of the caves, alcoves and stone caverns. He even had a stele erected by the sweet potato cellar, otherwise known as the 'water dungeon' where Huo Er'er had suffered so much. Only that he repackaged it and reinterpreted it by inscribing on the stele to read: "In search of elixir pills, Xu Fu practised asceticism in the seclusion of this cave for a decade before his eventual attainment of supreme enlightenment, hence the name 'Place of Xu Fu's Enlightenment'."

For a time, Tang Tong had wanted to take away the captain's uniform from Xu Haunches but later gave up the idea. He saw him as intriguingly fatuous and regarded his fabricated 'ancestor' story as equally interesting. "Damn! The lousiest people in the world have the most wonderful ideas. This guy, for example, conjured up a Three Mountains of Immortals in a flash!"

Tang Tong spent a whole year working on the Trident Island project, to which he devoted most of his energy besides the gold mine and the Large Rampart Compound of Purple Smoke.

The Tiantong Group printed a great number of brochures with colourful images to depict a fascinating prospect for the islanders. They said it would become an 'Oriental Hawaii plus Venice' and 'The First Maritime Amusement Park in Asia'. It would welcome guests from every part of the world, and eventually the wealthiest bosses with the biggest bellies would keep going there. Life on the island would be more interesting and enriching. If they wanted to, the islanders could go out to fish occasionally or just lounge around in the park. Everyone has the opportunity to secure a decent job. Those with good looks could work as servers, while those less easy on the eye could become uniformed gardeners. The Fish Opera troupe was the most important part of the project. From now on, it will act locally and think globally. It will visit various places and represent the Tiantong Group to enthral all kinds of audiences with the opera's tunes and melodies. Amusement arcades with various gaming devices like pachinko and fruit machines will be constructed on the island. The arcades will need to be staffed by a lot of young men and women. Some of you young men and women think you will have no chance to use your talents and looks, don't you? Now, here is your opportunity! In this great age, men can be as relentless as they can; women can be as horny as they wish. As long as you have an outstanding talent, we at Tiantong Group will guarantee you a place to demonstrate it. Real gold doesn't fear being tempered in fire, and, for that matter, a fake anvil fears a hammer. Those young men who have brawny arms and eyes that shine with fire and who are eager to steal or rob, hurry and join the Tiantong Group's public security team. Those young women who wear heavy makeup and revealing clothing, have one tuft of their hair dyed blue and another red, and loiter in the streets with their shoulders exposed even on cold days, hurry and come to work in our hotel massage salons or fitness centres, which are in dire need of unusual talents and are thirsty for geniuses. The more, the better…

The three islets were all re-planned and rebuilt, with the original alleys and streets either combined or rearranged to highlight the carefully constructed entertainment and amusement zones. The original suggestion to relocate all the islanders from the islets was instantly rejected by Tang Tong.

"No matter how wonderfully built the islets are, they can't be deprived of their own people. Without them, who would fish, grow vegetables, build houses, dig ditches and do all the other difficult jobs? Who can survive without the people? People are the real masters of the island. Whoever forgets this must be a fool who has grown up drinking head-muddling water!"

Trident Island used to have a leader, referred to as 'director'. Tang Tong disliked him very much. He therefore meant to give him the sole duty of rallying the islanders to work. Each of the three rebuilt islets would then be placed under the administration of an employee from his Tiantong Group. He had seen films about the Qing dynasty's navy that referred to a captain as *guandai*, similar to a battalion commander. He preferred the title name and wanted to confer it to the 'director'. One day, he mentioned this plan to Xu Haunches, but Xu was not convinced.

"The title *guandai* doesn't sound good on this island of immortals."

Xu Haunches remained sober despite having just drunk a flask of liquor. "Damn!" said a grinning Tang Tong. "We'll never succeed if we act upon the advice given by muddle-headed people like you. I figured it out long before. Tell me all the good ideas you have."

Xu Haunches took another sip of the liquor and, illustrating his point with his open hand, said: "To my mind, the leader of the island had better be called 'island master'. I've heard that all the islands in the seven seas, be they large or small, each has a master, only that they're wild creatures instead of men."

"Is that true?" Tang Tong asked with alarm. "Tell me more."

"I've heard that island masters included a rabbit, a Siberian weasel and a quail. It depends on the size of the island and what wild creatures are in the majority. An island master is the supreme leader as well as king. Islanders treat them as protectors of their islands. Everyone at sea knows that, upon landing on an island, one must first pay a formal visit to its master."

"I believe it. How can't I believe it? But how can we find wild creatures today? With the world turned upside down, I'm afraid all of them must have fled in fear."

"Those who have been scared away will return for sure," said Xu Haunches.

"Fuck! We're hard pressed for time. Besides, they're lurking in the dark, and I can't communicate with them in their language. Where can I find an interpreter that knows their language?"

"No, no, you're wrong," said Xu Haunches shaking his hand. "Island masters have all been incarnated in the mundane world. They speak through the mouths of human beings. Boss, you may as well appoint a human island master, and probably the spirit of a wild creature will be incarnated into her body someday. But such a person should not be frighteningly ferocious, which would scare away wild creatures. Think about it. Aren't all incarnates of the wild creatures on the hills and plains female? They find it easy to get things done with their pretty faces..."

"You're perfectly right!" Tang Tong said, slapping his knee.

In order to search for the masters of the three islets, Tang Tong's castle ship was moored at the Bay of Trident Island for many days. Accompanying him on this trip was Old Woman Shan with her narrow-faced adoptive son once more. A group of girls were also shipped to the island to work in its hotels. This time, only two guards were left on board to watch over the ship, all the others being allowed to stay in the amusement park. As if by magic, the three islets had been transformed overnight beyond the recognition of the islanders. As they remembered it, the changes had been marked by the appearance of a man in the early summer of that year. He was dressed in a white uniform embellished with gold threads and fringed shoulder boards. Old customs had greatly changed, and the population had significantly increased. The first heliport was under construction. It was said that the island would have the honour of being visited by the president of a country, a special envoy from the Pope, a high-ranking official from the United Nations and the most famous football player in the world. The number of unfamiliar girls wearing clothes that reveal the navel was on the rise. Then came girls who exposed half their buttocks, to the astonishment of the aboriginal islanders. One afternoon, two fishermen were sitting on a rock platform smoking, when they caught sight of a woman walking by swinging her hips and ostentatiously showing much of her bottom. The two fishermen dropped their pipes onto the path of the stone steps under their feet.

The selection of islet masters went smoothly; three beautiful and graceful girls were chosen. Two of them were from outside the island. The local one was none other than Young Shaliu'er, the famed lead actress of the Fish Opera. It might have been great news to her, but her mother Yuyu was cautious. "Don't become a master even if they threaten to kill you." Young Shaliu'er shook her head.

At the inauguration ceremony, the newly selected masters were dressed up, and each wore a garland around their neck. They were invited to sit stiff on the platform so that people would pay homage to them, offering incense and kowtowing. Tang Tong's staff repeatedly asked Young Shaliu'er to come up and sit with other masters but was rejected each time. As Maoha was always nearby, these people did not have the guts to pester her further.

Consequently, only two young women sat on the platform when the rite of worshipping the island masters started. Tang Tong felt a bit disappointed, but the ceremony had to go on. He led all the employees of the amusement park to the front of the platform, where they burned incense, bowed and finally dropped to their knees, followed by all the attendees. Someone was chanting a prayer with rhythmic cadence. Since it was the first time the two young women had experienced such a grand occasion, they sat on the platform trembling all over. Xu Haunches perceived their uneasiness and whispered to Tang Tong: "Boss, they're freaking out. Maybe the spirit of a wild creature is about to possess them."

Maoha and Young Shaliu'er stood among the spectators. Maoha's hands shivered when he spotted Old Woman Shan kneeling in the crowd. For a moment, he forgot to protect Young Shaliu'er. He elbowed his way little by little towards the front. When he was only three to four metres away from Old Woman Shan, he was still unaware of the narrow-faced young man who was only a step away from her. Having been following him with his cold eyes all the time, Narrow Face now stood up, a hand in his pocket. Maoha saw him too late. He scurried away through the crowd, with Narrow Face hot on his heels.

Narrow Face chased Maoha straight to the seaside without any of the ceremony attendees noticing.

Panting noisily, Maoha hopped and leapt and stumbled several times on the soft, sandy beach, thereby getting himself covered with sand. Jeez! This guy wants to kill me. Sure, he will, Maoha said to himself as he scampered with all his might.

Narrow Face aimed his flechette launcher at Maoha and fired off three darts. Maoha dropped to the ground, but in an instant, he sprang up. In the sun, blood was seen oozing from his side and upper arm.

Narrow Face stopped to aim again.

Maoha narrowly escaped the darts by jumping and somersaulting. Thank goodness, he was finally reaching the water's edge. Screaming desperately and panting heavily, he threw himself into the sea.

Casting away his flechette launcher, Narrow Face lost no time in following him into the sea.

Maoha swam towards the deep-water zone, feeling excruciating pain in the arm once he started paddling. He had to use his legs and the other hand to propel himself forward. Holding his breath, he dived to the bottom, where he laid low behind a large clump of seagrass.

Narrow Face rose to the surface to breathe from time to time and dived back into the water to search for Maoha. He found a mat of thick seagrass waving like wheat stalks. He was about to explore further when he saw a large fin wagging among the seagrass. When the dark mass turned around, it revealed a broad chest covered with brown hair. It was Maoha!

Before Narrow Face had time to feel horrified, a big hand had already caught his neck. It was so powerful that he could not resist it. Like a snake with its backbone broken, Narrow Face wriggled awhile and hung his head down motionless.

Lying face down by the seagrass, Maoha watched for a few minutes and saw the guy's limp body start to float up. He took a closer look and caught sight of the eyes on his narrow face. They were extremely frightening. Maoha worried that it would scare the islanders if, one day, tidal waves should wash this guy's body up to shore. He pondered a while before he tied a bundle of seagrass around his neck and pulled it tight.

He did not leave until he tested the seagrass to make sure that it was sturdy and secure.

FOURTEEN

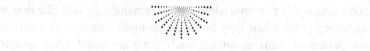

SHREWS

FOR DAYS, Liao Mai had been feeling a throbbing pain in his jaw and hands. The veins on the back of his hands bulged like the roots of an old tree and felt firm to the touch. He kept sighing and said to Mei Di: "I'm as sick as a nag with Potomac horse fever. I know what's happening to me. Medicine won't help. Bloodletting might be the only answer."

Staring at her man who had not shaved for several days, Mei Di found his eyes reddened, his lips peeling and his breathing heavy. She urged him to drink a medicinal soup she had decocted with sweet flag and cogon grass and scraped his neck and temples with the back of a comb.

"It's no use because my blood flows too fast and hot," said Liao Mai. "You don't have to bother."

Mei Di directed her large bright eyes at the man through the dim light of the night and stuttered: "I know… you… you've changed since that Rabbit stayed in… in our home for the night."

Liao Mai spoke no more. He wanted to hug her, but he reached his arm so abruptly that she uttered a cry sounding like an exclamation.

During the night, the large *kang* felt as if it were lined with glowing charcoal. Liao Mai found it hard to go to sleep, so he suggested that they leave the house to spend the night in the Jerusalem artichoke grove by the lake. Mei Di complied with a sigh of resignation. Before stepping out, she picked up a sheet, which Liao Mai grabbed and tossed back. Some of the fish in the lake were jumping out of the water while a few other creatures were releasing bubbles. Liao Mai knew that, as long as Mei Di was nearby, those filthy, unsightly fish would rise to the surface to gaze at her with their small, bulging eyes. Liao Mai wondered if they could sense her body odour. It's true that some women emanate a smell like that of distiller's grain when they get a bit plumper. Some guys who are inexperienced drinkers would easily get intoxicated when getting near the women. As for Mei Di? She was herself pretty much like those women nowadays.

Stars lit up the night sky, like the previous night. The wind was saturated with moisture, and the temperature was as cool as autumn. The fresh scent of flowering narrowleaf cattails evoked the urge to plunge into the water stark naked.

Liao Mai said to himself: Mei Di, you may have forgotten the days of our nervous and timid rendezvous in the wild, with our hearts thumping. How passionate we were in that tryst! We lay on rows of freshly cut sunroot stalks and soon forgot everything around us. Tonight, the sunroot flowers are blooming again.

By the lake, some sunroot stalks cut down by the workers a day before appeared like rafts. Liao Mai leapt onto them and pulled Mei Di down at the same time.

"How dirty and prickly the stalks are!" screamed Mei Di. "They're making my back bleed."

Liao Mai snorted but he still said in a soft voice: "You've forgotten what we've gone through. You've become a rich lady! You were afraid of nothing back then."

It was dawn. When the sun rose to the height of the treetops, he woke up. Liao Mai had slept well for most of the night, but Mei Di did not sleep at all. The sunroot stalks had made her itchy all over. She began to sit up from the moment the sun appeared above the horizon. She gazed into the distance, where several men and women wearing sunhats were doing something. They had been showing up outside the perimeter fence around the same time for each of the past few days. Merely moving around the farm, they had never ventured into it. Liao Mai was aware that they were hired by the

Tiantong Group. Everywhere they surveyed must have been incorporated into the damned Tiantong Group. All dressed in jeans, the men and women carried tripods on their shoulders and equipment and rolls of blueprints on their backs. Each of the women had a large chest, a pair of bulging eyes and a mouthful of yellow teeth. They often peeped into the farm over the fence.

"You may look, but if you dare to sneak onto my farm and trample my crops, I'll break your toothpick legs," mumbled Liao Mai, staring into their eyes. More and more, he realised that it was these people who had caused his physical discomfort.

Around mid-afternoon, a female team leader somehow came into the house with Mei Di hand in hand. Both were beaming. Upon seeing Liao Mai, Mei Di said: "We've become friends. We're friends now. I'm inviting her home for tea."

The woman nodded politely and introduced herself. She then said something to the effect of it being an honour to meet Liao Mai, who immediately paid attention to her features and facial expression. This woman in her mid-forties had high cheekbones, a mouth with thin lips and sharp corners, and a head with a flat top as if its other half had been chopped off. Her occipital bone seemed to be absent. There were some fine hairs above her top lip and a few that stuck out like animal whiskers. As she chatted, Liao Mai likened her to a shrew.

"I'm an old acquaintance of many people here. I was also a leader in those years, in charge of one of the gold-prospecting teams. How young I was. That was how I came to know Boss Tang. Great changes have taken place in recent times. This place has developed enormously." She looked at Liao Mai while taking the tea from Mei Di.

Liao Mai moved his eyes down as soon as they fell upon the woman's prominent chest, only to settle on her thin legs. She was actually quite bony except for her breasts, but it was hard to tell whether they were real or fake. No one would be surprised to see her stand up and reveal a long, slender tail.

"The shrew is a wild rodent that has a long lifespan. It's a kind of mammal," said Liao Mai, sounding as if he were talking to Mei Di or simply repeating something from a textbook. "They're covered with long, sparse hair and often reside in moist, shady places, particularly sewers. They come out either by day or at night depending on the season and the availability of food. It has a gland in the centre of its body that gives off a foul-smelling, yellowish-white slime. Ordinary cats can't deal with them. That's what it says in a zoological book."

Upon hearing Liao Mai's remark, the woman smiled at Mei Di and then turned to him. "See how interesting your husband is! We – he and I – must have a lot to talk about."

After a while, Mei Di went to get something, leaving the woman to talk alone with Liao Mai.

The few whisker-like hairs on her upper lip quivered, and she started to sound rather outspoken: "We've been surveying for a new industrial park. Your farm is within its boundary. You're going to have to move after the new crops are harvested. Boss Tang is a really big entrepreneur and has achieved so much in such a short time. If I had not seen his business growing with my own eyes, I would never have believed it."

"Really? You're an old acquaintance?"

She nodded but changed the subject: "You'll get handsome compensation. The boss won't short-change you."

"He treats everyone fairly. He must've treated you the same way." Liao Mai slammed the cup that he had in his hand on the coffee table. The woman was taken aback and her eyes moistened, but she soon broke into a smile, revealing her purple gums.

"No," she said, slightly pressing her lips. "When he's happy, he'll do anything for you. But when he gets angry, all hell will break loose. When rogues drive him crazy, he ceases being prudent. Take relocation to make room for the industrial park, for example. Some residents cling to their homes obstinately and lie on the ground in protest. In the end, they have to drink a forfeit after refusing a toast, so to speak. They'll come a cropper sooner or later. It's said that some people try to secretly incite protests, not knowing what consequences they're likely to suffer. They inevitably end up being taken away in bondage – I've seen such things with my own eyes. In a village to the south, I encountered a situation where some people lay on the ground refusing to get up when a forklift rolled over..."

The woman took a sip of the tea, stuck out her yellowish tongue and glanced at Liao Mai beside her.

"That's terrible," said Liao Mai, staring at the floor.

"Yes, but they couldn't blame anyone else. They deserved what they got."

Liao Mai shook his head and looked into her sharp-cornered eyes. "When I was talking about shrews, I was referring to some women I know. Though no longer young, they're still as cheap as rodents. They only think of how to covet a little favour from people of power and influence. They can do anything, even sleep with them because it's the easiest thing to do. As they get older, they don't have much to offer and become anxious, regretting being born in the wrong time. After so much has happened, they finally see a new era when poverty, not prostitution, is laughed at. Looking into the mirror, they find their youthful colour already faded. The more they look, the more they see themselves resembling shrews that have shed their hair and are covered with filth."

The woman tried to sip her tea but her lips shivered violently. She tugged at the bottom of her blouse, a move that only served to reveal more of her prominent breasts. "How interesting. What a humorous analogy. I enjoy listening to you speaking."

"Really?'

"Yes."

Liao Mai slowly rolled a cone-shaped cigarette and lit it. As the smoke drifted in front of his face, he squinted at her, flashing a cold smile. The woman looked up at him with her mouth half open, trying to return the smile but in vain. He bent over a little, glanced around slyly and beckoned her closer. She nudged towards him, and he whispered in her ear: "Hey, in fact those women can still find ways to make big bucks, don't you think?"

"Me? I don't know..." The woman's face looked ghastly, and the whiskers quivered.

"All roads lead to Rome. There're many ways to contribute to Boss Tang, such as taking care of his businesses, acting as a bulldozer to intimidate people, or anything else."

"You mean..."

"If you're in a hurry and can't wait, then you can be more audacious. I have an old saying for you: 'You can't catch a wolf without giving up your child.' You can't be shy and bashful. You give me the impression that you're pretty straightforward, so let me be frank. If you hang around here long enough, you'll discover that every place has its niche to make a fortune. It's not hard to make money here. Because of the gold mine, we have many wealthy people who're very generous. Unlike Tang Tong, they don't have his lousy habit of being picky. You may want to try them out. You can't put all your eggs in his basket."

As she listened, the woman widened her eyes, and the cup slipped from her relaxed grip and dropped to the floor. She stamped her feet and looked around in a hurry, pressing a hand over her chest.

Just then, Mei Di returned and asked what was going on. As soon as she saw Mei Di, the woman shouted, pointing at Liao Mai: "Your man, he was insulting me! Just now, he was insulting me! How can an educated person…"

Mei Di was at a loss. Looking at Liao Mai, she asked: "What did you do?"

Concentrating on smoking the roll-up, Liao Mai did not respond.

The woman went on complaining tearfully to Mei Di: "I really didn't expect that he should treat me as a slut! He doesn't know how to respect women. All of us who've come here are experts, well educated…"

Puffing out a cloud of smoke, Liao Mai said in a booming voice: "You can say what you want, but you can't speak on behalf of all women. You're in no position to do so."

"What in the world is going on?" Mei Di asked again as she stepped to the side of her man.

Liao Mai cast the cigarette butt, one of his hands trembling slightly. He patted Mei Di on the back and said: "Nothing. She's right. She's an expert. She's got a good degree. She's been a diehard assistant to Tang Tong all these years."

Mei Di said nothing, feeling somewhat wronged. Shifting her eyes from Liao Mai to the woman, she was at a loss what to do.

"Have you ever seen a shrew, a mammal that emanates a foul slime?"

Liao Mai was still smirking. This time, he directed the question to Mei Di, but she ignored him.

UNDER THE STARLIGHT

"You must admit, Maizi, you were quite out of line," said Mei Di, referring to what had happened earlier in the day. She looked sullen the whole night. "Besides, she'll definitely tell Tang Tong about what went on between you two, and she'll exaggerate."

Liao Mai remained silent for a while before he said with a sigh: "It's better to let her have her way. But I was too impulsive, I shouldn't've said those angry words. But nothing I could say would help anyway. You know I've been feeling depressed over the past few days, so much so that I really wanted to grab a hammer and smash their tripods."

"Well, well," said Mei Di, who could say nothing more due to her sadness and despair.

Liao Mai went out of the house and leaned against a Chinese parasol tree. He was not aware of Mei Di when she went up to him. The stars today looked particularly bright, and somehow much closer. The moon had not risen in the cloudless, purplish-blue sky. The aroma of cooked clams wafted over from the work sheds. Big Tiger Head shook the chains that secured it to the fence. Crickets were chirping.

"I shouldn't've been so bitter and sarcastic, especially to a woman." Liao Mai turned to look at Mei Di, cracking his knuckles. Reaching out her hand, Mei Di asked him to return to the house. He shook his head. "You go to bed. I want to take a walk."

Mei Di lingered awhile and returned to the house after watching him walk away.

Liao Mai walked north along the L-shaped lake all the way to the garage. He leaned against the warm wall for a few minutes and headed west towards the row of poplars. Rustling in the wind, their leaves seemed to be whispering to one another or greeting him affectionately. He pressed his face against the trunk of a poplar tree to feel its intangible pulse. He had always believed that, like people, these trees also had blood circulating through them and were now in their verdant prime. He remembered clearly how it had looked here two decades before: a row of saplings the thickness of a thumb waving in the chilly spring breeze, each with a few small, punctured leaves hanging from them. Mei Di had planted them earlier in the day. He had straightened the roots and firmed the soil around them during the night.

What a wonderful woman, he said to himself. She had thought of planting trees as soon as she settled down in this wilderness. Without her action, there wouldn't be so many trees to cover this much of the farm and provide welcome shade. There wouldn't be such a row of youthful brothers to keep me company, either. He regarded the poplars as male and the cherry plum and papaya trees in the south as female.

The gravel road by the lake was sturdy and clean. The grass along the embankment that provided protection waved with the rippling lake, allowing the water to rinse the grass gently day and night. The fields by the lake were crisscrossed with straight ridges and narrow paths and interspersed with either trellises twined with tendrils or fences covered with bean plants. Permeating the moist air was the fresh scent of the crops and the sweet smell of the soil. A quail chick emerged from under the tendrils, only to catch sight of him. It threw out its breast and walked back, carefree and content.

Tonight, the soil was as warm as Mei Di's skin. Liao Mai couldn't resist taking off his shoes and walking barefoot. What a tract of fields! There was hardly a single clod of earth larger than an apricot kernel. Neither were there any dead patches that couldn't be covered by a bamboo hat. He had caressed and patted every inch of land here countless times, and Mei Di had even more physical contact with it. All the small creatures, including crickets, beetles and earthworms, had watched their every move over and over again and exchanged their breaths with the two of them. Therefore, they were familiar with their voices, be they joyous or sad, and able to detect from a distance the odours released by their sweat glands.

The moon had just risen. He had been walking for a long time and now sat down exhausted. Soon, he went to sleep against a giant taro plant.

His breaths were soon connected with the scent of the green fields. In the green mist, a naked old woman smeared with dirt emerged, taking her children with her in this God-given moonlit night. They were sweating all over, their long hair, dyed emerald by the plants, draped over their shoulders. Like their mother, the children were also stark naked. Crouching down by Liao Mai, the old woman looked at him, unbuttoned his shirt and closed his terrified eyes. Gesticulating at her children, she said: "See this man? He's the man and brother in your life. Come and say farewell to him. His days are numbered."

The girls, with bright eyes and white teeth, exuded a mint-like smell that caused Liao Mai to flare his nostrils. They crouched down, looked at each other and murmured: "Is this our man or brother?" If he were a man, they would kiss him wholeheartedly, but if he were a brother, they could only hug him and comb his hair stuck with bits of grass.

The old woman said: "I've already said, he's both your man and brother, and he's going to leave this world."

They took his clothes off piece by piece while the moon illuminated the soft hair on his body and stained his slightly parted lips with the scent of grass. Shyness swelled in the two young women like water from the lake, and they shut their eyes. They tore off his underwear and twittered like birds. They measured his height and chest with their handspans, running their hands over each of his ribs. Overcome with ecstasy, they planted kisses on him. Then they started counting his scars and came up with a number close to fifty. They came to realise that scars were the growth rings of a man's life. They remarked on his handsome features: the up-curving brows, the prominent brow ridges, the deep-set eyes, the lengthy eyelashes, the brawny arms, the massive chest, the smooth abdomen and the round navel filled with moonlight as if it were white wine. Everything was lovely enough to move them to tears. His long legs reminded them of a galloping stallion in open country, and his flowing hair like its mane. His body smelled of Chinese mugwort mixed with a field of wheat on a July afternoon. One of them started sobbing, before kissing every part of his body. Their long hair soaked with tears swept back and forth over his torso, causing him to tremble in his slumber on the soft soil.

While the young women enjoyed embracing him, the old woman looked towards the distant open country, to which she directed these words: "Soon, you won't see him any more. He's about to be exiled to the wilderness. You'll see him staggering at first, then shrinking into a black dot, and then vanishing altogether. He'll leave alone, without taking his family. He'll be an empty-handed stranger in a new land. From this day on, he'll become a great foolish beggar, with the earth as his mattress and the sky as his bed sheet. In and out of this world naked, he has nothing to worry about."

In a state of lethargy, Liao Mai felt his body heaving and drifting with the cadence of the indistinct prattle. Later, he was awakened by the cold. He opened his eyes under the giant taro plant and found he was alone but was startled by the presence of a chilly slime all over his body. He could not tell if it was the sap of the cereal crops, or dewdrops of the night or the saliva of a woman who had dipped her hand into her mouth before running it over his body.

He sensed someone staring at his naked body, the gaze of some faintly discernible eyes peeping out of the foliage. He wiped the slime off his chest and stomach. When he tried to wipe his face, he found it covered with a juice that slid along both sides of his nose down to his neck of throbbing veins and seeped into the soil beneath him. He had become immersed too deep in his dream.

Just then, he heard footsteps. It was Mei Di out looking for him. "Liao Mai. Oh Liao Mai. Where are you?"

The gentle calls and footsteps got closer and then disappeared. Unwilling to respond, he lay there motionless. He then squatted up, surveying the drought-cracked fields and ridges revealed by the moonlight. He thrust his hand into a crack and dug out a bunch of tender tuber roots. Milk-like sap seeped out from one that he broke, and he immediately put the root to his mouth and started sucking. Oh, how sweet the wild honey of the land! He sucked the sap from two handfuls of taro roots. He rose, wiping the slimy sap from his mouth and licking his lips. The wind from the sea washed over his chest neither hurriedly nor languidly. He felt something like a syrupy alcohol circulating his body, warming his limbs and enlivening his whole self. He could hear his heart thumping vigorously and steadily.

The starlit vault was rotating. He gazed at it and found the stars extraordinarily brilliant. He felt that tonight's starlight was somehow familiar – a heartfelt feeling suddenly overwhelmed him. He tried hard to remember and finally recalled that it was the starlight he had seen in his childhood.

He recalled an early autumn night. Yes, the starlight of that night was etched in his heart, and the mark would be indelible for the rest of his life.

To this day, he could still remember every second of the moment of sorrow and despair. That early autumn, he had just lost his father and become an orphan. He did not know how to continue living and where his future lay. At that time, he could clearly hear his father's last words and the old miner's cry of "Kick-and-kick! Kick-and-kick!" Right up until midnight, he was still wandering the streets of Jiwo, balling his fists so tight that the joints began to hurt. Behind him was the sound of clanking blunderbusses and the shouting and yelling of pedestrians on Stone Street. Instead of halting his steps, he roved on and on, his eyes gazing into the emptiness, until he walked out of town.

He arrived at some open ground to the north of the cliff. By the time he stopped at the edge of the forest, he had exhausted his tears. He raised his head to look at the sky, only to be amazed to find it filled with dazzlingly brilliant stars. At that moment, he seemed to be pinned to the ground. Closing his eyes, he sensed something magic – something like liquid or lightning – pouring all the way from the stars down to him, from the quivering hair on his head to his ankles and beginning to circulate in his entire body. At that moment, he heard a voice from his inner self telling him: Hang on there. Hang on there from now on. Fear nothing. Despise everything. From today on, from tonight on, go straight forward, and you'll be surprised by what's in store. Something's waiting for you. What on earth is it? You'll know when you approach it. Your life is not your own. You'll be astonished by what you'll become.

That was how he genuinely felt, and he remembered every detail of that feeling.

That starlight left such a deep impression on him that, from then on, he became clear-minded, decisive and inconceivably strong. Nothing was imagined out of thin air because that night was as distinct as yesterday. He would later vow that that night had been true and nothing but true.

But thirty years had elapsed in a flash. At some point, when he was alone, Liao Mai would recollect that starlit night, that shocking moment…

When he looked back later as a man with a tremendous breadth of experience, he came to realise that only one word could encapsulate what he had learned that night: spirituality. What had been puzzling him was that, up to this day, except for a dauntless and unswerving sense of love, everything else was insignificant, so much so that he thought he was not worthy of enjoying that moment of starlight. Fortunately, he had never suffered from a feeling of inferiority. Instead, he had often told himself that there was a great path ahead, and he prodded himself to move on and on.

At this moment, he stood looking up. He gazed at the night sky while combing his dew-soaked hair with his hand. He gazed so hard that his eyes felt hot. "Tonight, I'll ponder many issues here, all by myself. I'll think it through from the beginning and think without taking a single misstep."

As he was telling himself what to do, he scrunched his fists so tight that they became sore without him being aware of it.

A FLASH OF LIGHTNING

Qi Jin sent Liao Mai a message saying that their former classmates had toured Trident Island more than once during the previous summer and autumn – to watch the magic Fish Opera and definitely to be lured by him, the collector of the opera's repertoires. Qi Jin told him to wait and see, saying that they had been in different parts of the country for too long and were missing him, and all wanted to come and see him, a 'successful farm owner'. Liao Mai passed Qi Jin's remarks on to Mei Di, which made her very happy.

"Let them come," she said. "We'll be sure to take good care of them. I won't let my really fine man down."

Liao Mai said to himself: Of course! Once they see you, they're certain not to be disappointed.

Sure enough, about two weeks after receiving the message, the former classmates began to stream to the farm in twos and threes. On entering the farm, they pushed their bamboo hats to the back of their heads and exclaimed: "Damn! This is the best private farm I've ever seen. You're awesome! Where's the boss? Come out to receive your guest clients!"

Reunited after a long separation, the old classmates got into an emotional conversation before they started drinking. Having drunk to excess, some began to sob, others became quieter, and a bearded guy kept ogling Mei Di and then whispered to Liao Mai: "She's a matchless beauty!"

After the classmates left, only the bearded man remained on the farm. Liao Mai remembered that this guy had been quiet in college and too timid to raise his head whenever he met a woman. Today, he was an employee with a government department at the provincial level. Liao Mai had not expected his personality to have changed so much over the years. The bearded man said that it was his lifetime hobby to look at pretty women.

"When I speak of a large beauty, she must be big and tall. When we watched the Fish Opera on Trident Island, I found the widely popular Young Shaliu'er really beautiful. Unfortunately, she's a bit too short," said the bearded man while raising his head to leer at Mei Di.

Mei Di was perfectly content. Like a conqueror, she walked about the room happily.

At night, the bearded man stayed with Liao Mai. He kept sniffing as if he had caught a cold. He sniffed while he muttered. Liao Mai wished he would put his hands over his mouth.

"Do you know, your friends have been talking about you all these years," the bearded man said. "No one understood why you suddenly returned to your native place to become a farmer. I can see you made exactly the right choice. When you have a gorgeous beauty, you must keep a close eye on her. We'd rather give up gold and silver than a gorgeous beauty. You must be close to her wherever she is. Brother, it can't be easy because it may be a lifetime job. But you've got no alternative. This is your fate. Aren't you tired? Of course! But amid all the hardships, we must strive to enjoy ourselves." With that, he slapped his thigh and burst into a guffaw. Liao Mai saw a badger in this guy's face. His eyes, in particular, bore a striking resemblance.

The bearded man was finally ready to leave. Before his departure, he posed for many photos with Mei Di. In each, he grinned in the same manner. Mei Di could not conceal her excitement, staring at Liao Mai all the while during the photography. "I'll travel to the island every year in future, and each time I'll stop by here," said the bearded man.

Before parting from Liao Mai, he turned around to gaze at Mei Di, then suddenly tugged Liao Mai's hand and said: "Brother, I'm good at observing people. I must tell you this – my sister-in-law is not an ordinary person. Look at her expression, her eyes, her nose and her gait! Whoever sees her won't forget her. She's evidently blessed. Take good care of her. Never feed her a morsel of lousy food."

After he left, Liao Mai said to Mei Di: "Thank God that lech's finally gone."

"He's the funniest of all your classmates."

Liao Mai laughed. He had the same feeling when they said goodbye to each other. He had not considered the bearded guy as evil but just a little naive and unsophisticated. And too blatant! While telling Liao Mai about his observation, the bearded man was unaware that he had repeatedly touched a man's sore spot. Liao Mai felt truly hurt. The pain slowly fermented in him from the love and infatuation that he had accumulated in his heart for so many years. It was a flower, a cup of wild honey that he was keeping so carefully and gingerly in a world that was heading towards obscenity. But now, he often looked with horror at the back of his wife enshrouded in the nightly darkness.

At some time, or a time that he did not know when, Liao Mai began to feel overwhelmed by a feeling of loss and anxiety, which hurt him badly. Whenever it happened, he would bury his face in Mei Di's long hair. The feeling would go away in just three or four minutes.

Liao Mai's expression was rather odd. When Mei Di stared at him, he clasped her shoulders and buried his face in her hair. After a while, he raised his head, shook it and snorted: "Well, I remember, it's been two weeks since Little Beibei last returned home."

Mei Di knitted her brows and broke into a smile, saying: "This Little Fawn's Hooves! Little Fawn's Hooves has forgotten us."

Not long after the bearded man's departure, autumn in its true sense arrived. It was a busy time of year. The entire farm got down to business, getting everything ready for the new season. The workers put the farm machines in order, cleaned up the work sheds and made room for new hires. Liao Mai had been busying himself in the garage, his hands smeared in grease and oil. Little Beibei had been called back home for the last few nights. What she loved to do best was handing tools to her father while talking with him affectedly, opening her mouth wide like a spoiled child. This was her special way of attaching herself to her father.

"I'm going to have another raise," she said. "My salary will soon be doubled. So I'd like to get a new car. I've saved a lot of money."

Liao Mai's muffled voice came from under the tractor: "Your mum won't let you. Your current car is good enough."

"Mum said if I buy one, I should buy the best."

"My daughter ought to be the best, not necessarily the car."

One cloudy afternoon, Mei Di walked over from the east gate of the farm and hurried over to Liao Mai.

"Another guest has come, a female," she said. "She told the workers she was your classmate."

"It's entirely possible. Maybe she's one of those travelling to Trident Island," said Liao Mai. He took off his gloves caked in greasy dirt as he stepped from behind the back of a vehicle.

The first thing that Liao Mai spotted was the white scarf fluttering from the guest's neck, which stood out against the twilit sky. His heart skipped a beat. He paused, trying to identify her through squinted eyes. The slender figure sauntered like a swan in flight.

"Oh my, it's her! It's Xiu." He felt blood rushing straight to his head and immediately turned to look at Mei Di and found her eyes fixed on the woman walking up from a near distance.

"This is her, Xiu, our poet…"

Liao Mai introduced her to his wife as Xiu held each of them by the hand. Xiu's dark eyes had never blazed like this before. Although these eyes settled for longer on Mei Di, they felt more scorching on Liao Mai's forehead. Xiu smiled, her white teeth leaving a deep impression on Mei Di. Meanwhile, Liao Mai scanned Xiu from head to toe and found her to be plumper than he expected. Her childlike waist was a bit thicker but would still appear slender to strangers.

Sure enough, Xiu had come via Trident Island. "When I heard the bearded guy mention your farm on the phone, I decided to come for a visit while I can still walk. It is indeed wonderful – a picturesque farm and man, as well as a gorgeous sister-in-law." With that, she held Mei Di's hand, her face as enthusiastic as summer.

"Of all Liao Mai's classmates, you look the youngest!" Mei Di said. "The bearded guy who's just left is so funny and casual in his manners. We're so glad to see you here."

Liao Mai discovered that Xiu had changed somewhat. She was less talkative, and her eyes had become pensive and affectionate. Placing the feline tip of her tongue against her upper gum, she looked at everything in the farm with pleasant surprise. She waved at the swimming fish and, cupping a hand over her eyes, watched a magpie landing in front of her. Liao Mai noticed that the colour of her lips had changed to light pink, her chest had become a bit round and her belly a little puffy. Flat shoes appeared to reduce her stature, but generally, she appeared more good-natured and measured.

What a change from the person who used to be so garrulous and so ardent! Mei Di stayed with her for a little while before going to make dinner. When he was left alone with Xiu, she remained silent for a long time, only darting her eyes from him to the thick clouds above. Drifting from the sea, the clouds were unusually low, and the uppermost layer was even darker. The breeze was starting to become chilly. Usually, as the wind increased in velocity, rain would fall. Xiu walked ahead on the ridge trying to balance herself so that her foot would not trample the young shoots below. When they turned to the back of the sweet potato trellises, Xiu suddenly grabbed him in her arms. He was motionless at first, then he struggled a little but to no avail.

Like before, Xiu's mouth had a sweet taste like that of the black locust blossom. Tears seeped from her closed eyelids. She sniffed at his neck and hair, searching for the familiar cigarette smell that was embedded in her memory. When her hand touched his chest, he took a step back. Xiu then thrust her hands into the pockets of her coarse-cloth jacket, trembling gently as if she were afraid of the cold.

"It's outrageous of me to chase you here to your farm. I didn't think I would have the courage to greet her. But when I arrived, I found it wasn't so hard."

"Good Heavens! I never imagined. As soon as I saw the white scarf, my mind went blank. Later…"

"Later what?"

"I found you so pretty standing there, just like a European herring gull."

Xiu stepped up to hold his hands and pressed them against her chest, saying: "You've just created poetry. Unfortunately, you couldn't think of it at the time. I could tell you were somewhat nervous and thought of me as reckless. Yes, I was, but I couldn't help it. This is my first and last visit here, my farm owner!"

"The way you described me is so jarring to my ears."

"But it sounds better than 'landlord'. 'Farm owner' is a Western concept, but, in fact, we call him a 'landlord' here anyway."

Liao Mai looked up and around painfully, but the trellises of sweet potato blocked his view. Instead, he directed his eyes up to the cloudy sky. He then thought of something and asked: "Why 'the last time'? This is all too much. Besides… forget it. We'll talk about it another time."

She guided his hands in a circular motion over her chest and then placed his finger in her mouth, tears streaming down her cheeks and dripping onto the back of his hand. Led by her, his hand went into her blouse and immediately touched the blossoming chest, which felt as smooth as the feathers of a young chick. That smoothness, and the smoothness of the skin all over her body, was etched in his mind.

He repeated a secret whisper: "I try hard to forget you. I've tried ten thousand times to forget you, and I've tried the same number of times to denounce myself. But I can't, maybe because I'm a hypocrite. Now, it proves again how desirous I am."

His hands continued to run over her chest and her back. As he attempted to reach further down, Xiu stopped him. Liao Mai gasped and heard thunder rumbling in the distance.

"I bet it won't rain in the first half of the night," said Mei Di at dinner. When Xiu asked why, she answered: "Because the thunder is still far away. The rain is probably falling over the sea now, over Trident Island, to be precise. The Fish Opera may have to be cancelled this evening," she added with a smirk.

"It's high time we had some decent rain," said Liao Mai. "Unfortunately, we can't count on it. Both the mountains and plains are gripped by drought. The older folk are searching for the drought demon."

Blinking her big eyes, Xiu asked: "What's a drought demon?"

"It's a legendary monster, also recorded in a classic pre-Qin mythical text known as *Shan Hai Jing*. If the monster hides somewhere, disasters will occur for many consecutive years within a circumference of fifty kilometres of that place." Liao Mai explained the tale with great effort but still worried that she might not understand it.

"What will you do after you find the drought demon?"

"After we find it, we'll beat it to death, and the years of drought will come to an end."

"Drought demon," murmured Xiu with a look of astonishment. She stopped asking further. At dinner, no matter how much Liao Mai urged her, Xiu declined to drink any alcohol.

"You used to like drinking. Go ahead," said Liao Mai.

Xiu smiled but shook her head. Mei Di's question about the Fish Opera turned Xiu into a chatterbox again. She said that Qi Jin had done a great job over the years in collecting the opera's repertoires. This salvaging effort had in turn given impetus to the opera's revival. Today, Trident Island boasts a decent Fish Opera troupe, which is performing more and more frequently. This, of course, also has to do with the development of tourism on the island.

"The Fish Opera was previously unknown because it was staged in a small, remote island. Full of the flavour of the sea from its choreographic moves to its music for voice, the opera is considered unique, like an ancient but still novel lyric of the sea."

"Maizi, we must visit Trident Island. Despite its proximity, we've never watched a single performance of the Fish Opera. We owe it to ourselves," said Mei Di.

As they were talking about the Fish Opera, Liao Mai suddenly thought of Maoha. Tonight, he was worrying about him again. The image of this web-footed guy crying with his mouth wide open appeared vividly in his mind. He was passionately in love with Young Shaliu'er and still harbouring a hatred against the Fish Opera collector who had invited himself to the island. He did not think that this passionate love would be fruitless; a feeling and desire without rhyme or reason can seize a person whether he likes it or not. Indeed, passion and desire dominate the world, a world of despair. From the day of its birth, the world started making love, making love without much love. Liao Mai was gripped by a headache after drinking only a cup of wine.

That evening, Mei Di became rather excited. To Liao Mai's surprise, she drank one cup after another. When he tried to discourage her, she was already a little drunk. As a result, she had to go to bed early, leaving Liao Mai and the guest to clean up the table.

After dinner, Xiu insisted on going to the lake again. Liao Mai had to keep her company. The wind was getting colder, and the lake started to ripple. A row of small, bright eyes poked out of the ripples on the water's surface and startled Xiu so much that she stepped back.

"It's nothing. They always emerge as soon as they see women," said Liao Mai, who then made a threatening gesture at the lake.

"What are they?"

"Sargus, a kind of evil, adulterous fish."

Liao Mai's explanation caused Xiu to giggle. The lamplight escaping from the work sheds shone on her pretty face, her larger than normal eyes and her straight nose. Liao Mai was instantly fascinated.

Raindrops began to hit the surface of the water, as the weather hustled in from the northwest. "It's raining! It's raining!" shouted Xiu.

"It's only pretending to rain. The drought demon's still around."

He tugged her hand, but she didn't budge. Rainwater trickled from her concave forehead down to her cheeks and the corners of her mouth. Her eyes, which had never been so affectionate and kind, caressed him from head to toe. She whispered distinctly in his ear: "I'm already... carrying a child."

Liao Mai was stunned. He widened his eyes and kept them on her as she turned and walked ahead.

She had just reached the top of the small arch bridge when she announced: "Maizi, I mean, it's our child." Almost at the same time, lightning struck, embellishing the woman on the bridge with a dazzling halo.

Liao Mai fell silent for a full quarter of an hour. He walked up, took off his shirt and wrapped her in it. They leaned against each other, walked down the bridge arm in arm and arrived at a tall poplar tree.

"I can sense you're afraid. But I came just because of this, to tell you about my pregnancy. I don't think I have the right to hide it from you. In fact, I could stay in the south alone, give birth to him and nurture him to adulthood. Maizi, I'll be living by myself in future. How much I want to have a child of our own, mine and yours."

The light rain stopped abruptly. It was exceedingly quiet all around. So much so that Liao Mai could hear her clenched teeth chattering.

"Are you feeling cold?" he asked.

Xiu shook her head and held him closer. He repeatedly caressed her hair and back. She looked up at him, her mouth slightly open.

"Xiu, you're right. I've never been so scared. I'm scared by our cruelty. Call me a coward, a chicken. I am indeed afraid. Since we don't trust this world one bit, and we're going to bring a life to it... We're truly too rough, and too cruel."

Xiu's tears ran down, not to be wiped off. She pushed him away with great effort so that his back hit the trunk of the tree. "It's you who're cruel by treating your own child like this, even though he was conceived merely out of sexual desire. As for me, though, I'm feeling nothing but happiness. You'll never know what a woman thinks when she's carrying a child."

Liao Mai closed his eyes and shook his head. "I have both affection and compassion for children. Because of them, we have no way for retreat. Please don't misunderstand me. I'm not prepared at all. I mean, a man of my age is not supposed to have any illusion..."

"But you're a man. You must have courage. From the day we are born, our route of retreat has been cut off, and we must naturally move forward and forward."

Alarmed, Liao Mai stared at her face covered with a mixture of tears and rainwater. He reached out to hug her, intending to protect her from the north wind, but she struggled off. Eventually, he grabbed her and held her tight in his arms.

PROPERTY SELL-OFF

For days, Liao Mai found his daughter and Mei Di whispering to each other from time to time. Thinking that Little Beibei was soliciting her mother's support for the purchase of a new car, he said to Mei Di: "Her current car is good enough. Don't encourage her to buy a new one."

"Don't worry, I won't give her my consent."

All the surveyors around the farm had withdrawn, and the men and women wearing sunhats and sunglasses were no longer seen.

Liao Mai said: "They're the most ominous creatures coming to our beach, just like mole crickets emerging from the soil after rain."

"You're speaking more and more unpleasantly," Mei Di sighed. "This doesn't sound like your usual self."

"No matter what, that woman, or 'shrew' that you invited home, was simply disgusting." He paused before continuing: "Why did you invite such a disagreeable person home for tea in the first place? A snobbish woman will grow a moustache sooner or later. She'll grow it in no time and scare Tang Tong when he sees her. Then, she'll be of no help to him."

At moments like this, Mei Di would always knit her brows and say nothing. She never knew how to react to her husband's dry humour. She lost sleep for nights on end, which had never happened before. To her surprise, Liao Mai began to sleep better, snoring evenly. In the morning, she expressed her jealousy, but he said: "I've nothing to worry about. I can sleep peacefully because the route of retreat has already been cut off."

She stared at him, propping herself up on the *kang* with one hand. He then repeated what he had just said: "There's no route of retreat. It has been completely cut off."

"What do you mean?"

"I mean our route of retreat has been cut off."

"What 'route of retreat' is cut off?"

"Everything. There's nothing to go back to."

Mei Di was filled with tender care. While rubbing his hair, she listened to it rustling beneath her hand. He turned his head left and right for a while and moved her hand off him. He nodded and uttered a snort.

"My really fine man, you're so good at mincing words that you've finally put your wife in the dark. I can't understand what you're saying. Nor can I tell what's going on in your head."

At breakfast, Liao Mai pushed aside the omelette and milk that Mei Di had made for him and gobbled up half a steamed yam and a big chunk of steamed lotus root. As he munched, his Adam's apple bobbed, and he wiped his mouth vigorously with his hand. "These are what we've produced in our lake. They can build up our stamina. We must eat more of them."

Around midmorning, a rumbling could be heard a short distance to the south. When Liao Mai stepped out of the house, he found all the workers standing outside their work sheds peering at where the sound was coming from. He went up to the fence, where his presence excited the guard dog Big Tiger Head before it calmed down. Some distance to the south, a cloud of dust rose up, and it spread into the air with an orange halo against the sunlight. He immediately realised that the small village nearby was being relocated, and the demolition of its houses had begun. A new rampart compound of purple smoke was going to be erected, and it was closing in on the farm, or rather, pressing on towards the farm and all the way to the beach to confront the surging waves of the sea. Liao Mai focused on the dust cloud so much that he did not notice Mei Di's arrival. She asked him what the faraway cloud of dust meant.

"They're having a funeral," he replied casually.

The entire day saw no peace. As the small village in the south was under demolition, some of the itinerant great foolish beggars were heading that way. After rummaging through the village, they went straight north and towards the farm. As soon as they arrived, they leaned over the fence to have a look. Mei Di gave them some food, which they ate while grinning at her.

When Liao Mai came over, one of the beggars stared at him and asked: "Hey, when do you guys start moving?"

"Start what?"

The great foolish beggar clapped his hands and said: "Putting out your lamplight and moving out."

Restraining his anger, Liao Mai asked in a booming voice: "How will that help you?"

Another of the great foolish beggars scratched his head with one hand and hoisted a filthy bag with the other. "We can collect some rare stuff and different things," he replied. With that, he held the bag upside down and sprinkled from it an assortment of items including a roll of iron wire, a cloth strip, a bra and a badly worn brush pen.

The foolish beggars left singing and shouting. They went to the beach to collect fish and shellfish washed up by the rising tide. In a short time, the head of the small village arrived. He was an honest old man with a golden beard, and he was also an old friend of Mei Di. After greeting Liao Mai, he started up a conversation with her. He was talking all the time in a voice that altered in pitch. Sometimes, Liao Mai was able to overhear a word or two: "Tang Tong will go all out this time. It's said that he's going to build a new Large Rampart Compound of Purple Smoke as well as a Large Rampart Compound of Blue Smoke." "Mei Di, you're the shrewdest! If it were anyone else, the bulldozers would have rolled over long ago." "I know better. I can't refuse a toast to drink a forfeit. Don't you agree?" The rest of the conversation was indistinct whispers.

After the old man's departure, Mei Di looked awful. Liao Mai asked her if there was any breaking news.

"He said they were cheated. They were paid compensation of a few thousand yuan for each six acres of their land, a few ten thousand for each of their houses and a few hundred for each of their mature trees. They had to move despite the screams of their wives and the cries of their children."

"As a head of the village, what's the use of coming to you to complain instead of leading his villagers in a fight of resistance?" Liao Mai snorted. "If he had acted like Rabbit, Tang Tong couldn't have done anything to the villagers."

"Isn't Rabbit fleeing?"

"That's because there're too few people like him. There're too many shrews, foxes, jackals, field dogs and striped skunks."

Mei Di shook her head. "Forget it, Maizi. No matter what, we must get prepared."

"Yeah, get prepared for perishing together."

"No more angry words. Don't we always now hear that phrase – 'face reality'?"

"The reality is those beasts are going to build a Large Rampart Compound of Purple Smoke by the sea and on my farm of exquisite beauty and fill the place with methane day and night. Every inch of the farm here has been irrigated by our sweat and tears for the past ten, twenty, thirty years. This is the reality."

Mei Di wanted to say something, but when she saw beads of sweat breaking out on Liao Mai's forehead, she was so scared that she bit her tongue.

The rumbling sound kept drifting over. Dust from the clouds soared into the air and was swept onto the farm by the southerly wind, followed by a smell emanating from burning grass.

Little Beibei returned home at dusk. Liao Mai felt better as soon as he saw the burgundy car pulling up to the gate. Pressing his hand on his chest, he remembered that he experienced a joyful sense of rebirth and happiness when he had learned of Mei Di's pregnancy. At that time, his feeling of happiness was indescribable, and he was not afraid at all. Nor did he consider him and Mei Di as rude or reckless. But today, in the case of his relationship with Xiu, his conclusion and feelings were completely different. He now felt fear and guilt. Why was that, he asked himself, what happened? I will continue to ask these same questions, and I must answer them myself because I can't avoid the answers. The only thing I know and am absolutely certain about is that I love Xiu and I'm compassionate and care for her and the child deeply. What's more certain is that I'm not willing to give up a beautiful new life to despair – handing it over to despair from the hands of its biological father! I must admit that I wasn't so hopeless and dejected even on the perilous flight for my life two decades ago...

Then, mumbled Liao Mai to himself as he watched Little Beibei jumping out of her car, you've got one big job to do in the second half of your life, and that is to warm up your icy cold heart...

His daughter walked up to him, preoccupied with something, and her hair was flowing in the evening breeze. My lovely Little Fawn's Hooves, Liao Mai thought, but will the future match up to your perfection? He noticed that she was putting a stack of paper in her satchel as she walked. Mei Di greeted her but did not pat or hug her as usual. Little Beibei seemed to be in a hurry. Putting down the bag, she went into the bathroom.

Liao Mai said to Mei Di: "Little Fawn's Hooves is coming back home more frequently. She should've done so long ago."

Mei Di stared at him and reached her hand out to touch his hair, saying: "After dinner, let our daughter give you a haircut." Liao Mai nodded.

Over the past year or so, Little Beibei had been cutting her father's hair. He used to regard the task of having his hair cut as troublesome, but now he looked forward to it. He enjoyed the adorable motion of her tender hand squeezing and releasing the scissors and the loveable way she scrutinised his hair in the front and at the back. The first few haircuts cost him dearly because his daughter had insisted on trying a new style. He was stunned when he looked into the mirror: a tuft of the hair in the front bristled up whereas the hair at the back was so long that it covered his neck. Not only was the cut uneven, but she also left two or three shaved patches, each as big as an apricot stone.

After dinner, he put a cloth towel over his shoulders and was ready to enjoy the experience. However, Little Fawn's Hooves was no longer talkative. She concentrated on cutting and shaping his hair with extra caution. She had really grown up and behaved in a more composed manner. Beautiful, natural and graceful: these words may be clichés, but perhaps they were still the ones that best defined her.

"Look how well I've groomed Dad!" Little Beibei said to Mei Di, who was busy reading something.

Liao Mai saw Mei Di putting a stack of paper in a drawer and immediately thought of the stack that Little Beibei had placed in her satchel. He pulled the drawer open. Resigning herself to what was in store, Mei Di stood by nervously.

As Liao Mai glanced up, his eyes blazed with anger. The stack of paper was a copy of a printed list. Now it was clear to him: it was an inventory of all the buildings and trees on their farm: 458 Chinese parasol trees, 210 poplars, as well as countless cherry plums, pears, apples, grape vines... Even the ages of the plants were detailed. Good Heavens! What a job! So detailed! So meticulous! How long had it taken them to create the list? To whom had it been submitted? He looked around and dropped the stack of paper to the floor.

"Maizi! This inventory provides a justification for compensation..."

"It's the farm's obituary."

"Maizi..."

"It turns out that you were doing all this behind my back. Looks like you've got everything ready... Good Heavens!"

"Maizi, we're only getting things prepared. I haven't signed the title deed yet."

"You were preparing to sell off our farm long ago, ready to make way for those beasts. Well, such a day is around the corner. It's coming soon."

"Maizi! Maizi..."

"Whom did you submit the list to? Whom?"

"I submit... submitted it to, of course to...."

"Of course to the beast Tang Tong!" Liao Mai screamed.

"Maizi! Maizi..."

FIFTEEN

NAMED A THIRD TIME

IT WAS REMEMBERED THAT, a few years before, a guy had been dispatched by the upper-level authorities to conduct a general investigation into the names of places. He looked extremely disagreeable: protruding ears, small eyes behind a pair of glasses and nicotine-stained fingers. This unlucky man paced up and down Stone Street all day long, never without a cigarette in his mouth. Whenever he ran into an elderly person, he would accost them with the same disgusting question about the name of the town, thereby causing uneasiness among the residents; for they suddenly realised that, for generations, they had been living in an illusory town that did not go by its real name.

"Aren't we living in 'Jiwo Town'?" asked an elderly man, who, glaring at him, withheld the curse he had meant to utter: Fuck you!

While tapping his cigarette, the guy replied: "Not necessarily."

In fact, everyone in town knew that all the places here, from the hillside to the cliff, had been covered with thistles and thorns, hence the name of Jiwo, literally 'Nest of Thistles and Thorns'.

"Everything deserves a thorough investigation," the guy said. "I've been studying villages and all the residencies there for a long while. Each time, I discover that all names have different histories behind them. However, due to the high illiteracy rate, people in remote rural areas are neither scientifically informed nor civilised. Therefore, the practice of echoing what others say and incorrectly relaying erroneous messages runs rampant, leading to indisputable blunders."

The more the townspeople listened with their brows knitted, the more bewildered they became. Therefore, they simply cut him short. "There's no use you babbling on like this. Simply cut to the chase! Tell us what the heck our place is called."

Wagging his nicotine-stained fingers, the guy announced: "Qiwo Town."[1]

"What the fuck! Now, we're living in strange times! This damned old man has just wrung such a rare name from the guy!" The people around kept swearing as they commented in disbelief.

Adjusting his glasses, the guy said: "If you go out of town, climb the highest hilltop in the south, and look down from there, you'll understand at once. Surrounded by hills, there's a depression in the centre, which is crisscrossed by mounds and ditches. It looks exactly like a man's navel, from which this beautiful name derives."

When news of the name change reached Tang Tong, he burst out laughing. One employee said to him: "Boss, he's trashing us. I suggest we take his trousers off and club his backside in the street."

"We can learn something from everything," Tang Tong replied. "How can we be so imprudent?" With that, he unbuckled his waistband and inspected his belly button. Just then, a girl server came in carrying a cup of tea. She was dressed in the most contemporary fashion: navel-exposing garments. All directed their eyes at her navel and then they clapped and laughed.

With his foul mouth, Tang Tong ranted: "How depressing the name Jiwo [Nest of Thistles and Thorns] Town is! We'd better fucking change it sooner rather than later. With such a jarring name, what moneyed people would want to come to invest here, be they Japanese or Westerners? Besides, the one who gave the original name to the town must have been from the Huo family. That damned landlord did nothing but eat grass and sleep with wild creatures. It was only too natural for him to prefer the desolate 'Nest of Thistles and Thorns'! The Tang and Huo families are sworn enemies. We have to change the name."

The employees present nodded and looked at each other. One of them chimed in: "Everything must be determined by the times.

Look at those beautiful girls walking on the streets of our town or visiting our hotels – all bare their belly buttons. So, why can't our town be named Qiwo?"

Accordingly, the name was changed. However, the townspeople did not think of it as the result of the general investigation into the town's name but of Tang Tong's weighty decision. It was said that Boss Tang had held a grand banquet in honour of the guest. With such scrumptious delicacies as sea cucumber and shark's fin, the hospitality had so overwhelmed the man that he dropped his trousers and revealed his own unsightly belly button.

As if to live up to the new name, more and more people started to wear garments that revealed their navels. At first, elderly women would scoff at them, saying: "It's so ugly to bare one's body parts." But as days went by, even some grandmothers, taking the hands of their grandchildren, walked in the streets baring part of their abdomens, their navels as dark as eye pupils looking at the world uneasily.

Three or four years after the name change, many of the printed materials such as registers and account books still bore the town's former name. Before there was time to alter them all, a new name popped up: Jiwo (Chicken Coop).[2] The reason given for this second name change was that the previous change was due to a lack of understanding. It was also because Boss Tang, being preoccupied with his business, had been taken in by the swindler with nicotine-stained fingers.

Here was the origin of the new name. A tall and burly man with blue eyes toured an area of a few dozen kilometres around the town accompanied by an interpreter and then checked in at a downtown hotel. He complimented Tang Tong with a Chinese sentence he had just learned: "*Ji* [Chicken] *wo* [coop] Town sounds great!"

Before the interpreter had time to correct him, Tang Tong stopped him and went on to say: "Foreigners have seen the world, so we must do everything in accordance with what they say."

Perhaps it was from that day onwards that news of the second name change began to circulate with the justification that, situated at the foot of a hill, the tallest ridge in the south looked exactly like a golden pheasant[3] that had just landed on the ground. Facing west, this 'chicken' was ablaze with various colours against the afterglow. This was an auspicious place for the beautiful chicken to return, and it was surely only natural that a man even more successful than Lord Huo should emerge here.

The new name must have been consented by Boss Tang because it quickly replaced the older one on all the prominent gable walls in town.

"The saying 'Everything must keep up with the times' is totally correct. Look at our town. With a gold mine, it has become home to wealthy people who squander their money without questions asked. Women who want to find ways to make a fortune all come our way with the same goal. Even blonde foreign girls fear they're lagging behind and throw themselves into hotel rooms to do that kind of a job. It's only natural that our town's become a 'coop of chicks'."

"That's so true. Since ancient times, people have been looking down upon poverty instead of prostitution. Today, we have finally broadened our horizon." People discussed the new name widely in the streets and came to the consensus that, after all the changes, this time, they had eventually got it right.

The town that finally had the name it deserved was still the object of controversy both in public and in private. Some thought that it was keeping abreast of the changing times. They argued that the place used to be so poor that it was covered with thistles and thorns, and people strived to get away from it. Later, the townspeople became more civilised in terms of social customs and began to welcome new things and reveal their belly buttons. And today? Their minds are finally more open, and their conduct indeed more candid. They've learned the principle that business is business, so they simply pull their trousers further down – do they need any secret trick to do so?

One after another pointed out that the town was already buzzing with the phenomenon, as unstoppable as a storm. That being the case, they might as well turn a blind eye to what was happening. When they came together, they would share titbits of information and gossip about unusual events now perceived as normal. Aside from in the few branded hair salons and hotels, that kind of business was thriving mostly underground. Now, no matter how much effort had been made, cracking down on pornography and prostitution was a fruitless task. It's said that even an artless mason in his seventies hired a few young women from his distant extended families and opened a covert brothel in town. His business flourished by offering a high-quality but low-cost service. This kind of business was so lucrative that even the most decent women in town changed their minds where their career plans were concerned. Take one of them, for example. She was pretty, apart from a slightly crooked mouth, and she had dimples when she smiled. Smarter and more skilful than other women, she marketed herself through both direct and pyramid sales. While keeping a low profile, she sold herself as a rare commodity in secret. The men associated with her were all good at recommending her by word of mouth, saying: "Seeing is believing! You've got to hurry. Then, you'll know how great the woman is." As a result, within six months, she found herself behind the wheel of a luxury car and in the best house in town. Afterwards, she became more reticent and arrogant. All the townspeople knew that she only dealt with men of prestige. If a man with nothing but wealth went to her, she would take his money with her left hand and throw it out of the window with the right. Good Heavens! Nowadays, people had to be very particular about visiting a brothel! Those who listened kept sighing and wiping their eyes.

Perhaps inspired by what was happening in town, the only time-honoured veterinary hospital transformed itself into an 'animal paradise'. The change was caused by the retirement of the senile and old-fashioned veterinarian and his replacement by his young son, who had just returned from the provincial capital. The son decided to revitalise the business by promoting only those profitable elements. He thus changed the hospital's name and distributed flyers stating the revised scope and nature of its operation. Illustrated with colourful pictures, the flyers listed all the horrifying symptoms of various animals caused by their sexual repression, such as insanity, violence, attacks on humans, gnawing objects, severe illness, retaliation against their owners, poor appetite, and so on and so forth. The flyers also told owners to be empathetic and realise how cruel it was of them not to take their pets to a breeding station to mate unless they wanted them to produce young ones. The text read: "How mean this utilitarian practice is! In fact, when in heat, animals think of the opposite sex so much that they pass a day as if it were a year. You can imagine that, after copulation, an animal will be ecstatically happy. How romantic that will be! And how much that will reflect on you, the owner! So why not go ahead?"

When the townspeople read the flyers, they exclaimed: "Would you believe it, an animal brothel has opened!"

Tang Tong was Animal Paradise's first customer. He drove a brown dog the size of a lion to the centre in his car. After looking around the facility, he started conversing with the young owner. The young owner had a lock of his hair dyed golden and wore a ring in his ear. He snapped his fingers to call the attention of his employees after he took possession of the dog. Then a gloomy black dog was led out. It was particularly large and walked with measured steps. Wagging its tail, it kept sniffing at the brown dog. The young man with the golden lock said: "Boss, done!"

The two dogs were led to the other side of the wooden fence. Tang Tong asked about the operation of the paradise and the habits and characteristics of various animals. The young man answered each question, raving until his mouth foamed. He had taken a liking to writing prose and poetry since childhood. He had even produced a magazine in college. After finishing his studies, he began to worry about the loss of opportunity to show off his literary talent. As Tang Tong listened, the muscles in his cheeks twitched incessantly. With a slap on his knee, he said: "Leave the management of the paradise to your father. Come and work for me as a manager of my hotel."

The golden-locked young man blanched. He was dumbfounded, his mouth quivering for a long time without being able to utter a word. Finally, he muttered: "Boss, I-I am a veterinarian..."

"It doesn't matter. Maybe that's all to the good. Young man, you've unwittingly revealed a great talent. Come! Come with me! Don't be shy like a fucking girl. We are so eager to hire talents. You must be resolute."

Golden Lock hung his head down. With clenched teeth, he said in English with a Chinese accent: "Yes, sir! Yes!"

LEGEND OF A GLUTTON

The history of every place in the world is shaped by some unforgettable figures, who may not all be sages but are at least indispensable. Take a man from Jiwo (Chicken Coop) Town, for example. Due to his insatiable appetite, this man had reduced his inheritably wealthy family to one of poverty. Being reclassified as a poor peasant turned out to be a blessing in disguise because he was spared considerable subsequent hardship and misery. He looked grotesque: his head, eyes, nose and ears were all smaller than normal, but his mouth was incredibly large, with protruding lips and powerful chewing muscles. It gave any beholder the impression that he had been brought forth to this world to enjoy all the good food that it could offer.

He was born into a family that had owned dozens of plots of poor land on the hillside and a dozen or so bluestone houses. Being the only child of the family, he was pampered. His parents filled his mouth with the best food possible, no matter what the cost. While he was suckling, his parents discovered that he would cup his mother's nipples with his mouth and grapple her breasts with his little hands, bruising them all over. He bit and injured her nipples soon after he started teething. His mother had to feed him by expressing her breastmilk into a bottle. He began to eat many different foods before his weaning period. He would stuff almost anything into his mouth, including twine, a thimble, a wooden block and a pebble. He devoured what he could and spat out what he couldn't. He often swallowed repulsive objects that his parents, while screaming with fear, desperately tried to extract from his throat but to no avail. Then he would play as usual as if nothing had happened. He always excreted the object the next day. Despite this behaviour, his life was rarely endangered and he was never seen rolling on the floor with his hands pressed to his tummy. Therefore, no one was worried about his gluttony.

As he grew up, he became more and more omnivorous and had a horribly big appetite. Consequently, he was known throughout town as Glutton. While he ate a lot, he had a docile temperament. He was reserved and honest. He cared about nothing but eating. When he was twelve years old, his family found that they could not raise poultry or domestic animals because he would always steal them away to cook on a barbecue. In autumn, puffs of smoke would rise in distant fields, indicating that he was roasting something to eat. Someone said that he had seen him eating a single meal that comprised ten yams, two steamed buns, a ham, three bowls of rice wine, a large block of pickled tofu and an earthen bowl of cowpea porridge. When he was full, he would be in a good mood, his face ruddy and his disposition pleasant. However, he was incapable of doing anything on an empty stomach. On such occasions, he would search everywhere for something to eat. Once he caught sight of anything available, he would prey on it swiftly and decisively.

A year before they died, his parents had found him a wife, the daughter of a landowner behind the hill. His father-in-law had enough to afford his avarice for food. On the night of their matrimony, they filled the bridal room with delicacies that included eggs, steamed pork, fish, duck and sweet pastry, in addition to more than a dozen plates of fruit and snacks such as apples, chestnuts and walnuts. As was customary, youngsters sneaked under the windows of the bridal room in the dark of night to overhear the new couple's private conversation. To their disappointment, however, they overheard nothing but the sound of chomping and munching. The next night, the tearful bride asked that all the edible items be removed, but she had not expected that when hunger hit at midnight, her groom would start to toss and turn on and off the *kang* while screaming: "I'm going to eat you! I'm going to eat you!"

"Go ahead and cry," the bride said. "Even if you cry your head off, I won't give you a morsel. I've got an agreement with your parents."

With reddened eyes, Glutton reached his hands out, pounced on his wife and began gnawing at her. Bruised all over, she soon became breathless and too weakened to beg for mercy. Glutton held her upside down by grabbing her feet and paced up and down the room, grunting: "Your dad's a landlord. He's got all the food there is. Ask him to ransom you with three pigs, a big basket of steamed buns and two more baskets of sesame-seed cakes! If they refuse, you can't expect to have peace at night."

On a night like this, the bride could do nothing but sob silently. Finally, she whispered in his ear: "I'll do whatever you request, my destined lover. If you can, let me have a baby."

Glutton looked at her carefully in the candlelight, reached out to measure her belly with his handspan, pressed her back a few times, and said: "That's a cinch, provided you give me enough to eat. How many babies do you want?"

"The more, the better. Those with fewer children are easy targets for bullies these days. We can have as many as we like."

Spitting into his palms, Glutton said: "Damn it! We'll fill the town with kids so that they can roll on Stone Street like a flock of sheep coming down the hill."

Within a few years, Glutton exhausted all the ancestral family properties through his eating, thereby reducing the social status of his father-in-law from a landlord to a rich peasant, then to a middle-class peasant and, in another year, to a poor peasant. During the years of affluence, his wife gave birth to eight boys. Later, when times were hard, she brought forth a few others, mostly haggard due to malnutrition, and soon many of them perished. After the death of the fifth child, they still had eight in total. Lack of food turned Glutton into a man of short temper, the shortest, in fact, in town. But Tang Laotuo found good use for his temper. Before denouncing and beating bad elements such as landlords and rich peasants, Tang Laotuo would starve him beforehand so that he would bare his canine teeth, curse loudly and eagerly beat the objects of denunciation. Afterwards, Laotuo would reward him with a large plate of steamed buns and stewed bean noodles. Sometimes, Laotuo would add some meat dishes as well as a couple of shots of liquor and steamed yams or sweet potatoes with their peels cracked open. If Laotuo sent for Glutton and starved him for three days, he was certainly up for something big. That autumn, before Tang Laotuo had a few of the Huo family members put in jute sacks and cast into the river, Glutton had nearly been starved to death.

Glutton was often seen screaming half naked on Stone Street. "Give me something to eat. How can you expect a peaceful existence if I'm hungry?"

During the years when mounted bandits ran rampant, Glutton lived a life of grief intermingled with joy. Among the bandits, there were diabolic ones who killed without a care in the world. They also liked to try novel things. Wherever they were, they would ask which family had good-looking women, which households had money, and who had extrasensory perception or psychokinetic powers. Each of the bandits had a different personality; some loved wealth and women, some preferred alcohol and others liked to scream. Once, a band of mounted bandits arrived on the scene. Its chieftain stood on a crag and yelled at a crowd for twenty-four hours continuously. Then, an associate chieftain harangued after him until the audience was exhausted. The townspeople nicknamed bandits who issued a tirade with hands on their hips 'big-mouthed bandits' or 'long-haired chatterboxes'. One rainy day, another gang of 'long-haired chatterboxes' came after another had left. They sent for Glutton when they learned about him.

It turned out that the chieftain of the gang wanted to challenge him in an eating contest.

The bandit chieftain was beaten in the contest by this man of special ability. It was said that the chieftain was a bear incarnate. He had a long nose and was heavily built and moved awkwardly. He also had the peculiar habit of being able to fast for several days after a big meal. All in all, the man did resemble a bear. As soon as he met Glutton, he had two plates of pork served, one for each. The plate of pork given to Glutton did not have a grain of salt, which was certainly intentional. But to the chieftain's surprise, Glutton, who had not tasted any meat for a dozen days or so, was able to digest the fattiest dishes once they had been swallowed. After he munched the fatty pork dish, he grinned with pressed lips at the bandit chieftain. With a wave of the hand, the chieftain demanded two stacks of sesame-seed cakes, along with side dishes of spring onions and bean paste. Holding the pancakes in one hand and the onions in the other, Glutton chomped them quickly. In the end, he held the bowl of bean paste to his mouth and drank it up like rice porridge in one gulp. By then, the bandit chieftain had only finished half the sesame-seed cakes, and his forehead was covered with bean-sized beads of sweat. Meanwhile, the slurping and swallowing Glutton asked the chieftain's bodyguard: "Do you have any fruit dessert?"

After losing the eating contest, the bandit chieftain challenged him to a fast. They were locked up for three days running in separate prison cells, and each was served only a bowl of water each day. On the second morning, Glutton began to scream with anger. A few bandit guards clubbed him on the ankle to quieten him. On the third day, he was so hungry that he lay face down on the *kang* and ate all the padded cotton that he had torn out from the bed covers. On the fourth day, when he found nothing left to eat, he noticed a clock ticking on a wall. He took it down, dissembled it quickly and broke even the face and hands into coin-sized pieces. He then washed each piece down with a sip of water. He ate up all the pieces in less than half a day. On the fifth day, he was generally calm, lying quiet on his back on the *kang*. On the sixth day, the bandit chief next door went out of the cell, and then Glutton was let out as well. The two glared at each other. The bandit chief surveyed his rival from head to toe and hated him for not crawling out. Glutton, on the other hand, wanted to grab his opponent by the hair and give him a good beating. He only refrained from doing so when his eyes fell upon the short blunderbuss at his waist. Seeing Glutton walking listlessly, the bandit chieftain proclaimed: "We'll declare the contest a tie. I'll spare you this time. Get out of here!"

Glutton had walked only a few steps when a guard found the clock in the cell missing. He rushed over to search for him.

"Where's the clock? Where's the clock on the wall?"

"I ate it last night," Glutton said, sighing and blushing.

Despite being a famed omnivore, Glutton died in the years of famine, and his death was destined. The famine had previously claimed his wife and five of his children. Before he had had time to teach each a good lesson for being a good-for-nothing, they succumbed one after another. He fed the remaining three children with chewed corncobs, tree roots and hemp stalks. They were finally able to survive when the townspeople started eating clay.

One day, Tang Laotuo planned to make Glutton an example of eating clay. However, he had not expected that this guy should have been so rapacious. On smelling the aroma exuding from the oily black clay, he lost no time in kneading it into thin strips and gulping down a large basin of it. He belched incessantly before he crouched down, nonresponsive to anyone's call. He remained like this for about fifteen minutes before collapsing and writhing on the ground. In the midst of repeated calling, he rolled over on his back without any further movement. He was dead.

When he recalled the scene of Glutton's death a long time afterwards, Tang Laotuo would still reprimand him. "What can I say? Why were you in such a hurry when there was clay everywhere? What was the point of gulping it down? You were too greedy. You thought you were still young? Brother, you must know the limit of being old."

At least Glutton did not die without descendants. He left three sons. About the same age as Tang Tong, they did not have any spectacular capabilities. Two of them used to carry blunderbusses along with other youngsters. Later, they became foremen in the gold mine. The youngest had gone out of town at the age of ten to live with a distant relative of the same family name.

After a few years, a rumour came that the youngest son had been hired by a bank, doing a job that involved carrying the bank director's briefcase. His name was said to be Jin Tang. "But your family's last name isn't Jin," said Tang Tong to the other two brothers.

Nodding and shaking their heads alternately, the two brothers responded: "We hear that upper-class people all pick their names randomly. What's more important is that a name must sound resonant when it's spoken and look pretty when it's written."

Jin Tang had never returned to Jiwo since leaving, but his reputation grew with each passing day among the townspeople. They said that he now had an assistant to carry his own briefcase wherever he went and that he was protected by bearded bodyguards. Counting on his fingers, Tang Tong reckoned that forty-three years had passed since he left home, meaning that Jin Tang must now be fifty-three years of age. He asked the two brothers if their third brother was also gluttonous. "Our younger brother may not be able to match our dad," they replied, "but he can still eat twice or three times as much as ordinary folk."

Tang Tong grimaced. He spent a lot of time asking about how high Jin Tang's official rank was. "He's an official or not an official," the two brothers explained. "Maybe he's one level higher in rank than any official he sees."

Tang Tong was stunned and exclaimed: "Wow, in those years, only Lord Huo was one level higher in rank than any official he encountered. Isn't your brother a landowner in some city?"

The two brothers shook their heads. "He is and he isn't. Maybe he's the one who manages landowners."

Not knowing whether to laugh or cry, Tang Tong uttered one expletive after another. "Fuck! Fuck..."

"You dare to curse Jin Tang?" the brothers asked in astonishment.

"Nah, I'm cursing myself."

A WARM WELCOME

The two brothers' days of glory began. They left town separately to assume official posts. All the locals said: "Our Jiwo Town brings forth a respectable person every three or five decades. Now it's Jin Tang."

Tang Tong meant to say "What about me?" but did not have the guts. In secret, however, he could not help but feel jealous, saying to himself: At least Jiwo now hosts a respectable duo, doesn't it?

However, the latest news gave Tang Tong a shudder. It turned out that Jin Tang sent a paper note measuring only two fingers wide from a remote place. In response, local officials hurried in to pay their respects to his two brothers. It was said that Jin Tang planned to return to work in his native province. Like a relieved military garrison, Jin Tang's relocation would threaten to be the largest cloud hovering above Tang Tong's head.

"But what the heck is his official rank?" Tang Tong again asked one of the two brothers, a subject that was weighing heavily on his mind.

Tired of answering, however, the brother retorted: "I'll tell you once again – my brother is one level higher in rank than any official that he sees."

"How about two or three levels?"

"That's not necessary. Only one level higher is fine. When he sees a village head, he's a township head. When he sees a township head, he's a county head. When he sees a county head, he's the mayor of a metropolis..."

"When he sees a mayor?"

"Then, he'd be like the mayor's father."

"Good Heavens! You're so audacious to say that!" Tang Tong mumbled, although he was devising an important plan in silence.

It looked like Jin Tang had really 'relieved his garrison' because his two brothers suddenly became arrogant, speaking to nobody but spitting anywhere they liked. Bowing to them, Tang Tong said: "May I ask Your Excellencies to take the trouble of inviting the Great Official to pay a visit to his hometown? Please let him know how much his fellow countrymen are missing him since he left the town as a child. We miss him so much that some of us have lost sleep at night, forgotten to pee in the lavatory, and lost their appetite for food and sex. It's like that song: 'Oh, come back! Oh, come back, even if you're in the remotest corner of the globe.' He should come back to look around. Great changes have taken place here in the past four decades. Even foreigners rush over here barefoot. Many of them are women. We have built the Large Rampart Compound of Purple Smoke, and we're going to build the Large Rampart

Compound of Blue Smoke and the Large Rampart Compound of Red Smoke. Anyway, we've got everything to satisfy his needs. We've got so much money that you can squander it at will. We've enough gold to pave the roads and enough jade to tile the walls."

"Don't overdo it," the two brothers snorted.

"You're right, you're right. But the truth is, I'm very eager to invite Big Official Jin to pay a homecoming visit."

"Nonsense, what did you call him?"

"Then what, what shall I call him? It's tough. It's really hard to come up with the right name for someone who's neither an official nor a landowner."

After consulting with each other, the two brothers said: "You'd better call him 'Senior Official'."

Tang Tong entreated the two brothers from the icy winter till the blossoming spring, when they finally got him the news.

"Get prepared," they said. "Our younger brother is set for a visit. We'll let you know exactly when."

Tang Tong got down to business. He had the intersections of the main streets repaired and decorated, walls whitewashed, potholes filled in and slogans written in conspicuous places. Meanwhile, he also had the Tiantong Group's band expanded and retrained; his male and female employees, dressed in uniform, practised marching in squad formation; and all the hotels and building halls were spruced up. Finally, he went to see Old Woman Shan at the estuary, talking with her about enlisting her seven nominally adoptive sons to stay in the headquarters of the Tiantong Group in case their services were needed. Old Woman Shan reminded him that she had only six adoptive sons because the best one had died on Trident Island; he kind of died on duty. During their discussion, they thought of the Fish Opera. He was going to temporarily move the opera troupe to Jiwo from the island. The rustic tunes and melodies could be a big hit.

The only thing they found it hard to decide was whether to provide girls to accompany Jin Tang. They knew that they had to be cautious in matters like this. Girls were like that riddle about chilli peppers: 'Red pouches, green pouches. Some fear them, some love them.' They remembered a young VIP who had visited Jiwo. Tang Tong had sent the most flirtatious forewoman to take care of him during the night. As a result, the young man swooned in horror, lying stark naked. One year, a woman head in her fifties came here on inspection. She took an instant liking to a young man at the reception desk. She insisted that he play cards with her. The next morning, the young man said tearfully to his fellow employees that the bitch had bitten him... As for gifting Jin Tang with money, neither Tang Tong nor Old Woman Shan had any qualms. They both agreed that no one would turn their nose up.

When the weather became warmer, trees turned green and flowers bloomed. The lake in front of the hotel was azure blue. Girls dressed in *qipao* with slits up to the waist were bustling about. At the same time, good news came that Jin Tang was about to come back to Jiwo.

Tang Tong was impetuous, fidgeting with alternating joy and anxiety. He did not know the appearance of the man about to grace town with his presence, but he only felt that their fates would be intertwined for the rest of his life. He went to the toilet frequently, as if he were suffering from a urinary infection. In the meantime, he smashed two or three mobile phones and yelled at his employees to make sure that everything was perfectly prepared. In this highly charged and busy moment, he suddenly felt the need for a particular person and missed her very much. He tucked himself away in a hidden room and, after pondering alone in the darkness for a moment, began to beg the person on his mobile phone to join him. The person first found various pretexts for not coming and then hemmed and hawed for quite a while. His teary sighs travelled with the radio waves and, like a rising tide that just reached the coast, lapped her ears again and again. At long last, and always at the last moment, she gave in. A person of great restraint was thus defeated. Tang Tong's heart pounded vehemently. From this moment on, he huddled in this little room, waiting for his rebirth.

It was a sunny morning. Around ten o'clock, at an intersection on the boundary of Jiwo Town, twenty kilometres from the downtown area, several uniformed men got out of a car, walkie-talkies in hand. Sweating all over, they reported to Tang Tong sitting tight in his car that Jin Tang was coming. Tang Tong hopped out of the car, quickly combed his curly hair with both hands and stumbled forward, murmuring: "Hurry up! Hurry up!"

As the engine sounds got louder, a motorcade came into view at high speed. Surprisingly, it showed no sign of pulling over. "What, what's going on?" shouted Tang Tong, throwing his hands open.

A swarthy-faced, stout man nearby said sullenly: "The senior official is not getting off here. Get back to your car and lead the way."

Tang Tong suddenly realised what was happening as if he were waking from a dream. He waved his hand and got back into his car. At the same time, two police cars and a dozen motorcycles waiting on this side of the boundary started rumbling and led the motorcade forward.

Pedestrians crowded on both sides of the road. Villagers along the road came out helping the old and carrying the young. The spectators would not disperse even long after the motorcade had zoomed by. Tang Tong's car closely followed the motorcycles that rolled in advance. In the car, he kept calling people, using three mobile phones and a walkie-talkie by turns. With newly-built arches rushing backwards as the cars sped forward, the motorcade arrived in Jiwo proper. Banners with familiar slogans written in golden characters were hanging everywhere. There were also words of greeting among the slogans to the effect that the townspeople welcomed the senior official and congratulated him on his inspection visit to his hometown. The motorcade rolled through Stone Street and into the hotel zone. It had to move slowly at first and was eventually forced to drive in a stop-start fashion due to the number of people. A group of young women flanked the street, wildly waving plastic flowers while hailing loudly and jumping up and down. They soon started to sound hoarse. Tang Tong had been looking back, and now he saw three doors of a limousine opening and out from it stepping a few men. Tang Tong jumped out of his car at the same time, but he could not figure out which was Jin Tang. He felt that everyone from the limousine should appear aristocratic, totally different from the residents of Jiwo. Later, however, he spotted a skinny, haggard man among them. He was of a medium height and staggered as if he were starved. He immediately concluded that he must be a briefcase-carrying assistant. While he was still deep in thought, he caught sight of the skinny man cocking up his relatively small head with some effort and then raising one open hand to wave at the welcoming crowd. He waved as he left his limousine and walked ahead looking resolute. Meanwhile, the volume of the cheers increased. Tang Tong felt a chill running down his spine, thinking in secret: Good Heavens! That's Jin Tang! Good lenses, bad frames indeed!

When Tang Tong elbowed to the front and introduced himself, Jin Tang only nodded slightly and walked on, waving his hand. The motorcade followed slowly while a large group of armed men pushed the advancing crowd with their plastic spiked batons. After the senior official and his motorcade squeezed out of Stone Street with great effort, everyone wiped the sweat off their brows and breathed a sigh of relief. Jin Tang was the only one without a drop of sweat. A few of the escorts asked him to get into the limousine as many others did.

In the hotel zone, the scene of welcome appeared even grander. Entering the gate, the motorcade was greeted by a brass band, a squad of uniformed employees and flower-presenting girls from the Young Pioneers[4] wearing red scarves. When the girls saluted the senior official with their right hands raised above their heads, Tang Tong could not help shedding tears nearby. Jin Tang took the flowers and turned his head slightly in search of someone. When his eyes fell on Tang Tong, the latter hurried over.

"You're doing me a disservice, don't you think?" Jin Tang said in a hushed voice.

A DIVER

"I'm dying. Argh, no one is supposed to see me. I must sleep on my back with my limbs extended for three days and nights before I can get fully rested."

Tang Tong yelled and drove all those close by who were ready to report their work to him. He locked himself up in a room, cursing while pulling his tie off: "The inventor of this neck-choking junk must be a wicked son of a bitch for generations! And what is this fucking 'level higher in rank in the presence of another official'? I don't know what I've achieved by working so hard that I'm almost exhausted to death."

He had just laid down on his back when a forewoman sneaked in like a rat and said: "Boss, care for a massage?"

"Get the fuck out of here!"

"How about just a little kneading?"

Tang Tong rolled his eyes, muttered a few oaths and turned his head aside. The forewoman was a little over forty, good-looking and broad-shouldered. Tang Tong gave in to her humour from time to time. Now, with a wave of her hand, a young woman came, took off Tang Tong's shoes and socks, and started massaging his feet. Tang Tong screamed and then fell fast asleep. The forewoman and the younger woman tiptoed back out. The former, however, did not leave after they were out of the room. Instead, she stood by the door to prevent others from entering the room and disturbing him.

An hour later, someone ambled over. The forewoman was about to block her when she realised it was Old Woman Shan. She immediately broke into a smile and nodded to her. She then pointed to the inside of the room with her pouted lips and made a gesture of sleeping by holding her hands palm to palm. Old Woman Shan said: "He cares nothing but sleeping like a log. He's slept enough. I must wake him up."

He seemed to be really exhausted. Rubbing his eyes, he scrutinised Old Woman Shan as she stepped into the room. Putting on his shoes, he cursed: "What the fuck are you coming here for?" His eyes were reddened, and the corners of his mouth moistened with saliva.

Old Woman Shan lit a cigarette and said: "Now that the senior official is gone, we need to take care of our own business. Did you forget about the man you've locked up?"

"Now I remember! Yes, he's still locked up. Do you have any clues?"

Old Woman Shan puffed a cigarette from her large, dark mouth and said: "Just go and look, and you'll know. Where would you be without your tutor? If I were not around to keep an eye on things for you, your curly hair would have long been pulled out by others, and you'd now be bald."

Tang Tong nodded dully and walked out with a yawn. He was completely awake now. He remembered that the senior official had just reached the town boundary the other day, when someone alerted him to the discovery of a diver emerging from the lake in front of the hotel. Tang Tong was shocked and ordered that the diver be locked up. He was about to leave in his car when the man who had given him the alert hurried back, saying that an investigation revealed that the diver had been invited by the hotel management. As the water in an upstream lake was about to overflow and the tunnel connecting to another lake in the lower reaches was blocked, a diver was sent to investigate under the water. Tang Tong flew into a rage and yelled: "Let him investigate then."

"But the diver was locked up by Old Woman Shan's adoptive sons as soon as he emerged from the water," said the man who had alerted him to the presence of the diver. "Despite repeated and patient explanations, her malicious sons flatly refused to release him." Tang Tong fell silent when he learned that it was Old Woman Shan who had given the order.

"Boss, what on earth shall we do?" asked the man.

"Keep him locked up."

While walking out of the door with Tang Tong, Old Woman Shan tried to avoid being seen by the forewoman. She whispered to Tang Tong: "Thanks to my children's sharp eyes, they found something wrong about the man as soon as they saw him climbing out of the water dripping wet. He looked pale and kind of agitated. When he saw my sons, his hands kept shaking, and his teeth chattered though it wasn't chilly."

"Could he be an assassin targeting the senior official? He must be up to no good." Tang Tong stared blankly, feeling a tremor of panic and fear.

"That's exactly what my children thought. They escorted him somewhere, and he only clenched his teeth, trying to tell them that he was just assigned to work here. But why did his hands shake so much? When asked, the management said they had indeed sent for a man to work here. This one could be an imposter, a substitute for the real one."

"It's perfectly possible. We must keep a close eye and do a thorough investigation."

"Yes, that's exactly what we did. As soon as my sons pulled off his headgear, guess what?"

"What?"

"This man looked very much like that malicious thug Rabbit."

Tang Tong paused abruptly and shouted: "Rabbit? I'll skin him. That son of a bitch has never showed up since he scurried away. It's said that he made a stir last month. I've cast a net of informants to look for him."

"They look exactly alike. But we found them to be two different people after further interrogation."

"So it was a false alarm?"

"It's always better to err on the side of caution. My sons are meticulous. They did an investigation in light of what he had told them and found out he had nothing to do with that Rabbit. The case is closed."

"Then close it and don't make any more fuss. I've just taken a nap. I've been tired out these past few days. Instead of benefiting from the senior official's visit, I was dressed down by his two brothers. They said: 'The senior official always visits places in stealth, bringing two bodyguards at most. Look at what you did! You made such a fuss. Are you inviting trouble for my brother?' I complained that they should've told me earlier and asked if the senior official was mad at me. The two brothers told me that Jin Tang was not mad because he was never mad."

Old Woman Shan had been grinning broadly as she listened. Now she gave a sigh of relief and picked up Tang Tong's conversation. "Even though the diver had no connection with Rabbit, his uneasiness definitely betrays him. That's why my sons didn't let him go. They interrogated him in a backroom for a long time. He finally confessed."

Gazing at Old Woman Shan's heaving chest, Tang Tong found her increasingly plump figure to resemble a dugong.

Chattering her short, black teeth, Old Woman Shan went on: "Good Heavens, guess what? It turned out that when he was in the water and crawled into a few problematic pipes, he found them clogged up with a few dead bodies, all female and in our hotel uniforms. They might have been there for quite some time."

Tang Tong looked up into the distance and said: "Get the corpses out then, in the dark of night."

"You still don't understand! What do we do with the diver? He's a witness!"

"Can't we buy his silence with money?"

"I'm afraid we can't. My sons beat him and knocked out two of his teeth because he refused to confess at first. He only shouted that he was giving up the job. As he was trying to sneak away, my sons got mad and knocked another two teeth out with a couple of punches."

Tang Tong saw it was a delicate issue, rubbing his hands together helplessly. Glancing at Old Woman Shan, he said: "Average people may not be able to deal with him, but if you allow him to suckle your big breasts, I bet he'll be submissive and never dare make any trouble."

"How can you be in the mood for nonsense at such a critical moment," Old Woman Shan retorted, stomping her feet. "He's still in detention. We can neither let him go nor keep him."

"If my dad were alive, he'd have put him in a jute bag and drowned him. But times have changed. I've a better temperament and feel less inclined to kill people."

"But he has a bad temper and is still screaming."

"Aha, he's screaming," said Tang Tong. He paced up and down, pondering with knitted eyebrows, before continuing: "According to the theory of Golden Lock, the new manager of the hotel, the symptom of a very bad temper must have a name. It is 'sexual stress'. How about giving him more money and having him go to see Golden Lock with it. With this bribe, our new manager will surely cure him of his bad temper. Besides, the money can be a token of our apology for detaining him."

"What if he's not going to see him?"

"He'll have to. How can we allow him to have his own way?"

Old Woman Shan fell silent.

POSSESSED

Tang Tong spent ages reflecting on Jin Tang's return to his hometown, on the whole process and on its significance, but he still had a lot of mixed feelings. They arrived to a noisy fanfare but left in silence, leaving Jiwo with a sense of profound loss, which was extremely hard to describe. So much time and energy had been invested in crafting the arches, practising making salutations in squad formations, putting on rehearsals for the brass band and staging the Fish Operas, and everything had just begun when the senior official and his people vanished in a cloud of smoke. Tang Tong also recollected his encounter with Jin Tang. He could not remember him saying anything except the whispered reproof at the welcome ceremony and the three-word adage "Development is necessary" after his visit to the few mining enterprises. Two days after Jin Tang's departure, several leaders from Jiwo's upper-level administration came in haste. Upon their arrival, they blamed Tang Tong for not having alerted them to the senior official's visit. "So he left like that, and you didn't even give us a report?"

They had left for sure. What vexed Tang Tong was that he never got to discover Jin Tang's official rank. But from these leaders' subsequent hasty visits to town, he could tell that the guy was surely 'a level higher in rank than any official he meets'. When he was alone, Tang Tong could not help feeling amazed at the capriciousness of life and the wonders taking place under his nose. He never had the guts to mention to anyone his memory of Jin Tang's childhood, when he had been running around with snot streaming from his nose and his little cock sticking out of his open-crotch trousers. Besides, he also remembered this guy's unpleasant nickname. What a miracle! In the blink of an eye, a great man came into being in an unknown part of the world. He chanted the lyrics repeatedly: "Oh, come back! Oh, come back", until tears swelled in his eyes.

After his feeling of emptiness moderated, Tang Tong went to the two brothers again and asked them to invite Jin Tang to return to his hometown as often as possible. The two brothers said: "We will. Like anyone else, the older he is, the more homesick he becomes. While his last visit was quite a success, the one problem was that it was too pompous."

"What should I have done?"

"That's easy. He'll stay here so long as everything's done in secret. Our brother is tired after busying himself for most of his life. He really wants to recuperate here."

Tang Tong grinned from ear to ear. "Keeping secrets and revealing nothing to the outside world is our specialty. That's perfect! Ask the senior official to come quickly. We want to take good care of him, but we don't know what he likes — you know, everyone has their own hobby…"

As he spoke, Tang Tong gazed into the eyes of the two brothers, subconsciously making a money-counting gesture with his right hand.

"Pah," the brothers said, leering at him.

The Tiantong Group employed fulltime shamans for unexpected occasions. Tang Tong consulted them about Jin Tang's return to

Jiwo. "With Glutton as his biological father, it's easy to understand," they said. "Just think how much energy his father had garnered from all the things he guzzled in his life, and how wonderful the son would become after receiving all the energy from his father."

Suddenly enlightened like waking up from a dream, Tang Tong asked again: "How am I supposed to pay him due respect?"

"Wondrous people must have wondrous interests. You need to figure them out before taking any action. Don't be reckless."

Before long, Jin Tang did indeed come again. This time, Tang Tong was well prepared with meticulously conceived plans. He called the relevant staff to his office, particularly the hotel manager Golden Lock, and told them not to divulge any of the senior official's secrets and that capital punishment would be meted out without mercy to whoever should disturb his quiet repose. Golden Lock read his mind. This time, Tang Tong discovered that Jin Tang arrived dressed in casual clothes and with a much simpler entourage. Apart from a couple of stout bodyguards, he was accompanied by only a sallow-faced elderly man. This old-fashioned man was probably his steward. Dressed in dated clothes, he walked in cloth stockings wrapped in puttees, and swinging his arms while taking big strides, he looked like a Daoist priest. He spoke both pedantically and metaphysically. Leering at him from a distance, Tang Tong cursed in silence: I don't give a damn about someone like him. Let him go to hell! However, when their eyes met, Tang Tong still had to bow to him with a forced smile.

Tang Tong arranged for a grand banquet for the senior official because he had learned from his two brothers that it was his birthday today. At the banquet, Jin Tang was quiet but ate plenty. Afterwards, Tang Tong followed him into a small hall, where he beckoned over three pretty girls, who carried a small casket. When opened, it revealed a row of gold cast tiger statuettes, eight in total. Jin Tang was born in the year of the tiger. He beamed as he stared at the three girls. But when he moved his eyes down to the casket, he immediately drew a long face. In a subdued, hoarse voice, he demanded: "Chuck them!"

What he said was beyond Tang Tong's comprehension. As he looked up, he saw the elderly man walking up to him. "The senior official's unhappy," the elderly man explained. "He wants you to throw them away."

Tang Tong followed the elderly man out, the latter carrying the casket of gold tigers. Tang Tong saw him staggering out of the door, opening the boot of the car that had brought Jin Tang here and casting the casket inside with a thump. Clapping his hands, the elderly man said: "This is what he meant by 'Chuck them!'"

Tang Tong gasped with pleasant surprise. At this moment, the elderly man leaned closer to him and whispered: "Do you have the best girls? Go ahead and send a few to the senior official's room to play cards with him at night."

"Aha! That's great! I'll consult Golden Lock. We're never short of pretty girls here. How about foreign girls as well?"

Knitting his brows, the elderly man said: "He likes the best girls..."

For each of the three nights, several girls were dispatched to play cards with the senior official, and all were taken by the forewoman in person. At the helm of the operation, Golden Lock felt exceedingly pleased with himself.

When the senior official confined himself to his hotel room, the elderly man and Tang Tong drank rice wine together. When his face began to redden, the elderly man became garrulous and began to brag.

"I've been with the senior official for many years and know quite a lot about him. He practises a self-cultivating exercise known as 'the art of self-reconciliation to one's sexual desire'. The beauty of this exercise lies in the word 'reconciliation', which is by no means indulgence. All who indulge in sex will either degenerate or simply die. There's never an exception."

As he listened, Tang Tong opened his mouth wide. "Is that so?" he exclaimed. "Is there such a rare thing in this world?"

The elderly man put on an air of disdain, chattering his teeth and biting his lip. "Only by reconciling oneself to one's sexual drive can one feel free and natural and transcend mundanity in this world. Indulging in and restraining from sex are both forms of lechery. Think about it. How many men fail to be excited by the sight of beauties. Having sex quietly and unhurriedly every day cools one's temperament. Then one will be neither competitive nor emulative, neither happy nor angry, and neither hateful nor sorrowful. One can remain composed even in the face of a toppling mountain. Like our senior official, one will become peaceful, quiet, gentle and breathing as if one had only a tenuous hold on life. Then, one will evoke only compassion. Who will be jealous of such a person or wish him harm? That's why the senior official can grasp profound theories and extend his magical power far and wide while regaining his health in self-confinement."

Clapping his hands and slapping his thigh, Tang Tong said with revelation: "No wonder I shuddered at the first sight of him, wondering why this man looked so haggard, staggering as if he were walking on clouds and talking listlessly. It turns out that he was practising a mental and physical exercise! But, but, to me, he'll be finished... Oh, Good Heavens! Sorry for my slip of the tongue. I meant he looks like this because he's so exhausted."

"Agh, agh!" interjected the elderly man in wrath. Springing to his feet, he said reprovingly: "You're talking nonsense! Both his complexion and gait are the results of self-cultivation. Walking on clouds? Indeed! That's what an immortal does. He's reaching the Great Realm of Immortality."

Hanging his head in shame, Tang Tong mumbled: "Please pardon me, Master! Your Excellency, I mean, I could never master such art in my life. I'm a good-for-nothing. My sweat breaks out and my heart thumps as soon as I see a pretty woman. I'm a bumpkin beyond doubt. I've only one person in mind, so I can't hang out with anyone else."

This time, Jin Tang stayed longer, for a week in total. Only a month later he came again. Like the previous time, he remained quiet in the hotel room, with the arm-swinging elderly man walking like a Daoist priest on the front lawn. During his stay, he left the hotel only once. That was when he was escorted to a Fish Opera. During the performance, he fixed his eyes on the lead actress. The elderly man asked if she would perform in his hotel room, but the request was adamantly rejected by the actress.

Golden Lock often reprimanded the forewoman, which increasingly made her feel at a loss. Sometimes, she left straight after she took a girl into the senior official's hotel room, but on other occasions she was asked to stay by the official and was unable to leave after quite a while. There were times when she got into squabbles with the girls who came and went, some of whom eventually got accustomed to her tantrums.

Golden Lock would occasionally scold her: "Let me tell you, if something goes wrong, heads will roll."

The forewoman would sob and respond: "Some of them are too young to be reasonable. So I have to argue with them. Even the senior official says the older is the wiser, just as older ginger is spicier."

Golden Lock was so angered by her rebuttal that his face turned waxen. "You'll suffer the consequences and get more than you bargained for sooner or later," he said.

After repeatedly quarrelling with the girls, with Golden Lock and with some others, coupled with a proper lack of rest for several days, the forewoman was, to use a traditional Chinese medicine phrase, hit by the effulgent life gate fire. Rolling her eyes, she dropped to the floor unconscious. Both doctors and shamans were sent for. They worked on her for quite a while before she came to, but she was still not herself. Waving her arms randomly, she stared into space and then burst into laughter. After Golden Lock told Tang Tong about her condition, Tang Tong glanced at her and felt that he did not have the heart to let her go. She had been demure and good-looking, but now her uniform was torn so that her chest was exposed and her face smeared with filth. He said to Old Woman Shan who was approaching him: "She's been working for me devotedly for the past decade or so, loyal and honest. Poor thing!"

"There's nothing serious," a shaman said. "She's just possessed. She'll recover after a while."

Tang Tong had the forewoman taken to a small hotel room in the corner and ordered Golden Lock to watch her carefully and take good care of. He visited her from time to time, and only then would the forewoman calm down a little and be able to utter the word "Boss" correctly. As for others, she referred to them as animals. For example, she called Golden Lock a Siberian weasel, the senior official in his hotel room a cobra, and Old Woman Shan an old, colourful-faced demon.

"Boss, have you ever seen a cobra as thick as a fist? There's the character 'longevity' written on its forehead. It lunges forward to kill with a quick bite. A cobra and a man can intertwine with each other and coil up as high as a building. Hissing its forked tongue, it can scare you to death... Boss, you were also controlled by a spirit that day and couldn't move. The spirit's smooth body gave off a fragrance thick enough to make you cry again and again. You rolled and screamed stark naked, and the spirit caught up with you. She pinned you down on the floor with her foot and started peeing. Her urine moistened your curly hair so much that it looked as if you had just crawled back from the underworld."

Chuckling and shedding tears alternately, Tang Tong muttered fearfully: "I don't have the heart to kick you out considering that you're almost forty and still single. But you're so foulmouthed that even heaven is afraid of you!"

"I'm the senior official's fairy boy holding his portable charcoal stove, standing by his side ready at his disposal. With a Buddhist alms bowl in his hand, the senior official tends to chant: 'Pray thee harmonise the five basic tastes in me, right my bones, supple my sinews, make the *qi* and blood flow in me, close my interstices tight and prolong my life!' Grasping his glasses, he would recite: 'I'm lucky enough to have these objects that make my eyes clear and sharp.' Around midnight, the senior official becomes a cold cobra with squinting eyes and a comb on its head and starts to twine people and suck their foamy blood. He sleeps with his eyes open and snores like a blown whistle."

Tang Tong was astounded and screamed: "Good Heavens! She's really possessed. How come an illiterate virgin like her is able to recite such literary texts? Let me ask you, what spirit on Earth are you? Where did you come from? If you refuse to answer, I'll ask the shaman to kill you with his sword!"

Upon hearing these words, she chuckled: "Bring it on, Curly Hair! I'm afraid of nothing. I'm the nominal adoptive daughter of the Monkey King who boasted the title of 'Great Sage Equalling Heaven'. I'm also Old Woman Shan's grandma…"

"It's terrible! It's terrible! There's nothing we can do about her. It's like that saying: 'He who makes himself a sheep will be eaten by wolves.' I can't condone her just because she's worked for me for many years." Tang Tong darted out of the room and soon returned with a shaman.

The shaman poked the forewoman a few times, and she crouched down trembling. "Do you see, Boss? The spirit's asking for mercy." He quickly stripped her naked. Even Tang Tong could hardly bear the sight of him doing so. The shaman jotted down a few characters on a piece of paper with red ink, then set fire to the paper and burned it to ashes, which he mixed with a cup of liquor, and, after drinking it, sprayed all of it over the woman. As the liquor mixture dripped from her breasts, she flapped her hands like fluttering wings. Pointing at her with his wooden sword, the shaman shouted: "Confess or not?"

"I confess! I confess!"

"What spirit are you? Where're you from?"

"I'm a fox spirit, from Mount Lao, a cradle of Daoism."

The shaman whispered in Tang Tong's ear: "See? Another fox!"

Both curious and fearful, Tang Tong asked the forewoman: "Are you a fox spirit? If that's the case, then I was too rude to you."

"She's not a spirit at all. She's a demon." Turning to the forewoman, the shaman continued: "How did you become a demon to harm people in this world?"

The forewoman shivered violently, saying: "I mistakenly drank vinegar for wine and then I got addicted to it and couldn't help it any more."

The shaman threw away his wooden sword and said: "It's all clear now!"

SIXTEEN

A PRISONER'S MEMORY

"Maizi, you can't continue like this. Do you hear me? I know you're angry and sad, but…"

Despite Mei Di's repeated entreaties and admonishments, the door was still shut tight. This was one of the rooms in the house by the garage. Liao Mai had spent the last two nights in it. At first, he had worked in the garage in his uniform as usual, eating and drinking during breaks. When tired, he would nap in the adjoining room. Later, however, he also spent the night in this room.

"What do you want me to do, Maizi? Can you tell me?"

"I want you to shut up and go away!"

Staring at the rusted iron door, Mei Di's tears stopped abruptly and her hand that had been tapping at the door froze in the air. "You shouldn't be tormenting yourself like this, Maizi. Who are you mad at?" she asked, her voice trailing away. In the end, she looked at the dimming sky in the west and left.

Little Beibei came home at dusk. After chatting with her mother for a while, she went to the room where her father was staying and repeatedly knocked on the closed door. Liao Mai opened the door and said: "Go back, Daughter. You can see Dad is busy. I must make the best use of my time to fix the machines. Besides, I want to be alone for a while. Your mum's too noisy. She needs to be quiet for a few days, too… Go, Daughter. Don't worry about me here."

Little Beibei surveyed the room suspiciously before departing with pouted lips.

After the door was closed again, the unlit room returned to darkness. Beside the makeshift bed was a long bench spread with books, paper and some car parts. Towards the edge of the bench, there was a torch and a kerosene lamp. After a while, he lit the lamp, its illumination more pleasant than if the ceiling light had been kept on. He began to smoke a cigarette.

For a long time, he had not experienced any tranquil nights like this, and tranquillity is always a luxury for some people. To him, it would be a tragedy for humans to lose tranquillity. Sometimes, it was like self-inflicted injury, self-alienation and self-exile.

Liao Mai said to himself: My days of living as a vagabond and fugitive were even quieter than they are now. At that time, I was alone and had time to ponder until I figured something out. But I can't do that now. With a family, I've lost the opportunity…

He picked up a flatbread and took a bite. With his taste buds stimulated, he sipped some sencha tea and continued talking to himself: It's like this when you have a woman by your side. She's muddled my mind. I must straighten things out carefully, starting from the beginning. Let me turn back the clock.

Let's start from the night of my escape, continued Liao Mai. Oh, no, from a time even further back: from the eyes of my father on his deathbed, from that encounter in the alley extending all the way to the endless wilderness, to south China, to the provincial metropolis and to the present – the cursed present. Such a long time seems to be compressed into a flash, in which a big chunk of life has passed, and the most precious part has been squandered. I am no longer young. How shall I vent the anger that has accumulated and is swelling inside me? To whom shall I relate my current sorrows and anxieties?

Of course, the decades of my experiences by no means constitute a history of repentance, although it contains little in which I can take pride.

I've enjoyed a great love. It may be the cause of all my shortcomings and of all the problems that have been haunting me. Although I'm a man of dynamic personality, I've been doing almost nothing for the past three or four decades. I've imprisoned myself in a two-person world of sweetness, narrowness and infatuation. So much so that I haven't found time to do anything else.

Reflecting on the past caused him to shudder, but he went on with his silent soliloquy: It was like my current punitive confinement, which I've subjected myself to of my own will... Oh, Liao Mai, you've eaten so many bowls of gunpowder-scented, golden-scaled crucian carp soup, but what achievements have you made? You still can't struggle out of the prison cell that you've built for yourself.

As he mumbled to himself, he drank some more sencha tea and, leaning over the sill of a small window, looked into the distance. The humid air from the lake assailed his nostrils while the smell of cooked clams whiffed over from the work sheds.

He had been stunned by Mei Di's unrestrained shout of ecstasy in the throes of passion and then began to hate the ugly fish in the lake. He had spared no effort to exterminate them, but to no avail. The main cause of his failure lay in the fish's horrible propagating fecundity; they leave their black eggs tangling all over seagrass, and the eggs hatch in strings of fries after being exposed to a few days of sunshine. The strings of fries are not eaten by other fish but instead are carried like necklaces as the fish swim. However, this type of fish was a favourite of Mei Di and she enjoyed eating them every once in a while. Each time she did so, beads of sweat would break out on the tip of her nose, rashes would appear on her cheeks and armpits, and her breathing would accelerate. He reckoned that she must have been severely poisoned on several occasions with the symptoms of being short of breath and squinting. Despite being at a loss what to do, she refused to see a doctor. After a brief display of fortitude, she suddenly took a deep breath and turned both strange and libidinous.

Tonight, the smell of barbecued clams reminded him of Maoha once more. He remembered Mei Di calling him over in a hurry; covered all over with mud from the lake, Maoha slept in the shade of a tree by the lake, his chest a mass of dense, brown hair; his webbed-feet extended, and his huge testicles exposed through his tattered trousers. At that time, Mei Di had just returned to the farm exuding a strange, pungent odour that even the cooked clams failed to mask. Maoha seemed to have sensed this smell of hers before.

From time to time, she would take Liao Mai by surprise. The

most unforgettable moment was when Mei Di presented him with the ambitious plan for remodelling their house. He had been genuinely stunned at the time because he suddenly discovered that his supposedly delicate wife had completely changed from within and without; her shoulders were now round, her waist plump and her buttocks conspicuously bigger. Along with the physical changes, her voice turned decisive, her gestures sweeping and her opinions obstinately overbearing. When they were discussing the details of the architectural structure and the interior decor, she demonstrated unexpected knowledge and exceptional vision. During their visit to the hotel, the lobby manager was over-courteous. When she ran into a forewoman who appeared from behind a wooden lattice sliding door, the woman seemed to freeze momentarily before putting on a weird expression, that is, her wide-open mouth too slow to close and her indescribable smile solidified on her face – all these things failed to escape his observation. On the night of returning home, he rewound what had happened, and the scenes flashed by in front of his mind's eye before he fell asleep.

During the sleepless autumn nights, he gradually began to face the frightening reality of being unable to sever ties with the Tiantong Group; for the company that employed his daughter belonged to Tiantong, and most of the produce from the lake had to be purchased by a Tiantong company. Even worse, his farm had become an isolated island as a result of Tiantong's encroachment on the surrounding farmlands, roads and buildings.

He imagined a man holding fast on an isolated island, risking everything including his own life. This current night was one of yearning for someone and one of writing. As usual, he went to bed very late because he was busy writing down what was on his mind – all that concerned him and was hard to forget, words that he wanted to say and events that had happened in the past. He had vowed to his wife that he would live an ideal life of farming on sunny days and reading on rainy ones, a life of decent labour, and a life of purity, sobriety and honesty. He particularly stressed that he would accomplish one thing in his spare time, that is, to write a book entitled *A Secret History of the Jungle*. This had to be done. He felt an urgency to finish all the jobs that he needed to do by making the best use of the precious time before the isolated island sank.

He was too ashamed to recollect what had happened during the initial days and nights of his return: the intense excitement, the tender affection and the freedom enjoyed by an unrestrained galloping mustang – certainly every unspeakable happy moment. His own land and home, in which there was an unquestionable beauty, a woman who had gone through trials and tribulations without the slightest regret. All of these had come as a dream, whose joy was beyond his expectation. He often held her face in his hands, and they gazed into each other's eyes that swelled with tears of happiness. At that moment, he silently pledged: Remember. Remember we're a couple who have been through many ups and downs. If, in future, I should commit any act of betrayal, I'll die a deserved death by my own hands.

They had cancelled out their extravagant joy with exceedingly hard work. To be exact, they had worked untiringly, busying themselves for an entire day under the sun. They weeded and ploughed the fields. They pulled up twisted wild hops and rolled them to the edges of the fields like mats. Their faces were covered with scratches and, if they felt unbearably itchy, they would rub at each other's itching spots with their saliva. One evening, Little Beibei cuddled them by turns, and they decided to reciprocate her tenderness with a show. Later, they also performed the show, seriously and attentively, when their daughter was not home. The performances were impregnated with their unspeakable love and intimacy.

He had never thought that all the affection and happenings would become memories that he would be least willing to recall. They made him embarrassed, unhappy, guilty and full of self-pity. Their performance was from the repertoire of amateur shows left from those heartless times. It depicted an elderly rural couple studying the *Little Red Book* one evening… Under Little Beibei's smiling gaze, he and Mei Di each put a white towel over their heads, and, a *Little Red Book* in hand, they came on 'stage' from opposite corners, tottering like old folk. They sang as they walked: "Back from work and after supper / An old couple sit tight on the *kang*. / We begin to study – the *Selected Works*."

They beamed at each other and continued in a loud voice: "My old woman! Yes. / My old man! Yes. / Which passage do you suggest studying? / I suggest we study this one."

They still remembered how Little Beibei looked at them with

amazement when they started the high-pitched part of the performance: "Well, that second son of ours / He's too lazy to work hard."

Further into the show, Mei Di sang her affectionate and yet serious criticism: "I say, my old man, / You're a little subjective / And hate to listen to others' advice."

At the end of the performance, the three family members hugged together, and the two adults chanted in chorus: "United, we'll defeat the enemy / With our firm revolutionary will!" They each scrunched a hand into a fist and swept it vehemently downward.[1]

The scene of that night was still vivid before his mind's eye. Now, he felt his face burning with embarrassment. Indeed, that scene had been an illustration of their relationship, which could be described as love-struck, or, to borrow a Chinese proverb, 'sticking to each other like glue or lacquer'.

Wait a minute! Tonight, he had to remind himself that that ugly breed of fish had appeared in the lake even then. They lay on their bellies at the edge of the water staring towards the bank with their wide-open eyes as small as mung beans.

A LETTER

It's another silent night. I'm at the desk as usual. I'm smoking a cigarette and drinking sencha tea – both are bad habits, but I just can't help myself because I'm a man by the sea. Fortified with alcohol, I can stand up in the face of the strong north wind. Of course, I'm missing you. But my surging, romantic heart is under control, and I'm missing you and enjoying the night of dim chaos and warmth with a heart that already knows the fate decreed by the heavens. Everything about you that I've deposited in my heart and blood constitutes the real high-proof spirit, with which I'm fending off the north wind of my life.

One must keep what one treasures close to one's heart. One mustn't reveal it because it's one's indescribable secret.

Your real life is too short because it's withered unexpectedly. But your fragrance has ruined my sense of smell, and the mellow alcohol in your mouth has killed my taste buds. I'm entrapped in a deep love akin to hatred and can't escape, thus subjecting my simple and promising life to endless torment. The hopelessness is like the gaze of a blind man or the behaviour of a foolish beggar. The black age spots covering my hands are the marks of a harmful spell you've cast. These hands now shiver whenever I reach them out. With these shivering hands, I have to hold your face and run over your thick hair, in which I have to bury my face deep. Your blood of twenty-odd years has been injected into me like the sap of the white water snowflake plant, fermenting tonight, this year and for the rest of my life. It has nurtured my teeth-gritting hatred that gnaws my love to death little by little.

On your face, which can withstand repeated scrutiny even at close distance, your eyes shine and sprinkle gems to fill the purplish-blue sky of my heart. That breathtaking, innocent and naughty nose, curving down regularly from your forehead, infuses a kind of supernatural beauty. I can't help thinking of the noses of all the love-evoking creatures being licked by the wrapping tip of a rosy tongue. Beneath it is the philtrum and the lips, as well as their implicit deterrence and seduction. As soon as I glance at them, the silk of my desire will be spun into a yarn to twine around your neck and choke you till you swoon. Then, I'll ensnare you surely and steadily like I do with a hummingbird with its wings broken.

Unfortunately, you've crossed over from spring to a frosty morning with a single stride, giving yourself no time to produce blackish seeds, so that we'll have to face the freezing cold winter together. I'm honing my sword without knowing where to wield it. In my empty embrace, I'm always holding an exceptional beauty. Like an ancient warrior galloping afar on a war horse, I'm going to the endless kingdom of illusion. Then I'll be gone, leaving behind only a vain stele of public praise.

The person that is the realistic you is already dead, and in the absolute sorrow of death, I'm committing many soundless words to paper throughout the night.

In the murky light of the kerosene lamp, I've taken the unavoidable decision to turn over a new leaf. Without you, I've lost my touchstone, my orientation and my time to pour out my heart. Under your eagle eye and on your dusky face, I'm reviewing my ideal vision for the future. Your fingers, concealed in the humble darkness of the night, inspired my imagination. Since then, you've turned everything vulgar and caused me to lose my endurance, indomitability and constancy of purpose. For you killed my hope, oh my hope, too early.

My craziness and self-esteem co-exist. My miserable yesterday has taught me to shut my mouth but open my eyes and to keep my secret at the cost of my life rather than frivolously casting it away for nothing. The best of my best love, my delusive and dejected departure is about to come like that.

I remember that we questioned and answered each other like strangers only once. It was the mingling and handshaking of voices, which have come to a precipitous mountain pass to meet after travelling separately in the past decade or two on a road of thistles and thorns. Then, in the light of static arcs, my face blanching, I turned around, crouched down and vanished.

Since then, I've always been looking up to you, listening to you and steering clear of you. I'll be turning my back on you for the rest of my life. I won't utter a word, or even a syllable, because this is the last grain of gold-bearing gravel in my heart that I don't want the water of time to wash away.

As life repeatedly attempts to prove the humbleness of the physical body, so I'm tenaciously trying to testify to its stubbornness. Now, unimaginable faithfulness and triumph are coming my way. In those days, I was quiet, abstinent, impoverished and depressed, like a monk in a religious habit. But devoting myself to penance and living as an ascetic has turned me, a man in his prime, into an eccentric. My eyes sparkle with a kind of bewitchment, and my thick, dark hair curls as a result of abstinence, its tip sticking closely to the forehead and the nape like an ancient man of the Roman Empire. My hands, pale, strong, large and with glossy nails, are symbolic of my exceptional vitality and good health.

It was on such a day that I'd be enveloped and gripped by your deep love and good intentions, by the light of your desire, and by the fullness under your casual, loose garment. With neither suspense nor imagined feelings nor so-called physical intrusion, I was instantly and abruptly pushed to the edge of a cliff and, standing there, engulfed in the surging clouds. I was all tears in the invisible mists. I've said that I, too, have a humble physical body, or a weightier outer form. The moment you held the petals of the orchid blossom in your hands, I experienced the climax of shock.

With an unbearable, gentle scream, I turned around and departed. The petals falling from your hands, you gazed at me with surprise.

This is the history of an immaculately clean piece of paper of me with ink not yet bleeding all over it. In this midnight, while praying for my double faithfulness, I'm also struggling and feeling abashed. If I lost this state of mind, I would enter a dangerous situation of exile. Today, tonight, at this moment when this world is submerged in a tide of desire, oh my fatal love, I still want to be an isolated island. I love you both as well as every inch of my distinct yesterday. That's exactly the memory of a human being, and that's exactly me.

I want to divide my loved ones into day and night, into the living and the dead, into the symbolic and the realistic, and into the above-the-clouds and the on-the-ground. But I can't deceive myself as well as others. No, I can't. Yes, this isolated island has not been submerged. It's still above water, neither fragmenting nor collapsing in the surrounding tidal waves crashing against it.

That was why I sailed over to you, like a weather-beaten boat reaching a familiar bank. You lowered the sail for me, untied the mooring line and pointed me to the quay. This was the first time I sailed into a harbour in a strange land. South China is as fragrant as the irresistible scent of cloves. Nothing was in my way. I might have been too late. I was intoxicated and faltered in the harbour.

At this moment, I don't know how to look back. Let the fate that has given me a second chance to grow depart without hindrance through the only pass that I can't bypass and where I can't feel sorry for myself. I remember the first morning after my return, when the sun shone on the green land. I had just opened the window to look out when suddenly a wave of gratitude hit me. With mixed feelings of happiness and sadness, I was instantly at a loss for words. I thought of you and that night, when we had given ourselves to each other, going further than we had imagined. We are the ones that have a journey and a tomorrow ahead of us.

You denounced my cruelty. Indeed, on the arched bridge, the unexpected lightning frightened me. For I knew what would be in store for a new life. Alright, move forward. None of us will balk or retreat. On a midnight such as this, I'm thinking of you, blessing you and looking up to you more than others. Only I know why you have chosen to be a mother now. Just as you expected, I'm still an isolated island, not submerged. I'm looking up to you amid the increasingly strong waves crashing against me. That's because I love you. I love you very much.

FISH OPERA

Liao Mai finally came out of the little house. Mei Di found her husband less haggard than she feared except for the stubble on his face. She immediately started to make him a golden-scaled crucian carp soup. The sight of her with her sleeves rolled up finally brought a smile to his face.

"I've been praying to the heavens to protect my really fine man from catching fever during this autumn season and from becoming crazy and ill again. I also prayed that we'd both be happy and nothing bad would happen to us." While she was clearing the table and murmuring, her eyes never left him. "My really fine man looks more handsome with his beard untrimmed." She served him a bowl of fish soup filled to the brim.

For a whole day, he toiled with the workers. Before it got dark, some of them talked about going downtown, saying: "It'll be the last show of the Fish Opera. It's said the opera troupe will go back to Trident Island."

Caught by surprise, he learned what was going on from the workers and returned to Mei Di. "Confined as we are to the farm, we know nothing of what's going on outside. It turns out that the Fish Opera troupe has been here for several days. It's the opera that Qi Jin mentioned. Let's cancel our plans tonight and go to watch the show."

Although the opera had been staged for several days running, there was still a full house. Liao Mai and Mei Di sat in seats near the stage – seats that Mei Di had solicited from the theatre's manager. As soon as gongs and drums sounded, Liao Mai started scanning the theatre for something or somebody. Meanwhile, his mind was filled with Qi Jin's description of the opera as he hoped that Young Shaliu'er would soon appear on stage. Sure enough, the exotic music, from gonging to drumming, was like nothing he had heard before. An oboe-like instrument made from a large fish bone sounded loudly, reminding the audience of surging waves on a rainy day. There was also the roll of fish-skin drums, the twanging of fiddles, the billowing of sails punctuated with shanties, and the screams of marine creatures. Liao Mai wished that sitting beside him would have been the Fish Opera collector Qi Jin, who was familiar with all the repertoires on Trident Island. Today's show was one of the classics. Its title *Red Porgy Girl* was projected onto a side curtain on the stage.

Red Porgy Girl was played by Young Shaliu'er. He had not expected her to be so small. All her features were clearly visible to audience members in the first three rows, even her pretty, heavily powdered face and the slender figure like a little boy. Dressed in red, she danced with her hands moving like fins. Swimming close to the surface or amid the waves, her image tugged the audience's heartstrings. Against the background of shoals of fish darting back and forth through thick seagrass and seaweed, she frolicked with a huge squid and rode a killer whale as if it were a horse.

Red Porgy Girl
Who doesn't envy me, Red Porgy Girl? I look exactly like a mermaid. I'm picking flowers here and there. Big Clam is opening its shell to reveal pearls. Old Turtle is wearing a summer hat in spring. Moon Snail is sprinkling apricot flower petals. Corals are like precious *lingzhi* mushrooms. While Young Anchovy is peeping at me, Rajiformes comes waving a big fan.

Rajiformes
Anchovy is chasing and Catfish is ogling, flirting with her with sweet words. Abashed by their harassment, Red Porgy Girl is fleeing on a seahorse, in the direction of the chilly west wind. Longfin Batfish shows off his archery skills above the water, thus revealing his mastery of martial arts. But the real master is Young Killer Whale. With shiny armour, he looks smart, and his big eyes sparkle like the moon. One look from Red Porgy Girl, and he hangs his head low, blushing.

Red Porgy Girl
I think of you and your awesome stature day and night. Your cloak is draped over a white shirt, and your round head makes you look wise. With your sharp snout pointing at me, I'm blushing while my heart is beating hard. Oh no, I'm babbling like a fool. Red Porgy Girl's too shy to speak, and I find my hiding place in the seagrass.

Young Killer Whale

This killer whale is young and heroic, a handsome man with a reputation. Who doesn't praise me, saying I'm good-looking and kind-hearted? In the East Sea, I've rescued a woman in danger. In the West Ocean, I've sent a pirate to the netherworld. Time flies without my notice, and I need to marry a sweetheart. I can't wait till my hair turns grey, I can't wait till the end of the world. [Speaking] Hey Killer Whale, you're imagining things with your blinking big eyes. You're wasting your time and worrying for nothing. Then, you try to chew a piece of meat, only to find your teeth gone! Anxious and teary-eyed, I bump my head at regular intervals.

Red Porgy Girl

Really good Young Killer Whale is an introvert, pondering all day without a word. Your nonchalant parents are smoking water pipes, whose stems are as long as wooden clubs. Visiting neighbours from door to door, they really look like a pair of prunes. Red Porgy Girl is an expert at needlework. I've embroidered a pair of lovebirds on a handkerchief. With a crystal stone wrapped inside, I give it to Young Killer Whale as a keepsake.

Young Killer Whale

I, Young Killer Whale, was only eighteen two years ago, and I'm no more than twenty now. She's said to be better than a fairy lady, with her face as pretty as a picture. Her skin is as smooth as a jellyfish. Her mouth has two rows of white teeth. She gives off fragrance as she breathes, and she hides in deep water upon seeing a stranger. I've tried to grasp her a couple of times but to no avail. She flees, flexing her body back and forth. Back and forth with a flower on her head, she is the amorous bride in my dream. With happy tears swelling in my eyes, I have the confidence to venture into the world.

Rajiformes

Happy is Young Killer Whale, joyous is Spanish Mackerel, and laughing and clapping is Squid. Old Turtle sings, stroking his beard, and he sings about the marriage of a handsome young man and a pretty woman. Seagulls and storm petrels mew in the sky. Seething with anger, a hawk hovers short of breath. It reaches its iron claws out but catches nothing. Here comes delicate Porgy Girl beaming.

An otherwise scrumptious dish, with a leap the red porgy is nowhere to be found. Filthy Dragon stomps with jealousy, viciously swearing a death oath: While a beauty rare in a hundred years, she'll come to no good. When the door of her bridal room opens, she'll be too old to marry. Filthy Dragon is sordid, gluttonous and lustful. But his power is beyond description. When he becomes ruthless, he will loot and plunder. At a word of his command, his shrimp and crab soldiers fanned out. They yelled and captured Young Killer Whale. They tied him with a thick rope and constrained him with shackles. They whipped him three times despite his innocence. After lashing his chest and back, they took off his trousers. They clubbed him until he was motionless. Meanwhile, they captured Red Porgy Girl. They carried her into the Crystal Kingdom on a sedan chair.

Filthy Dragon
I, Filthy Dragon, am rustic but smart. Every night, I dream of Red Porgy Girl. I'm strong enough to lift a thousand-kilogram bronze tripod. I'm powerful enough to conquer the East Sea. My shrimp and crab troops stand ten kilometres long. My fishy concubines hold my precious vases. My wedding bed is made from ivory, the walls are tiled with the shells of hawksbill turtles. With rows of luminous pearls, I have no need for lanterns on dark nights. As long as you touch my bearded face, I'll cast all my gemstones before you. As long as you give me your dimpled smile, I'll give you a pair of gold bracelets. As long as you obey in every way, I'll take you on an outing, holding your waist. Whoever dares to hurl abuse at you, I'll seal his mouth for the rest of his life. I'll cover you with lotus quilts every night, so that you'll always beam with happy smiles.

Red Porgy Girl
Red Porgy Girl has only one life, but I've promised it to Young Killer Whale. If he's hurt, I'll bleed. If he dies, I'll follow him. You may have enough gold to fill the sea, but you can never bribe me to agree. You may have a sharp sword, but you can never use it to end our relationship.

Filthy Dragon
I'm a king in my royal court, but a little killer whale is nothing. My beard turns white when I'm angry. I kill demons without the need of

a wooden sword.[2] I get up early after I drink, then I'll pee upon the killer whale's head, one pee after another. I've a broad sword on my naked back. I'll wield the sword in excitement, and it'll slash and bleed the rebels to death. I can chop the god of the land in wrath. Killing you, she-demon, would be a doddle. Don't refuse a toast only to be forced to drink a forfeit, let's live happily till our hair turns grey.

Red Porgy Girl
Don't you be proud of your nonsense. You're but a foul-mouthed bastard. My life is one of a chaste body clad in a red dress. How can I allow you to assault it? You, Filthy Dragon, have maggots crawling beneath your scales. Your vicious heart is wrapped in a viper skin. Your stench contaminates all rivers and pollutes the entire land. [Speaking] Oh, this life of mine! I swear, you'll have bad luck even in the afterlife, you'll suffer from scabies and diarrhoea. And you'll be shot by a three-muzzled gun when you leave your residence, each bullet penetrating your forehead. Young Killer Whale, please wait for me, I'll be yours till the sea's turned dry.

Rajiformes
In his rage, Filthy Dragon darkens the sea. Waves are surging with black sand. With a raised voice, he calls the executor. He'll kill Young Killer Whale in bondage. The corals sob while seahorses weep, and the turtles drop to their knees. Longfin batfish are shrieking, and porpoises and whales are leaping and jumping. I, old Rajiformes, am crying so bitterly that my tears add salt to the seawater.

Filthy Dragon
So long as you can change your mind, so long as you sleep with me for one night, I promise to set him free with expensive clothes, and he'll ride all the way to the South Mountain. Think straight by counting on your fingers. Don't miscalculate and leave it too late. I'm waiting for the sun to set, then you'll see his blood at my command. I don't care if he's handsome and has big eyes. I don't care if you two are lovebirds. I always get what I want by nature. If we babble on like this, he'll give up the ghost in no time!

Red Porgy Girl
Here I come to the Crystal Hall, where I caught sight of the monster
sitting by. To be tarnished tonight, my life would be worse than
death. I wish I could trade my ordeal for my lover's freedom. When
the wind abates tomorrow, I'll re-dress my remaining self with tears.
The night is long and so are the tears of the candle wax. I know my
Young Killer Whale is agonising, as if a thousand arrows pierced his
heart. Candles are out and curtains down, the fishy smell is pressing
close, and I feel the earth sinking and the sky collapsing.

Rajiformes
Young Killer Whale is agonising, riding back and forth on
horseback. Pray you Mazu, goddess of the sea, protect my wife, and
I ask the Goddess of Mercy to help me. In the moaning wind and
under the bleak clouds, ghosts scream and spirits howl. Even the
mountains shake and the earth sways. These signs bode ill, not well.

Red Porgy Girl
The morning glow looks bloody. With Filthy Dragon, I spent a night
of torment. Shrimp spirits carried me out of the palace, and I called
and shouted myself hoarse: "Young Killer Whale, hurry back, back
to your wife swimming with tears. Each tear is a drop of blood. I'll
never wear my red dress." My Young Killer Whale puts me on his
horse, with my body still covered with the bruises from last night.
I'm washing away the filth in the East Sea. I'm vowing to be your
wife forever.

Young Killer Whale
May the fire of thunder hit the earth, may it burn us two into ashes.
May we become brother and sister, may we be husband and wife no
more. It's but a dream of love and hate. Now our blood relation is
known to the gods. Follow me to the end of the Earth. We'll settle
under the Chinese parasol tree. Your single brother is tilling the
land, while my sister weaves and embroiders at home. There will
always be a fine and lucky day, when I'll marry my sister away.
After you leave in a sedan chair, I'll return to the fields with my
bamboo hat.

Rajiformes

His words hit Red Porgy Girl like a thunderbolt. She can no longer stand with the sky swimming before her eyes. Rain pours down. Young Killer Whale alights his horse and cries. Widening her eyes, Red Porgy Girl sobs: "I want to be your wife, not your sister." To Young Killer Whale, virginity is important, but Red Porgy Girl's faith is leading to her death. Asking his beloved to take good care, she throws herself over the cliff. All the creatures wail in the pouring rain, and the Jade Emperor issues his thunders of indignation. Her grievances fill the surging tide, and from now on her cries become its rumbles.

A TRIP TO TRIDENT ISLAND

Liao Mai might not have begged Qi Jin ten thousand times, but he did put in a lot of effort to persuade him. Finally, Qi Jin agreed to take him to Trident Island. Liao Mai was bent on paying the island a visit not only because he wanted to watch more Fish Operas, but also because of some other reasons. The unique vocal music as well as the peculiar acting and speaking were fascinating, even stunning, making people wonder what customs and traditions had nurtured this type of art. He had been worrying that the Tiantong Group would obliterate many of the cultural relics on the island in its savage dash for development. For days, a kind of unspoken urgency, pent-up anger and anxiety had been accumulating in Liao Mai. He only expected to be cooled down by the penetrating, chilly wind from the high seas.

Liao Mai knew that all the reasons given by Qi Jin not to visit the island were but excuses. This sullen guy had left his true love, confusion, taboos and other vital issues on the island. That was why he hesitated and finally decided to go anyway; Trident Island would be a permanent magnet, and he would be but a small pile of iron filings in future.

With his own eyes, Liao Mai saw how this swarthy scurf was magnetised upon reaching the island. Qi Jin started fidgeting before the boatman steered the boat into the bay. He shifted his feet, smacked his lips, craned his neck and kept on picking up and then putting down his backpack. On the island, he rushed ahead with his involuntarily quick footsteps, almost disregarding his companion Liao Mai. On the first night, he tossed and turned, and several times he rose and leant over the window to look out. And when day broke, he went so far as to set off alone, leaving his companion behind.

Liao Mai had ample time to saunter about. He did not want Qi Jin to introduce him to others too early. Neither did he intend to look for Maoha in a hurry. He planned to take a rough tour of the three islets that were not far apart from one another. This was pretty easy to do because small docks had been built to ease commuting between the islets. There were also punctual, scheduled shuttle boat services. This mode of transport was primarily designed to facilitate tourism. Thanks to the new service, the islanders did not have to take their boat out to sea except for fishing. It was now hard to imagine how the three islets were previously connected and how big the single island used to be. It was equally unbelievable that the big island should have been home to a large square, busy streets and an old Fish Opera theatre.

Today, however, everything except the people had changed, or rather, even the people had changed as well. Apart from the elderly, no one still cared about the past. Those who had been born a little over a decade before, no longer handled boats. They would rather earn a small wage from the Tiantong Group by working in its tourist zone. When the square of flat ground that had connected the three islets was mentioned, youngsters would grimace and say: "That's bullshit!" They only knew white yachts, bars, working girls, fruit machines and domestic and foreign tourists with their hair dyed in various colours. They looked forward to the huge castle ship pulling into the bay once a month, its glistening appearance giving the impression that the ship was simply a recast of what was described in a fairy-tale. By mooring there, it proved its own value as well as Trident Island's. It's said that the big boss himself and various other respectable persons were on the castle ship. But no one could see them because they only landed on the island to have fun at night, fearing that ultraviolet radiation would tan their faces[3] on the island. It was said that the social elites of this era had inverted their daily schedule: sleeping soundly by day and being wide awake at night, when women put on lipstick and eyeshadow, and men wore ties and walked with fashionable canes. Instead of looking half-awake, they widened their eyes as large as those of bulls.

Liao Mai found the area of the three islets smaller than he had imagined. He had learned from Qi Jin before that this was the result of the rising sea level. The three islets were, in fact, the tips of three mountains. He wondered where the local residents and the numerous immigrants were crowded. Then, he learned that many of the early islanders had emigrated to other islands, leaving behind only two types of people – youngsters who loved new-fangled things and elderly people who were either extremely nostalgic or who would rather die than give up their fishing boats.

On the subject of fishing, some would sigh: "Look! We can't even find a place to moor our fishing boats." It turned out that the best locations had been turned into small docks that denied access to fishing vessels. "We suddenly have so many gluttonous outsiders, begging to eat our fish, thereby doubling the price. We use our hooks and nets and take our boats to sea even at the risk of our lives," shouted an old man with age spots on his face and exposing the two remaining teeth left in his mouth. He asked Liao Mai where he had come from. Liao Mai told him that he was from the mainland. The old man immediately cursed. "From Tiantong? The people there are all beasts." After Liao Mai said he was not from the group, the old man gave a sigh of relief. He then whispered: "Those people don't do what humans ought to do."

Under a cliff, Liao Mai saw a man in oilskins clambering up from the sea with a basket, in which there were some conches and other shells. He asked him about Maoha.

"Maoha?" the man said. "Ahh, this type of work is too easy for him because he's not a human being at all. He's a fish spirit. He can even sleep in the sea without any trouble. He has no problem catching fish or finding conches, but he can't be bothered to do it. He's a lazybones. Nowadays, he wants to be a millionaire and says he can become one in six months. That's very strange since he's so lazy and listless all the time. His hairy balls are growing bigger and bigger, though. Maybe he's suffering from a strange illness."

Liao Mai was concerned. One day, he stopped what he was doing and went to see Maoha. The guy was indeed lethargic. As soon as he saw Liao Mai, he gave a loud cry, grinning from ear to ear. After a while, however, his eyebrows drooped. Yuyu was not home, but, in reality, she was the one that Liao Mai wanted to see the most on the island. He did not ask, but started a conversation with Maoha instead: "Long time no see. I've often thought of you.

Look at you now, so unkempt. Since you're not fishing in the sea, does that mean you've given up work altogether?"

Maoha was lacking in spirit and looked a little older. Pouting his lips as an angry person might do, he said: "Someone's going to kill me. Someone..."

"Going to kill you? Why?"

"I don't know. A narrow-faced man from the castle ship, always by the side of Old Woman Shan... They're gone now. They won't come because my mum won't either."

"What on earth happened? Could it be your illusion?"

Maoha chuckled and wouldn't answer the question. Then, he twitched his mouth and burst into tears, saying: "I miss my mum, but she refuses to accept me as her son. I don't understand why."

Liao Mai tried to calm him down but to no avail. He realised that he was obsessed.

"So, you still want to look for her outside the island?" he asked.

"No, it's too early. I must stay put on the island." Maoha rubbed his eyes and turned his head to look out of the window.

"I heard that you're sick, is that right? What's wrong? Can I have a look at your crotch?"

Not feeling in the least abashed, Maoha immediately took off his trousers. Liao Mai found his testicles many times bigger than normal. They appeared to be terribly swollen. "Gosh! You must see a doctor. They're the cause of all your misery, Brother Maoha."

Maoha shook his head. "Nothing serious. I only feel uncomfortable on cloudy or rainy days. When it's fine, I feel better having aired them in the sun by the window."

When the conversation turned to the Fish Opera troupe's performance in town, Maoha pulled himself together. Widening his eyes, he said: "Well, I followed them to their shows. It was me who pulled the curtain for them. Later... later, when I saw Old Woman Shan's adoptive sons running here and there, I returned to the island."

Liao Mai was astonished, but he knew that Maoha wouldn't lie.

The sun shone violently through the window. Out of habit, Maoha moved closer to dry his crotch in the sun.

This man is being tormented by an impossible love. He may even know the consequences, thought Liao Mai, while running his hand over Maoha's shoulder.

"Qi Jin came with me," he whispered.

"I know."

"Did you see him?"

"Nope. When Sister Yuyu felt uneasy, I learned about his arrival from her pale face."

Liao Mai fell silent. After a pause, he could not help asking: "Where is Yuyu?"

"She went out early this morning. She must be chatting with Qi Jin at the water dungeon."

Liao Mai wanted to wait for her there. He asked Maoha about his ailment. Maoha said that he had had it for three years. He then told him why Wandu, the physician who had received both Chinese and Western medical training, had failed to treat him.

"He's a good doc. It was the bogus drugs that caused his failure and tarnished his reputation." Speaking of quack medicine, Maoha dwelt upon one of the oldest traditions observed on the island and a never-failing prescription: "Once stung by a stingray, a fisherman is doomed unless he can rush back to the island, turn over a rock in front of any of the houses and take out a small paper package. He must burn the hair found in the package and apply the ashes to the wound. Then it will heal for sure."

When asked, Maoha told Liao Mai that it was the body hair of unmarried girls from the island. It was at this point that Maoha flew into a rage: "Since the arrival of the Tiantong Group, all the packages beneath the rocks have been replaced by no one knows what. Consequently, three fishermen have died in a year. They all died because of the bogus contents in the packages."

"I'm afraid the prescription is an ignorant folk custom, isn't it?"

"It's you who is ignorant! It's a matter of life and death. The prescription is a hundred years old, so who dares to mess around with it? Nowadays, some people are paying hugely inflated prices to buy the drugs on the black market. They are colluding with each other in secret."

"Are you sure such a strange thing is happening?"

"Yes," Maoha said, shifting his posture. "The priest in the new Daoist temple is one of the collaborators."

THE NEW DAOIST TEMPLE

Liao Mai finally saw the legendary woman Yuyu. Like her daughter Young Shaliu'er, she was relatively small. But her looks quickly caught Liao Mai's attention. Although she was at least fifty and her hair was starting to grey, there were no wrinkles on her oval face. Her eyes were unforgettable: alert, sharp and yet very pretty. They lingered on Liao Mai's face awhile and gradually became warmer, as if to say: Yes, you're Qi Jin's friend. Qi Jin stood by, rubbing his hands together uneasily.

Liao Mai had run into the pair on his way back from Maoha. Yuyu invited him home for dinner, but he declined, saying: "I saw Brother Maoha. I'll come and eat some other day."

Instead of following Yuyu home, Qi Jin went back to where he was staying with Liao Mai. Liao Mai did not ask this quiet man any more about Yuyu, and for his part, Qi Jin seemed to have no intention of saying anything.

Liao Mai had actually been expressing his thoughts in silence and even felt that Qi Jin could somehow hear him: She turned out to be such a woman! Yes, Qi Jin, you're really quite a guy! You got married and divorced, and then you went from the plateau in the west to the mountains in the south to live the life of a wanderer and ascetic. Today, however, you've finally run into someone you can reckon with. Apparently, she's experienced the hardships of life and possessed a personality of fortitude. She can be described as a cold beauty emanating a special strength, which Liao Mai had felt upon seeing her…

A man of austereness akin to indifference, Qi Jin had never found it easy to like anyone.

What was particularly troubling and even embarrassing was that her only daughter Young Shaliu'er had a persistent and yet unrequited love for Qi Jin. The whole affair was like a cheap love drama.

"Is she older than you?" Liao Mai finally broke the silence.

"Three years older."

"You've got to talk with Maoha… and Young Shaliu'er."

Qi Jin shook his head. "Maybe the worst thing to do is explain. I'll wait and see."

After a moment's rest, they went out. They had wanted to visit the Fish Opera troupe's rehearsal arena, but Qi Jin walked around it. On Liao Mai's list of places to visit were the legendary 'water dungeon', the theatrical stage and the Daoist temple.

Qi Jin said: "The Tiantong Group builds Buddhist or Daoist temples wherever it has its development projects, with a view to entreat divine blessings and promote tourism. These places are popular with both foreigners and Chinese, including us." Liao Mai did not say anything. He was only curious about the Daoist priest.

Liao Mai noticed that there was a rock in front of each household. He could not help lifting one to take a look. Sure enough, there was a paper package beneath it. He replaced the package to its former position. Qi Jin knew about the rocks and paper packages, the story of which echoed Maoha's account.

On the peak of the islet, a blue-bricked building flickered behind the foliage. It was a midsized Daoist temple, appearing very new. As soon as they entered it, a pungent whiff of burning joss paper greeted them. It was a very familiar smell. As he had expected, everything was the same as what Liao Mai had seen elsewhere: somewhat crudely constructed buildings that copied ancient architectural styles, crude clay sculptures and coloured drawings, large incense burners coated with gold, an altar table spread with bundles of incense sticks and stacks of joss paper, and a box for the donations from believers.

A young Daoist priest was sweeping a brick path in front of the side-rooms. He did not stop to greet them.

A main path led from the side-rooms to the rear hall. They were about to reach it through the main hall when the young priest blocked them with extended arms. He told them that visitors were admitted into the main hall only.

"Is the abbot in?" Liao Mai asked.

The young priest did not answer. He raised his head, measured them a minute with his eyes, and, discarding the broom, rushed to the rear hall.

Before long, an abbot in his sixties came out in a brand-new hat and gown. On his glossy face, he wore a long beard. The abbot politely led his guests to one of the west side-rooms, where he started a conversation with some questions. Liao Mai had just said that he was from the southern beach when the abbot chuckled and stroked his long beard. "Big Boss Tang is a friend of mine, a friend."

Liao Mai glanced at Qi Jin and said: "May I ask you, venerable abbot, where you are from?"

The abbot beamed but avoided answering the question. He only said: "I resumed my secular life for eight years before coming out to carry the mantle of abbotship. Well, I couldn't say no to Boss Tang. I taught myself Daoism and cultivated myself accordingly, so I'm well versed in the Daoist doctrines from Wang Chongyang, one of the founders of the Quanzhen School, to Qiu Chuji, the leader of the Seven True Daoists of the North. My birthplace is only one and a half kilometres from Qiu Chuji's native Binduli, Qixia,[4] which was divinely destined. I've served in the Qixia Taixu Palace and the Daoist temples in Laizhou, Hantong Mountain, Daji Mountain, Weihai and Tiecha Mountain, as well as the Taiqing, Shangqing and Bailong temples on Mount Lao." He finished his self-introduction in an archaic tone: "I am did satisfy with what I has't gotten in this life."

"It's mine own first timeth to cometh here to seeth the ven'rable abbot," said Liao Mai, mimicking his tone.

"Welcome to the treasure place of feng shui! The treasure place of feng shui!"

The abbot cheered up and signalled a young priest to serve tea. He rubbed his nose and went on: "The temple may be small and have few people, but when the tourism industry flourishes in a year or two, things will get better. Men must have beliefs. To be frank, since my childhood, I..."

"I'm a believ'r, too," said Liao Mai, still aping the abbot's pedantry.

As they were chatting, they heard a commotion, and a young priest burst through the door, saying: "Your venerable abbot, she's kicking the door again! She said it was time for her to get out to refresh herself."

The abbot sighed and said with a wave of his hand: "Let her out, this burden!" Turning to Liao Mai, he continued: "A woman from Boss Tang. She's possessed and was banished here after she made quite a scene. In fact, more than one spirit has possessed her. I count a dozen in total."

Just then, the woman screamed and rushed to the front of the main hall. To prevent her from escaping, the young priest banged the temple gate close. Liao Mai and Qi Jin hurried out of the west side-room, only to see a woman with dishevelled hair.

The woman turned her face towards Liao Mai and was transfixed with surprise. Liao Mai also recognised her. She was none other than the forewoman from the Tiantong Group, the one that he and Mei Di had seen before. The forewoman stared at him, then lunged forward and burst into laughter with her hand covering her mouth. She jumped and screamed: "You know the hedgehog spirit?"

Liao Mai felt his face pricked by her gaze.

"I'm a fox spirit, and she's a hedgehog spirit. We're a duo! I'm a bosom friend of the hedgehog spirit. You're her husband, so please get me out of here. I want to go to my bosom friend. I don't want this damned abbot harassing me every night."

Right at the moment, the abbot leapt to her presence as if from nowhere. Pointing a peach-wood sword at her, he shouted: "Boo!"

With that, the forewoman shivered all over. The light in her eyes dimmed, and, staring at Liao Mai for the last time, she crouched down.

Liao Mai walked up to her, attempting to pull her up. But she trembled more violently, her teeth chattering audibly.

"Boo!" The abbot thrust his wooden sword closer to her face.

She huddled into a tighter ball, shivering continuously.

Qi Jin and Liao Mai exchanged a look of alarm. They called her again, but she seemed not to hear them.

SEVENTEEN

GOLDEN LOCK GIVES A LECTURE

"I JUST SO HAPPEN TO BE AVAILABLE today. So, I thought I'd take the opportunity to present a lecture to you. Our boss always encourages us to get professional training. He's right. To my mind, our consciousness is more important than our skills. Since we're having a private conversation within our group, we'd better be frank. I've made a draft, and we can discuss it as I read it. The topic for discussion is 'Sexual intemperance means patriotism'. Don't grimace. When you hear what I have to say, you'll find I'm not trying to get your attention by deliberately creating a sensation.

"The ancient maxim of the sage 'Desiring food and sex is human nature' really hits the mark. We all know the old adage 'Man is iron while food is steel', don't we? Is sex also steel then? I don't see there's any difference. In the feudal era, the ruling class tried every means to satisfy their sexual desire while making the labouring class work hard on an empty stomach and erect stone arches to honour chaste women widowed at a young age. The consequence? The country became weak and vulnerable, unwittingly allowing the Eight-Power Allied Forces into the capital. At that time, foreigners compared us to 'a sleeping Asian lion'. That is to say, each of us Chinese was listless. Sexual love between men and women benefits both the self and society in general. It enlivens and energises the entire nation. Then, why can't our country be strong and prosperous?

"Don't you see that men and animals are the same, and the laws of nature apply equally to both? Both become aroused when attracted to the opposite sex. Modern medicine explains the phenomenon in terms of the endocrine secreted from the pineal gland and seeks evidence from hormones such as gonadotropins. As a consequence, scientists understand that sex is an objective need. As dialectical materialists, how can we bury our heads in the sand? As modernists, we should not be embarrassed to get to the truth. This is not the age of the Manchurian Qing! But we often say one thing but mean another. While our hearts are pounding hard, we strive to remain civil and are reluctant to admit our desire. This is like the popular saying: 'We suffer from our pretence by keeping up appearances.'

"A modern person must have a sound personality, be straightforward, keep forging ahead courageously and strive to blaze a new trail. It's hard to change the habits of several thousand years. Therefore, up to this day, some people still see sexual intemperance as an arch enemy and charge over trying to restrain it with rubber batons, foaming with anger and arrogance. But what's the fuss? A nation is similar to a rocket, and its desire is like the fuel. Without the best liquid propellant, how can you fly? If all of us are fettered or do things in stealth, then foreigners will certainly leave us further behind and put us in the miserable situation of passively receiving their blows. This is a frank forewarning. In short, if our nation can't have a positive attitude towards sexual intemperance, it will be almost impossible for it to revive.

"The shackle of abstinence is easier to break than anything else. Who can remember a single word of the stereotyped speeches of those dressed-up hypocrites who, after receiving thunderous applause, sneak into red-light districts? To say that Western countries are powerful and prosperous is not spreading rumours. Instead, their success is based on a relationship of mutual promotion. Only by being filled with sexual desire can one love beauty, desire material comfort, heighten the imagination and be the most creative. Don't you see that countries of extreme absurdity dotted with red-light districts are the most powerful hosts of advanced technologies, dense woodland, wealthy people and verdant lawns? Don't you see that countries that treat promiscuity as great scourges are full of impoverished individuals, wanton evildoers and public-deceiving, hypocritical preachers? The truth is that food and sex are interlinked. Abstinence leads to material shortage and starvation. Those who suffer from hunger find it harder to take off their clothes, and those who're deprived of sexual activity are prone to melancholy. This is a vicious cycle and testified by the ancient Chinese saying: 'A frost is added to snow', which means 'Calamities occur in succession'.

"Now, let's talk about national quality and character. The libido of an ascetic doesn't necessarily disappear altogether. Instead, it shoots here and there in the body and will eventually be released one way or another. That is why, in previous years, our country saw so many group scuffles and gang fights, various threats to inflict physical harm, and all kinds of cruel torture and instances of harsh law enforcement. The reason why so many in our communities are sinister and narrow-minded is simply because our character has been disfigured by the suppression of sensual enjoyment, generation after generation. On the other hand, those who give way to their carnal desires are always affable and unrestrained. Devoting their energy to love-making, they don't have to persecute and brutalise others. So, my principle is to guard against making friends with someone who is too chaste.

"To sum up, the barrier between men and women has to be dismantled. This is a responsibility we must face in the current era. Technology is progressing exponentially, and we're hard pressed for time. As everyone embraces change, we must work hard to catch up. There're many drugs to boost the sex drive. Pornographic material is rife across all media. Women talking provocatively on the radio, live sex phone calls and online dating services are competing for market share. New products and formats emerge in response to the prevailing needs. Whereas some people avoid them by covering their eyes, others clap their hands and embrace them with joy. This reflects the progress of the times and is a bliss of the nation. Feasting, revelry, pornographic language and vulgar music – all are auspicious. As heavy snow promises a good future harvest, so romance reflects a glorious age. The 'spirit of the paupers' is no match for delicious bread. No matter how aspiring a young man is, he'll give in if he remains single for a decade. No matter how pretty a young woman is, she'll become haggard and tongue-tied if she remains a virgin for a protracted period of time. Truth is covered by a single piece of thin paper, and, with a poke of the finger, you'll see through it.

"Ideological dogmas are omnipresent and ensnaring. Treating sexual affairs between men and women as common occurrences is the way to govern the country and boost the economy. The traditional culture of our country is one of asceticism. Everyone who practised it was set as an example to be emulated by others. As the situation worsened, talk of sexual desire became a taboo. In the end, anyone who sought but a little true love had to resort to stealing. It was absurd to discredit those things that are the most beautiful and decent and treat them as poison. Those who were extremely libidinous had been born at the wrong time. They either had to suppress their desire or were beaten black and blue if they should make a small attempt to express it. In the worst scenario, they could have even been put in shackles and deprived of their freedom for the rest of their lives. Women suffer the most. Under great pressure, they have no alternative but to behave decently. Forbidden from looking at handsome men when they run into them, they're subjected to a life without pleasure.

"All the disagreements in this world have resulted from mundane desires, of which sexual desire is the most fundamental of all. From my observation, even great historical and literary figures, as well as incarnates of the Literary God, have to make love, hence the proverb 'Even a hero cannot resist the temptation of a beauty'. After a few thousand years of enforcing the policy of asceticism, our people haven't become any stronger. Instead, our intelligence has been blunted, and we're becoming increasingly half-witted. Look at those countries in the West! With confidence and assurance, they boldly open their brothels to the public, provide medical care like injections to combat sexually-transmitted diseases, and pay people for the amount of work they do. The result is self-evident, so I don't have to waste my time. Just look at the number of technological innovations that lead to an abundance of high-tech products ranging from electrical appliances to aircraft carriers. In those countries, decent men have women to comfort, while decent women have men to love. Everyone mutually exchanges what he or she needs in their societies. Each touts sexuality as their leading daily activity and indulgence in sex is encouraged as the best qualification of a community member. Therefore, they have talents in large quantities and in almost every area. Even those whose faces are as ugly as crooked melons or cracked jujubes don't have to suffer loneliness so long as they have money in their pockets. It's apparent that they're rejuvenated at heart. With a ready supply of nectar, a nation is no longer lifeless. Nations like this that are fabulously wealthy can bully others with military prowess. Moreover, they can also peacefully enjoy themselves with their big houses and beautiful gardens, their aromatic coffee and cocktails, famed dancers and singers, porn stars and macho men – all those with beautiful bodies born to have more money than they can squander. They are the movers of this world with profits rolling into a mountain of wealth! We often refer to Western countries as *huahua shijie*.[1] How can they be so successful without being sensual?

"Although these words don't carry much weight from a person in my humble position, I dare not shirk my responsibility to worry about our country's future. I often debate with my dad, and we always end our conversation in unhappy discord. Today, however, I'm telling you all my comments bluntly because they're based on what I've been feeling. So, don't blame the messenger, but be forewarned by what the messenger has said. Correct it if you've done something wrong and guard against it if you haven't. Of course, being a veterinarian, I don't know much about anthropology. But if you can follow what I've said, you'll understand everything else by analogy. Thank you. It's been a great honour to give this lecture."

TO TIANTONG

To whom it may concern in Tiantong,

I'm the father of my undesirable son Golden Lock, to use his popular nickname. I'm writing to you because my unworthy son spoke a lot of nonsense in the meeting hall of your respectful company's hotel at three o'clock in the afternoon on the fifth day of the third month in the spring of this year according to the Chinese calendar. His nonsense caused everyone in the audience to leer at him in exasperation. My grandniece came teary-eyed and told me everything in detail. I'm so angry that I can't sleep. So I got up and turned on the light, and I'm now writing this letter to express my indignation and to show my feelings of shame and remorse. I'd like you to read it to your employees in public in the hope that it may eliminate the damaging effect. The title of my letter is 'On lechery being the evil of evils'.

Throughout the history of China, all sages have treated the libido of men and women as crucial to the governance of the country. The maintenance of social norms and the eradication of licentiousness are crucial to a country's rise and fall. My unworthy son shamelessly used words of falsehood to befog the minds of your employees with superficial knowledge, parroted assumptions and blindly copied remnants of Western theories. It's really unfortunate for an old and infirm man like me, at the stage of having my five wind types being intersected,[2] to see rare and grotesque phenomena emerge. In those years, I read veterinarian classics extensively and studied many veterinarian technologies. Having received a good education, I pursued a career as a vet with a view to making a contribution to agriculture. I worked hard to serve my fellow villagers until my unworthy son returned home unexpectedly with his hair dyed blond and earrings hanging from his lobes. He took away his father's clinic and perpetrated whatever evils he pleased, thus resulting in pandemonium. Sadly, the rascal is a perfect conman. Later, he deceived you, the boss, and usurped the power of the concierge service, thereby making him many times more pernicious.

The affairs of men and women conform to the laws of nature and the way of yin and yang. In a narrow sense, they're private matters, but in a broader sense, everyone in the world can talk about it. The flames of sexual desire can destroy public morals and mores, thus causing great harm. What can happen in China can also occur abroad. Every country that encourages sexual desire is bound to look strong while being fundamentally weak. Their people must be in a constant state of anxiety, getting lazy, making no attempt to aspire higher, breaking norms, lacking a sense of right and wrong, drowning themselves in carnal pleasures and loathing the correct way of the human world. There are some opportunist barbarians in those countries who repeatedly arouse amorous feelings, craving nothing short of keeping the flames of sexual desire burning. While touting it as sexual liberation, they aim to weaken the ruling governments. What a pity! Don't you see scoundrels running rampant at the cost of the common people in this morally confused world? Don't you see rulers indulging themselves in carnal pleasures behind curtains in thick-walled palaces and enjoying drinking with coquettish girls in the innermost recesses of palace halls? At the same time, however, they mete out severe punishments and enforce harsh laws. How can we average people learn from their example? For us, happiness means peace and safety, and joy means being fed and clad. How can they bear obscenities? Straw shacks and thatched huts that shake even when the wind isn't blowing, how can they stand the fierce gusts of lechery? Therefore, being hardworking, law-abiding, willing to suffer poverty and unwilling to deviate from the right track are the traits of normality. With limited food supply and bent on learning from the West, those young country rascals who wear gold and silver earrings indulge themselves in gambling or whoring. I'm certain that they'll come to no good.

I've been worrying for a long time. People of this world may have various shortcomings, and that has been true during all dynasties in history. Nevertheless, lust is something that must be guarded against because sages have always been concerned with the detrimental consequences of its proliferation. When lust is on people's minds, there'll be an absence of discipline, trust and fortitude. The line of defence between men and women will be pounded day and night. As a result, people are no longer solemn and respectful, but instead they become indolent, flirtatious and irresponsible. Ridiculous people fail to exercise due care and instead try to make their gains by trickery. Success comes from thoroughness, and failure stems from merrymaking. Restraint is harder than indulgence. Like the human body, the human world will display strength of character, keen intellect and an abundance of wisdom when practising abstinence. The results of years of hard work can be squandered in a few days. A country's protracted deficiency leads to delirium, hysteria, vacuity of yin and yang, and dangers lurking on every side. Therefore, from a town, a township, a city, a country down to a village, a household, a couple and a single person, everyone must respect each other like guests with dignity and abide by the law. It is in keeping with the law of heaven for men and women to enjoy and love each other and then do what nature calls to carry on the family line. What is there to be denounced? By contrast, what one must be wary of is the confusion of truth with falsehood and the lack of a sense of honesty and shame.

This useless old man is seventy-two years old. I went through the clamorous years when spiritual wholesomeness was advocated. I might occasionally be narrow-minded and often went to the extreme, but I harnessed my sexual drive, lived a simple life and worked conscientiously. As a result, I constantly added to my curiosity to learn and worked whole-heartedly in an effort to help build the country. I could summon a lot of people worthy of praise very quickly, but we often went the wrong way and got half the result with double the effort. Today, however, everything has been turned upside down. People have dissipated their vital essence and no longer believe in elixirs of immortality. Many of them are swathed in luxury and go from bad to worse. Men and women have barely exhausted their means to expose their bodies in outlandish clothes on and off stage. Nowadays, people vie for attention with their useless Western-style gadgets. They oppress the weak with sheer strength, sell their souls for money and betray their friends for personal gain. All of these traits can be traced to the promotion of sex and the loss of sincerity and honesty. Letting loose lust would destroy all the traditions. It's like a frayed jumper. Once the yarn starts to come loose, its end can be pulled and pulled, and eventually there will be nothing left of the garment.

Anyone abandoned to erotica will find their eyes fuzzy and see the landscape of the country drained of colour. Immersed in a sea of lust, one feels one's tendons and bones softened, and breath shortened. How can one fight for the truth as well as one's survival? One is bound to muddle through work or throw oneself into another's arms. A cynical and flippant person is obsessed with personal gain. Everyone tries to be smart and in the process becomes sophisticated and fainthearted. Consequently, only the ambitious and bold rise to vie with one another, causing evil forces to run rampant while plunging the average person into misery. Under the protection of walls and armour, bureaucrats and aristocrats fear no robbers, whereas the owners of small businesses and residents of the poor parts of town live in fear every day. Every time I go to the central business district, I feel my heart thumping because the world is transformed, and danger lurks everywhere. What comes into view all around is the sight of women baring their large breasts, individuals who are androgynous in appearance, men with dragon tattoos on their arms and women with nose rings, and some women, in particular, swaying as they walk because two thirds of their buttocks are exposed. All of these phenomena are signs of the end of the world. Each time I make such an assertion, my son Golden Lock foams with anger. As a result, he tends to harangue me for half a day.

We began as an agrarian nation and once stood as an example among all nations with our pastoral landscape and literary achievement. On the other hand, many of the other countries, being constantly looted by foreign bandits on horseback, were bound to struggle desperately for survival. Unfortunately, giving themselves up without loving themselves later, they dumped what was precious and picked up what was stinky garbage and thereby ended up on the path of decline. Our people, nevertheless, conforming to Confucian ethics and rites, following Buddhism and Daoism, and making studying pilgrimages to the West, restrain themselves from sexual indulgence. What a great tradition it is! But it was ridiculed by my awful son with his irresponsible remarks. The human experience has been bumpy and laden with misery. Now, it's incurring the wrath of heaven – don't you see those succumbing to a strange disease called Aids? It's a nasty, terminal disease originating from promiscuity. This warning stuns even fools, but the average person still sticks to their old way of doing things, unaware of the imminent catastrophe.

There will be some youngsters who regard my letter as rubbish and sweep it away with the tempest of the anti-Confucian May the Fourth Movement, not to mention the many revolutions in Western history. Generation after generation of sexual liberation movements have done nothing but deplete their ancestral properties. They are doomed to bankruptcy despite their solid family assets. Today, all the merrymakers have become penniless and are merely scraping a living. I may be senile, but I'm by no means an unenlightened, austere apologist of the Middle Ages. I just want to ask for the return of basic human dignity.

Thinking me senile, my worthless son Golden Lock dismissed me as a moralist. But he's dead wrong. I may know only a smattering of Confucian and Daoist doctrines, but I respect and follow them. I always maintain that only men of great stature are real heroes while emperors and their generals and ministers can follow. Being troubled with the people and the world, I've been taunted and hurt. I'm but a sacrifice dedicated to the world by way of cleansing absurdity and monstrosity with faith and integrity. I'm afraid that I may become a laughing stock as I can't expect anyone in my family to uphold moral standards in the last stage of my life. Rogues gang up to raise hell with an irresistible force. And after the pandemonium, the land will become desolate everywhere. The common people will be left with no alternative but to start from scratch and irrigate the land with their blood and sweat.

Pornography runs wild despite monthly crackdowns. The reason is that it has become habitual among the odd and capricious. In those years of class struggle, it was suppressed with an iron fist. But today, everyone turns a blind eye, as if they were idly watching the house of their next-door neighbour burn. Why is it so? Our country's prosperity after a century of weakness is to be expected, but it must take the precaution of looking hard at the past and the future. Why should it bow to anything foreign? A civilised country with a literary heritage and a long history can achieve success by being calm and unhurried. Don't you see that major waterways change their courses, heavenly bodies move in order, and changes become the norm? Therefore, panic and self-abasement are unnecessary. Besides, not everything in the West is the same, and even countries in Europe and North America are as varied as the spectrum of colours. Therefore, we mustn't appropriate any element of Western culture of which we have only a superficial understanding.

As a humble old man, I am being so bold as to write to your magnificent Tiantong Group. I humbly think that I have no alternative. Whether to advocate virtue and accumulate morality or vice versa is crucial to a company with funds raised in the hundreds of millions. After thinking for a long time, I feel so disappointed with Golden Lock's promotion to an important position. My worthless son may have the blood of common people circulating in his body, but he was so poisoned in other places that there's no antidote to cure him. As part of a workforce, he's more qualified to herd sheep and cows than men and women. Since this is a grave matter, I wish that your respectful group gives it serious thought and makes the right decision. Although I'm feeble, my will is still strong. I therefore have rebuilt the seriously damaged veterinarian station. The guesthouses of Tiantong Group are beautiful and accommodate visitors from foreign lands. That means it plays an important role in showcasing our national character. I wish you could consider my request seriously and remove Golden Lock from his post as a warning to others against following a bad example. Please take my request into consideration.

Respectfully submitted by your humble servant

RUMBLING THUNDER

"Oh Heavens, you haven't thundered so loudly for a decade. It's so scary! The clouds are also gathering. We'd better run."

A middle-aged man carrying something on his back looked at the sky sideways. His companion, a lanky man, taller than he was, now cast a glance at the sky in the northwest, saying: "It's not going to rain anytime soon."

They had not known each other until now, being merely travel companions. The one carrying something tugged the other, looked at the surging dark clouds and took to his heels. The lanky man laughed. He rolled a cigarette and lit it. The man ahead had already run a good distance. He called him, hoping that he would wait. But that man did not show any sign of stopping. Taking a puff of his cigarette, he started to run as fast and as light as his legs could carry him.

He soon caught up with the man ahead, and both slowed down a little.

"Brother, you don't have to be afraid. The rain won't fall until the wee hours. It's going to be a heavy one, so it needs time to get into position. Heaven is the most patient."

"How come that thunder was so loud? It's scary!" He looked into the sky and then at the dark shadows of the stretches of buildings in the north. The Large Rampart Compound of Purple Smoke was puffing up clouds of purplish-red smoke of varying dimensions.

They sat down to rest. The taller man rolled a cigarette and handed it to the other, who took it and said: "You're a fast runner!"

"That's why people call me Rabbit!"

The other man stood up abruptly and exclaimed: "So *you* are Rabbit?"

The taller man smiled, nodded and directed his eyes at the roll-up in his hand.

"Oh man! Everyone in this area knows you! Are you really that guy?"

"A real one can't be fake. You can just call me Rabbit."

"It's said you're a master of martial arts, can launch an explosive palm hit with a flick of your hand and run like the wind. Oh Brother, could you launch an explosive palm hit now so that I can see?"

"I'm not that all-powerful," Rabbit laughed.

The thunder rumbled louder, and the dark clouds surged right above. The colour of the smoke puffed out from the Large Rampart Compound of Purple Smoke flickered like will-o'-the-wisps against the sky.

"Look there, Brother Rabbit, the monster's foaming with anger!" The man appeared to be in a trance when a loud peal of thunder caused him to turn his head back, saying: "I think we must run again. The rain is really coming this time. Hope it'll rain hard. We haven't had a decent dowsing for the past decade because of the drought demon."

Rabbit nodded. "We've been suffering terribly at the hands of the drought demon. It's time to settle the account with him. You'd better rush back to your village. You don't want to be late and miss the campaign of fighting the drought demon."

"We're fighting the drought demon today?" the middle-aged man asked as he rose to his feet.

"Today. We've looked for him for six months and finally found his den. The demon was the culprit of the decade's drought. If we can't get rid of it, the farmers won't be able to continue. At mid-afternoon today, the villagers all around will come out to quietly hem in the drought demon, and nail it, so that it won't have a chance to escape."

"Good Heavens! I see... Then, we must hurry, Brother Rabbit," said the middle-aged man, who had become so excited that his teeth chattered. Patting Rabbit's shoulder, he continued: "You're a good man. I wish you luck for the rest of your life."

"Hurry and go! Thank you for the good words. Bye now. See you during the fight against the drought demon!"

It was early afternoon. Rabbit went into a village, where the street was quiet and still, as if everyone were taking a nap. He took a turn down an alley and caught sight of a man coming out carrying a large hoe. When he took another look, the man retreated. Silence reigned everywhere, without even the cries of domestic animals or chickens. The front door in every house was shut.

"It's about time. Yes, I can just make out the smell of the smoke and fire," muttered Rabbit as he ventured deeper into the village to pay a visit to an old friend.

This was the largest village in the hilly area, only a few kilometres from the villages on the plain in the north. There were few trees in the village, and the slate-paved surface of the streets glistened. Large areas were worn away by thousands of feet over several generations. The sun was finally setting. It seemed that someone uttered a muffled cry, and with it, footsteps started to thump on each of the slate-paved streets and roads. A wave of hues and cries lapped over.

All the young and middle-aged men of the village swarmed into the widest street from the various alleys carrying hoes, spades, picks, three-pronged rakes, as well as iron bars, shoulder poles and large hammers.

"Let's go and fight the drought demon!" a husky voice shouted. "It's high time we settled our account with it. Go! Let's go! People from the surrounding villages all come together. No one can slack!"

His call to arms was followed by others: "Let's go! Only sons of bitches slack."

"Let's go. Give the old drought demon a good kicking!"

"If we don't castrate the vermin this time, we can't expect to have a drop of rain!"

As the crowd surged to the entrance of the village, peals of crashing thunder could be heard. Cupping their hands over their eyes, they saw dark figures thronging the paths in the fields ahead. Behind the kicked-up dust, people appeared from other villages, also armed with farm tools.

"We'll teach the drought demon beast a good lesson this time. We must run quickly, though, before others get to it first. With our big hoes, we'll break the demon's gate open."

"Yes, whoever is soft is a coward. Whoever has shaking legs is a chicken."

"We've been suffering from this drought demon for ten years. There's no turning back."

In just half an hour, people converged to the open field from all sides. "Let's encircle the Old Graveyard," a voice boomed. "Surround it with multiple layers!"

The villagers then formed into several groups, each following a leader. The Old Graveyard consisted of tombs of the ancestors from the biggest village, known to all the locals. It had taken the villagers six months to figure out that the drought demon was hiding in this graveyard. It had betrayed itself by keeping a patch of soil moist while everywhere around it was as dry as a bone. The findings were circulated secretly, and a shaman had also surveyed it clenching his teeth and nodding his head. Then, a circle was drawn a couple of kilometres from the spot, and peach-wood swords were planted on the circumference. The shaman chanted incantations day and night, waiting for the chance to besiege the demon... An hour had gone by before people sneaked around, arching their backs and soon surrounding the graveyard so closely that not even an ant could escape.

A hubbub arose again in the open field. Shouts erupted in the middle of the graveyard, but it was not clear what they were shouting about due to the commotion. The surging crowd sometimes shaped itself into multiple groups and sometimes into a single diamond or oval formation. An even louder clamour burst out from the centre and farm tools of varying lengths were hoisted like trees swaying in a strong wind. The pandemonium lasted until mid-afternoon, when a stream of people darted diagonally from a shady place. As they ran, they screamed, followed by the remaining horde.

"No! No! The demon is running away. Towards the wilderness. Hurry! Let's go after it."

"Does the demon still want to slip away today? We'll catch it even if it throws itself into the sea." The crowd swarmed here and there, chasing an indistinct, whitish figure.

"Where in the world is it?"

"Look! Look! It rises like a misty cloud and falls back."

"In the form of an inverted V?"

"Well, it's a demon after all, so it changes form all the time."

"Hey, I can't see it any more..."

The crowd looked up in unison, searching the sky for the fleeing drought demon as they shouted and reached out their hands to scrabble wildly.

Some of them said that the fierce sunshine scared the demon and forced it to shrink into a white streak, which was discernible only to those with the best eyesight. Look at it, swaying and twisting and tumbling forward. What's ahead is nothing but death!

"Do you see it? That's the head. Those're the arms. Hey! It's on all fours and leaps towards the east, then towards the north. Aha, son of a bitch, it's scampering towards the Large Rampart Compound of Purple Smoke. What shall we do?"

"Yes, yes! I saw it dashing that way. My God! It's running into the compound. What shall we do?"

A man in the lead leaned upon his hoe. He shouted only because he did not have the guts to continue the chase. Everyone looked in the same direction, gasping. As they approached it, they found the large, black rampart compound sneezing and belching. They all covered their noses to repel the intensifying stench. The rampart compound was surrounded by high walls, with an electric accordion iron gate on each side. Each gate was topped with a flashing police siren and was manned by guards carrying spiked maces.

"Open the gate! Open the gate!" shouted the man with the booming voice, hoe in hand.

"What're you up to?" asked one of the guards.

"The drought demon has just sneaked in! You didn't see it even with your glasses on?"

"What drought demon?"

"Damn! We don't have time to explain. Hurry and open the gate."

"My God! Hurry! Report to the supervisor straight away. Report to the supervisor…"

Before the guard could finish, a dozen or so hoe-carrying villagers had pushed one side of the accordion iron door forward, and the crowd stormed into the walled rampart compound.

The screams, curses and shouts of the chasers could be heard everywhere. Soon, an object was broken, sending shards of glass flying and cutting a villager's face, from which blood oozed out. Ignoring his injury, the guy screamed: "Look! Look there!" Everyone scanned the place where he was pointing, trying to make out what it was. Finally, they spotted a white figure creeping out from the roof of the largest and tallest rampart, baring its teeth and glaring at the crowd down below. "Jeez, the drought demon has crawled back in. Now we've seen it clearly with our own eyes."

Clamour arose on three sides within the walls, and the dust was so thick that it overwhelmed the purple smoke. Putrid gas permeated the air. A uniformed man rushed out to shout through a handheld megaphone, but his voice was drowned by the uproar of the crowd swarming over. After a while, sparks twined into a fiery ball like a thunderbolt and rolled here and there, issuing one muffled rumble after another and sending out cloud after cloud of thick smoke into the sky.

After about an hour, the Large Rampart Compound of Purple Smoke that had been growling all the time now began to pant with great effort amid human voices and a strange, muffled sound audible from time to time. Just then, police sirens coming from all directions added to the hubbub.

"The police are coming. What are we going to do?" someone shouted in the smoke and dust.

"We're waiting for them. The sons of bitches should've come earlier. They've just remembered to help us fight the drought demon."

"They're in time! They're in time! They have guns. We can deal with the demon now."

"Hold on. Are they from the Tiantong Group or the police station? They may be coming to protect the drought demon."

"Let's move close and ask them if they're from the police station," roared the guy with the booming voice.

Someone passed on his order and said: "Our leader told us to go over and ask."

The police sirens sounded ever closer. Some of the villagers rushed towards them and soon returned, announcing: "They're not from the police station. They're from Tiantong. They blocked our way and forced us to stop fighting the drought demon."

"Whoever stops us from fighting the drought demon is our sworn enemy! Guys, wield your hoes but be careful not to accidentally injure our own people," the booming-voiced man roared.

"Good Heavens! Our leader is so combative he's become crazy. Let's follow him anyway."

The police cars lined up to form a barrier within the walls, and a large group of helmeted men in new uniforms stood facing the crowd with their legs apart and police batons or firearms in their hands.

Those charging in front of the crowd whispered to one another: "Looks like they're from the regular police stations."

"No! It's evident they're from the Tiantong Group. They got their uniforms by trickery. Don't make wild guesses. Besides, how can policemen be on the drought demon's side?"

"Right. You're absolutely right."

With the blast of a whistle, several helmeted men started shooting.

"Aah! They dare to pull the trigger. Looks like they're not going to live till supper!" As soon as the booming man uttered the curse, the other villagers charged forward after him with hoes in hand.

The helmeted men dispersed in an uproar. Some of them cast their weapons aside, only to picked up by the onrushing villagers. The remaining helmeted men darted out of the compound and galloped like crazy. None of them wanted to fall behind. Seeing them scurrying into the distance, their pursuers turned back, and the first thing they saw was the row of police cars. While cursing the drought demon, the crowd began to smash the vehicles and soon reduced them to heaps of scrap metal.

"Hey guys, I don't care if you're old or young. Let's go and seek the drought demon now that we've smashed their cars and caused the Large Rampart Compound of Purple Smoke to exhale its last puff of smoke. We won't give it time to catch its breath," yelled the man with a booming voice and with a murderous look on his face. In the flickering light of the storm, he seemed to be rocking violently from side to side.

"Let's charge, leader. We'll charge with full force. We'll pull apart anything that's in our way. Let's go! We'll press forward. We'll attack savagely without looking up," shouted a young man with a teary voice, his face covered with bloodstains.

The crowd spread out and pressed on from different parts of the Large Rampart Compound of Purple Smoke. Occasionally, people rushed over from the other side, each carrying combat gear. Though strangers to each other, the two groups all knew that they were here for the same purpose. They exchanged what they knew about the rampart, saying: "Don't worry. Just forge on. It's said the workers on watch have all gone. They've suffered enough for too long, and each is as thin as a toothpick."

"The part of the rampart compound there has become a heap of metal. We heard that a white-haired demon was dragged out of the debris and was hoed to pieces. Could that be the drought demon?"

"It must have been. Where's it now? Where is it? I won't believe it until I see it. Take us there so we can have a look."

The news that the drought demon had been killed circulated amid the bustling crowd. Their cheers rippled like waves. It was pitch-dark, and the wind was increasingly chilly. The clouds were both dense and thick. Instead of darting back and forth from the north to the south, the thunder now stayed overhead. The muffled noises in the distance and the hubbub close by echoed each other. Fire bolts outstretched in the sea of clouds and soon lit up half of the sky.

"The clouds are really patient. We'll see how the rain falls tonight. If we've killed the drought demon, all the rainwater pent up for a decade will pour down at once," said someone who was looking up and panting with fear, his weight supported by the hoe standing beneath his pressing hands.

"What a vicious drought demon it was, denying us a decent rain for more than a decade."

"Listen! What makes that sound?"

"Well, the thunder – oh no, police cars. Why are we hearing gunshots before seeing the cars?"

"How come? I only hear the police car engines."

"'Bang, bang'! If those aren't gunshots, what can they be? They're from semiautomatic rifles, semiautomatic rifles…"

The people gathered together. They all said that their leader was so combative that he had total disregard for the consequences. Now that he was nowhere to be found, they wondered what they could do next.

"I assume a whole army is closing in because Tiantong has all the people it needs. It can summon an entire regiment or even more from the villages."

"Nah, I think it has more than a regiment. They won't take their losses lying down. Since they can launch a counterattack, they must be fully prepared."

"Maybe they're from real police stations. If they are, they'll sure help us."

"Whoever they are, I think we've done enough. The drought demon has been killed, and the rain is about to fall. As the old saying goes: 'A wise man doesn't keep on fighting when the odds are against him.' It's time to retreat."

"Hey leader! Did you hear that? It's time to pull out."

The shout was echoed by the crowd in unison, and their footsteps also sounded as one. Meanwhile, the police cars, blasting their sirens, roared loudly with their headlights shining on the crowd. A loudspeaker sounded: "You're surrounded. You're surrounded. Put down your arms. Put them down! Place your hands over the back of your heads. No one is allowed to escape. You're surrounded, surrounded…"

"Fuck you sons of bitches who work for the drought demon! If you're here to arrest us, we'll make you as helpless as a dog with mustard in its mouth. Everyone, old and young, let's pierce their backs through with the tools in our hands. Charge!"

The crowd surged like a tide and rolled on with thunderous cries. At the same time, tons of rain poured down and hit the crowd to the ground. They fumbled to recover their tools and then forged ahead, arching their backs. As they plunged forward, they shouted: "Look what we've done! We've killed the drought demon for sure. Look at the pouring rain! It's worth it even if we die."

FIGHTING THE DROUGHT DEMON

The sound of the lashing rain drowned out everything that night. It even masked the gunshots and the rumbles of thunder behind the rain curtain. The crowd was dispersed by the rain like ants. The opponents of the conflict could not distinguish each other and had no option but to fumble their way back to their shelters. Unfortunately, many of them lost their bearings. They bumped into each other and scurried here and there and eventually to no one knows where. The abandoned spiked maces, rifles, hoes and shoulder-poles were washed away by the torrential rainwater, all the way to the lowlands.

Everyone was talking about the incident in which a legendary drought demon had been dug out the previous day. This monster had incarnated itself into the corpse of a human being and sneaked into its burial ground. By doing so, it left a moist mound on the thousand-kilometre drought-stricken land. It was unknown whether villagers on the plain or those from the hills located the demon and thus could claim credit for achieving the best outcome in the world. Whatever the truth, after being besieged and deprived of the chance to escape, the demon plunged itself into the wilderness and then sneaked into Tang Tong's Large Rampart Compound of Purple Smoke.

No one doubted that the drought demon was killed last night. Otherwise, there could not have been such rain after a decade-long drought. When the sky cracked, it began to spew water unstoppably like a wailing old man opening his mouth wide. The rain was determined to fill up all the ravines and valleys. That night, the farmers fled from the rain rather than from the Tiantong people, and they were relieved not to be washed into the ravines to become frogs and toads.

The rain had been falling incessantly for a day and a half. The women of all the villages had prayed with tears for the whole night and finally they were able to see their husbands and sons come back home. Those who had failed to see anyone return home threw themselves on the *kang* in despair, unwilling to get up. The rain had both merits and demerits. While it dispersed the combatants and put out the raging fire, it made it difficult to address the situation. The rain might have fought the drought demon, but in the process, it had also damaged the Large Rampart Compound of Purple Smoke. The employees of Tiantong would not forgive the farmers. It proved impossible to arrest all the fleeing people involved in the act of fighting the drought demon. A pack of police dogs was unable to cope with the roads washed by rainwater, and it would take various police vehicles days to drive into all the villages in the flooded open country. Meanwhile, people scattered in all directions, and it was impossible to rein them all in.

The weather was now clearing up. Wherever the police vehicles went, they were greeted with silence, as every household shut its door. Vivid, detailed rumours were circulating far and wide on the plains and hills in a matter of a few days. While sharing more or less the same outline, varying versions of the rumours each had their own added detailed descriptions. It concerned an incident that had originated from the heavy rain. Years of drought had inflicted misery on the farmers a few dozen kilometres around. Both the rocks and soil were so dried up that smoke started to rise from them. Luckily, a fox spirit often visited people's dreams to tell them the existence of a drought demon in the area. It was the culprit of the drought. Residents from the surrounding villages were eager to find the demon. They decided to accomplish this life-and-death task at all cost. Sons followed fathers, who in turn consulted their sons, leaving only the women behind to watch their homes. Then, carrying pot-baked flatbread in their clothes, they went out to search everywhere. They repeatedly scoured the desolate graveyards and every inch of the hills.

They searched and searched until they finally tracked it down to a thousand-year-old graveyard. The elderly folk all knew that the demon was entrenched in the ground and sneaked out only at midnight, when it would sweep the clouds away in the sky with a gigantic broom, leaving not even a wisp. It had the habit of working at night and sleeping by day until the land cracked and was unable to yield a single crop.

"Good Heavens! We've finally found this demon. Look at the scorched grass around and this wet spot above its hiding place. How creepy! It's still snoozing in the den." While the discovery was passed around, a shaman was hired to decide on an appropriate time for action, and everyone was notified of the date. When the day came, villagers from all around swarmed to the graveyard.

The result was a botched job due to a prevailing sense of anxiety and impatience. The pitter-patter of footsteps shook the earth and startled the demon. It rolled in the ground half asleep. Some men were busy digging the ground holding their breath while others watched in rings that spread into the distance, all waiting restlessly for the demon to come out so that they could exterminate it with their concerted efforts.

That day, a pent-up wrath exploded and shot into the sky, thus alerting the Lord of Thunder to the war that the humans on Earth were fighting against the drought demon. He beat his drum to render his help. In response, clouds gathered from all around and got ready to rain as soon as the drought demon was terminated. But the people on Earth were growing increasingly agitated, hoping to flush out the demon with one swipe of a hoe and smash it with more, random strikes. However, none of them had seen this notorious creature. As they dug deeper with diminishing confidence, their hands began to tremble.

Knowing it was besieged, the demon played dead. When the diggers reached the bottom of the pit they had dug, an extraordinarily pungent stench nearly overwhelmed the diggers and the crowd, who had to step back covering their noses with their hands. When they ventured forward again and craned their necks to look, it was too late. The drought demon, in an incarnated human form wearing an armour of jangling copper coins with its white hair sticking out of the crevices, suddenly sprang out of the big pit and, with a single stride, scurried a kilometre or two away. Unlike average beasts, it was too fast to capture.

The crowd stood dumbfounded for more than ten minutes, at a loss what to do. By the time they collected themselves, the drought demon had broken through many layers of the encirclement. But thanks to their significant numbers and their tools as numerous as the trees in a forest, the farmers, young and middle-aged, from the plains and hills eventually cornered the stinking demon. It was forced back to the north and then the west. Hot in pursuit, the crowd zigzagged on the open fields and, in the end, darted into the Large Rampart Compound of Purple Smoke.

"Fuck! So you guys smashed the rampart compound as well, did you?" a man in uniform asked, notebook in hand.

Some of the elderly villagers chuckled so much that their few remaining teeth shook. "Impossible! It's said that, after it got into the Large Rampart Compound of Purple Smoke, the drought demon was almost overpowered by the fart smell spewed from the ramparts. It couldn't stand it, so it trembled and hopped. The worried villagers feared that it might damage the large rampart compound in doing so. And that would have been serious! So, they cried loudly together, trying to scare it out."

"How did they scare it? What did they shout?"

"I shouted: 'Hey drought demon, you think you're bolder than the God of Heaven? How dare you harm the rampart compound! This is a big farting machine built by Tang Tong and the foreigners. If you dare lay a finger on it, we farmers from all the villages around won't give you a chance to live. Be good and come out. Or may the fart kill you with its stench.'"

"What happened then?"

"It couldn't help it. The smell was too strong for it to endure. It struggled hard and, with a few punches and kicks, ravaged the rampart compound. The villagers then started to hoe and pick the drought demon in retaliation. In the end, they killed the demon while breaking some of Tang Tong's machines in the process."

The uniformed man chuckled: "Granddad, you may be good at fabricating stories, but that won't prevent us from taking you to the police station."

"What did I fabricate? The big rain is a testimony to what I told you. If we hadn't hoed the drought demon to death, how could there have been such a downpour?"

The man put away his notebook and jerked his head as a signal. His colleague cuffed the old man.

"I'm wronged. If my wife knew I'm being taken away, she would cry herself blind."

Instead of listening to the old man's appeals, a few officers pushed him roughly into a car with blue stripes, and it drove away blasting its siren and flashing its light.

For a whole month, a search was conducted for the leader of the fight against the drought demon. The villagers said that it was too complicated to tell who the leader was. They argued that it was the fox spirit instead of any person of fame or esteem that started the fight. They had been sworn enemies for between eight hundred and a thousand years. If the police wanted to take care of their conflict, it would have needed a magic power. The villagers asked the policemen: "Do you have shamans and thunder-stricken, peach-wood swords in your station?"

A policeman took out a mugshot from his pocket and showed it to the people near and far. Then, he asked: "A fox spirit that looks like this?"

Quite a few of the villagers recognised the image as the man nicknamed Rabbit, but they pretended to be confused, saying: "Officer, you're joking, aren't you? This image is of a real person."

"Well, a wild creature can be incarnated as a human being. If we catch this motherfucker, we'll teach him a good lesson. This scoundrel is so vicious that he can create havoc." The policeman holding the picture opened his mouth wide in astonishment.

Tang Tong's police cars drove here and there, sometimes cruising silently through the alleys, sometimes accelerating away with their sirens turned on. When this happened, villagers would look up and scream: "They've arrested another one. Another one!"

Various rumours were flying around. Some said that, on the day of fighting the drought demon, the farmers wreaked havoc on Tang Tong's Large Rampart Compound of Purple Smoke and caused human casualties, wounding thirty of his people and killing five of them. The casualties of the villagers were more than fifty wounded and over a dozen killed, who fell victim not only to bullets and clubs but also to the fart of the ramparts. Some of them were so severely wounded that they could not run fast enough to survive the torrential flood in the ravines. It was said that Tang Tong regarded his own people's lives as worth more than those of the villagers. To be exact, one of his people was worth three villagers. In total, he had sustained more than a hundred casualties. Therefore, he was capturing enough villagers to make up the difference.

"Good Heavens! As the proverb goes: 'A case involving human life must be treated with the utmost care.' Foreigners own half of the Large Rampart Compound of Purple Smoke and share half of the profits with Tang Tong. Now, the foreigners were mad! Glaring at the curly-haired guy with their cat-like blue eyes, they questioned him: 'What did you promise us before? Didn't you thump your chest and say OK?' The male and female *tongzuizi* were kept so busy that they ran back and forth. They had used to kiss the foreigners before starting to translate, but now they didn't have the time or inclination to observe the ritual."

"Who had the time to perform the foreign ritual? It's said that Tang Tong even sobbed. While rubbing away his tears, he said: 'I don't usually shed tears. If my memory serves me, I cried only when my dad passed. I must capture Rabbit and his like. Then, I'll skin them, put them in a pot and cook them into a soup on high heat with the help of electric bellows. I'll pluck all the hairs off his body!' Listen! That's real hatred."

"We farmers have been suffering endlessly, from both the drought demon and the Large Rampart Compound of Purple Smoke. Some of us also say that the demon and the compound are allies anyway. Otherwise, the demon would not have run into the rampart compound. If there was a way out, who would leave their family behind and rush out with their hoes held high? They knew if they stepped out of the village, they might not be able to return in this life. This is what we call 'Fight the drought demon at the risk of our lives'. It's not like going to a temple fair with our hair all done up. It's like having one's head tucked in the waist belt – by going out, they've already given up half of their lives. Oh, Heaven, pray you protect the villagers. Protect Rabbit. The spirits of foxes, Siberian weasels, hedgehogs, as well as the gods and goddesses of the sea, you must know that our villagers are suffering enormously. Please help us with your concerted efforts. We villagers are all grateful and will sacrifice twelve big hogs to you. After our prayers, we'll offer incense to you from the early morning."

With teary eyes, old women stood at the entrance of their villages expecting their family members to return. Once they came back, the old women would burn incense. Even the dogs were seen to move with their backs hunched. Drawing a long face, none of the animals had the heart to bark. This autumn would certainly not be forgotten for a long time. But the mysterious, filthy, sly and surreptitious demon of Earth will remain in legend forever.

After many, many years, someone might say: "My loved one was a fighter of the drought demon. He died in that battle."

EIGHTEEN

BESIEGED

ON A SUNNY MORNING before the rain, Mei Di was already restless.
She paced up and down inside and outside the house, reluctant to
do anything. At around ten o'clock, she took a hot bath. She
intentionally turned the temperature hot enough to feel her skin
scalding so that it became red in patches. She put on her bathrobe
and a towel around her head and went out of the bathroom, only to
see Liao Mai hurrying in from the outside.

"Why are you in such a hurry? What's going on, my fine man?"

Casting a glance at her, Liao Mai did not respond. He poured
himself a mug of water and drank it in big gulps. Shaking his head
and pounding his back with his hand, he said: "Maybe it's going to
rain because my back aches. You've got to go to the side of the lake
to take a look. Those fish are crying and leaping. They're calling
you!" With that, he swigged the rest of the water from the mug.

Mei Di planted a kiss on his forehead, but he remained
unmoved. "My really fine man, I've been extremely fretful. I really
feel like biting you to give vent to my vexation." In saying these
words, she pinched and twisted a muscle on his chest and gave a
gentle bite on his upper arm. Liao Mai untied her bathrobe and
examined her chest and armpits to see if she had rashes there, but

the moist, smooth skin was back to normal and free of any blemishes.

"Go! Go to the fields," he said. "We still have a lot to do before the weather turns."

Mei Di did not follow him out. Instead, she leaned over the windowsill and watched him walking towards the side of the lake, hoe over shoulder and waving at some of the workers. She knew that he was going to dredge the waterways by removing the slush and sedge caught in the sluice railings. She did not want to work. She just wanted to lie next to him, to bite him, to cry and to babble away. They had barely spoken for the past ten days. He was now consumed with hard work. At the end of the day, he returned covered with mud and sweat, yet he still went to bed without taking a bath. As soon as she started complaining, he would go to the room by the garage to sleep by himself.

In the middle of the afternoon, the dark clouds and the rumble of thunder heralded the rare certain prospect of heavy rain. Drought had seized the entire plain and hill areas for the past decade. The farmers complained constantly and cursed the drought demon in unison. This was the only farm to be spared the worst of the drought because of the L-shaped lake and its advanced irrigation system. Toiling away for the whole morning with the workers, Liao Mai finally made the water flow freely and started to reinforce the work sheds by staking the rickety wooden frames to the ground. Later, wearing overalls and white gloves, Mei Di joined him and worked in high spirits. Liao Mai looked at her when the lightning lit up the night sky, discovering that she might be a bit plump but not at all clumsy. Instead, not only did she look nimble, but she also appeared extremely graceful.

After midnight, rain started to pour, and it was surprisingly heavy. Leaning out of the window, Mei Di mumbled: "Gosh! Maybe the drought demon is indeed dead. Now, we'll have a flash flood."

Liao Mai put on his clothes and sat on the kang. He was listening to the thunder rumbling and the guard dog Big Tiger Head barking. Gradually, he began to feel impatient. He had an urge to tear everything around him to pieces. Mei Di paced up and down as the lightning flashed outside, her buttocks swaying as she did so. In anger, Liao Mai blurted out a swearword, a really obscene one. Even he himself was scared by his brazen insolence. Mei Di turned to gaze at him with tears swelling in her eyes. From midnight to dawn, neither of them fell asleep. The rain continued. By six in the morning, it was still pitch-dark all around.

"Maizi, look what's going on in the south," Mei Di cried on the porch. Liao Mai jumped off the *kang*, dashed to the porch and caught sight of a piercing light beam sweeping horizontally. It was the spotlight of a police car, and it was apparently mired in a muddy road. The other intensive beams waving constantly were high-power handheld torches. The beams of different light sources probing up and down and left and right reminded him of the scene when Rabbit was being rounded up last summer. "I must go out. I must take a look," said Liao Mai as he grabbed his jacket and stepped out of the door. Mei Di urged him to put his raincoat on.

Only when he had almost reached the end of the farm did he realise that there were people shining torches to the east, west and south. They were gathering towards the north, followed by many barking police dogs. It was evident that these pursuers were trying to corner the fugitive against the base of the fence wall over here. Liao Mai stared at the base of the south fence wall. He did not see anyone climbing over it even when the pursuers were drawing nearer. Some of them wore raincoats while others did not. Covered with a greasy, blackish dirt and mud all over, they looked exceedingly scary. Without saying a word to him, they scaled the fences one after the other and seemed unstoppable.

An exhaustive search began, first of Liao Mai and Mei Di's house and garage, then of the work sheds and the groves and farmland. Soon, horrible cries were heard from among the giant taro plants. A gang of club- and rifle-carrying men found three bleeding fugitives. They pounced upon them, grabbing their arms, kicking them and hitting them with clubs that they wielded horizontally. Liao Mai overheard them yelling their questions: "Where's that scoundrel? Tell us!" The three men clammed up.

After another search of thirty minutes yielded no more fugitives, the pursuers left, taking the three captives in cuffs with them. Each time he watched them trampling a pumpkin or a giant taro plant in the fields, Liao Mai's heart sank, but his efforts to stop them either physically or verbally did not work. Concentrating on their search, they paid him no heed.

The rain stopped. Liao Mai found himself sitting in the loose mud by the reeds at the curve of the L-shaped lake. He sat there dazed for a while when all of a sudden he heard water splashing behind him. He turned around and was stunned. A man with a large lotus leaf on his head and mud and bloodstains on his face was waving at him and whispering his name. Liao Mai screamed in silence: Good Heavens! It's Rabbit.

After sunrise, all the workers came out from their work sheds with ghastly faces. They had been scared by the rain falling throughout the night and by the horrifying searches and arrests. They approached the fence wall, only to become more frightened. They saw a huge stretch of shiny water surrounding the farm that had now become an island.

The water besieged the farm for three days without receding. Some armed men paced around the farm and changed guards at intervals. Police cars with their flashing red lights were parked on high ground above the water. There was a checkpoint at each intersection. People were stopped, interrogated and examined on the paths leading to the small dock from around the farm. All the workers who went outside the farm and the drivers of vehicles that transported goods out of the gate were questioned on their way as well.

During the first few days, Rabbit and Liao Mai stayed in the garage and then relocated to the attic above Liao Mai and Mei Di's master bedroom. It was used to store various items. Along the attic wall, there was a row of moveable boards that had originally been used for the installation of heating pipes. The space could now be used for a hiding place in an emergency. Rabbit and Liao Mai seldom went downstairs. If something happened, Mei Di would inform them by tapping the pipes.

"We have ample provisions here anyway. We've got everything. You just wait here patiently and see how long those sons of bitches can stand on guard out there," said Liao Mai.

The cuts on Rabbit's face had formed scabs, but one of his eyes was still swollen, and he felt terribly sore in his left ribs. Clenching his teeth, he said: "I'm very anxious. I've been worrying about my people. I must find a way to get out of here as quickly as possible."

During the three days of his stay with Liao Mai, Rabbit told him what had happened in detail, specifically the whole process of the fight against the drought demon. "Many of us were wounded, and four or five were killed. Perhaps there have been more deaths. That's something I must figure out when I get out of here. Tiantong's people and those who helped them also suffered losses, but they had fewer casualties. We had no alternative but to launch the attack. We had planned to do it a long time before, but it was inevitable sooner or later. But for a few glitches, we would have done it at the beginning of spring."

Rabbit asked Liao Mai for a cigarette. As soon as he took a puff, he started to cough, but he continued smoking anyway. "Damn!" he said. "The villagers are now certain to suffer from the aftermath of the drought demon. Tiantong's Large Rampart Compound of Purple Smoke is going to be expanded and will be followed by the rampart compounds of blue smoke and red smoke. Tang Tong is desperate for the expansion. The water from the large rampart compound is killing fish when it flows into the river and reservoir, and destroying crops when it overflows onto the farmland. If someone dares to lodge a complaint, he'll be mugged by masked thugs. Tiantong has bribed all the village heads with cars and houses and turned them into its running dogs and moles embedded among the villagers. No matter what the villagers plan to do, they must keep it a secret so that it won't be divulged by those running dogs."

Liao Mai nodded. "The corrosive power of money is ten times stronger than sulphuric acid. If money is not powerful enough, other means would be used. The Large Rampart Compound of Purple Smoke is pressing northwards, towards this farm... Those beasts!"

"They are beasts! The workers in the large rampart compound are all poor folk from the surrounding villages and children from places outside the area. There's no worker protection and they're paid unbelievably low wages. Each month there're workers who die of accidental intoxication or commit suicide. If the relatives of the dead workers come to claim their bodies, they'll be paid little indemnity. If they're lonely migrants, their bodies will be buried in secret. The villagers all say that the Large Rampart Compound of Purple Smoke has been built with the white bones of workers as bricks and their blood and sweat as cement."

As he spoke, Rabbit pressed one hand against his left side and reached out the other for a painkiller. Liao Mai shook his head.

"You've already had too many." But Rabbit refused to withdraw his hand. Liao Mai sighed and gave him a tablet reluctantly.

Rabbit continued: "The villagers had planned to rise up at the beginning of spring. They had prepared for a few months while keeping the village heads in the dark. Who would have expected there to be an eccentric among the rebel leaders who was obsessed with religious activities? But a Daoist priest that he had enlisted was a fake. He was an associate of the Tiantong Group and had done many evil deeds within a radius of fifty kilometres. He built a Daoist temple to profit by collecting money and to fish for information about the rebels. He thus caused two of the rebel leaders to be taken prisoner and the rebellion to be called off. They were sold out by the Daoist priest and are nowhere to be found even today…"

"Have you seen the Daoist priest?" Liao Mai interrupted. "What does he look like?"

"He's of medium build – a big, round, glossy face and a sparse, golden beard. He's under sixty."

"That's him! There can be no mistake."

Pulling Liao Mai's shoulders with his hands, Rabbit asked: "What are you saying?"

"Um, I'm thinking of a man." Liao Mai recalled the new Daoist temple on Trident Island and the demonic priest who tormented the forewoman. "Most probably, that's the guy." He went on to tell Rabbit about the Daoist priest that he and Qi Jin had seen.

"It must be him!" Rabbit said. "It's said that he'd been urging Tang Tong to build a new Daoist temple and make him its abbot. This guy's hands are soaked with the blood of farmers. Someone will settle accounts with him sooner or later. Let's wait and see."

It was late at night. Neither of the two men could sleep. Their constant pacing also prevented Mei Di from falling asleep down below. Instead, she went up to listen to them talk and cooked some snacks for them in the kitchen.

After she left, Rabbit said: "I've never seen a woman as beautiful as my sister-in-law. Brother, I can't imagine your luck. Everyone in the world must envy you. It's true!"

As Rabbit's pain in the left side intensified, Liao Mai and Mei Di suspected that he might have broken his ribs. They wanted to send him to hospital but considered it impossible on second thoughts because police cars were still cruising back and forth outside the fence wall. Mei Di collected some Chinese violet grass that has the property to heal the symptoms of injuries caused by knocks and falls. She remembered that her father used to apply this medicinal herb to himself. She pounded the herbs into a paste and plastered Rabbit's left side with it. She changed it daily.

Every time Mei Di changed the herbal paste for Rabbit, sweat would break out all over his body and stream down from his forehead. Occasionally, the opposite would happen; feeling cold, he would shiver and chatter his teeth.

"Are you hurting badly?"

Rabbit shook his head.

"Then what's wrong?"

Rabbit fell silent, biting his lip. Whenever Mei Di was close to him, he would smell a strange scent, like the raw smell of something in the wilderness, like Siberian cocklebur or Datisca. The scent was so strong that he could barely endure it, but he still said holding his breath: "Don't worry, my sister-in-law. I'm... I'm much better."

The night seemed extremely long. Neither Liao Mai nor Mei Di could sleep. It was after midnight, but Liao Mai was still drinking. Rabbit began to worry about him.

"Brother Rabbit! I want to tell you. I'm quite sober tonight, so please don't think I'm talking as a drunkard."

His face scarlet, Liao Mai held Rabbit's hands tight. However, it was now two-thirty in the morning and Rabbit knew that he had been drinking on and off for the past three or four hours. His eyes were reddened, and the bloated veins in his temples throbbed – he looked wretched. Rabbit heard from Mei Di that these hours had been the most difficult time for Liao Mai over recent days. He sometimes awoke, seized by a bad mood and could not easily shake himself out of it. When he was in such a state, he would feel dispirited and hopeless and believe that only death offered the most reasonable and beautiful outcome. She tried her best to shake him out of it and reminded him again and again that this was a kind of illness. Sometimes, his face blanched, and sometimes sweat broke out on his forehead while he was feeling restless. At this point, he had to bury his face deep in her thick, coarse hair until he got better... With Mei Di's help, his symptoms had not recurred for the past month. But now, tonight, Liao Mai was fidgeting again. He paced, leaned over the sill of the small window to look out, and listened to Mei Di's breathing downstairs.

He turned abruptly to Rabbit and said: "I want to tell you that my wife, Mei Di, is the offspring of a hedgehog spirit. She's not an ordinary person. When my father-in-law took her out of the forest, she was still wearing a straw raincoat, and she didn't take it off until she was over ten years old."

Rabbit gasped, staring at Liao Mai with wide-open eyes.

With his head hanging low, Liao Mai recounted the story of his father-in-law, Liangzi: how he left the forest and how he parted with a woman who also wore a straw raincoat at the edge of the forest. "I've been worrying that Mei Di may leave without trace one day. Our relationship may not endure…"

The dumbfounded Rabbit took the cup of alcohol. Before Liao Mai had time to stop him, he had gulped a big mouthful, then stuttered: "Are, are you sure? Are you talking this nonsense because you're drunk?"

Liao Mai shook his head. "She still has the little straw raincoat stowed away. I'll show it to you."

SISTERS

Since Rabbit's departure, Liao Mai came downstairs at night. He began to indulge in excessive drinking, which worried Mei Di immensely.

During the day, apart from toiling with the workers, he would hang out with the foolish beggars. As soon as Mei Di came by, the foolish beggars would scream and grimace at her, which perversely made Liao Mai happy. The number of vagrant beggars streaming from the south increased with each passing day. Some of them lingered for days at the base of the fence wall. Liao Mai would then offer them food and alcohol, and he'd eat and drink with them. "Do you know?" he told the foolish beggars while pointing at Mei Di in the near distance. "She's a hedgehog spirit." He continued to drink until his face turned purplish-red.

One of the foolish beggars burst into a guffaw and clapped his hands. "Good Heavens! No wonder there's a wild, fishy stench. Buddy, it's lucky we've run into each other. I prefer coming to your farm. So long as I lie down at the base of the fence wall, I'll do nothing but think of the past and the old forest that we can't forget for the rest of our lives. I won't tell this to anyone except you." With that, the foolish beggar grabbed the liquor bottle with one hand, grasped his dishevelled hair with the other and fixed his eyes on Mei Di in the distance.

Liao Mai knew that this guy was already inebriated. The foolish beggar lounged there holding the bottle. While scratching his itchy body, he said: "I'll tell my story bit by bit. Please don't think I'm making it up just to please you. I would compare what I'm going to tell you to a steamed bun, eaten in a dream but its aroma still lingering in your mouth when you're awake. In other words, it may leave a lasting, pleasant impression on you.

"I was a teenager at the time. One day, I followed my third uncle to the island to visit my maternal grandma. The island was relatively near, and my third uncle soon boated us there before lunchtime. He then steered the boat away, leaving me in the care of my grandma. I ate black-carp balls three times a day and collected clams on the beach. No one cared about me, and I could swim as well as fish.

"One day, I lay face down on a patch of sand reef and ate oysters from their shells. I was enjoying my meal when suddenly I started to throw up. I felt dizzy and was hit by cramp in my leg. Jeez, as soon as I left the reef, I was dragged away by an undercurrent. I panicked. Although I could see the island, I couldn't swim across to it. While floundering anxiously, I was choked with a few mouthfuls of seawater. Then I passed out.

"Good Heavens, when I came to, I found myself on a white-sand beach. I was lying on a layer of flowers called ladybells. Two girls were chattering. 'See! He woke up and opened his eyes. Told you he wasn't dead!' 'Not at all!' I saw them crouching nearby. They were about the same age as me. They reached out to touch me, with wild berries in their mouths. Beside me was a heap of seagrass and mud. It turned out that it had been scraped from my body. I wanted to say something, but when I opened my mouth, I couldn't utter a sound. My throat had been inflamed by the salty seawater.

"The sisters soon got themselves into a squabble. After listening hard, I figured out they were fighting to own me: 'Since I found him first, he belongs to me!' 'But without me, how could you drag him up?' 'He's mine! I gave the little seal up to you last time, but you failed to keep it alive.' 'That was because it was already wounded!' 'This creature isn't a seal. With its slimy body, it may be harder to keep alive.'

"After quarrelling for quite a while, they crafted a makeshift stretcher with kudzu vine and carried me into an old forest. Only then did I notice that they were both wearing straw raincoats over their naked bodies. I remember clearly that they smelled of water deer. Even the scent of ladybells and jujube flowers were not able to mask it... The old forest was really thick and full of spiked animals. I can still see their faces covered with fuzzy hair. They would pop up along the way to sniff me all over. I overheard some of the conversations clearly: 'What is it? Where did you pick it up?' The sisters answered: 'We don't know. We're going to take it home to show Mum.'

"I saw a thatched hut that was the same colour as the straw raincoats they were wearing, and its big roof drooped to the ground. Its window was as small as a basket. The vines of Indian beech plants crawled all over the ground outside. There was a pile of firewood against the west gable wall, where there were also two sleeping cabins. They carried me into one of the cabins instead of the big house. Crouching there, the sisters talked about what to do with me – whether to show me to their mother or keep me in hiding for a while. Finally, they decided on the second option.

"A little further away from the cabins, there was something like a pile of firewood, which contained a nest of cogon grass. They carried me into it, gave me water, and fed me with some plump, white worms, which I immediately threw up. Then, they offered me ladybell seeds, pine nuts and taro juice that they called 'wild honey', but I was still hungry. Homesick at night and missing my grandma, I kept crying while tossing and turning, my body covered with bits of grass. The two sisters came to see me in the morning. They crouched down and murmured: 'Who knows. Maybe this creature prefers sleeping in a cage like a bird.'

"They wove a bird's nest to fit my frame and hung me up from the bough of a Persian silk tree.

"Many wild creatures came to view me during the first couple of days. The sisters bragged to them that they had captured me with their own hands and, pointing at the badgers and foxes, said: 'It's bigger than you are!'

"I wanted to speak, but I had lost my voice because of the seawater. Eating wild berries and honey and sleeping in the cage on chilly nights, not only did I suffer from a bad throat, but I also had a high fever, and my body was as hot as a glowing fire poker.

"The sisters said in panic: 'We can't let such a lovely pet die like the others. Let's tell Mum.'

"A woman in her fifties or sixties came wearing a straw raincoat. She approached the cage. As soon as she saw me in it, she was stunned. She turned to reprimand the two sisters. 'This is a terrible mistake. You have a man in there!'

"The two sisters stuck their tongues out, pulled their heads into their straw raincoats and fell silent. The grandmother dismantled the cage and held my trembling body to her chest. She then carried me to her large room, humming all the way. It was a real human abode because it was furnished with a chest of drawers and a bed with sheets and pillows on it. Lying in bed, I took the medicinal soup concocted by the old woman and felt much better. She also made me a bowl of Job's tears porridge and some boiled sweet potatoes. She then set two plates on the chest of drawers, one filled with strawberries and the other with mulberries. Apparently, she was treating me as a human being. The day I was able to speak, the first words I uttered were: 'I want to put on my trousers.'

"I was given a straw raincoat, the only available garment. My genitals were exposed every time I moved. It was easy to pee, though. I had to make do with it. I told the old woman where I had come from and said I was homesick. She said my home was in a village outside the old forest, far away from here. She asked me to stay and relax and not to go out until I was stronger. At night, the two sisters would sneak into my bed, tear off my straw raincoat, and say: 'He's naked! He's naked!' They touched me up and down and planted kisses on me all over. They commented that I was better-looking than a hare. They frolicked nonstop, pretended to sleep when their mother came in, and resumed frolicking when she left. Later, when the old woman found my straw raincoat likely to fall off all the time, she teased me with a threat: 'Weasels will bite your private parts', which made the sisters giggle. They reached out to pinch me. One of them jeered: 'Wow, it's still there!' The other gibed: 'This pupa is something else! It can get bigger and smaller!' After midnight, they lit the lamp, and compared their private parts with mine and said, pouting their lips: 'We prefer that pupa after all.'

"On a moonlit night, the sisters took me out. They swayed as they walked. As soon as they saw a creature twinkling its bright eyes on the winding path, they would tap it on the head. They climbed to the crown of a poplar tree and started singing as they swayed. The sea wind carried their squeaking tune a great distance, and it was echoed by the wild creatures everywhere.

"'The old badger must have caught a cold. Its voice is hoarser than a wild boar's!' said the elder sister. Seeing a goat coming to the base of the tree, the younger one urinated. Rubbing its head, the goat wondered why it was raining on such a fine day. As soon as the goat left, they burst into laughter.

"The sisters ran around, hopping and leaping on the beach. Their crisp singing cut through the sound of the lapping waves. They ran holding my hands, followed by a big, panting wild boar, whose tusks looked like two tree branches in the moonlight. Before bedtime, we had collected a lot of wild berries. We put them on the bed and chomped them beneath our quilts. As the bright moon shone through the window, the sisters gazed at me silently and then sniffed me all over. Sometimes, they screamed unexpectedly while pointing at my body: 'Look!' At that moment, I shut my eyes and held my breath. While I felt as happy as could be, I was rather timid. When the moon shone right through the window and illuminated every part of the room, it was my turn to observe their naked bodies. They both had glistening fuzzy hair on their backs, and the golden hairs on their tummies sparkled when I brushed them. 'Jeez! What's going on?' I sat up, and they giggled, baring their broken teeth.

"Early one rainy morning, the old woman took me with her while they were still fast asleep. She walked me out of the forest.

"But when I returned to my village, I had no peace any more. Seeing me always staring blankly, my parents thought that I had been possessed in the wild. So they invited a shaman home. He held a mirror over me and pointed a peach-wood sword here and there while repeatedly exclaiming: 'Hey, hey!' In the end, he said: 'It's a shame for such a good boy to have been laid by a spirit!' My mum asked what he meant by this and he replied: 'I mean he's been molested, assaulted or raped.' I couldn't understand a word, but, glaring at him, I decided that he had become my enemy. My heart thumped and thumped.

"The shaman made me drink a bowl of blackish liquid. Strangely, I recovered after that day and I no longer thought of the forest all the time. Like other boys, I started working in the fields and going to school until I grew tall enough to reach the back of a cow, my hair turned black and shiny, and my face was covered with acne.

"Then, one night, I suddenly felt hot and dry all over my body. I found it so hard to go to sleep that I sneaked out of the village. As if being pulled by something, I lunged forward and forward to the west. The moon was really big that night. Looking at the endless wild country and forest, I could not help gasping. In the northwest wind, I could hear the rumble of the surging waves and the rustle of the swaying trees. Then, I clearly heard the two sisters singing far away. I was sure. The singing soon merged into a sweet and agreeable chorus. It turned out that all the wild creatures were opening their large, whiskered mouths.

"I had to go to the forest. Unable to sleep for nights on end, I cried in secret and said to myself: Let me go to the forest. Let me go, or I could die. So, one day, I found an excuse to leave home. I plunged into the old forest and vowed never to return. I got lost as soon as I stepped into the forest, where kudzu vines tripped me, and thistles and thorns caught my clothes. My hair was a mess, my limbs got scratched, and my blood dripped into the sand, where it would nourish the growth of ladybells in early spring. I walked for a whole day until the bright moon rose again. I leaned against a tree, and sure enough, a gentle creaking sound wafted over. The two sisters had started singing again! Tears swelled in my eyes. I darted towards where they were singing.

"At sunrise, I spotted the thatched hut and two young women in straw raincoats. The sisters had grown so pretty that my throat tightened and sweat broke out on my palms when they turned and glanced at me. They blushed and covered their mouths with their hands...

"Her back already stooping, the old woman recognised me straight away, crying: 'My child!' I responded: 'Yes.' The two sisters were of a medium stature, with the elder one being slightly taller and prettier. As if they had transformed into different people, they became reticent, communicating only with their big eyes. Oh, Moon, rise sooner at night! Under the moon, in a place where many wild strawberries grew, I thought the sisters would become their old selves. Unfortunately, I was wrong. When we went out of the thatched hut, they remained silent. When we reached the place overgrown with mulberries, the elder sister picked a handful and gave them to me. The younger sister walked behind flicking the heads of wild creatures with her fingers.

"I sat with the elder sister by the sea. She smelled of water deer all over. I closed my eyes and felt her kissing my hair. I leaned my head against her breasts and watched the moonlight streaming over her body, seemingly to wet her clothes, and flowing down to the fuzzy hairs on her abdomen. She trembled while cuddling me and whispered in my ear: 'Tonight! Tonight...'

"I slept on the same big rattan bed. In the middle of the night, the elder sister came closer, and I smelled the same water deer scent. A hand touched my head, and I held her tight. In the dark, I felt the smooth hairs like those on the belly of a kitten. My heart pounded. Remembering what the shaman had told my mother, I mumbled: 'Let me get laid. Let me get assaulted. Let me get raped.' She covered my mouth with her hand while I reached out mine and ran it over her back, and as soon as I touched that patch of peach-fuzz, I trembled violently. I was so nervous that my hand shook and wriggled like a leaping carp. Just then, I heard footsteps and the cry of the old woman: 'Guoguo! Guoguo!' She came wearing her straw raincoat and holding a candle in one hand. The sister called Guoguo took flight, arching her back.

"'My child,' said the old woman, who lifted my quilt and looked. Running her hand over my face, she continued: 'You're a grownup now. I must tell you that you can't sleep with her.'

"'Why? I'd like to be with her for the rest of my life.'

"The old woman tugged her straw raincoat up a bit and said: 'We're hedgehogs. We must live in the old forest generation after generation.'

"I jumped up saying: 'So what? I can stay in the forest all my life.'

"The old woman shook her head. Looking up and out of the window, she continued: 'My child, people and hedgehogs are different. People must return to their ancestral home no matter where they are, just like a tree's fallen leaves must finally settle with the roots of the tree. So, when you leave here, you'll never come back...'

"'I won't leave! I don't want to go.'

"'My child, I'll walk you out at daybreak.'

"As the old woman hung her head and clenched her teeth, all the straw stems on her raincoat stood on end. She nearly scared me to death.

"Day broke. I had to leave. It was no use crying. But I didn't know where to go.

"Once out of the forest, I had no intention of returning to the village. So, ever since, I have become a homeless tramp wandering on the wilderness. Whoever sees me will call out: 'Hurry and look! The big foolish beggar is coming again.'"

YOUR PREDESTINED LOVER

Jiwo (Chicken Coop) Town welcomed its special guests – The Publicity and Lecturing Team on Eliminating Superstition. At the request of the town, the team was formed by the higher-level authorities to include scientists and professionals from the provincial meteorological observatory as well as college students studying hydrometeorology. The team spent a month on a publicity campaign in the town and its surrounding villages. The experts gave lectures on subjects in accordance with their own academic backgrounds. They tried their best to explain profound scientific knowledge with simple and intelligible terms. To attract the public, they staged theatrical performances before and after the lectures. In addition, a man specifically responsible for investigating the drought demon incident addressed the audience. This man looked stern and talked in a harsh voice, as if every word he uttered was as definitive as a nail hammered into a board.

"Some people spread rumours by exploiting the situation, saying that a few dozen people from both sides were wounded or killed," he said. "Who told you that? People from several villages participated in the fight against the drought demon, but where there're more people, there's more mess! It was only natural for them to bump into one another and it was unavoidable that one or two got hurt. When did you see people killed by gunshots? After more than thirty days of investigation, in which we checked each of those who were involved in the incident, I bet on my career that I can tell you, my countrymen, no one was wounded or killed by gunfire. Of course, among the wounded, some were pretty serious. But the blame must be placed on feudalistic superstitious ideas."

No applause followed his admonitory remark; silence reigned like death itself among the audience.

Those who lectured on science sweated profusely each time they talked, as they had to make every effort to make believe that years of drought were inevitable and were the result of scientific causes, such as 'strong airflows', 'troughs' and 'air convection'. All were phenomena related with the sky, not with the earth. Besides, how could there be evil spirits like the drought demon?

The publicity and lecture work went smoothly during the first few lectures before problems arose. One day, a woman who looked like an administrator went onto the stage to denounce the stupid act of fighting the drought demon and then to talk about the contribution that Tang Tong had been making as a role model of the times and the huge losses that he had suffered from this superstitious act. As she talked, she even rubbed her teary eyes. An audience member recognised her as a local resident and instantly exposed what she was: "We don't believe you. When you used to sleepwalk, you ran along the ditch every night wearing a sailor's cap with a ribbon."

A hubbub broke out among the attendees because many of them knew what she had been doing. Someone slapped his thigh and echoed: "That's true! That's true! We've heard about this young woman. So it's you!" The woman burst into a crying fit. Then, she murmured a scarcely distinct four-letter word and darted off stage.

Following that day, the publicity and lecture team ran out of steam and was disbanded after two or three more lectures. The reason for its failure was simple – it was alright to talk about anything else in these plains and hills, but it was no use trying to deny the existence of the drought demon. Elderly people said angrily: "It goes against heavenly principles to deny the existence of the drought demon and ban the effort to fight against it."

After the publicity and lecture team left, many jokes were made and circulated. Because of the team members' bias against the drought demon, some of its vowed enemies would retaliate by harassing them in secret. The fox and weasel spirits all went into action as they were invisible anyway. They had gone up to the stage unseen to slap the lecturers on the face. They had even dragged their trousers down. A man nicknamed Blabbermouth Liu came up with a doggerel about the incident of fighting the drought demon, and it spread to several of the surrounding villages in a few days. In his doggerel, he identified Tang Tong with the drought demon and, for that matter, the demon's den with the Large Rampart Compound of the Purple Smoke.

When drunk, he would alternate between chanting the doggerel and swearing: "The son of a bitch kept cursing and scolding Lord Huo in those years. But, in fact, Lord Huo did nothing but eat grass. You, however, chomp delicacies from land and sea. It's true that Lord Huo lusted after women, but you've fucked many more, even girls from the West. You've also raped minors. You're a true beast that deserves dismemberment."

Every time Little Beibei came back home, she would bring various snippets of news with her. Liao Mai was astonished at how much she knew – for example, the specific number of participants in the fight against the drought demon, the detailed figures of the losses that the Tiantong Group had sustained, how a man known as Jin Tang allocated emergency funds and how the injured criminal of great importance had made good his escape.

"The man's name is Tuzi, meaning Rabbit. He may have been hiding by the sea for quite some time and fled after recovering from his wound," she said while sucking her ice cream and grimacing at her father.

Liao Mai cast a glance at Mei Di but remained silent.

Tonight, for some reason, possibly to look for an old book, Little Beibei went up to the attic. She had just got there when she screamed. Liao Mai and Mei Di rushed up, only to find their daughter crouching on the floor, her eyes darting from the cigarette butts to the bandages smeared with herbal ointment and bloodstains.

"Your dad just got injured in a fall during the heavy rain that day," said Mei Di as she set about tidying up the floor.

"Dad, oh Dad!" She inched close to him, attempting to lift his shirt to take a look.

Liao Mai stopped her, saying: "Nothing serious, Little Fawn's Hooves. Let's go. Let's go downstairs."

After they went downstairs, Little Beibei remained quiet for a long time, glancing back and forth at her mother and father. Then, she moved close to her mother and whispered something in her ear. Mei Di looked a bit nervous. Liao Mai asked: "What happened?"

Mei Di did not respond. Only when he pressed with the same question did Little Beibei tell him: "Something happened to Blabbermouth Liu. A woman from our company saw him on her way to work. Blabbermouth Liu was lying in a ditch with his hands bound behind him and his mouth stitched together with jute twine. He was taken to the hospital to have the twine removed. But he was fine apart from that."

Banging the desk, Liao Mai roared: "See how brutal they are! But can they stitch up all mouths?"

Little Beibei looked serious, fixing her eyes on her father. She cried timidly: "Dad, some people are brutal, but I bet on my life that our Tiantong Group didn't kill anyone that night. Some people are rumour-mongers. They're anxious to see the world in disorder. Indeed..."

Liao Mai gave a shudder and suddenly uttered a scream. He shook a little before standing firm. Glaring at Little Fawn's Hooves, he panted: "Your, your group? Which group do you belong to?"

"By our, I meant Tiantong."

"Your group?"

Mei Di hurried up, pulled Little Beibei behind her, and said: "Maizi, our daughter's company also belongs to the Tiantong Group."

"Mei Di, did you hear what she said just now? She said: 'I bet on my life!' Did you hear? Who asked her to bet on her life? Who? She said someone is rumour-mongering, but I think that someone is her! She's spreading rumours! She was not there at the time, but she still dares to say that no one was killed!"

He exploded and lunged towards Little Beibei. Mei Di pushed and held him back, saying: "Calm down! Calm down, Maizi. She's still a child. She was babbling like a child, Maizi."

"I think she's the one who deserves to have her mouth stitched up! She's a child, but she should've known how much the victim must have bled and how much pain he must have felt when jute twine was passed through the flesh of his mouth."

"Maizi, oh Maizi…"

However hard he tried to push and pull Mei Di, he still failed to separate mother and daughter. He pointed at Little Beibei and bellowed: "Get out of here! Get out! Get back to your group. Get the hell out!"

Little Beibei trembled all over. She struggled hard and finally freed herself from her mother's hands and burst into tears. She dashed out of the gateway, into the courtyard and towards the burgundy car. Before Mei Di could catch her, the car was driving away.

Mei Di returned to the room, only to find Liao Mai sweating profusely; large beads were breaking out on his forehead, streaming down his neck and onto his collar. She withdrew into a corner in silence, weeping in her heart.

Mei Di stayed there till midnight when she smelled the intense reek of alcohol. She rushed out to look and found Liao Mai having emptied a bottle of *baijiu* liquor. In an attempt to grab the bottle, she knocked it to the floor and it smashed into pieces. One of the shards cut Liao Mai's thumb. "Good Heavens, Maizi!" She was going to bandage him, but he declined. He went to the sink to wash the wound and immediately the water turned red.

She stood by shivering, then said as if to herself: "Please pardon her. She's still a child."

Liao Mai's bleeding finally stopped. He sat at the table, put the bottle to his mouth and drained it in one gulp. Feeling short of breath, he panted. He rose, his chest heaving wildly. Mei Di went over and, staring into his pale face, said: "Maizi, you've drunk too much. Are you feeling sick?" She ran her hand up and down his back and chest. She kept doing so, then pressed his face into her dense hair.

Liao Mai took a deep breath and sat down. "Nothing serious. I'm feeling better." As he turned to look at her, she found his eyes reddened. He looked down at his injured hand and gripped it hard, as if wanting to squeeze the blood out again. "Perhaps, it'll happen soon," he said in a deep voice. "It's high time we came to a final conclusion. It'll happen soon."

"What will happen soon?"

He did not respond but kept gazing out of the window. "I must make the best use of my time and do something," he said. "I've promised them. I must do what I've promised..."

"Maizi, what in the world are you talking about? Do what?"

"Pay the workers. I said before that we and they are not simply in an ordinary labour relationship. If we balance the accounts each year, we should pay them more – much more than what we're doing."

"So that was what happened to you. You're still having this stupid idea." She raised her voice: "Maizi, you're paying them much more than others. How much more do you have in mind? They're only migrant workers and don't have a stake in the farm. Besides, ours is not a joint-stock company. I, I can't let you have your own way any more... after we've invested so much in the farm."

"You've invested! You've invested too much! But do you think because you invested at an early stage, you must make sure that you can continue exploiting your workers again and again for the remainder of your life? Haven't you seen the effect of the sun – layers of skin on their backs peeling and their faces cracking? You want to be a female Tang Tong? Who in the world are you, after all? You tell me. You tell me now!"

Liao Mai leaned closer to her with reddened eyes, scaring Mei Di, who took a step back, gasping and yelling: "Who am I? I'm your wife – your, your predestined lover! Who am I? Maizi, you tell me yourself! Tell me who I am."

Liao Mai reached out his big hands and got hold of her, then with a jerk, dragged her into his arms. He held her dense, velvetleaf fibre hair tight and twisted it in a way that made her face look up and her mouth open wide. He could see her wriggling tongue. She gazed at his eyes quietly.

"You may cry and shout and say the savage is beating his wife!"

"I'm not going to."

"Go ahead, offspring of a hedgehog spirit. You hurt me with your spines, and I must teach you a good lesson."

As he said these words, he abruptly withdrew his arms and pressed her face hard against his chest. She didn't move for a long time. Then he felt her biting him, biting his pectoral muscle, one bite after another.

It was pitch-dark and extremely quiet. Even the sound of a

scuttling mouse would have been heard. But, no, they did not have mice in their home. Neither did they have cats. The sound of the fish leaping out of the water came from the distance. It was the golden-scaled crucian carp, which, when made into a soup, would exude the overpowering smell of gunpowder.

"Maizi, Maizi, you've never been as drunk as this before." He held her motionless, gazing at the dark window, knowing that he was completely sober.

"I love you, Maizi, my really fine man. I love you to death. I've said I can't live without you. We two are truly predestined lovers..."

READING ON A RAINY NIGHT

Dear Qi Jin,

I'm not sure where you are or what you're doing tonight. I'm missing you so much that I'm talking to you with my pen. It's after midnight again, and I'm sitting comfortably at my desk, enjoying the feeling of plain beauty, a kind of antique beauty, all by myself, of course. I'm here with neither a beautiful companion nor a gaudy reputation. My dear friend, hemmed in by wind and rain on this silent night, what I'm thinking most about are the days when we were together. I'm not referring to those days when you, Xiu and I were with each other. I'm referring to the time when I conversed with you in the mountainous areas of southern China and on the island in the sea. Your strange abode, the stone cavern on the hillside with a huge roof, was so mystic. It reminded me of a hawk, the nest of a hawk. I can imagine how you protected yourself against the mountain storms. At the time, you could probably hear the cry of the wolves in the mountains. You needed a good helping hand, but unfortunately, that man did not get to your place safely. I must tell you the bad news – he was intercepted on the way.

I empathise with his situation – I treat as my brothers all those who can't find their footholds on the plains and in the hills. But I still feel uncertain about that earth-shaking fight against the drought demon. I fear the potential catastrophe underlying the incident, which is not what you wish to happen, either. You disdain empty talk and are less willing to be caught in a quagmire. Exploration, courage and hard work are your mottoes.

You know that I've always been craving for a life of farming when it's sunny and reading when it's rainy. This is what I've promised myself to do and have been doing so persistently. I thought this to be the most honest and easiest thing to do, but today it proves that I was totally wrong. Since my father's generation or even earlier, many people had the same promise, but all found it hard to fulfil. Life is neither simple nor easy because it's full of upheavals, exile, separations or something else. Mei Di can read my mind. The first thing she did on the farm in which she's invested so much of her hard work was to build me a study, for which I've been forever grateful. I even believe she's the representative of such a lifestyle. We've settled down. Yes, I work in the fields on fine days and read on rainy days. We've been suffering from the drought demon for years, so that I've been farming under the blazing sun almost continuously and reading in the dark night. Well, it's all the same. They're the two parts of one verse.

Such an arrangement here might not have won the approval of the Eight-Nation-Alliance.[1] Landlords, however, may not oppose it. Both of them are powerful, but their worldly ideals are totally different. Today, it's difficult to breathe while making a living under the influence of the Large Rampart Compound of Purple Smoke. I often talk with Mei Di about the blue-eyed people coming and going, but she's very open-minded, saying: "They're better than the Eight-Nation-Alliance." When I mentioned to her the stench of the ramparts, she said that it's better than being shot with bullets. I replied: "It's true! While we could be killed instantly by bullets, we're being killed gradually by the stink of money, by the rising seawater, by the permeating purple smoke and by the heartless people who're murdering us with either force or emotional provocation. Anyway, we'll die slowly, although the ways of dying may differ."

We're both facing such a sad moment, but we're still living in different situations. You have your hawk cave while I'm on my solitary quest at midnight and in the small hours. I found that I can't keep up with my dark childhood, when I knew what lay behind the darkness. Now, things are different. I can't get rid of all the muddy water that soaked me during my early years. I don't have the heart to think of the eyes of my father and the old mother in the mountain. From their eyes, I saw only love and hope. They placed all their hope on a lad. How young I was then! In the darkness of a moonless night, when I swept back my bristling dense hair it sent out blue, static sparks. I lunged towards the wilderness with no fear at all.

What lies in store for me? Looking from a distance into the eyes of my two close relatives, I want to say that I desire neither wealth nor wisdom endowed by time. My only yearning is the blue sparks produced when I use my hands to sweep back my thick hair – the lightning of adolescence, without which I can't kindle the flame in my heart.

My friend, I didn't participate in the fight against the drought demon – I either did not have the chance or I hesitated profoundly. I was caught in a dilemma. You can imagine the people crowding the fields in great numbers, whose power equalled ten million tons of TNT. Yes, each individual had a pinch of the powder on his or her mind, but…

Farming on sunny days and reading on rainy ones? Hey, my friend! You sit smoking a pipe on a mountain showing no emotion. You surely can't be completely indifferent towards the things you witness, can you?

I'm trying to figure out what has done me harm. I know it's a slow process. Mixed in the wind, it's weathering me away without my notice. A farm and a house with books and bathrooms, as well as a modern mode of farming – they are indeed 'new concepts'. I'm sleepwalking into it… At midnight, I suddenly realise that it's like a poison – we're in an age of being silently poisoned.

The night is murky. I'm feeling hurt, badly hurt.

You've paid attention to me and helped me. So has open-minded, beautiful Xiu, who's become physically close to me and has fished me out of troubled waters. She's touched my heart profoundly with her vibrancy, romanticism, as well as her attitude of being led forward by her sincerity and poetic ardency. Her love for me is unequivocal, and I wish I could live up to this innocent love in future. When I saw her off that morning, I felt unspeakably touched and affectionate at the sight of her burgundy check blouse and her fair, exposed neck and chin. I told myself what a perfect woman she was, and how happy I was!

The rain is pitter-pattering tonight. I'm opening my book and giving free rein to my unspeakable addiction to reading. Tonight, I've come to this chapter: in the chaotic wars between ancient states, a bookworm was so obsessed with reading at night that he was completely oblivious to the besieging troops. By dedicating himself to reading aloud, he forgot everything and was unaware of the imminent disaster. All around him that night, blood ran like a river, while every house was reduced to ashes by fire. Only an area of a hundred steps around him – where his reading voice could reach – was intact. It was an amazing sight. One version of the story tells that a boy with double bun hair came in to pay respect to him, saying that his master in the mountain was not feeling well and wanted to send for someone who could read to him. Without much thought, the bookworm followed the boy out with his books and into a thatched hut in the mountain valley not far away. Sitting upright on a mat, the bookworm read aloud, and two hours later, the door in the next room opened, and out came a white-bearded old man walking with a cane. The boy said: "This is my master. Sure enough, he's feeling much better after hearing you read aloud." The old man returned to his room without saying a word. Before the bookworm's departure, the boy came to say goodbye, holding a tray on which there were some silver ingots, a prescription for a herbal medicine and a bundle of incense sticks. On his way, the bookworm asked the boy who his master was. The boy held his hand and wrote a name on his palm with his finger: Sun Simiao. After his return, the bookworm took the prescribed medicine, kindled the incense sticks and started reading addictively as he had been doing before. One autumn day, the one-hundred-and-twenty-year-old bookworm thought of the thatched hut in the mountain valley. He followed the original path, attempting to revisit it, only to see an endless plain. The valley was not there at all...

Tonight, I raised my head to listen to the pattering rain. I pushed the window open to watch the darkness of the night, which was as boundless as my feeling of emptiness and despair.

I began to read aloud. Yes, tonight, the voice of reading could reach a radius of a hundred steps...

NINETEEN

THE DARKEST NIGHT

IN THE CAVE of a gold mine, deep under the hilly area, five people were getting ready to sleep. At least it felt like night, time to go to sleep. But, in fact, they had no idea what time of day it was. The three veterans had been in the cave for two years. One of them was sight-impaired and served as the teller of time. When he said that it was dark, it was considered dark. They had a pecking order based on age and the date of their arrival in the cave. They called themselves Eldest Brother, Second Brother and so on. Eldest Brother suffered the eye problem a year after entering the cave and eventually was unable to see even dazzling electric bulbs. However, he was getting smarter and could, through mental calculation, reckon time, figure out what was happening outside the cave and predict the date of his own death.

Eldest Brother foresaw that he would die on the eighteenth day of the second lunar month. No one had quibbled about the predicted date of his death, but they weren't sure in which year this particular date would fall. For, due to their carelessness, they did not record the exact time of their entrance. Later, they realised the significance of chronicling their underground life and started to carve regular marks of the days they had spent. The problem was that they did not have a clock so they had no idea whether it was day or night. With the complication of leap months, it was even harder for them to tell a specific date. Nevertheless, Eldest Brother told them that he had made a great effort to reckon the date mentally, and his date of destiny would occur among the next dozen days or so. It was near at hand, he said.

"May heaven eliminate this date! We would rather die than see Eldest Brother leave us. Once he passes, the cave will collapse and nothing will be left," said Second Brother to the two who had arrived recently.

One of the newcomers was a young guy. He stared at Second Brother for a while before asking: "Why?"

"Because he's our eyes. He tells us everything happening outside the cave, making us feel as if we are seeing things as we walk by. If he kicks the bucket, we'll become blind and never know what's going to happen out there."

The young man thought this was nonsense, though he bit his tongue. He chattered his teeth gently as he stared at Eldest Brother's stony eyes in the dim light. After suffering from a stye, the old man had to keep his eyes open as wide as the size of an egg, day and night. His eyes eventually turned the colour of stone. Some of the miners pressed them gently when he was sleeping at night and could not help exclaiming: "Good Heavens, stones!"

Five men lay face-up on the same bed, covered with straw sacks, empty concrete bags and cardboard. Their bed cover was greasy and dark blue. Thirsty for information, the three veterans kept pestering the two newcomers over the past few days for more stories that had taken place outside the cave. They gave them no time to take a break. What was wrong with Eldest Brother? Was he losing confidence in his capacity of mental calculation? No! He was only trying to prove himself. After listening to him telling a few things that had supposedly transpired outside the cave, the newcomers were stunned, for they had really happened! Just a month before they were thrown into the cave, the old man had been mumbling: "We'll have new members added to our family." However, he had not mentioned the reason for their arrival. He only pointed at his mouth a few times.

Lying on his back and looking at the dark rock ceiling, the young man said: "At present, the person I hate the most is not Tang Tong or anyone else in the Tiantong Group. It's the old Daoist priest. It was this ruffian who tricked me into telling him what he wanted to know. When I see him one day, I'll pull off his beard and cut off his tool!"

"I hate him. I hate him with a passion," said one of the newcomers who was slightly older.

"You'd better watch your mouths," warned Eldest Brother in the dark.

Wiping away his tears in secret, Fourth Brother could not help asking: "Eldest Brother, my good brother, could you tell me what my wife's doing at the moment? When I left her, she was sewing a pair of cotton-padded socks for our second son, and she'd just finished one of them."

Eldest Brother snorted, as he did whenever he was asked a difficult question. "She's finished making the socks alright, but now she's just taken off her padded coat and is getting ready to sleep. She's holding your son's little foot. A good wife and a good person." He went on to issue a series of compliments.

Fourth Brother sat up and asked: "What's happening to her?"

"'A day as husband and wife means friends for a lifetime.' Less than a month after you left home, a single man visited her holding up his trousers by the waist. Guess what she said to him? She said: 'I'll gouge the grease out of your body with my poker! For as long as I live, I'm the wife of my son's dad. When I die, I'll be a ghost lingering with my husband!' At present, she's breastfeeding your baby, who is suckling her large breasts with his monkey-like eyes twinkling. That's what's happening to her."

Fourth Brother sobbed, and the others sighed. Fourth Brother went on: "I know who that single man was. I'm confident that he'll never succeed in seducing my wife for the rest of his life. Right! You really have sharp eyes! My wife does have large breasts. All the villagers call her 'Big Bags'."

His dry humour did not evoke any laughter. Biting his lip, the younger of the newcomers finally asked: "How about my woman? What's happened to her?"

The snorting was audible again. "About you, son? Let's be frank since we're as close as family and share the same fate of soon becoming the ghosts of wrongful death under the earth. Let's stop being evasive and be forthright by telling the truth. Your date has not been faithful. With her long braids flowing and her ample bottom swaying as she walked in the market, she looked left and right at nothing but young men. She sobbed a little after you left alright, but she soon wiped her eyes dry and had no more tears to shed."

"She's not waiting for me?" said the young man as he jumped off the bed.

"Waiting? Till when? You've just arrived. We three have been here in the cave for two years and we still can't see any hope of seeing the light. We work in the dark mine every day while they send us food down the shaft. There's no end to our life here. The foreman has a heart as vicious as venomous snakes and scorpions, and he kills people without batting an eye. Well, Son, you've only yourself to blame for the fruitless relationship between you and your girlfriend with the long hair. You had your fire irons at the time, but why didn't you stoke up her fire when you had the chance? Now, the fire has died down only a couple of days after you're gone…"

The young man was heard sobbing in the dark, and his sobs soon turned into wailing. He jumped and cursed: "The heartless foreman, the debased great-great-grandson of Tang Tong, and that fake Daoist priest – you and your later generations will all go to hell! I'm being buried alive so young without anyone knowing it. What am I supposed to do? What's the point of living? Let me die! Let me die!"

As he cursed, he tried to bash his head against the cave wall, but his suicide bid was stopped by the others who pinned him to the floor. Eldest Brother crouched closer and pressed one of the young man's hands over his head, saying: "My friend, can you feel the big scar on my head? You can? Like you, I wanted to bump my head open and die. I saw no point in living. It was the two brothers that prevented me from killing myself. They reminded me of an old saying to put things in perspective: 'So long as the green mountain remains, we don't have to worry about a shortage of firewood.' Now, I'm trying to do the same with you. Live and live on even though we don't know if it's day or night. You're different from us. You're so young! How can't you have a chance to see the light?"

"But who will know we're buried alive here except the few beasts? When will such a life end? Good Heavens, are we going to live in this cave like rats?"

"Lie down and go to sleep, my friend. It's very late. Lie down and I'll tell you what's happened recently above ground so that you won't feel bored. Please lie down." Stroking his back, the old man finally calmed the young man.

The only thing to break the silence in the cave was the pitter-patter of the rain. "Wow, don't you see? I'm seeing rain pouring down amid thunder and lightning and a group of people following a mountain torrent rushing down the hillside with extraordinary force. The white head of the torrent swept Tang Tong and his people off their feet while they were busy mating asses and horses. A foreigner came out of the Large Rampart Compound of Purple Smoke with an interpreter, both smelling like farts, and they were talking about having some fun with the boss when they were greeted with an onslaught of spiked maces. It turned out that the thugs had been disoriented by the floodwater and seen everything as monsters swept over by the torrent. Wielding spiked maces for a whole day, they killed quite a number of people. Puffing and panting, the Large Rampart Compound of Purple Smoke finally ran out of steam. Those women who had an intimate relationship with Tang Tong were so desperate that they darted out naked and milled aimlessly on the streets until they became dazed and were finally taken home by the singletons of Jiwo."

"Old Brother, what you said does help vent our spleens alright, but I'm not sure if it's true..."

"Have I lied to you before? I'm an honest man, and I said what I saw."

"Indeed. Old Brother is an honest man."

As they chatted, the five men fell asleep in no time.

No one knows when the old man woke up and, stretching out his neck, mimicked the crows of a rooster to herald the arrival of another morning. The miners washed their faces with the water from a pool, relieved themselves in another corner, and crouched down beside the shaft to wait for the food and drinking water to be lowered down from above. They unloaded the food and water from the basket and, in exchange, filled it with orcs.

Eldest Brother was pleased to smell chilli pepper in the breakfast this time. Clapping his hands, he said: "I've been expecting the eighteenth day of the second lunar month to come, but this delicious dish came instead! Dig in! Dig in! Ow! Augh! It's really delicious! To my mind, whoever sent down this food cannot be bad. Let's pray for that person. If it's a man, we wish him to hold a pretty girl in his arms. If it's a woman, we hope that a young man might take a fancy to her... Let's eat. Tuck in. Ow! Augh! It's really delicious!"

After breakfast, the three veteran miners tried to allay the anxiety of the two newcomers, telling them to be patient and make long-term arrangements. They led the pair into a narrower cave around a corner and through a space with water dripping from above into an open ground lit by yellow incandescent light bulbs. It used to be an artificial cavern. Good Heavens! There were three reliefs of human figures on the walls, all sculptured from a mixture of clay and rock powder. Life-sized, they were all female. The two young miners were stunned into silence.

"They're statues of my wife," said Second Brother in a booming voice.

Pointing at Second Brother, Eldest Brother said: "This guy is really talented. How can you work underground without your family? You two can tell him what your women look like and ask him to sculpt their images into statues. After a bit of trial and error, I'm sure you'll be satisfied."

Today, Fourth Brother did indeed start working with Second Brother on a statue with rock powder and clay. "Her chin is pretty big, and so is her mouth. Her eyes are like apricots, and she has two dimples when she smiles. Let me see... when she crouches down, she looks like a calf."

"My brother, your description makes my job difficult. You must give me more details."

"To be more detailed, well, she's got broad shoulders..."

The young man was unable to concentrate on mining. He went to the cavern to take a peek from time to time. Finally, he said: "She may be unfaithful to me, but I've still been thinking of her at night. How about this, Second Brother? How about making a statue of her for me, too? She has long hair, a large bottom, rabbit eyes and she's about one point seven metres tall."

As Second Brother was now tasked with sculpting clay, the other four miners shared his quota of the mining work. After thirty days and repeated corrections and improvements, Second Brother had by and large finished the sculptures. Now, they had five women gazing at them with their mouths wide open. One of them, the one with long hair, was the prettiest. There was a slate in front of each with the same sacrifices set upon them: a morsel of steamed bun, a little preserved vegetable and some dried fish.

On the afternoon following the completion of the statues, Eldest Brother felt tight in his chest. "Well? The day is finally here, eh?" With that, he calculated by counting on his finger joints. The other four miners hurriedly carried him onto the straw bed.

That night, the old man panted violently. About midnight, his stone eyes stopped moving. The other four miners cried as they huddled together.

"Today turns out to be the eighteenth day of the second lunar month. Son of a bitch! We'll never forgive this day!"

TURTLE DOVE AVENUE

"Old Tang Tong has a Turtle Dove Avenue, / Trying to walk on it many gluttons queue." This popular doggerel had been circulating in town in recent years. The new residential and commercial area was next to the hotel, occupying an area as large as that of the old town. The once busy Stone Street was overshadowed. It was said that seventy per cent of the population in the new area came from outside town. They spoke a variety of dialects and wore different styles of clothes. The names of the streets in the new area had been borrowed from familiar slogans, such as Progress Road, Ascending Street and Pioneer Alley. Today, however, they were changed overnight by Golden Lock, Tang Tong's favourite employee.

Golden Lock had a really smart head. It was the most valuable asset he possessed. He suggested to his boss that the street names be changed, saying: "The names are not only rustic but also hard to remember. They're dull and obscure. Besides, they show our ingratitude."

This last word stung Tang Tong, who asked: "What do you mean?"

As Golden Lock spoke, the platinum pendants swung from his ears. "We can never forget the contributions made by the ladies! Coming from all parts of the country, they have helped us enormously."

Tang Tong seemed to understand what he was talking about and listened with his mouth half open.

"As I see it, the most easterly street is studded with hair salons, and their business is getting more prosperous with each passing day. It should be named Wild Chick Street. The one in the middle, in which our waiters and waitresses, company employees and ball boys all live, ought to be called Turtle Dove Avenue. The one in the west, flanked by flash apartments occupied by the wives of important people, should be named Phoenix Road. Then, not only will the names be easy to say but they'll also be easy to identify. The residents along each street will feel uplifted, and we won't have to worry about which apartments to assign to different people."

Tang Tong clapped his hands and complimented Golden Lock even before he had finished. He accepted the suggested names except Wild Chicks, which he changed to Golden Pheasant. He had meant to consult Yi Bo, an adviser to the Tiantong Group, about the name change. But now he has changed his mind: "We're not going to ask that old guy."

Yi Bo was the brother-in-law of a high-ranking official and worked as an associate professor at a university. His sideline job with the Tiantong Group earned him a handsome allowance. He lived in the group's guest house most of the time.

Glancing at Tang Tong, Golden Lock said: "Well, this guy Yi Bo..."

"Forget it," said Tang Tong, knowing that he was going to lodge a complaint. "Everyone has their own shortcomings. Live with them."

"But this I can't live with..."

"Put up with it then!"

Tang Tong left. He did not want to talk about Yi Bo at all. Golden Lock knew that he feared that guy's brother-in-law. The mere thought of the name Yi Bo disgusted Golden Lock. In his fifties, the guy wore a white suit and a wide-brimmed hat popular among the gentry of Southeast Asia. He held a Western-style cane as a symbol of good breeding and wore a pocket watch with a gold chain.

"Pah!" Golden Lock spat with contempt.

Walking on Turtle Dove Avenue, Golden Lock was exceedingly happy. Pink silk trees lined both sides of the avenue. They stayed in flower for a long time, and both the fragrance and colour of their blossoms were delightful. Behind the trees were buildings of various styles and heights. Most of them were residential apartments for the employees hired from different parts of the country. Seventy per cent of them were female, and they all lived in this designated residential area. When they were out, they dressed in either special uniforms or outlandish clothes, both pleasing to the eye. They chatted and giggled like young turtle doves. Many of them worked in the hotel. Therefore, when they saw Golden Lock, they were very courteous, and when they called 'Manager', the word sounded as sweet as honey. He nodded in all seriousness. When he saw groups of young women swarming out of the entrances of their apartments, he would linger to watch. Among them were textile workers and waitresses coming off their night shift. Despite having worked the entire night, they did not show the slightest sign of fatigue. After emerging from their hot morning baths, they came out rosy faced, their heads still wrapped in towels. He might not know eighty per cent of the young women, but each of them evoked in a him a feeling of caring love.

How nice, he said to himself. What great assets! You little turtle doves, fly with the cause of the Tiantong Group. Where else could you find such a bright prospect lying ahead of you!

Two women under a pink silk tree ahead of him caught his attention. As soon as he saw them, his feet were nailed to the ground. One of the women facing him was about forty or perhaps a little younger. Facing slightly to one side, the other was about twenty and had a beautiful figure, tall and with long hair cascading over her shoulders. The older woman, however, was more intriguing to him because he was not sure if he had seen her before. He couldn't take his eyes off her. She was slightly plump but not at all heavy. She looked dignified but could not conceal her coquettish charm. It seemed that anything caressed by her eyes would be blessed. Focusing on the younger woman, she was unaware of someone sizing her up a few metres away. Her look was sincere and warm, and she was talking in a gentle voice. The younger woman began to wipe her eyes; she was apparently crying. Shaking her head again and again, she seemed hesitant or adamant in refusal. The older one looked disappointed and frustrated. She stepped aside and then walked ahead.

Fearing that he might never see her again, Golden Lock followed her for a few dozen metres, seemingly unaware of everything else.

He was tagging after her when suddenly someone called from behind: "Golden Lock!"

He was taken aback. Whoever in the whole Tiantong Group had the nerve to call his nickname on Turtle Dove Avenue would be considered defiant of human law and the divine! He turned around, but before he found his target, a second call sounded: "Golden Lock, you scoundrel! How dare you shadow someone! What're you up to?"

It turned out to be the younger woman who had been with the one he had followed. Her name was Liao Bei, an office staffer of a company affiliated with the Tiantong Group. She sounded angry. Sure enough, she had been crying, as shown by her bloodshot eyes.

"Oh, Director Liao. I was only looking at her because I thought I knew her. Well, who is she? I saw you crying as she was dressing you down – is she your mum?"

Liao Bei appeared to be in a very bad mood. Pointing at his nose, she said: "It's none of your business. Don't be so conceited."

"Aw, Director Liao. I was just expressing concern. See how angry you are... 'Turtle doves are cooing, / My family a good aunt is visiting.' I have to go now. Bye!" Golden Lock did not take the scolding to heart. Instead, singing a nursery rhyme, he took to his heels.

Liao Bei quickened her pace and strode onto the pavement. She stood under a pink silk tree awhile and looked down at her shoes smeared with mud. Her mother had been trying to talk her into returning home. She hadn't been back since her father drove her out. What a frightening scene! The thought of it still made her cry. It was genuine wrath, as powerful as a thunderbolt, which she had never experienced before. Now, she asked herself whether she should go back. Then, she shook her head and said to herself: Father, oh Father, I dare not. I'm scared. You're no longer the father you once were.

She replayed the conversation she had had with her father earlier that day, trying hard to find any mistake she might have made and the rationale behind her father's fury. But nothing she could think of or dredge from her memory could surely explain her father's rage. She had repeatedly asked her mother the question: "What in the world has happened to my father?"

Mother had said a lot in an attempt to persuade her to return home but she failed to provide a convincing answer to her question.

Liao Bei plodded towards her office building with heavy steps. She stood on the balcony looking at the hustle and bustle of human traffic on Turtle Dove Avenue. It was a sunny weekend morning, and the traffic was somewhat heavier than on weekdays. She leaned over the railings, and an unprecedented sense of dejection and being wronged took over her. Everything on the street was blurred. This would be her last day on Turtle Dove Avenue because she was soon moving to another location. Her small dormitory room had been vacated. This cramped, untidy space had given her much happiness. While she had to share with three other roommates, it was still a lodging place and much better than her college dorm where eight of them had to sleep on four bunkbeds. After her promotion to the position of department director two years later, the other three roommates moved out, leaving her to enjoy the entire dorm on her own. Today, however, she was about to move to a high-grade suite with five bedrooms and three other rooms on Phoenix Road.

Everything was happening like a dream, one that filled her with indescribable happiness and excitement. But now, as she was saying goodbye to Turtle Dove Avenue, she felt deeply sorrowful. So much had happened so fast that it was almost scary – misunderstanding, censure and jealousy would come one after another. Besides, she had something pressing to worry about: what if her father traced her here? He would have to knock at the door of an empty room and stand there waiting for ages. It was just as likely that Father would rush over here today as Mother had done.

ENOUGH IS ENOUGH

Turtle Dove Avenue looked splendid in the fading light. All those familiar with the changes to Jiwo over the past few years quietly shied away from Golden Pheasant Street and kept a respectful distance from Phoenix Road. But they showed special favour to the sweetly innocent Turtle Dove Avenue. "Turtle doves are cooing, / My family a good aunt is visiting." Whenever he came here, Golden Lock would chant the same nursery rhyme. He seemed to think that the entire avenue was, like its name, the work of his creation.

A smartly dressed man in a white suit came along. One glance told Golden Lock that it was Yi Bo. Golden Lock deliberately turned his face to one side. Looking from this angle, he saw a balcony, on which the most beautiful turtle dove occasionally perched. Of course, she would soon become a golden phoenix. Right at this moment, he was stunned once more because the person on the balcony appeared again. But after casting a few glances in his direction, she just looked away.

Yi Bo poked him with his Western-style cane. Golden Lock immediately bowed and greeted him: "Hello, Professor!"

"I've been trying to contact you for ages. Is your phone turned off? What a weekend! Would you care for a drink at my place?" Yi Bo was polite and modestly gentle.

Golden Lock smirked because he had two mobile phones on him at all times, but he often turned off the one that was known to Yi Bo. Shaking his head, he said: "Professor, I must go back to my office. I've been out the whole day and have a lot of catching up to do."

"It's been a while since we talked. No matter how nominal my title title of consultant is, I must do something concrete, don't you think?"

You son of a bitch, Golden Lock cursed silently. You've already done enough. But instead what he said was: "You're right. You're right."

As soon as Golden Lock spoke these words, Yi Bo reached out and linked arms with Golden Lock. They talked as they walked. Golden Lock tried to free his arm, but the professor held tight. Yi Bo's occasional mention of his brother-in-law – the man of great importance – gave Golden Lock goosebumps.

The two arrived at the hotel zone in no time. Yi Bo was staying in a large suite, but he had made a mess of it. Its untidiness and noxious smell repulsed Golden Lock, a man in the hospitality profession.

Wearing an affected smile, Yi Bo served tea. Golden Lock received the cup with a forced smile. Photos of effeminate men clipped from magazines lined the walls. One glance was enough for Golden Lock. He had been here before, and the initial memory was still vivid, and his hair stood on end whenever he recalled it. He stood up to leave, but Yi Bo stopped him by pressing his hand on his arm. Golden Lock looked up, only to see the muscles on his cheeks twitching and the corners of his mouth quivering.

"I am, as you know, Professor... averse to this sort of thing. From a scientific point of view, the consequences of being forced to do it... are really bad."

"That's true, but you know... well, you know everything. Only you can truly understand the distress I am in and... well, I'd better stop talking." With that, Yi Bo's eyes froze for a second, and he seemed no longer hesitant.

Golden Lock struggled to suppress the swelling tears of grief and indignation in his eyes. He wanted to say "It won't happen again", but it was too late. The professor's sudden assault did not leave him any chance to say no.

It was dark when Golden Lock stepped out of Yi Bo's lousy suite. He staggered listlessly and felt a chill all over his body. He stood awhile under a Chinese parasol tree and made up his mind to see Tang Tong. He dialled the number and plucked up the courage to mention Yi Bo's name. Unexpectedly, Tang Tong agreed to see him straight away. Golden Lock heaved a sigh of relief.

Whenever he stepped into Tang Tong's office, Golden Lock always felt emboldened. In addition to being spacious, the office was situated at the top of the building, which meant that no one could be above him. The layout was complex yet not extravagant. It consisted of a spacious study, a large bathroom, a meeting room, a bedroom and a room for office assistants. The office suite was accessible via a special lift. There was a door for the use of the office assistants and guests only. To them, the other rooms of the suite were mysterious and out of bounds. To Golden Lock, however, the layout of the office was not only stylish but also auspicious: it was a deliberate setting that portended infinite hope and possibility and displayed a kind of royal prestige enjoyed solely by the kingdom of Tiantong Group. As soon as he entered, Golden Lock seated himself in the meeting room as usual and turned off his phone.

About twenty minutes later, the boss came out. He surprised Golden Lock since he was still in the middle of a haircut. Only one side of his head had been trimmed of his curly hair, and he was still wearing a white cape. Beaming with smiles, he was clearly in a good mood today, and he was extremely interested in anything involving Yi Bo. Sure enough, as soon as he sat down, he asked: "Lockie, he did that to you again?"

Golden Lock drew a long face, cracked his knuckles and remained silent for a while.

"Tell me what happened, from the beginning," prodded Tang Tong, who appeared extremely amiable.

"That motherfucker! I've had enough of him. Boss, you told me never to offend him. So I decided to humour him on the last occasion. He makes advances to all the male housekeepers and even the male guests. I always have to stifle my indignation to avoid trouble. But, to my surprise, he also persists in harassing me and he did it again today. You may not know, but scientifically speaking, it is a genetic problem. I simply don't have it in my genes. So what I've been suffering is more than anyone can appreciate. But, considering…" As he struggled to finish his complaint, his voice became teary. "Boss, I've really had enough of him!"

"I'll consider what you've suffered to be your contribution to the group," said Tang Tong with a straight face. But he soon started laughing and pushed him gently as if he were a child that needed coaxing. He inched closer and asked: "Lockie, tell me about it in detail. You know I may be a pro when it comes to affairs between men and women, but I'm totally ignorant of Yi Bo's sexual conduct. What did he do exactly? Did he start assaulting you while you were chatting? I'm afraid it sounds a little far-fetched to me. In fact, I still don't believe it!"

Golden Lock rose, wiping his tears and said: "If you don't believe me, you can go and ask him. This is my ultimatum – I won't let him off next time because enough is enough."

Tang Tong chuckled. "But someone's also lodged a complaint against you. In fact, she also said 'enough is enough' – you were shadowing her and her mother. Besides, you peeped at her several times outside the building…"

"This… I have to explain to you… where do I start? This little turtle dove – oh no, she's a golden phoenix today. I respect her from the bottom of my heart, but I'm just curious. I don't know her mother, and I've never seen any woman like her mother! To use a cliché, I'd say she's 'gracefully attractive'. I'm telling the truth. I couldn't help following her a few steps. That's all I did."

As he listened, Tang Tong became teary. He asked in a raised voice: "'Gracefully attractive' – it means she's overwhelmingly beautiful, doesn't it?"

"Yes, boss."

"Well, I'm granting you amnesty!"

Dumbfounded, Golden Lock asked: "What do you mean?"

"You're off the hook. Go now. As for your encounter with Yi Bo, I'll get in touch with him. I promise he won't mess you around again. Go, go! I must finish my haircut."

As soon as Golden Lock went out, Tang Tong skipped into the inner room. Addressing a young woman holding a pair of scissors, he said: "My daughter, come and finish cutting your dad's hair."

The young woman combed his curly hair and checked his appearance in a mirror. She then pressed the left side of his curly head and turned on the electric clippers.

"My daughter, whenever you turn them on, the clippers sound like a buzzing bee."

The young woman placed a hand gently on his curly head and muttered: "Yes. Don't turn your head around in future."

"I promise I'll behave. I'm totally obedient. Continue cutting your dad's hair, there's a good girl. Take it easy."

Close to midnight, Tang Tong took a light meal and went out. After leaving the office, he walked up to Phoenix Road and strolled back. Looking up into a window for four or five minutes, he then headed towards Turtle Dove Avenue. A group of young women passed by like a flock of birds, which cheered him up. He chanted the nursery rhyme again: "Turtle doves are cooing." Finally, he arrived at Golden Pheasant Street, where the streetlamps were dim and pedestrians were few. Occasionally, he could see some seductively dressed girls loitering in front of the few hair salons that were still open. They were pretty in their red clothes against the background of verdant holly trees.

Look how orderly the area has become under your management, Tang Tong congratulated himself. Maybe you do have superb talent and ability. Golden Lock often compliments me like this. I presumed he was just kissing my arse…

He continued to saunter while thinking these thoughts when he found himself arriving at Yi Bo's building. He remembered his promise to Golden Lock and went upstairs. He casually knocked on the door. Yi Bo opened it listlessly and suddenly became alert when he saw the visitor to be Tang Tong.

"Hope I'm not disturbing you, Professor."

"No, Boss. Please come in! Please!"

"Your rooms are a bit of a mess. So, you've been busy?"

"I've nothing to busy myself with. I'm just lazy. Tea or a proper drink? I've got some whisky somewhere."

Tang Tong asked for a cup of water while Yi Bo fixed himself whisky on the rocks. This son of a bitch really enjoys himself, thought Tang Tong. He eyed him, trying to find out what exceptional traits he possessed. He finally settled on his bulky chest, so bulky that he appeared to be wearing a large bra. Hah, he's unusual indeed, Tang Tong exclaimed silently as he bent to take a sip from the cup. On looking up, he found Yi Bo blushing. Clearly, Tang Tong's scrutinising look had abashed him. To deflate the tension and to come to the point as soon as possible, Tang Tong spoke: "Professor, you must feel terrible, living here all by yourself. Am I right?"

Yi Bo stared at him in silence, his eyes burning as if he had taken a fancy to his smart new haircut. Tang Tong felt his own eyes scorched as soon as they met those of Yi Bo. Tang Tong rubbed his eyes and cursed in a muffled voice. He looked at him again and felt burned a second time. He had to turn his back on him. He was standing like that when he heard deep breaths and sighs from behind. In a few seconds, he felt a hand on his back – strangely, it was also scorching, hot enough to penetrate several layers of clothing. The hand was ironing his back! Tang Tong turned around, only to see the guy winking at him and reaching both his hands out in an attempt to touch him, and in a very flirtatious manner.

"Argh! This is indeed bizarre behaviour, isn't it?" groaned Tang Tong.

"Bossy! Bossy! I've been thinking of enjoying… a talk with you. I find your curly hair irresistible! How about…"

It was the familiar term "Bossy" that he hated the most. Besides, this son of a bitch was really coming on to him, something that he would never have imagined happening. Veins bulging on his forehead, Tang Tong evaded his clutches while digging out his phone.

"Anyone there?" he shouted into it.

In just two or three minutes, police sirens sounded. A car stopped outside the building. Several fierce-looking men jumped out carrying spiked maces, and they stomped upstairs and stormed into the room.

Yi Bo was taken aback, shouting repeatedly: "Boss... Tang Tong, what are you up to?"

"Take him, take this gentleman, out!" Tang Tong ordered, pointing at Yi Bo. "Take his trousers off and give him a good beating. Beat him to a pulp!"

WATER WORLD

Liao Mai had been sullen for days. Nor was he willing to speak. Mei Di did everything possible to cheer him up but without success. Mei Di felt concerned for their daughter Little Beibei. She had been feeling restless ever since she ran away from home.

"She's still only a child. You scared her to death. Go and get her back or give her a call. I went and talked to her, but she was too frightened to return. She's afraid of you."

Liao Mai refused to commit himself. Early one morning he went out, satchel over his shoulder. Mei Di watched him walk away, a look of relief on her face. He wandered along the coast, enjoying the squawking of seagulls. Some of them were on the sand beach and wouldn't fly away until he went up close. His attention was drawn to their surprisingly large breasts. "Damn," he mumbled, "they're just like Mei Di's. Her chest is agitating the neighbours!" He continued to walk on and found himself not going to the town's shuttle bus terminal. Instead, he was heading east – then he realised that he wanted to go to the small dock, to catch a boat to Trident Island.

Yes, from the day of his return from the island, he began thinking of a certain person. He was tormented by the thought. That person was the forewoman. She might have unleashed a tirade in her state of madness and might have been quickly interrupted by the Daoist priest, but the few words she uttered and the single surreptitious look she gave were etched in his mind and caused him to shudder. He always wanted to know what in the world was meant by the confinement of the forewoman on the island.

Travelling across the sea, Liao Mai became increasingly anxious. He had never been so anxious in all his life. He started to wish that this passenger ferry could grow wings and fly.

After disembarking, he headed straight towards the Daoist

temple. As he climbed up to the hilltop, his feet pounded the slab-stone steps, and beads of sweat trickled down from his forehead.

It was still early, and the courtyard was empty. He had just opened the half-closed gate when a young Daoist priest appeared from one side. "Hey, who're you?" The young priest took a while to recognise him as the man who had visited the temple before. He continued: "Please, please wait. His Reverend is still sleeping."

The young Daoist priest trotted to the rear hall.

About twenty minutes later, the round-faced abbot came waddling out. He had gained weight, his face was more haggard, and his thin beard was long and filthy. Liao Mai was repulsed by his conventional greetings. He just wanted to vent his anger with a few hard punches, but he managed to keep his composure.

"How are you, Your Reverend Abbot?"

"As a Daoist living a simple life, I'm fine. Thank you. Thank you." The abbot languidly led his guest into the west wing.

"I'm intrigued with the architectural structures here. That's why I've come back. I didn't get the chance to get a good look at the rear hall and the side-rooms."

After some more small talk, Liao Mai stood up. The old abbot stood in front of him, blocking his way while stroking his beard and squinting his eyes.

"You're the most learned man, the most learned man," the abbot said. With that, he placed his hands upon Liao Mai's shoulders and pressed him down as he seated himself. Seemingly perking up, he continued to chatter away.

"I hadst did survey the site before we did start building the temple. It was no easy job! Lumber was scarce on the island, and it would have taken us a long time to ship it from outside. The short-tempered boss couldn't wait. I thought of Qiu Chuji's feat of building the Qixia Bindu Daoist Temple in Shandong Province. He was a founder of the Quanzhen Daoist School. He ordered that a water well be dug in the yard and fished from it the timber felled in southern China. Therefore, I asked people to go and cut down trees in faraway northeastern China, and on the island, I had a big well sunk. The trunks of pine trees from the northeast floated to the well here via rivers above and under the ground. Then we were able to obtaineth as much lumb'r as we needeth without exhaustion."[1]

"Really? Then I might not but taketh a behold at thy rev'rend abbot's large well," Liao Mai said mockingly.

Lifting the front of his robe, the old Daoist abbot rose and walked ahead to show him the way. They arrived at a well with a brick opening behind the main hall. It didn't look anything special. Liao Mai said to himself in silence: This demonic priest is blowing his own trumpet.

Tired of beating around the bush, Liao Mai pointed at the rear hall and asked: "Where's the forewoman I saw staying there last time?"

The old abbot shook his hands and responded: "She's left. She's left. After I chanted incantations for several days, I exorcised her of the demon that was possessing her. She left soon afterwards."

"Where's she now?"

"Well, eh," said the old abbot rolling his eyes, "that is not a question we're supposed to ask. Hmm, hmm…"

Pretending to be interested in the architecture, Liao Mai strode into the rear hall. It was partitioned into a bedroom, a study and a utility room, but there was no one around. It was filled with a strange odour, like a mixture of burning incense and air-freshener.

After consideration, he decided that the smell was from a poor-quality perfume. He suspected that the forewoman was still here. For the rest of his stay, he inspected the few structures in the courtyard and examined all the accessible space. He finally concluded that it was hard to hide a living person in this small temple without a secret hideout.

After he left the Daoist temple, he went to see Maoha. He was missing him and thought at the same time that Maoha would be the best person to probe into the secret of the Daoist temple. As long as the old abbot had not sent her away, it would be hard for him to hide her from the eyes of any conscientious islander.

Maoha was not home, and his door was locked. When asked, his neighbour said that he had gone to work.

"Gone to work? He's gone to sea, right?"

"No, he's performing in Water World. He's been making big bucks for the management of the tourist area."

Liao Mai asked for directions to the tourist area and eventually found Water World. It turned out to be a comprehensive entertainment park offering the attractions and thrills of canoeing, diving, a marine mammal park, water slides and much more. A group of near-naked young women were getting ready to get into the water to perform a ballet show. Their skin had turned ruby-red under the scorching sun. It somehow seemed that the deeper the colour of their skin, the prettier they appeared and the more excited they became. Beaming, they stood in a neat line, looking straight into a distance where visitors were queueing up to purchase admission tickets. After making inquiries, Liao Mai found out the specific attraction where Maoha was working. Then, he headed towards the most crowded part of the park.

This was a dolphin show theatre. Three lovely dolphins were frolicking with a man, who turned out to be none other than Maoha. Like waves lapping the shore, cheers and gasps erupted intermittently from the spectators. Liao Mai stood among them and watched, knowing that it was only too easy for Maoha to perform these breathtakingly 'difficult and intricate' stunts in the water. Liao Mai was soon able to discern that the man performing under water was becoming increasingly lethargic and melancholic. He could tell from his noticeably drooping lower lip. Maoha looked like this whenever he felt distressed. In contrast, the three dolphins were joyous and lively. They kissed Maoha sincerely and whispered in his ear. Maoha played with them half-heartedly. However, the more disengaged he felt, the more alarming the stunts he would perform. He could even spend half an hour sitting cross-legged at the bottom of the tank as if on a *kang* at home, playing with the naughty dolphins. When he was tired of sitting, he would glide like these aquatic mammals. He swam more like them than human beings.

In the eyes of Liao Mai, Maoha did nothing but return to his own world in the water. This was no performance. Liao Mai waited and watched among the cheering spectators. Then, he discovered that something else was going on. One of the reasons why the spectators were gazing so attentively at the creatures frolicking in the water was the sight of Maoha's extremely large testicles that he unwittingly exposed once in a while. They peeped out of his loose shorts like huge sea urchins or jellyfish. Liao Mai gasped, because he discovered that the men and women cheered every time they became exposed. Apparently, the marketing of Maoha's huge testicles, just as much as his extrasensory ability in swimming, was part of the tourist area's money-making appeal. It was rather cruel. Did the man in the water realise what was going on?

The thirty-minute show was over. After Maoha climbed out of the water, many of the spectators went up to take photos with him. The staff from Water World tried to stop them. "Beat it! Beat it! You must pay if you want to take pictures with him. Five yuan a photo." The men and women followed the fatigued Maoha, looking at his webbed feet and his chest covered with thick, brown hair. They also stared at his bulging crotch. A blonde foreign girl asked her girlfriend in somewhat awkward Chinese: "His testicles really big?" The girlfriend nodded seriously and gestured by making a circle the size of a large bowl with her forefingers.

Liao Mai's sudden appearance enlivened Maoha. He pulled up his lower lip instantly, thereby concealing his strong teeth. "Brother, I've just been to the Daoist temple. Let's go. We'll talk as we walk." Liao Mai pulled him out of the crowd. Seeing a few youngsters following him, Maoha paused, turned around, and, widening his mouth, forced a hissing sound between his teeth and sent them scurrying away screaming.

"Brother Maizi, I dreamed of you. See, my dream has come true!" Maoha gestured him downward with his hands, and they sat on a flight of steps.

Liao Mai almost revealed what had fascinated the spectators but thought better of it. Instead, he urged him to wear tailored shorts when he performed in the water. Spreading his legs apart, Maoha said: "They're too tight! Damn it! If I don't air them in the sun, they'll get itchy and swollen. They'll be the death of me."

After a brief conversation, Maoha began to mention Young Shaliu'er. "She's an actress. I'm an actor now as well – she's on stage while I'm in the water. We're in the same line of work, so she can't reject me as a good-for-nothing any more."

"No, she's never rejected you."

"You're right, but she's missing that dark-faced son of a bitch!"

Liao Mai fell quiet and swallowed a sigh. After a moment, he broke the silence and told Maoha the reason why he had come to see him – he wanted him to find out where the forewoman was hidden or if she had really been moved out of the Daoist temple.

"I've seen the mad woman," said Maoha, biting his lip.

"When did you see her? Recently?"

"About ten days ago. When Young Shaliu'er went to offer incense to the temple, I tagged along. The mad woman ran out, but the young Daoist priest shooed her back and locked her up."

"Let me get to the point. You should know that this person may be very important to me. She'll be able to answer many of my questions when I see her. I'm worried that the old abbot may have confined her in a secret place."

"You may rest assured, Brother Maizi."

A DRENCHED MAN

Maoha gnashed his teeth in anger whenever he laid eyes on the Daoist temple on the hillside. Sometimes, he would mumble: "It is you, Abbot, that I hate the most. I want to strangle you to death! I'll strive to accomplish the task Brother Maizi has entrusted with me. That damn old abbot plays dirty tricks in the dark. I'll catch you and feed you to the fish."

One day, Young Shaliu'er was going to the temple again. Maoha intended to follow her as usual, but Young Shaliu'er stopped him and said: "Please go back. If you're there, the old abbot won't tell me anything."

Maoha did not say a word but followed each of her steps. Young Shaliu'er was seething and sat down on a rocky slope. Waving his big hand, Maoha said: "So, go ahead by yourself. Hurry and go!"

Young Shaliu'er entered the temple gate while Maoha waited on the stone steps outside.

When she last came to offer incense, Young Shaliu'er had repeated a name in silence. As she started to mutter aloud, the old abbot overheard her. He astonished her by giving her a sudden low bow with his hands held in front of him.

"When I have time, I'll exorcise you of the evil spirit that's possessing you, my poor child," he said. She was stunned into silence and then she dropped to her knees to thank him and asked him when she should come.

"The next full moon," the old abbot replied, "and outside your menstruation period."

It was the afternoon on the sixteenth of a lunar month, when the moon was full. The old abbot was sitting upright in the rear hall. On the floor was spread a piece of white cloth with a bagua diagram drawn on it. He was chanting something with his eyes squinting into slits. Seeing her arrive, he waved but remained sitting. Young Shaliu'er stood aside while holding her breath. The old abbot chanted for more than ten minutes before he stood up by supporting his weight on a wooden sword he held against the floor. He opened his eyes, which shot out a bright, piercing beam. Resting the sword on his shoulder, he walked around the white cloth several times at an exceedingly slow pace. Young Shaliu'er dared not look up. The abbot walked and walked when he suddenly hesitated. Turning around, he pointed the sword at her.

She trembled out of fear, not knowing what to do. She remained in that state for a long time until her body gave up on her and she collapsed to the floor.

Only then did the old abbot stop and reach out his hands to help her up. "It's sinful," he said.

"Your Reverend Abbot..."

"It's sinful."

The old abbot looked extremely stern, biting his thick, moist lip. Young Shaliu'er sobbed. "Cleanse your body," demanded the old abbot in a hushed yet determined voice.

"What does body cleansing involve?" asked Young Shaliu'er, who raised her head and looked at him timidly.

The old abbot turned and shut the door in the hall and returned to the inner room. When he came out, he was holding a shaving knife. He came close to Young Shaliu'er and whispered in her ear: "None of the body hair is to be kept. It's the first step of the exorcising process known as 'body cleansing'."

Looking at the closed door in the rear hall, Young Shaliu'er started to step back. The old abbot closed the shaving knife, stroked his beard and said: "All right. To avoid suspicion, just follow me." He led her to the utility room across the hall and shoved aside a folding screen to reveal a shelved shadow box behind.

Young Shaliu'er hesitantly inched closer and noticed a small paper package placed in every square. Each package had a young woman's name written on it: 'Young Flower', 'Second Girl'...

Pacing up and down in front of the shadow box, the old abbot explained: "Each represents a person that has had the evil spirit exorcised of her. And the packages contain their hair removed during the cleansing procedure. Come on, my child. Let's get this done." He opened the old-fashioned shaving knife and tried it on his beard. Young Shaliu'er's face turned ghastly white. She swung around and fled to the outer room. There she shook and banged the door with the old abbot pacing and occasionally sighing behind her.

At this crucial juncture, the door crashed open. Before they had time to collect themselves, Maoha had already planted himself between them.

Young Shaliu'er was shocked, but before she gave out a scream, she squeezed nimbly out of the door and dashed straight towards the temple gate.

The shaving knife dropped from the old abbot's hand.

"Agh, you demon! You demon! What're you up to?" the old abbot shouted, gesticulating with his open hands.

Maoha swung his leg and swept the old abbot to the floor. He then pounced upon him and held the abbot's throat firmly with both hands until white foam appeared around his mouth. The old abbot rolled his eyes and gasped for air.

"Where's the forewoman?"

The old abbot shook his head, swallowed and gnashed his teeth.

Maoha crouched over his head, his huge testicles hanging down to cover his face and preventing him from breathing through his nose or mouth. Kicking and twisting his legs, the abbot was almost suffocated. He stuck up a quivering forefinger. Maoha sat up to allow the abbot to gasp for air.

"I, I'll tell you. She... she's gone."

Maoha scolded him and sat upon him again. After another round of painful kicking and twisting, the abbot stuck up a finger, and Maoha sat up once more.

"I, I..." The old abbot picked himself up by pressing his hand on the wall. He staggered to a pillow and fished out a greasy key from under it.

It turned out that there was a small rusted door behind the shelved shadow box. As soon as the door was opened, a gust of moist air swept out. Maoha went down the staircase, grabbing the old abbot with one hand and pressing the wall with the other. Below the staircase, he found a cellar built along the slope of the hillside. The only light came from a small window and a single electric bulb. A person was huddling in a corner. Maoha peered at the person and could not help bursting out an exclamation.

That person rose upon hearing the scream. She was none other than the forewoman. Her face covered in matted hair, she threw herself into Maoha's arms and wailed loudly. "I'm the nominal foster daughter of the Great Sage Equalling Heaven. I'm a fox spirit, and I've a hedgehog sister. She can get me out of here."

"I'm taking you to your hedgehog sister."

"I've a hedgehog sister. I have…"

"I know, Fox Spirit, you poor thing."

Looking back, Maoha caught sight of the old abbot crawling towards the small door and almost reaching it. Screaming, he dragged him back and pinned him between his legs. Clenching his teeth, Maoha called out Young Shaliu'er's name. Then, he mumbled with rage and urinated over the abbot involuntarily. The old man twisted his body, kicked his legs and eventually passed out and lay still on the floor.

Maoha sat up, examined him, and jumped up with a scream of horror. The abbot's face was blue and his teeth were sticking out. After staring at him awhile, he inched a few steps closer and reached out his hand over his nostrils. Realising he was still breathing, though feebly, he took the forewoman's arm and said: "Let's go! The faster we go, the better. We can't allow this dirty abbot to get us into trouble."

Maoha locked the small door again, returned the shelved shadow box to its former position and rushed out of the hall, pushing the forewoman in front of him. There was no one between the main and rear halls. He hesitated a little, then carried the forewoman onto the wall and, with a single bound, leapt onto it himself.

"Damn! It's dark! We've missed the last passenger ferry. We have to take a ferry on another islet. Fortunately, it's a bit closer to your hedgehog sister." The forewoman squinted and nodded. She was overwhelmed with fatigue.

Holding her hand in his, he ran by the darkening bay. In the end, he simply carried her on his back. While he was boarding the ferry, the other passengers made way for him, thinking that he was taking a sick person to a doctor outside the island.

"Go to sleep. When you wake up, the ferry will pull into shore." Maoha held her tight beside him to prevent her from falling. "I wish that old abbot had suffocated. But I was in too much of a hurry.

Besides, I didn't really mean to kill him." Throughout the journey, he smelled the stench of urine exuding from her body. "Jeez, maybe you really are a wild animal spirit!"

The ferry was moored by a large island. Maoha carried her off but was unsure where to go. He did not slide her off his back and sit her on the sand beach until all the passengers had dispersed. From here, he could see lamplights on the other side, and they seemed so close. The dark sea stretching into the distance reflected the glistening lights of the lamps and stars. Maoha knew that the lamps shining brightest must be from Jiwo. He looked at the person slumbering next to him and wondered: Are we going to sit here till daybreak? Then, we'll have to wait here the whole night. Maybe it's better if we swim over. It'll only take a little while. I'll have to carry you on my back like a turtle, but you must promise to hold me tight and not tickle me... Wake up! Wake up! If you're still sleeping by the time we enter the sea, you'll drown immediately.

Maoha woke her by patting her on the back. After giving her instructions, he slid into the sea by kicking his feet against the sand. With one arm holding her on his back, he started swimming and he continued despite her screams and contortions. When they reached open water, she was so scared that she kept quiet.

"You're enjoying yourself more in the sea than on land," he mumbled. "But mind you don't fall asleep. In half an hour, I'll guarantee that your hedgehog sister will be standing in front of you. I'll leave as soon as I let you down – I have a lot to take care of on land. I must go and find my biological mother. She lives at the end of Xihe."

While muttering, Maoha alternated backstroke and sidestroke and had to prop up the forewoman every now and then. "Damn it. You're a real burden. Without you, I would have covered several kilometres under water with my eyes closed. Damn it... At last, we're approaching shore. Hey! Open your eyes, you crazy, urine-smelling fox spirit! We're almost there. Here we are. Here we are. I'm not in the least tired but I have caught a fucking cold. Now, I'll be coughing for sure..."

He helped her to the shore. It was due west of the small dock. Liao Mai's farm was not far away to the south. The forewoman started running and screaming. Finding it hard to persuade her to stop, Maoha simply grabbed her, put her on his shoulder and hurried south.

It was exactly midnight. Neither Mei Di nor Liao Mai were asleep. Mei Di was making fish soup and Liao Mai was reading. They were interrupted by a banging on the door and they both went to open it. Liao Mai got there first and was confronted with a drenched man. It was Maoha, carrying a dishevelled woman on his shoulder.

"Here's your hedgehog sister." With that, Maoha dropped the woman to the ground in front of Mei Di.

Mei Di and Liao Mai were too shocked to say anything. The woman leered at them and suddenly threw herself upon them shouting: "Help, my hedgehog sister! Only you can help me. We're sisters after all…"

"What, it's you! It's you…"

"Yes, it's me, my hedgehog sister. We're both the boss's women. We're both his women. Let's go back together. Let's go back to him together. Let's go back…"

Mei Di tried to cover the forewoman's mouth but she kept on jumping and screaming while repeating what she had said again and again.

Trembling all over, Mei Di said: "See how crazy she's become! How crazy…"

Liao Mai fixed his eyes on the forewoman.

She was still screaming, still repeating those same words.

MEETING

Liao Mai stood in front of the mud houses on the estuary. He had counted five young men here, no more no less. They all looked sullen and reticent. Upon seeing him, they walked slowly up among the sampans and fishing nets that were heaped by the water's edge. Some of them were wearing glistening chest waders, poised to go fishing. They were now approaching him, thumping and squishing.

"I'm here to see Old Woman Shan," Liao Mai shouted to them.

None of the five men responded. Instead, they stared straight at him. The silent stalemate lasted more than ten minutes. Liao Mai was about to walk straight up to the small courtyard when one of them picked up an oar and bashed it against a sampan. The banging startled the seagulls in the near distance, and they took flight over the sea.

A plump woman with a blue cloth around her head appeared from her mud house, peeping at the visitor by cupping her hand over her eyes. Having made sure who he was, she beckoned him over.

Liao Mai approached.

He had walked to within a dozen steps of her when she turned around and plodded slowly ahead. Liao Mai caught up. They crossed one courtyard and into an adjoining one. Both yards were filled with old boat planks, rolls of torn fishing nets and bits of broken floats. Unlike the other fishing households, no dogs were kept here. With a gentle breeze caressing the calm sea, it was oddly quiet all around.

They sat down in front of a mud house in the middle of the courtyard. It smelled fishy as usual. It was a typical fisherman's courtyard. A large mud-clay stove was positioned against the south wall with a huge, empty, rusted iron wok set on it.

Old Woman Shan spoke first: "I wasn't in the mood to move around after my husband's death. Everything here looks the same as it did during his lifetime."

Liao Mai produced a roll-up, lit it and took a puff.

"I often saw you when you were young, very young. You were a handsome boy. I've seldom seen you since you left town."

"You've been too busy. You've been the one that's always doing great deeds."

Old Woman Shan chuckled. "I've been doing nothing but rearing a few adopted orphans, and fishing and farming sea cucumbers. I don't have more than a few years in me."

"Your orphaned sons are all masters of martial arts."

"Nah! They all lived hard, parentless lives until they had the good fortune to be adopted by me... Well, it's been our fate. We're just trying to make ends meet."

"You're pretty wealthy. You're very lucky."

"Nobody in town has done better than you. You have a beautiful wife and own a big farm..."

"The big farm's coming to its end. As for a beautiful wife, she is indeed beautiful. But, unfortunately, she's not a human being."

Old Woman Shan widened her eyes. "What? What did you say?"

"In fact, you know everything – she's the offspring of a hedgehog spirit originally from the wild forest."

"Good grief! You're a learned man, and yet you also believe what's said about her? It's nothing but a groundless rumour."

"Is it? I do believe that Mei Di is indeed an incarnated hedgehog."

"Maybe. You know her better since you're her husband. Perhaps, you've discovered something strange about her after so many nights together. If you don't mind, would you tell me something about it?" Old Woman Shan's interest was piqued and she bent her head closer to him.

Liao Mai scolded her in silence: You're daydreaming, you bitch! But what he really said was: "You actually know everything about what she's been doing over the past two decades. Everything about me and her. Which townsperson can hide anything from you?"

Old Woman Shan shook her head. "Oh my! Oh my! You're trying to flatter me. I'm only an ignorant widow." With that, she sucked in the corners of her mouth, wrinkling it like the tightened neck of a fabric sack. Looking up and smacking her lips, she asked: "So, you're here about Mei Di?"

Liao Mai shook his head and said: "Anything concerning her has become the past. Our relationship can't go anywhere further. I've come here today for another person – it's Maoha. As you know, he treats you as his biological mother. He's been here twice and will come today and tomorrow again. Your nominally adoptive sons are going to kill him, to rid him of this world. I'm here to tell you that my friends and I don't care if he is or isn't your biological son. But you must restrain your nominally adoptive sons and make sure they don't kill him. They're being watched by people far and near. I'm here just to give you a warning – leave Maoha alone! Anyone who dares harm this poor man will die a violent death and can't even expect to have a burial ground."

Old Woman Shan remained silent for a whole quarter of an hour. Then, she began to repeat the words "friends" and "near and far" in a hushed voice. She broke out into a chuckle and, staring at him while slanting her head, responded: "Well said, my smart child. Some of the things have to do with retaining my privacy. Yes, each unfolds as a long story and defies clear explanation. Take my seven nominally adoptive sons, for example. No one knows their personalities and temperaments like I do. They're so wretched. They know nothing but to work hard in silence. They'd feel wronged if anyone out there should misunderstand them. I'd like you to straighten things up for them on my behalf."

"I've nothing more to say to you. I just want you to remember what I've just said – rein them in."

Old Woman Shan started to become a bit vexed. "Who knows anything about that creature crawling out of the sea? Kill him? For what? In reality, someone's trying to kill my sons. Out of seven, I've only five left…"

"That's right. That's why I'm here to give you my warning. Make them behave. You want to keep some alive so that they can support you when you are senile, don't you?"

Her teeth chattering, Old Woman Shan asked: "You know their whereabouts? One disappeared at sea, and the other went missing one stormy night. My poor sons! I miss them dearly." With that, she rubbed her eyes.

"It's said that many people were struck dead by thunder on the day of fighting the drought demon. Your sons must have been targeted by the God of Thunder since they had blood on their hands."

"Well, can't you say something that'll sow virtue for your future generations?"

"But I must tell you one more thing today – Tang Tong is also marked by the God of Thunder."

Old Woman Shan sucked in the corners of her mouth again, as tightening the sack neck even more.

Liao Mai rose and saw himself out of the door.

TWENTY

A GOLDEN PHOENIX

"WHAT ARE YOU LOITERING HERE FOR?" she asked. "Why do you always hang out here?"

The woman was in her fifties and had walked over from the other end of the hallway. She seemed to have been keeping an eye on him for a long while.

"I'd like to wait a bit longer. Maybe she'll be back. I'm sorry…"

The woman snorted while jiggling a wooden key ring in her hand. "Who are you waiting for? And who are *you* for that matter?"

"Oh, sorry! You must be new here – I've been here many times before. I'm her father."

Knitting her brows, the woman tried to size him up and asked: "Her father? It's strange a father doesn't know his daughter has already left. You could've called her before you came here."

"I had no idea. Just moved? Where to?"

"Phoenix Road in the west. Hey, your daughter's now a successful woman!" she said, all smiles, while continuing to jangle the wooden key ring as if it were a tambourine.

Liao Mai had never been to Phoenix Road. He asked for directions along a few alleys that led to a new area that wasn't all that big. Everything that came into sight was brand new, including all the paving stones and trees that flanked the road. Among the trees were several tall and thick London planes, Japanese pagoda trees and Canadian poplars transplanted in order to provide shade earlier in the year. Many of them were still clad in protective straw ropes. This newly constructed, north-south thoroughfare was really beautiful and clean. A succession of five-storey buildings lined the west of the road with plenty of space between them. Gardens and lawns covered all the other parts of the zone that were not taken up with roads and parking bays. Pristine fescues and other flowering grasses appeared like velvet blankets.

Liao Mai was stopped by the uniformed guard at the zone entrance. After giving him a salute, Liao Mai explained that he was visiting his daughter. The guard phoned the office and immediately put on a smile, telling him that the office was on the top floor of the second unit in Building Number Five.

Liao Mai climbed up to the fifth floor, panting slightly. Liao Bei had just put on her jacket and was coming out when he was about to knock on the door. He had paused to inspect the coir door mat, admiring its exquisite workmanship and patterns. He then raised his head to examine the door. It was a reinforced, wood-imitation steel door with a peep hole and video doorbell. Standing by the door, Liao Bei uttered a barely audible "Dad".

The floor was carpeted, and slippers were laid out for guests. Liao Mai, however, neither took off his jacket nor removed his shoes. He just looked around with ostensible attention. He found it to be a two-level penthouse with a wooden staircase covered with an oxblood-coloured carpet leading to the upper floor. The foyer was oval shaped and contained a separate, shallow-stepped spiral staircase. Each floor consisted of three living rooms, five bedrooms and two bathrooms. The larger of the bathrooms had a floor space of more than ten square metres. It was equipped with a whirlpool tub and gilded taps. There was a separate shower unit and a vanity area, where the marble basin countertop measured three metres long. The entire bathroom was floored with thick carpets and was adorned with two seemingly genuine oil paintings on the walls, although they did not bear close scrutiny.

The dining room was spacious, as much as thirty square metres, and contained a Western-style dining table with carved edges. Rows of dazzling bottles of wines and spirits, most of them imported, were displayed in a glass-doored wine cabinet console table. Along with the racks and bottles were sparkling wine glasses and complete sets of silverware. The roses planted in ceramic vases gave off a faint fragrance. A coffee-maker and bean grinder set was displayed on an end table. A maroon wicker basket was filled with apples, grapes and oranges. He was taking in the contents of the room when he heard "Cuckoo! Cuckoo!" as a little velvet bird popped out of a small wooden door in a wall clock.

The upper floor was equally spacious and also high-ceilinged. Its layout was less conventional and more exquisite than that of the lower floor. The windows offered a view of the garden in the zone; on the lawn, there were several enormous cedars, beds of lush Chinese peonies and a tall papaya tree heavy with fruit.

After scanning the apartment, Liao Mai withdrew into the foyer and sat down. Liao Bei served him tea, but he pushed the tea set to one side. "Dad," Liao Bei said timidly, but he did not respond. "Dad," she repeated, raising her voice a little.

"Liao Bei, now that I've seen your apartment, we can get down to business. I'll ask you some questions and I hope you'll answer me honestly because what we need most at the moment is honesty. Maybe I won't ask you the same questions any more after today. Do you understand?"

"Yes, I do. I'll... definitely," said Liao Bei, who was trying hard to keep her voice from trembling.

"All right. First, you must answer me – is it me alone that you call 'Father'?"

The question caught Liao Bei off guard. She froze and gaped, at a loss what to say. Staring at her father, she bit her lip, feeling a chill running over her face.

Liao Mai was waiting.

"I..."

Liao Mai looked to one side.

"I... I must say, being honest, that I have called Tang Tong 'Godfather'. Maybe I omitted the 'God' bit..., but I only did it once or twice. I called him that with great reluctance. I must admit he likes me and cares for me because he's childless and always wanted to have a nominally adoptive daughter. He suggested it repeatedly, and he also asked me to talk to my parents about it... Mum... she gave her consent, of course."

"Is that all she did? Didn't she tell you to do something in addition to that?"

"She said that if others knew about the relationship, they'd misunderstand me. She asked that I call him that only when he and I were alone together."

Taking a sip of the boiled water, Liao Mai continued his interrogation: "What else did she tell you to do?"

"She didn't want me to tell Dad."

"Why?"

"Mum said that Dad would get angry – mainly because feuding with Tang Tong for two generations, you absolutely wouldn't allow me to endear myself with him. I think Mum's forewarning makes sense. That's because I find Dad's view of Tang Tong is sometimes very..."

Liao Mai stood up and placed a hand over his chest, as if he was suffering a heart attack. He sat down again and, hanging his head down, fiddled with the glass attentively. When he spoke, he began to sound hoarse all of a sudden. "When did this happen?"

"Eighteen months ago. It wasn't long after my promotion to the position of department director. I was giving a colleague a haircut when the boss came in. He looked awhile and asked me to give him a haircut. Later, I was chosen as his designated hairdresser, and he asked me to become his nominally adoptive daughter..."

"You cut his... hair?" He stood up abruptly and started to speak in a slightly louder voice. He gasped and sat down again, pressing his hand over his chest.

"Yes, in his office. No one could see us. As Mum said, if others saw us, they'd get the wrong impression..."

Lounging on the sofa, Liao Mai kept his eyes closed. Without opening them, he asked in his hoarse voice: "How much is this apartment worth?"

"I don't have any idea. Maybe, maybe it's worth between one and two million. It was bought after it was refurbished."

"You had the guts to move in without knowing its worth?"

Sweat broke out on Liao Bei's nose. She sat with both hands pinned between her legs. "Along with company shares and other fringe benefits, the group rewards all middle and senior administrators with mortgage payments. I really don't quite understand all of it... it'd be too complicated to keep track of everything."

"Really?" Liao Mai rose again. "I don't think it's complicated at all. So long as you do the big deals, all the other problems will be readily solved, just as bamboo splits as soon as it meets the edge of a cleaver. It's really that simple. You must have made such a big deal yourself and know what it takes for a turtle dove to become a golden phoenix. But what you neglected to consider is that you'll be debased and impure for the rest of your life. And there's no way you can get your old life back."

"Dad! Dad! Oh Dad..." Covering her face with her hands, she leaned forward as if to hold her father, but without the courage to do so. She collapsed onto the sofa.

Liao Mai continued in his hoarse voice: "This is ten times dirtier and filthier than I imagined. I've had enough! We've nothing more to discuss because you've made your choice. You've bet everything on it... you yourself, your parents' dignity, two generations of blood and tears – cost plus interest – everything. Your life of sin has thus begun. Enough! That's it. I've nothing more to say."

Giving his daughter a grave look, he headed towards the door.

Her face covered with tears, Liao Bei screamed and stood between the door and her father. "Dad, if you leave like this, I'll bash my head against the wall. I'll definitely kill myself because you've wronged me. You've wronged me. I've done – I've done absolutely nothing like what you're imagining. Nothing has happened between me and Tang Tong. I call him Father only because he likes me... this is really what's happened."

"Calling him 'Father' gets you rewarded with two million yuan? Plus the position of department director? You think Tang Tong is the kind of person to make such a deal?"

"I don't understand it, either. I had my suspicions and was vigilant at the beginning, but Mum said he was childless and yearned for a daughter. I gradually discovered that he's done nothing to me that crosses the line. Nothing! Believe me, Dad."

Looking up at the ceiling, Liao Mai seemed uninterested in his daughter's explanation.

"The boss wanted to give me a luxury car, but I declined because you said there was no need for one. He gave me this apartment as compensation, I assume. Dad, if you still regard me as the person you imagine, then I must prove my innocence by killing myself…"

Liao Bei cried so hard that she could not continue and would have stumbled to the floor if her father had not caught her. In his arms, he caressed her hair, which was as thick as her mother's. In his arms, Liao Bei cried out: "Dad, oh Dad, how dark a heart one must have to imagine one's daughter a slut! I'm frightened."

"My daughter, it's not your father whose heart is dark. It's here, this world that's dark and dangerous."

"Dad! Dad…"

"I'm responsible for your degradation. I've said a lot before but only about the hatred we've had with Tang Tong for two generations. While it was necessary, it also caused misunderstanding on your part. It was not a hatred between the families of Liao and Tang – things would be much simpler if that were so. My mistake was to be too blunt when I told you about the hatred and in a simplistic manner. Of course, all my mistakes can't account for what you've been doing. You've taken a terrible and unforgivable step."

Looking up tearfully and shaking her father, Liao Bei pleaded: "Dad! Dad! Please forgive me. So long as you tell me what to do, I still want to be your good daughter!"

"It's too late, unfortunately, because you've already taken the first step."

"What step? What first step have I taken?"

Staring at her, Liao Mai removed his caressing hand from her hair. "Taken your father's enemy as your father."

WAR

The rumbles increased in volume with each passing day. Although they seemed to come from the ground, their sheer velocity and deep-reaching, echoing tremors turned people's heads up towards the sky. Some foolish beggars in tattered clothes were still heading north, carrying bedrolls on their backs. When they passed by the farm, they would stop for a while, and Liao Mai would greet them. They would respond by either smirking or uttering something that they did not mean to say. Most of them were reserved, though. The number of various kinds of foolish beggar had increased in the past few decades on the paths and roads and in the towns and villages. Each time he saw them, Liao Mai would silently chant a verse about tramps written by an author whose name he had forgotten:

> *Wandering free in this mundane world,*
> *We sleep between the sky and the earth.*
> *Why can't others enjoy a life so free?*
> *Because they don't have the liberty.*
> *Since everything we need costs us nothing,*
> *Why do we worry about financial spending?*
> *We beggars fill the streets and alleys,*
> *We roam the farmland as we please.*
> *Just as we don't have to get money,*
> *So about losing it we need not worry.*

"There's going to be a war," said a middle-aged foolish beggar leaning against a wall.

"How do you know?" Liao Mai asked.

He rubbed the filth off his cheek and grinned, baring implausibly white teeth. "The rumbles are coming from all directions. People are beating a hasty retreat into the wilderness."

By the time Liao Mai looked around, the beggar had already left, chanting and carrying his bedroll. Liao Mai said to himself: Yes, it's war. It started long ago and nothing now will stop it. Like all wars, it will involve a scramble for land by both sides. Some villages will be laid waste and some land taken. Then, there will be the construction of defence works. Impoverished, forced labourers will emerge, and so will military engineers, battleground-inspecting commanders along with their orderlies, saluting privates, as well as women on the battlefields.

Liao Mai was sensitive to the role of women in battle as he looked back from time to time at his two-storeyed house, which appeared maroon in the mid-morning sun. Its large gable roof seemed stately and magnificent, giving the impression of what the ancient poet Du Fu had described as 'a palatial mansion'. This was a personalised building deep in the wilderness, a building where people of different genders and levels of intelligence were fused together, a building that appeared from a distance as decorous and profound. But at this moment, he felt its profundity to be somewhat elusive.

He was expecting that woman on the battlefield to come out of the house. He felt that the time had come. He was imagining what those traditional army women would look like in their uniforms. They must look the part somehow, not pristine, and they must wear an army cap. Such a military outfit should always exaggerate the female form and beautify her figure and hair, a lock of which, sticking out of the cap, should be enough to prove its allure. Stomping along in a pair of big boots might make her look like a ruffian soldier but only enhance her feminine beauty with her lightly dusted cheeks, rouged lips and pencilled eyebrows. Beneath gloves, her soft, delicate hands should invite anyone to shake them. She should never appear overtly sexy and she must speak in a brusque and forceful manner. She should prefer talking about cannons, enemy deployment, military conduct and discipline, as well as gossiping about senior officers... Anyway, as soon as they appear on the battlefield or at a command post near the front line, the charming smell of war would be intensified.

On this rumbling morning, Mei Di got up late. She had been as active as a hedgehog the previous evening, busying herself in the kitchen, on the first floor, in the utility room, guestroom and other parts of the house. She had begun making midnight snacks, a strange habit of hers. The snacks included a thick soup and some vegetable pies that Liao Mai had never come across before. They were filled with burning bush and sweet potato plant leaves or a kind of wild herb or the leaves of a tree that irritated the nose with their pungency. She had tried making more than a dozen kinds of pies to pique Liao Mai's appetite, but about half of them tasted repellent and had a throat-burning, peppery flavour. Surprisingly, however, Mei Di was able to munch them with gusto.

The previous evening, she had stayed in the kitchen for a long time before going to the bathroom, where she bathed for two hours. Sometimes, the sound of gushing water could be heard, sometimes it was quiet, but Liao Mai was able to imagine how she was killing time. Nobody loved to play in the water as much as she did. She would lounge there, lifting her legs and sticking her head out of the water, reading magazines, reciting doggerels or eating snacks. Her body, and even her head, would be covered with grape seeds or some kind of dark-green mud paste. Then, she would lie on the floor, wrapped in a bath towel until she dozed off. She would wake up with a yawn and plunge herself into the bathtub again. She repeated nonsense verse such as "Glossy socks and leather shoes / Walking as if on turtle shells" and "As fast as his bowlegs him can carry / Out to the street he would desperately scurry". When she felt particularly happy, she would trick Liao Mai into the tub and shock him with her naked body. In the warm, moist air, her skin turned from the colour of honey to something that was hard to describe and gave off the aroma of Korean mint that caused him to flare his nostrils. Once, he found her eyes bloodshot, which must have been the result of prolonged crying. He thought that she had been using anti-ageing eye patches because she often wore them around the house and would scare him at night when they bumped into each other in the hallway. When she accidentally left the patches on for too long, they would leave red marks on the skin. But she had long run out of eye patches. She looked around in panic and at him from every angle in the mirror as if she were searching for something, her face sullen and ghastly white. He remembered that the last trace of her hedgehog origin, the V-shaped golden fuzz on her back, had now vanished.

Mei Di got up at ten thirty in the morning. She didn't have the energy to rise earlier. She used to be in the habit of making Liao Mai, her really very fine man, a sumptuous breakfast. But recently, since Liao Mai always rose very early to eat breakfast, she simply stayed in bed.

She glanced at the sun by the door and walked towards Liao Mai amid the sound of rumbling. She leaned over the fence wall and saw, in the distance, a dark red cloud of smoke rising, its edges thinning and mingling with the colour of the sky.

"What... what's going on?" asked Mei Di.

"It's war. The first shot has been fired – you're one of the planners of the campaign."

Mei Di did not respond, probably to avoid conflict. She turned her head aside and said: "The noise is too loud."

"Several dozen armoured vehicles are advancing from three directions – the south, the west and the east. They want to win the war as quickly as possible. You should've helped them in the frontline battles as you did before."

Mei Di ignored him. Liao Mai left the fence wall. As he was heading towards the house, he called: "Come back. I want to talk with you about something important."

She was still leaning there. She did not follow him until two or three minutes later.

After entering the house, Liao Mai went straight into his study to wait for Mei Di. She came, her footsteps heavy and slow. She paused at the door a while before entering the study. Only then did Liao Mai notice her slightly swollen eyes. He took out a few sheets of paper from a drawer and put them on the desk.

"I've spent quite some time on this document," he said. "It shows the investment we have made – you and me, and the workers as well. The incalculable investment is not included of course. I'm not doing this out of anger. You know that I've been thinking of coming up with a new relationship with the workers, and we've been squabbling over it a lot. Please go through it. You can make any changes you like."

She did not even glance at the few sheets of paper.

"This matter must be resolved. Didn't you hear the rumbling? The war is taking place almost under our nose. When the smoke starts appearing on our farm, it'll be too late to address this matter." Liao Mai pushed the sheets of paper to her.

"Maizi, must we do it like this? Is it necessary? Haven't you been driven just a little bit crazy by what the forewoman, or rather the lunatic, said to you?"

"It has nothing to do with her."

"So, you mean we must do it?"

"Yes, if you think you're being short-changed, you can distribute my shares among the workers as their compensation. As for our emotional account, we can settle that later."

"You think we can settle our account thoroughly?"

"There's no alternative. Since you disagree with me, we must divide the funds first." Liao Mai looked serious as he rose and trained his eyes out of the window. Out there, the rumbling sounded even louder.

He mumbled as if talking to himself: "It's coming soon, the day of wedlock between a hedgehog and a porcupine…"

Mei Di took the sheets of paper and returned to the master bedroom.

The rumbling got louder and louder throughout the afternoon and evening. Many of the workers from the sheds cupped their hands over their eyes and were looking over towards the south to watch the dust being kicked up into the sky, cloud by cloud.

Waking up the next morning, they were all surprised to see countless bulldozers and power shovels moving like tanks on a battlefield to within five kilometres of the fence walls. "Good Heavens!" the workers shouted. "They're rolling up here, the armoured beasts, so many of them."

ROSES FROM WEST OF THE RIVER

The magnificent spectacle of bulldozers and power shovels had never been seen before. A group of roaring armoured monsters glittered in the sun. On the dust-shrouded site, not a living soul could be seen. Just moving steel bodies and arms. Now that the small villages in the south and the east had all been levelled, the view was clear. So much so that the huge, dark shadow of the Large Rampart Compound of Purple Smoke loomed large in the distance, dwarfing the insignificant villages that surrounded it.

The incessant rumbling from far and near gave the people on the farm not even a second of respite. They had no chance to sleep. As soon as the south wind sprang up, thick clouds of dust assailed their faces and covered everything around. Unable to go outside, the workers had nothing to do but squat in their sheds smoking or playing the board game 'five in a row'.

"Fuck! I've never seen so many metal objects assembling together in my whole life! There're at least forty or fifty."

"Yep. Nothing can stop these monsters. I saw with my own eyes how one of them ran over a tall tree and knocked down a section of a stone wall. They drove over ditches and through pools of water like they weren't there."

"If these iron monsters can wade into the sea, I wonder if the dragon king would be afraid of them. If he is, he may retreat a few dozen kilometres and cough up some land to the old Tang Tong."

"Such a greedy and hard-to-please man is sure to turn his attention to the sea once he has occupied the vast land here. That's no joke. It's said that dykes have been built in the sea somewhere, enabling water to be pumped out and earth filled in to form land.

Buildings have already been constructed on this land. So, you think it won't happen here..."

Liao Mai counted a total of forty-two machines in the west, east and south. Was their deployment in preparation for an engineering project or simply a show of strength? Liao Mai suspected that it was both. He was sleepless the whole night. But neither was he in the mood to go out. He did some reading and wrote in his study instead. Strangely, he wasn't sleepy at all. There was an overcoat on the couch that he could use as a blanket if he wanted to lie down. He put it on in the small hours when he started to feel chilly. Before entering his study, he had visited the guard dog Big Tiger Head in the south of the farm. He ran his hand over it without saying a word. The dog had been silent for days, only looking into the distance, first sitting up and then lying down. At moments like this, even dogs are quiet.

That night, Mei Di was particularly agitated. Not in the mood for a bath, she mooched around, moving from room to room. She covered the household objects with cotton sheets and newspapers and then spent most of her time on the huge wardrobe, trying to keep out any permeating dust. She took particular care of that small, golden straw raincoat, running her hand over it again and again before wrapping it in layers of cloth. At last, it was daybreak, and she took a light breakfast, left a note on the table and drove the passenger truck out of the farm. Liao Mai did not find the note until long after she'd left. He picked it up and read it: "I've gone to reason with those hooligans!"

Liao Mai quickly changed the plural pronoun "those hooligans" into the singular "that hooligan" and put the note back down on the table.

A veteran worker with his face covered in dust approached the house and stopped Liao Mai as he was exiting the front door.

"Old Liao, do you think the iron monsters dare to bulldoze our fence walls?"

Liao Mai was smoking a roll-up and handed one to the worker. "I don't think they dare for now."

"No, looks like they don't..."

"Because I have an Amazon in my family!"

The veteran worker grimaced and soon corrected Liao Mai with a compliment. "Nah! What you have is a great wife. How gentle she is. You're so lucky to have such a wife, Brother."

"No matter how great she is, a woman can still turn into an Amazon if you let your guard down."

"You're kidding, Brother! Your jokes go a bit too far."

For the whole day, they did not feel like working. They waited around, though no one knew what they were waiting for. It was getting prematurely dark as the dust blotted out the sun. It appeared like evening yet it was only four or five in the afternoon. Liao Mai was eating supper with the workers in the dining quarters of a work shed. He ate many barbecued clams, a favourite food of the workers. He had tasted them before and felt nothing special. Tonight, however, as he ate the clam flesh removed from their shells and drank beer with the workers, he was able to savour the unspoken taste of charm. Cooked in their shells, the flesh seemed more tender and gave off a special aroma. Chewing them and washing them down with cold beer, he felt a freshening delight going straight to his heart.

"Take some to your better half, Brother," suggested the veteran worker. Liao Mai shook his head.

It was completely dark. Mei Di drove her truck back into the farm, the headlights struggling to pick through the thick dust. She clacked her way through the doorway in her leather shoes. Liao Mai saw that her leather handbag was under her arm instead of over her shoulder. He also noticed that she looked much happier. Perhaps she had eaten dinner already because as soon as she entered the house, she went straight to the study, glanced at him and put the handbag on the desk.

"I went to reason with them. They gave me such a hard time!"

Liao Mai leered at her and found her a little nervous but much relieved. "You found Tang Tong?" he asked.

"I went to the office under his administration. He's got a whole bunch of people to take care of the business. An entire team."

"Well, negotiation representatives. When you came in, you were looking more like an army representative. But I just can't figure out which side you're on..."

"Don't make such jokes," Mei Di replied, knitting her brows and twitching her mouth. "The final moment is about to come. It's almost too late. I've been fighting hard with them. We must fight them step by step. We must make them commit everything to paper. I just talked with them without signing anything. I needed to come back to discuss it with you. You know, it's not just a matter of money, both to them and to us…"

"Well said!" complimented Liao Mai, with a smirk on his face.

Staring at him, she said with a tight, dry voice: "They've promised to take our requests into full consideration as long as we move out of the farm. The new site for our farm has long been decided upon. It's much bigger than it is here, just west of the river – five or six kilometres west of Old Woman Shan's sea cucumber farm. Of course, most of the land is waterlogged, full of reeds and sand, not arable at all. But they told me that when everything is settled, they'll drive the forty-some machines to the west of the river, where they can open up a new farm in a matter of three or four days. What's important is to transfer all the soil here to the new farm, and it's guaranteed that crops will grow next year. As for the house, they'll build a new one in accordance with our plans and add or deduct things as we will – anyway, they want us to be satisfied."

"Well, sounds good. Anything else? Any other considerations?" Liao Mai was all seriousness.

Mei Di exhibited an excitement that she could hardly contain and answered in a lively voice: "Maizi! They've agreed to plant trees on our new farm! Just like the ones we have now – cherry plum, poplar and various other kinds. And also, a lake, an L-shaped lake. Most important, they're going to plant some really big trees for us so that we'll have large areas of shade in two years at the most. I've also laid down some conditions, and they've accepted all of them…"

"What conditions?"

"I want them to plant some roses! Our flower garden's too small, but we'll have more space there. I want to have a large rose garden! Maizi, just imagine a large bed of red roses."

"Fantastic!"

"Yes, how wonderful it would be! Besides, we'll also have tree peonies and Chinese herbaceous peonies…"

Liao Mai rolled a cigarette and twiddled it in his hand without lighting it. He glanced at the colourful leather handbag covered with a layer of dust and said: "It seems that Tang Tong is going to make a considerable sacrifice. This guy's really generous – and as an army representative, you've done a good job."

"The most important thing, Maizi, is that we don't have to be bothered in the days prior to our relocation. They said we'll move only when everything is finished on the new farm and only when we feel satisfied having inspected it. We won't be bothered by the noise of the machines, either, as they'll work far away from us."

"Good. That's very considerate!"

"Maizi, don't be cynical, OK? It sounds cumbersome, but to the Tiantong Group, it's as easily done as planting a tree. It's true. The contract will soon be ready, and all we need to do is sign it."

Liao Mai lit the cigarette and took a deep drag before saying: "I'm not being cynical. I've said already: 'The day when a hedgehog marries a porcupine will soon come.'[1] I haven't been suspicious for a long time. But what I'm going to say is that, since you're acting in the capacity of a negotiator, I must tell you this – Tang Tong is miscalculating. He can plant roses, large beds of roses with beautiful blooms west of the river, but I'm still determined not to be lured there."

A PIECE OF PAPER

Dust fell layer upon layer, covering everything – the roofs, the lake, the trees and the cereal crops, turning them a dusty grey – and still it kept falling day and night. There was no wind, which might have swept the dust to the south. People were forced to stay inside and shut their windows and doors. Even so, they had to change their clothes every day. Mei Di washed hers twice a day. Liao Mai simply stopped washing his face. He was covered with dust all over, including his brows. He acted as if he were slow-witted.

"Maizi, what happened? Talk to me! Don't do this! Don't do this…"

Liao Mai was sitting in the study reading and writing, and occasionally reading aloud. Other than that, he was silent. Once in a while, he would look up with dull eyes and seem not to hear anything. She was scared. The handwritten manuscript of *A Secret History of the Jungle* was taking him forever to finish. The draft was tied into stacks and stowed in the drawers. To Mei Di, there was no reason to write the book, and the few draft pages she had leafed through seemed puzzling to her. This made her lose interest in the manuscript.

My really fine man, you can do whatever you like so long as you're happy. It's for you, no one but you, that I've endured so many hardships. As she spoke to Liao Mai in silence, she could not help feeling a great deal of painful tenderness.

The iron monsters were closing in, and the increasingly loud rumbles became unbearable. The gloss on Mei Di's face was gone. She had been losing sleep for days. She found the lamplight in the study on all night long. Liao Mai did not want to sleep at all.

My really fine man is gathering dust, sitting there like a statue, without eating, drinking or speaking. What shall I do? She paced up and down outside the study and peeped in through the keyhole, seeing him reading and writing alternately while sitting upright. My fine man, you're still so handsome even though you've been working yourself so hard. Look at his big deep-set eyes and straight nose. His mouth, shaped like a snow-pea pod, is always pleasing to the eye.

Mei Di did not know how to make him eat or sleep. He remained silent, saying nothing. She cried. He never touched the soup that she made and had placed on his desk.

One day, Liao Mai went out. When he got back, he put a package on his desk. From the smell, Mei Di instantly knew that it contained barbecued clams. She peeped through the crack of the door and saw him removing the flesh from the shells while fixing his eyes on the draft of the book. She could not help looking in and asking: "Maizi, shall I fix you a bowl of golden-scaled crucian carp soup?"

Saying neither yes nor no, Liao Mai looked up, and she caught a flashing glimmer in his eyes.

In less than a quarter of an hour, a gunpowder smell started wafting from the kitchen. Drawn by the smell, Liao Mai staggered out of the study and into the kitchen. Before the soup was poured into a bowl, he picked up a ladle, scooped some liquid from the pot and put it to his mouth so that he could blow on it before eating. He ate until sweat broke out all over.

Before Liao Mai stepped out of the kitchen, Mei Di decided that talking to him was better than putting up with him. "Maizi, we can't go on like this. We don't have any time to lose. I lost count of the number of times I scolded them while standing by the fence wall all yesterday. I scolded them and demanded that they stop, but it was no use. Don't be difficult. We've done all we possibly can to resist them. I think we'd better leave while the going is good."

Liao Mai did not say anything. Nor did he return to his study. He stood on the veranda for a while and headed towards the work sheds. She saw that he was now walking more steadily. She went back to the study and fumbled through the stacks of his draft manuscript, hoping to find something that might account for his behaviour. Each stack was still covered with dust, and each sheet was covered in his handwriting, and the text was still kind of enigmatic to her.

As she walked out of the study, she called a number on her mobile phone. She called repeatedly but couldn't get through. She wanted to speak with Little Beibei, just to listen to her voice.

"Little Fawn's Hooves..."

"Mum, are you still up?"

"Yes, I can't sleep."

"Mum, Mum!" she sobbed.

"Don't cry, my daughter. My good daughter..."

Mei Di heard her hanging up after crying heartily. She was extremely grieved. Looking up at the stars, she yelled to herself: I can't take this any more. I'm being driven almost crazy.

Not until dawn did Liao Mai come out from one of the work sheds, stumbling and smelling of alcohol. He leered at Mei Di when he ran into her and staggered into his study. Mei Di followed him in.

"Maizi, what shall we do? We can't wait and do nothing like this."

Liao Mai raised his head to look at her and said with a smile: "Yes we can! With a vast sea and a large tract of the wilderness here, how can I be pricked to death by a hedgehog and a porcupine!"

"What're you talking about? Are you drunk?"

"I don't believe it! I don't believe..."

His body wobbled slightly as he stood there. Mei Di caught him, helped him lie down on the couch and covered him with the overcoat.

It was broad daylight. Mei Di walked out of the house wearing a piece of blue cloth to protect her head from the dust. It attracted the attention of all the workers in the sheds. Without greeting any of them, she hurried into the truck and drove away, kicking up a cloud of dust behind.

Following her departure, no one came to the courtyard in front of the house. In the early afternoon, someone from the work sheds came carrying a large package of barbecued clams and a case of beer. Checking to see if there was movement in the house, he left the items on the step and left.

Night fell, but Mei Di had still not returned. Liao Mai woke up and noticed that it was already nine in the evening. He had been startled awake by a sudden sense of calm. He rubbed his eyes and sat up. Sure enough, it was completely quiet all around. Huh? What's going on? He opened the window and looked out, only to find that outside the fence walls, the iron monsters far and near had stopped moving and their headlights were turned off. The rumbling sound had stopped.

He walked out of the house, and as he gained pace, he began to feel a throbbing pain in his head. He steadied himself by pressing his hand against a column on the veranda and paused. In front of him was the farm shrouded in total darkness. The only light came flickering from the work sheds in the near distance. Just then, he heard the sound of an engine, and a pair of headlights shone through the gate and right towards him. A person got out, and, to his surprise, it was Mei Di. When had she left, he wondered?

"They've stopped, they've stopped! Finally stopped!" murmured Mei Di, removing the leather handbag from her shoulder and rushing over to Liao Mai. Staring at him, she continued: "I've just signed it."

Liao Mai struggled to open his eyes. After trying a second time, he finally woke up: "What? Say again."

"The contract, I signed it a moment ago. You were terribly drunk. Take a look and you won't believe it. You can't imagine how cost-effective it is. They kept their promise. See the machines outside? They've stopped and have been instructed to drive to west of the river at dawn."

Liao Mai was listening attentively to Mei Di, but before she finished, he started to feel tired. He turned slowly and plodded back to the house.

Mei Di followed him in. She took out a stack of paper from her handbag and pushed the sheet with signatures, the most important part of the contract, in front of him. "Look! Apart from the funds for our relocation to the west of the river, the Tiantong Group has also compensated for our farm – the trees, the house and all the losses we're going to sustain. Altogether, it's eight million three hundred and sixty-five thousand…"

"Plus Liao Bei's luxury suite," Liao Mai added, his eyes closed. "That must be counted in because it's part of the deal."

"Of course! Maizi, it turns out we have a good deal. There's no other way of looking at it. This deal is good enough."

Liao Mai grabbed the signed contract, glanced at it and threw it back on the desk. "Good enough," he said. "This is the money you've sold your body for. This large sum can finally recompense you for your services over the past twenty years."

Mei Di froze for several minutes. Then she gave a sharp scream. Straightening up, she shouted at him with wide-open eyes: "You! Are you drunk or crazy? Good Heavens! What did you say?"

"No more crying. I've been sober all the time. You must be sober as well. You can't yell away what you've done over two decades. We must be honest tonight. We must tell each other everything we know. Mei Di, I may be too aggressive, but I really want to know how many times you've slept with Tang Tong."

Mei Di pressed hard against the desk. She picked up the handbag and was ready to leave, but the bag dropped to the floor. "You tell me!" she shouted. "You tell me! You've been confused by that lunatic, and you'd rather trust her."

"Answer me. I've a nasty curiosity, you know."

Mei Di's tears fell like a torrent, and she leaned over the desk. After a long while, she looked up and said: "Maizi! Maizi… He and I only… nine times… yes… only nine."

"Nine times, ahh, nine…"

Mei Di bolted up and shrieked: "No, no! Maizi. I meant 'none'. I could never do such a thing. 'Never,' 'never'…"

"Numberless times?"

"'Never'! I mean I've never done anything wrong."

OH, FAR, FAR AWAY

"Mei Di, your explanations and attempted cover-ups are feeble. You'd better stop trying. We are two poor souls. In fact, I've been thinking a lot about how we can get over what's happened between us, but in vain. You may have figured that I've long suspected something fishy has been going on. I just didn't have the evidence. I felt so unbearably painful at the time that I resorted to violence, for which I'll condemn myself forever. Besides, I must tell you tonight that when I was away from home last time, I was feeling the most painful. You remember my trip to southern China and my being together with Xiu, don't you? We fell in love. That was true. We have a child already."

"What? Is... is it true?"

"It's true."

Mei Di started wailing. She howled so uncontrollably that Liao Mai found it impossible to go on. She leaned on the desk again.

Placing his hands over her shoulders, Liao Mai said: "I had to let you know because I absolutely can't hide it from you."

Mei Di stopped crying. She thought of something and asked: "You said you'd devote your *Secret History of the Jungle* to an 'unrivalled beauty'. I've always remembered those words – were you referring to Xiu?"

"No. I was referring to the you of two decades ago."

"Oh, Maizi! Maizi..."

"I've been trying to make a decision all these days, but I haven't made up my mind because it's so hard. Now, after six months have passed, I find it impossible to put off making the decision any longer. I know we can't be together any more. I must leave."

"Going to Xiu?" Mei Di threw her head up.

"No. I just need to leave. As for where I'm going, I haven't figured it out yet."

Mei Di tried hard to suppress her tears but failed. Her voice suddenly turned old and strange. "Oh Maizi! Please stay. The only thing I want is for you to stay. I'm not begging you, but I'd like you to consider Little Beibei and think of how I brought up this illegitimate daughter and waited for you in the wilderness and how our daughter nearly froze to death in an ice hole. I'd like you to think of the ordeal I went through. At that time, if I had refused Tang Tong, he and his father would have killed you... You should've thought of those things. You should have."

"Those are the things I've been thinking of these past six months. Mei Di, you don't have to say anything. You've tasted the wealth of Tang Tong, his enormous wealth, one or two hundred million or even more – a fabulous amount of money. You knew your choice long ago. Of course, I'll remember what you said for the rest of my life. I'll leave deeply in love with you. I'll leave grateful and indebted to you. I'll never be so infatuated with anyone else as I've been with you. Therefore, I must leave. I've been pondering it for more than six months. How can I change my mind so easily? I'll leave before the start of the relocation to the west of the river. Except for a few small things and books, I'll take nothing with me."

"Good Heavens! Good Heavens! What's going on? Am I dreaming? This must be a nightmare."

Liao Mai was about to continue saying something when he started trembling all over, his face turned sallow, and his forehead was drenched with sweat. He held Mei Di tightly and buried his face deeply in her thick hair. She stood still and remained that way for a full quarter of an hour. Then, he lifted his head and took a deep breath. She remained immobile. Gritting his teeth, he placed his chin upon the top of her head while she looked up and asked softly, as if she were merely exhaling: "How can I go on living?"

"Live a good life. We both need to continue living and live a good life."

"Are we in a dream?"

"No," said Liao Mai as he picked up the signed contract. "It's there, not a dream. I'll make a copy and take it with me so that I can look at it from time to time. It'll help remind me that this is not a dream."

"This is a dream! Believe me, Maizi, it is a dream."

"No, no! We are waking from our dream… Sit up, Mei Di. Sit up. It's rare for us to be so quiet together. We've been arguing too often. How nice it is to be quiet. I can't stay in the house at present. I was short of breath and nearly choked. I'm better now. Please let me take a walk outside by myself. Let me be alone outside the house for a little while."

"Maizi! Maizi…"

He did not respond.

Mei Di rose. As he stepped out, she put an overcoat over his shoulders. After he disappeared into the darkness, she leaned on the couch, which still exuded the lingering odour of Liao Mai.

Liao Mai cast a glance at the sheds where the workers, after prolonged fatigue, were fast asleep. Even the fish in the L-shaped lake were at rest. There was no wind, and the sky was a perfect purplish-blue. Meteors were streaking across the sky like sprinkling flowers of starlight. He gazed up, his heart pounding audibly. This night sky reminded him of one in his childhood. He remembered how he had endured the sorrows of his adolescent years that night, when he had also fixed his eyes at the starry sky.

It had been a sudden revelation, a shudder, shooting through his entire body. How could he forget that moment? It might have confused and surprised him at the time, but it was still fresh in his memory to this day and to this night...

He gazed at the bright, starry sky, finding it mysterious, beautiful and yet distant. What was more unforgettable tonight was the remote starry night of his childhood – oh, far, and far away! It was remote and indistinct, like boundless pity and compassion.

It was four o'clock in the morning when he returned to the house, which was pitch-dark and silent. Mei Di was nowhere to be found. Liao Mai was rather surprised. He hurriedly searched every room and even the attic, as well as the truck... "Uh, where is she?"

He even removed the protective panels covering the radiators in the attic. "Are you playing hide-and-seek with me?" he mumbled while stumbling downstairs. Standing in the foyer, he suddenly remembered the spacious wardrobe. He banged the doors open, only to find everything in place. Each item of Mei Di's clothing was hanging neatly in it. On closer inspection, however, he found that the small, golden straw raincoat was missing. He was struck by an awful feeling, and his heart sank... He had just closed the wardrobe doors with his head hanging down when he screamed in surprise – a large mass of thick hair, like velvetleaf fibre, was at his feet...

It had been cut from the nape and still felt warm. Holding his breath, he gingerly pulled the dyed tresses apart and caressed the hair beneath gently. He noticed some silver, broken and dry locks. This was the first time he had been aware of them. He pressed his cheek against them.

"Mei Di! Mei Di..." He scurried from the attic to the kitchen, to the garage and to the lake, but he found no trace of her.

The night was thick, dark and endless. He could not help screaming. However, none of the workers stirred due to their extreme fatigue. Liao Mai trudged forward and felt a sharp pain in his ankle. Only then did he realise he had somehow sprained it. He panted as he limped towards the Jerusalem artichoke grove and paused with his hand upon one of the plants for support.

The starry night was bright, remote and endless.

He gazed at the distant and vast starry sky. Something dropped pitter-pattering into his eyes, but he kept on looking up, allowing the droplets to roll off from the corners of his eyes.

Through this crystal coat of liquid, he saw the star clusters bursting out like rapeseeds, seemingly rotating and blossoming. He stood transfixed while chilly dewdrops dripped from the tall Jerusalem artichoke plant.

He reached out his hands and received them.

NOTES

ONE

1. Mei Di added the suffix 'zi' to Liao Mai's given name to show her affection
2. The toothless old man is unable to pronounce 'TNT' correctly and instead cries out 'Kick and Kick'

ELEVEN

1. Literally, 'mouth-to-mouth communicator'
2. In his ignorance, Tang Tong mistakenly thinks that all foreigners speak the same way and therefore could understand his manner of speaking
3. Ancient Chinese used the orbit of Jupiter to reckon time and created their calendar on the basis of major sexagenary cycles of repeating minor twelve-year cycles. Jupiter orbits around the sun once every 11.86 Earth years. To compensate for the difference, ancient Chinese created the imagined Tai Sui, the star of 'Great Year', directly opposite Jupiter and made it orbit exactly twelve years around the sun. In the Chinese zodiac and *feng shui* tradition, both Jupiter and Tai Sui are regarded as the gods of the year. The Chinese believe that wherever Tai Sui passes above Earth, there will appear an eponymous supernatural mushroom in the ground of the corresponding location. And this supernatural Tai Sui fungus is considered to be the earthly manifestation of gods of the year. To break ground where Tai Sui appears is blasphemous and disastrous and is therefore a taboo

FIFTEEN

1. 'Qi' in 'Qiwo' means 'umbilicus' or 'navel'. Hence the name of the town Qiwo means 'Town of Navels' because many girls wore navel-exposing clothes to look fashionable
2. The Chinese character 'Ji' in this newly changed town name shares the same pronunciation as in the original name of the town that meant 'Thistles and Thorns'. The sound *'wo'* can mean a place in the sense of a house or a 'coop'. Hence the latest name of the town Jiwo means 'Chicken Coop', which the author uses as a pun to indicate that it is a place teeming with prostitutes
3. The golden pheasant is known to the Chinese as 'bright and beautiful chicken'
4. A national organisation for Chinese children, similar to the Girl Guides and Boy Scouts

SIXTEEN

1. During the Cultural Revolution (1966-76), Red Guards often put on shows in streets or on stage to assert their loyalty to Mao Zedong and their revolutionary resolve. Such an abrupt and rigid gesture is typical of the shows

2. Traditionally, a Chinese shaman uses a sword made of peach wood to exorcise demons or evil spirits
3. Unlike Caucasians, most Chinese and other Asian women avoid exposure to the sun to maintain a pale complexion
4. Binduli, the seat of the Qixia Taixu Temple, was located in today's prefecture-level city Qixia under the jurisdiction of the metropolis of Qingdao, Shandong Province, China

SEVENTEEN

1. Meaning, literally, 'a world of sensuality'
2. According to *Huangdi Neijing* (*The Inner Canon of the Yellow Emperor*), an ancient classic that has been treated as the fundamental doctrinal source for traditional Chinese medicine for more than two thousand years, there are eight winds in nature and five winds in human meridians. The eight winds in nature can be external pathogenic evils capable of invading the meridians. Then they will follow them to the five internal organs, causing them to develop lesions. What the author of the letter means is that he is at an age when all his organs start to develop lesions, which in turn means that he is senile and vulnerable to various diseases

EIGHTEEN

1. A multinational military coalition that invaded China at the turn of the twentieth century

NINETEEN

1. Being pedantic, the abbot spoke in Classical Chinese from time to time. He meant to say: "Then we were able to obtain as much timber as we needed without exhaustion"

TWENTY

1. Here, Liao Mai is comparing Tang Tong to a porcupine. In Chinese eyes, a hedgehog and a porcupine look similar in the sense that both have spines. It's akin to the English phrase: 'Birds of a feather flock together'